TO FREE THE RISING STORM

THE ReEmergence Chronicles

C.N. MAXWELL

XALADOR
ELROS
SERPENT S
FAIREGROVE
LATERA
LIV
MIREFIELD
GO
THO
LAKE WILLA
DRAKE'S SPII
HOLLEYVILLE
GREAT
PLAINS
CRESTHILL
NEZRYN'S
RESPITE
RAVEN'S
BEAK
SHADE'S CRESCENT
SILVER S
BOILING FALLS

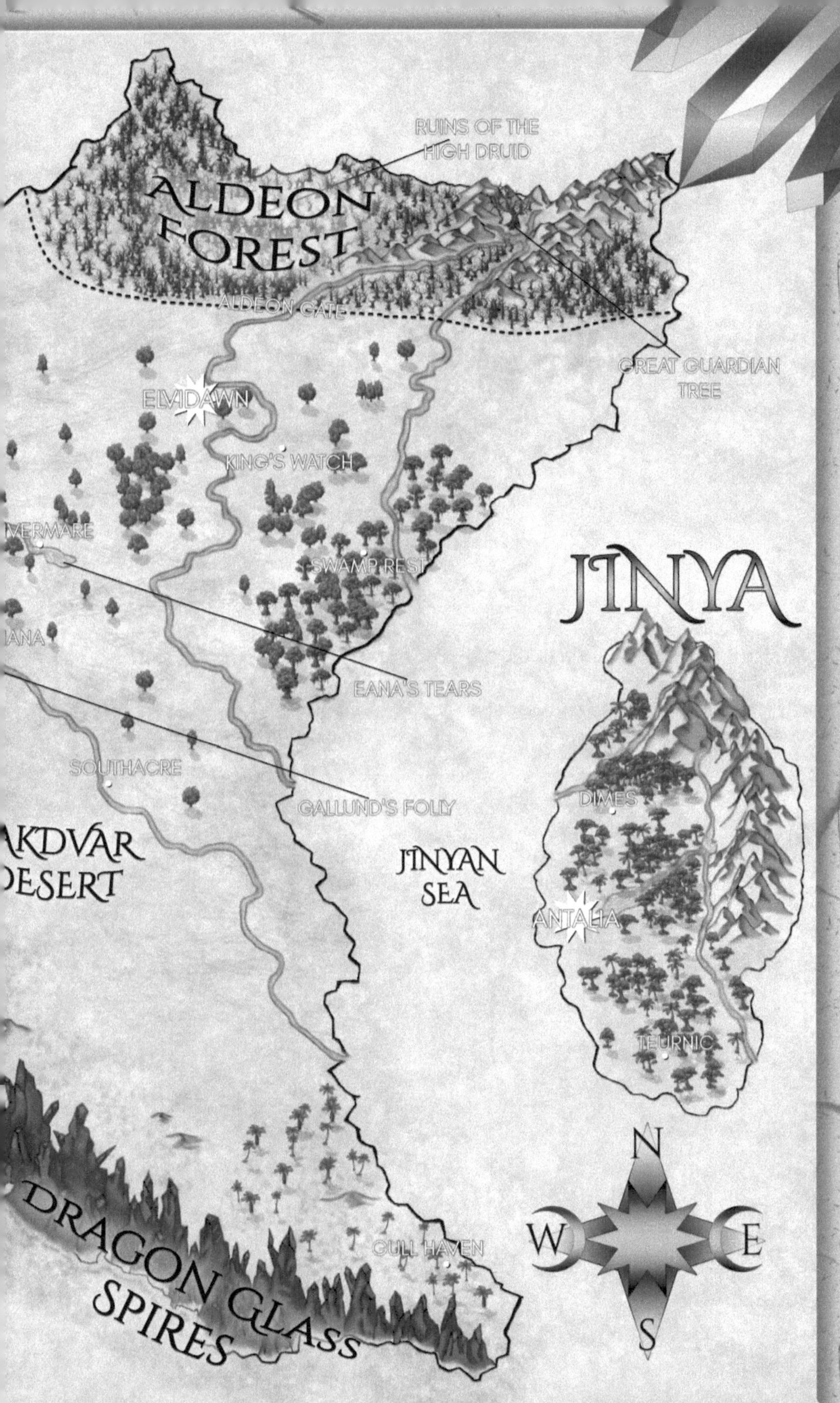

RUINS OF THE
HIGH DRUID
ALDEON
FOREST
ALDEON GATE
GREAT GUARDIAN
TREE
ELVIDAWN
KING'S WATCH
JINYA
VERMARE
SWAMP REST
EANA
EANA'S TEARS
SOUTHACRE
DIMES
GALLUND'S FOLLY
AKDVAR
DESERT
JINYAN
SEA
ANTALIA
DRAGON GLASS
SPIRES
GULL HAVEN
TEURNIC
N
W
E
S

Edited by Juniper Ink and Co

Edited by Black Quill Editing

Cover Design © Fantastical Ink

Part 1-4 Artwork by Lauren Hamlin, Black Cat Print Co.

Chapter Header Crystal Art by Lauren Hamlin, Black Cat Print Co.

Chapter Background Art by C.N.Maxwell

Map Design by C.N.Maxwell

Published by © Arcantus Worlds Publishing

ISBN (Hardback) 978 1 7347348 4 3

ISBN (Paperback) 978 1 7347348 1 2

ISBN (Ebook) 978 1 7347348 8 1

www.authorcnmaxwell.com

TO FREE THE RISING STORM

The ReEmergence Chronicles

C.N. MAXWELL

THE ELVEN LANGUAGE OF XALADOR

Attention, Xaladorians! Upon The ReEmergence, you may find some Elven-blooded speaking amongst each other in a language you've never heard before. Fear not, and pay no heed. This language cannot be learned. However, if you are eager to try, here are the basics that may give you a more insightful reading experience. Note: if you find yourself already understanding this magical speech, congratulations on your reemergence. Be safe, *yrçen.*

VOWEL SOUNDS:

Where these real diacritics are used in many languages throughout universes, they are used as such in Elvish.

Á á - /'a/ (as in *apple*)

A a - /ă/ (as in *ah*)

AE ae - /ā/ (as in *fate*)

E e - /ə/ (as in *pet*)

Í í - /ē/ (as in *eat*)

I i - /ī/ (as in *eye*)

Ö ö - /ō/ (as in *oath*)

Uu - /ū/ (as in *root*)

Y y - /'i/ (as in *ill*)

CONSONANT AND DIGRAPH SOUNDS:

While most of the consonants stay the same as they would be in Common, some make different sounds depending on the diacritics or notes below.

Ç ç - /'k/ - (as in *kid*)

J j - /zh/ - (akin to the French *ji* like in *bonjour*)

LL ll - /y/ (as in *you*)

R r - when at the end of a word, /'aər/ (as in *air*), otherwise tapped, not rolled

Ś ś - /'sh/ (as in *shop*)

AR ar - this digraph also makes /'aər/ (as in *air*)

ELVISH RUNES
AND THEIR COMMON COUNTERPARTS

Á A AE B Ç D E

F G H Í I J K

L LL M N O P Q

R S Ś T U V

W X Y Z

ELVISH

DICTIONARY

FEEL FREE TO BOOKMARK THIS PAGE—YOU'LL NEED IT.

álaçarna - fire

adöneś - courage

arí - love

aríma - darling, sweetheart (pet name between lovers)

aryn - fate

Arynáthi - fate bound

çlíöça - disguise

çor - ball/sphere

çruthi - create

çli - in

çlina - into

dias - come

dö - of

dras - venom

eçor - a magic circle; visual representation for a wizard's spell

et - she

ethari - ground (as in to root something or someone)

fich - bring

gasi - this

graeśta - help

hara - great

hart - soul

hirul - permission

ieth - a sound of exasperation (oh, ah, etc.)

ignaes - ignite

íjaç - banish

ít - the

jdimen - forgive

kevlla - dance

kríev - blooded (as in Elven-blooded)

Kríevas - Veins (The Veins of the Arcane)

ladrön - thunder

lla - where

löth - stop/cease

maer - rain

medaes - magic

medaesí - spell

nánöweth - nexus

na - to

naev - up

nen - we

neśta - heal

neváçína - invisibility

ni - me

ölst - rise

ölsta - rising

ölsty - wake

öpstupae - dazzle

örö'hith - reemerge

öśnív - spider

philam - vial/bottle for holding potions

praeśte - grant (as in approve)

rö - is

rynd - shield

rys- change

saeör - free (as in liberate)

sam - room

sçölith - ward

shöni - gods

śíçaevr - frost

Śi - I

te - and

thryng - wring out/draw out

tul - may

váöd - from

vadák - cast

vadáki - casting

vatha - confine

víd - see

vi - my

vŏ - you

vŏlat - have

vyl - elf

vyl'kríev - Xaladorians with elf ancestors (Elven-blooded)

Vylaryś - Elvish

wyn - light

wyn'kevlla - lightning (*light dance*)

xera - storm

xutha - bind

ylustrís - illustrate

yrçae - arcane

yçaedös - arcane energy

yrçen - mage

DWARVISH

THE LANGUAGE OF GOR THORÜM

The dwarves are very proud of their culture and have encouraged (quite loudly) Xaladorians to learn the basics for communication over the ages. Best get to studying if you want to be on good terms with the adamant folk of Gor Thorüm.

VOWEL SOUNDS:

Most are similar to what is found in Common, but with some exception. More on these in another lesson. All vowels must be pronounced in the very back of the throat.

Ö ö - /ō/ (as in *oath*)

Ü ü - /ū/ (as in *root*)

CONSONANT AND DIGRAPH SOUNDS:

Like the vowels, these are similar to those in Common, with exception.

J j - /y/ (as in *you,* or *fjord*)

R r - heavier tap than that of Elvish, but not quite a roll of the tongue

D d - pronounced as /d/ but instead of speaking with the tongue behind the teeth, it starts between, almost creating a /th/ sound.

Ei ei - /īē/ (spoken like eye-ee)

DWARVISH

DICTIONARY

FEEL FREE TO BOOKMARK THIS PAGE—YOU'LL NEED IT.

alöfheim - farewell

arn - her

da - father

delva - going

elskairn - toddler

elskairv - toddlers

fenoth - dishonorable

galdarth - burns

garz - damn

garzül - dammit

gef - with

ilrn - to

jünoc - you're

kar - it

knül - try

lanza - flirt

ret - not

svitoth - family; one that is not of blood, but found

CONTENT WARNING

This book, and *The ReEmergence Chronicles* as a whole, is not intended, nor recommended, for anyone under the age of 18.

To Free the Rising Storm contains the following possible triggers:

Domestic abuse of a parental figure, thoughts of suicide, attempted sexual assault (not carried out by any romantic interest), mentions of rape, conversations about infertility and miscarriage, parental death, and grief.

To Free the Rising Storm contains the following explicit content:

Graphic sex scenes—including heavy foreplay and oral sex, all which are written in detail and are not censored— language and profanity, gore and blood.

This is a work of fiction.
Please proceed with these warnings in mind.

For Lance,
because you freed my storm.

This is our world. Let's watch it take flight.

PART I: BEGINNINGS

CHAPTER 1

Mae

I didn't fear death. I begged for it. Nightly.

Wax dripped onto my hand, down my wrist, hardening over the fresh bruises adorning my skin. I ignored the burn as I drifted into my thoughts, watching the dancing flame atop the candle in my hand, the only source of light in my bedroom tonight save the distant flashes of the oncoming storm.

Although I knew they'd fall on deaf ears, I said my prayers. The gods had been silent for generations, so why would I be any different than the rest of Xalador to receive divine intervention? Still, praying made me feel less alone sometimes, if only because my whispering drowned out the voices from downstairs.

Mother was still yelling.

Father was still drunk.

Nights like these seemed unending. I lost track of the moments I'd been sitting here under my window, staring at the bruises my father had left on me for being the demon I was not. A drip of wax fell to the hardwood floor and for a moment—for a critical beat—I pondered what would happen if I just...let the candle fall. Wondered if the flames would hurt as bad as the pain I dealt with daily.

1

I would watch without remorse, see this house turned to ash if I could burn one final time.

But the wind blew in from the window and snuffed the fire, the draft cold and saturated with the smell of rain. I breathed in the air, then let out a sigh in defeat, awaiting my afflictions to begin their nightly torment.

The fighting downstairs died out, the front door opening and slamming shut.

He must have left again…

Left to go elsewhere. Somewhere he could drink more, fuck more, spend more.

It was another hour before I decided to change into my chemise. Goosebumps rose all over my body as the chilly and humid air kissed my bare, ashen-white skin. I preferred this temperature though—couldn't deny the strange tingling and satisfying feeling that came over me right before it rained.

I went to lock the window, glancing up just as lightning scattered across the midnight sky.

And with the first clap of thunder, a screech tore from my throat.

My veins seemed to course with liquid fire, racing up and down my arms, pumping into my chest until I couldn't breathe. The roaring throb of my heart pounded in my ears. I gasped and groaned, crawling to my bed, gripping the quilt and screamed for Mother.

What seemed like hours later, keys jangled outside my door before it was unlocked. She came in, hair tousled, eyes swollen and red. "What is it now?" she growled.

I couldn't respond. I felt like I was burning from the inside out.

With an exasperated huff, she came to my side, pressing her hand against my sweat-drenched forehead. "You do not feel fever-ish, Mae," she said with narrowed eyes.

The pain raked down my shivering torso into my stomach. I curled around myself and managed, "It hurts so bad."

I hardly noticed her leave my side, coming back with a wet cloth she lazily laid over my head as she reminded me, "We've been to the physician. He told us there is *nothing* wrong with you."

But there was. There had to be.

I buried my face in my hands, muffling curses on my tongue. "Then, just…leave me alone."

Mother scoffed. "Leave you alone? You're the one who screamed for me. Gods' sake, girl, I won't put up with this attention-seeking ruse much longer and neither will your father."

I almost laughed at that one. He hadn't put up with it since it began.

She went on after a yawn, "Between you waking me up at *tormish* hours of the morning, and worrying about your father's where-abouts, I'm exhausted."

I couldn't hide the snarl on my face—I'd long since forgotten the last time I'd slept through the night without torment.

One more sharp jab down my spine left me hunching over.

And then the storm brought rain.

Release swept through me. My tight chest loosened. For a moment, my blood went cold before washing with warmth and bringing relief. As if the storm itself had been my cure.

Mother eyed me. "Gone so soon?"

I turned on my side away from her, curling up beneath my quilt. I said nothing in response. She stomped out, the slam of the door bringing fresh tears to my eyes. I was left in the dark, the silence a reminder I was suffering alone.

I had always been sickly. I often came down with colds, and meals didn't always agree with my sensitive stomach. I'd gotten used to those hindrances, but then some sort of illness had overwhelmed me two years ago, bringing me painful flares nightly. No one could give me an explanation of what it was, or how I had developed it. At one time, I thought it was a lingering symptom due to falling from a tree and breaking my left arm as a child, for the flare always seemed to be worse in my wrist and lower arm. But oftentimes, it would start in my chest or stomach, flowing through my body like a boiling river.

Elros's physician diagnosed me as *deranged* when his tonics did nothing for me. A trip to another city to see a different physician was costly, and my father was too stingy with his coin, even though he took a merchant trip to the Twin Cities every season. Besides, my parents didn't believe I was in pain.

Relishing the cool mattress against my clammy skin, I tried to find sleep as I lay and listened to the wind rattle my window shutters, the rain dripping down the glass. Lightning brightened my room in flashes, tagged with roaring thunder.

Being born on the autumnal equinox, it was no surprise I found peace within storms. They were quite frequent during autumn in this region of Xalador, rolling in from the northern coast of the Serpent Sea and providing rain for the evergreen hills Elros nestled between. Nature's chaos was like my own lullaby, rocking me to sleep like a babe in her mother's arms.

Although I wasn't sure I knew what it was like to have a mother whose touch was so gentle, her arms made all right in the world. My mother loved me in her *own* ways. She loved dressing me up in lavish gowns, covering my pale face with rouge and kohl, pulling my corsets so tight they forced my gaunt figure to have hips, and decorating my neckline in jewels. She loved buying expensive things, leaving them in boxes and chests for me to find as she awaited my expression of gratitude. I always gave her what she wanted—a bright smile and an ear to listen to her newest lecture. Indeed, every gift had a price tag as she'd often remind me by saying, "I'm trying to prepare you for marriage, Mae. You're beautiful, but that white hair of yours does nothing but ward off men. You need something to *distract*."

She also loved pretending I didn't have the features I possessed.

I was born with the *Pallid Curse*.

According to an old fable, a rare demonic bloodline had been passed on to certain Xaladorians throughout the land. A quiet, inherited curse that only appeared through the children born with white hair. Evidently, most of the babies were stillborn, the tale claiming the gods chose to smite them of their demonic spirit before they took their first breath. Those who lived were thought to be pillars of chaos, their blood monstrous enough to even deny the gods' will.

I was the only Pallid Cursed in Elros, and my white hair set me apart from everyone around me. However, my purple irises were as bright as the citizens born with boldly colored hair and eyes—Elven-blooded. Because neither of my parents had the curse, nor did they have any unusual hues to their hair and eyes, I often wondered where my elven blood came from.

That unanswered question had always kept the lips of Elros's citizens thick with gossip and rumors ever-growing.

In the eye of the public, I was Rucas Mordaunt's shy, sheltered, strangely beautiful daughter he doted on, and he was the benevolent martyr; a man who graciously fathered a woman with the Pallid Curse. Behind closed doors and drawn curtains, I was the abomination he was obligated to foster; the alleged demon he beat and slapped when I stepped outside a line he drew, or when he was drunk enough to want to.

His unadulterated loathing for me began when he returned from a yearlong merchant trip to find I'd been born. Mother had been told she was barren after years of trying to conceive, but had indeed fallen pregnant and was unaware for many weeks after Rucas left. No amount of denying she'd laid with another convinced him otherwise—my white hair was all the evidence he needed to believe Mother had cursed our family with her actions.

As a child, I often felt like I was just going through the motions, obeying him no matter what he told me to do. I grew into a fortress full of cold secrets, unable to make many friends. Those I did have remained unaware.

But ever since I developed my affliction, I had become someone different. A fight that didn't belong to me seemed to brew within my veins, my very bones.

He was just always one step ahead.

When I turned of marrying age a week ago, Rucas quickly reminded me I was not available to just *anyone*. I wasn't allowed to tryst. Frankly, I was surprised he wanted to marry me off at all, given he'd lose control over me after I was wed.

But when I learned who he had chosen, who I was *allowed* to marry, I recognized his plot set in motion. The bastard he deemed worthy was the son of Elros's physician. Wylan Welch had always kissed the path Rucas walked on, and also owed him a great amount of money. What better a debt paid than a guaranteed husband for his usurer's wretched, cursed daughter?

But marrying Wylan's son was just locking me into a life of more torture. Willem Welch had already proven what he would do to me once he *owned* me. This was nothing but Rucas's chance to finally get rid of me.

I couldn't let it happen. I wanted to choose love for myself. There was someone else who had held my captivation for too long to just give up.

I wanted happiness.

I wanted freedom.

I just didn't know how I was supposed to break my chains when I was so powerless.

I didn't sleep much after my flare. My head swirled with the same nightmare I'd had every night for two years. Images of ominous, violet clouds and a thunderous voice screaming the same thing over and over. It always ended with crystals shattering across my vision, the flashes of lightning reflecting every color imaginable. I only pulled myself from the bed when the sun demanded I rise, my heavy limbs and burning eyes begging for more sleep. Unfortunately, that was never an option for me.

Limping on sore legs to my vanity, I found myself astounded by the woman staring back at me in the mirror. With dark circles under my eyes, and pale hollowed cheeks, I hadn't realized how much the sleepless nights were starting to take their toll. I practically glared at myself, not in anger but because opening my exhausted eyes was still difficult. I made no effort to straighten my posture as I began to braid my hair, still sticky from sweat. I had to make sure I looked presentable to help Rucas and Mother at the shop. Truthfully, I didn't know how I was going to manage that. I was already in a horrendous mood. Not to mention the walk to town, the people I'd have to smile at even though I had nothing to smile about…

Finding that strength, that *will*, was almost as hard as getting out of bed.

But asking to take the morning to recover would bring me more harm than good, so I pushed myself from the chair and wobbled dizzily over to my wardrobe. I was just about to pull on my favorite violet tunic when Mother allowed herself into my room without so much as a knock on my door.

"No, no, no. Off with that. You're wearing a dress today," she tiffed, shooing away the tunic.

I was too tired to argue, so I chose a magenta dress instead. Mother tried to hide her wince at my choice before she carped, "It's about time you got up. Half the morning is gone and we need you at the shop."

"I'm aware."

I turned to see she had placed a small box on my bed. She pulled me back in front of the vanity and made me sit, the bright smile growing on her face telling me she had another gift for me from Latera.

The smile also told me she would be ignoring the happenings of the night before.

As she lifted the top off the box, the first thing that caught my attention was the diamond-shaped jewel, iridescent in colors of reds and oranges. The morning sun beamed off the facets of the gem as Mother lifted the piece—a circlet—causing red shimmers to dance around my room.

I took a shallow breath as she nestled it upon my brow. "It's beautiful."

"Quite so." She sighed. "Your father and I are so very sorry we were away for your birthday. I hope this makes up for it."

"Yes, of course," I replied, surprised at the mention of my birthday at all. They had been absent on my birthday for the past six years. "Thank you, Mother. I will wear it often."

As I went to take it off, she smacked my hand away. "What in Xalador are you doing, girl? Leave it on."

I blinked. "Don't you think this is a bit much for working at the shop?"

"Of course not. Think of the people you'll see. Your future husband."

Acid pooled in my stomach. Always a price tag, indeed.

"You're a Mordaunt, Mae," she reminded me as she pulled stray white curls from my braid and twisted them around the silver wiring. "Nothing short of nobility."

I huffed a laugh. "A crown is not what I seek, Mother."

She scoffed. "No, just laziness and a wasted morning." She turned her nose and began to walk out. "Your father needs your help with some items we purchased on our trip. Be downstairs soon."

The door clicked behind her, leaving me to stare in the mirror once more. I ground my teeth, biting back the fight building in me as I glowered at the headpiece.

I don't want to do this anymore.

Then don't.

I pinched the bridge of my nose, thoughts aggravating the ache in my head. Since the pain had started, it was as if there were two separate beings up in my consciousness, battling over the last word.

I looked into the mirror, lips pressed together, but I couldn't smile.

You are powerful. Prove it.

CHAPTER 2

Mae

Mother's scribbling on parchment was the first thing I heard as I stepped off the stairs, followed by Rucas's deep guttural voice bellowing as he counted. Coming into the dining room, I had to blink twice to make sure I wasn't still in a dream state.

The large table's surface was buried in new merchandise, but these weren't necessities or goods for the people of Elros. It was as if my parents had dredged up an ancient king's tomb and the treasure that had been buried with him was now piled up where we should have been eating breakfast. Books with intricate spines were stacked up higher than Rucas in his hunched position. There were pieces similar to the circlet on my head, and necklaces and bracelets set with sparkling gemstones I'd never seen before. Scrolls still sealed with wax stamps lined the floor under the table.

I crossed to the other side, coming into view of several bottles and vials in front of Mother and her parchment, each one filled with liquids of every color, bubbling and spewing within their glass as if they were boiling. As Mother lifted one, I realized they weren't hot at all.

"What...is all of this?" I whispered to Mother.

She only pressed a finger to her mouth. Rucas's voice rose as he counted, glaring daggers my way. I knew better than to disrupt him; his loss of concentration would have me locked in my room.

They had just returned last night from their third merchant trip this year. Since Elros was located in the northwestern part of Xalador, the chilly temperature from the Serpent Sea made our summers mild and our winters long and bitter. Growing sugarcane was nearly impossible, and the ground stayed too cold for too long to germinate good wheat crops. So, Rucas and his merchant guild traveled often to trade fish, tools, and lumber for stock Elros required. His merchanting business had always kept Elros afloat and kept my parents above the rest financially.

But the things in our dining room displayed a different side of my parents' wealth I'd never seen before. None of it was essential. The greed was almost palpable in the air, the smells of metal and dust overwhelming.

"287, 288, 289…" Rucas counted slowly, with emphasis, every gold piece falling into the chest beneath him with a clink. More gold for the Mordaunts. Two hundred more pieces for us instead of the poor.

The headpiece on my brow suddenly felt very heavy.

I had to step over more scrolls to get to the kitchen. Dirty plates were piled in our water basin, and by the looks of the leftover oats and half-eaten fruit, I realized the owner of The Alderbright tavern had come to serve my parents breakfast. They ordered food to be brought to them often, especially on busy mornings.

"Is there any left for me?" I asked.

Mother didn't look up from her parchment as she chided, "You slept in."

I took a deep breath, nails digging into my palms to seize the crude gesture on my fingers. Sleeping was the last thing I was doing.

Searching the pantry left me more frustrated. The shelves were practically bare, minus a few of Rucas's favorite sausages hanging from hooks in the ceiling. I wouldn't have dared to eat those. I settled for a pear I grabbed from a bowl on the countertop.

"Mother," I murmured. "I'm ready to help Father."

Her head lifted, lips pursed together in a tight line. "You can wait," she said through her teeth, glancing at Rucas gravely.

A rough sound came from his throat as he looked up slightly from the gold in his hands, shooting us both a dark glare before continuing his counting. I waited as patiently as I could, careful not to seem like I was fidgeting. Finally, his chair skidded on the hardwood floor as he rose to his feet, fists clenched at his sides as he glared down at Mother.

"We didn't make enough this trip, Fantine," he growled at her, as if the fault fell to her alone.

Mother's mouth parted and closed twice before she answered, "We sold so much—"

"We'll have to go back in a fortnight. Make the arrangements."

Mother didn't argue.

Rucas snapped his head in my direction. His chin dipped. "You gave it to *her*?"

He was looking at the circlet on my brow. One step forward had me backing into the counter.

Mother stopped him. "Rucas, dear, you know I purchase things for our daughter every trip. Besides, we *were* gone for her birthday again."

He snarled as he looked me over. "Something so exquisite doesn't belong on someone with the Pallid Curse."

I bit the inside of my lip, hard enough to keep the expletives snuffed. My blood ran hot, stinging under my skin.

Mother scoffed. "Even with her curse, she's still a Mordaunt. She *is* exquisite."

Rucas ignored her, uncorking the bottle beside him and taking a swig of ale. Another day, another bottle.

Picking up a stack of strange books, he shoved them into my arms, then grabbed more for himself and sneered in the direction he wanted me to follow. "Come."

It was then I realized Mother hadn't stood. She wasn't coming with us. My body buzzed in alarm. I always tried to avoid being anywhere alone with him.

Giving her one last pleading look—which she ignored entirely—I followed him out the door.

It was a chilly morning, but the sun's rays brought warmth to the slight breeze blowing through the hills, petrichor rich and strong in the air. Raindrops still dripped from the manor rooftops in our neighborhood as we took the road toward the market. I dug my feet hard against the gravel road as the path came to a slope, struggling to balance the books in my arms. Every step I took made them wobble, and the pile was just high enough to prevent me from being aware of where my feet landed.

Relieving some of the cramping in my arms, I shifted the stack down a bit, glancing at the book on top to make sure it wouldn't fall. A silver-inked title spread across the dark-blue cover, the letters bearing interesting marks above and below certain curves and strokes, reading the words—

My breath hitched.

I stared at the first word. Then the second.

I could *read* them. Perfectly.

I had never learned how to read. Not in our common language, not in *any* language in Xalador.

And this language, I had never seen, but I *knew* it. It was the same of the words I'd heard in my nightmares for the past two years —screamed at me by someone concealed in the folds of my mind. And I comprehended all of it; the letters and marks and principles as if I had known how to read and speak this tongue my entire life.

My heart slammed against my chest, the silver ink enchanting me. *Ít Nánöweth. The Nexus*—

A hot jolt suddenly coursed up my left arm, scattering through muscle and nerve. I cried out, the control over my impulses failing entirely. The books tumbled downhill, tripping Rucas when they landed in his path. His stack went to the ground as well and he whirled around.

"What in Torm are you doing?" he hissed, jaw tight in a menacing scowl. He grabbed my arms in a brutal grip, shaking me as he barked, "You dare to put on this ruse now? You cursed bitch!"

I was thrown aside to my knees. As I gazed through tear-blurred eyes, down to the books scattered along the slope, a sharp, high-pitched ringing pealed in my mind. My shaking hands reached up to cover my ears—

I took another shrill gasp, reeling myself away from the book I could somehow read. It was radiating with glittering light, pulsing with every blink. The terror that swelled in my stomach was something I'd never felt before.

This...

This seemed all wrong.

Why are they glowing? Why do I know this language?

This is what you seek...

Shut up. Shut up.

But something about it all felt familiar. And *right*.

I tasted blood, realizing too late I had been biting down on my lip through a wave of pain. It was bad enough to make me want to rip every layer of my skin off, to bone and muscle, to get out whatever in Torm was making me hurt.

Neighbors in the surrounding houses began to emerge and look toward the scene I was making. Only then, when we had an audience, did Rucas kneel before me.

The harsh expression on his face became dramatically soft as he purred, "My dear Mae..." He reached out for me. "Let's get you back to the house for a bit."

And even through the pain, all of the resentment for the man before me was visible in the icy glare I granted him. "Don't. Touch. Me."

He matched my anger with his own, the mask of care he'd plastered on not a moment before melting off completely.

Someone called to us, asking if we needed help. Rucas told him no. But that person rushed up to us anyway. I looked up through my blurred vision at the masculine figure wearing familiar clothes, throwing an evergreen cloak over me as I gasped out, "Eryx...help me."

I couldn't remember a damn thing.

As I blinked the last of my tears away, my awareness came back with a strange displacement. I was sitting on my knees, hunched over, hugging myself tightly in the middle of the storage room of

Rucas's shop, *Mordaunt Treasures*. I wasn't sure how long I'd been here, or who had brought me here.

But I was surrounded by more books.

I stilled when my memory of the flare and the glowing book came back to me, gaping at the tomes and novels as if they might jump out. Despite the aching of tense muscles, everything was...normal. As I lifted a book written in Common, only recognizing the letter *M* because I knew my name started with that, I contemplated if it had all been a figment of my imagination.

There in the doorway leading to the front of the shop, Eryx stood with his hands crossed in front of his chest like some bloody guardian statue before an ancient portal. By the look on his face, that outlandish, conscientious temper I absolutely despised in him had been roused.

"Are you all right?" he asked, voice so stiff I almost didn't catch the worry for me in it.

I huffed in response. "Did I pass out?"

He shook his head. "Not exactly. It was the same thing as last time."

He was talking about the flare he'd witnessed two weeks before. What he had described as a "distant stare" was more than a few moments of being in a daze for me. It was when the pain began to wane, the heat ebbing from my blood as if it was being called away somehow, and for an indefinite amount of time, all I knew was an unexplainable nothingness. I could sometimes remember colors and shapes. Voices, even, but no conversation.

These were new symptoms of my affliction and didn't happen with every flare. However, I'd never suffered one so close to the other.

"You've been staring at nothing for almost an hour," Eryx told me.

Or for so long.

They were getting worse.

I stood on shaky legs. It was then that Eryx moved, instantly at my side to support me. "You need to not be so stubborn and ask for help."

I stifled a laugh. "Sorry. I forget you give a damn."

"Of course I do," was all he said. My friend was a man of few words and small smiles.

And of course he cared. Eryx had always been like a brother to me and was often there when I found myself in trouble. Small troubles, like disputes I had with sellers in the market or impudent customers. He didn't know about my abuse. For side work outside of hunting, he was employed by Rucas as an escort on merchant trips, and had always thought my father was a great man.

His mother had been my wetnurse, and eventually my nanny when my parents went out of town. Those days I always looked forward to, even though the RothHall's house had been cold and I often had to sleep beside Eryx to keep warm. There had been many times I'd wanted to tell him about what happened behind closed doors, especially since he had always been so protective of me. But even though we had been friends since we were young, there had always been something I didn't quite trust about Eryx. Not to mention he had already lived with so much heartbreak.

After his parents died of a sudden illness, his brother Darrick left for Elvidawn, leaving him to bury them alone. Then a few years later, his wife, my friend, Kendra died unexpectedly. The light behind his amber eyes had been snuffed out by a shadow and the length of it stretched with each passing season. It had been a year last spring.

My problems...he didn't need another thing on his shoulders. I'd be rid of Rucas eventually.

Maybe.

"What happened to the books I dropped?" I asked.

"I helped your father get them inside," Eryx replied, pointing to the far corner where books lay in many stacks and piles. It occurred to me Rucas had more books to put up for sale in his shop than he'd ever had before.

"I don't know why Father is trying to sell all of these when everyone can just go to the Wynharts' library," I said to Eryx as I picked up a book on top of a stack. This one didn't glow, but the language was the same.

Eryx shrugged. "His explanation was that some people like to *own* books."

"Or maybe he's just trying to get under Professor Wynhart's skin," I grumbled.

Years ago, when Professor Mattis Wynhart proposed the idea of a free school and library within his own home, Baron Kenrad granted him such. The school would be funded through taxes, allowing anyone to come and gain an education. Rucas put up quite the argument; his prudish, elitist mentality deeming education a practice for only those fortunate.

However, he had just proclaimed himself head merchant and made sure the Baron knew his newly assembled merchant guild would become the foundation of Elros. If the town needed something, the guild would see it through. He didn't realize that meant the school and library as well. Forced into a partnership he didn't agree with, he had remained unkind to the Wynharts all these years.

Though his grudge wasn't the reason I couldn't read Common. He had never said it, but I knew even though I was part of a fortunate family, an education would give me tools I could use against him. If I knew how to write, I could easily slip a note to someone explaining my situation. He kept me ignorant for the sake of control.

When the topic of my education had come up over the years, I was always forced to lie. Even Eryx believed I couldn't read because I had chosen not to learn. It was just one of the many fabrications I'd created to prevent Rucas's wrath.

But looking down at this strange language I could indeed read, a small spark of hope ignited inside of me.

Eryx and I moved up front, and I began to tidy up trinkets and antiques on the shelves. Rucas was outside washing the windows as he did every morning when I heard him growl, "What do you want?"

My heart tumbled over itself, a smile trying to rise. Rucas's large stature blocked my view from the person he was grumbling at, but I knew. I always knew.

"I've come to place my usual weekly order, of course," a man's rich and steady voice replied, sending my pulse racing.

Rucas shifted and crossed his arms. "You can wait until I'm finished out here."

Eryx lifted his head from a stack of books he was organizing. "What's going on out there?" he asked me.

"It appears Varys Wynhart is pissing Father off early today," I said coyly as I turned back to my dusting. It was quite the coincidence Varys was here now when we had just spoken of his father.

"Bah," Eryx grunted. "Your father would have less pests bothering him if he designated another merchant in the guild to handle the Wynharts' orders."

I made no effort to hide an eye-roll. "Divvying out control? Father would *never*."

He raised a brow, and I bit my tongue, then changed the subject, "So, all of these new items are an investment or something? I've never seen Mother and Father bring back such strange things."

His eyes avoided my face—a telltale sign he was trying to avoid the truth. I crossed my arms and stared at him hard.

He shot me a matching glare. "I hate it when you look at me that way."

"Then don't hide things from me. I'm not stupid and I'll find out eventually." I tossed my rag up on the front counter. "I feel like I should know what makes these things so important to my family."

And why in Torm there were bubbling bottles and glowing books with a language I could somehow read.

"Investments, yes," he surrendered. "Don't be surprised if your father decides to take several more trips this year."

"He mentioned something like that this morning. He didn't make enough profit?"

Eryx shook his head. "No, he did not. Or at least…not enough to buy necessities."

I stifled a mocking laugh. "Then why exactly did he buy hundreds of gold's worth of trinkets and jewelry?"

Eryx didn't respond to that.

I huffed after a beat, turning to a table in the corner piled with bottles similar to those I'd seen earlier. I raised one up to the sunlight and froze. There it was, the same language I could read.

Ösnív Dras.

Spider Venom?

I swirled the thick black liquid around and watched the dregs slide down the inside of the glass. "Where did these things come from?"

Eryx perched himself on a stool. "From what I understand, earlier this year, a wealthy halfling family and their caravan came through the docks of Latera, their stock overflowing with things Xalador has not seen in ages. Before long, word spread, and apparently, all of these items were said to be magical."

I snapped my head to him. *"Magic?"*

He pointed to the circlet on my brow. "Rucas bought that from a woman claiming it could send a ray of light bursting from the jewel if the wearer has the affinity to do so." He scoffed. "She also threatened your father when he wouldn't pay her what she wanted, claiming the piece was much more valuable than what he offered. She gave in when her companions talked her down. Mad woman…"

I placed the bottle back on the table, the glass tinkling as I ran my fingers over the many different corks of the others behind it. "So, magical jewelry and baubles. Sounds like Father was swindled."

A nod. "I warned him of the same. He…" His eyes dodged mine again. "He didn't agree."

I frowned. There was apprehension written all over my friend's face, his gaze blank, distant, and pensive as he stared forward. I was familiar with that sort of look. I often found myself dazing when a memory hit me. Recollections of yelling, a slap setting my ears to ring, the pain of Rucas's grasp, his smile when I begged him to stop…

It seemed his mask was beginning to slip.

But before I could ask, Eryx said, "Doesn't matter anyway. Your father believes people are going to buy this stuff whether they know what it is or not. In Latera, there's a fascination among the merchants. They're trading these bottles and sticks wrapped in beads and crystals—taking them in payment over gold. Problem is, it's causing the prices of normal goods to rise. We had several merchants refuse to sell to us because we didn't have any of this magic shit to trade with. So…Rucas started buying it all. And before long, he was out of money and hadn't made profit."

I smirked. "That will come back to bite him, I'm sure."

I hoped.

"Perhaps. But the Fest of Change is coming up. He'll make it all back then."

I didn't respond. Everything on my tongue was cruel and couldn't be said.

Eryx came to my side, looking down at the bottles. "The merchants said these are potions," he said as he picked up a small vial of red liquid. "Mr. Welch smelled and examined them. They are possibly medicines from hundreds of years ago; tonics and potions to cure some of our deadliest plagues." His words became tense. "Shit that probably could have saved my ma and pa, or…"

I looked up to him. I knew what was running through his head as his words trailed off. "Eryx…"

He held up a hand. "Don't need your pity."

"I know what you're thinking." I took his shoulders. "If magic was ever real, even then, it wouldn't…"

I couldn't finish my thoughts aloud. *It wouldn't bring her back.*

He shrugged my hands off. "Perhaps *your* cure is in here though."

I raised a brow. "If Mr. Welch's tonics don't work, I doubt the bubbling gruel in these bottles will prove to be much better."

"I bet they taste better." Eryx only grunted at his joke.

I watched the sparkles and specks of light slide down the glass as he capsized another bottle. I could read that label as well. *Wyn Philam. Light Vial.*

"I don't believe drinking an ancient potion would do me much good," I said, thinking of all the possible things a vial of light could do to one's insides. "Unless my sickness is linked to my curse. Maybe it would finally put the demon inside of me out of its misery." It wasn't something I'd necessarily thought of, but on the other hand, there wasn't anything in the old tale stating cursed people had strange illnesses come over them either.

Eryx rolled his eyes. "Curses aren't real. Neither is magic. You have white hair because someone in your family did long ago and that's that. I really wish you'd stop believing such idiocy."

I frowned. He was extra moody today.

He took out his pipe, packing it with a blend of green and

cream-white leaves. "I'm leaving to hunt. I don't know when I'll be returning, but I'll see you then."

I only nodded in response. As he lit the pipe and walked out, the lingering smoke drifted toward me, the smell sweet and ripe. I waved it away when my eyes began to sting. I knew very well what was in that blend of pipe-weed.

He hadn't smoked moonshadow in two years.

CHAPTER 3

Mae

"It's barely noon. Come back later," Rucas's grumbling voice rang out through the shop as the door opened and shut.

The door opened again as someone cleared their throat. "Per our agreement, Mr. Mordaunt," Varys started with an instructional, yet flippant tone, "I'll remind you, once again, I come on the second day of the week, every week, before the library opens and right after the school lets out for the day."

I pressed myself against the wall of shelves in the back room. I wasn't supposed to be listening—I couldn't help it. My chest swelled with warmth as I dared to look over, catching a glimpse of dark-blue hair. As he followed Rucas, Varys's brighter blue eyes flicked to mine, just like they always seemed to do. I bit my lip to restrain a bashful grin.

He was the son of the man Rucas hated most—glancing at each other was just asking for trouble.

Despite Rucas's unwillingness to be kind to the Wynharts, Mattis and Varys were always around us. Varys and I had barely spoken to each other besides a few shop-related conversations, and had only shared secret looks in the market. We had no friendship, no memories together, because nothing was allowed between us. But he wasn't necessarily a stranger, and lately, when our eyes met—wherever they met—there was this undeniable connection. Something I couldn't explain. And my curiosity to have a longer, prohibited conversation with him had grown over the years as much as it scared me to know what consequences I would face.

"What do you need?" Rucas halfway mumbled the question.

"Twelve rolls of parchment," Varys relayed to him. "Each student has been tasked with some research—"

"I don't care *what* is going on in that school," Rucas sneered, "just tell me your bloody order."

Between their words, I had sidled my way to the door and peered around just enough to get a better view of them. They were at the counter now. Varys wove his fingers together behind his back before taking a long, steady breath, never dropping that sly smile he often wore. "The parchment. Three more bottles of ink. Our quills are about worn out, so let's order twenty more of those. We also need a few of those arithmetic books we received back in the spring. Four of them."

Rucas lazily wrote down what Varys told him before asking impatiently, "Anything else?"

Varys swept a few loose strands of his blue hair back. He'd always kept his hair a bit shaggy, but I wasn't sure why he didn't cut his bangs so they didn't hang in his sight so much.

His throat bobbed. "I was also sent to ask about my father's new spectacles—"

Rucas cut him off, "Yes, yes, they'll be ordered soon."

"You said previously at the end of summer you could get them in Latera, and since you've just returned from your trip..."

Rucas stilled, glancing over to the corner where several chests of new merchandise lay. "I...was forced to make some unexpected purchases instead."

"That's a shame." Varys's shoulders squared before flattening his hands on the counter surface. "We've already given you coin for them, so will we be getting a refund?"

Rucas's eyes dropped to where Varys's hands lay, nostrils flaring as he sucked on a tooth. "Your father can have his money back when I make time to fetch it from my coffers."

"Wouldn't fetching the coin now be easier than having to notate it in a ledger?" Varys asked coyly. "Do you really want to be in debt to the library?"

Rucas's jaw tightened as he pressed his fists into the counter, the wood creaking beneath his weight. "I go back in a few weeks," he said in a low, cold voice. "I can get the spectacles then."

I held my breath. I'd seen them argue before, but it had always been cordial, no matter what bluff Rucas pulled or how many forced smiles Varys presented. Varys had a way of getting under his skin, whether it be his words or the way he questioned Rucas's integrity when no one else would.

But the room was tense—*Varys* was tense as he shook his head and said through gritted teeth, "I think until you are ready to fulfill our order for sure, I'll be taking our money back. I would hate to have to inform the Baron of this poor excuse of extortion."

I pressed my hands to my mouth to hide the gasp as Rucas straightened, arms falling to his side. It was the first time I'd ever seen him stumped. Varys used to be a bit sheepish and socially inept, but his confidence now was admirable. I could not lie to myself. Seeing the man who dragged me through Torm every day and night backed into a corner, unable to escape...I enjoyed seeing him crumbling.

Rucas's mask was down, the darkness I often endured twisting his features, his fists clenched, knuckles white, eyes blazing. The very thought of him showing the same cruelty to Varys as he did to me—

I stepped into the room. Varys whipped his head to me as I met Rucas's gaze with my chin raised.

"M-Miss Mordaunt..." Varys said by way of greeting, as if he didn't already know I was here. "Good morning."

Rucas let out a very obvious cough before flinging open a small chest on the counter. "Here's your damn five silver, *boy*."

Varys's eyes trailed from where I stood to the coins. He sighed and pocketed the money, barely tipping his head in thanks before turning to leave. Rucas grumbled under his breath and marched out the side door.

My heart thundered as I watched Varys walk away with a stiffened back. I always seemed to have that effect on him. "Have a good day, Varys."

He paused in his steps and began to turn toward me when his eyes caught something on the table beside him. He lifted a bottle of thick, green liquid, thumb running over the label. Beneath his bangs, his eyes widened and he asked, "Where did this come from?"

"Latera," I said in a bored tone of voice, moving closer. "Father acquired some new merchandise."

He smirked. "I gathered that. This potion is...very old."

I tilted my head at that. "How do you know it's a potion?"

He swallowed before uttering a few incoherent words, then replied, "I mean, it's a bit evident such bottles would hold a solution akin to a potion or some sort of ancient elixir."

His eyes skimmed the label. Left to right.

Reading it.

"Though of course that is only an educated guess," he said, placing the bottle down and picking up another. "These labels are in Elvish. The dead language of magic and the elven race."

I couldn't stop the gasp, nor the paling of my face. His words hit me so hard, I took a step away from him. "I beg your pardon?"

Elvish. I could read *Elvish*?

Varys combed his hair back, eyes narrowing on me. "Are you all right, Miss Mordaunt?"

I regarded his radiant sapphire irises and hair as blue as the sheet of sky behind the stars just before dawn. Features determining his elven blood. That strange connection between us thrummed the longer I stared.

Pointing to the label of the bottle in his hands, I asked in a strained whisper, "Can you read that?"

He blinked at me. Then, at the label. With a cocked head and that sly smile of his, he asked, "Can you?"

I was about to respond when the store door flew open. My heart fell into my stomach.

With a sneer on his too-squared jaw, Willem Welch strode in as if he owned the place. Given that he was the man I would be forced to marry by the end of the season, he would eventually absorb the business, so his arrogance was right as rain.

He didn't, and would never, own me though.

My legs shook with the need for flight as Willem came closer.

"My, my...today is my lucky day," he drawled as his eyes scanned my body slowly, then glared at Varys. "I was coming to talk with Elros's finest merchant and managed to stumble upon Elros's finest amusement as well."

I inclined my head. "I'm glad you've found Father's array of mirrors."

His jaw tightened. Varys hadn't moved from his spot, nor had he taken his eyes off Willem, watching him carefully.

I bowed my head to both of them, quickly returning to the counter. If I made myself busy enough, Willem would go find Rucas, and I would be—

He was behind me suddenly, pressing my body against the counter. One hand snaked up to cup the underside of my breast, and I lost a breath in panic.

"I'll have you soon, sweetling," he whispered in my ear. "Out of that dress, that snobbish mouth on mine, and this white hair in my grip."

I snarled, pulling in my shoulders to force space between us. "You're a sick pig." I twisted my body, attempting to push him away. He didn't budge.

"*Hey!*" Willem was grabbed and whirled away. "Leave her alone, asshole."

Varys.

Oh, thank the gods.

I spun around just in time to see Willem jerk Varys toward him by his shirt, inches from him as he spat, "You need to mind your own fucking business, Wynhart."

A roguish smile played on Varys's lips, his eyes dropping to where Willem's hands gripped his collar.

I started, "No, Willem. You need to go—"

My words halted as I watched Varys force his arms up between them. A brief flash of shock crossed Willem's face before Varys twisted his arms and hurled him across the room. My hands shot to my cheeks as I watched Willem stumble, body slamming into a table of baubles and trinkets. Down each one went, clinking and clanking to the floor, glass shattering.

A muscle thrummed along Varys's jaw. Now towering over

Willem, he said ever so casually, "Don't make it my business, then, Welch."

Willem groaned and sat up on his knees.

Varys turned back to me. "Are you all right?"

I was absolutely speechless. As I stood there gaping at him, I realized how little I had seen him in the last few seasons. I'd been preoccupied with my own problems. Something about him was different. Something about the way he looked at me was different. Whatever it was had my heart pounding, my entire being wanting to stay beside him.

But when the side door opened and slammed shut, reality sped up. Rucas had come back into the store. He looked to the broken wares, to Willem, then narrowed his eyes on Varys. "Are you responsible for this, Wynhart?"

"No," I insisted, pointing a shaking finger at Willem. "He was defending me from this *snake*."

Willem feigned innocence as he looked at Rucas. "I was only making my advances of romance known, Mr. Mordaunt. I guess Wynhart here became rather envious."

Varys chuckled. "You're a damn coward, Welch."

Willem shot to his feet, and every march toward Varys was full of a threat.

I stepped between them. Willem's eyes widened, as did Rucas's. "Leave," I demanded. "Before I make you remember that night behind the butcher's shop. How I shoved my boot so hard into your bollocks you couldn't stand for a week—"

"That's *enough*," Rucas barked. I flinched at his tone, all courage banished from my blood.

Too far. I'd gone too far.

Rucas refused to meet my gaze, fists clenched at his sides as he came forward. "Wynhart, get out of my damn shop," he growled, "before I decide your father owes *me* money for all the shit you broke."

Varys's eyes darted between me and Willem before he took his leave.

There was something cautious and hesitant in his gaze as he went. It made my nerves writhe with warning.

The market at this hour was a melting pot of Elros citizens bustling about. Women gossiped as they shopped for vegetables, paying no attention to their children running circles around shopkeepers shouting about their great sale of the day. I dodged in and out of the crowd, combatting judging eyes from every direction. All semblance of pleasantries from me were gone, out the door the moment I bid Willem nothing more than a crude gesture before I left him and Rucas to talk about my obnoxious behavior. The scowl on my face deterred anyone from crossing my path, turning away the appalled stares of onlookers. Unfortunately, I could still hear them—their whispers were harsh enough to stop any other person in their tracks. I was used to it, and I didn't care anymore. Not when this day had gone to shit the moment I rose from the bed.

I came to the edge of the market and continued straight at a sharp decline. The path branched off in several directions, leading to the houses settled up on the hills off to the east.

When Elros was established, the Baron had priced the land depending on how level the terrain was. On the northwestern side, the wealthy bought up a massive plateau and built their manors on its flat top, never having to worry about sharing a hilltop with their neighbor. However, that was not the case for the middle or poorer class, who had been left to purchase slopes, building houses and farms practically on top of each other. This required heavy maintenance and those living in poverty usually couldn't afford to make repairs. In autumn, especially when it rained almost daily, houses slipped off their foundations or became circumstance of a mudslide.

It wasn't ideal how most of the citizens lived, and with the neighborhoods keeping the financial classes separate, it was no wonder there was an underlying tension throughout Elros. Especially when there were men like Rucas claiming power and superiority.

I stopped at the top, looking down into a small valley of wildflower-covered hills and quaint houses. From here, I could see the forest that spanned for miles north and south, the reds and oranges of autumn painted on every leaf, and the log walls around the perimeter of Elros. I would have to exit through the east gate to reach the stream, the main source of water for everyone in Elros. I knew from there, I'd cut through another passage, one that led me away from the possibility of encountering a group of women and servants gathering to wash laundry. I had no interest in their gossip, nor their judging stares.

Besides, I was going this way to escape for a moment. From people, from Rucas, from pain. Just for an hour or so. Enough time to clear my head, but not so long Rucas would wonder where I was. After my little outburst, he'd told me to go home instead of helping in the shop.

But I wasn't going home. I was going to my tree.

It had been a couple of years since I'd visited the tree I had climbed during a thunderstorm. The same tree I'd fallen from and broke my left arm as a young girl when lightning had struck its canopy. I still had the scar from my bone tearing through the flesh, though it had faded. And the tree itself had since died and fallen, leaving a clearing that had always felt like a place of peace and wonder.

The guardsmen paid no mind as I walked through the gate, the sound of crisp trickling of water growing louder with every step. Across the stream and deeper into the wood on the other side of the stream, the hills became cliffs with sharp drop-offs into the Serpent Sea. Built into one of these cliffs was a large manor where Elros's only dwarf citizen, Duros Cauldücen, lived with his wife—and daughter, a mean brute who was hostile to anyone she came near. I hadn't crossed her path too often because I had my own troubles and certainly did not need more.

But the only way to cross the stream was hopping along the same small boulders I knew the Cauldücen family used to get to town. During this season and with the constant rain, the stream's water level sometimes rose above those stones, making it impossible to cross without wading through icy water. I hoped the stream had receded since the storm last night.

I cut left and strayed from the path into a passage of higher grass and brush. Just beyond a spruce tree ahead, I could see the bank of the stream, relieved to find it low and crossable. I couldn't wait for the quiet, anticipating the relief in my legs when I could finally sit down.

I came around the wide rim of the spruce when something pulled my arm and spun me around. Panic sliced through me as I looked up into Willem's eyes, but I couldn't move, as if my feet had planted themselves.

"What did you find, Willem?" a voice asked. Theon Brooker, the mayor's son, stepped out from behind the spruce.

Willem chuckled, his breath heavy with ale. "Just a snob." He traced the entirety of my frame, licking his lips. "Come, sweetling. Let's have some fun."

I tugged away from him. He only gripped me harder. "Let me go."

Willem pulled me against him as Theon pressed himself into my back. I shoved my hips into both of them—I was locked in between. I was *trapped*.

"You fucking snakes!" I shrieked. "Let me go—"

Willem's hand slapped over my mouth.

Fear barreled down my spine.

"Let's not spoil those lips," Willem sneered. "Not *yet*."

My shouts were muffled as they dragged me over to the bank of the stream. I kicked and writhed, screaming as loud as I could, scraping my throat raw. They lowered me to the ground, taking the circlet off my head and tossing it away. As Theon held my arms above my head, Willem began to untie his trousers. I squeezed my eyes shut, his cold hands groping my legs, my thighs—

My arm surged with pain as I was suddenly overwhelmed with a flare. Desperation took over, my muscles spazzing, filling with a strength I didn't recognize. Theon's face scrunched as he struggled to keep my wrists pinned, and with another twist of my arms, I got free and struck his face. He fell backward into the stream, and I sunk my nails into Willem's neck. But another wave of pain made me go rigid, leaving me unable to stop him from locking my legs under him, his hands everywhere I didn't want. My stomach convulsed as he stroked himself with a wolfish grin.

"*No! No! No! Get off!*"

He gripped my bare hips.

I screeched, the outer rim of my vision exploding in white. An intense buzz vibrated in my bones as I shot up, clawing into his face and neck and chest, my fingers suddenly hot—

And from underneath my nails, a spark of light ignited. A snap cracked the air.

Willem was off—*blasted* off with a yelp of pain.

There was a voice crying out from the edge of the tree line, but I could barely hear anymore, deafened by the ringing in my ears.

My world spun, white blurring to violet stars until all I knew was blackness.

CHAPTER 4

Mae

Maelawyn...
      Why are you sleeping when you should be storming?
Maelawyn...
Maelawyn!

"Miss Mordaunt?"

I shot up, instantly throwing punches. "Get the fuck away—"

Bright, sapphire eyes shrouded in midnight-blue hair gazed into mine, robbing all air from my lungs.

Him.

Varys Wynhart sat on his knees before me, tightly gripping the strap of a book bag slung across his chest. He seemed guarded, and it didn't take me long to realize why. His pinched expression spoke of everything that had happened.

I looked down at the dusty gray cloak laying over me—his cloak. He must have covered me to conceal the bareness of the lower half of my body. Tears stung my eyes. Willem's touch lingered in places where I had only graced myself, the feeling like a thin coating of grime.

"Did he…" My throat was too dry to sort through all the questions looming over me.

Varys shook his head, watching me carefully. As if he was waiting for me to do something. "No. No, I don't think he got too far." He gulped.

Intense relief flooded through me, drawing out a sob with my shuddering breath.

"Are you all right?" he asked. "Are you...are you hurt?"

I shook my head as I made myself decent under the cloak. Varys immediately turned away to give me privacy. My cheeks burned when I handed it back to him. "Thank you. Another man might not have had the decency."

He tied the cloak back around his neck. "Of course. I only wish I would've been here sooner. I'm so sorry."

I wrapped my arms around myself. The tremors moving in waves across my bones wouldn't stop. I could have tamed them if I hadn't been struggling to breathe from the heaviness of my chest.

We both fell silent, the only sound the constant rushing of the water behind us. As I turned to the bank and cupped my hands to fill them with water for a drink, I noticed the red-angry marks that still banded my wrists where Theon had pinned me. When I splashed another handful on my face, I realized the circlet was missing from my brow.

I couldn't think of that right now—couldn't think of the trouble I would be in when Mother learned it was missing.

None of that mattered right now.

"Did you scare them off?" I asked Varys as I wiped the water from my eyes.

"Hardly." He ran his fingers through his hair. "It seems I arrived just in time to see them fleeing from *you*."

My neck tightened. "You're not suggesting *I* assaulted *him?*"

"No, no." He waved his hands. "I meant you hurt him before he ever managed to hurt you." His eyes narrowed, searching my face. "Do you remember anything?"

I looked away. "I don't."

Liar.

My stomach curled, the *snap* still echoing in my mind. The flash of light was still burned into my vision. What I'd done to Willem...I wasn't sure how to explain that. I wasn't sure where that strength, that *power*, had come from. Something had sizzled beneath my nails and expelled. Released.

From *me.*

When I had fainted, the pain of the flare lingered in my unconscious state until the voice from my nightmares spoke to me. It hadn't screamed at me in what I now knew was Elvish. It had spoken to me as if it was an old friend. Someone who cared if I woke up. And for the first time, it addressed me as if…it knew me.

Except, it had called me by a different name. One that felt like it belonged to someone of power, not me.

"What do you think I did?" I asked Varys at length.

I realized he might've seen the entire thing when the question left my mouth. Maybe he'd asked if I remembered anything because he knew what I did. But he only crossed his arms, those sapphire eyes blazing into the ground before us inquisitively. "I'm not sure. When I arrived, the two of them were running off. Willem seemed to be injured because he was weeping."

I almost laughed at that.

"After what happened in the shop," Varys continued, "I couldn't just go about my day. I felt sick. I had a feeling he was going to try something. So, I closed the library temporarily and went into the market to hopefully find you." He let out a long breath, as if steadying himself. "Unfortunately, I didn't until you had already passed through the east gate. Theon and Willem weren't far behind you." He glanced at me with a look I couldn't read. "Following you. So, I followed them."

Ice formed in the pits of my stomach. "Bastards," I rasped.

A nod. "I lost sight of them due to their pace but then heard you screaming. I thought I was too late once I realized what was happening."

He gave me another quizzical look, as if I were an arithmetic problem he couldn't quite find the answer to. "You're absolutely positive you don't remember what happened to make Willem run off like that?"

"I wouldn't have asked what you thought if I knew." My tone came out much more cutting than I wanted it to.

He lifted one eyebrow. "Or…you're not giving me the full story."

My mouth parted. "Are you calling me a liar?"

I expected some sort of glare from him. Eryx would have snapped back quickly, forcing us into an argument that would go around in a never-ending circle.

But Varys just…*smiled*. With a small chuckle in his throat, he replied, "No, Miss Mordaunt."

He adjusted his book bag and seated himself in a more comfortable position, clasping his hands. Even sitting down, he was half a head taller than me. "What you just experienced, I would consider traumatic and thus be difficult to talk about openly with someone you haven't spoken with much before now." He paused, as if to let me acknowledge his words before continuing in a tender tone, "I completely understand your apprehension, and I'm not trying to force you to say anything. However, I think it would be best if you told me so I can be an advocate for you. You can trust me."

I stared at him. For the past few moments, everything had been confusing and in one solid speech, he made everything make sense.

But what would he say if I told him I believed I had some sort of light come from me?

I dodged his gaze. "I was hitting and scratching him as hard as I could. Perhaps he just gave up."

Liar. *Liar.*

"But," I continued, "if you hadn't followed them…" My gut twisted. "Thank you."

I couldn't find anything better to say.

"This wasn't the first time, right?" Varys asked.

I knew what he was insinuating. "No. It wasn't."

"There have been rumors. I wasn't sure they were true. He's hurt you before." His eyes darkened.

"*Tried*," I quickly amended. "He's *tried* to hurt me before. He's never succeeded. Including today."

There was no victory in that statement. I suddenly felt like I might vomit.

"Will you tell your parents?" Varys asked.

I couldn't respond to him for a moment. I squeezed my arms tighter around myself, throat constricting at the thought of going back into town, knowing there was a possibility Willem had already brewed up some story. The forest beyond the water, beyond Elros, had never called louder.

Varys seemed to sense my discomfort. "They do know about what happened last time, right?"

"They do." My body began to shake again, the events of that night replaying in my mind. My sobbing pleas. Rucas slapping and shoving me until I agreed to say the whole thing was a lie. Mother watching as she tidied up her hair to go and apologize to the Welch family for my dramatics. "They didn't believe me."

Varys's breath hitched.

That had been the night I first realized my abuse wasn't always because he was drunk or because he hated me. Sometimes it was to shut me up and keep secure connections with the people who made him rich.

I couldn't hide the anger on my face and spat, "Unfortunately, my father wants me to marry the pig. Gods know, they probably have some sort of coin pinned to my chastity."

A sudden rigidity seized Varys's composure, all pleasantries in his beautiful features turning cold. "Rucas wants..." He seemed like he couldn't finish his sentence. With a deep breath, he continued in a low voice, "I apologize, Miss Mordaunt, this is all too frank of me..."

He sat forward a bit, as if to make sure I was paying attention, his jaw tightening as he beheld me. "I don't believe your father comprehends the difference between what is immoral and what is plain villainy."

My eyes and cheeks burned as I looked away from him and breathed, "I can't disagree with you."

If only he knew.

"So, what can I do to help you?"

I snapped my head to him. His words had jarred something within me. "W-What?"

Help?

I watched a genuine smile lift the side of his mouth, compelling my heart to race. "Tell me what I can do to help you, Miss Mordaunt. What do you need?"

I didn't have words. I didn't have an answer.

His questions were foreign to me.

He pressed, "I can escort you home. Or, I can leave you to yourself. Whatever you need, I'll do."

"No, don't leave," I said too quickly.

His smile widened. "Then I will stay."

I breathed out slowly—in relief, I realized. I'd been attacked by two men. I hadn't had time to fully process the disorderly blur in those few, terrible moments.

But every nerve that had roiled with fear had been soothed by Varys's presence alone.

I was...*safe* with Varys.

I knew sitting with him, having a conversation with him—something I'd wanted for a *very* long time—was breaking every rule Rucas had laid down for me. Rules that if broken, mandated bruises. Or worse.

I had not yet seen what *worse* looked like. This, disobeying Rucas like *this*...

Was it worth it?

"I'd love an escort home." My voice wavered as if it was the bravest thing I'd ever said. Maybe it was. "Fair warning though. If Willem's informed anyone, I'm sure we'll be questioned upon arriving."

My words seemed to amuse him. "Willem is a coward, and if we refer to our encounter earlier today, he's just going to hide the wounds of his pride until you say something."

I didn't respond to that. I knew myself well—knew I wasn't saying a damn word to anyone. Who in Torm was I supposed to tell? Who could I trust enough to not twist it or make it less than what it was?

Not my parents. Not even Eryx.

It would stay here, between Varys and me. If I stayed quiet, Willem would stay quiet. Rucas wouldn't find out either.

But that light—that changed things. I had to hope Willem was the coward Varys believed him to be. Too scared of *me* to say much of anything.

Because if he wasn't...

"I'm just saying to prepare yourself," I warned again, "in case we get bombarded by people ready to twist things around."

Varys only shrugged. "I decided years ago not to be bothered by the opinions of these pompous clowns. I've always known there was something different about me anyway. I'm content with that."

I stifled a laugh. "Easy enough for you to say." I pointed to my white hair. "You're not cursed."

His eyes traveled from the top of my head, down the unraveled braid, then he said gently, "We are all cursed with something, Miss Mordaunt."

His words left me speechless again. He just gave me another smile. "I actually have several. One, in particular, is my search for knowledge."

"Why is that a curse?"

"Because I don't ever stop asking questions." He eyed me. "However, it's a curse I bear proudly, because I *always* have answers."

He unbuckled the lapel of his bag and pulled out a book, placing it before me. "Take this home and read it. There have been findings, especially of late, which trace Xaladorians with white hair to be similar to those of elven descent." He pointed to his own blue hair. "Genealogies are complicated. The science behind what makes us look like our parents—or what decides if we don't—has yet to be discovered."

I stared at the title written in Common, all of it gibberish in my head as I looked over the letters. "I...can't." I gently pushed it back to him. "I couldn't read that if I tried, Varys."

"Oh, don't worry. I know I tend to sound like I'm giving a blasted lecture at times," he said candidly, "but I assure you, it is not a difficult read."

I straightened and cocked my head. He didn't understand. "I trust you. However, I still can't read it. I can't read...at all."

His eyes widened in disbelief. "You can't read?"

"Never learned." Never *allowed* to learn.

He shoved the book back into his bag, replying quietly, "I apologize for insinuating."

I sighed, smoothing out the wrinkles in my dress. "You didn't know. I've always wanted to learn, but I've gotten this far in life without reading, so I guess it's not too necessary."

He scoffed. "My life would be tormish if I were illiterate."

I frowned.

"I just…" He acknowledged my furrowed brows, my narrowed eyes. "I couldn't imagine…" Incoherent words escaped his lips as he began to amend himself. After clearing his throat, he managed, "I-I only mean I am the man I am today because of reading."

He flashed a quick, apologetic smile and I watched his hand make its way up into his hair, combing it back behind an ear—a nervous tick, I realized.

"And not just because I'm a scholar and love to learn," he continued, "but because the things I've learned in books have allowed me to understand this world much better than I ever could without. My beliefs, my values; they all stem from taking in the words written from different times, cultures, and points of view. Discerning and analyzing everything, making my *own* assessments on the wonders of our world." He studied me curiously. "What we know of our existence is not limited to what we see and hear throughout our lives, nor is it limited to what is here in Elros." A quick laugh broke his speech. "Certainly not what is merely housed here in these isolated hills. Books give me a piece of the outside world, and I think everyone should have access to that."

I gaped at him. "That sounds a lot like freedom."

Now it was my turn to catch him off guard. "What do you mean?"

I gulped. "To be able to make up your own mind, to have your own ideas…"

I didn't allow myself to finish. I was treading in deep water suggesting I *wasn't* free.

"I want to learn," I quickly followed up. "I want to know things I don't already know. I want to have conversations—like this one."

He nodded quickly, responding breathlessly, "As do I."

I couldn't stop the bright grin rising on my lips and spreading across my heated cheeks. His breath hitched, eyes glancing at my mouth for just a moment. "I've never seen you smile before."

He was right.

Because unless it was pasted on, I didn't have a reason to smile. Not *this* kind of smile. There was no one who deserved such a look from me.

This man, my new friend, the man whom I shared an unexplainable connection with...he deserved the real me.

"Varys?"

A nod.

I smiled for him again. "Call me *Mae*, please. You're my friend."

"*Mae*," he said with a grin. "No more formalities then?"

My chest fluttered and warmth blossomed over my skin. "No." And the word felt final.

I couldn't avert my eyes from his gaze, unable to hide my attraction, every part of him mysterious and gorgeous; from his brilliant irises like fragments of sapphires, to the small scar cut vertically down his left eyebrow. His dark hair shrouded those beautiful features I'd never seen this close before, and when he combed it back in a nervous manner, it was as if he was allowing me to catch a glimpse of that connection between us. There was no doubt it was real, even if I wasn't sure what it was.

The pieces he'd given me today were enough to make my decision.

"You asked me how you could help me…"

He nodded.

I was shaking, and there was a part of me that knew the moment I asked for it, reality would hit me over the head.

Too close. We were *much* too close.

"Can you teach me how to read?"

He let out a happy laugh. "I had hoped you would ask, Mae."

CHAPTER 5

Mae

I didn't meet Varys for my first reading lesson.

It had been three nights since the incident at the stream, but I was still allowing the swelling in my cheek to decrease after Rucas had slapped me for my insolence in the shop that day. Three nights, and I could still feel Willem's hands on me.

So even though I had agreed to meet Varys earlier today, I knew I wouldn't have been able to focus. I just hoped I would have another chance.

Mother entered the house and said by way of greeting, "Your father won't be home tonight."

I knew what she meant; the strain in her voice said it all.

There were often nights Rucas didn't come home. Those nights, Mother would sit in the gathering room chair for hour, letting silent tears roll down her face.

She flung her cloak aside, not bothering to drape it over the coat rack, and went straight to the chair, avoiding me altogether.

We didn't talk about where he was. I never told her I knew he was between the tavern and the brothel.

We didn't talk about how Rucas sometimes came in at four in the morning reeking of ale and would force Mother to her knees to pleasure him. She never questioned why on those nights I pulled my

40

vanity in front of the door to bar it in case he ever got the idea to force me to do it instead.

We didn't talk about my abuse.

We didn't talk about hers either.

And I felt selfish for being relieved he wouldn't be home—that he wouldn't be hurting *me* tonight.

There was never a night in the Mordaunt home where someone didn't suffer.

As I sat in front of a very large slice of apple pie I had baked, I mulled over everything Varys and I had talked about at the stream, including what to expect in lessons. He had discerned that I already knew several letters—those that made up my name—and that I had memorized words like "shop", "bakery", "butcher", words I knew would help me navigate around town. However, I didn't understand *why* they were spelt that way, nor why certain words were pronounced the way they were.

Varys had told me we would start with *vowels*, and that learning those were crucial to reading because the *consonants'* sounds would be determined by the vowels' placement. It had all given me a bit of a headache, but I had been excited to learn.

He'd written out every letter of the alphabet for me on a piece of parchment. I was to memorize them for our lesson, but I'd already forgotten the names of half of them.

I wished it came to me as easily as Elvish did, which I hadn't let myself think about too much, nor the glowing books, the magic items and potions. I still hadn't been able to sort out my thoughts; they'd all been replaced with Willem's attack. The unhinging awareness of what could have happened to me. What would he have done after? Would he have hurt me more? He had to have known I would say something.

Except I wouldn't say anything. Not after I had tried to expose his crimes before. Not after Rucas and Mother had called me a liar. Maybe he knew that. Maybe that was why I hadn't heard a single thing about him or any gossip about what I'd done to him.

There was a tightness in my chest I couldn't describe. Not a pain attack. The walls around me felt too close. Too dark and shadowed.

I didn't feel safe where I was. Not in this house.

But I couldn't leave. I knew what consequences that led to.

I couldn't get out. I was just...stuck.

Caged.

I'm not safe.

I couldn't go to my mother. She didn't care, not really. She'd abandoned the gathering room chair for her bedroom. She hadn't even said goodnight, nor had she made sure I was well.

I had nobody. Even Eryx was away hunting.

No, I had one place: the library. But the recklessness...the thought itself was just asking for Rucas to hurt me.

You could be safe.

"*Godsdammit!*" I whipped my arm across the table so fast, I barely registered making contact with the plate and fork before they both crashed to the ground. The leftover pie crumbled, and for a moment, I just stared at it.

Originally, learning how to bake was a necessity for me. I realized very early in life that I would have to feed myself a lot since my parents were so busy. But then, I realized I had a talent. I turned into quite the artist when cutting my lattice strips, flowers, and leaves out of the dough to decorate the tops of my creations.

However, baking became a form of escapism. I always turned to making desserts to take my mind off of everything, and sweets made me feel better.

The pie itself was proof I had been repressing everything, like I always did until I erupted with rage. Usually, Rucas was the recipient of my anger, when I threw violence back at him, when my fright turned to fight.

He deserved every bit of my storm and fury.

The outburst mellowed my anger, the shadows on the walls had shortened, yet my body still quivered with uneasiness. I swept up my mess, then I decided to bathe for the third time today.

I heated a few buckets of water over the hearth, tossing in lavender stems, and then dumped them into the tub. Wincing at the heat, I slid down the body of the tub until everything was immersed but my face. I didn't like hot baths, but ever since the stream...I couldn't rid myself of the lingering unwanted touch. Making the water hot enough to nearly peel the skin from my bones seemed to be the only way I felt clean.

I began to whisper to myself, "A...B...C...."

I paused after a few letters. I couldn't remember the next one.

Illiterate. I was struggling not to take offense to the word. For some reason, it had made its way to stand beside a few other terms I had heard used against me: cursed, nothing, ugly, stupid.

Perhaps *stupid* and *illiterate* felt like the same thing.

Varys hadn't meant to hurt me, but it had. If he only knew I would have loved to have grown up within the library's walls— would have loved to have grown up with Varys, too.

But that wasn't my reality, and it was why I hadn't allowed him to walk me all the way home after the incident. The guilt made me sick to my stomach. After all the laughter, all of the smiles and long gazes, I had still stopped him at the foot of the hill where the plateau began. I'd still insisted I walk myself back home from there.

I couldn't get the disappointed look on his face out of my head. He had to have known my insinuation—to be seen in my neighborhood with Varys would raise too many questions.

If Rucas had been home...

I was being pulled in so many different directions, I might rip apart. I wanted Varys's friendship, but if Rucas discovered our meetings, all of Torm would break loose. However, the fighter spirit I had developed over the past couple of years demanded I rebel.

And the idea of Varys encouraged that rebellion. I couldn't deny the pleasurable heat that had curled within me just from being near him, nor had I been able to avert my eyes from staring through his tunic at the tone of his powerful arms.

Our one afternoon together had changed *everything.* I wasn't sure if I was scared of the rising feelings, or if I was scared that I knew I was allowing them. I was definitely afraid of what I would *do* with those feelings and those fears made me nauseous.

I couldn't entertain the thought. Not of him. Not of our reading lessons. Not of the connection I felt between us.

"I can't have him."

But something inside me rattled against those words, sending my blood boiling. For once, my fury roared louder than the pain.

And I was *done*.

I hauled myself out of the water, threw a towel around my body, and stormed for my parents' suite. I didn't know what I was going to say, or what my demands would be.

But as I reached to open the door to their bedroom, a thin streak of light jolted from my fingers to the metal doorknob. I jerked my arm back. The shout that tried to leave my throat ceased when all air escaped my lungs.

Up and down my left wrist, beneath my thin, pale skin, my veins began to glow like violet rivers of fire.

I felt the warmth leave my face as I stepped back—far, *far* from my parents' bedroom—and slumped down to my knees. Before my eyes, I watched the glow expand up, past my elbow, to my bare shoulder and across my chest.

I let out a breathy sob. My veins looked like lightning when it webbed through a stormy sky.

I sprung to my feet and ran up the stairs as quietly as I could, shutting the door behind me and bracing my shaking body against it. The glow in my veins bathed the darkness of my room in a violet sheen, dancing on the walls like rainbows after light filtered through the prisms of crystals.

My heart slammed against my chest as I discarded my towel to the floor and pulled my vanity over to bar myself in. I couldn't catch my breath, and tears poured down my face as I curled onto my mattress and pulled my quilt over my head.

My body was radiant beneath the covers. I tucked my arm in close, tracing my veins with my fingers. Nothing was hot. Nothing hurt.

It was just...beautiful.

It was *magical*.

The panic in my chest and belly eased, my often disjointed thoughts beginning to click together like pieces of a puzzle. Everything from the last few days had left me confused.

But now, everything was beginning to make sense.

I had been told my entire life I was nothing. Weak. Worthless.

But as I looked at the streaks of lightning under my skin, I knew I could be powerful.

I just didn't know where to begin—if this even was a beginning. If I should try to run away. Or find someone to…

Help.

Varys had said the labels on the potions at Rucas's shop were in Elvish. I wondered how much he really knew about the elves. What I knew of their history, I had always doubted, such as the tales of magic and the claim they'd been created by the gods themselves.

But my veins were *glowing.* There was no doubt this was some kind of power. Whether or not it was mine or an effect of coming in contact with the magical items, I was determined to find out.

Even if that meant I was going to have to hide it.

Because if this was a power I'd been given, I had no idea how to use it. I didn't know if I would accidentally allow that light to discharge again like it had on Willem.

What if I did it to Rucas next?

He'd kill me.

He'd *kill* me.

But if I asked my questions carefully, if I could sneak around, if I could manage to get one step ahead of him this time, maybe I wouldn't have to worry about him hurting me ever again.

The glow began to fade as I drifted off into sleep, my last thoughts on Varys. I had reason to feel reckless and unbridled around him.

There was attraction. Desire. Connection.

And if I planted the right seed…

My freedom.

CHAPTER 6

Varys

I was severely distracted, and had been since that day at the stream. My nerves were still set on edge, her shrill screams still ringing in my ears. I had never run so fast, never pulled my dagger with intention to kill.

But when I had come to the edge of those trees, reciting an incantation in my head, the wind had ceased.

The quick flash of light was still burned behind my eyes. There hadn't been a cloud in the sky, not since the storm the night before then, but I knew what I had heard rumble across the hills. The sound of thunder after lightning had struck.

And when her screams died out, I felt it.

I hadn't been able to throw up my wards in time, let alone think of the word needed to do so, before a pulse of energy had washed over me and the forest surrounding.

I knew what it meant. Gods, I'd researched enough to know, despite never feeling it myself. There was not a doubt in my mind.

It had been an expulsion of power.

Of magic.

Mae Mordaunt was a mage. Like me.

And she had lied about all of it.

Given her circumstances at the time, I hadn't tried to force the

46

truth out. I'd wanted her to trust me, and I still wanted that, but I couldn't deny it was due to other reasons entirely. Reasons I couldn't focus on now. Not when I knew she was a mage and the danger that entailed.

Two years ago, everything I had known about myself, and what my future promised, had changed in an instant. I could still recall every detail of that morning when I woke up on the anniversary of my mother's death. She'd died a decade before.

I had decided to climb up to the attic to look over all the things Father and I kept in her footlocker after her untimely passing, to pay homage of sorts. Her armor, favorite clothes, jewelry.

And most importantly, her journal.

I'd read through the worn pages a hundred times before, filled with entries from a time of my grandparents and their parents, records of marriage vows, and my mother's writings of her travels with my father before they settled in Elros.

But when I had reached in to retrieve it from its place at the bottom of her footlocker that morning, a warm glow from within its binding spread up and over my hands. Inside, its usual content was no longer present, each page delineated with the formulae of specific spells written in *Vylaryś*, or Elvish in the Common tongue. A language that could not be learned, the speech itself magical and inherent, lost to all when every elf in Xalador died after the great war almost a thousand years ago.

Yet suddenly within that treasured journal, I could read every word, every rune, knew every diacritic and why accents were placed above specific letters. Before I could determine what in Torm was happening, an envelope tumbled to the floor. My mother's name was on the front but when I picked it up, the letters faded and a new script appeared, addressing it to *me*.

Inside, the note simply signed as *F* revealed Xalador's most vital secret.

The ReEmergence of Magic.

In legends, Xaladorians were told magic was lost when the elven race was eradicated, when in actuality, it had only laid dormant for ages. Something had triggered the magic back, and like the buds of flowers rising amidst the melting snow, magic awakened inside of me and everyone else across Xalador that was born of elven blood.

Whether they knew it...or not.

In the time of the elves and magic, there were three different streams of mages: wizard, druid, and sorcerer. All of them drew their magic from *the veins of the arcane*, the ley lines of arcana that coursed through all of Xalador, ebbing and flowing through everything and everyone—even those not of elven descent. It was creation, life, and the force of all existence.

The mages' differences were mainly dependent upon how they pulled their magic from the veins. Wizards were usually highly intelligent and conveyed magic from esoteric study. Spells were written into spellbooks, runes and shapes drawn accurately within, creating formulae that broke down the elemental and metaphysicality of the arcana. It was a science—calculated incorrectly, the spell would fail.

Druids pulled magic from organic resources and used their surroundings to their advantage. They had a natural affinity for understanding how everything was touched by the veins and were able to create magical potions and salves. Legends told of powerful druids that could change their form or command their surroundings at will.

Because the veins flowed through all life, it was no wonder certain elves were able to access the magic within their very blood and thus, producing sorcerers. In history books, they were described as rare—and powerful. Unlike the other types of mages, sorcerers did not require any sort of study or physical component; their magic was instinctive and raw.

All spells required a command word—or in more powerful spells, command verses—to execute the incantation, and they could be exhausting. The more powerful the spell, the more energy it required from its caster, both mentally and physically. It was important to know exactly what intention lay behind the purpose of every spell before casting altogether; the same as drawing a blade, as one doesn't do so unless they have a need to defend or have settled within themselves the intent to take a life.

Of course, this was all information I'd learned from ancient

Elvish text, and I'd gathered there was now a bit more to magic than there was a thousand years ago.

Because I was different.

I was what *F* called a *war sage* in the letter. How this person knew who and what I was still bothered me immensely. I'd only found a few mentions of war sages in my research; wizards who were proficient in both spellcasting and martial arts. The discovery had made me quite apprehensive because I'd never felt like I could follow in my mother's footsteps of swordsmanship.

But since I was part of a lesser-known channel of mages, it made me wonder how many people out there in Xalador had discovered newer forms of magic. It only added to the mountain of mysteries and questions. What had revived the magic? Why had it lain dormant for almost a thousand years? I had spent the next several seasons after my reemergence devoted to nothing but solving the puzzle, only to come to countless dead ends.

Upon learning that The ReEmergence was linked to the elven bloodline, I immediately attempted to seek out the other few in Elros that I knew were of elven blood like myself, deducing such possibilities because of their colorful hair and eyes. I'd learned from *F* we were to be known as *Vyl'kriev*, which translated to "Elf blood" in Common—though it meant something closer to "descendant" in Elvish.

Alas, I found no one in Elros anymore. Those I suspected had left—had uprooted their entire family. I had come to the conclusion that if they knew they were magical, they had been scared and decided to seek wisdom in the capital. And that was my plan, too. I had already decided I would be leaving for Elvidawn early spring, especially if my admission essay was accepted at the College of Elvidawn.

What I hadn't expected was *her*.

There had always been a forbiddance as solid as a brick wall between me and Mae, keeping me from getting close to her. Of course, I'd never voiced the want to have anything between us or given the slightest hint that I'd always been enamored by her. Our frustratingly-short, commonplace greetings were a constant reminder of the feeling that I wasn't good enough for her.

However, I'd always been aware of the looks full of simmering curiosity she gave me from across the market, tempting me like a siren song calling me out to sea I knew better than to listen to. It seemed every time she realized it, she'd look away and break that connection before it could ever become something more.

For years, I'd been fine with that.

But after witnessing what I did and discovering she was a mage, after our afternoon of genuine conversation...

How could I leave for Elvidawn now? I couldn't leave her behind knowing I had answers to any questions she might have.

I'd already decided what books I would be rereading when I returned home from dinner with our family friends tonight, and I knew I wouldn't be getting much rest, not until I was ready—

"Fawkes, where's yer bloody head?!"

I only saw the sheen of a blade swipe down inches from my nose before the metal sole of a boot slammed into my armored sternum, sending me to my back, out of my inner thoughts, and to reality. A shrill chime echoed through the Cauldücen's basement as my sword bounced off the stone floor. Another boot stomped down and pinned the cross guard to the ground before I could retrieve it. I looked up to the heated face of my best friend, Leona.

"Nah, ye aren't gettin' this back until ye get yer damn flighty head out of yer arse!" she shouted. The lilt of her accent was always heavier when she was angry.

I only grinned apologetically. She blew out of her bottom lip, wisps of her fiery red hair fluttering out of her face. Both our fathers, Mattis and Duros, were howling with laughter, our only, but eager, audience sitting upon a table with their pints of mead sloshing around.

"You get lost thinkin' about your rendezvous with that erotic dancer back in Fairgrove?" my father shouted in slurred speech. I shot him a glare.

"Aye, such a time that was, lad," Duros spouted. The dwarf had a much better handle on his speech even though he'd drained half the barrel of mead to himself. "We haven't drank like this since then." He paused. "What should we celebrate t'night, ol' friend?"

"Apparently..." My father hiccupped. "The loss of Varys's pride!"

The two burst into a joyful fit, Duros landing a playfully stoic elbow into Mattis's ribs, nearly causing my slender father to fall from his perch.

Leona slowly cocked her head toward the two of them with a fearsome glare. "Out with the both of ye! If I needed two soaked birds drippin' on my trainin', I'd head to the fuckin' guard barracks m'self, ye bunch of useless fops." She whipped toward me and thrust a finger into my now aching chest. "Fawkes, ye were doin' fine before ye fashioned ye'self as some starry-eyed droll. What in Torm was that?"

I lifted my arms in surrender and stood to my feet. "Sorry, long day."

She glowered. "Ye did nothin' all day."

I stifled a chuckle. Working at the library was hardly nothing. I felt her eyes follow me as I went to my water skin on the table. She let out a frustrated sigh and marched over to grab hers as well.

"Bah, we're done for the week," she spat, unbuckling her plated bracers.

"You're grouchy tonight."

"And yer fightin' like a fledglin' squire boy." She took a swig. "We both know ye've got more in ye. So, what's yer problem?"

I paused after my drink to watch Father and Duros head upstairs, off-kilter like two boats on the Serpent Sea during a storm. Once the basement door shut, I looked down at Leo. "I don't exactly know where or how to begin. Some things happened a few days ago, on the 8th, and then...I spent the afternoon with *her*."

Leona's demeanor drastically transformed from heated to exaggerated thrill as she practically jumped up on the table. "Well gods-be-damned, did ye now? That explains why ye're fightin' with the wrong head." Her smile was wide and bright as the sun.

I chuckled and shook my head as I sat down in a chair nearby, unbuckling my greaves. "Sorry in advance to disappoint you. It was hardly romantic."

"Ye said ye spent the day with her." Her accent was already thinning as she calmed. "Ye've got a beauty of a story to tell then, I'm sure."

I grimaced. "It certainly didn't start off pretty. I'll get to that in a moment." Her smile fell slightly. I sighed. "Mae's a mage."

Her emerald-green eyes widened. "What? Ye saw her use magic?"

I rubbed a knot in the back of my neck. The soreness from training was beginning to set in. "Not exactly. I felt the presence of her magic. There was this...light, and then thunder." Her incredulous expression made me realize I wasn't making a lot of sense. "She did *something* to hurt Willem Welch when he…"

Leona snarled. "What'd that goat fucker do?"

I couldn't help but sigh at her choice of words before I continued, telling her first about the shop, then the incident by the stream. Before long, I was pacing with clenched fists, wishing I would have struck Willem harder in the shop. I'd never been the type to enjoy confrontation, and my loathing for both Willem and Theon dated back to childhood when they would push me around and throw my books into the mud. I had never fought back.

Unfortunately, I was not their only victim. Part of me knew they had hazed Mae as well, but I never saw it. I also knew Rucas had both of their fathers strung up in debt, so I never thought they'd go too far.

They didn't believe me.

My father wants me to marry the pig. They probably have some kind of coin pinned to my chastity.

Mae's words kept repeating in my head. I knew I hated Rucas for how he treated my father and me, and I found a slight enjoyment in outsmarting the asshole. So many people of this town sang his praises, but hearing Mae talk about her father the way she did confirmed he was no idol.

As I continued to describe to Leo what I had heard upon coming to the stream, I found myself shaking in a mix of anger and resentment of myself for not following those bastards more closely. I couldn't even make eye contact with Leona, too disgusted and infuriated. My aching heart slammed against my chest, thinking of how

I'd found her upon my arrival. Exposed, unconscious. Her thighs marked with red abrasion. I'd assumed the worst. I would have stayed there all night, until she woke up if needed. Never before had I wanted to kill a man, but if Willem had succeeded in his assault, he would have made it an easy decision.

"Ye're as white as the linens, Fawkes," Leona said, yanking me from the dark depths of thought. I didn't know when I'd stopped talking.

"I'm sorry. What did I say last?"

"Ye don't need to continue. I get the picture," she spoke through clenched teeth.

"I would have killed him, Leo. Theon, too."

It would have been so easy.

Leo stood and grasped my shoulders. "Hey, ye did the best ye could, yeah?"

"I would have killed them."

"And I would have helped if I were there, Fawkes." She patted my cheek. "But it sounds like Mae handled him herself."

"It appeared so."

"So, here's a question then. Why didn't ye ask her outright if she used magic?"

"I...did. Sort of." I scoffed as, again, in hindsight I wished I'd been more direct. "Leo, you know how I get around people. Around anybody. I'm—"

"Awkward, apparently in even the direst circumstances."

I huffed, rolling my eyes. "Yes, that."

"Aww." She pouted mockingly. "So, what was her response?"

"She lied. She told me she wasn't sure what happened."

She clicked her tongue. "Ye beat around the bush about yer question and she gave ye half the truth. What did ye expect?"

I growled under my breath. "I don't know, Leo. I've never met another mage before and *now* it's the one person I least expected. It's...her, and every little bit I thought I knew about her has changed completely."

"Fawkes, ye've never actually known her at all. Ye've never had a conversation with her without chokin' on yer balls."

"Leo. Please. I just now know she's something else besides a wealthy, beautiful maiden from The Flats I've always been taken by." The Flats were what the rest of Elros called the neighborhood that belonged to the richer citizens. "There's just...something off about her. I don't know if it's magic or something else."

Leona crossed her arms. "Maybe she's scared, Fawkes. Maybe she's tryin' to hide it. Like ye are."

I glanced at her with narrowed eyes. Leona had been trying to get me to tell my father about my magic. She believed it best if my close family and friends knew in case anything tragic happened in a magical accident.

But the letter from *F* had stated I was to prepare myself for a threat against the *Vyl'kriev*. Until that threat came and was hopefully eradicated, I'd decided to keep my magic a secret. The fewer loved ones who knew about something that would put them in harm's way, the better.

Though, I had to tell *someone*, and had practically ran to Leona to show her the first spell I'd learned. A simple spell of creating a small light and making it float beside me like a personal, intangible lantern. She'd sat with me for hours as I went through every charm, enchantment, and other forms of prestidigitation in my new spell-book. We only stopped when I had accidentally turned Leona's greatsword invisible. I had been sure she would kill me, but thankfully the spell only lasted a few seconds before she could become irate.

"Maybe you're right." I finally breathed. "Maybe she realizes her father would use her or something. I won't know until we see each other again—"

Leona gasped, every bit of girlishness she possessed spreading across her freckled face. "Ye two have plans? Ye should have told me that at the beginnin', ye oaf! And here I thought ye fucked up yer one chance."

"Thanks for the confidence."

"Give me every detail. What do ye two plan on doin' next?"

"Nothing that would interest you, I'm sure."

She was swinging her plated legs like a child, grinning brightly.

"I could always make suggestions. If I were ye, I'd have already swept her off her feet."

"Of course, you would. You don't understand boundaries."

She shrugged. "I'm just sayin' if ye don't hurry up and claim her, I might. The lads and lassies I've had yet aren't strong or able enough to fulfill my desires."

I stared at her deadpan. "And...she would be?"

"Nah. But I might be strong and able enough to fulfill hers." I rolled my eyes when she winked, crossing her arms under her breasts and pushing them up purposefully as if to assert a dominance I was not aware I needed to compete over. She cackled. "I for sure wouldn't pussyfoot around."

I groaned, waving my hands in a placating manner. I knew she was joking about it all, but I wasn't quite in the mood. "Leona, stop being so crass. Given her circumstances that day, I just wanted to know she was all right. She was scared. Any advances of romance would have been severely inappropriate. I helped her in every way I could and that was that. She's the one who brought up more meetings. I'm going to teach her how to read."

If she would actually show up for a lesson. We had decided that today, on the eleventh of autumn, would be when we would begin. I'd waited for hours earlier.

Leona let out a long, exaggerated sigh, letting her head roll back dramatically. "What. A. Snore."

"Leona," I hissed. "I have to put The ReEmergence first. If by teaching Mae how to read I subsequently help her understand the power she has, and she trusts me enough to tell me the truth, that's all that matters. Despite what I think of her. She's not some prize to be won just because I'm choosing to help her. I want to assist her because she needs it and because she is most assuredly a mage which can be incredibly dangerous if left unknown."

She stood and returned to the center of the room to grab her greatsword *Thorn* from where it lay on the ground. She swung it a few times in the air before she responded, "I think she's...sick."

My heart stumbled a beat. I lifted my eyes to hers. "Sick?"

She nodded, brushing her thumb over the rose that had been

carved into the silver of Thorn's pommel. "Ye know, Mum hears things here and there when she speaks with the herbalists who are involved with Rucas's brown-nosed gits. Someone told her *'Rucas's daughter had some sort of fit'*. One of the neighbors overheard her screamin' like she was in pain. Ye said somethin' was off about her. That may be why."

As I listened, my gaze became confined to an imperfection on the stone floor—a spot that had not been ground smooth. One would miss it if they weren't looking hard enough. I suddenly felt that way about this new information—like I hadn't looked hard enough.

Sick. She'd always been pale, gaunt, and seemed feeble. Sometimes I'd find her walking through the market holding a basket of food and seeming unable to hold on to it. Other times she walked in a daze like she was half-asleep. Her amethyst eyes were striking and left me breathless, but they had always seemed to house a chilling vacancy. I was starting to understand why.

How could I have not noticed?

With those thoughts, my mind was roaring with so many possibilities of what her sickness might be. It explained why I rarely saw her. Perhaps she was sheltered because of the illness.

What was Rucas doing about it?

I gulped down an overwhelming disquiet in the pit of my stomach. Something wasn't right.

I looked up to find Leona studying me. "She is Pallid Cursed," she said.

"Bah." I shook my head sardonically. "She has white hair as I have blue and yours is red."

"So, magic's real, but curses aren't?" she bit back, cockeyed.

I breathed out heavily through my nose. Too many questions, not enough answers. "I don't know." I stood. "I need to do some reading. Maybe I can find something regarding a correlation between illnesses and magic. Tell Father I'm not hungry and I'll be back at home, please."

I started for the door—her sword came down in my path, making sparks as the edge connected with the stone floor. "Excuse me? Am I yer trainer or yer maid? I did not relieve ye."

I blinked at her. "You said earlier we were done."

She muttered to herself in Dwarvish before commanding, "Put yer greaves back on and draw yer sword. I've decided yer story earned ye some more time in the trainin' circle."

I huffed. "Leo, I really want to figure this out—"

"Before I put ye on yer arse, Fawkes. Yer books can wait."

Blood dripped from the fresh cut across Leona's upper arm. She paced in front of me, Thorn gripped tightly in her hands, eyes sharp on my movements. I'd accidentally nicked her—for the first time ever—and now the only thing that stood between her vicious blade and my life was the too-tight training armor I wore and a bit of sheer luck.

She feigned a step, but I never dropped my eyes from her stance. She let out a short laugh—she was absolutely pissed.

"Don't make me wait all night, Fawkes." She crooked a finger, beckoning me to come at her. "It's neither fun in the bedroom nor on the battlefield."

I scoffed. "And here I thought women liked a good tease."

"Aw, is that what Elise Carrington told ye back then? Ye need to get back out there and learn what a real lassie wants."

I grimaced at the mention of my first lover, whom I'd trysted for two seasons before I found her riding another man in the woods. "I prefer to focus on what makes my lover tick."

Leona groaned with annoyance. "Ye take too long to do so. Fight me, Fawkes. In and out. No more teasin' cuts!"

I lowered my guard for a moment in disgust, scrunching my face. "It's a bloody fight, not sex!"

"They have more in common than ye realize, slow-boy."

Through every part of our conversation, I'd studied her. She was too loose, overly confident. Faking it. She was never like this, so I could only assume the cut I gave her had dampened her otherwise aggressive fighting spirit.

She let out an exaggerated huff—then a formidable warcry, charging me. The speed of her rush put great force behind her blade as she swung up to meet mine, causing sparks to flicker and fly to the stone floor.

She shoved her shoulder into me. I held, pushed her back, and watched as she caught herself clumsily. I'd never been able to match her strength. Something was definitely off.

Or...was it me?

We had stopped using dulled practice swords a couple of seasons ago, and I hadn't picked up a wooden sword since my training began. For Leona, swordplay wasn't playing or practicing at all. In the training ring, I was her enemy and she was mine. Necks would be spared, limbs would still be intact, but I had received countless bruises and welts, a few jammed fingers, and enough slices and stitches to let me feel pain and avoid it as much as possible. And that was the point. Dancing with the possibility of injury and bloodshed had made me a stronger fighter. Leona's massive blade against my longsword was like a trunk against a twig and even though she was much shorter than me, Thorn made up for it in length.

It was why I'd also realized my style of combat was to avoid, parry, and use my opponent's strength against them.

For the first few weeks of training, my muscles had burned, cramped, and wanted to recoil every time she swung and made contact. My callouses had bled, my skin was lashed, and fingers lost feeling from gripping the handle so hard. But soon, the amount of disarming decreased. Today had been the first time I had let my guard down and to Leona, it was an embarrassment and great dishonor—not just for me, but for her. The fact that her trainee had been disarmed after weeks of improvement—by the gods, I was not going to let that happen again.

Leona dodged backward from my diagonal slash, a sneer on her face as she returned the attack with an overhead swipe to my neck, only to be met with my own blade and held in a clinch. She screamed a Dwarvish curse, heaving me away and centering her blade to quickly guard her open stance.

"Damn, Fawkes," she said through heavy breaths. "Where was this earlier?"

I rushed forward, feigning an uppercut only to slide to the

ground, sweeping her legs from under her. She dropped to one knee, but she wasn't down for long. "Yer playin' dirty!"

I rolled to my feet, then shrugged. "I thought you'd like it."

Her nose twisted as she lifted her blade. "Gross." She swung back down and I dodged.

We would be here all night if I continued to evade, feign, slash, repeat. In real combat, she would have already beaten me. I knew it too. It wasn't that she was necessarily going easy on me, it was the fact that she wasn't able to do what she did best—severing her opponent in half.

But I had never tried bringing in what *I* did best. Being a war sage, magic was just as important in my style of combat. It was the only real reason I had started training to begin with, but I hadn't learned how to blend them properly yet.

After shifting back out of reach, I raised, "One spell.'"

I watched the bob of her throat as she angled Thorn before her face like a vicious mask. "That won't be fair."

"What's wrong? Is the great Princess Leona Cauldücen afraid of a little sparkle?"

She smirked, sucking on her teeth in thought. "All right, Fawkes. I guess since ye've had to spend the last few seasons learnin' to take a real hit, I can learn to not let pretty lights bother me."

I chuckled. Frankly, I wasn't sure how I'd be able to do both. Since Leona's sword was much larger than mine, I usually gripped my own blade with two hands so I wouldn't lose my hold on it if our blades made contact. But with magic, I required one hand free to cast.

Holding my sword in my dominant hand, I extended my left to cast. Leona held Thorn high in defense.

"Are ye gonna tell me what ye'll do?" she asked.

"Wasn't planning on it. Maybe I'll light my blade on fire, or maybe I'll make yours disappear again."

She swallowed as she watched my hands. "Just 'cause ye can see through it doesn't mean it'll keep yer limbs on."

I began to think through every spell I had learned over the last two years, each falling into different schools of magic, some drawing from the elements, others mere tricks of the eye. Some spells could latch onto my blade, or I could make myself invisible for a short duration to move unseen from my attacker.

Focusing on the spell's command word I had memorized, I breathed out sharply and brought my arm out fast—Leona jumped. My fingers danced and flexed, repeating the movements instructed in the spell. Magic eddied through my consciousness as my book bag on the opposite side of the room began to glow, my spellbook inside coming to life.

Leona watched carefully, whispering a hasted mix of awe and curses as she squinted up at me. A smirk crept up on her lips. "I will never get tired of watchin' yer eyes start glowin' like that."

Indeed, a blue light glinted off my blade. Whenever a spell of any kind was cast, a mage's eyes glowed a color unique to their characteristics. Everything about me seemed to be about the color blue, from my hair, to my preferred clothing choices, to my eyes—even when they weren't glowing with arcane light. I'd stood in front of the mirror before and watched my blue irises ignite as if a blue flame danced behind my gaze.

"You will when you know it's a sign you've become a mage's challenger," I said coyly. "But first—"

I charged at her. She let out a screech as she slashed, her eyes sharp with a glare and pure panic, avoiding the glow of my spell ready to be cast. But I was waiting to activate the spell with its command word. Waiting, looking for an opening because that's what I was good at. Watching, listening, and preparing for a window of opportunity. She swung wide at times, especially when off guard.

I jumped back, watching her blade move right to left. Her gaze followed and turned from me.

There it is.

I planted my feet and uttered, *"Öpstupae."*

Leona gasped as a blue cloud of glittering dust blasted toward her head. She shouted, swinging aimlessly—blinded. I slid out of Thorn's reach. When she cleaved in the opposite direction, I rushed forward, gripped her wrist and shoved my shoulder into her.

Thorn clanged as it hit the ground. We went down with it.

I landed on her, pinning her sword arm to the floor as she struggled.

My sword pressed to her neck.

Leona's chest heaved, even as my knee pushed against her.

The impact was final. A blow to a teacher from her apprentice. Her eyes were still glazed over—an effect of the spell. Seconds later, they cleared, and she blinked rapidly up at me, frowning at the blade on her neck before she smirked. "Some fuckin' sparkle."

CHAPTER 7

"Stop being so proud, Leona. Let me help you bandage your cut," I told her as we came into the gathering room. "I'm really sorry—"

"Don't ye *dare* apologize." She picked some of the dried blood off her arm. "I'm just pissed ye don't have one to match."

"I have plenty in places I'd rather not have."

She snorted, eyes glancing to the exact spot I was referring to. She'd accidentally sliced my hip last season during one of our training bouts. "Oh, ye wee *elskairn.*"

"Did you...just call me a toddler?"

She flicked my nose. "Aye, gettin' along on yer Dwarvish, I see. Besides, Fawkes, I'm just doin' ye a favor. Ye need some roughin' up. Lassies *love* battle wounds."

"*You* like battle wounds. There are plenty of other women who may not."

She laughed. "The women I've been with do. They get all giggly, askin' where I got them. I've made up the wildest shite."

We came to the foot of the Cauldücens' dining table and she handed me a pre-poured goblet of wine, courtesy of her mother, Natalia.

I took a drink just as Leona stated, "I bet ye *Mae* would love to caress that scar on yer hip."

I choked on the wine and spilled the rest down my chin. Leona laughed out before tipping back her own goblet, metal boot up on a chair.

You'd never know by just talking to her that Leona was a mad romantic. She often spoke of her future spouse, and bearing children if she were to marry a man, but right now, she was just enjoying her youth. I often found her walking home from the tavern early in the morning after a long night of drinking and other frivolous activities that concerned a man or woman. Usually, someone who passed through on their way to the northern fishing docks, or a mysterious merchant or storyteller around the Fest of Change, which was approaching rapidly.

Very rarely had she been with anyone in town. Everyone in Elros knew her as someone else—someone *false*. I'd heard everything from *brute* to *half-breed thug*. This started when she was very young. She had only spent one week at my father's school before she got into a fight, defending herself when a boy teased about her short, stout shape. But of course, gossip and rumors spread, twisting the story into a tale of Leona hurting the boy without provocation.

They knew little of the woman I claimed as my sister and best friend. The woman who held herself in a brutal demeanor when needed and had a smoldering temper that could easily become a devastating flame when stoked, but was also a kind friend with an understanding heart.

"What're we havin' tonight, Mum?" Leona asked as I finished patting my tunic dry.

Natalia spun to us, long auburn curls swaying with her movements, bangs tucked behind a Jinyan scarf wrapped around her forehead. She smiled warmly, holding a tart freshly pulled from the stone oven. "It's getting a bit chilly out there, so I decided to warm us up with some pumpkin soup. And a plum tart for dessert."

Leona let her tongue hang out, rubbing her stomach beneath the plated waist cincher she wore. "I'm starvin'. Let's eat!"

Natalia sat the tart down and waved away her husband when he tried to pull a sugared plum off the top. "Duros darling, that tart is still piping!"

He chuckled as he looked at his wife—tilted his head up, for the woman he'd married was so much taller than him. He kissed her knuckles before drunkenly meandering over to the barrel to pour him and Father more mead.

Natalia wiped the sweat off her forehead with her apron, chuckling to herself when flour residue smeared over her golden tan skin. "I've also got bacon and poached eggs if you want something hardier."

Duros sat at the head of the table as master of the house with Natalia to his right. Father sat to his left and Leona sat across from me. She didn't wait for Duros's blessing before she snatched a grape from the cheese board.

Duros began, "Hail Victors, our champions of past! Thanks be to tha warriors who gave their blood. May tha only fire we face be of hearth for feast, drink, and love. Hail Victors!"

We all repeated, goblets and tankards high, "Hail Victors!" and drank.

It still surprised me Duros could recite that entire ode inebriated. Granted, drinking, feasting, and hearth-warmed homes were all part of the culture he'd grown up around living in Gor Thorüm, the dwarven kingdom.

Especially since he had once been heir to the throne.

As we began to eat, I couldn't help but smile as I watched Natalia and Duros exchange romantic glances, apparent and exposed for anyone to see, still just as in love as they were when they had first laid eyes on one another. They wouldn't hide it and didn't when he was a prince either. It was why he was here in Elros and not seated on the throne.

The dwarves were a proud race and refused to procreate with any other race besides their own. Duros's father, King Dajorn, was angered and disgusted by his son's relationship. He had given him a choice: Natalia or his crown. He chose her and his father banished him from the kingdom.

An exiled prince, never to set foot on dwarven territory again. With no place to go but into his lover's arms, Duros took Natalia to Elros where they eventually made a home for themselves and their newborn daughter. The friendship Leona and I shared was built upon our parents becoming friends first. Natalia and Duros had settled down in Elros within a week of my parents moving into our home. Both couples met at The Nook and Cranny, a tavern where the Cauldücens had stayed until Duros finished the manor.

The Cauldücen manor was the most architecturally exquisite building in northern Xalador. Hewn out of a sheer cliff north of Elros by Duros's hand alone, most of the manor was underground, much like his former home.

Banished or not, Duros was proud of being a dwarf and even though we weren't dwarven, Father and I made sure to follow every custom, say every blessing, and drink to our heart's content when we supped with the Cauldücens.

We also respected Natalia's Jinyan morning ritual of quiet reflection and herbal tea. She'd allowed me to join her on several occasions, and I'd found my love for tea and solace because of the tradition. I hadn't joined her for a while though—not since The ReEmergence. My inner thoughts were much too loud now, always screaming for answers.

"I received a letter from Kenrad this morn," Duros mentioned after a moment of silence while we ate.

"Ah, will the baron be joining you for your annual hog hunting trip I'm never invited to?" Father asked with a devilish grin.

Duros barked a laugh. "I'd be daft to find yer arse in that forest!"

Father only chuckled lightheartedly. "You're right." He lifted his pint for a long drink. I think I was the only one who caught the melancholy that filled his eyes, leaving as quickly as it came on. He hadn't been off-road in the southern forest since Mother died out there. "Though the two of you could at least join me for a night of dice and drink at The Nook and Cranny while he's in town."

Duros let out a belch which Natalia quickly scolded him for. "Aye lad." He wiped the mead from his red beard. "That'd be a night. Unfortunately, tha letter stated he may be late for tha Fest of Change this year. Some...complications within tha fiefdom."

I snapped my head to him. "What kind of complications?"

Duros eyed the four of us. Father put down his bread. Leona stopped her smacking.

Duros cleared his throat as he leaned in and braced his arms on the table, lacing his fingers together and showing off his burn scars from his years of blacksmithing. "These dinners bring me much joy. So, don't be troubled by me words."

The hairs on the back of my neck rose. Leona and I made eye contact, both of us making the same wry expression.

Duros continued, "He's informed me that in tha southwestern region of Xalador, there've been many sightin's of strange creatures runnin' amuck. Large beasts and men up to no good."

"Beasts?" Father asked. "Like bears? Or wolves?"

I caught the flicker of pained anger in his eyes. Mine burned.

Too many accidental nods to Mother's death tonight.

Duros shrugged. "I don't believe it would be much of an issue if it were tha common mutt. Unfortunately, Kenrad didn't say *what* they were."

Shit.

F's forewarning played in my head.

"He's enlisted several of the King's Guard to track these threats down," Duros went on. He twisted a gold bead at the end of one of five braids plaited into his long, red, and frizzy beard. "No word of that sort of thing makin' its way north just yet. The Duke has been up his arse to make sure he has it under control."

My stomach turned over on itself. The weight of *F's* words were heavy now. Two years ago, I would have been thrilled to learn that in my lifetime there was a possibility I'd see magical creatures and beasts return to Xalador. Reemerge like magic had.

But along with the warning, a question had quickly formed among the many constantly ringing in my head.

Where had the creatures gone after the fall of the elves?

Besides what a map could show me, the northwestern side of Xalador was what I was most familiar with. The furthest south I'd traveled was Fairgrove, and I knew traveling any further would lead to leagues of uninhabited plains besides the smaller settlements that weren't large enough to be marked on the map.

Xalador was split down the center by a massive mountain range known as Drake's Spine, leaving the western and eastern lands of the kingdom separated as though they were the two wings of a gargantuan dragon. No one had ever climbed over the blizzardous summit and lived to see the other side. Not to mention if they did make it, they would only die in the treacherous, orc-ridden Hakdvar Desert. The tail of the mountains, The Dragonglass Spires and legendary home of the dragons of old, were too sheer and smooth to climb over. Historians believed the dragons had used their sharp scales and fire breath to grind the mountains into huge, jutting pillars of black crystalline earth so that no one would be able to find their homes—one would have to fly to do so.

There was nowhere to hide in the Great Plains, nor did I believe anything could survive in the mountains.

But past the grasslands and fields, to the east and following the edge of Drake's Spine, a vast forest stretched from the beaches of the Serpent Sea all the way south to Shade's Crescent. I had read many dark and twisted faerie tales which spoke of the gigantic spiders that had once overwhelmed the wildwood. The forest had also been a fae realm, where faeries, dryads, fauns, unicorns, and other magical creatures had roamed. Creatures that with the elves, vanished nearly a thousand years ago.

So, if creatures like those were returning now, could they be coming from that forest? Had they truly been hiding there for thousands of years? I doubted that. In fact, I had speculated most of these magical creatures had retreated to another forest entirely. Aldeon Forest, the home and kingdom of the fae. Once ruled by the High Druid, the great woodland crowned the northeastern land of Xalador, a few leagues above Elvidawn.

But there was another problem with that theory of mine. The forest was dead now, and had been since the war of the elves. Even the map of Xalador showed the forest as brown and gray leafless trees. An Xaladorian king of the past had built an iron gate along the guardian oak tree lines, history books stating he did so to protect the once magical forest from people who may try to build homes on such ancient, sacred land.

But thinking about the whereabouts of the fae and the rest of the magical creatures of the days past, I wondered if the king knew something the rest of Xalador didn't, and had built the gate for something inside to remain *safe*.

None of my speculations gave me answers, and I knew very well I probably wouldn't get those answers until I learned from a fae creature myself.

The thought of that was just...astounding.

"And I'm assumin' the baron's not talkin' about those damn bandits of Raven's Beak who've practically claimed the south-western plains?" Leona asked with an eyeroll. She and her father had a run-in with one of their clans a season ago when they went to Fairgrove to stock up on blueberry mead.

"Nah, but it could explain why tha bandits were that far north," Duros told her. "Perhaps these strange men and large beasts are forcin' them to move."

I gulped. The bandit clans were vicious, almost as territorial as the orcs. Yet, they had kept to themselves for years. The last time they had tried to raid the southern part of the fiefdom, the Duke's army quickly ended the problem. They retreated to the furthest corner of western Xalador, claiming it as Raven's Beak.

Duros went on, scratching his chin, "Kenrad mentioned these men were...different." He glanced at everyone but his gaze seemed to linger on me. "Almost elven."

I sucked in a breath. "The elves are dead."

Duros shrugged. "Tha elves were also long-lived. They could live a thousand years or more. Maybe some of them have been in hidin'."

It was Father who shook his head before I could respond. "No, No. The elves are definitely gone. I've done enough research myself, and Varys is doing his entire admission essay on them. If they were still around, magic would be too."

I shifted in my seat, refusing to make eye contact with Leo, who was boring a hole in my head with her stare. I hadn't told her I was still planning on sending off my essay yet.

Father went on, "Besides, the elves were a peaceful race. The war was brought on by the dryamorn—who are gone as well."

"*Banished*," I corrected. "They were locked away in the Ever-shade. With magic."

Father lifted his palms. "Don't let bedtime stories warp hard facts, son. Magic is gone. Has been since the elves died off. If there ever was a magical barrier keeping the dryamorn in the Evershade, it would have diminished the moment magic did."

"My recent findings find banishment to be true."

Father only shrugged again. "Your findings are in old elven books you have roughly translated."

Roughly. I kept my face blank. Leona pressed her lips together hard, failing miserably at hiding a laugh.

"I'm learning," I stated. "I'll find the truth and I'll add it in my admission essay. That will guarantee my acceptance into the College of Elvidawn."

Father grinned proudly. "I have no doubt about that, son. However,"—he twisted back to Duros—"I don't believe these men to be dryamorn. The kingdom would be in an absolute uproar by now."

As Father and Duros continued their back-and-forth conversation about what the strange men could be, I could only focus on how the very mention of dryamorn felt like nails had been dragged along my nerve endings.

Somewhere deep under Drake's Spine, deeper than even the dwarves of Gor Thorüm had dared to dig, lay the hidden realm of the Evershade, home of the dryamorn—the very race that eradicated the elves from existence.

The spawn of Lithia, Goddess of Death.

After the war, the dryamorns' history had been warped and watered-down, turning into legend and faerie tales just like the elves' history had. It wasn't until I began to do my research, now equipped with the ability to read Elvish text, that I learned the truth.

I knew magic had only lay dormant, so a force field of some kind was most likely still active, and the entire dryamorn race still flourished somewhere deep within the Evershade.

But...what did that mean now that magic was reemerging?

Did it make that barrier stronger? What if it did the opposite?

Had I been warned of enemies because The ReEmergence could somehow—like the rest of the magical creatures—bring the dryamorn back as well?

"Varys, are you all right?" Natalia snapped me from my daze.

I looked up, trying to hide the shakiness of my hands as I picked up my goblet and downed the rest of my wine, then grabbed the pitcher to pour myself more. "Of course. Long day."

Leona snorted. I looked to where my spellbook lay inside my bookbag which was hooked over an armchair by the hearth.

"Father, if it's all right with you, I will be heading home after dinner," I said, looking to him. "I have some things to attend to for my admission essay. Rewriting and such."

Father's features tightened, and he gave me a hard smile. "I guess that's fine, son. At least you told me this time and I didn't have to find you gone from your desk at the library...like I did three days ago."

I opened my mouth to say something and shut it. Twice. I had closed the library when I went to follow Willem and Theon.

I could only stutter out, "I-I'm so sorry."

"It's not like you to just leave," he said. "Where did you go anyway?"

I noticed Duros's scrunched face, trying not to laugh at me.

Leona giggled. "Fawkes has had a long week—*oof!*" I kicked her shin under the table, glaring daggers her way. She scoffed, picked up a half-eaten bit of bacon and tossed it into my fresh wine. I snarled in disgust and she stuck her tongue out.

"*Children,*" Natalia groaned.

Leona gave me a haughty smirk and said, "It's my fault."

The entire table turned to her—and suddenly, I realized my reaction to her response put one single thought into our parents' heads.

"You two?" Natalia asked.

Father's words tumbled over Natalia's, "Wait. What?"

Duros just started laughing. "I told ye we should've never let them bathe together!"

Krayd's chaos.

"No!" Leona and I both cried out, waving our hands.

"That's not what she meant," I said as I pinched the bridge of my nose.

"Mum, Da, ye *really* think I'd bed my best lad?" Leona crossed her arms. "Even for shits and gigs, I've found better things—and people—to do."

I huffed when the two fathers burst out laughing.

"Then what did you mean, dear?" Natalia asked.

I eyed Leona, hoping she had a good lie. "I made him leave the other day for a spontaneous trainin' session," she fibbed. "One of our lessons not too long ago was to always be on yer guard. I didn't expect it to take so long." She shrugged. "He's still got a bit to learn."

I shook my head, rolling my eyes to the stone ceiling. I couldn't necessarily be mad at her for berating me, and she knew it. She was saving my ass.

But...why was I hiding anything? Every single person at the table knew I was interested in Mae Mordaunt.

Our folks didn't know of Mae's magic though. Or mine. Or magic in general.

"With all that bein' said, *look!*" Leona held her arm across the table, her red cut still unbandaged and swollen. "He finally kicked my arse tonight."

My best friend's eyes were sparkling with something I'd only seen a handful of times: pride. Not because she wasn't ever proud of me, or proud in general—she *was* half dwarf—but she'd never had that sort of look about our training until today.

She hadn't wanted to train me initially.

I'd given my mother—*her* trainer, mentor, and idol—strife about training when I was a child. Mother wanted to start me young, so by the time I was an adult, I'd know how to defend myself in case I was ever attacked by bandits or thieves. I had no interest then; I'd much preferred reading about knights wielding swords over dragons than actually using one myself.

So, when I asked Leona to train me ten years after Mother had passed, she almost refused. Taking Krystan Wynhart's son under her wing had been unsettling for her.

But Leona had a belief in destiny unlike any other person I'd ever met. Her faith wasn't in the silent gods, or even the dwarven belief of their Victors giving strength to those in battle. She believed that every person had a destiny written out for them and no matter the path we took, our fate would find us. We could not run or hide from it.

Upon learning I was *Vyl'kríev* and that Mother would have been one as well, Leona discerned it was part of her destiny to teach me. It only made sense; she had learned from the sword-maiden who had given birth to her best friend and then given her the knowledge to teach him when his own destiny would reveal itself.

"That was tha first time he bested ye, aye?" Duros asked as he examined the cut. Natalia had at some point left and came back with a medicine chest.

Leona nodded, giving a quick wink only I could see.

"I can't believe you're showing this off like you're proud of it. You're just like your father." Natalia chuckled as she began to rub the wound with an herbal ointment.

Leona winced, giving me a disturbing grin—some sort of promise if I had to guess.

"Lassies *love* battle wounds, Fawkes."

Three glasses of wine was all it took for me to accept the invitation to join Father and Duros in singing a few ridiculous and loud tavern songs. The third one had me and Leona laughing hysterically on the floor when Duros decided to take the lyric "Until the summer moon" out of context to quickly present his ass to my father.

"All right, that's enough of you, dear." Natalia strung a chord on the lute sitting across her lap.

I immediately recognized the progression she began to play, drawing me out of my laughter and into an exaggerated groan. "Natalia—"

"Please, Varys?" Her fingers danced up and down the fretboard, every chord plucked deep and moody, the melody romantic and sad; that of a dark sea ballad. It was one of my favorites, despite my apprehension. I loved to sing, but Natalia thought me to be the real Deity of Music if Formos hadn't already been given that domain so long ago.

I wasn't *that* good. There was a difference between a pastime and a talent—and besides magic, I'd yet to reveal my true talent to anyone.

"Sing for me?" Natalia pleaded. "I have to deal with those two the rest of the night."

She gestured to Duros and Father who had both sat down in an armchair. Two moments ago, they were hollering like animals, now they were practically passed out.

Leona elbowed me. "I want to hear too, Fawkes. We both love it when ye sing."

I sighed, not giving them a yes or no. Natalia knew me well enough. She continued to strum and pluck, an eerie progression filling the gathering room, seeming to stoke the cinders in the dying hearth fire as I began to sing:

> *Thunder, Thunder*
> *Crash, here comes your storm*
> *I don't want your cold embrace*
> *Your voice, I can't afford*
>
> *You'll command the waters*
> *And wake the sky*
> *Drown my troubles*
> *Take my life*

Mae's face surfaced in my head, scared and frantic as she was at the stream. I wasn't sure why the melody and lyrics made me think of her, and I wasn't sure if it was the wine or just the thought of her that sped up the beating of my heart. Maybe it was her eyes, a kaleidoscope of amethyst fragments, the lavenders and blues reminding me of the umbrous clouds ever-hanging above the northern Serpent Sea.

> *Thunder, Thunder*
> *Crash, here comes your storm*
> *I am sailing on a wave*
> *And cannot make the shore*

Maybe it was the whirlwind of emotions she gave me, those of concern, others of passion and desire.

> *The one I love*
> *Waits for me*
> *Spare my life*
> *I beg you, please*

All I could focus on was what I'd witnessed at the stream. The crash of thunder I'd heard echoed in my head until my hands were shaking. Willem's scorched arm—burned by that flash of light.

My pitch wavered.

Not just light. Lightning. Expelled from her out of fear and rage. Empowered by *emotion*. I was right. I had to be right.

If I was, there had to be only one conclusion to what stream of mage Mae Mordaunt belonged to.

A sorcerer.

But there was more—so much more. I knew what I'd have to find.

> *Thunder, Thunder*
> *Crash, here comes your storm.*

"Her *strain*…" I whispered after my last note, my voice barely audible.

Natalia's playing ceased, her and Leona both looking at me as I stared forward, both the wine and my thoughts leaving me dazed.

As if on cue, the sound of thunder rolled above us, quiet and muffled through the stone ceiling.

Leona went to the front window and huffed. "It's raining again."

"'Tis the season," Natalia chimed.

My heart wouldn't slow down. I stood to my feet, balancing myself against Leona as I watched lightning flicker through the clouds. "I need to leave," I told her. "I need to know."

CHAPTER 8

Varys

The rain was as cold as death. I pulled my cloak over my head, wincing as Leona and I stepped into the manor yard. My cloak was fine for windy days and cool spring mornings, but I desperately needed something thicker for the colder seasons. Unfortunately, that would all depend on our finances after the Fest of Change starting on the eighteenth of autumn. Father and I weren't merchants of course, but we did acquire some donations from travelers who were happy to see our quaint little school and library thriving. The truth was we had always struggled to make ends meet, especially after Mother died. Most of our money went to the school, then food. Other necessities we required often fell into luxury. Being the librarian, I was paid whatever was leftover, which was meager and often gone before I could save. I'd had to spend a lot of my earnings the past two seasons on new tunics from wearing them out during training, not to mention growing out of them when I gained muscle. So, I would have to deal with my thin cloak for another season.

"*Wyn,*" I muttered with my palm turned toward the dark and cloudy sky. Gold light bathed my hand, blinking until it fabricated into a floating orb.

Leona grimaced. "Ye sure that's a good idea?"

I nodded. "It's after midnight. Who's going to be in the forest at this hour?"

As we came to the edge of the tree line, my *Wyn* spell illuminated frost sparkling on the leaves and brush beneath us. I stopped at a low-hanging branch, running my finger over the twigs, tiny slivers of ice melting at my warm touch. Somehow, it was not nearly as chilling as the realization that fell over me.

"This...can't be the first frost," I said incredulously, guiding the ball of light around to brighten a few feet before us.

"That's early." Leo pulled her fur cloak tighter around herself. "The first frost is always six weeks after the equinox, around the thirty-seventh of autumn or so."

I shook my head with a gulp. "Last year came earlier as well. But not *this* early."

Apparently, I had something written on my face because Leona said, "Not everything has to do with the ReEmergence, Varys."

Her use of my real name caught me off guard, making me look at her quickly. She only called me *Varys* when she was serious.

She smiled warmly and patted my shoulder. "Don't let all of this stress ye out. Just probably means a bloody cold winter is comin'."

I chuckled. "I won't let it get to me."

"Promise?"

I hesitated in my response, provoking her to glare at me.

"Varys, I *will not* let ye kill ye'self over some magic bullshite *or* Snow."

"I'm not worried about the snow, I promise."

She shook her head. "Not the *snow* I'm talking about." I paused in my steps, frosty leaves crunching beneath my feet. She chuckled. "Mae. Ye know I give everyone a nickname."

I sighed. "Indeed."

She'd given me the nickname *Fawkes* when we were young. My dark-blue hair had always grown strangely. Why I kept it shoulder length and choppy now was another story entirely, but when I was a child, I had two cowlicks that forced a few shorter layers to stick up on either side of my head. Leona had decided they looked like fox ears—fox spelled and pronounced as "fawkes." The misspelling in her Common language studies was quickly corrected when learning to read, but due to her inherited dwarven accent, it was a challenge for her to understand when she was young. So, the spelling and pronunciation stayed—if anything, due to her stubbornness.

"Mae might take offense to that nickname, though," I said just as we ducked under a low branch. "She's been labeled as something she isn't because of her hair color."

"I don't mean it rudely. I mean, when ye look at me, don't I resemble a beautiful rose with thorns?"

She blinked her lashes as girly as she could. She'd never been much of a lady.

"The thorns, maybe." I grinned deviously.

She elbowed me. "I'm fuckin' gorgeous and ye know it."

"Sure. But I still call you Leona."

She huffed. "Oh, fine. If it pisses her off, I'll just find a better one."

I snorted, knowing if she pissed Mae off, she may not get the chance to redeem herself. "How about you just call her *Mae?*"

"No!" She laughed out. "That'd be weird."

I rolled my eyes with a chuckle and continued forward.

The path came to a downward slope and we trudged heavily, careful not to slip. The night was quiet besides the rain and the occasional rumble of thunder. I'd walked through this part of the forest between Elros and the Cauldücen's manor a hundred times. The path we took was probably created by me and my father alone. I'd always felt safe here, unlike the southern part of the forest where Mother had died—we shouldn't have been there to begin with.

But tonight, every hair on my body stood on end. The feeling of hidden eyes staring at me from every angle compelled my hand to stay ready to draw my blade. The chill on my skin wasn't from the temperature, but from the panic rising up my spine to the crook of my neck.

"Relax," Leona said. "Everythin' is fine."

"You don't feel it?"

"No, Fawkes," she drawled. "I don't have a weird connection to the *blood of the earth* tellin' me somethin' wants to eat me—"

The brush ahead rustled.

Leona and I both stilled and shifted into guarded stances. With a quick curse, I dispelled the light. I gripped the handle of my sword tighter, both of us watching and squinting through the darkness. All was silent again. We held our breath as we listened. There was a crunch of leaves and twigs, then someone stepped into the path ahead. They could see us as well, staring silently for a beat too long for comfort until a man's voice asked, "Who's out there?"

I glanced at Leona, looking for some sort of approval. She only kept her gaze forward and I responded, "Who wants to know?"

The man walked closer until we could see him well enough. "Wynhart? What are you doing out here?"

Before us stood Eryx RothHall.

I didn't know much about Eryx besides the tragedy that occurred two springs ago when his wife passed away. I'd purchased leather from him that made up the trousers I currently donned, and I knew his meat sold at the butcher at a price my father and I could never afford. I also knew he was an acquaintance of Mae's.

Seeing no immediate threat, the grip on my blade loosened. "Ah, good evening. We're traveling back to town."

He looked me over. "At this time of night?"

"What's it matter to ye anyway?" Leona sneered. "Ye're not patrol."

Eryx snapped his head toward her, a snarl on his face as if he were shocked she'd spoken to him. "No, but as a citizen of Elros, I find it my duty to report any suspicious activity in these woods."

She smirked. "Then why don't ye run along and find somethin' suspicious?"

I shot her a displeased look, shaking my head. I was in no mood to make enemies. "We were at her house, and I realized I needed to get something I had left back at home," I explained as the two continued to scowl at one another. "What brings you into the woods this late?"

"Hunting." Eryx slowly dragged his glare from Leona to me.

"Well, good luck. We'll try our best to be quiet and not to disturb anything you may be hunting." I bowed my head. "I hope you find the rest of your night well."

He nodded, and I believed we'd made parting ways apparent. But just as I passed his shoulder, his hand caught my arm, jerking me a bit. Leona shouted a Dwarvish curse, but Eryx raised his other hand to stop her as he asked, "What was that light?"

My stomach dipped. "W-What?"

"I saw a bright light when I came around the bushes. Now there is no light." His brow furrowed. "What was that light, Wynhart?"

"It was my bloody torch, ye dolt." Leona pulled a previously used torch stick from her belt I didn't realize was on her.

Thank the gods—

"It's raining. Do you think I'm stupid?" Eryx growled.

Shit.

Leona scoffed. "The tree cover isn't lettin' enough rain on the road to extinguish a torch! We panicked when we heard something rustlin' and put the torch out." She snorted. "Just a busybody, apparently."

"Why were you panicked? Up to something?" Eryx tilted his head.

My jaw tightened. This bastard was getting on my nerves—

Eryx snatched the torch from Leona's grasp, hands palming the top of it. "Interesting. It's cold as if it hasn't been lit—"

Leona cocked back her arm to take a swing. I shouted and rammed my way between them. "*Stop it!*" I ripped the torch back from Eryx. "RothHall, I don't know what your problem is, but please let us pass. We don't want any trouble."

His eyes met mine, narrowing as he searched my face. I didn't know what he was looking for, but he stepped back and adjusted his cloak. Leona still braced herself against my arm as if it were a gate and if I dropped it, she'd pounce.

Eryx glanced between the two of us. "No trouble to have."

Leona laughed darkly, shaking her head. "Ye're fuckin' right about that—"

"I wouldn't travel this forest at night anymore," Eryx cut her off as if she didn't exist, speaking directly to me. "It appears you are well armed. But the forest is...not the same as it was."

I would have asked him to elaborate if he hadn't already pissed me off. Besides, I was already aware of how I felt walking tonight.

"We'll keep our guard up." I eyed him. "As we would with anything. Good evening."

I linked my arm with Leona's and dragged her past Eryx before she tried to stab him.

Eryx didn't follow—he disappeared as if the darkness had swallowed him whole.

Leona and I were quiet the rest of the way to the stream. My face was hot with anger, no longer bothered by the cold. Leona was glaring forward most of the way, every once in a while glancing back as if Eryx might jump out.

We wouldn't be discussing *anything* until we got to the library. Which meant I wouldn't be using magic either.

Thankfully, the rain had stopped, leaving a sharp, chilly temperature in its wake. Leona broke the silence with a curse, pointing forward. "Look."

I huffed. We could see the stream now, the waters higher than they'd been earlier that day due to the rain. We would have to cross it by wading through.

This was a constant problem we dealt with every autumn. Years ago, there had been a bridge connecting Elros to the forest but was demolished during a storm. Coincidentally, it was the storm everyone in Elros knew as the time Mae had gotten herself caught up in a tree and lightning struck the branches, causing her to fall and break her arm. The Mordaunts and their rich advocates had voted for the bridge to not be rebuilt since Mae wouldn't have been able to cross to that side of the stream without it. This became a huge issue for the Cauldücens whenever they would go back and forth between Elros and their manor.

Unfortunately, it wasn't as if the people of Elros really considered my friends a part of the town anyway.

Laying my cloak on the ground, I rolled my sword and book bag into the material, then held the bunch above my head, keeping everything I didn't want wet out of the water when we crossed. Leona snarled as she watched the rushing stream.

"This is fine," I said to her optimistically. "This time, I have a spell that will dry us off and warm us up in no time."

She rolled her eyes. "That's convenient. Could've helped me out last year when I came down with hypothermia."

"Honestly, that was your own fault. You could have stayed at the tavern."

She scoffed. "The man I'd just slept with told me he *loved me*. Fuck that. The moment he passed out, I ran home. I didn't care if the stream was cold."

"Not just cold. Almost iced over completely. You could have *died*."

She shrugged. "A risk I was willin' to take. Better an iced fanny than a narked one." But as she looked at the water with a grimace, I wasn't sure I believed her. "That spell better work."

A roguish smile lifted my lips. "Hope so. I've not tried it out yet."

She whipped her head to me, scowling. "Ye aren't serious? There's no way in Torm I'm lettin' ye cast a spell on me ye haven't tried out!"

"Relax." I stepped to the edge of the stream. "I'll use it on me first. Let's just get to the library."

She blew out her bottom lip. "Fawkes, I swear to the stars, if ye don't find what yer lookin' for and we came all this way for nothin', ye can forget about your bloody charms and lights 'cause I'll hide that fuckin' spellbook for a week."

I ignored her and stepped in, hissing at the iciness that immediately seeped through my boots. With every step further and deeper into the stream, my muscles stiffened and burned down to the marrow. I gasped when the water hit the bare skin above my waistband. At the deepest point, it was just past my ribs.

Leona on the other hand, whose head barely came to my shoulder, was going to have trouble.

I turned to see if she was coming, my legs tingling and numb. Leona had her bundle of things above her head, watching me with tight lips. "That water's goin' to come over my tits," she said deadpan.

I grimaced. "I-I promise my spell will dry you off in no time. Just—" I shivered. My spine felt like it was trying to curl into my shoulders and my legs were beginning to ache. "J-Just hurry, p-please."

She growled a few Dwarvish curse words under her breath. "This lass better be worth it."

She stepped in. The shriek she let out probably woke every person in Elros, but she was in and *running* through the water. She passed me and didn't stop until she was on the other side. She pulled herself onto the bank and wrapped her arms around herself with chattering teeth. "Fawkes! Y-Ye bloody idiot! Ye stupid, l-love-sick git–"

The rest was in Dwarvish and I thanked the gods I could only decipher bits and pieces.

I, too, finally made it to the bank, shivering to the point I thought my bones would snap if I didn't stop. Leona wrapped herself in her dry cloak and slung Thorn over her shoulder, too cold to strap it back on properly. "I-I will require a hearth and yer f-father's finest mead when we get to the library."

"Fine. But let's cut through the alleys. It's quicker."

We found ourselves jogging stiffly into town through the east gate, cutting corners and into the back roads we generally didn't go out of our way to use. But we were too cold to care, not stopping for anything.

We turned into an alley just as a large person stepped into the road, coming from the opposite direction. They stopped, letting out a wet, throaty cough before vomiting onto the street. Swaying to our right, light from the nearest house window shone upon him, and my pulse skipped when I identified the blue and gold cape over his shoulders.

Leona scoffed. "The fuck—"

I grabbed her and pulled her behind some stacked crates, finger to my mouth. "Shh. That's Rucas Mordaunt."

"What?"

We peered around. His feet seemed to drag as he ambled along. With a tip back of the bottle in his hand, he steered left, came to the door house, and banged.

"Come on, Fawkes. It's freezin'," Leona whined. "Who cares about that bastard?"

I shook my head. My nerves were roiling, heart racing. "I didn't know Rucas was a drunk."

"A drunk? Shite, I've had nights like that after too much ale——"

"But you don't find your way to a less fortunate family's home after midnight."

The door creaked open, firelight bathing the alley road. "Mr. Mordaunt," a man said, sounding surprised—nervous.

Rucas slumped against the doorway. "I've come for yuh payment, Whitaker."

I froze. Leona's eyes widened as she looked at me.

"Rucas." Mr. Whitaker, a livestock farmer, tried to laugh off his obvious apprehension. "It's a bit late. My children are sleeping and my wife——"

"Yes, yes…" Rucas tipped back the bottle. "Yuh wife, indeed. Are ya going to invite me inside?"

Mr. Whitaker was silent for a moment. The wind shifted in our direction—I could smell the reek of Rucas's alcohol on the breeze.

"All right." Mr. Whitaker nodded once, and Rucas was led inside. The door closed.

Leona and I both let out a heavy breath. "What in Torm was that about?" she asked.

I stepped out from the crates, noticing quickly the window to the left of the door was open. I could still hear the murmuring of voices.

Leona whispered my name as I crouched and crept over to the window, plastering myself against the wall beneath it.

I could hear everything.

"Rucas, I promise I will have half of my debt repaid after the Fest of Change," Mr. Whitaker said, a pleading tone in his voice. "I thought we agreed on that at the tavern the other night."

I could hear the bottle tip over, liquid sloshing around, and then Rucas let out a gasp when he stopped drinking. "Ya, but the guild ran into some…financial issues. The trip to Latera cost me *greatly*. Being part of this merchant guild has its benefits, Whitaker. But only if ya pay yuh dues. So, I've decided—tonight. Tonight, ya pay, or ya can kiss yuh shop goodbye." He hiccuped and belched.

"I…don't have the money." Mr. Whitaker's voice shook. "Rucas, we agreed——"

"Then perhaps we can come to another sort of agreement."

A door opened from within the house, a woman's voice asking, "What's the meaning of this?"

Rucas laughed out. "Perfect timing." The bottle tipped up once more. "Whitaker, I'm willing to cut yuh debt in half, here tonight, if you grant me this one request."

My insides turned, the already too-thin air becoming harder to breathe. I pushed up, just enough to where I could see into the room.

Rucas stood in front of Mrs. Whitaker, twirling one of her golden curls around his finger. "I get her for the night. You keep yuh shop and yuh debt is cut in half."

By the gods.

All the blood left Mrs. Whitaker's face. "You *can't* be serious."

Rucas turned to Mr. Whitaker, who was gripping the back of a chair, knuckles white. Rucas smiled. "Do we have a deal? Debt is halved. More food for yuh children, better clothes on their backs. Ya can pay the rest after the Fest of Change."

My insides twisted. I couldn't believe what I was hearing.

"Maire, it's...we have no choice," Mr. Whitaker whispered.

"You sick bastard! Get out!" Maire shrieked. "I'll tell every soul in this town what kind of criminal you are—"

Rucas's hand clamped over her mouth. Mr. Whitaker stepped forward, hands waving in a placating manner. *"Wait!* Rucas, don't hurt her."

"Oh, I won't." Rucas chuckled. "I'll be *very* gentle with this one."

Fuck this.

I sank down and thrust both of my hands out from underneath my cloak before I began to rotate them around each other as if I were creating a ball of air. I heard Leona whisper something, but ignored her, hands glowing white hot. I muttered, "Śíçaevr..."

Despite my already frozen fingers, frost crystals formed between my palms. I continued to swirl them, creating a small, spiked orb of ice. One glance to Leona motioned for her to start running before I jumped up and threw it into the house. The orb hit Rucas in the side of the head, knocking him over. He went down, crashing to the floor. The Whitakers gasped when the ice shattered, and by the grace of the gods, never looked in my direction as I took off running behind Leo.

We didn't stop until we were a block from the library, halting to catch our breath.

"Fawkes! What in Torm—"

"Rucas..." I huffed and sucked in the cold air, my lungs burning. My use of magic had tired me more than I'd expected. "*Shit...*" I coughed and waved my hand to tell her to keep walking. "I'll explain on the way."

I filled her in and what seemed like several torturous and cold hours later, we made it to my house. I quickly built a fire in the library hearth.

Leona shivered as she curled under her cloak. "H-Hurry and use that damn spell already."

"Give me just a moment." I shuddered as my knees hit the cold hardwood floor, laying my opened spellbook before me. I flattened the pages down and scanned through the spell. My eyes went blurry for a moment, but cleared when I blinked. "I just need to find the command word."

She groaned. "I'm goin' to freeze to death—"

"*Thryng.*" Springing up from my palm, an *eçor* appeared. This was a visual representation of the makeup of the spell, something only wizards could truly understand and produce in their magic. If present during the casting—as they weren't for all spells—each *eçor* housed a different color devoted to the school of magic cast, shapes and images symbolizing the ruling elements and celestial bodies, and Elvish runes. The *eçor* floating above my palm was orange and made up of circles and the symbol for the element of air. It ticked and turned like a time-teller.

With a flick of my wrist, the *eçor* expanded and I guided it over my body. It pulled water out of each thread of my clothes and every strand of my blue hair. The water collected until it became a large bead of liquid. I dismissed the water into an empty bucket by the hearth.

Speaking the command word again, I sent the spell over Leona. She watched it with a grimace as it expanded and fell over her, exhaling with relief as the freezing water left her skin and slid off the metal plates of her greaves and bracers. The moment she was dry, she started for our kitchen down the hall.

"That. Was. Shit. Find yer damn book, I'll find the mead."

"So, are we just goin' to ignore the fact we almost witnessed Rucas Mordaunt take another man's wife as if he doesn't have his own back home?" Leona questioned.

"Of course not," I said, grabbing yet another book as the last two hadn't given me any viable information. "But...I hit him hard enough to knock him out. I think—I *hope*. He'll probably come to, sober up, and realize he made a complete ass of himself."

Leona shook her head. "Such a lousy excuse."

"I'm positive that's the game he'll play. He'll make some grand apology, pay the Whitakers off, and we'll never hear a word about it. As if it never happened."

Leona drank from her tankard of warm mead. "But it *did* happen, and ye saw it."

"You're right." I flipped a page and huffed. I wasn't finding anything I hoped to.

I looked up to see her glaring my way. "Ye *should* be writin' Kenrad a letter explainin' what ye saw."

I threw my hands in the air. "Yes, and I'll be sure to add that I hit Rucas with a ball of ice I conjured *myself*. I saved Mrs. Whitaker and I'd do it again, but I..."

Leona inclined her head. "Ah. Ye wish ye hadn't used magic."

I tossed the book aside with a rough exhale. "I wasn't thinking. I just...I had to do something to help. I can only hope the Whitakers didn't notice anything magical about the ice. But unless they come forward about the incident and need a witness, I'm going to stay low." I paused. "Does that make me a coward?"

Leona sighed. "Not a coward. Ye did the right thing by stoppin' Rucas. I guess I just can't wait for the day when ye can use yer magic openly. If people like Rucas knew there are people like ye willin' to use yer gifts to put people like him down, there'd be a lot less evil in the world."

"And I'll confess if the Whitakers need me to. I will."

She nodded. "I know ye will. Ye're a good man, Fawkes." She moved the tankard to her mouth. "A hero even."

I shook my head. "Heroes don't let villains walk free."

"Ye're being way too hard on ye'self." She gulped down the rest of her mead, then put the tankard aside and stretched out on the settee like a sleepy cat. She had removed her armor, now relaxed in her tunic and breeches. Propping her head up on her fist, she looked at me with bored, hooded eyes. "Are ye done yet? I'm knackered."

I clicked my tongue. "I've barely started." I gestured to the stack of books in front of me. "You can always go to sleep."

"I don't sleep well on this settee," she whined. "And I'm not sleepin' with ye anymore. Ye hog the blankets."

She was the one who hogged the blankets.

"Ye should just put a bed in yer room for me," she said. "I come over enough anyway."

"Yes, that'd be a real sight for my future wife. 'Oh, by the way, love of my life, this bed is for my best friend who will sleep here on occasion.'" I lifted my palms. "Well, won't you look at that, I'm a bachelor again."

Leona only smirked. "Fawkes, whoever yer future wife is— whether it be Snow or some other lucky lass—they'll have to accept that I'm not goin' anywhere. And she'll have to like me whether she wants to or not."

I snickered. "You're still not getting a bed."

She grumbled something under her breath before standing and walking into the rows of books.

I knew exactly where she was going and counted down the seconds before—

She shrieked, and I heard what sounded like jumping up and down before she raced back to me, dropping a book before me and shouting, "Why didn't ye tell me?!"

I laughed as I looked over the roughly bound book, title reading *The Dragonhart Series: Book 2.*

"We received it the other day." I'd prepared for this conversation. "That's the only copy, for now, so be diligent with it."

She held the book to her chest and sighed ardently as she

slumped back down to the settee. "I won't be sleepin' t'night when I've got Kiren to read about. I thought ye said ye didn't know when Y.T. Fillen would be done."

"I said I didn't know when the books would arrive. You know how it is in this town. If you don't order through the merchant guild, shipments take a little longer." I smiled. "Plus, I may have wanted to surprise you."

She crossed her arms. "I hate surprises."

"I know." I winked, then returned to my work.

I didn't hear another sound out of Leona for a while after that. She began to read and by the looks of it, devouring every page with wide eyes, chewing on her lip.

I couldn't help but smile—watching someone read and obsess over their work was what every author loved to see.

Y.T. Fillen: citizen of Elvidawn, recently betrothed, and Elros's favorite author of *The Dragonhart Series* and a few other short stories on the shelves of the library.

In secret, he was a twenty-year-old man still living with his father, who wrote late into the night up high in his bedroom when he should be working on his college admission essay.

I was Y.T Fillen.

I started the series when I was sixteen and was currently in the middle of the final drafts for book three. From the start, I wanted to write under a pen name to hide the fact I was the one writing these stories. I didn't enjoy being center stage.

But when I'd bound together three copies of book one and placed them on the shelves of the library, I had no idea how popular the series would become in town. The copies were always checked out. And my little web of white lies was getting out of control, especially around Leona—I hadn't told her I was the author and didn't intend to.

She was constantly daydreaming about Kiren, one of my main characters who was a dragon disguised as a human. Of course, I had taken the inspiration for his character from old fables of dragons within our world. There were many tales, even in history books, that dragons possessed the ability to transform themselves into humans and live among us with relative ease. I often wondered, knowing what I knew now about magic and The ReEmergence, if those stories were fact and if I knew anyone who was a dragon in disguise.

The thought was both amusing and frightening.

Hours passed, and before I knew it, dawn's soft pink and turquoise light began to flood the library through the windows as birds sang their song. The fire had died in the hearth, and Leona had fallen asleep right in the middle of one of my more erogenous scenes—which was *so* unlike her. My eyes were burning and heavy with exhaustion.

"Aha!" I jammed my finger onto the page. Leona stirred and cursed me, shifting onto her other side. I ignored her. I finally found what I'd been looking for.

It seemed that of the three streams of mages, sorcerers were the most complicated. One could say every mage had their complications, with wizards being a mental practice and druids requiring specific components. But sorcerers were complex because they were never *just* sorcerers. Their strain was determined by who they were.

Their magic was raw and often, wild. Emotions could play a part in their spellcasting, anger being like air to a fire, where sadness could shut down a spell entirely.

"Sorcerers are encouraged to focus on what brings them joy when casting," I read aloud, "as happiness is powerful enough to empower a spell if one needed to do so. Often, sorcerers abandoned worldly attachments so nothing could hamper their abilities."

There was a short excerpt about a mage accidentally setting half of the Great Plains to flame when his lover was found dead. I thought about how Mae must have been feeling when Willem attacked her. The fear and anger she must have felt. How her emotions could have overwhelmed her and caused that great expulsion of power. Perhaps in her state of panic, she burned or jolted Willem.

I realized…it might have been an accident. Maybe that's why she seemed to avoid my questions. Why she lied. She wasn't even sure what had happened.

All in all, it pointed to her being a sorcerer, but didn't give me any clue about her strain.

For another hour, I searched through every strain the book mentioned, keeping in mind the power I'd felt, the thunder I'd heard, and the light I'd seen. Everything I'd witnessed pointed to some sort of storm magic.

I read on, the excitement pounding in my chest slowly starting to ache and feel empty with every paragraph and word. Eventually, it came to another great historical piece about a sorcerer once flooding the entire city of Livohka in order to drown the dryamorn during the war—at any other time, I'd be interested to read more.

However, the chapter ended. The pages moved on to another topic.

And I came to a dead end once more.

I didn't have any other books on sorcerers. Especially not on strains.

I let my head fall to the table, thumping my brow against the wood a few times. My eyelids felt raw and swollen as I turned to the window, the sun now just above the horizon.

Leona yawned and sat up in the settee, her eyes widening when she saw my face. "Ye haven't slept?"

I barely had the energy to shake my head.

Her brows lifted. "And did ye find what ye were lookin' for?"

I stood and dropped my spellbook down on the table before I trudged upstairs to sleep off my defeat.

CHAPTER 9

Mae

The gods wouldn't give you something you couldn't handle.

The gods were silent and didn't give a shit about what I could and could not handle. And if they had decided at some time—wherever they remained—that I would be inflicted with this illness because they believed I could handle it, I wasn't so sure they were entitled to my prayers and worship.

But Mr. Welch had still told me such years ago and had made many other undercutting remarks whenever my parents had taken me to his infirmary. It did not matter whether I was sick with a common cold or if I came in with concerns about my menses, any problem I had was always blamed on the Pallid Curse and was disregarded because it was *the gods' will.*

I had tossed and turned all night with my typical nightmares and pain attacks, but this time Mr. Welch's words had added to my misery. I wasn't entirely sure why they were bothering me at all. I hadn't been to the infirmary in two years, since he'd dubbed me deranged. Maybe it was just because of what his pig son had done to me.

But I didn't truly believe the gods had anything to do with that. However, they did have a lot to do with the elves. And their magic.

I didn't know much Xaladorian history. I'd absorbed what I did know from Eryx—who claimed to know little—and from tales I'd heard whilst shopping in the market. I knew we were in the second age, and that humans and halflings came from a distant land in the middle of the first. The dwarves had their own history and kept it to themselves, or so I'd been told, and the orcs came to the land much later.

But the elves...they were supposedly god-made. Due to a war some thousand years ago, their history had become strewn and not much more than a faerie tale. It was why so many Xaladorians in this age didn't believe in the magic of the elves to begin with. We only had legends that spoke of the gods creating the elves as the first inhabitants upon Xalador's inception, giving them features mirroring their own: skin, hair, and eyes in any and every color imaginable, tapered ears, and tall, lithe bodies. And of course, the tales spoke of magic and how their powers bathed Xalador with a prosperous, golden first age.

The end of the war brought the second age, and evidently, complete genocide to the entire elven race due to Lithia's fiends, the dryamorn. However, everyone in Xalador knew that the elven lineage was passed on. Over the course of the second age, humans and halflings had begun to show features of elvenkind; entire families with brightly-hued hair and eyes. Sometimes, the aspects only showed up in a son or daughter.

But *never* pointed ears. And *never* magic.

So, maybe that's why my dreams had spun of those words. Maybe my own consciousness was reminding me I didn't necessarily have elven features—features that were supposedly of the gods.

But I did have magic.

A small part of me believed it was the circlet that passed the abilities to me. Had somehow changed me into someone who could shoot bolts of lightning from my fingertips and read Elvish as if I was an elf myself.

But there was a large part of me that knew, and maybe an even bigger part that hoped, that I was given this ability. I thought over what had transpired the night before. How my veins had glowed as if the same blood that had been burning me alive finally became fire. But it wasn't fire. It was light and radiance and color. It was *power*.

Maybe giving me magic was the gods' way of giving me something I could use to handle everything I couldn't.

I slipped deeper under my quilt, groaning and curling up around my nakedness. The temperature of my bedroom this morning reminded me that my skin had always been unnaturally cold. It was only two weeks into autumn, but the freezing air promised winter was coming early this year.

I needed to get out of bed, but I swore I could see my breath even under the covers. Had the entire town froze over? What I wouldn't give for a bedside hearth, or...

With the thought of heat, my mind raced back to my dreams. I'd dreamed of Varys last night as well, wanting everything I couldn't have here in reality. Even there within my mind, his touch was warm and soothing. But that...that was a different kind of heat, and one I was not accustomed to. Allowing those images to repeat in my head, I found myself short of breath, imagining him behind me, caressing me. And that heat, like liquid fire, burned and throbbed in places I wasn't aware of before, and I couldn't help but to push all of those pulsing aches against the mattress. It wasn't enough, so I...imagined my hands were his, my fingers his as I stroked between my thighs. Until I was no longer cold. Until I had release.

But as if my mind had a will of its own, as my pleasure ebbed, I was reminded that those dreams of desire had been devoured by nightmares and screaming. I had watched his face shatter with those crystals, and the feeling of anguish was still so palpable.

She had shattered him.

Ripped him from my dream state as if those damn words she always screamed were more important for me to hear than to feel or see him. She had to know he had become someone important to me so quickly. Whenever she had screamed those words before, it had always been out of desperation or warning. This time, they had been laced with a threat. As if she would continue to break him over and over if I didn't do what she said.

I didn't know who or what she was, but it was clear to me she wasn't just part of my nightmares. She had to be a separate being.

But I would never abandon the happiness I'd had as I slept. Nobody could take that from me, nor remove the flashes of his lips pressed to mine, his voice decadent as he'd spoken my name.

And there was something else I had felt when I'd dreamed of him. *Still* felt even now.

The connection I'd always sensed between me and Varys had become something stronger. Like a chain trying to wrap itself around me and the more I evaded its grip, it clamped down. It wasn't holding me prisoner, it just...*wanted* me. To keep me if I allowed it to begin its binding, heat curling within and filling me with...

Feelings I shouldn't be having for a man I barely knew.

In an attempt to will away those prohibited desires, I shoved the quilt down. The temperature of the bedroom hit me as if I'd dumped a bucket of ice water over my head. I hissed and cursed at myself for not dressing in a chemise the night before.

I lifted my left arm, held it in the dim morning sun—

All air left my lungs. I jolted upright, ignoring the cold and instant lance of pain through my muscles from my flares. Following every blue and purple vein, a dark stain now streaked in thin, jagged lines, affirming my former enlightenment that veins looked like lightning. My instant reaction was to try and rub it off, but I couldn't. It was as if I'd had this mark my entire life, like a birthmark. Eryx had a large triangular-shaped birthmark on his right shoulder, but these marks weren't raised and reminded me more of a tattoo.

The marks started from the middle of my lower arm and stopped just at my wrist. A knot formed in the pit of my stomach when a thought hit me. *What if they spread?*

I had to hide it.

I slid out of bed, shutting out the shock of the icy temperature despite how it made my body pimple with goosebumps. Ignoring my stiff muscles from my restless night, I padded softly over to my wardrobe, knowing if I made a single sound, Mother would wake and be up here before I could come up with an explanation. Teeth chattering, I quickly donned a tight, long-sleeved, white chemise to go under a dress I'd yet to pick out. The sleeves covered the marks—

it was a chemise I often wore whenever I had bruises I needed to hide.

But it seemed a new fear surfaced with every shallow breath I took as I stared stupefied at myself in the vanity mirror while combing my hair, worst-case scenarios playing in my mind. Perhaps if anyone saw the marks, I could tell Mother and Rucas they'd appeared after I touched that circlet they gave me. But then, my parents would demand to see the circlet, and I still hadn't figured out how I was going to tell them I'd lost it. Doing so would bring up what had happened at the stream and eventually, Willem and Theon would be questioned. And knowing Rucas, whether I received the powers from the circlet or not, there would be consequences.

A small, rough sound escaped from the back of my throat as I stood with my hands on my hips. My plans were slipping through my fingers. I knew they weren't well-thought-out to begin with. Gods, I wasn't clever in the slightest, but I was desperate.

I braced the sill of my frost-covered window and gazed out to the pink horizon. The hills of Elros rolled and dipped past the main gate in the south and didn't seem to end even as they were devoured by thick forest. I knew the land eventually flattened into plains of grass and heather, and stretched for leagues until inclining once more into great mountains, the peaks of Drake's Spine so high they were lost beyond the stars—just more things I'd been told. I'd never witnessed them. For all I knew, there was nothing beyond the forests of this small piece of Xalador.

Something flittered across the window, snagging my focus. A small white butterfly had perched itself on our roof. Given that it was so cold this morning, I was surprised to see a butterfly at all, as most insects migrated to the south where it was a milder winter. But it was still, technically, autumn. I just hoped the poor thing didn't freeze to death.

For a moment, I found myself lost in watching it, its black speckled wings opening and closing slowly as if it were showing them off. A smile tugged on the corner of my mouth. Such freedom the creature had. To go anywhere it desired.

I wanted that. I wanted to somehow wrap myself inside my very own chrysalis and sprout wings. To no longer be stuck in a family that didn't want me, in a home I was caged inside. Even in my bedroom, a place where most people would find rest, I was in a constant state of disquiet. I was always pacing in here, or staring out the damn window, anticipating when I'd be hurt again or have another pain flare.

My gaze shifted to a clay shingle-roofed building that sat just beyond the outskirts of the center of town. The library. If I looked hard enough, I could see Varys's window.

I couldn't lie to myself. There was so much of me that wanted my plans to work because they involved him. Meeting with him and finding out more about the elves was crucial for me to understand my powers, but it was dangerous for us to become anything else. But, I wanted it. I wanted him and always had. It made me feel incredibly selfish, as if I might accidentally use him. How could it not look that way when he had information that would help me get what I wanted?

But despite everything I felt, time was of the essence. I didn't know how long my powers would stay dormant, nor did I know how to tame them if I lost control. The storm beneath my skin felt so wild. *I* felt wild.

These marks were only unforeseen obstacles. This power was a second chance, and life barely offered second chances. I suddenly had another choice instead of deciding between pain or death.

Today, I would hold my head high, gather every amount of courage I possessed, and set my plan into motion. I pulled a crimson overdress from my wardrobe, hands shaking as I tied the corseted front's strings tight. The color seemed like a proper pick; the rays of light from the morning sun beaming in streaks of gold and red. Eryx always told me mornings of this color were a promise of good luck for hunters, the red for the blood of their kills to come and the gold for the money they'd earn.

I wasn't out for blood or money. But...I was on the hunt.

CHAPTER 10

Mae

I spent the next three hours of the morning making bread in complete peace. Mother had woken, checked the gathering room to see if Rucas had come home, and when she saw he was still missing, grabbed her cloak and left. No good morning. No greetings.

I was fine with that.

I sat down to eat my freshly baked bread, spooning out a greedy amount of honey to drizzle over the slice on my plate. I let out a sigh, breaking the deafening silence of the house. There weren't many silent moments within these walls. The mahogany chairs lining either side of the dining table had often found their high backs on the floor in times of drunken rage. Sometimes, they were thrown at me, but only once had one of the chairs ever hit me—a leg across the back of my shoulder.

The very chair I sat in I had claimed as my seat long ago because it was the only one he'd never swung at me. It was the only non-matching chair at the table, a gift to my mother from my maternal grandparents long before I was born. No matter how many times Rucas had wanted to get rid of it, Mother fought him about it, so it stayed. And I knew why he never picked it up. It was wrought iron with a thin, pointed arch back, and if used as a weapon, it would assure injuries too difficult to hide.

A thud on wood echoed through the entry hall behind me before the front door swung open and then slammed shut, propelling my heart into a quick race. I swallowed, slowly lowering my next bite of bread, squaring my shoulders, bracing the iron armrests. I knew who it was before he ever stepped into the dining room, all of the fresh air suddenly snuffed out with the bittersweet stench of liquor. The wood floor groaned as he shuffled, steps haphazard and heavy.

Rucas was still drunk.

Keeping my eyes forward, his presence pressed down on my skin as he moved from behind me. I went taut, preparing myself for anything. My left arm tingled, but I couldn't tell if it was the start of a flare or if my powers were reacting to my situation. As much as I wanted to look down, to see if my veins were glowing, I was...godsdammit, I was too scared. I needed to remain still and unnoticed.

My lungs ached and burned as I prevented myself from breathing normally or in his direction. He had hit me for less before. Left bruises for glancing at him a few years ago. He normally went for my shoulders or arms, sometimes my shins and ankles, but he'd slapped me in the face many times for walking past him.

But along with the iron chair he'd never reached for, he'd never struck me with his fists in the face. I often wondered if it was because I'd never made him truly mad enough to do so. He hated me, but I didn't infuriate him often. He just hurt me because he could.

I watched him from the corner of my eyes as he trudged to the kitchen, glass clinking as he placed a bottle of whatever was seeping through his sweat down on the countertop. He grabbed two eggs from the egg basket and cracked them onto a skillet.

I wasn't focusing on his struggle to light the tinder, nor the curses as they left his mouth sounding just as soaked as he was. My gaze had settled on the swollen, bloody wound on the side of his head.

He wet a rag and winced as he pressed it on the blow. I wasn't proud of the smile that tugged at the corners of my lips. Deep inside, somewhere in my chest, a sensation wanted to rise behind that smirk. Amusement, laughter, rejoice. All of it laced with a vile, bitter taste on my tongue.

He deserved that injury, however it had happened.

I continued to eat, slowly, soundlessly, wincing when the metal spoon *tinked* the glass jar as I scooped more honey onto another slice of bread. But he never looked my way, never growled at the noise I made. It was like I was a ghost, completely invisible.

I...preferred this, I realized. To be transparent and intangible rather than the porcelain object I was to him—constantly thrown from the shelf and broken, then put back together as if my worth was still the same.

Someone came through the front door and Mother gasped as she emerged from the entryway. "Rucas, dear, your head."

She glided across the dining room, arm outstretched as she made her way to him, to take his face into her hands—reminding me that somewhere, deep within her, there was care for him even if all love and romance had been extinguished long ago.

He gripped her wrist. Shoved her away with a growl. "Don't."

For a moment, she stood there gaping at him, throat working on a gulp. He went back to his cooking, the smell of eggs now mixing with the stench of him, banishing my appetite completely.

Mother turned to me, her smile not meeting her eyes. "You made bread, I see."

Something in the way she stated it made me gulp. As if I shouldn't have done so. I glanced at Rucas. Anything out of my mouth could set him off.

"Yes," I said. "We were out—"

"Ya *ate* all of it," he snapped.

I breathed out of my nose, trying to compose the anger wanting to rise. Assessing his disposition was always part of the game—and it *was* a game. A dangerous one. I'd learned that long ago. I just often lost.

But today was different. Felt different. Maybe it was because *I* was different, given my new abilities even though I didn't know how to bring them forth. Maybe it was because he was drunk and injured. Whatever it was, in this match I felt like I had the upper hand.

I held my head high and stared straight at him. And I shouldn't have, but that torrential sensation that had been stirring within since my feet hit the ground this morning was demanding me to do everything I knew would get me in trouble.

So, I let loose the grin I was holding back and sneered, "Am I not a resident of this house?"

Rucas snapped his head to me, face contorting into a snarl, flames of the stove burning in his bloodshot, hazel eyes. He opened his mouth to spit something…but stilled as he regarded my face. My body went rigid, but I refused to drop my gaze. The grin remained, every nerve dancing with alarm as I clenched my hands together under the table. Twinges of pain lashed up my wrist. I ignored them. All the courage I was trying to display would be rendered false if he saw I was shaking.

Rucas's baffled expression was familiar and I realized where I'd seen it before. *Varys.* The day Varys stood up to Rucas in the shop, I'd watched him remain dignified and courageous as he demanded his money back.

Any other day, Rucas would have flown across the dining room and slapped me across the face. Today, he only lifted the rag back to his head, free hand pointing a finger at me. "Better be glad yuh mother still *wants* ya, filth. Ya don't know how many times I've thought about dumping yuh cursed, wretched ass on our front porch, locking the doors, and calling it a godsdamn day."

Empty words. It was all just empty threats. Because I did know how many times he'd thought about throwing me out. Or at least, I had a pretty close guess. Yet, I still sat at his table. Still ate the bread made from flour he purchased. Whether that meant I was truly a member of this house was debatable, but throwing me out, he wouldn't do. Not because of Mother, but because throwing me out would reveal that *he* didn't want me. And that was a much more dangerous, reputation-destroying path for him to walk, drunk or not.

"Rucas, please," Mother sighed, eyes closing as she pinched the bridge of her nose. He only glared at her, lifting his middle finger in response.

A pungent, unpleasant smell of something burning replaced all the putridness of the liquor that still churned my stomach. For a moment, I was thankful that the smell was gone but, *damn*, this new stench was foul and—

"Your eggs are burning," I blurted out, seeing the smoke rising from the skillet behind him.

Rucas jolted in surprise, whirling from us both to lift the skillet off the flame. More curses spilled from his mouth as he scraped the burnt eggs onto a plate, a mean, cocked eye on me. "Ya best be shutting yuh godsdamn mouth, else I'll force these down yuh throat."

I perked a brow up, a strangled laugh I couldn't hold back escaping. "At least I'd get to eat."

If Mother hadn't stepped in the way, he would have hurled that plate of eggs at me. She ripped the plate out of his hands. "I'll make you more. Sit *down*."

I wasn't sure he'd obey her. A dark anguish was written all over his sweaty face as he slumped into a chair, ignoring me once more.

I sat back in my iron seat, crossed my arms, made damn sure my sleeves were down, and watched him scowl at the table awaiting mother to bring him breakfast.

Besides the sizzling fresh batch of eggs, the silence of the house returned. For several long moments, I breathed normally and continued to eat the bread I'd made. Rucas's blinks were slow and heavy, like he would pass out right there in his seat. A stream of blood rolled down his cheek and he lazily wiped it off with a grimace.

Mother placed the eggs in front of him, bending down to whisper something under her breath. I only caught the words *dinner* and *help*, watching Rucas's scowl erupt into a wide-eyed, puzzled expression. Mother nodded once and hurried down the hall. For a moment, Rucas's gaze shifted around as if searching for something before it darted to me. I looked away quickly, finding anything to look at other than him.

It didn't take him long to finish those eggs, chasing them with a swig of whatever was in that bottle. He called for Mother, the chair screeching as he rose and followed her down the hall. I took the moment to rise and walk my breakfast plate to the basin.

From the kitchen, I could hear them whispering. I washed my plate, then opened a cupboard and pulled out a small amber bottle—

"Put that down. Now," Rucas hissed from behind me.

My spine locked. I could feel his dagger-edged glare in the back of my skull, sending my nerves racing. I turned to him slowly, clutching the bottle tight.

"Why?" I managed.

He took a step toward me—I was instantly against the counter, bracing myself.

"I'm not paying for it anymore."

My heart fell into my stomach. I sidled against the counter, knowing damn well I was getting close to the stone oven. Knew he was cornering me.

"It protects me." My voice was too weak, all of that courage I'd had simply vanished before him. I'd been taking the thistle-pink contraceptive every week since I'd had my first blood.

"I don't care." Another step closer.

I was against the stone base now, the heat of the cinders blazing my back. I couldn't go anywhere else. Further back, I'd be...

He knew that.

The cruel smile on his face left me weak in the knees. My eyes were darting behind him, hoping Mother would come around the corner. Save me. Sometimes she did.

Sometimes...

He was so close, the stench of him burning my nostrils. I clenched the bottle tight. Even through the fear holding my bones hostage, I still couldn't—*wouldn't*—go down without fighting him. I didn't care if I lost. I didn't care if I got hurt. He needed to know I wasn't weak anymore. He could lock me up. Marry me off. But this was the last thing, the *very last thing*, I had control over.

"I *won't*," I proclaimed. "My body is *mine*."

He chuckled at that. "Surely ya know that it won't be forever. You'll be married before this season ends."

I couldn't prevent the whimper in my throat, his eyes locked on the bottle as he prowled toward me. Before I could do anything, his large hands gripped my wrists. He dipped to my ear, the strength of his hold tightening until tears stung my eyes. "Have I taught you *nothing?*" he growled, the liquor on his breath churning my stomach with nausea.

With one quick rip, the bottle was out of my hands. Anger flooded my veins. I screamed and sunk my nails into his arms. When he hissed and pulled back, I clenched my fists and pounded on his shoulders. He held the bottle out of my reach and with a firm shove, I was pushed back against the stove, heat licking my backside before my instincts thankfully took hold and I rolled myself to the floor. He laughed out and chunked the bottle across the room, the glass shattering as it made contact with the floor.

No.

I drew back from him, into the corner of the kitchen, among the broom and buckets. I heaved, my chest rising and falling in sharp, quick spurts, the burning in my stomach as hot as the cinders in the stove.

As I stared at the liquid spilling out onto the floor, Mother rushed into the room, eyes widening at the mess. Rucas stalked past her and demanded she clean it up.

I barely acknowledged her take the broom, eyes confined to the broken bottle, no longer able to hold back the ragged sob in my throat as I watched Mother clean up the contraceptive that protected me from what scared me most.

Pregnancy.

Clenching my hair, I crumbled and wept into my knees. Memories of Eryx's wife's death washed through me like a flood, drawing out more cries, reminding me of one reason why I took that contraceptive.

"I need you to get groceries today," Mother said as if nothing had happened. She paused her cleaning, pulled a few gold coins from her coin purse and laid them on the table. "Father and I must meet with the Welches. We were going to have them over for dinner, however, that won't be the case anymore."

I didn't care.

I didn't fucking care.

But something in her tone made me ask, "Why?"

She didn't respond for a long moment, finishing cleaning. After returning the broom to the corner I sat in, she knelt before me. Her hand closed around mine softly as she swallowed. It was probably the softest touch I'd ever received from her. "Willem Welch and Theon Brooker are missing."

A grin that shouldn't have been on my lips was trying to rise. I found myself gripping the armrests of my iron chair, holding back. The wait for Mother and Rucas to leave was excruciating, every moment ticking by adding more and more tenacity to the smile wanting to slip out. But I waited. Waited for them to leave out the front. Close the door.

Then, I let it all out.

Unbridled, vicious laughter turned to violent hysterics.

Willem and Theon are missing.

Willem and Theon are missing.

I had to hunch over, gripping my belly as I laughed, and laughed, and laughed, plunging me into a spinning, out-of-control, wicked torrent. A storm without a mass of land to conquer, so I just went on. And on. Until tears came and drowned out my glee.

Because it wasn't funny.

My cries choked me as they came out. I gripped harder on the armrests so I could anchor myself to it like I did often. But my breaths were coming in too short, too shallow. My stomach felt like a ball of lead, expanding painfully, swelling into my lungs. I couldn't breathe. My heart was exploding in my ears, head spinning like a vortex, around and around and—

Something snapped within me and I began to scream.

For a moment, it was unadulterated fear. Then it turned to cold fury, sweeping through my body with such a burn, such a rage it obliterated all sensible thoughts. I jolted from the seat hard enough it tipped the iron chair backward, sending an ear-piercing clang through the room. And before I could wrap my head around what was happening, before I could swim up as the waves crashed down, pushing me under, my consciousness went black and still.

Blades were scraping my throat. The ground was cold beneath my hands. That's all I knew as my senses slowly came back to me. I was breathing in slow, thick gulps.

They are missing.

Pieces of my shattered mind were reconstructing themselves.

They're gone.

Things before me took shape. Colors, smells, feelings, and sounds appeared once more, and as they did I realized I was still weeping. I breathed out one last, defeated huff and looked up.

My blood iced over in horror. Books had been thrown across the room, some of them laying open, others on their face. Mother and Father's lounge chairs had been toppled over. Glass littered the hallway leading back into the dining room. It was when I realized that during my moment of blackness, I ended up here in the gathering room. I'd blacked out and still moved, still...destroyed.

I stood, my legs weak and heavy. Dizzily, I stepped over the glass and followed the trail into the dining room. My eyes widened as I recognized the glass: a vase Mother had on the table with fresh-cut mums. The plate of eggs Rucas had eaten from was shattered along with it.

I'd thrown these things. I didn't remember grabbing them, didn't remember the feeling of glass against my hands. But how else would they have broken?

I came to the tipped-over iron chair and pushed it upright. I'd left my breakfast plate alone. Hadn't touched the bread or jar of honey. I realized the bread knife was gone and I glanced down and around, drawing my eyes to the chair across the table.

I stilled. There, sticking out of the pillowed backing of Rucas's chair, was the knife. I'd picked it up and thrown it with enough force to puncture through.

I released the held breath, shuddering as it came out. Fresh tears stung the reddened, raw skin around my eyes. I didn't know what scared me more. The blackout rage I'd just displayed, or that I'd thrown the weapon with such...accuracy. Rucas had been sitting in that very seat only moments before.

As I swept up the glass, I tried to piece my worried, unhinged thoughts together. Willem and Theon had probably gone missing after they attacked me. Maybe they had run off and were hiding, or maybe they had left Elros altogether knowing what they'd tried to do and failed.

But that didn't make much sense. Perhaps I was just used to the circumstances twisting and it becoming something I was at fault for, but it was unusual for no one to find out about the incident for this long. Of course, I'd kept my mouth shut, but it was completely out of character for Willem to do the same thing.

There was also the question of how someone from Elros went missing in the first place. It was unheard of. Elros wasn't a large city. Everyone knew everyone, or at least everyone knew every person who was of great importance. Someone would have to know where they were.

Looking down at the pile of glass, I started to devise a story I could use as my excuse for the vase and plate breaking. I could have told them I'd fallen due to one of my flares, but wasn't using my real problem as a means to lie proving their claims?

Unfortunately, it was the only excuse I had.

Burying the shards out back had only brought more hindering thoughts. I hadn't expected the smell of dirt on my hands to evoke memories of the assault. I still hadn't allowed myself time to process any of it. I hadn't given myself the chance to pin down all the emotions whirling around. I needed to cry. To scream. Maybe even talk about it with someone.

It was why such a frenzy had come over me. It had been born of stress, anger, humiliation…

Trauma.

I still couldn't focus on how it made me feel. How I felt knowing when and if Willem finally returned and told everyone of my actions, revealing this new crazy power I had no control over, it would still be me suffering the consequences, not him.

Maybe that's why I'd laughed. It was sweet, twisted irony that *missing* possibly meant they'd received what had been coming to them both for a long time. There wasn't a single speck of remorse inside of me. I'd never feel bad for thinking—maybe even hoping

—that they were dead, that I'd avoided another unfair consequence.

Unfortunately, there were others I needed to focus on now.

The awareness of my marks lying beneath my sleeves was almost tangible. I pulled back the material and wondered what made them light up. I'd thought they might be triggered by my emotions because I was always scared or angry whenever I'd had any surge of power. But...they hadn't lit up all day, so perhaps it was more complicated than that.

Nothing was going to make sense until I learned more about elven magic.

After I placed the books back and pushed the chairs upright, I went to my room momentarily to buckle a belt around my hips, then tied my coin purse to it. When I returned to the dining room, my eyes fixed upon the spot where the contraceptive had fallen. Feeling another round of tears threatening to form, I huffed and gathered the coins on the table, placing them inside the purse. I hesitated to drop the last piece in. If it wasn't going toward groceries, it could buy another bottle of contraceptive.

I didn't start bleeding until I was seventeen. Because I was late, Mr. Welch believed I would have fertility problems like Mother, and still wasn't sure if I could bear children since I had only bled again once since my first time. He also blamed it on my curse and reminded me that if I ever had children, according to the legend, my baby would be stillborn.

But now that there was a possibility I could get pregnant, Rucas asked for me to be put on contraceptive. I knew it was only so I couldn't have children with someone other than *his* choosing. And I obliged because, for a small amount of time, I knew it would also protect me from bearing children I didn't want to have with the man he chose for me.

I couldn't stop Willem from forcing himself on me—that was clear—but I could prevent the posterity that came with it. I would never have a family with someone like that. I refused. And I had planned to take the contraceptive in secret for the rest of my life if I married Willem, hoping someday he would throw me out like Rucas always threatened to do with Mother. Except, I wouldn't beg to stay.

No, I wasn't sure what I'd do if that came to pass and how I'd survive. I wasn't good at coming up with plans and escapades. I knew that. I just hoped, even if I had to struggle, I would be free eventually.

Only then would I want children. When I had the ability to choose who I wanted children with.

However, two springs ago, I'd witnessed something that made me fear childbirth even more.

Kendra, Eryx's late wife, had only been pregnant for a season. Usually, it took two and a half seasons before labor would begin. Sometimes my nightmares tormented me with her screams as she gave birth to a babe born too early and too small. I had held her, sat in her blood, cried with her until she went limp in my arms.

The possibility of bringing a little, fragile child into the world and dying frightened me to the core. Not to mention the possibility of it being stillborn because of some curse I didn't even know if I believed in.

The contraceptive kept all of those thoughts quiet. It kept my hopes of the future bright. When Rucas had thrown that bottle, it was more than a means to control me. It was a possible death sentence. I was now fighting for my life.

As I turned to head out the door, my eyes flicked to the glint of something silver lying ahead of me. I drew closer—it *was* silver. Six silver coins lay carelessly across the entry floor. Dropped, I realized.

My parents' money.

I scooped them into my hands, the next thoughts rendering me still. I could buy more contraceptive.

Another particularly exciting and frightening revelation made my pulse skip.

I could easily pay someone to take me to the next town.

With a heavy, thick breath, I dropped the silver into my coin purse.

You are chaos, indeed...

The words hit me just as I opened the door, spinning to look behind me. I realized quickly that no one had spoken. I was alone— alone with my thoughts.

But that one thought...had been so loud.

CHAPTER 11

Varys

"K*rayd's chaos,*" I muttered irritably as I came downstairs. Blue shimmers washed across the cold hardwood floors, pulling my focus to the mantle where my mother's sword had remained inside a glass display since she'd died. The sapphire set in the silver pommel was practically a beacon this morning—like a godsdamn allegory since I'd just woke from the reoccurring nightmare of her death.

Another would stare up and marvel at the weapon's beauty, but I looked upon it and felt as if I was standing on the edge of a cliff, petrified and haunted by her memory. Not once had I unsheathed it, not even when Father informed me it was mine now. I hadn't seen it brandished or cleaned since we found it covered in the blood of wolves, and...nothing more of her. No body. No trace.

Had she died quickly? Did she fight until the very end? Out of all the questions in my head, I didn't know if I wanted those answers.

I knew I would never be able to ignore the sword and the weight of it. Just like this house was a constant reminder that she was gone. Even when the library was full of students or people browsing books, it felt empty. As if the rooms were too big for just two people to live here.

Her absence didn't make me hate the house. I couldn't. It was my family home. The house Father bought in its fixer-upper state and poured all the love and passion for what it would become into improving it. I'd heard many stories of how he and Duros struggled replacing beams and the stupid arguments they'd had over dimensions when cutting wood, all because the original layout was so unconventional and disorderly.

We had been told the halfling who assembled the building had married a very tall, human woman and had built to her accommodations over his. Halfling houses—or hovels, as they called them—were typically one story with ceilings no taller than six feet. Apparently, it'd been his first attempt at constructing any sort of residence as he'd been an astronomer, and it showed. There were no perfect angles, the foundation was unstable, and there were many drafty windows. Granted, it was another home built upon uneven land, a feat even the greatest builders and masons in our town had trouble working around.

It was all of those aspects of the house which had made my mother love it so much.

She had loved how stepping inside was like walking into a small cave and finding a massive cavern. She had adored the small, humble kitchen and how it was so close to the master bedroom. *"Such a halfling thing to build,"* she used to say, as to suggest tea and bacon had been the first things on the halfling's mind every morning. I used to tease and say she had that in common with him.

She had always been amused by the great room, that it was supposed to be a massive dining hall for parties and Father had turned it into a place of education. He would remark that his teaching was grand fun, to which Mother and I would pretend to snore.

She had even loved the closet-sized bathing chamber. Had pointed out that the tub took up most of the room and was big enough for the wife, while the latrine was over in a corner and small enough for him, implying what was important between the both of them.

But out of all the house's quirks, her favorite place was the room upstairs for its window. It'd been the halfling's work space and he'd put the large window there for his telescope. At one time, a rocking chair had been placed in front of the glass. I could still recall the melodies hummed to me as a babe while Mother and I rocked.

She'd taught me the names of the constellations by the light of the moon. The window had the best view of Willa's Crown, a five-star constellation that crested above Elros, usually at its fullest lumination around Hearthswreath, a holiday celebrated on the sixtieth day of winter.

The space turned into a playroom, where I'd sit and listen to stories of her time as a sword-maiden. How she'd taken down an orc chieftain when his tribe tried to attack a helpless caravan at just fifteen years old, or when she'd helped a homeless child find the care he needed when she lived in Elvidawn.

The playroom then turned to a child's bedroom. Toys turned into books, the crib turned to a bed. Eventually, the bedroom turned into a bachelor's space of study and rest as I turned from a boy to a man. But that window never changed, as constant as the stars and the love my mother had for me, even now.

I was only eight when she left this world. Taken too soon, in a way she didn't deserve. I could still hear her laugh, and how it glittered like the night sky she loved so much.

Krystan Wynhart had been starlight herself, the brightest light in my life.

A shiver pulled me from my thoughts. I'd been staring at the sword for too long again. I often thought it had some sort of enchantment over it. Other times, when the house was silent, its presence was so palpable I could almost imagine it screaming at me. I refused to truly listen though. I was afraid if I did, I would find all of those answers I didn't want, or maybe some sort of enlightenment I wasn't ready for.

Someday, I would unsheathe it. Someday, I would take it as my own.

But not today.

I glanced up to the small, dwarven time-teller Duros had gifted my father a few years back. It ticked as the gears turned. An arrow with a sun as its tip pointed to the top of the device, while a similar arrow with a moon pointed down. This told me it was noon. A longer, thin arrow pointed to one of the eight moon phases cut into the time-teller's metal faceplate, circling the sun and moon arrows. Right now, it was almost on the full moon. Tomorrow would be the first full moon since the autumnal equinox, which didn't mean much to many. But Leona and I reveled every full moon, and spent most of our night at The Nook and Cranny—the *other* tavern, as many called it.

No, The Nook and Cranny wasn't as clean as The Alderbright, nor did it have fancy dishes and wine that had been aging for longer than Duros had been alive. But The Nook and Cranny did have a warm, joyful air about it, and was a much more comfortable place for kicking back and enjoying fellowship. It was our favorite place to listen to the bards sing and play. The meat was always tender and marinated in the richest of sauces, the stews were so hearty they could fill an orc for an entire day, and the mead was sweet, fragrant, and no one ever knew how much was too much until they were on their ass.

Of course, the tavern did have its faults. The cleanliness. The late night perusing of escorts trying to entice men into their brothel next door, which always infuriated The Nook and Cranny's owner because they stole customers away. The obvious moonshadow dealings and mercenary exchanges were a problem too. Leona and I never found ourselves in trouble; everyone at The Nook and Cranny, unless they were passersby, knew Leona Cauldücen wasn't one to mess with, and I had no interest in any business besides my own. As for the escorts next door, I wasn't interested in being entertained by them. I'd been with a woman for entertainment once— once was enough. Simply holding a woman for an evening wasn't what I desired. I was ready for a deep and intimate relationship where I could invest my heart into a future.

There was a *clank* from behind the door at the far left of the room, then a Dwarvish curse. It drew a chuckle from me as I began to walk to the kitchen.

Leo must be cooking again.

She hadn't learned a thing from her mother. She was always burning bread, overcooking meat, and scalding soup. She couldn't even make tea correctly.

More curses sounded as I opened the door and jogged down the short hallway. She came into view, waving her hand around before sticking a finger into her mouth. *"Garzúl! Kar galdarth!"*

"There's plenty of freezing water in that stream now to help the burn—"

Silver flew past me, something metal clanging off the wall and to my feet.

She'd thrown a bloody fork at me.

"Shut it, Fawkes," she spat before I could really process what had just happened, her accent as thick as the smoke in the air. "I'm not goin' near that stream 'til it's lower and can get m'self home without yer sparkles."

"I'm sorry you didn't sleep well, princess." I was fully aware I didn't sound genuine in the slightest. I didn't sleep well, either.

Surprisingly, she didn't retort as she turned back to the steaks sizzling on the stove. I sighed and leaned against the counter. All of the usual, familiar smells of char filled the kitchen. I glanced at the meat. One side was blackened, past the point of thoroughly cooked and edibility.

"Leo, I can take over," I offered.

She huffed. "No. I went and bought 'em at the butcher this morn. I'll cook 'em."

I shook my head at her stubbornness. "Smells good."

"It smells like *shite*," she growled. "But I'm starvin'. And I'm sure ye are too."

I gave a slight shrug, eyeing the meat. Oh gods, had she planned on cooking one of the cuts for me?

"I'll be fine," I said quickly. "I'll just drink some bergamot tea."

She turned the second steak over. It was somehow darker than the other. "Damn."

I had to bite the inside of my lip to keep myself from saying something she'd smack me for. "Just need to take them off sooner is all."

I still expected her to hit me, but she only nodded. "I did manage to boil some water in the kettle. That's what I burnt my finger on."

"Well, lucky for you, water for tea is supposed to be hot." I winked.

She rolled her eyes, stabbing her fork into the charred meat as if she was thinking about doing that to my hand.

I reached for a teacup and a clay jar stored up in the cupboard on the wall. Bergamot tea was a staple in the Wynhart household. For a long time, Elros didn't have merchants for tea of any kind. Xaladorians didn't drink a lot of tea because it was imported from Jinya and only places like Elvidawn and the trade cities carried it. But over the years, Jinyans had found their way to Xalador and settled down across the continent. About five years ago, a tea merchant moved his family to Elros. My father purchased the tea in bulk from him every autumn.

I opened the jar and frowned, seeing only two tea bags left, instantly reminded it was about the time to buy more. However, I wasn't sure if that would be happening. This year had been tough on us financially.

"You know, on second thought," I said, putting the jar back into the cupboard, "I'll just wait for dinner."

Leona had sat down at the rickety dining table. The chair I took a seat in was held together by scraps of burlap and nails hammered into the joints. Leona and I had been pretty rough on them as kids from building forts and pretending they were shields against imaginary monsters. Father had never been able to replace them.

"Well," I started, folding my hands behind my head and looking to the ceiling. "What to do today?"

Leona was quiet as she cut into the meat, rocking the table as she did so. I gave her an arched look. "Free day, I guess. The library is closed, and Father doesn't teach today."

She remained quiet. Raised, haughty brows and pursed lips was the only expression on her face. I noticed she had put all of her armor back on.

"Do you want to train?"

Another beat passed before she answered, "Nah. Already promised my da I'd help him in the forge."

I tried hard not to laugh as she stuffed a piece of gray meat into her mouth, forcing it down with a grimace. She glanced me over. "I'm assumin' ye know yer spellbook's been hidden?"

"I figured since it's not on the table where I left it," I said wryly.

She let out a scoff, shoving another piece in her mouth and chomping down. She didn't swallow, speaking through the bits between her teeth, "I knew it'd be the first fuckin' thing ye'd come downstairs for." She made another face of disgust before grabbing her mug of water and taking a drink. "I take it ye dragged me all the way here for nothin'?"

I hung my head in defeat. "I'm sorry. I didn't find what I was looking for."

She rolled her eyes. "Victors, Fawkes. Ye really do need a day off."

I sighed and nodded. "Fine. But tomorrow—"

"T'morrow, we are goin' to The Nook and Cranny and havin' *fun*."

"Yes, yes." I waved my hands to placate her. "But before any of that, I want to ask Mae if we can start her reading lessons tomorrow."

A wicked grin curled on her lips as she sat her fork down with a slow, intentional clink and then crossed her arms. "Why don't ye call it what it is?"

I cocked my head. "And that is?"

She batted her lashes dramatically. "A secret tryst."

I snorted at that. "No. It's giving her an education, something her prick father is too busy sniveling his way into good men's pockets and marriage beds to do."

"Of course. But don't, for one second, tell me ye won't"—her tone went excessively languid—"enjoy takin' her to school and teachin' her *all* those careful strokes and sounds on yer tongue."

"We're talking about reading and writing, correct?"

A wide grin scrunched up her freckled nose. "Of course, Fawkes."

She definitely was not.

I pulled a hand through my hair. "She needs this, Leona. That has to be my focus tomorrow."

Her lips thinned. "Ye're hopeless. This'll be the closest ye've ever been to her and ye're not goin' to try to...to, uh…" She started to snap her fingers, lips moving without sound. "Ah *garzúl*, what is the Common word for *lanza?*"

I repeated the obvious Dwarvish word under my breath a few times, attempting to translate it as I stared at her. "I'm not sure you've taught that one to me."

"Ye know…" She tapped her lips in thought. "To...make an impression. Give her long, sensual looks." She clicked her tongue, and then repeated what she'd initially said but in Dwarvish slowly so I could understand.

I still didn't. "Knowing you it probably means *lay with*," I said with a snort.

"It *doesn't!* Shite. What do ye say when ye're playin' with a lover?"

My eyes narrowed. "Foreplay—"

"No." Her head lolled back in annoyance. "This is why I hate Common. There's so many bloody words that mean the exact same fuckin' thing." She crossed her arms. "Give me words that mean seduce."

My eyes widened, but I began, "Lure, entice, entrance, enthrall—"

"Less pretty."

I scoffed. "Woo, toy, dally, flirt—"

"Flirt!" she exclaimed, pointing a finger at me. "Da says it all the time. Flirts with Mum every chance he gets. Like in the kitchen the other—"

I waved my hands. "Yes, I've seen that enough." And, I had seen it *too* much.

"Okay, so Dwarvish lesson for today." She cleared her throat. "Answer my question: *Júnoc ret delva ilrn knúl ilrn lanza gef arn?*"

It took me a moment to translate. When I understood, I answered with a sigh, "No. I don't intend to make any sort of romantic advances if we meet tomorrow. It's too soon."

Leona blinked at me. "Why?"

"Because…" I took a breath. "I want her to trust me enough that she'll tell me the truth about her being *Vyl'kríev.* Or if she doesn't know what that is, she'll at least tell me she has magic. She's a mage, Leo. There's no doubt about it."

Leona was quiet for a moment, lips pursed to the side in thought. "Here's somethin' I've been thinkin' about, and I tried to ask yesterday. Mae has that Pallid Curse—"

"Mae has white hair," I said deadpan.

She swallowed. "All right. So, elven blood shows up in certain features. Bright colored hair and eyes, like ye, yer mum, a few others around here—"

"Who have left town—which has always been a bit odd to me. Because what if like Mae, they discovered their magic but decided to leave town because they were scared—"

"Godsdammit, stop cuttin' me off," she snapped with a glare. "I'm not like ye and can hold a billion different fuckin' questions and ideas in yer head at once."

I grimaced. "Sorry. Please, continue."

She huffed and bit into another piece of her foul meat. "Mae doesn't have Elven-blooded features."

I lifted a finger. "I had always assumed that as well. If she had obvious ones, I would have sought her out two years ago about this—"

"Ye should have sought her out two years ago anyway." I shot her a glare. She winced. "But go on."

I snorted. "Her eyes… They have to account for something. Plus, the other day I was reading through a newer dissertation written by a former student of the College of Elvidawn. Her findings suggest that these Xaladorians born with white hair are just another elven family's line."

"And this is someone's theory or truth?"

I sighed. "Theory. It's all theory. My father's research was labeled as theory. But it just makes sense to me."

Leona nodded. "So, here's the big jar of worms. What are ye goin' to do if ye find yer own theory of her bein' a mage is wrong?"

With my elbows braced on the table, I rubbed my temples. "Then I will teach her how to read and...and that'll be that. Because what do I have to offer someone like her?"

She put her fork down again. "What?"

"Leo, this is Mae Mordaunt we are talking about here. She's beautiful, wealthy, and has a powerful family." Every word was thick and I found it hard to swallow. "This is the daughter of the man who truly runs this town with his wealth and guild. The man who would do anything to see my family's livelihood crumble, who has tried in the past to destroy our foundation. He despises us, and honestly the feeling is mutual. It's gotten to the point where we can barely put in orders for the school. He gives us such tormshit about everything. I am nothing but the dirt on his boots, and no matter how much I don't care about what he thinks, he'd never allow Mae and I to become anything. He barely allows conversation—it's blatant. Taking magic out of the matter renders me that poor, lowborn man who doesn't deserve his daughter."

She was shaking her head by the time I finished, eyes thin with scrutiny. "Who gives a fuck about Rucas? What matters is how Mae feels about ye."

I crossed my arms. "And she has yet to show any signs of what you are speaking of—"

"Any signs?" Leo's frown deepened. "Did I just imagine the times I've seen ye two look at each other in the market? Am I goin' mad, or have I told ye I've seen her glance up at yer window when she passes? It seems to me, the only people who are blind to the romance that has been brewin' for years is ye'selves. It's about time to finally push things along."

Well, she was right about all of that. I knew there had always been something between me and Mae. I knew I hadn't been able to deny my attraction to her, and the looks we'd given each other at the stream hadn't been those of friendship.

Mae *had* given me the signs.

Still, I knew real romances didn't end with captivation. There needed to be so much more to the kind of relationship I wanted with her.

I relaxed back in my seat, looking down at the rickety table, aware of the splintering chair I sat in. "But what kind of life do I have to give her?"

Leo's shoulders slumped, a flicker of astonishment in her eyes. "Fawkes…"

I went on, "I still live with my father. I don't have a trade. All I have to offer are these broken table and chairs, a library of musty books she can't read, and...magic. I guess her having magic as well connects us so I have a better chance."

Leona studied me for a long moment through narrowed eyes before she said, "I don't understand why someone as smart and selfless as ye can't see their worth. It pisses me right off." She shoved the plate away from her, leaning forward. "I think she likes ye, Varys. And what if the reason she does is because of who ye are? Is that so hard to accept?"

It...was.

She huffed. "Fawkes, I didn't know askin' what ye would do if she isn't a mage would bring ye down like this."

"I'm a man with my head in the clouds." I shrugged. "I need to be pulled down every once in a while."

Gods, she did not like that. She snarled, picked up the knife she'd used to cut her steak with, and began to clean her nails. A habit executed when she felt like she wasn't taken seriously, or to distract herself from throwing out harmful words.

"You're not wrong for asking," I assured her. "It's something to think about."

"Maybe." She spun the knife in her fingers.

"Besides, I have another dilemma. And this does, and does not necessarily involve Mae." I made sure she was listening because I knew my words would ultimately change her future too. "I've decided I will be sending off my admission essay to the college."

Leona stared at me. "I didn't realize ye still wanted to go."

"Why wouldn't I?" I lifted my palms. "Leo, the college was the original source of elven education. It probably still houses vast amounts of knowledge that *I can read.*"

I stood and began to pace, her wide eyes on me. "I'm more qualified now than I was two years ago. I know what they're looking for, and I've used The ReEmergence to my advantage and poured every amount of knowledge I've learned on the elves and Xaladorian history into my admission essay."

Relief seemed to cross her features. "Victors, I'd hoped..."

"I know." I smiled. "I know what that means for you."

We'd made a pact of sorts a few years ago that if I was going to go to the College of Elvidawn, she'd leave with me. It wasn't like she couldn't go on her own before, but she felt that if my time to leave ever came, it would be hers as well. We were both ready to see the rest of Xalador.

"But…"

Leona's jaw tightened.

"How can I send in my essay to the college in the hopes of being accepted knowing Mae might be *Vyl'kriev*? How do I leave knowing I have the answers to questions she may have? And what if I'm not accepted? I'll have to stay here in Elros and rethink my future. I still won't have a trade."

Leona's head jeered back. "Ye can't balance yer entire life on uncertainties, Varys. You need to do what ye want and yer fate will find ye. And if Mae is in yer destiny, it will be so."

I looked away from her, annoyed with her rant of destiny and fate. Part of it was because I had no idea what in Torm I wanted. The other part…

"Oh, don't worry Leo. I feel…" Oh gods, I was going to feel as stupid as it sounded. "I feel all of that damn destiny and star courage Mother used to talk about whenever I think about Mae."

Leona only smiled warmly.

I went on, "But…not because of my obvious feelings for her, but because of the fact that I have answers to a mutual future that comes with a brand new world." I dragged my lip in between my teeth as I worked on my thoughts. "It may come with new ways of life and culture, but it could come with fire and blood. And when I think of what my destiny entails, if I look at those stars…" I wasn't expecting the emotion to settle in my voice, but Mother had been on my mind all morning. "And allow them to guide me, I am always left with this…*need* to help anyone and everyone I can before this world changes, however it may."

"Then there's yer answer." Leo took a breath. "Ye *will* help Mae, Fawkes. Maybe in magic. Maybe just in education. Either way, ye're helpin' her prepare for that world that's inevitably comin'. Ye are givin' her a life, Varys. Ye are not incapable of givin' her, or any lass, a life to proudly live."

I sighed. "That's all lovely to think about, but I currently can't put food on the table."

Leo's foot tapped, her face pinched with incredulity. "Yer actin' as if *yer* magic goes away if she's not a mage." She gestured down the hall, to the library. "Varys, ye've talked my ear off about how these powers brought prosperity to the time of the elves. That they had things we could only dream of."

She was right about that. The things I'd read about still stunned me just thinking about them. Magic could move hot water through pipes leading to faucets installed over tubs, so there was no need for heating water in buckets, or broilers when using dwarven fixtures. It could clean the water, so there was no need for constant trips to haul it from rivers. The elves could light hearths without flint and stone, send messages without birds, cure illnesses with magic potions.

And then, there was the transportation system. Gods, I'd read the information I'd found on the *Gates* over and over so many times, I could easily recite the passages. Once a person stepped through the large archways that had once been active all around Xalador, they were instantly taken from one city to the next, like a shared doorway. People could live in Shade's Crescent, pass through a Gate, and be in Elvidawn in seconds. It was how Xaladorians managed to travel even with Drake's Spine cutting off the land as it did.

Alas, all of the Gates were sealed shut or ultimately destroyed during the war.

"Poor in coin, not in power," Leona said, as if to remind me.

I sighed heavily, my hands laced behind my head. "Magic doesn't yet equal gold in this age."

She eyed me. "But it may impress Rucas."

My stomach dipped at the thought. "I don't like thinking of my magic like that. Especially not in conversation about who I…"

My words failed.

"Go on. Spit it out, Fawkes," she ordered. "I know ye've got a gamy vocabulary. Don't think I didn't hear all the things ye said to that erotic entertainer in Fairegrove."

An annoyed huff left me. "I wish everyone would stop bringing that up."

"Just teasin' ye."

"Semantics." I took a breath. "Leona, you know how I feel about Mae."

"That I do." She stood and walked her plate to the basin, continuing, "Which is why ye should *lanza* her first." She winked. "It will get ye what ye want to know naturally, despite yer insecurities and the *ifs* concernin' her magic. Instead of meetin' with her and then askin' all these outrageous questions that may in fact scare her away forever."

I pursed my lips. "I hadn't thought of that."

With a smug smile, she grabbed her cloak from the back of her chair. "I do know lassies, Fawkes."

I swallowed. "If you know women, then why do you think she's lying to me?"

She finished pinning her cloak with a metal rose brooch before she looked up at me. "I know, Fawkes…"

I tilted my head at that. "Know what?"

Her lips thinned. "I know why ye're desperate to know why she's lyin'."

My insides turned acidic. "I promised myself…"

And I didn't declare promises I couldn't keep. When it came to romance, I had made promises, and promises had been made to me. But those whispers in the dark, words of a future, of marriage, of children…all of it had been a lie. Elise Carrington had only said what she had to lure me into bed. I should have known then, but I thought I loved her. I should have known she had just wanted me for sex, but I was still learning how to feel again—

I shut down that train of thought.

Elise had lied to me. It was why I had to know the truth from Mae—I promised myself I wouldn't be lied to ever again.

Leona clapped me on the shoulder. "Varys, I don't know why she's choosin' to lie and hide this from ye. But I do know there is a difference between lies to hurt and lies to protect. If ye take my advice, I think ye'll eventually learn the truth, and when it comes, it's not goin' to hurt. Not like last time."

She crossed the kitchen to where her sheathed sword leaned up against the wall. Strapping Thorn to her back, she continued, "Fate knows what it wants, Varys. Yes, I'm usin' yer real name because I want to make damn sure ye're not goin' to fuck this up."

"I'm not going to fuck this up," I said with a sigh. "It means too much."

Mae meant too much.

An annoyed noise came from behind Leona's teeth. "Invite her to The Nook and Cranny, ye eejit."

I perked up. "What?"

"Tomorrow." She drew out the word as if talking to someone brainless, which was definitely how I felt at that moment. "After yer reading lesson, invite her to tag along with us. I'll leave ye two alone." She held up a hand. "Promise."

My jaw dropped open. "Why didn't I think of that?"

Her face screwed up, hands on her hips. "I don't fuckin' know. Ye've had romances before. And ye've been besotted by Mae since yer balls dropped—"

"Good gods, Leona."

"I'm not wrong."

I refused to agree with her, but...she really wasn't wrong.

⁂

"I'll be finishin' up somethin' at the forge today," Leona said suddenly as we walked into the road leading to the busy market.

"Oh?"

She nodded. "Been practicin'. Ye'll find out."

"You're not going to tell me? I thought you didn't like surprises."

She grinned, her curls bobbing as she moved her head back and forth excitedly. "I don't like surprises for me, I like surprises for— *Fawkes!*"

I hadn't seen or heard a rider coming up behind me. Leona grabbed my arm and pulled me toward her, allowing a black horse to continue.

After I found my composure, I glanced up at the rider and gave an apologetic bow. "Sorry about that."

The man atop the horse was cloaked, every piece of clothing he wore black as night. I could hardly see his face, but when he inclined his head, my stomach turned over. His eyes were silver, almost colorless.

"Careful, good sir," the man warned, his voice smooth as silk with just a touch of grit. "My companion comes down this way as well."

I apologized again and the man went on. Another horse strode toward us, this rider perched atop the saddle in the same manner the falcon on his shoulder was. The small bow of his head he gave us tossed his short and shaggy chestnut-colored hair in his eyes for just a moment. I took in the sight of the saddle's leather, the breed of the horse. Both the same as the black rider.

A cold sensation raced down my spine. I wasn't sure when my pulse had picked up its pace, but my heart was slamming against my ribs to a near-painful point. I looked to Leona, my hand involuntarily sliding down to the dagger on my hip.

When the second rider's eyes settled on her, another chill worked its way through me. His dark brown, almost black irises warmed as he beheld her. Nausea threatened to rise up my throat as I watched a wolfish grin rise.

She can take care of herself. She can take care of herself.

"'Ey there," he drawled, pulling back on the reins. "You're dwarven, aren't you?"

Leona hadn't even noticed he was there until he said something. A small snarl lifted on her nose. "And?"

He shrugged. "I heard there's a dwarf living in these parts who makes the finest weapons."

Leona dropped her taut composure. "Oh, aye. That's my da. He hasn't set up shop for the fest, but he will be soon."

The man *tsked*. "That's a shame. I was hoping I could purchase some things from him now. My partner and I have been traveling for weeks. I need a few blades sharpened and replaced."

Leona straightened. "Oh, well, I was on my way to his forge. Da doesn't typically take commissions outside of his shop, but if ye're willin' to pay, I could take ye to him—"

It was the dumbest thing I would ever do.

In an attempt to silence her, I flung out my hand. *Gods*, I meant to hit her arm.

But I smacked her chest.

She gasped, hunching over as several Dwarvish expletives spewed from her mouth before her own hand launched out and found my groin.

"F-fuck…" I rasped, pain lancing through my crotch, up to my stomach. And the nausea I'd had come over me just moments before was now real, promising more embarrassment to this situation.

I could hardly think through the pain, one eye opening through a grimace to find Leona glaring down at me. "What the bloody tormfuck is yer problem, Fawkes?"

I looked to the man, who was chuckling softly and still hadn't continued on. "I just got here and I'm already thoroughly entertained."

Leona left my side, reaching out to shake the man's hand. He had to bend down a great deal to take it.

She smiled, shifting her weight to one side—a move I knew all too well. She stuck out her hips and ass just like that when she saw something she liked. "Leona Cauldücen."

Dammit. Don't tell him your godsdamn name.

"Find me some other time," she said, drawing out each word as she looked from his eyes to his arms. Lower. "I'll get yer weapons taken care of."

The man bowed with a wink at her. "The name's Orin. Looking forward to doing business with you, milady."

Gently spurring the horse, Orin caught up with the man in black. The two never seemed to acknowledge each other as they turned and headed deeper into the busy market.

Leona spun back to me. "Are ye goin' to explain ye'self?"

I rocked back onto my ass, legs spread apart to hopefully release tension off my groin. "Sorry. I got a really bad feeling about those two."

She knelt in front of me. "Varys…Ye've had maybe three hours of sleep," she reminded me. "Even my head is feelin' fuzzy, and I'm snoozin' the moment I get home. Da's gonna want me at my full strength in the forge."

She helped me to my feet. "What have I told ye about my tits?

Even in our trainin'. Not only is it completely shameful, but it's the biggest prick move ye can make—"

"I was going for your arm. And didn't you say the same thing about you going for my balls—"

"Ye make a prick move, ye get the prick hit."

My head fell back in annoyance. "You told him your name and I was having...I don't know. Bad feelings."

She shook her head. "Follow me to the stream, then I want ye to take it easy and don't think another damn thing about magic or bad feelin's for today."

She began to walk but then gave me one last smirk. "He was...attractive, wasn't he?"

CHAPTER 12

Mae

My arms shot around my stomach when an embarrassing growl declared I was still hungry just as a group of people passed by. I instinctively threw up the hood of my cloak and sped up my pace. The sooner I got to the bakery, the sooner I could possibly sample some of Mr. Flax's baked goods. Not to mention walking into his bakery was the breath of air I needed after this morning.

When I began baking, I often reached out to Mr. Flax for advice. Eventually, he became a mentor of sorts and taught me everything I wanted to know whenever I visited his bakery. I enjoyed his company and our conversations about secret recipes. He often spoiled me with lavender honey biscuits, apple danishes, and my favorite fig tarts. Whenever he came up with a new creation, he had me sample them first as I was "experienced in my sugar".

Lately, I'd been trying to get over to the bakery as often as I was able to help him with meager chores. Work he used to have help with, but his son had just moved out of Elros for reasons never said, and his wife Hildith had tragically died in a fire a year and a season ago.

A small *ching* swelled through the bakery as I entered through the blue-painted door, warm and toasty scents filling my nose and making my mouth water.

"Ah, good afternoon, good afternoon," Mr. Flax shouted cheerily from the back.

I smiled softly, looking around the bakery so familiar to me. Built into the wall behind the front booth, rows of honey-colored oak shelves were filled with a variety of pastries, breads, rolls, and pies.

The male halfling emerged from an archway to the right, the stone oven's blaze behind him casting a faint red and orange glow to his deep umber skin. A broad grin spread across his face as he looked up to me, patting his sweaty forehead with a handkerchief. "Miss Mordaunt! I was hoping I'd see you today. Have a seat."

I slid into one of the several chairs set up in front of the booth, ideally for Mr. Flax's customers who came in regularly to eat a pastry and indulge in small talk. He stepped on a stool behind the counter, gaining a full head in height, but his shoulders were barely over the edge of the surface. He'd told me many years ago he didn't *want* a halfling-sized bakery. Tailoring to humans meant much more business. Every Xaladorian knew halflings were great salespeople and honest merchants, however, most turned their nose to halfling shops with short ceilings and narrow doors, unwilling to stoop their heads for a few moments to acquire better stock than they'd find from a sniveling merchant like Rucas.

Mr. Flax had never said it, but I knew he built his bakery to "human size" to make sure Rucas didn't overlook him in the merchant guild.

A glass dish was set before me and he lifted the dome lid off, revealing several small, round desserts. The sweet was dark brown and speckled with powdered sugar.

"Chocolate?" I asked with wide eyes. Chocolate was a rarity and could only be imported from Jinya.

Mr. Flax nodded excitedly and edged the plate closer to me. "I purchased cocoa right after the summer solstice. I call these *chocolate darlings*. Please, try one."

I took one between two fingers. It was just small enough that I could fit the whole thing in my mouth in one bite, but I nibbled a small amount off, savoring the flavor I didn't get to enjoy often. The rich sweetness of chocolate made me instantly sigh and I devoured the rest.

"It's delicious," I commended as I brushed the remaining powdered sugar off my fingers. "In the winter, you could even add crushed peppermint on top for a seasonal treat."

Mr. Flax winked. "Now, that's an idea. Have as many as you'd like. I made twelve more batches in the back."

I thanked him and took another from the plate. He turned from me for a moment, pulling a few loaves from the shelf. "I'm assuming you've come for bread."

I finished chewing quickly and nodded, clearing my throat. "Yes, let's do three loaves today."

I untied the coin purse from my belt, the gold and silver jangling as I sat it on the counter. I was reminded of the extra coin inside, sending a jolt of unease through me for no reason—it wasn't like Mr. Flax could possibly know I'd stolen from my parents.

His eyes were already on me when I handed him a gold piece. "Mae, are you...well?"

I looked at him, the uneasiness continuing to blossom in the pit of my stomach. "Yes."

He gave me an arched look, took the coin, and began to bag the loaves I'd purchased in cheesecloth. "Eating enough?"

I pulled my hand away from the chocolate darlings. "Yes. And my stomach hasn't been against me too much as of late."

A nod. "Well, I beg your pardon if I come off as intrusive, Miss Mordaunt, but..." He turned from me, as if he wasn't sure what to say next. Then, "Mr. Yearn, you know, the tailor? He was on his way to his store the other morning and stopped by here for break-fast. He told me that he saw your father and Eryx RothHall standing around you while you were in some sort of fit. He said he would've stopped to help, but the looks your father gave him...well, who could blame him for not? Were you having one of those spells again?"

I studied my pale hands, wondering if they'd soon be covered with lightning marks.

"The attacks have become more frequent." My voice was strained. "Mr. Welch doesn't know what's wrong with me. I have tried just about every tonic and medicine he has made up. A brew to delay pain. Some sort of cream to ease it when it comes on. Both were utterly useless."

"Nah. I personally doubt Mr. Welch's remedies will do much good for what you're dealing with." His gaze flicked upward momentarily, his foot tapping. "What do your folks think?"

I gulped down a sudden lump in my throat. "They…don't think I need to worry."

His brows furrowed, and he was quiet for a moment, eyes fixed on the window behind me. With a shake of his head, he finally said, "You're suffering, Mae. It's all over your face."

My mouth parted. "I-I'm all right. I just don't get much sleep—"

"If you were my daughter, we'd get to the bottom of what is causing you pain. It broils my skin to think your father is just ignoring this."

I frowned and looked away before he could catch any truth in my eyes. If I were his daughter, I would no doubt be free from this disease or illness, whatever it was. I'd most certainly have a future. Maybe even a trade in baking. I could make my own money and leave Elros eventually.

I would be free from abuse as well.

"Thank you for your concern, Mr. Flax," I told him.

He clasped his hands and leaned forward. "There is no need to thank me. My concern is no heavy burden." His voice was thick with emotion. "You remind me so much of my youngest, and sometimes I see Hildith in your passion for baking. She adored you."

My chest tightened, Hildith's face forming in my mind. *Gods*, her hair had been tangerine orange. She'd never braided it, only tied it back with a coif when she worked, and it had fallen down to her ankles. You could spot her anywhere in Elros, hair billowing like a sea of flames. Her eyes had been yellow and almost feline due to the halfling trait of larger, angular eyes. Those Elven-blooded traits, coupled with the hint of red to her skin, and her quick-to-anger nature, always made me think she was made of fire.

It was a terrible irony that she'd died in the fire that burnt their house to the ground. Last time I had asked, Mr. Flax was still living at The Alderbright, waiting for his new house to be built.

The plate of chocolate darlings was pushed closer to me, and I realized I'd fallen silent.

"Eat," Mr. Flax said with a warm smile.

I nodded absently and popped another in my mouth. Four pieces of silver in change were set before me. I went to grab them and he cupped my hand gingerly in his. There was a glossiness to his eyes as I stared at him. "If you ever need anything—*anything*—you know where to find me."

Anything?

It had never dawned on me that Mr. Flax would be someone I could run to if I needed help. But I quickly realized why I had never given it a second thought when he got down from his stool and hobbled away to the other side of the storefront with a wince as if he'd stood a bit too long. He was getting along in years. I wasn't sure how old he was, and halflings lived much longer than the average human.

I would never put his livelihood at risk. There were other ways I could escape now.

I was just about to take my leave when the door swung open. A newborn's cry filled the bakery as a young woman made her way inside, shushing the infant sweetly. I instantly envied the woman's lavender hair cascading down her back, the burlap cowl on her head barely enough to keep her ears warm. She wore a plain, dirty dress and held her baby wrapped and tucked in her arms safely. With heavy eyes and a sleepy smile, she looked at him as if he was the most amazing thing she had ever seen.

The baby's cries fell silent and no sooner than they did, she was up to the counter. "Please, sir. One loaf."

Mr. Flax obliged with a nod, turning to grab a loaf of golden-brown bread. He sacked it and laid it on the counter. "What a beautiful baby," he cooed softly.

The woman timidly thanked him before pulling out a small coin purse.

"It will be two silver today, ma'am," Mr. Flax said as he smiled down at the baby.

But the woman stilled. She sat her purse down and pulled the string to open it, all while cradling her child in her other arm. She shushed as the baby began to wriggle.

"Two silver," she whispered, looking down at Mr. Flax with wide eyes. "I'm…I'm sorry. Have you gone up in your prices?"

Mr. Flax's brows drooped sadly. "I'm afraid I did have to go up."

Her mouth parted, shaking her head. "Gods help me, I can't even afford bread anymore."

My breath hitched.

The woman's eyes shimmered with tears as she drew her purse back. "Thank you for your time, good sir," she muttered, holding her child close as she slowly turned away.

I felt frozen in place as I watched her walk toward the door. Her ragged clothes hung on her thin frame, and the child began to cry as a sob escaped her throat, reaching for the doorknob.

She couldn't afford *bread*, the cheapest source of food in Xalador. How were her living arrangements then?

The silver pieces I'd stolen suddenly felt like lead.

The misery that emanated from her…I couldn't bear it—

"Put it on my bill," I said so firmly, I almost didn't recognize my voice.

The woman turned to me with wide, confused eyes. Mr. Flax's were the same.

"I beg your pardon?" she gasped.

"Mr. Flax, put the woman's bread on my bill," I repeated. "How much will get you through the quarter?"

The woman's jaw went slack. She shook her head. "Miss, I can't let you—"

"How much will get you through the quarter?"

She was leaving with food if I had to stuff a bag with loaves myself.

The woman stared at me, then down at her child before she let out a breath. "We use about four a quarter."

My pulse stumbled because…well, surely four loaves of bread was not enough. I ate four loaves every two weeks. And that thought made me feel really appalled by my eating habits.

"It's just my husband and me. Our baby doesn't eat solids yet, of course," she continued, sounding as if she was drawing up every explanation she could come up with. "He's away right now. At sea. As soon as he gets paid, I can pay you back—"

"There is *no* need, miss," I said as I nodded to Mr. Flax. A smile tugged on his lips and he began to sack up the loaves.

The woman's eyes welled with tears as Mr. Flax handed her the bag full of bread. Even holding the baby and now the bag of bread, she still managed to use her free hand to grab mine, her head bowed in gratitude. "The gods bless you! May they not remain silent to such a wonderful woman like yourself!"

She squeezed my hands for emphasis, thanking Mr. Flax and me once, twice more before she left, the door clicking shut behind her.

Mr. Flax chuckled as I turned back to him and handed him the silver in my purse. "Mae, you've made me look bad in my own store."

I stiffened, my eyes wide as I looked down at him. "What? Why?"

He shook his head with a grin. "I'm joking. I just would've done the same for that woman, but—"

The bakery door flung open once more so hard, the bell's ring dulled. A tall, stocky man trudged inside. My pulse skipped as I watched two guardsmen walk in behind him, bearing the Xaladorian royal crest: two crescent moons flanking the symbol for our sun.

The King's Guard.

The man made eye contact with me first. Reynard Lethlity, the tax collector. He turned to Mr. Flax, looking down with a hard, focused expression.

Mr. Flax just smiled, like he always did. "Ah, good afternoon Reynard. Here for the usual I assume?" he inquired as he began to climb a ladder to reach the top shelf filled with trays of rolls.

Reynard cleared his throat. "No, Tobias. Not today, friend." The word *friend* sounded a bit forced. "Just business today, unfortunately."

Mr. Flax's brow furrowed as he stopped midway up before climbing back down. He crossed his arms. "Reynard, I already paid my taxes for this quarter. On the 3rd, I think. I can show you my receipt—"

"It's been raised. I have the notice here. I'm sorry, you know I'm just doing my job."

Mr. Flax's eyes widened as Reynard handed him a piece of parchment. He took it and read it over, hands visibly shaking.

Sweat had formed on his brow when he handed the paper back. "Another two gold? It went up again? So, that makes the tax four gold a quarter? Is King Elyon mad? People can't afford this. Especially not in this town."

The two guards shifted and glanced at one another.

"Tobias, I'm sorry," Reynard said, sounding slightly sympathetic. "The King has ordered more soldiers out of Elvidawn. Along with this notice, we got word that he's sending guards here to Elros as well." He gestured to the men behind him nonchalantly. "Things are…getting dark out there. There's talk of an unknown evil."

Mr. Flax's tongue clicked. He glanced up at me. "What? Bandits or something?"

Reynard pulled at the collar of his coat. "I am in no such position to elaborate. However, the King raised the taxes to pay for more soldiers. He's readying forces."

My stomach turned over.

Mr. Flax muttered something under his breath but nodded. "Fine."

He pulled a chest from under the counter, taking out two gold pieces before letting them fall into Reynard's hand.

The tax collector pulled out a small notebook and feather pen from his belt. "Here's your receipt," he said as he wrote onto the page, pulled the parchment from the book and handed it to Mr. Flax. He bowed his head. "I do pray this is the last time I do this until next quarter. And, uh…the next time I come in will be for some of those delicious rolls, Tobias."

Mr. Flax nodded absently, looking up to the shelves. "I'm afraid they won't be the same price as last time."

The tax collector sighed. "I do understand," he murmured before he and the guards headed out. The door slammed shut with a devastating thunder and the bell fell off its perch, landing with a *ting* that rained over the chilling silence.

The air felt tense. Like it did before a storm.

CHAPTER 13

Varys

After crossing myself, I watched Leona skip across the rocks and small boulders above the water, the stream lower now than it had been the night before. She gave me a quick wave, then a roguish grin as my spellbook appeared in her hand from virtually nowhere, making my magic look like child's play.

"Keepin' this to make damn sure ye take a day off," she called as she started for the edge of the trees.

I rolled my eyes with a smile. "Oh no," I drawled exaggeratedly. "Whatever shall I do? I hope you don't find all the dirty poetry I've written in the back."

Her eyes went wide as she twisted back to me. "What?"

"What?"

She snorted, and my spellbook disappeared once more somewhere within the flaps of her cloak. "*Alöfheim,* Fawkes."

She trudged into the wood and I waited until I couldn't see her red hair among the evergreen branches before I continued down the stream.

With my hands behind my head, I walked along the bank. Breathing in the smell of fresh water and pine, I tried to allow myself to think of anything but magic and The ReEmergence. I'd spent a lot of time out here, sitting up in trees or beneath their limbs and writing my *Dragonhart Series*. After all, this wasn't a *bad* place, despite the recent events and its ever-changing water level. It was a gorgeous piece of Xalador that reminded me Goddess Willa hadn't held back on her gifts when covering the world in her domain. Birch and cypress trees clung to the bank up and down for miles, the branches sometimes so heavy they hung into the water and when winter came, they'd become frozen in the stream for the entire season. In the spring, ivy and moss always grew in spiraling towers up the trunks, often overwhelming the trees entirely. The water was always cold and refreshing to drink, and in the summer it was nice to swim in.

I passed one of the many rapid falls and decided to cut back into the forest. Apprehension always knotted my insides when traveling into the woods, but I knew where not to venture. I often examined the ground as I trekked, searching for prints I recognized. Deer, human, rabbit, fox, any of those were fine. But I still had the urge to run whenever I saw wolf tracks, even though I wasn't that small child anymore and I was more than capable of handling myself in a fight—especially now with magic. I wondered if those haunts would always be with me.

I came to a spot I recognized from my many trips this way, pulling my book bag from my shoulders and dropping it to a patch of soft grass. Today I'd work on the next installment of my books.

But before I could get comfortable, a strong gust of wind swept through the area, the tendrils of air whipping through my hair and cloak. I spun to the woods, facing the gale's direction. When I inclined my head to the trees, my spine went rigid, heart pounding. In the remnant breeze, the branches swayed for a moment before bowing inward to form a natural archway leading deeper into the forest.

Another gust burst forth. I dug my feet into the ground, bracing myself only for it to blow gently over my face like a light kiss and with it the smell of...

"Rain?"

It was a cold day, but the rain from the night before had long since passed. The sun was bright in the sky, sitting just above the forest which told me it was just a few hours from sunset.

Another gale rushed from the forest, this one strong as it blew around me. My pulse stammered as it swept up the fallen leaves at my feet, seeming to intentionally circle around me before changing direction, dragging the leaves back into the boundless wood as if the forest had taken a deep breath.

I remained planted for a moment before instincts took over and I sunk into a wider stance. Something beyond nature, beyond the disposition of weather, was creating this wind. Something deep in the woods, into similar places I'd dared not to venture since my mother had been ripped from my life.

The winds blew back to me once more. The scent still promised approaching storms, but this time it brought with it a chilling, disembodied whisper. One that hurled my thoughts right back to magic and for a reason I couldn't explain, *her*.

I swallowed. I knew what could find me if I ventured deeper into the forest. And this time, it could very well not be wolves. This was something magical and possibly stronger in power against my small spells of light and frost crystals. But that whisper—the familiar rasp on the back of the indistinguishable words. It was her voice. Beautiful and mystical, icy and smoky all at once. The voice that sent warmth through me whenever my name rolled from her tongue, and yet left me with goosebumps as if I were in the presence of an otherworldly queen. It was the voice that stood out in the crowd, her greetings and small-talk with merchants like a strange descant above the repetitive, never-ending melody of monologues and gossip.

I was no longer fearful of wolves finding me, no longer apprehensive about encountering powerful magic. This voice—*her* voice— was for me, guiding me. I'd be a fool not to follow.

Squaring my shoulders, I began to move inward, watching the trees overhead bow into an arch with the wind once more. The whispers became a ghostly presence, the words soft, obscure, and lifting the hairs on my neck as they teased the air around my skin. Wind continued to whirl, dead leaves brushing my pants as if it were an invisible entity toying with me, inviting me in.

The sound of rapid water died off the further I walked. Soon, the forest took on a wild and estranged scene filled with guardian oak trees, the kind of trees I knew had filled Aldeon Forest at one time, twisting branches so low I had to duck under them. The sky overhead disappeared completely, covered by the thickness of the limbs spiraled around each other. I couldn't tell how high they grew and the path before me was narrowing with every step.

A familiar alarm was resurfacing, the shadows and blanched twisting branches extracting every nightmare in my head and displaying it before me. Memories of large gold eyes and snarling growls as I found my eight-year-old self backed into a small, tight space, in a forest parallel to this one. A shuddering breath escaped my throat and I went to turn around—

Dias…

My spine went rigid, insides turning somersaults as the hair on my skin stood on end. The voice had been so clear I half expected someone to be standing before me.

Dias çli…

I let out a choked laugh. This voice, whoever or whatever it belonged to, was elven.

"I hear you…" A smile tugged my lips upward.

Dias çlina ít xera…

My eyes widened, heart pounding so hard my breathing was ragged. Something within demanded me to pick up my pace, the voice repeating the words over and over, beckoning me. I ran, kicking up red and orange leaves and acorns as I dashed, twisting around knurled trunks and ducking beneath low branches.

The sudden separation of trees forced me to halt entirely. I'd come into a clearing. The canopy overhead was parted, allowing sunlight to pour in, the rays casting down onto the very reason there was a clearing here to begin with. In the center of the wide space, a guardian oak tree lay dead.

Come into the storm.

I stepped out of the shade, into the sunny area—

The wind stilled.

The leaves rustling around me dropped to my feet and the voices died entirely.

This was too familiar. I'd felt this sudden stillness before, the other day when she'd—

I held out my hand quickly, fingers outstretched as I jumped into a guarded stance. "*Sçölith.*"

With the command, a golden *eçor* began the spin before my palm, a blue aura rippling down in front of me, small lights dotting the pads of my fingers. I could feel the shield of magic brush against my hands as if I were bracing myself against a thin sheet of glass. My *wards*.

I waited for several moments, expecting another wave of energy. But nothing happened except for a tangible tension against my wards. I glanced around and thought to another spell I had memorized, keeping the command word on the tip of my tongue in case I needed it.

My headspace felt light and open as I took another step into the clearing. It was quite extraordinary, the feeling of magic expanding my consciousness. My mind often felt compacted with knowledge and theories, but the moment I cast a spell, it was as if the magic compartmentalized all of those things and allowed me to concentrate on nothing but the spell and my surroundings. I also noticed that while I was casting, my nervous ticks weren't a problem. I hadn't tried to speak much when using magic, but I didn't stutter when speaking Elvish.

Using magic was liberating and made me feel like I could truly do anything, despite the doubts and anxieties I had.

I lowered my arms cautiously, keeping my wards up mentally—a feat I'd been working on. The pressure was not entirely malevolent but undeniably magical. Why in this place?

As I slowly made my way toward the dead tree, the weight against my wards intensified. Beads of sweat formed on my brow, my eyes fixated on a black burn along the trunk.

Realization hit me hard enough, I staggered back. Lightning had struck this tree and scarred the bark in rivulets of light and heat.

"Come into the storm."

A trapped storm.

This was the tree Mae had fallen from when it'd been struck by lightning all those years ago.

I could still remember the crowd outside the physician's infirmary awaiting the news of her wellbeing. She'd broken her arm and was unconscious. Mr. Welch hadn't been aware of the use of a splint. Back then it was a newfound practice. So when Mr. Welch announced her arm would need to be amputated, Rucas had flown into a rage. I'd never forget the venom in his voice, but his words...perhaps they had been the start of my unadulterated distaste for the man. Because Rucas hadn't been angry at Mr. Welch's decision.

He'd been angry at *her*.

She'd been eight years old. A child. He'd screamed about her stupidity, her behavior, expenses. But it wasn't even those words that had left some sort of deep scar on my consciousness. It was how much she deserved becoming disabled for being Pallid.

I wasn't sure how Mae's arm was ultimately saved, but she'd left the infirmary several days later with a splint.

My skin rippled with goosebumps. This pointed to everything I'd seen. The light and thunder and pressure. I'd even tried to read up more on storm magic early this morning. It was the answer I'd been looking for. It was...almost too good to be true. Was it possible that whatever dwelled here knew Mae's path had crossed mine?

As always, I began to ask more questions. Mae had fallen from this tree back before The ReEmergence had ever begun. Maybe some residual sorcerer magic remained here, having been expelled from Mae when she was young. But how could that be possible if magic was dormant?

I thought about the wave I'd felt the other day. It had to have come from her. Maybe that expulsion of power had awakened this place.

The center of my head was starting to ache. My wards were starting to wear on me. I'd have to come back when I was well rested, maybe bring Mae if she felt comfortable.

I decided to survey the area where the tree's crown would have been if the branches had not splintered and decayed with time. Everything was calm, soundless. I couldn't hear the birds chirping anymore, and there was no wind. Just an eerie serenity. If this was a trapped storm, I supposed that this clearing was akin to the eye. If I hadn't left my book bag by the stream, I knew I would feel safe and peaceful sitting here and writing. For a moment, I contemplated doing just that but quickly thought against it given the nature of normal storms. What would I do if it suddenly evolved into something that would sweep me away?

I was just about to head back when my focus snagged on the glint of silver beneath the leaves. I came closer, identifying it as a small, silver pendant. Kneeling before it, I made sure my wards were still up. Having done a vast amount of research on magical items, I knew not to touch it before inspection.

"*Vid Medaes.*" There was always a slight burning in my eyes whenever I cast this particular spell. As if I had donned a pair of magical lenses, the world before me transformed. Colors brightened, every shade rich in saturation, but within everything around me tendrils of rainbows danced. I knew this was the essence we mortals could never touch, never feel, never truly see without magic—the veins of the arcane.

But with *Vid Medaes* cast, I could also see magical auras if present. And before me now, gold swirled around the pendant, sparkling with iridescence. I grinned, sheer excitement bubbling up as I reached out and picked the pendant up, the chain connected to it following. Gold auras were found when abjuration magic was present, usually a sort of protection spell or something similar to a ward.

But it wasn't just a plain silver charm attached to a dirty chain. Beneath clumps of mud embedded between the settings, I could see gemstones.

I took one last glance at the tree. I would return. *I'll get answers.*

As I made my way back to the stream, I was a bit surprised there was no wind or whispers beckoning me to stay. My heart clenched when I thought of how my mother would have reacted had she been alive and learned of my findings today. How proud she would have been that I decided to follow the path of wind and voices—a path of destiny, as she would have said.

Finding my bag where I'd left it, I unbuckled the flap. I could clean the pendant off with the same spell I'd used on Leona and me, but I didn't have the formula memorized just yet. I reached inside for my spellbook—

Realization dawned on me later than I wanted to admit. I didn't *have* my spellbook.

With a huff, I carried the necklace to the stream, muttering to myself about the fact that I hadn't done a single thing that Leo wanted me to. Now instead of a clear head, there were even more questions running through my mind about The ReEmergence.

I washed the pendant and chain, holding it under the water for a few seconds before scrubbing the mud off with my fingers. Upon pulling it out of the water, the sunlight glinted off a gorgeous, iridescent gem set into the center. I tilted it left to right, watching it shift from blue to purple to red.

But my breath caught upon observing the several tiny stones set around the middle gem. Transparent like quartz, but reflecting with every hue imaginable.

My blood heated the longer I stared at it. I knew exactly who I'd give this to, who deserved such a beautiful amulet. Problem was, gifting necklaces in Xalador meant more than just a token of adoration. Most of the time, there were promises of marriage involved. A betrothed person wore a necklace as a symbol that they belonged to the person who gave it to them, and then when the two wed, another necklace was made for the person who initially proposed. Usually the necklaces matched.

But it was much too early to be pondering these things, about whether or not Mae and I would become lovers. No matter how beautiful the necklace would look around her neck.

I blinked away the burning in my eyes only for it to come back with a vengeance. Pain shot through my sockets, the gold aura swirling in between the gems seeming to glow brighter and brighter—

"Shit!" I hissed, snapping my eyes shut and rocking back on to my ass. "*Löth Medaesí.*"

The feeling of an open headspace shrank down until I was sure my brain would be pressed to a pulp. All of the bright colors vanished, ripped away like a torn veil. I yelped, my heart pounding in my ears, muscles slacking as a heaviness fell over them. I could hardly breathe through the feeling, unable to stop my strength from pouring out of me, vision blurring as I toppled back onto the bank.

But just as unconsciousness began to overwhelm me, the bout subsided. I stared up at the sky, unseeing, unable to think about anything but *you fucking idiot.*

I'd never canceled *Vid Medaes*, nor my wards. I wasn't at all strong enough to hold two spells at once for that long. Any other day it wouldn't have affected me this bad, but I had only slept a few hours.

I knew better than to be this reckless—what it could have cost me.

After several moments of feeling like I could pass out right there on the bank, I dragged myself over to sit beneath a low branch of a beech tree and dozed for maybe an hour, waking to a late afternoon sun. Feeling refreshed enough to work, I pulled out my quill and inkpot, opened my notebook, and began to write.

I was there until sunset and only wrote four sentences, too distracted by the questions I didn't have answers to.

CHAPTER 14

Mae

"Pull!"

The shouting of men drew my attention up to a banner being stretched across two log pillars—the same one raised every year that I couldn't read but knew what it said. With everything going on, I had almost forgotten that starting on the eighteenth of autumn, the Fest of Change would transpire here in Elros. A festival welcoming the harvest and giving thanks to those who worked hard to provide necessities, supplies, and keep our lands and town from falling into profound poverty. For three days, we would feast on food, drink the mead that had been aging all year, dance with bards, and most importantly, spend gold. The merchants of our town depended on the festival to bring in the largest portion of what they'd make all year. And because it was a festival known for spending money, we had attracted merchants from all over western Xalador, making the Fest of Change larger every year. I could remember the year before had so many travelers coming in, both The Alderbright and The Nook and Cranny were completely booked. This year, given the early arrivals who had already pitched tents on the outskirts of towns, I knew it was going to be the biggest celebration we'd seen yet.

However, as I weaved my way in and out of booths to finish up my shopping for the day, the people I came across who were obvious travelers showed no nature of anticipatory celebration. There were enough scowls and dodging eyes to coerce me to pull up my hood and keep to myself. The very air had felt ominous and tense ever since I'd left my visit at the bakery, and Reynard Lethlity's warning of evil and raised taxes hadn't left my thoughts.

Something about it all rang of an importance I couldn't place. As if something deep inside of me already knew this was coming. But Xalador had always been peaceful. Besides the stories of bandits I'd heard from Eryx, and the orc problem on the eastern side of the kingdom, Xalador had no troubles.

Or was I just ignorant of them? It wasn't like I could read the town's news bulletin, nor was I ever involved in town meetings. Mother had always told me to stay home, that kingdom troubles were not our problems.

That train of thought reminded me why I wanted to learn how to read to begin with. Even though I hoped to discover more about myself through Varys's possible knowledge of the elves, learning how to read Common was essential to my freedom too. I wanted to be like him—enlightened and no longer in the dark about the world around me.

Twilight washed the market with vivid blues and purples, mixing nicely with the decor and shop wares throughout that proved autumn was in full swing. Garlands of dried oranges and pine cones were strung across the doors of flower shops that had begun to display their seasonal plants: chrysanthemums, croton leaves, and magenta asters. Farmers were selling golden squash and big, bright orange pumpkins.

My stomach churned with hunger as I walked, thinking of the smaller pumpkin within my bags I'd purchased to make my delicious pumpkin soup for dinner tonight. Rucas hated it—I didn't give a damn.

I passed a group of people hovering around a jeweler's booth and sighed in relief when I saw this section of the market had emptied out. Usually, this was where the fruit stands were set up, but it seemed today they had sold out early. Going this way would be a longer trip home, but I was ready for a little quiet after today's incidents and revelations.

My hood was ripped from my head as a brisk wind rushed through the streets. On it, a smell of burning wood and bergamot tea leaves had me halting in my stride. I knew that smell, and as the wind blew it to me again, a familiar sensation roamed over my skin.

A feeling only felt when I was in the same vicinity as *him*.

It was the connection, running through me, lifting my gaze and yanking my head, beckoning me to turn.

With unerring accuracy, as if he'd already been searching for me, I locked eyes with Varys as he stood from the bench he'd been resting on. A tender smile lifted on his lips, a hand waving in greeting. The space between us seemed to shrink the longer his fervent gaze fastened to mine.

He was beautiful, and those eyes spoke of what that connection between us meant. What it did to him, to me, and what we would do if we both let it sweep us away.

"It probably sounds ridiculous," he began before I could say hello, "but I was just thinking about you." I could do nothing but stare at him as he walked toward me. He let out a small chuckle. "I've just been concerned."

"I'm all right," I breathed, taking in the sight of his wind-blown hair. There was a dullness to his usual bright sapphire irises, and I realized his retinas were bloodshot, patches of dark circles beneath his lashes. I recognized that disposition all too well—lack of sleep. "Are *you* all right?"

He blinked heavily. "Tired. I didn't sleep much last night."

"I figured as much." And I was *never* so assertive, but my blood ignited as his gaze dipped to my lips and then quickly ran over my frame. "Though I hope it wasn't because you were thinking about me."

He beamed, a breathless laugh escaping as he stepped closer. "I'd be lying if I said you weren't at least some of the reason, Mae."

My body hummed with approval at the sound of my name on his lips, my grin broadening as he took another step, the toe of his boots brushing mine. This was the closest he'd been to me yet and *gods*, I adored how my head had to tip back just the slightest when I looked up to him. His broad shoulders shielded me from the wind sweeping his blue hair off his eyebrows, revealing that thin scar down his left. For a moment, I pondered what might have happened to him to receive that scar, but his scent hit me again.

My eyes went wide as I breathed it in, the woodsy, spicy aroma filling my lungs and stroking through me as if it were his hands brushing over every sensitive area, conjuring the images I'd conceived in my dreams last night. With a step back, I turned my head away, trying to hide my astonishment.

"What is it?" he asked.

He was so close to me. Places on my body ached and pulsed, the connection pulling and wrapping around me as if I'd been embraced by him. I couldn't breathe through it. I didn't know what I'd do if I let it bind me, and his furtive watch was setting my body ablaze.

I'd burn for him. To utter ash if I could just get his hands on me, his lips on mine, his tongue on—

"Mae?" he asked again.

My heart leaped against my ribs. I snapped my head back to him and forced out, "I should let you get home and sleep."

I went to bow my head in farewell.

"Wait," he said with a smile in his voice.

His hand found mine.

"Don't leave me so suddenly, again."

My eyes shot to where our skin met, where his fingers curled around mine, his touch like a brand as he tugged me closer.

A sudden pulse passed between our hands, a jolt racing up my arm fast enough to make me gasp and rip away from him, anticipating a flare of pain or power. Nothing came, but the connection was now as tense and charged as the air before a storm.

Varys's eyes had gone wide by the time I looked up and realized how strange my reaction had been. "I-I'm sorry." He rubbed his scarred eyebrow. "I shouldn't have done that."

"No, that's not...you didn't..."

A question lingered on the tip of my tongue.

Had he not felt that pulse?

But his words rushed back to me before I could think of much more. "What do you mean 'leave you so suddenly, again?'"

He straightened, looking like he had realized something very wrong before he stuttered out, "Oh, I-I was referring to when you'd…" Taking a steady breath, he tilted his head, studying me like he'd done the other day, as if trying to solve a puzzle. "I was just really enjoying your company the other day and didn't want it to end so soon, but I understand you were probably eager to get home."

My chest fluttered. "Truthfully, I didn't want it to end either. And I'm sorry about not showing up yesterday for our reading lesson. I just…"

As the lie formed on the tip of my tongue, my jaw stiffened. I didn't want to lie to him.

But I couldn't risk anything else right now.

"I wasn't feeling very good."

His throat bobbed. "Well, if you're feeling better now, we could always—"

Varys suddenly swayed, and before I could grab hold of him, he collapsed to his knees. My heart plummeted to my stomach, the connection that had been so taut now slacking, the heat curling turning to ice.

"Varys!" I knelt before him to brace his shoulders.

He leaned into me, murmuring as he pinched the bridge of his nose, "Damn." He rubbed his eyes and then looked up. "Sorry. I…didn't realize I was as tired as I am."

I gaped at him, insides hollowing as I watched the warm colors drain from his skin. "Have you eaten anything today?"

He grimaced. "I haven't."

When his eyes closed, I shook him. "Varys, hey, stay with me."

Relief swept through me as he nodded and chuckled sleepily. "Always…"

Holding him closer, I cupped the back of his neck and tilted his limp head up to watch his face for any signs of lost consciousness. His blue hair was soft against my fingers.

He looked at me with a bleary focus and took a deep breath. "Your eyes are beautiful, like torrents of violet stars and storms."

I snorted. "You can't be serious."

"I've never been more serious in my life."

My cheeks heated—I couldn't help it. It was a bit ridiculous in the moment but endearing. "Is this just from sleep deprivation and lack of food, or is something else going on?"

He sighed. "Did something dumb. Used a lot of strength."

I tilted my head at that. "What did you do?"

His neck slacked again, eyes rolling backward before shutting.

"Shit!" His body started to slump over onto mine, and I braced him as I shook with all my might. "Stay awake, Varys!"

It was a chilling moment too long before his eyes snapped open. Incoherent words left his lips as he grunted and pushed off the ground. I shot to my feet, steadying him with a tight grip on his forearms. His legs and arms shook, muscles protesting as he stood. For a moment, I thought he was going to be sick, eyes wide and hand plastered against his mouth.

"Chaos," he gasped. "I really fucked up."

I gulped. "Varys, what did you do?"

He couldn't respond, breaths coming in shallow as sweat beaded his forehead. My mind was everywhere, trying to form some kind of plan to get him to his house or somewhere safe, but I couldn't help to notice the hard and taut biceps beneath my hands. Not because I was focusing on what that knowledge did to me—that he was probably gorgeously delineated under this thin tunic—but because of the intense realization that started to settle over me. Varys had the arms of someone who didn't just read books all day, of someone who didn't just sit up in a room and study all night. There was strength, *power* in his body. And that didn't happen with maturity alone, nor did it happen quickly.

And if his body was this strong, what in Torm had he done to make him this exhausted and weak?

I didn't have the strength and muscle to lift him, but there was no one else around us to help. "Come on." I wrapped my arms under his shoulders. "Lean on me. I'll get you home."

The dim glow of the quickly fading sun was the only light in the library before us. In his delirious state, Varys had instructed me to help him to the sitting area before the hearth. He was hanging heavily on me as we walked, his eyes closed as I guided him to a chair. He sighed an apology as he sat down.

"Don't apologize," I told him. "I'm just happy I managed to get you here." We hadn't been too far from the library, but I'd been pretty sure the incline up was going to be the death of me. I rotated my shoulder around to get the blood flowing and ease the ache.

As Varys dozed, I roamed around half-blind, searching for a means to start a fire in the hearth. Finally, I came to a large desk with so many books and papers, I wondered how anyone could work at it at all. But there beside a quill and inkpot, I found a firesteel.

Varys jumped upon the first spark, his eyes wide as he watched the fire roar to life. "H-How did you light that fire?"

I arched a brow, showing him the firesteel. "With this of course, I found it on that…"

My words ended with a gasp, the sound echoing through the room around me. I knew the old house up on the hill was the library and school, but with the light of the fire illuminating the room, I was sure I'd stepped through some sort of portal. The place was definitely bigger on the inside. *Gods*, I'd never seen so many books. The shelves went all the way back to a row of windows, and I could only guess there were stairs that led up to the balcony hanging over the room. Every wall was covered with Xaladorian maps, star maps, shelves displaying rocks and agates, paintings of landscapes and buildings I didn't recognize, and another above the mantle of what looked like the Wynhart family when Varys was a child—which made me grin, especially seeing him beside his mother whom I knew had passed away years ago. Next to the painting was a beautiful sword on display, and more books that looked like they might be collector's editions since they weren't on the shelves.

The desk I had grabbed the firesteel from sat in front of a large board marked with numbers and writings I couldn't read, and there were seven small desks, neat and clean, with wooden signs hanging in front of each and scrawled with words I could only imagine were students' names.

"This place is…" I started in a murmur.

Varys's gaze was like a thin slice of sapphire. "Ah, you've never been here have you?"

I sat in the chair across from him and shook my head. "It's magical."

His brows perked up. "Really?"

I nodded, breathing in the smell of burning wood and the unique scent of books I'd only ever smelled in Rucas's shop. "There are so many books."

He smiled, eyes hooded as he rested his chin on his fist and beheld me. "There are eight hundred and forty-two new books since our census two years ago, making a total of seven thousand, five hundred and sixty-three."

I blinked in surprise. "Exactly that many?"

"I'm the librarian. I just…have to know these things," he replied idly. "We've been quite fortunate to add so many. Donors have been forthcoming with books recently, sometimes even just laying them at our doorstep, discarded."

I relaxed back in my seat, smiling when I realized some of the strength in his voice had returned. "You're talking better. I hope that means you're on the mend."

He pressed his lips together. "Sorry, I probably bore you to tears with all my talking."

I scoffed and crossed my arms. "No, you don't. I told you the other day I enjoy our conversations. I know they've been few, but I've enjoyed them nonetheless."

His sly smile appeared, and it was the first time I noticed that when this particular expression crossed his features, his scarred eyebrow popped up just the slightest.

Gods, I couldn't lie to myself. I could watch him do that all damn day.

"Well, let us make sure they don't return to small talk and short greetings," he suggested.

I laughed. "That would be what bores me, Varys."

"Then allow me to always entertain you."

The heat from earlier returned with a vengeance, warming my skin with a delightful burn. I bit my lip as if it would throttle the dizzying current racing through me, and his eyes were instantly on my mouth. For a heartbeat, an expression I'd yet to see fell over his face, a maddening eagerness that had me writhing within, those sapphires simmering.

We were...well, we were alone. In a warm room, speaking words we both had to know were laced with searing promises.

But his stare turned heavy, and when he blinked, his eyes stayed closed. I stood to check on him, and the action had him straightening up in his chair.

Snickering, I bent down and took his shaking shoulders. "You are going to fall over, Varys. You need rest, but I'm worried about you not eating. Where's your kitchen?" I looked around the dimly lit library. "If you don't mind my intrusion, I can cook you something."

His head hung limply as he met my concerned gaze. "Thank you, but I'll be fine. I've gone without eating before."

I gave him an incredulous look. "I doubt that."

His lips quirked to the side. "Well, winter gets hard sometimes, you know." He chuckled. "Father and I have a stew recipe that has enough meat and vegetables in it to hold us over for a few days. Besides, I don't think we have any food at the moment."

Guilt fluttered through me. "Oh...I'm sorry. I didn't realize you meant..."

He tilted his head. "What?"

"Your family...struggles."

The glaring ignorance of my upbringing made my face burn. Even though my stomach was sensitive at times, and the pantry was empty more than it was full, it was never because my family couldn't afford food. I was privileged enough to know I would never starve.

He sighed, pinching the bridge of his nose. "Mae, no. We're not *poor*. It's just a hard season is all. M-My father is probably out getting dinner supplies now. Last night, we had dinner at a friend's house. We are not struggling—"

"Varys." I clenched my hands to my chest. "You don't need to explain. I'm sorry."

He frowned, his gaze dropping to the floor as he shook his head. "I do though. I need you to know you're the last person I want to think my family is struggling."

My face screwed up. "Because of my father?"

A short, bitter laugh escaped him. "No. Because...I care about *your* opinion of me."

My mouth parted, and I suddenly understood. The Wynharts weren't farmers who could store up their produce, and I knew the school was mainly funded by donation. I also knew Professor Wynhart was paid by the Baron out of the community taxes, which used to be a problem for people like Rucas who didn't agree with the school opening at all. Perhaps Varys thought I had the same mentality as Rucas.

But he couldn't be more wrong. The thought of the Wynharts struggling in any degree lit a fire in my chest. People like Rucas were bathing in gold, getting more and more wealthy by the day, and people doing great things for our community like the Wynharts were getting *nothing*.

"Well, my opinion of you is that I believe you are a kind, good-natured man," I told him. His breath hitched. "I have more opinions, like how I love listening to you speak. You make me laugh and smile—which is a feat not many possess. And...I feel safe around you and like I'm with someone I've known for years despite this only being our second longest meeting."

He had gone utterly still, and I felt like I might combust where I stood. But I continued, "None of those things have anything to do with your money. Because, frankly, I don't give a shit about money. I'm *not* my father."

He shook his head frantically. "No, no, you're not. I didn't—I didn't mean you were like him."

My lips thinned, noticing his nervous stutter, something that had seemed to have subsided over the years. Perhaps he had more confidence now. I didn't want to be the reason for its return—someone who made him uncomfortable—so I softened my tone and said, "I am the furthest thing from a Mordaunt, Varys." My heart still slammed against my ribs at that declaration. "And I want you to know that, because I, too, care about your opinion of me."

The breath he took came out shuddering. "We'll be here all night if you're giving me the chance to unravel my thoughts about you."

I could barely breathe or think around his words, desire beating in rhythm with my unsteady heart.

"Maybe another night," I murmured in an attempt to regain my composure. I still had no idea why he was so weak, and that was much more important than the heated thrill still curling within me. "Because you still need to eat, and I haven't figured out a way to thank you for helping me at the stream. But I think I have something small to achieve both problems."

I pulled out of my bag the small bundle of chocolate darlings Mr. Flax had given me before I'd left the bakery. Sitting it on the table beside the chair, I untied the string. Varys arched a brow, seeing the determination on my face, and then looked inside.

"Is that...chocolate?"

I gave a curt nod. "Yes. For you."

He shook his head frantically. "These must have cost a fortune—"

I scoffed. "No. I'm friends with Mr. Flax. Besides, even if they did, you deserve them. You deserve *so* much and this is just the start of paying you back for everything you've done for me." My heart twisted as he gaped at me. "Please. Eat."

He suddenly stood, swaying as he did. Before I could protest, he took my hand in his and held it to his strong chest. "First off, you do not owe me *anything*—"

"I do." I swallowed. "And until I feel like my debt is paid, I will continue to make sure you are rightfully acquitted."

He squeezed my hand. "I don't want that from you, Mae."

My pulse quickened, heart throbbing in my throat. "Then, what do you want from me?" I inclined my head, neck feeling suddenly exposed and hot. "Anything."

His eyes traced my features, his chest breathing hard beneath my hand, his body taut. "Only you as you are."

"You already have that." I smiled. "Pick something else."

He shuddered, pressing his fist to his mouth for a moment, breathing deeply. "F-Fine. I want...just two things."

I stepped closer. His pupils flared, and I felt a gentle brush on my other arm. His hand cupped my shoulder, giving just the slightest nudge. I took another step, the space between us closing almost entirely and my focus honed in on his lips.

"Tell me," I murmured.

He took a breath. "I want you to join me at The Nook and Cranny tomorrow night."

My stomach flipped, spine steeling in his loose embrace. A nervous laugh escaped my throat. "For a…reading lesson?"

"No." He tapped my nose. "I was going to try to make up for our missed session tomorrow and ask you then, but since you're so insistent on knowing what I want from you…" He leaned in closer. "I want to get to know each other and have a little fun together."

I grinned. "That all?"

"Among other things." My heart was tumbling over itself again. "Dinner. Drinks. The bards are playing, and since it's so close to the Fest of Change, merchants have already begun to book the place and there are always fascinating stories told."

My chest swelled and I smiled so brightly, a laugh escaped me. "I've never been to The Nook and Cranny." I eyed him playfully. "Pardon me and my stuffy upbringing, but I've always been told it's a place of precarious characters and blackmarket dealings."

"Well that's not too far from the truth," he said candidly. My jaw dropped and he chuckled. "But you'll be just fine. I have no enemies, no debts, and don't have any illegal habits." He smiled, brushing the side of my face with his fingers. "You're safe with me."

"I know." And, gods, did I.

But the kind of trouble this spoke of…this was no longer prohibited conversations. This was a means of becoming something greater than friendship, and deliberately ignoring the fact that if Rucas found out, the consequences would be something so severe, they might change my life forever.

If I went through with this—and there was no way in Torm that I wouldn't—I knew that by the end of tomorrow night, I'd have to make the decision to tell Varys everything or never see him again. I knew people didn't go to The Nook and Cranny to sit around and mingle. They went to find entertainment, carefree pleasantries, and romance.

He didn't have to say it. Varys wanted me. It had been written all over his face tonight, it had been there at the stream, and it had been in every look, every smile, every greeting for years. It was no surprise that the moment we were able to really speak to one another and enjoy each other's company, it would move so quickly, so wildly, nothing could stop it.

But apprehension still held fast, the fear of being caught lingering as I reminded myself that I wholeheartedly believed Rucas knew what would happen if I were allowed to get close to Varys. There had been many times Varys and I would find each other in the market and Rucas would scoot me along so we couldn't say hello. The many times in the shop Varys had come in and Rucas would interrupt any conversation that had started. Varys was a threat to him.

Varys was waiting for my response—my *yes*. And I knew it would be hard and dangerous, but I wanted him more than I feared Rucas.

"Will there be...dancing?"

"Absolutely. Usually becomes a madhouse." He paused. "You like to dance, don't you?

I sighed with a nod. I did. It was the only thing that made the fancy parties I was forced to attend sufferable. It was another reason I was looking forward to The Fest of Change. Rucas and Mother were always so busy with customers, I was often able to sneak away to secretly dance with the traveling entertainers. For a few songs, I would let my hips sway and explore a sensual side of myself that I kept buried so men like Willem would never see.

Warmth spread to my ears with that thought. Varys had never attended the parties, yet he knew I loved to dance. "How did you know?"

It was his turn to redden, his nervous stutter returning full force. Oh gods, he'd seen—

"Hearthswreath," he said with a firm nod.

Oh.

He'd seen *that* dance.

Last year had been my first Hearthswreath I'd ever celebrated. I had quickly thrown together a wreath crown, a headpiece everyone wore decorated with small things their loved ones had given them over the year, and attended the festivities with Eryx. Mother and

Rucas had been out of town, and usually, Rucas always made me work the shop during the holiday.

Eryx had taught me the winter waltz everyone danced during the celebration. He ended up with blisters on his feet from me wanting to dance all night under the gleam of the constellation Willa's Crown. I remembered seeing Varys's window glowing with candlelight, and him and his father enjoying the festival from afar.

I smiled softly. He'd been watching me.

"And..." He cleared his throat. "Last year at the Fest of Change, I was walking down the same alley the traveling entertainers often dance and...well..."

I squeezed my eyes shut. "Oh, gods."

He scratched the back of his head with a nervous chuckle. "Don't be embarrassed. Just promise you'll dance with me? I'm awful, but I can try."

I grinned. "I can probably teach you a few things."

"I have no doubt."

His hand moved to the side of my face, snagging a strand of loose hair and tucking it behind my ear before his fingers traced the line of my jaw. My heart pounded in sync with the strange pulse I felt within his touch, and as he lifted my chin, my eyes fell closed.

"You are beautiful, Mae Mordaunt," he whispered.

My hands lay on his chest, leaning into him as his arm curled around my waist, his other hand keeping my head tilted, aligning my lips with his. His breath was warm on my mouth and cheeks, nerves roiling with anticipation of his kiss—

Varys went heavy against me, body falling into mine, lips meeting my chin instead of my mouth. It wasn't until he sagged I realized what was happening. I shouted, pushing against his shoulders. He only groaned and sunk to the floor. I went down with him.

"Varys, what in Torm did you do to yourself?"

He didn't respond. I shook him, calling his name, eventually shouting it. He'd fallen unconscious.

I cursed and stood, whipping around to look for anything to help me. I knew I could run and get the physician, but that would mean I would have to tell Mr. Welch I'd been with Varys. Then, Rucas would find out—

Damn the consequences. I needed to get help.

I had started for the front when a door behind me in the back squealed on its hinges as it opened.

"Varys, I'm home," a voice called out.

Oh, thank the gods. It was Professor Wynhart.

He halted when we made eye contact. "Miss Mordaunt?"

"Hello," I greeted sheepishly, wringing my hands. "I'm actually in need of your help."

With stiff legs, I turned to Varys and rushed back over. The professor followed after he tossed his cloak over an armchair.

"I don't know what's happening to him," I said as I knelt, watching Varys's chest raise with every shallow breath. "He just keeps fainting on me."

Professor Wynhart stared down at his unconscious son, looking much more calm than I felt. "Well," he said with a smile. "He owes me money."

I blinked. "I beg your pardon?"

He chuckled as he knelt as well, his rich laugh a parallel to his son's. "I told him years ago, maybe when he was fourteen or fifteen, that if he ever managed to work up the nerve to ask you over, he'd probably pass out. He of course argued he was much more brave than that. I told him to bet on it."

I stared at him. "Professor Wyhnart, I think Varys is actually really ill, or severely famished."

As I continued to explain what had been happening to Varys, Professor Wynhart checked his pulse, strangely composed the entire time I spoke.

He let out a sigh. "Well, I doubt he's famished. This man ate twice as much as I did last night at dinner with our friends. I don't understand why he's collapsing so suddenly, but he has been training hard."

I almost choked on the words as they spat out, "Training?"

He looked up at me, giving me a familiar arched look behind his spectacles. Professor Wynhart didn't have blue hair or eyes, but his eye shape, nose, and jawline were almost identical to those of his son's. "From the way you spoke, it sounded as though you and Varys have had a few conversations. He hasn't mentioned his training with Leona in swordsmanship?"

My eyes widened. *His arms.* Strength compared to that of a swordsman. A warrior—

"Wait...Leona?"

The only woman I knew who went by that name was...

Oh my gods. Not *her*. The cruel half-dwarf woman who lived outside town?

"Yes," he said. "Leona is Varys's best friend and trainer."

I didn't know how to process that information. Did that mean what had been said about Leona Cauldücen was a lie? I couldn't imagine someone as caring and friendly as Varys would want to be friends with someone like her.

Professor Wynhart pushed his son to a sitting position. Varys let out a few incoherent sounds, head lolled to the side.

"Should we get him to bed?" I asked.

"It would be best. Think you can get his legs and I under his shoulders?"

I snickered. "That would be a lot easier I think than how I carried him here earlier."

He sighed. "You poor woman. I hope he wasn't too much trouble."

I smiled, kneeling and lifting Varys's legs in my arms. "He gave me terrible trouble, but nothing I couldn't handle."

Professor Wynhart laughed.

I made sure it didn't seem like I wanted to linger as Professor Wynhart pulled a blanket over Varys.

"I hope you two are able to discover the source of his issue," I said with a smile. "Please let him know I'll see him tomorrow."

His eyes went wide. "Really? Tomorrow?"

I was sure I could trust Professor Wynhart with that information. It wasn't like he'd find Rucas—the man he equally despised—to tell him his son was seeing his daughter. "Varys is teaching me how to read."

Realization crossed his features. "You two weren't together the other day, were you?"

I gulped. "Yes. For a little while."

He only chuckled. "That explains a lot. Well, thank you, Miss Mordaunt—"

"Mae, please."

He bowed his head. "Thank you, Mae."

As if my name had jolted him awake, Varys sat up in bed. "Wait, Mae—" He stilled, eyes growing to the size of small saucers when he looked upon his smirking father. "Oh, shit."

Professor Wynhart snorted, eyeing us both. "I'll be downstairs preparing dinner. Goodnight."

Dinner.

I was already supposed to be home.

Professor Wynhart left the room. I kept myself against the frame of the door. Varys breathed in deeply, both of his eyes red and puffy. "Tomorrow?"

I nodded. "Tomorrow."

He sighed and laid back. "Would you like to have your first lesson then?"

I still didn't know how I was going to get away with this. "Yes. But let's meet at the stream."

He blinked. "Really?"

Even though I wasn't sure how I would be able to handle going back so soon after Willem's attack, it was still safer than anywhere else. Even here, where I was in the company of safe people. "Yes. In the morning? Before the library opens?"

He nodded, seeming a bit leery still of my place suggestion. "Deal."

"Promise me you'll sleep," I said as I came forward, sitting the bag of chocolates on his bedside table. "And you'll eat these."

He snorted. "So insistent…"

I shrugged. "They made me feel better after everything that happened. The only reason I've smiled besides you."

His throat bobbed. "I promise I'll eat them. And then tomorrow, I promise to keep you smiling all night."

My heart throbbed. I bent down and pressed my lips to his forehead. His fingers toyed with the ties of my cloak for only a moment, whispers of his skin brushing my collar bone. When I pulled away, his sensual gaze nearly pulled me back down.

"I…" He sighed.

"Yes?"

His fingers stroked the side of my cheek, down the length of my neck. He stopped at the white curls, twisting a strand between his fingers. "You need to know what else I want from you. It doesn't have to be tonight. It…can't. It can wait. But you need to know nonetheless."

Everything in me went taut, my mind racing with possibilities. "What is it?"

He looked away momentarily, but when his gaze returned to me, his brow was pinched, eyes more serious than I'd ever seen them. "I want answers."

CHAPTER 15

Mae

Answers.

"*About what?*" I had asked Varys. His words had stolen the warmth from my blood.

He'd only replied with closed, tired eyes, "*Tomorrow, Mae.*"

And as I rushed home, my stomach felt like a boat on the northern Serpent Sea, sending waves of nausea through me. How in Torm was I supposed to rest easy tonight not knowing how to prepare the answers he wanted from me? Were his questions about my family? About me?

I found myself halting in the middle of the road trying to catch my breath. Tears pricked my lashes—I didn't know why, but I felt guilty of something.

I tried to convince myself to walk, but as I took a step, another thought stilled me. What if he was just trying to get me to confess something? It could be anything. Rucas's abuse, my affliction—

I gasped, hands flying to my cheeks. *My magic.*

Something inside told me he already knew. He had asked if I was giving him the full story.

And I had *lied.*

About everything. It didn't matter whether or not I planned on telling him tomorrow. He was one step ahead.

So why didn't he just come out and tell me?

I didn't like this. I didn't like being kept in the dark. It felt...it felt like another cage. It felt like what Rucas had done by keeping me from education, from leaving this damn town. Sheltered equaled ignorance.

Thunder roared over the hills. The sound itself lifted the hairs on my skin, an unbridled thrill shrieking through my veins. I shuddered, releasing a harsh breath.

And then my blood began to burn.

The pain tipped me over, to my knees. *No, not now.* I was almost home. I needed to make dinner. I needed to get home before Rucas—

My eyes went wide with horror. From the opening of my sleeves, light cast a violet sheen on the ground. A drop of rain kissed my cheek, then another before the sky broke open and water poured down, drenching me and my groceries.

Quickly, I grabbed my bag and stuffed it beneath my skirt. My veins were a beacon of purple light, the pain only mild as I rose to my feet and began to race up the hill. My boots kicked up water and mud, soiling the back of my dress as I held the front up to protect the groceries. I let out a sob when my house came into view, fear beginning to bubble up from deep within. I was late, the food was wet, I had ruined my dress—

"You bastard!"

I halted before the porch, sucking a breath in. That was my mother's voice, from within the house.

The sound of a mattress creaking rang in my ears, as if someone had sat down on a bed right beyond the door. I recognized it as my parent's bed—the metal coils in the featherdown mattress had always been noisy. But my parent's bedroom was well down the hall, and yet I could hear the mattress, the stomping of big boots, and the ruffling of paper as if I were standing outside their bedroom door.

"You will say nothing."

"You're a monster. This is too far."

My heart throbbed in my throat. Between the silence, a ring pealed in my ears, the same sound I had heard when I dropped that glowing elven book. It wasn't near as bothersome, but I still shoved my fingers in my ears to make it stop. It didn't.

A chair scraped across hardwood. *"You should be thankful the gods are silent and won't strike you down where you stand——"*

The slap against skin was so loud, it might as well have been to my face. *"Know your place, or you'll find yourself on the streets. And I mean it this time."*

"No. Rucas. Please. I'm sorry."

A door swung open. Footsteps marched toward me, but the sound was like a drum in my ears. Each step, a kick to my head. I gasped, crying out with every contact to the floor. It was too loud. I squeezed my ears closed, pain lancing through my head as the steps grew louder, *louder.*

Thunder cracked the air. I shrieked, crumbling to the porch floor. "Stop! Stop! Please for the love of the gods, *löth!"*

The rain stopped pouring.

The fire in my veins was extinguished and the light beneath my sleeves flickered out.

My tongue was still tingling from the word when the front door opened, the ringing in my ears fading.

I lifted my head to find Rucas glaring down at me. "You're late."

He gripped my arm and dragged me inside.

I shook as I wept, standing in nothing but my chemise, arms wrapped around myself and head bowed before Rucas. The groceries were ruined. The bread was soggy, the eggs were cracked and had dripped all over the herbs and spices. The only thing saved was the pumpkin, but when Rucas had learned I'd planned on making the soup he hated, he'd thrown it at me. It didn't matter that I'd decided on my walk back before my flare I would make him something else. He took the decision as mutiny, and the pumpkin had hit me in the center of my thigh and then he'd crushed it with his boot.

I sobbed, sniffling back the moisture that threatened to drip from my nose. His dark glare was a blade through my spine, pinning me in place as all my fears bled out of me. My plans of rebellion, all of the courage I'd had, all of my power...vanished. Gone, as if I'd never had them.

"I'm sorry," I murmured.

He raised a hand—I recoiled so hard I almost tumbled backward.

Rucas grinned, a dark chuckle in his throat as he twisted to the bottle he'd placed up on the mantle of the gathering room hearth. Mother was sitting in her armchair, her hands in her lap. She hadn't met my gaze since I'd been pulled into the house.

"You cost me money tonight," Rucas hissed before taking a swig.

"I know." I could hardly speak more than a whisper.

"However, you may not be the only one in deep tormshit."

I looked up just in time to see Mother shuffle in her seat. Rucas's glare narrowed in on her. He held it there until she began to shake and shrink back into her seat.

"We are missing six silver coins," he stated, looking back to me. "Have you seen them lying about, Mae?"

Gods strike me down.

I could lie about this one. I could. The money was gone without a trace, spent on a woman who needed it, and I knew Rucas didn't know who she was. He would never associate himself with people of her financial class.

"No," I said, surprised how steady the lie came out. "I only found the money Mother left on the table this morning."

Mother's head dropped to her hands. Rucas took another long drink. "How sure are you?"

A shiver ran through me. "Absolutely sure."

He nodded slowly. Before I could understand what his intentions were, Rucas ripped Mother from her seat and pushed her across the room. She cried out, knocking into the gathering room archway. Breath left me as he stormed to her, gripping her arms. "You lied to me, wretch."

She stilled. "Rucas, no—"

"Where did the money go then?"

Bile rose in my throat and I stepped forward, words tumbling out of my mouth. "*No!* Don't you fucking *touch her!*"

Mother's eyes went wide. Rucas snapped his head to me, glare blazing with a murderous promise. He released his hold on her, and time seemed to slow entirely as he prowled toward me instead. I started to back away, blood running thin. My hands bumped into the fireset on the hearth, the chimney shovel and brush clanging to the ground. Desperation seized me as I grasped the ornate topper of the fire stoker and tore it off its hook, pointing it forward—toward his torso. "Don't touch me either."

Rucas froze where he stood. Mother's breath hitched on the beginning of my name.

The room went cold as that tragic darkness brewed between us, something like tormfire burning in the fireplace instead of a cozy flame.

"You bitch," Rucas growled. "What are you doing?"

"Fighting back!" I yelled, tears pouring down my face. And I realized they weren't born of fear or sadness, but absolute fury. "Something I should have started doing years ago." I jabbed a warning blow forward. He backed away. "I lied. I did find those coins."

Mother stepped toward me.

"They were on the floor. I took them."

"Mae," Mother warned.

"I took them and I—"

The words ripped from her, "Shut your mouth, girl."

Rucas snarled as she stepped around him, lifting her chin high with all the poise and grace she'd tried to instill in me. "Do not cover for my mistake."

My jaw fell open, mouth going dry as I held her gaze. Anger and silent pleads overwhelmed her expression. I recognized her stance between Rucas and me, only because there had been many nights I'd begged for this reaction from her. It was enough to drag a sob from my throat.

She was trying to protect me.

But I was caught off guard, and Rucas saw my reaction as an opportunity. The stoker was ripped from my grasp, tossed toward the fire, the sharp end finding flame. In the same swift motion, he clenched my arm and pushed me to the floor. Burying his boot into my stomach, he pressed down until I thought he'd grind himself through.

And then he reached and grabbed the fire stoker once more.

I went cold as he revealed its red hot tip, dread rippling down my spine as I squirmed to get out of his pin.

He held it before me. "Maybe I should give you six burns on your disgusting face. One for each coin? Or shall I carve out your demonic eyes?"

I breathed hard, whimpers escaping my throat as I tried to focus on the fear and panic. Tried to will the power I had forward. Why would it only come to me when it wanted to?

Like lightning, he was shoved off of me. The firestoker clanged to the floor as he fell back into a bookshelf.

"Rucas! Stop it!" Mother cried. She made no movements to help me up, but she stood between us.

The murderous gaze he cast over the both of us chilled me to the bone. "You treacherous woman."

She jabbed a finger in his direction, as sharp an action as I'd done with the stoker. "This is not Mae's fault. It's mine. You've had your temper tantrum, but if you need to let out more hysterics, we can do so *later*." She lifted her chin. "Just remember what I know."

He growled, gripping her arm again. "And you just remember what that means I'm capable of."

She scoffed, breaking from his hold. "You wouldn't dare." She stepped closer, inches from his face. "It was six pieces of silver, Rucas. Whether I dropped them, spent them on accident, or I was pickpocketed, we will not miss six pieces of pauper money."

I gulped.

"We are the Mordaunts," she continued. "We are a legacy of fortune."

I wanted to laugh. I wanted to remind her that our legacy was only gilded. That we could adorn our home with gold and jewels, but it would never mask the wickedness within.

PART II: CHRYSALIS

CHAPTER 16

Mae

The crystals wouldn't shatter.

I couldn't wake up no matter how hard I tried to yank myself from this dream. Violet glimmers danced in and out of the opalescent shards. It would all be so beautiful if the thin points weren't pinning me to a tree, slicing into my flesh. My blood trickled out of me in rivulets, seeping into the crevices of the bark beneath me. There were only storm clouds beyond the mass of crystals pushing down on top of me, aiming straight for my head as they sank lower and lower.

My screams came out as thunder. Jolting cords lashed out from me but only whipping at air, unable to conduct to whatever material these crystals were made out of. Glass, quartz, I didn't know. But a point was now piercing into my chest—

As if my ribs had hinges, my entire torso split open. Hundreds, thousands of butterflies expelled from within me, taking flight as if my body had been a chrysalis for all of them. Their wings glittered with rainbows, flying into the stormy sky above.

I want to go with them.

A shard on my forehead was pushing itself in.

I want out of my shell.

Laid open, bleeding out, the crystals pressed in, in, in…

I want to be free.

Warm blood splashed across my vision as the point ripped its way through my skull—but then the screaming began. I could hear her shouting those words just as she always did. Tonight it was a desperate cry, a pleading request.

But I was already lifeless, my body pinned to a tree, ribs exposed to the charged air.

She whispered once more, a beg on her lips.

Then I saw her.

As if her visage had given me life once more, I blinked up at her face.

My face. But I'd been painted violet and given black eyes as dark as the night sky.

"Speak, Maelawyn…"

And so I did.

The crystals exploded, a thousand violent cracks shrieking through my head-space. And once I was loose, I slid down until I was falling..falling…

Falling like I had that evening, when lightning had struck the tree I'd climbed to find a safe space from danger…

Maelawyn…

Why was she calling me that?

I wasn't sure how long I'd been staring at the ceiling, but had been doing so since waking from that dream. My head spun, nausea rising, but my body was too weak from the flare I'd apparently suffered in my sleep to go and heave in the bathing room. So, I just ignored it, concentrating on my heart rate and breathing in the cool air of my room.

Eventually my thoughts wandered to the conversation I had overheard between Rucas and Mother, how odd it had been that I'd heard it at all. I couldn't figure out what triggered my powers to come forth or how I manifested them. They were always borne of my emotions, but I couldn't control which ones. Anger seemed to be the strongest, but why couldn't I bring them forth to protect me?

And really, I'd only seen the lightning-like magic. That ability to hear beyond walls seemed so accidental.

I thought of the woman in my head, how she'd had my face in the nightmare. How was she connected to all of this?

I looked over to my door. I had pulled my vanity in front of it the moment I'd left the gathering room. After Mother had protected me, it seemed Rucas had forgotten the ruined groceries and our scuffle with the fire stoker. That I'd threatened him, that I'd initially lied, that I took his money and did what I wanted with it. Out of all my crimes committed that night, Mother's was worse.

The cold silence of their room downstairs hadn't allowed me to fall asleep easily. A dread I'd never felt before had kept my nerves on edge. I'd never been more scared for my mother's life.

Not to mention the argument I had heard on the front porch hadn't felt like a normal dispute, on strange accounts or no. Those words exchanged had seemed like Rucas had done something terrible and Mother had figured it out.

There was a bang on the front door. I laid there quietly, counting the seconds that went by before my parents bedroom door creaked open and heels clicked down the hall.

Mother.

Relief flipped my insides and swelled through me as I slowly sat up in bed, breathing through the pain. Dawn hadn't arrived, but the birds had begun their song. I stood and creeped to my door.

A man's voice spoke into the house. Mr. Welch. "We must leave at once, Fantine."

My pulse skipped.

"Yes, of course," Mother replied. "I'll go wake Rucas and Mae."

I recoiled from the door. Rucas *and* Mae? My jaw tightened as I stared forward, awaiting the swift and hard footsteps ascending the stairs.

I wasn't going *anywhere*. I had…

I had my lesson with Varys. And then dinner with him.

She tried to open the door. It hit the back of my vanity, the bottles of rouge and eye-dust rattling around. I heard her huff in frustration, then, "Mae, open this door right now."

For a moment, I didn't move. Every breath I took was quicker than the last. She knocked and made her demands again. All I could think about was the night before and what she had done. How much I had always wanted protection from her.

She had saved me. From his wrath. From more pain.

What had it cost her?

I pulled my vanity back to its spot with a quick jerk. Mother opened the door the moment she could, rushing in without a greeting.

All air left me, my jaw dropping open in horror. Mother had always kept her thick, dark-brown hair long, stopping just before her hips, and normally left it down with the front pieces pinned back with jeweled combs.

Her hair had been chopped off—no, *seared* off. It now stopped at the nape of her neck, the ends crisp and uneven. Instantly, my thoughts went to the fire stoker and its red hot tip.

He had burned her hair off.

My eyes stung with the onset of tears. "Why?" I rasped.

She halted in her rummaging through my wardrobe, turning to me with her head held high. "I wanted a change—"

"Why do you let him do this? Your hair was beautiful."

Her gaze snapped away from mine, returning to the clothes. She pulled out a dark green knee length skirt, my black leather breeches, a white tunic, and a floral embroidered vest I'd never worn because it had been purchased for traveling—and I had never traveled anywhere.

"Put this on," Mother said curtly. "I'll pack your bag. We will leave in an hour."

"*Leave?*" I stepped forward, shaking my head. "Mother, in case you've forgotten, you and Father have never allowed me to travel outside of Elros. Ever. And now you expect me to go without telling me where we're going?"

Her brows knitted together, but she said, "Willem and Theon have not returned. The Welches and Brookers have gathered whomever they can, and at daybreak we are riding out to search."

I gulped, pressing my hand to my heart as if to still my erratic pulse. "Why do I have to come along?"

She threw her arms up. "Willem is your future husband, Mae. You are going to show his family support, compassion, *worry*." She shook her head. "Are you not?"

"Am I not what?"

"*Worried*," she bit out. "Worried that the only man you are allowed to marry is missing?"

I couldn't stop the laugh that rose from deep within, from where I kept all of my apathetic sentiments for that bastard. "I'm not marrying him. And I'm not going."

Her pupils flared. "Excuse me? Since when do you make the decisions?"

The wicked grin that didn't belong on my face continued to broaden. "According to Rucas, I make a lot of decisions, including the nature of the weather."

Her scowl deepened, and the glaring daggers she sent my way were so similar to that of Rucas, I stepped back—

Then she rushed me. My breath hitched in surprise when she gripped my wrists, tightly, painfully. She'd never—*never*—grabbed me like this before. She had never tried to hurt me as he had.

"Your defiance is going to get you *killed* one day," she growled in my face. "Do you not understand that?"

I cried out as she shoved me away, seething at me. "Mother—"

"I do everything I can to keep you away from him. *Everything*." Her eyes welled with tears. "Your lies. Your recklessness. Faking a godsdamn illness. One day...he's going to lose it on you. I cannot promise I will be able to step in and help."

I rubbed my wrists, suddenly aware of the lightning marks beneath my chemise and thanking every silent god she hadn't seen them. Her eyes were devoid of all things I had ever wanted from her. There was no care, no affection, nothing like motherly love.

"Then why did you help me last night?" I asked hoarsely.

She looked away, rubbing her neck, the crisp bristles of her hair brushing across her hand. "You are already a tragedy."

My mouth parted, chest grinding as my body flooded with warmth and ice at the same time. "You protected me because you were afraid the burns would add to my cursed looks."

She didn't respond.

"You already believe I'm ugly." I wrapped my arms around myself. "It wasn't because you were scared for me. It was because burns across my face wouldn't make for a perfect bride."

She refused to look at me, the shame written across her features as clear as crystal. "I suffered for my actions more than you will ever understand—"

"You're right, I will *never* understand." Every muscle in my body quivered in anger. "I will never understand how you can go on and pretend that he isn't hurting us. You wake up everyday and ignore his deception. His adultery and abuse. The fact that every single coin he's touched has become breadcrumbs back to his villainy. I know where he goes. That he leaves to be fucked by younger women."

"How dare you—"

"I know he comes home well past midnight and forces you to your knees."

"Shut your mouth."

"And I know that you are scared of him. That's why you continue to let him hurt you." Tears were threatening to form, and my throat knotted up. But I shut it down, swallowed my sobs. "It's why you don't protect me. Why you've never tried to get yourself or me out of this house. I know, because I'm scared of him too. But I'm *done*. I'm ready to fight back. Because I know the truth."

She didn't respond, staring at me as if she had forgotten who was in front of her.

"I know why I'm cursed. Why I'm a tragedy." Every word felt like venom on my tongue. "I know that you stay because if you left, he would know the truth too. That he's not my real father."

Mother's eyes went wide. *"What?"*

"I am done being controlled by a man who's not my father. I'm not going today because I'm *not* marrying the bastard he chose for me. From now on, I will do as *I want*."

Mother was still, unmoving, face flushed. "Why do you not believe he is your real father?"

I stifled a laugh. "I hear everything you don't want me to. Rucas believes you had an affair. It's why I'm Pallid. It's why he hits me. It's why he *hates* me—"

"That's a lie."

I lifted my chin. "A lie? Which is the lie? That he hates me or that you had an affair?"

She snarled. "Know your place."

"I do know my place," I snapped. "It's right here, demanding the truth. Because everyday passes by, and I get older, and I look at this white hair and my purple eyes and pale skin, and there's not even a drop of Mordaunt in my looks." I matched her sinister gaze. "What's the real story, Fantine?"

Her fists clenched at her sides. "You're a Mordaunt."

Another one of those malicious laughs escaped my mouth. "I'll never be like you and Rucas."

She scoffed. "You are a wicked, *vile* girl." Her lips tilted up. "You already are."

All of my wrongs flashed before me with her words. My lies. My ploys. Who I had wrapped into my own little web. I shook my head in denial, avoiding her glare as if locking eyes with her would reveal my deceit. Would prove her right.

"If that is the truth," I rasped, "then I will do everything in my power to eradicate it."

I would stand by those words until the bitter end. I would lose myself to make it so.

Mother's eyes only rolled. With nostrils flared, she turned from me and began to head out my door, gritting out, "Get dressed. Be downstairs—"

"I'm not going. I thought I made myself clear."

She halted in the doorway. "And I thought you understood that I cannot protect you. I cannot help you if you choose to rebel."

I let out a shuddering breath. "You did. I don't need your help. Don't think for another moment that I will ever ask for it."

She didn't turn back as she said, "Then do not beg to be let out."

Before I could comprehend her words, the door slammed shut. Breath left me when I heard the jangling of keys from the other side, and then the click of the lock.

I sprung to my feet and rushed for the door. The handle wouldn't turn.

"*No!*" I screamed. "You can't do this!"

The only response I received was the clopping of Mother's boots walking downstairs from the other side.

Fury ignited my blood, hurling me into a flare. I could hardly feel the pain beyond my ire, beyond the growling shrieks that spewed from me as the outer region of my vision became a vignette of white. My left arm pulled back, sharp heat racing through my veins. Energy gathered, a breeze blew through the room, lifting my white locks. The air churned of a smell that I was sure had to be that of storm and sky—some part of me knew it was *ether*. My fingers curled in a devastating, distorted flex as charged bolts began to jump between my nails.

I would free myself, even if I had to hurl jolting power through the door, into my mother's back—

Saeör...

I went as still as time suddenly felt. My blood washed cold, the goosebumps rising on my skin banishing the heat.

Saeör ít ölsta xera.

And the lightning in my hands flickered out.

No.

"That wasn't me."

I looked up, glancing around my room as if I would find the host of the voice standing in one of the four corners. No one was here with me.

My heart throbbed, throat feeling thick as I swallowed. It was the first time I had heard those words outside my dreams, the same ones constantly screamed at me. I'd never said them out loud. They scared me more than anything, not only because I still didn't understand why I could translate them, but because of what they demanded.

Saeör ít ölsta xera.

Free the rising storm.

"Who..." I was shaking. I was afraid to ask. "Who are you?"

But there was only silence in my head.

"What does it mean? Why won't you tell me?"

Nothing.

I sank down to my knees, my stomach feeling like a chunk of iron. It had been two years since I'd heard those words for the first time. Before last night's nightmares, I had never seen her face before but wasn't convinced she was some alternate version of myself. And yet, that dream had been different from all the rest. In two years they had only changed twice—the one that included Varys, and then the last one.

She had contacted me in another way, I remembered. In my unconscious state, after Willem had attacked me when I'd...

When I'd defended myself with magic.

She was there. She'd made me wake up.

My pulse quickened as I thought to all the times I'd had thoughts in my head that didn't feel like my own. How I'd attributed it to my pain, my lack of sleep. I'd believed I was going crazy at times.

She was real. She was truly inside my head.

But how in Torm did she get there?

Why was she always demanding me to free the rising storm?

My anger twisted, abandoning my fury toward my mother and focusing on the being in my head. I snarled. "Who are you?"

Silence.

"Why are you not speaking anymore?"

Nothing but the song of birds perched in the trees outside my window could be heard. No matter how long I held my breath, stilled my muscles, and silenced my own thoughts.

Pulling my chemise sleeve back, I inspected the lightning marks. I wasn't surprised to see them glowing, but they were already fading.

Saeör ít ölsta xera.

I shuddered, an angry sob ripping from my throat. "I don't know how."

Saeör ít ölsta xera.

I pounded on my skull.

Saeör ít ölsta xera.

"I don't know how to help you. I don't even know how to help..."

I lifted my head, sucking in a sharp breath. A weightlessness fell over me, the realization filling me with such peaceful clarity I started to smile. "I don't even know how to help *myself*."

Saeör ít ölsta xera.

My head began to nod, the words seeping in as I repeated them over and over in my mind.

Her words weren't a cry for help. They weren't a threat.

I was in a cage and the words were my key.

She was demanding I free *myself*.

There was a rising storm within me. Rising up from beneath my skin, from under my fears and weaknesses, and manifesting a change in me everyday. But it was out of control. *I* was out of control. The magic I'd almost called forth would have sent a blazing jolt of energy through that door if I wouldn't have stopped. If she hadn't stopped *me*, I realized.

Closing my eyes, I focused on all of the images I'd seen in my dreams, trying to sort through each one to find that one clue that would help me unlock my power. Crystals and storms, butterflies and trees...none of it made sense, but maybe now that I knew she was trying to relay a message to me, I would be able to unlock the secret eventually.

But none of that was helping me get out of my room.

Rucas's voice outside tore me from my thoughts. I rushed to the window, seeing Mother and him along with most of the neighborhood circled around Mr. Welch and our mayor, Mr. Brooker. Theon's older brother stood with his wife. Willem's younger sister, Wrenly, was draped over her current lover, Lucan Ward—a man I knew had no intention of marrying her. Several guardsmen were mounted on horses, except the one seated on the bench of an open carriage currently checking the reins of the horse chosen to pull it. Mrs. Welch sat inside the carriage next to Mrs. Brooker, both of their heads high with determination.

It was their sons missing after all. I could at least pity them.

I caught sight of Mother. The burning resentment I had for the woman who had birthed me made my chest and throat feel tight. She had locked me in here. Without food. Without water. Without means of relieving myself. And while I had experienced being locked in here before, it was only ever for a night. Even when my parents left town, I had the entire house to myself. I had food. I could use the bathing room.

And I knew better than to run away. Not after what happened the last time. I was smarter than that now because I knew it would all be in vain. I knew I would never be able to outrun him. Not until

I could get a hold of this power and got the help I needed. Not until I freed myself.

I watched as the search party headed south toward Elros's gates. Morning had arrived, another red and gold sun rising as it had the day before.

The minutes ticked away. I spent several of them jiggling the door handle, pulling it with all my strength, hoping the door would give way to no avail. My room was the only one up on this story. There were no loose boards in the walls or floors—I'd checked a hundred times before. The only way out was through the window.

And, gods, it was a straight shot to the ground. A fall that promised a broken spine or snapped legs.

But there was a tree. I had never jumped to it before—had never been desperate enough. I could make the jump to one of its branches, but I had no idea how I would be able to get back into my room. I didn't have any rope and I didn't trust tying my gowns together to make one.

I would worry about it later. I wasn't going to remain here, caged in like an animal. I was going to free myself and this wasn't going to hinder that. I was stronger than this. I could fight harder. I would. *I will.*

I picked up the traveling clothes Mother had pulled out and decided today they would get some use after all. The tunic sleeves were a little loose but hid my marks well enough. The vest was snug and gave my figure the appearance of hips and larger breasts. Omitting the skirt, I belted my purse around my breeches, then pulled my hair up into a high ponytail, braiding the loose hair and securing it with a black ribbon.

As I looked over myself in the mirror, I realized this was what I needed to be wearing the last time I tried to run away. Maybe I would have succeeded. I could run, jump, even roll if I needed. And I decided right there that when it was time for me to leave because I had the power to do so, I would put this on and never look back.

I opened my window, climbed onto the sill. I didn't look down as I took a breath, focused on the branch a few feet in front of me, and leapt.

CHAPTER 17

Mae

I hung there for a moment, a screech lodged in my throat. My stomach had made contact with the branch first, knocking the breath from me. It required every bit of strength I possessed to curl my legs and arms around the limb as it shook from my weight.

This was stupid—the dumbest, most foolish decision I'd ever made. I held my breath until the swaying stopped, but when I moved even the slightest bit, the tree creaked, eliciting tense whimpers from me.

If I could just get my foot onto the trunk—

The branch gave way. My stomach dipped, and I held onto the limb for dear life, falling and landing on a branch below. But the sudden stop made me lose my grip, ripping the leaves and bark from my fingers. I screamed, flailing my arms in midair to grab hold of something, *anything*, only finding air as I dropped. My spine tensed, anticipating the impact, the pain of a split skull and broken back.

And in that moment, the memory of falling just like this crossed my mind. When I had fallen from my tree in the woods as a small girl awaiting the same fate, watching lightning strike through the branches. Such a destructive force of nature and storm and yet I'd never seen anything more beautiful.

A sense of clarity hit me with that memory, coming too late. I couldn't die now. Not when I was so close to finding the source of my power. Not when I was so close to being free—

My body collided with a firm form, arms catching me as if I were weightless. A cry of relief tore from my throat as I was lowered to the ground softly, shocked I was still alive. I started to shout my thanks, finally gathering the courage to open my eyes, looking into those of my savior.

I stilled, my insides lurching as I stared up at the person. An eerie elegance twisted his devastatingly handsome features, his kohl-lined silver eyes almost colorless as if I were looking into a pool of moonlight. His lips were full like mine, his skin the same ashen tone. I suddenly realized this was how people felt when they looked at me. Shocked. Taken aback. Because cascading from the crown of his head, down the back of his black fur cloak, and tangled with the red rubies around his neck, was wavy, white hair.

He was Pallid.

I'd never seen someone who looked so much like me. And as if he could read my thoughts, the first words he spoke were, "By the look on your face, I suppose you have not seen many akin to yourself?"

Good gods. I didn't expect the voice that came out, deep and silky with a touch of rasp, his accent just as otherworldly as his clothing. The rubies on his neck were the size of a quail's egg, four of them on a chain with long spikes in between each. A long, thin blade adorned with a light green jewel in its pommel was sheathed at his hip, held by a belt around his waist riveted with silver studs. Despite the colors of the jewels and metals, every piece of clothing was black, from his heeled boots, to his collared shirt.

I realized I was staring, and I looked away as I responded, "No, I haven't. I'm the only Pallid around here."

Those silver eyes studied me for a moment, head cocked like a pigeon watching people in the market. "And I'm going to assume jumping out of windows and falling out of trees is something special about you as well?"

My face flushed as I stood on shaking knees. "Not usually." I bowed my head. "Thank you. You...saved my life."

A small smile rose on his pale lips. "The pleasure is mine. Though, I'm still not entirely sure why I needed to."

I grimaced, looking up to my window. "I locked myself in that room. It was a dumb decision."

The stranger chuckled, clasping his hands behind his back as he surveyed me. "Where is your spouse?"

I pushed a lock of my hair that had fallen from the braid behind my ear. "I am unwed. This is my parents' home. They left a while ago and have the key."

An incredulous expression crossed his features. "Well, it is not my place to be in the business of a stranger, I am just glad I saw you falling. I can't imagine how long you may have waited there for help with an injury."

Something about the way he said it made me feel absolutely stupid. But before I could amend myself, he said, "*Pallid*. Now there's a term I've not heard in a while."

My brows shot up. "What do you mean? You don't call yourself that?"

He flipped a lock of his white hair off his shoulder and inclined his head. "Absolutely not. The term came from old, religious fables. Specifically heard in the Churches of Eana. Are you one of her devoted?"

I stifled a laugh. "I pray to all of the gods equally and none of them answer, so mostly I just waste my time."

A smile that didn't reach his eyes lifted his porcelain features, "I cannot say I blame you. Most mortal-kind have become rather agnostic and have turned their devotion to gold and wicked games of survival."

I gulped. That was definitely the truth for most of the people in this town. "I didn't mean any offense by calling you Pallid. It is only what they have called me my entire life."

I wasn't sure if he heard me at first, too busy picking at his lacquered nails. "None taken. But perhaps I should ask, who's *they*?"

When his eyes caught mine again, my heart began to thunder in my chest. There was something terrifying and magnificent about him, leaving me feeling as if I were in the presence of a dark prince.

It was hard to look away, but not in the same way it was with Varys. I couldn't decide if I was intimidated, or intrigued.

I realized the feeling was similar to how I felt about my powers. Which made me wonder if he had powers like me.

"My parents call me Pallid," I replied. "But they heard the term originally from our town physician. When I was born, no one in Elros had seen anything like me. The physician informed everyone of what I was. That I was cursed, and demonic blood flows through my veins."

The man scoffed. "I'm going to assume this physician is the one whose infirmary has the large altar of Eana perched outside the doors? The altar where he also claims offerings as donations to his infirmary, much like a cleric would take a tithe?"

My eyes went wide. This man was not from Elros, that much was clear. It wasn't too far-fetched to believe he was a merchant who had stopped in town for the Fest of Change. And yet, his words made me wonder if he'd lived here for a few quarters at least. Even I had always believed Mr. Welch would be a better cleric of Eana over a physician. He had a booming voice, even when speaking quietly, and I often imagined he was preaching from a dais when listing off all the things wrong with me, or when he would tell me it was in the gods' plan for me to be the way I am, even if the Pallid Curse was something of demons and treachery.

"The Welch family are specifically devoted to Goddess Eana, yes," I replied to the man. "Eana's domain was life and health, and he is a physician."

He rested his wrist on the sword at his hip. "Do you believe you are cursed?"

I only shrugged, not comfortable with spilling all of my insecurities to a complete stranger. Instead, I said what Varys had told me. "We are all cursed with something."

He crossed his arms. "Wise words, but not a yes or no. Sooner or later, you're going to have to decide if you truly believe you are cursed, or just something different from everyone else. Humans are such judgmental creatures, full of such prejudice for those who do not look or act in the same manner they do—even among their own kind." He paused. "And although I am human, I am different. That, in no way, makes me cursed."

And I thought maybe that's what Varys had tried to say, too. That he was different, that being different was a good thing and not at all something to fret over. That I should let my differences shine and allow myself to love and cherish who I was. I longed for the day I was no longer ill, for when my bright purple eyes wouldn't be crested with dark circles. When I could finally gain muscle and weight because my stomach was no longer sensitive or I was forbidden from eating as punishment. I didn't want to wear my hair in some fashion to pretend it wasn't there.

"You're right. It doesn't make you cursed." I paused, taking a breath. "And I think I'm done believing I am as well."

And tonight, I would prove that to everyone in that tavern.

The man nodded, looking me over once. "I'm glad to hear my words had such sway over you. Don't forget them." He bowed his head. "If you are no longer in need of catching, I shall be off."

I wrung my hands as I watched him begin to turn. "Sir…"

He stopped, a perfect eyebrow arching. "Yes?"

I took a deep breath. I needed help. I didn't know if this man would be willing, but I…*shit*, I was desperate. "Well, I do have a bit of a dilemma."

For a moment, his face looked as bored as Eryx's did constantly. But then, "What do you need?"

"I'm locked out of my house." I smiled, lacing the expression with as much sweetness and charm I could muster. "You wouldn't happen to know how I could get myself back in?"

He only smirked, turning back to me fully. "I'd be obliged to help you, but how about a name?"

I kept my smile wide, refusing to look away from his colorless eyes. "Mae Mordaunt. Thank you for your help, Mr…?"

I didn't have time to react before he snagged my wrist and pressed his lips to the back of my hand, white locks spilling over his shoulders as he dipped down. My breath thinned as he lifted his head, a cloying cordiality dripping in his tone, "The pleasure is mine, but please no sirs or misters. Just call me Vamir."

Vamir.

I wasn't sure I'd ever heard a name like that before, and it chilled my blood when he said it, reminding me of creeping fog.

He also hadn't given his last name when I'd given mine. For a moment, I thought about making some kind of excuse to leave altogether, but he rose to his full height and snapped open the buttoned pouch on his hip. He reached inside and pulled out a small silver key. The green stone set in the intricate design of the key's bow was similar to the one on his sword.

"This key"—his eyes searched my face—"is magical."

A jolt of excitement went through me, but I made no such expression. I had wondered if Vamir had magic, but that didn't mean I needed to tell him I did. "Oh?"

He gave a slow nod. "It will open a door with a warded lock."

A laugh of disbelief escaped me—this was exactly what I needed. All of the doors in the house were like that, even my own.

But why someone like Vamir would have such an item? Was he using it to open doors all over the town? That was really suspicious.

He had just saved my life though, and I didn't think someone suspicious or criminal would go out of their way to help someone in need.

"Show me," I said.

Without another word, Vamir twisted from me, the buckles of his heeled boots clinking as he glided to the front of the house. I followed cautiously, skimming the houses around to still find no one watching.

He stopped before the front door and turned to me. My stomach dipped then, and I realized how foolish I was being. Allowing a stranger to open my own home—I knew better than this. I didn't know his intentions. I wanted to believe the same man who had saved my life moments ago would merely open the door and leave. But I also knew how easy this would allow him to corner me if he was the kind of man like Willem and Theon were.

Perhaps I had just been groomed to worst-case scenarios, but I wasn't about to enable a situation like that to even arise. "Why don't you show me on another door first?"

Vamir looked at the key with a frown. "Well, magic has rules as you know."

I took a steady breath. "No, I didn't know that."

He nodded, twisting the key between his nails. "Every spell has limitations. This one will only allow the person access if they live there. And they must use the key themselves."

Well, that made much more sense than what I initially thought it could do—which was that it could open *any* door with a warded lock that ever existed, and well, that was too fantastical. A good thing, too. I couldn't imagine what would happen if a person with ill intentions got their hands on it.

Vamir inclined his head, holding the key out to me. "Well?"

My stomach dipped. I was more nervous than I thought I'd be about taking a magical object in my hands. What if it set my power off? What would I do?

My hands trembled as I slowly went to take it. Vamir snickered. "It's not going to hurt you."

"I know that," I muttered, and took the key between my two fingers. Nothing happened, but it felt warm against my palm.

I breathed out and moved around him, stopping before the door. I looked back when he stepped away, only surveying me, waiting for me. Telling myself to stay calm only made me more nervous.

But I needed to make it look like I had never left home. I needed inside so I could come back if my plan failed, or my parents returned early.

This had to work. I was going to that tavern tonight.

I inserted the key and twisted. There was no catch as the lock clicked and I lifted the handle. As easy as it was with any other key, the door swung open. I gasped. "It really is magic."

A small snort came from Vamir behind me. "Your father sells magical items, yet you're so surprised to see one in effect?"

I slammed the door shut and whipped toward him. "How do you know I'm Rucas's daughter?" I demanded. "You're not even from around here. How do you know so much?"

His silver eyes lit with surprise as he held up his hands in a placating manner. "I was a customer yesterday. I talked to your father for a long time before I purchased some goods. I did not make the connection until you gave me your name a moment ago."

I frowned. "And how do you know they are magic? Can you read Elvish?"

He cocked his head. "Can you?"

There was that damn question again. Both he and Varys had asked it, but why was I the one that had to answer?

I rolled my eyes and handed the key back to him. "Of course not."

He shrugged, holding up the key in the sunlight. "Well given that I am in the market for magic items being a merchant myself, I have learned that most things with Elvish script have magical properties, and those that don't may or may not be. It's a gamble entirely. But there are certain pieces that I know have to be magical because they are not from this time. I am well-versed in the matter, as it is my profession."

I looked away. Gods, he sounded a lot like Varys in the way he spoke. Elegantly, intelligently; every word brought some sort of resolution.

I tried to open the door again and sighed when I found it locked. "The magic isn't permanent."

Vamir shook his head, picking his nails again, this time inspecting them as if they'd been scuffed. "The key only has so much magic enchanted on it as well. The next use could be its last, or the next. Only an elf would be able to tell you, and they are long gone."

My heart was slamming against my ribs, eyes focused on the key as he went to put it back into his pouch. It was exactly what I needed, and there was a chance I could use it two more times—once to get into the house, once to get into my room. I could even prop the doors open once unlocked. Then, after my night at the tavern, after dancing and drinking and laughing with Varys, I would come back and lock myself inside.

I *was* that desperate.

"How much do you want for the key?"

He grinned. "A merchant's daughter indeed."

I asked again, "How much?"

He flipped the key between his fingers once more, and then in one quick motion, the key was in my hand. "It's yours. You need it more than I do."

My eyes went wide. "I insist on paying you something."

He shrugged. "I am a very wealthy man, Mae Mordaunt. I am no longer in need of gold coins to spend or jewels when I can easily adorn my neck in them myself. I am now constantly searching for intriguing experiences. This was definitely the highlight of my stay thus far in Elros, so it is I who should be thanking you." He closed my fingers around the key, his touch just as cold as my own. "It is a gift. Use it well."

I fell back on my bed, a smile on my face as I stared up at the ceiling, holding the piece of parchment with the Common alphabet written out to my chest. Joy was bubbling through me, eliciting giggles as I held up the magical key.

I did it.

I couldn't believe it still. I couldn't believe I'd been stupid enough to jump out a window, couldn't believe I didn't *die*, and that the man who saved me ended up having a magic key that would allow me to get in and out of my house with ease. I wasn't sure if this had been the gods' doing, or some prewritten tale in my fate, but as I laid there I found myself sending thanks to whatever decided to intervene.

The magic key had its limits though, so I had propped my bedroom door open with my vanity. Upon entering the house, I had also found the key to the side kitchen door still hanging in the entryway and decided to use that exit tonight instead of propping open the front door and risking the chance of someone entering the house while I was out.

My plan had felt so incredibly loose and foolhardy, but it all came together. All I had to do now was wait.

So that's what I did.

I lived a normal morning. My only concern through breakfast was that I needed to make sure I didn't make my presence known with crumbs or dirty dishes. I wished I could bake something, but I wasn't an organized baker by the slightest. I used too many bowls, dirtied up more utensils than necessary, and was always left covered in flour.

There was evidence of last night's scuffle everywhere in the gathering room. Mother's chair was still crooked from when Rucas had ripped her from her sitting position. The pumpkin had been cleaned up, but my dress still lay in a crumble near the window. Rucas's bottle of liquor remained on the mantle, and I looked to the fireset on the hearth to find it still toppled over, but missing the firestoker—confirming my assumption Rucas had seared off Mother's hair with it. A black burn marked the hardwood floor in a couple of places from where the hot stoker had fallen, and I realized the entire house could have gone up in flames if it'd been left on the ground too long.

The lingering chaotic ambience in the air sent a shudder through me. At first, I went to clean it all up, but realized that would give away that I'd been down here. It wasn't like the walls could store memories, but the longer it all sat here, the longer it would stay in mine.

I sat down in Mother's crooked chair and opened the folded parchment. The letters were so sharp and there were too many lines. I thought to myself how much easier it would be to learn Common if the letters were pretty like the runic system of Elvish.

A strange, out-of-body sensation washed over me. How did I know Elvish worked off of runes and not letters?

I breathed out my nose and spoke into the silence of the room, "A...B...C..."

The market bell sprung me from my doze, striking an hour before noon. It was time.

I rushed to the bathroom, quickly glancing myself over in the mirror. My stomach was in knots and my heart thrummed quickly as I slipped out of the kitchen door, tucking the key into my empty coin purse. I pulled my cloak hood up and looked around to see if anyone was watching. The neighborhood was still empty of people and for a moment, a haunted feeling passed over me. Either everyone was truly in the market, or everyone had really gone to search for Willem and Theon.

It was a cold reminder that people were sheep and flocked to power, corrupt or no.

But as I went down the hill, I could see the swarm of people. The entire outskirts of town were covered in tents, more than the night before. Campfire smoke left the air smelling ashy, and a thin haze had settled over the crowd as I pushed my way through. Out-of-town merchants weren't supposed to be selling or trading yet, but I saw faces I'd never seen before barking at our resident sellers, holding up strange scrolls and bottles—magic items. Eryx had been right; this was just like what he'd seen in Latera. These merchants didn't want to spend gold, they wanted to trade these supposed magical objects for goods.

This would be detrimental for a town like Elros if these outsiders didn't leave or start spending gold. Elros was dependent on gold, especially if taxes were being raised. I assumed most of Xalador was like that too.

I thought of Vamir and how he'd mentioned being a merchant of magical items. Surely he hadn't been in that sort of business his *entire* life. Even Eryx had said the original stock had come from a halfling family earlier this year. But where had they found it all?

And why had all of these merchants decided to gather here for the Fest of Change? Yes, it was a big celebration, and we'd been attracting more and more outsiders over the past few years. But this was overwhelming the town.

I audibly scoffed, pushing by a man who stood in my way and refused to move aside. He only let out a grunt, and I pulled my cloak around me tighter. The way forward was much more clear. I found myself picking up my pace, hoping I could get through before another swarm of people blocked me in.

I reached the path into the hills, not surprised to see it too had been filled with campsites. Frustration lay heavy in my chest, but determination tugged harder so I pressed forward without remorse, weaving in and out of tents, stepping over sleeping rolls, and watching out for tarp ropes.

I made eye contact with a man busy stoking a fire. His bright green hair told me of his elven heritage. A woman with hair the color of the sky sat behind him just inside the tent, breastfeeding her baby who already had locks of blueish-green hair.

I gave him a quick smile—the man frowned and retreated to the woman's side, the two of them watching me. I glanced away and continued on.

Maybe I wasn't *cursed*, but I was still uncomfortable with the way people looked at me. I probably wouldn't ever get used to that.

I reached the edge of the temporary campsites and started on the decline down into the valley of houses toward the east gate. The closer I came to the stream, my skin began to tingle with apprehension. I hadn't been able to prepare myself for this moment, for when I would come back to the spot where I'd been attacked. This had been my idea but…I wasn't sure I could handle it anymore. Had I known Rucas and Mother were leaving, I would have been fine with having the lesson *anywhere*. Anywhere but here.

Memories began to combat with reason, every limb shaking, eyes darting between branches and searching for quick exits. I picked up a small, fallen branch and held it over my shoulder, watching and ready for any movement that wasn't Varys.

I'll be safe this time. I told myself those words over and over, but the closer I got to the spruce Theon had been behind, the more clear my memories of the attack became. How I'd missed the bushes to the left and realized that was probably where Willem had been hiding. I gripped the branch tight, slowing my steps, tears threatening to form.

I passed the spruce, taking in the familiar scene as those memories still tormented me, my own screams threatening to deafen me. His callused hands on my thighs that reminded me of snake skin running along the softest parts of me.

Why did I come here? Why didn't I tell Varys to meet me somewhere else?

But my memories also reminded me of what didn't happen. My fear had called forth my powers, and had been the ultimate refusal. Had forbidden him from touching me when I said no.

I would be safe this time. Not because Varys would be there, but because I could protect *myself*, and that awareness was much more significant to me.

Not a moment passed before the wings of several birds rustled as they took flight behind me. I jumped and spun around, the branch in my hands swinging outward. Beyond the bushes and the line of trees past them, someone said something I couldn't understand.

My heart dropped as I held the branch tight. I didn't know what I needed to do, but I focused on my fear, how it was laced with anger and annoyance. Maybe it would be enough to make something spark.

I stepped slowly toward the brush, peeking between the sticks. I couldn't see anyone, but I could hear someone walking, swishing fallen leaves around. The person was beyond the wood ahead—

Leaves fluttered out from behind a tree.

Someone was hiding from me.

I moved around the bush, stepping lightly, holding the branch over my shoulder, and prepared to swing.

The person sighed roughly, and more leaves were kicked around. My heart was slamming against my ribs, fear flooding my bones. I trembled, but I would not run. If it was Willem or Theon, they were going to wish they'd never tried coming back here.

I inched closer, closer—

The person stepped out so suddenly my only reaction was to swing.

"The fuck?!" They grabbed hold of the branch before it made contact with their face, ripping it from my grasp and throwing it away.

My spine went rigid.

I swore I felt my very soul leave my body, knees wanting to buckle, blood rushing cold.

I looked—looked *down*—into her green eyes. She, too, had gone still, gripping the handle of the blade strapped to her back.

It was the half-dwarf woman, Leona Cauldücen.

CHAPTER 18

Mae

I had repressed a lot of my childhood memories, mostly because a lot of happy moments were replaced within the same day by nights of abuse. But one memory in particular I had carried with me throughout my life was the first time I saw Leona Cauldücen. I had been one of the several people that had rushed toward the school to see why a boy was screaming, and why she had pinned him down in the mud, punching and slapping him in the face. Varys had tried to intervene, only to get slung away in time for Professor Wynhart to arrive and drag her off. She still lashed out and kicked in his grip, and I remembered thinking to myself how she reminded me of a feral feline cub, claws out and teeth bared.

I never learned of what had caused her to attack him like that, but I'd been warned to stay far away from her if I didn't want to meet the same fate. For a while, I had a pretty terrible opinion of her. That she was like Rucas; just another person who hurt people.

But she had faced consequences. And people like Rucas never did.

I didn't see her for several years after that. Not until one afternoon when we were teenagers. We both had become small women, but where I had stayed willowy, Leona had erupted with curves. It didn't matter that she wore baggy tunics and breeches, she had the kind of features I envied greatly. But there were other characteristics she'd developed I knew weren't necessarily because of maturity. There was girth to her arms and thighs, all of it lean, hard muscle. And I hadn't understood why she had emerged from wherever she'd been hiding looking like that until I had noticed the sword strapped to her back, the knives on her belt, and the foulest scowl on her face she offered to anyone who dared to look her way. A look that had earned her the title of "the town brute", middle fingers, and doors slammed in her face.

But she had been...a *child* when she hurt that boy. I knew now how much this town twisted stories, and that people believed whoever held the most gold over their head. After all the judgment I'd received over the course of my life because people believed I was cursed, I wondered if perhaps Leona and I were on similar ground.

But I couldn't have weapons on my hips or snarl at everyone who hated me. I was a Mordaunt. When people spoke about me, it was spread in whispers and rumors. When they spoke about Leona, it was to her face, sometimes in cruel shouts from across the market. The difference was who our parents were.

What if her display of arms and emblazoned glares were a means of guarding herself? The thought heated my already reddened cheeks, embarrassed and flustered as she stood there looking up at me, already loosening her grip on the handle of her blade. There was no disdain in her eyes, nothing that made me feel threatened. Her reaction to grab her sword was justified considering I'd swung at her.

"What in Torm were ye doin' sneakin' up on me like that, Snow?" she asked, and it was the first time I realized how thick her dwarven accent was. "I could've split ye wide."

I stepped back a bit, trying my hardest to steel my resolve. I was still shaking from my memories and how they'd led me to this encounter, but I didn't want her to think it was because of her.

"I'm sorry. I thought you were..." I paused, thinking back to her initial question. "Wait, *Snow?*"

Her freckled nose crinkled and she crossed her arms. "Ye like it? I wanted something that'd suit ye, but Varys thought ye might hate it."

"I don't hate it," I told her with a small smile. "My hair *is* white."

She laughed out. "Thought ye'd understand." Her smile dropped as quickly as it came on, and she eyed me hard enough I took another step back. "Seriously though, what were ye doing? Out here mindin' my own business, takin' a piss—"

"*What?*"

She blinked at me. "I was takin' a piss."

I gaped at her in horror. She scoffed. "What don't ye understand? Relievin' myself. Peein'. Ye do pee, right? Or are ye too fancy for that sort of thing?"

I frowned. "Of course not. I just…" I looked around, back to the tree she'd been behind. Oh my gods, I really had walked up on her trying to do business. "This was definitely the most uncanny way of meeting someone for the first time. Can we start over? Properly?"

She blew out her bottom lip. "Bah, damn the propriety. Ye're Mae, I'm Leona. I'll call ye Snow every once in a while when I feel like it, ye can call me Leo." A roguish grin lifted on her lips. "I'm just glad to finally meet the infamous Mae Mordaunt."

Infamous. Did she mean that because she had heard a lot about me? Or was she referring to what Varys had told her? Both of those questions made me nervous, but I said, "Glad to meet you, too. I am sorry for sneaking up on you. I thought…I thought you were someone else."

She tilted her head at that. "Who?"

Just thinking of their names threatened my fear to rear its ugly head. "Nobody friendly."

Surprise overwhelmed her features and she uncrossed her arms. I watched as she looked away, her lips parting. "Ye…think I'm friendly?"

I saw it there then. Beneath the hard expression, behind the massive blade and the armor over her tunic and breeches, beyond the stone wall of her demeanor, there was a woman who had been mistreated all of these years, deemed as a monster she was not.

Abused.

I didn't know what came over me as I stepped forward and gently placed a hand on her shoulder. Her eyes widened at the gesture, but I only smiled. "You've never given me a reason to believe otherwise, Leona."

She went still beneath me, and a silent understanding settled between the two of us. What we knew of each other was only the surface.

A sudden determination filled her emerald eyes. She took a breath, clenched her fists, and blurted, "I could train ye."

My mouth went dry as I glanced at the hilt of her sword. "For...what?"

She chewed on her lip. "I'm a swordswoman, but I also know how to get m'self out of a situation I declined to be in."

I gulped down the sudden nausea, feeling like I'd been stripped naked. She didn't have to say it. She knew what had happened here, which meant Varys had told her. My heart wrenched at that, not because he'd said anything, but because Varys...he'd been scared that day, too. Along with those awful memories threatening to overwhelm me still, I saw Varys's face when I had regained consciousness, full of fear, concern. Anger. I hadn't been able to really think about how disturbed he'd probably been after finding me unconscious and exposed.

I was glad he had someone to talk to about it. That was something *I* needed.

She stepped forward when I didn't respond, gulping. "If ye wanted, that is. I don't want to scare ye, or intrude on yer business. I'm just sayin'...I know how that sort of thing feels."

My mouth parted on the breath I took, tears pricking my eyes. Leona didn't lower her unwavering stare up at me, but she offered a comforting smile. "When it happened to me the first time, even with a little training in me, I couldn't stop it. Fear takes hold when ye're trapped."

My chest tightened, thoughts caught on her first few words. *When it happened...I couldn't stop it.*

"We have a sayin' in the Cauldücen household, though," she continued, then enunciated slowly, "'Bones may shiver, mind may shake, but steel your heart and turn fear to flame.' Fear is power, capable of keepin' a child awake at night and equally strong enough to dethrone a king. Transformin' that fear into power is why I decided to train. It's not just slingin' a blade around, it's breathin' through the fear, and havin' the ability to defend m'self. When that situation came again, and it did—another person, another age—I held strong to those words and my trainin'. Even though I was scared, I didn't allow the fear to overwhelm me. I turned my fear into power, and I got away."

My eyes were wide, my throat tight. My powers didn't always come when I needed them to, but turning my fear into power was how I'd escaped my situation with Willem and Theon. Maybe training with Leona could not only help my body gain the necessary strength to defend myself, but also help me find the courage I needed in any situation—with Rucas especially.

"Thank you, Leona." My voice wavered and I couldn't stop a tear from falling down my face.

Leona winced, a hand extending to my shoulder as I'd done to her but stopping. "Oh, Snow. I didn't mean to make ye cry."

I shook my head. "It's not a problem. I haven't…" I took a breath, hands pressed to my chest. "I haven't really been able to process it all. And coming back here was something I needed to do —*had to* do. And before I found you—"

"Snuck up on me pissin', but go on."

I laughed and the tears spilled down my cheeks. "Before that, I was thinking about how I managed to, I guess, turn my fear against them. It's how I got out of my situation. My heart, my very being, said no and I found the power to stop them."

She lifted her chin and studied me for a moment. I didn't know what she found in my face, but she said, "I think I understand, Snow. But my offer still stands. It's great for a person to know how to handle themself in *any* situation."

I nodded. "I'd love to be trained. I don't believe I would do well with any sort of weapon, but if I could learn how to defend myself with my hands or legs, I would feel safer overall."

She beamed at my response. "Exactly! Then maybe along with yer readin' lessons…" Confusion crossed her features as her words trailed off. "Ye're supposed to be with Varys today, aren't ye?"

"We are supposed to meet here, yes."

She turned to look behind her, toward the main path. "Well,

where is he? It's not like him to be so late to somethin' extremely important to him." A glance to me. "And ye are, I hope ye know."

I couldn't hold back my grin, the fluttering feeling in my chest made of such raw joy and sparking recollections of the night before. To when I'd left Varys with promises of dinner, conversation, but most importantly, a promise of tomorrow.

My smile waned. Tomorrow was here, but he was not.

"Oh, wait." I pressed my hands to my mouth. "Yesterday, Varys wasn't feeling too well."

Between all the discord with Rucas, Mother, being locked in my room, and focusing on getting out so I could even make my reading lesson, I had forgotten Varys's sudden condition that had come over him the night before.

Leona cocked her head. "No? He was doin' fine when I left him. When did ye see him?"

"Last night at the market. I was shopping and we happened to meet by chance."

Her smile was wide and lewd, showing a bit of her tongue clamped between her teeth. "Ye two happen upon each other in the market far more often than not. What did ye two *do* last night?"

A blush crept across my nose and cheeks, my mind instantly on that almost-kiss and everything I'd desired. "Nothing at all. I helped him get home because he kept passing out on me."

The brightness of her face died like I'd snuffed out a candle. Struck with obvious concern, she stepped away from me, muttering a few words under her breath. "Tell me what happened."

I felt like we shouldn't continue to stand there. That maybe I should've gone straight to the library instead of coming here. Maybe he was still unwell.

"Let's go to him. I'll explain on the way."

At a fast stride, we made our way back through the woods. I told her what I had witnessed with Varys, just as I'd done with Professor Wynhart. Her steps grew more and more rigid as we walked, tension bracketing her mouth.

"I assumed it had something to do with your training," I said as we started up the hill into the market, then quickly informed her of all the tents ahead.

Leona seemed too interested and concerned with Varys's well-being to care. "No. I told him to take the day off yesterday."

"He also told me he didn't eat yesterday."

Leona smacked her palm to her forehead. "Fuck, ye're right. He didn't eat breakfast because he slept in, and then he didn't eat lunch either. Godsdammit, I should have forced him to eat. He stayed up all night. Victors, we were *both* up all night."

My heart flipped enough to make me slow my pacing. "Wait. You were...with him?"

Her eyes shot to the sky. "Yes. His antics will be the death of me I swear. Wouldn't give up so I could get some shut-eye." She laughed and crossed her arms. "It's yer fault, too. He doesn't stop thinkin' about ye. It's sweet."

I blinked. "I'm sorry—what?"

Just as my stomach knotted, Leona's face burst with revelation. "Oh gods. No. *No*, Mae. It's nothin' like that." Her accent was suddenly heavier. "*Garz*, don't ever run yer head that way again."

A nervous chuckle escaped, but I nodded. "Sorry."

As we stepped around campsites and tents like I'd done earlier, Leona's eyes were wide as she looked around. "There are...a lot of Elven-blooded this year."

I pulled up my cloak hood. "I don't think they've seen many Pallids either."

We were silent and I noticed the both of us were keeping our heads down as we entered the market. When we came to the path leading to the library, I asked, "What is something stupid Varys would do?"

She looked up at me with an incredulous expression. "What?"

"That's what he told me. He did something dumb and it used a lot of his strength. I assumed it was just whatever he did coupled with lack of food that made him weak and tired to the point of absolute exhaustion."

Leona's face went cross. She was no longer looking at me, eyes up to the library roof we could now see. I didn't know why, but my words had made her angry. "That damn fool."

I tried my best to keep up with her as she marched forward. We were on the inclined path up to the steps of the Wynhart home when we heard someone shouting Leona's name behind us.

We turned to see Professor Wynhart jogging our way. I noticed a slight limp in one of his legs, something I didn't know he suffered with.

"Mattis?" Leona stopped in her tracks. "What is he doin'? It's a school day."

I looked to the front door—to the large sign hanging over the door handle. "Leona, what does that sign say?"

She spun to it, her jaw dropping. "No school today. At the… physician?"

Mattis caught up to us. "Leona. I'm glad you're here." His eyes seemed to linger on me as if I was out of place standing beside Leona.

"What's wrong with Fawkes?" Leona asked. I assumed *Fawkes* was some sort of nickname she had for Varys.

Mattis's chest rose and fell for a moment, catching his breath. He fixed his spectacles and rasped, "I don't know. But he won't wake up."

CHAPTER 19

Varys

I couldn't get out.

    The viscous darkness surrounding was permeated with air too thin for my small set of lungs, burning and begging for me to take heavier breaths. But I needed to stay quiet. I couldn't afford to gasp.

A monster was hunting me.

I wondered if it could hear my heart beat, how it pummeled painfully in my chest and roared in my ears just loud enough to drown out its hungry growls.

Momma...

Come save me...

But she didn't know where I was. The lie I'd told would forever haunt me. I'd gone too far into the dark woods, had been too ambitious and determined to draw the strange mushrooms on the mossy floor. My lantern had been too low, and within moments of it extinguishing, bright yellow eyes started to prowl toward me.

I'd thought this hollowed log would protect me, but now I was trapped. I was too scared to look out the small hole in the bark.

The monster wanted to eat me.

Momma's scream tore through the air. She never screamed like that, she was much too brave to sound so scared. "Mattis! Run! Find Varys!"

She sounded close. She could save me now. Looking through the hole, I *watched as my parents backed away from the trees. There were more monsters now, their golden eyes gleaming in the moonlight, growls curling the night air.*

Momma raised her sword, tossing her head in the opposite direction. "Go."

Dad's eyes were wide. Scared. "I'm not leaving you, Krystan—"

Momma kissed him, pulling him to her hard by the collar of his tunic. The sight was like something out of a story. Her face was filled with fear, yet her kiss was hard and full of so much love.

"Go," she said firmly. "You keep our son safe, Wynhart."

His hands pleaded, staring in horror at the pack of wolves encircling them with rabid barks and hungry snarls. I still couldn't move. I couldn't get out. He wouldn't find me here.

"Dad! Dad, I'm—"

Teeth appeared from nowhere, a snout snapping into the hole. I shrieked for Momma, claws tearing at the bark as I pressed myself deeper inside. Dad yelled my name, but I could hardly hear him over my own screaming. I kicked at the wolf, its claws catching on my pants and shirt, tearing at them, slicing at my face. There was a sharp pain through my brow and warm blood seeped into the crevices of my eyelid.

I was trapped.

It was so dark and tight, and I couldn't breathe.

A sharp whimper left the wolf's maw, its blood trickling down through the gap, staining my ripped clothing. The mass of fur was yanked off the log, and Momma's hands found mine. For only a moment did I see her bright, starry smile before she was ripped from my grasp.

No.

NO.

I was still there, pinned in that log I should have never climbed in. Places on my body hurt, my pants warm and wet. I couldn't get out.

"Varys!"

I couldn't get out.

"Someone help me. Please."

"Varys!"

I couldn't get out—

"I CAN'T GET OUT!"

"Varys!" Hands were on my shoulders, shaking me. The weight was too heavy, too tight, pinning me just like that beast did. Just like those wolves probably pinned her before they—

Instinct seized me. I wasn't a scared little boy anymore. I was armed. I would kill. I gripped my dagger, a mangled shout scraping my burning throat as I slashed, but my arm was snagged by small, strong hands. A familiar voice cursed, "Fuck! Fawkes, it's *me!*"

My eyes snapped open.

Instantly, my senses returned, rushing over me like a wave. Goosebumps broke out over my skin as I became aware of the cold sweat that drenched my body and pants. Wide emerald eyes met mine—Leona. It was her who had been shaking me, but I didn't quite understand why she was gripping my wrist. Nor why my dagger was mere inches from her neck.

Nightmare. It'd been another nightmare.

A strained cry escaped my throat and my hand went lax, dropping the dagger to my mattress. I gasped out, pushing away from her, crawling back until I was braced against the headboard.

Leo gaped at me, arms still raised in defense. "Hey, hey, it's just me. Are ye all right?"

I couldn't respond. This room was my shelter, my escape, and now its walls were closing down on me.

"Varys, breathe."

I could still feel the bark on my skin, a phantom confinement. I heaved and panted for fresh air. "Window."

Leona shook her head. "What?"

"Open. Open it," I gritted out. "Open the godsdamn window."

Without another word, Leo spun from me. My curtains were drawn back and golden light beamed into my bedroom—a light that instantly began to soothe me. Leona pulled the latch up and then swung the window open. Cold air wafted into the room, but I didn't care about the temperature. I could hear people and the birds—*life*. The tightness in my muscles eased.

Leona came closer, slowly, as if she were approaching an injured animal. I stared at her, forcing myself to take deep breaths. "It...it felt real." My voice was so hoarse, I wasn't sure if she could understand me.

But she shook her head. "It wasn't though."

"They're...the dreams are getting worse." Leona took my face in her hands. "Every night now. It's like I'm back there. It's like I'm back in that space and I can't get out and that wolf is—"

"Stop. Stop it." I was trembling as she held my face. "Ye're not there. Ye're here. With us."

I blinked at her. *Us.*

There was someone in the doorway—dammit, I *knew* who it was. And when Leona let go of my face to push strands of my sweaty hair off my forehead, I all but crumbled into my arms from the sheer embarrassment. How much had she seen? How long had she been standing there, watching me while I'd dreamed of my rawest fears? Had she seen how destructive I could be, how I'd almost hurt my best friend, how I'd flown into something I couldn't control?

What did she think of me now?

Leona patted my back. "He's all right."

I heard Mae take a breath. "I'm going to cook then—"

"You don't need to do that, Mae," I muttered from my hunched position.

I heard her scoff, and then boots clicked across the bedroom floor. The weight on my mattress shifted when Leona stood, then it sank down on my left. Cool hands found their way through my arms, lifting my chin.

My heart throbbed. Fierce, violet eyes gazed into me, and I felt more than saw the tenderness within them. I found it suddenly easier to breathe as the look she gave me seemed to consume every single fear still roiling around in my head and replaced it with...with *courage.* It was such a foreign feeling, to be able to just will away the terror as if it could never touch me again.

Chaos. As if looking into her eyes was all it took to reshape me into everything I wanted to be.

I watched every movement she made, those beautiful, full, plum lips lifting into a warm smile as she stared right through me. Just as it had been the night before, her touch was cool but it wasn't unpleasant. In fact, it was just what my skin needed, like a refreshing rain after a blistering summer day.

She moved in slowly, lips aligning with mine. My entire being went still. I wanted that kiss. I wanted to pull her into me and give into the evident desire we both shared. But she only pushed more of my hair off my clammy face and told me, "I am making you food. And you are going to eat it."

I nodded once, hands tingling with the need to feel her. "Yes, I am."

She left my side—too fast and too soon. I watched her as she began to walk out, a swelling ache in my chest as I took in her delicate form. I'd never seen her dressed in something like that, the breeches allowing me to catch a glimpse of her slender legs.

She stopped in the doorway and turned back slightly. Her eyes met Leo's first and the two seemed to have a conversation without words for just a moment before she lowered her gaze to my floor. "I have nightmares, too. Every night." With pursed lips, her brow scrunched as if she was trying to determine what to say. "It is a torment not many people can understand. But I do, Varys."

Her gaze found mine again. It may have just been the light, but I could have sworn tears had formed in her eyes as she said, "I only wish I could have been here sooner to help you."

My breath hitched. I realized, whether on purpose or not, she repeated what I had said to her at the stream.

She continued down the hall. Every part of me wanted to get up and go after her, but when I found Leona scowling at me from the edge of my bed, the fire in my blood was stamped out.

"What?" I asked her.

She glanced toward the door. It was clear she was waiting to say something until Mae was out of earshot. Then, "So why are ye sleepin' with a godsdamn dagger under yer pillow?"

I gulped. "Leona, I am so sorry—"

"I'm not mad about that. I knew better than to try and shake ye awake when ye were havin' a nightmare. I—I don't know. I panicked. Because Snow said some shite about ye passin' out on her yesterday and—"

"Wait. What time is it?" I sat up straight and whipped my head to the window, to where the afternoon sun beamed in and cast a golden tone over my bookshelves and messy desk.

Leona scoffed. "Yer stomach should tell ye that one. Ye've skipped five meals."

"Five!"

"Ye've not eaten since dinner at my place."

As if on cue, an almost painful growl slithered through my stomach. "Damn." I wasn't sure what Mae would be cooking for me, but I was eager to find out.

I grumbled as I rolled out of bed, scanning my room for my tunic. There was a heaviness in my head as if I'd spent the entire night drinking. A thick, frothy feeling coated my tongue. Memories were just as clouded as I felt, images of my night no more than flickers of shadow and color.

When I turned back to Leona, who was holding my tunic in her hands, it all rushed back to me. I'd taken the tunic off after Mae had left last night. Had placed it there on the nightstand where I'd knocked a few books off in the process, but I'd been too tired to pick them up. An involuntary doze had found me before dinner. Father had tried to get me to eat; I could remember his voice asking if I was hungry. I didn't know what I'd responded, if I did. But then I remembered waking to a sweat-drenched bed, so cold and hot I could barely breathe. My vision had danced and spun as I'd made my way to the bathing room, barely able to hold my stomach back before I vomited, then again, and again. Remembering that, I was suddenly aware of how sore my abdominal muscles were, leftover pain I'd experienced when my insides purged an empty stomach. I had fallen unconscious over the latrine, but I'd made my way back to the bed at some point.

That was when the itching started. I didn't know how long I'd laid there, tormented with worry as I scratched my right hand raw. I knew what had caused it, and the tips of my fingers still felt like I had minuscule cuts beneath the surface of my skin. However, besides the red marks where my nails had dug, nothing was there.

It was my casting hand, suffering the itch of arcane decay. I'd used two spells simultaneously for a long period of time, and I knew better than to do so. Not only had I heeded instruction in my spellbook from the mysterious *F*, I'd read enough Elvish text about famous wizards who'd sacrificed entire body parts during the war to cast spells they weren't strong enough to perform. Though, it wasn't just wizards who suffered from arcane decay, and full-blooded elves wouldn't have had as much difficulty unless the spell was borderline world-changing, but I was more human than I was an elf. I knew I would have to strengthen my body, but more so my mind, in order to achieve powerful spells and be able to sustain incantations for longer.

Not to mention I shouldn't have dared to use magic at all with my spellbook being so far away from my person. A wizard's spellbook was like a reservoir of magic to siphon from. When a wizard learned a spell and cast it for the first time, arcane energy was pulled from the veins and then stored within the ink. Then, when the spell was cast again, the wizard used the energy stored in the spellbook, but like a constant stream of water, the veins replenished the energy for the next cast.

Because my spellbook was in Leona's possession when I had cast my wards and *Vid Medaes*, the commands pulled from the closest source of the veins—*me*. It was why I'd been sapped of all energy and strength, and why now my hand was healing from the internal damage of arcane decay. If I ever tried to cast a spell I wasn't yet ready for, if my mind and body failed, the magic would rip my mortal body apart.

"Fawkes?"

I shook my head from my thoughts and took my tunic from Leona. "So...the two of you met, then?"

Leona nodded once, still glaring at me with knowing eyes. She was just waiting for me to say the very thing that would set her off. Gods...I was much too tired for a lecture.

"I need to go and apologize for missing her reading lesson," I told her as I laced the strings of my collar.

"Ye still have plenty of time for that before dinner t'night." Her monotone response had a bite to it and when I turned around, she was still studying me through that thinned gaze.

I swallowed. "Is she mad?"

She snorted, her head shaking minutely. "No, *she* isn't mad because *she* is oblivious to yer problem."

There it was.

"Leona, can we talk about this—"

"What the fuck did ye do yesterday, Varys?"

I let out a long huff, rolling my eyes to the ceiling. "I had every intention of doing *exactly* what you told me to do. I needed a break, and you were right about that."

She inclined her head. "Of course I was."

"But—"

"There's always a damn *but*." Her brows pinched together, eyes like emeralds under a forge. "Is that *but* why ye've been unconscious and vomitin' all night?"

I grimaced. "How—"

"Mattis informed us. Said ye didn't sup with him, then found ye passed out in the bathroom early this morn."

Her words snapped the last puzzle piece of my fragmented memories together. Father had helped me back to bed.

She went on, "Mattis went all the way to Mr. Welch's infirmary to get some possible help, but no one's there."

I scoffed. "I'm *not* sick. Especially not on a last resort level as to getting Mr. Welch to look over me."

I took a deep breath and spun from her, heading for the hall. Leona started to protest, only cutting herself off when I closed the door instead.

"We need to discuss this in private," I muttered.

When I turned back to her, she was no longer glaring. She had gone completely still.

"What's goin' on with ye?" she asked, and there was concern in her voice again, the fires in her eyes dying out. She knew now this wouldn't be light conversation. Not when I was ensuring the woman I had feelings for wasn't involved.

"I'm all right," I told her, slumping against the door. "I did something stupid on accident, but I would've never needed to if…" I made sure she was looking at me. "If a voice hadn't called out to me."

Trying my best to remember all the jumbled details of my encounter yesterday, Leona stared at me as I disorderly relayed them to her. She stayed quiet, eventually taking a seat in my desk chair.

"My wards were going to shatter under that pressure, Leo." I was pacing at this point, eyes between her and the door. "But something was definitely calling me there. Something knew who I was.

Because in the middle of all of that pressure, in the clearing, lay the tree Mae fell out of when she was young."

Leona's breath hitched. With a nod, I continued, "I didn't recognize the area because the last time I'd come across it, I'd traveled from a different direction."

Her eyes shifted to the door. "So, somethin' magical is happenin' to it?"

I shrugged. "I don't know exactly. I don't even know if it's linked to Mae in any way. It's possible that it was something magical back in the time of the elves, and with The ReEmergence its power is coming back. Perhaps it was home to faeries, or some other form of the fae."

"Perhaps it still is." She chuckled.

I nodded again as I went for my book bag and reached inside the small outer pocket to pull out the necklace by its chain. The opalescent stones glimmered in the gold light of my room. "I found this in the clearing."

Leona gasped. "That's *merlite*—a dusk stone, there in the center. Has to be." She took the necklace by its pendant and held it a few inches from her face. "Ye can't find merlite in these parts of Xalador. Dwarves have to dig *deep* to find dusk stones." An incredulous expression crossed her face. "They're said to glow in the dark— in *true* dark. In places never touched by sunlight."

I pursed my lips, my stomach taking a small dip. "Like the stones that were spoken of glowing in the Evershade?"

Leona shook her head. "No, those stones are called somethin' I can't pronounce. Da's not even sure it has a direct translation either. Dusk stones, though, are very rare. Ye'd have to be a dwarf to mine one, or be wealthy enough to purchase one in Gor Thorüm."

"And what of these?" I asked, pointing to one of the opalescent stones.

She tilted her head back and forth. Leona had a knack for identifying stones and gems. Of course, her dwarven father had mixed it in with her education when she was young, but even I had studied geology extracurricularly and couldn't name them at first glance like Leo could. She was just a natural.

"The colors shift like that of an opal," she said, curiosity in her tone. "However, this stone is vitreous, almost like quartz. Most opals, even in their rawest form, are cloudy. But it's possible this is just higher quality since whoever had this pendant made was wealthy enough to afford merlite as well."

"Do you feel how warm it is?" I asked. "It's got some sort of protection spell on it, although I haven't been able to…"

My words trailed off when I realized Leona had a familiar expression on her freckled face. *Oh boy…*

Her emerald eyes sparkled as she brushed her thumb over the pendant, fingers tightening around it. "This is a beauty."

"It is," I murmured, watching her cautiously. "And *I* found it."

Her eyes didn't leave the necklace as she *tsked*, "Of course, Fawkes." She held it in the light, turning it back and forth. "It would look gorgeous with my—" I folded my hand over the pendant. She blinked at me. "What?"

"Your *dwarf* is showing," I told her, pulling the pendant out of her hands with a smirk.

She balked, and the exaggerative drop of her jaw told me she knew *exactly* what I meant. "I wasn't goin' to take it. I was just— what are ye goin' to do with it, anyway? Wear it?"

I shrugged. "Perhaps. Maybe the blue in the dusk stone will bring out the color of my hair and eyes."

I blinked rapidly—stupidly—and she smacked my arm. "Eejit. It belongs around some pretty lass's neck."

"And that means yours?"

"I am a pretty girl, yes." She flipped a few of her red curls back. "But perhaps someone else with pretty purple eyes. Someone who's currently cookin' yer lunch."

"I know. I intend to." I tucked the necklace back into my book bag with a smile. "Why do you think I was so quick to take it back? You and your dwarven greed would have me in need of a new token of adoration."

She scoffed. "Dwarven greed…"

"You're right, that's not appropriate." I turned back to her, a shit-eating grin on my face. "I should have called you a greedy dragon."

A sly, feline smile appeared. Flashing her teeth, she nipped in my direction before purring, "I like that *much* better."

I rolled my eyes with a groan, then chuckled as I was reminded of the pure irony of Leona's obsession with dragons. Before the fall of the elves, before humans even came to Xalador, a war had broken out between dragons and dwarves. Duros had a song he liked to sing whenever he was hammered about how the war ended—how a half-dragon and dwarf fell in love and showed the two races they were equals. Once, I'd told Duros that I was sure the battle didn't end merely on the count of lovers. He'd only looked to Natalia, smiled, and then told me, *"Never underestimate the strength of a bond between two people, lad. There is no greater power than love. It can build entire kingdoms, shake them when it is questioned, or bring them down when it is ripped away."*

Natalia and Duros were testimony of his words. Their love *had* shaken the dwarven kingdom, and they'd built their own here in Elros, the entire Cauldücen manor a semblance of their strong bond. Built into stone as if to say, *"Nothing will bring us down."*

My mother had shown that power too in her sacrifice. Beyond death, her love for me and my father was strong. It held our family together, held this house together. And even when she was ripped away, we didn't fall. Yes, we'd been wrecked. Shattered. Both my father and I were still piecing parts of our metaphorical kingdom back together, each of us working on our own separate walls and cornerstones. But we'd been doing so for over a decade now—we weren't falling to ruin anytime soon.

"Anyway, back to the tree," I said, slinging my book bag over my shoulder. "Or really to the necklace."

I hesitated in my next words. I hadn't yet told Leona about arcane decay, and knew she wasn't going to react well. She seemed to have cooled off during my explanation of my strange journey to the fallen tree, and she had been very understanding of magic and my discoveries thus far—as much as anyone could be who *wasn't* a mage. But...Leona didn't like to see me hurt, in any way, shape, or form. Minus, of course, the cuts and bruises *she'd* given me while training. And that was only because they were small lessons learned, reminders of who I was before I got them and how strong I was now.

Could I prove to her that arcane decay was similar? Lessons learned?

I took a deep breath. "There's something I need to tell you. Something I haven't filled you in on about magic and its...occasional consequences."

She didn't look too happy about that. Her jaw was taut as she gritted out, "I'm listenin'."

"I used two spells at once yesterday," I said slowly, "and I shouldn't have. The pressure in that area was heavy so I had to keep my wards up, but...then I saw the necklace. I wasn't going to pick it up without knowing if it was magical. I wouldn't have picked it up at all if there was a dangerous spell over it."

Her eyes were cold, lips turned down and nostrils flared. I knew that look. She'd given me that look from the hilt of Thorn.

"I had to use a spell to determine the enchantment over the necklace," I continued, "but I couldn't let my wards down. I didn't know what that tension would do to me. Not to mention, you had my spellbook—"

"Yeah, to keep ye from usin' magic." Her eyes lit with fire again.

I grimaced. "Leo, that's not exactly how it works. When I learn a spell, I can cast that spell but...it's harder to do so when it's far away."

Her head jeered back. "Ye've never told me that."

"I'm sorry. You've seen how tired I get after using a lot of spells. Using those two for a long period of time, away from my spellbook...it was a mistake."

The sigh she released was laced with a growl. I swallowed, assessing her disposition. I knew underneath all of that fury, Leona was truly concerned for me. She was constantly worried about how magic was affecting me.

Today wasn't the day to talk about arcane decay. I'd save it for another time.

I placed my hands on her shoulders. "I'm sorry I made you worry. It won't happen again."

She looked up to me, jaw tense. "How can ye prevent it from happenin' again?"

"The same way I prevent cuts and bruises when I'm sparring." I smiled. "Training. Once I get my spellbook back—of course, on your accord."

She rolled her eyes. "We'll see."

I went on, "I will need to make sure I take baby steps and just practice. It's a mix of exercises to strengthen my body and mind simultaneously. I underestimated what two small spells could do."

She didn't respond for a moment, her shoulders beneath my hands as tight as a strung bow. Then, "Would it have killed ye?"

My blood went cold. "If I hadn't caught it in time...perhaps—"

"Yes or no," she snapped.

We held each other's gaze for a long moment. I was the first to look away, looking over to the door, then to the ground and sighed. "Yes."

Her body made no movement beneath my hands, as if my words had frozen her solid. Then she stepped away from me, a lifelessness to her usually spirited eyes. Turning toward her pack she'd placed beside my bed at some point, she unbuckled it, each sharp movement a bitter word left unsaid. From beneath a mound of crimson material—some sort of outfit, I presumed—she pulled out my spell book.

She didn't hand it to me. She placed it on my bed and muttered, "Here."

"I'll be more careful," I rasped.

Her eyes were downcast when she turned back to me, cheeks taut with streaks of red that spread down her neck. My stomach turned over. I knew that look. Even though I had seen it only a handful of times, I *knew* that look. The knot that grew in my throat barely allowed the plea to escape, "Leo..."

Leona hated seeing me hurt, and it absolutely gutted me to see her cry.

"I didn't know takin' that bloody thing away would be dangerous." She shook her head and sniffled. "I can't keep ye from doin' everythin' ye can to help her, nor can I keep ye from discoverin' more about this magic. I don't understand everythin', even when I want to. But if ye'd had yer spellbook…"

She lifted her gaze slightly, enough that I could see the line of silver beneath her molten stare.

"Leona, this is not your—"

"I didn't know that ye'd be hurt because I took that fuckin' thing away!" she shouted in such a fury, her tears seemed to evaporate the moment they hit her face. "Why not tell me that?"

Pressure clamped down on my chest, the twisting feeling enough to suffocate me. "Leona, I didn't know this would happen."

"But ye didn't turn around either," she seethed, prowling toward me, jamming a finger in my chest. "Ye didn't think for one gods-damn moment that ye were without yer spellbook. Yer *weapon*, Varys. It *is* a weapon. But ye just—" A growl of frustration broke from her throat and she spun from me, blazing for the window. She gripped the sill, letting out a huff as a breeze wafted through the room.

I sat down on my desk chair and waited, giving her the silence she needed to snuff her fires. More tears must have fallen, but she wiped them away before she let them show.

Finally, she let out an exasperated sigh, tucking her hair behind her ears. "Ye are the most intelligent man I know and yet…ye don't use yer head sometimes, Fawkes. And ye're so damn impulsive."

I let my head fall back against the chair and took a heavy breath. "I know. I'm just—"

"Tryin' to do everythin' to help her."

"Yes. And I know you want me to slow down," I told her. "I know I can only do so much. I'm not sleeping. I'm not thinking. I've barely eaten. And I'm…"

With her hands on her hips, she finally faced me. "Ye're what?"

I blew out, my heart picking up its pace. "Leo, I'm falling for—"

"Don't." Her jaw tensed and she bit out, "Don't say it. Not yet. Don't allow ye'self to break so easily. I know ye've had feelin's for the lass for a long time, but…" She shook her head. "Ye're bein' reckless."

I gulped. "Sometimes love and recklessness look like the same thing."

The look she gave me could have set me on fire. She leaned down, bracing the arms of the chair on either side, trapping me under her glare. "Pretty words. Just remember not to love so recklessly that ye lose ye'self."

CHAPTER 20

Varys

To the War Sage, Varys Wynhart,
keeper and inheritor of this tome,

My brethren and I were not prepared. Not yet ready.
But nevertheless, The ReEmergence of Magic has begun.
I do not have much time, nor can I write many words
to express the direness of your discovery. If you are reading
this, then the magic of this spellbook has revealed itself to you.
No longer will your life remain the same, for you are Vyl'kriev.
Born into a family of elven heritage,
you, my child, are one of Xalador's next generation of mages.
This is no mere coincidence for you.

You are a War Sage, inherently skilled in both magic
and the ways of the blade.
This spellbook is both your weapon and your compass.
Follow the instruction I have left on each spell.
I have written a simple breakdown of a few spells for you.
But furthermore, I bid you to research and learn more
of the elves and their history. You now possess the ability to
read our language—use this to your advantage, Varys.
Know that there are others like you. Maybe around you.
But also know that with The ReEmergence of Magic,
a great danger will come. One that you can only prepare
yourself for, and cannot avoid.

I bid thee well, Varys Wynhart. I do hope we meet in time.
Sincerely, F

There were now thirty small tally marks along the bottom of the page. I'd only realized by the fourth mark a new one appeared every time I opened the letter. Something—or someone—was keeping track of how many times I read it. I wasn't exactly comfortable with the knowledge I was being watched, but assuming it was *F*, perhaps they had reason. But it made me ask questions. Was I only supposed to read it once? What would happen when the tallies reached the edge of the page? Was there an enchantment cast over the letter that would cause the parchment to disappear or burn up?

I paced the length of my room, the edges of the page held tightly between my fingers as I read. I hadn't been able to sit still after my dispute with Leona. She'd left, claiming she needed to blow off steam and told me not to come downstairs until I was damn sure her words had sunk in. I'd laughed, replied *"Yes, Mother,"* and well, that had thoroughly pissed her off. She had slammed my door so hard, a few books had fallen off my shelves.

That was about when my train of thought began to spiral, problems and troubles bringing on an instant headache, and as of late my cure for that had been taking my mind off all of it and focusing on learning a new spell. I had practically lunged for my spellbook.

When I had opened it, just as it had the first time, *F's* letter had fallen out.

Upon my reemergence, I had started to see the world differently, as if my eyes had been opened wider. Nature and the weather was nothing but raw, uncontrolled forms of magic to me now. Everything happened for a reason, despite my internal fight with destiny and fate. I also had found myself having a hard time trusting people initially, wary of every word, every conversation. It was why I'd been apprehensive about the man riding into town yesterday. Whether those bad feelings I'd had were a figment of my delirious imagination or they were an omen radiating from him and his comrade, I wouldn't ignore it.

When the letter had fallen to my feet this time, it hadn't felt like an accident. It had *wanted* to be read again. And so I'd acquiesced, looking for something that stood out, something specific. I had gone over the letter twenty-nine times and now there was suddenly something different about it, as if the very nature of the penman was no longer an enigmatic character behind a curtain. That *F* was a real person trying to communicate something to me through this letter.

I halted in my pacing only to slump down on my bed, letting out an, "Oh my gods."

I found it.

You now possess the ability to read our language.

Our language.

Our.

I had believed that sentence implied *F* was *Vyl'kriev* since all of us could speak Elvish now. It had never occurred to me that *F* had actually left a tip-off, whether by accident or for this very purpose. That perhaps *F* was insinuating they weren't *Vyl'kriev*, but just a *Vyl*. An elf.

A pure-blooded, genuine elf.

I didn't know how that would be possible, but it would make sense. It would also explain how the letter magically appeared in my mother's old journal that just so happened to also be a dormant spellbook.

Or maybe it wasn't a spellbook to begin with. Maybe *F* had changed it somehow.

But wouldn't that mean *F* would have had to have been near the book itself at some point? Or...close to my mother?

There was no one with a name that started with "F" on either side of the family. Besides, if they were still alive, they all resided on the eastern side of Xalador and we had no contact with them.

It would've had to have been someone here in Elros, or someone who had passed through. Which meant the true identity of the mysterious *F* was staying hidden, elf or no.

I tucked the letter back into the folds of my spellbook and rubbed my temples. My headache was worse now. Although I needed to eat and I'd had a rough night, I knew the headache was from neither of those things. This discovery had added to the mysteries of The ReEmergence and I just wasn't sure how much longer I could handle having so many questions in my head. Alongside everything that had happened with Leo and Mae upon waking up after my magical accident...I was a mess.

So I locked my door and knelt in the middle of my room, knees hitting the hardwood in sheer surrender as I laid my spellbook before me. Light glinted off of the flat red stone in the center of the cover, surrounded by intricate designs of leaves, feathers, and crescent moons embossed into the thick, brown leather. This was of course the true form of my spellbook. It hadn't revealed its magical form until I had cast my first spell and stowed arcane energy within. Most of the time, I had a spell cast over it to disguise the book as a rudimentary journal—Mother's diary. But the spell only lasted a few hours. Being in the hands of Leona, it had transformed back.

With my palms up and eyes closed, I took a deep breath and shifted my focus to my spellbook alone.

"*Vadáki Rynd.*"

Immediately, the ache in my head ebbed with the inward flow of magic, the Elvish words I'd spoken commanding a casting shield, or circle of protection, to manifest. I opened my eyes when I felt the warmth on my skin, looking down to see the glowing *eçor* beginning to form. Twisting and ticking shapes and images appeared beneath my bent legs. In the spaces where figures did not meet, Elvish runes blinked in, pulsing like a heartbeat for a moment before the colorless light washed gold. A thin, shimmering barrier began to rise around me, following the edges of the outer circle of the *eçor*, closing me into a pillar of energy. I smiled and relaxed my tense shoulders. Even though the space was small and tight, I didn't feel confined. My fear of enclosed spaces couldn't touch me here.

All outside sound was muted inside the casting shield, which I currently welcomed. Eventually the barrier would strengthen as my magic did, and right now anyone could come through. But it would disrupt my focus and spellwork, causing something called *shattered spell*. It had only happened to me once. Leo had been in one of her more childish moods, purposefully picking at me to be a brat. We'd been by the stream and I had begun the process of learning a new spell, only vaguely aware of the pebbles entering through the barrier. In the middle of speaking the command word, Leona had tossed a final pebble in and it hit my nose, causing me to burst out laughing. But my laughing had instantly turned to cold sweat, nausea, and then my vision *broke*. Everything around me had looked like I was seeing through fractured spectacles. I had to wait several moments before my vision returned to normal, and it had taken me a week of reading to find what had actually happened.

My spellbook began to glow, blue light blending with the gold. I turned the pages to another minor spell I wanted to try. These spells were usually small and required little effort. Sometimes they were mere tricks of the eye. Sometimes they were spells to help someone around the house like animating a broom to sweep the floor.

This one would allow me to create optical illusions that did not have any influence over the mind as most illusions did. What I could conjure was entirely up to what my imagination could create. And my head was pretty talented at creating things I wished and did not wish to see.

But first I had to mentally construct this spell's *eçor*. *F's* instructions were thorough enough, but if I didn't structure it correctly, the spell would fail. It was similar to solving an arithmetic equation, but instead of numbers to work with, I had to piece together an image that represented the spell in every aspect. The symbol for the ruling element of fire—a geometric triangular shape—had to be on the left. The celestial body's figure had to sit perfectly parallel, in this case it was connected to the moon in its crescent phase, the symbol sitting inside a circle. Both the element and celestial body's symbols needed to be resting on the border of a thin ring that would spin in orbit around two hexagons sitting offset from each other. Other shapes were required, all of them so impossibly twisted and overlapping each other, it was hard to tell what was a square and what was the beginning of an octagon.

For several moments I worked, my magical aptitude allowing me to mentally envision the *eçor* as if I was drawing the image within my mind. When I felt like I had it correctly structured, I extended my second and middle fingers toward a blank page in my spellbook and muttered, *"Ylustrís."*

The Elvish word commanded the magic to illustrate, the orange light of the transmutation school washing over my spellbook, bright enough I was forced to close my eyes and wait for it to fade. In its wake, the *eçor* was now perfectly—magically—inked into the page as if I'd drawn it with a quill. I was now ready to begin casting the spell for the first time.

I sat down all the way, crossing my legs and resting my hands on my knees. I took a breath, focusing on the *eçor*, on the element of fire, the moon, the shapes.

"Tul ít yrçaedös ölst váád ít kríevas…"

May the arcane energy rise from the veins…

"…te praeste Sí, Varys Wynhart, Vyl'kríev te yrçen…"

…and grant I, Varys Wynhart, Elven-blooded and mage…

"…hirul na vadák gasi medaesí."

…permission to cast this spell.

Like water bubbling up from a fountain, arcane energy rushed over the page, channeling through the lines of the *eçor* with light sparkling in an array of colors. I focused on the Elvish runes pulsing with a glow as they spelled out the answer to the command word.

I set my intentions—I knew what I wanted to conjure before I'd ever begun to learn this spell—and waited until the final rune lit up. *"Çruthi."*

Darkness devoured the room as the spell-light ceased in its glow. As minuscule dots of stars began to twinkle among the curtain of sky I'd created right here in my bedroom, the effects of the casting circle continued to fade out, sound returning until I could hear the birds, the wind—

A shrieking from downstairs, flooding my veins with an icy-horror.

And Leona shouting and pounding on my locked door, *"Varys! Godsdammit, open the door! Mae needs help!"*

Mae's body arched off the kitchen floor as she screamed in wild agony. I lunged for her, knees sliding on the ground to her side. "I'm here. What do you need, Mae?"

For a moment her scream continued to ring out, so shrill my eardrums spasmed painfully before it ceased, as if whatever had hold of her was coming in waves. She panted, beads of sweat rolling off her forehead.

Her eyes opened, a shake to her head. "No. No. I don't—" She sobbed, arms flinching, fingers flexing out uncontrollably. I went to take her hands but she pulled away. She bit out, "I didn't want you to see this."

I took her shoulders. She quaked beneath my hold. "What is this? What is hurting you?"

"It's—"

A shriek tore from her lips. Her feet pounded the wood floor in a tantrum of pain and fear as her muscles spazzed and tears poured from her eyes.

I spun to Leona who hadn't moved from the threshold of the hallway entry. Her wide emerald gaze met mine and she shook her head. "She was gettin' lunch prepared and then just collapsed and started to…*this*."

"Go get help—"

"*No!*" Mae's icy fingers gripped my arm. "It will pass—*it will pass!*"

Another scream left her, and gods, it sounded like she was burning alive. I wrapped my arms around her, pulling her into my chest. The chill of her skin bit through me as she buried her face into my shoulder, nails sinking into my back.

Her convulsing in my arms sent panic through my own body. I didn't know what to do. I didn't know how to help. I didn't know what in Torm was going on.

"Mae, breathe."

"It *hurts*," she hissed. "Everything...is..."

Her breaths were too quick. The plum color of her lips had washed to a blue, eyes bulging as she stared up at the ceiling.

"Mae, please." I couldn't stand to see her like this, but couldn't focus on the qualm of my stomach. "Try to breathe through it."

"I c-can't."

"You can. You *must.*"

She shook her head. "It's never been...it's never been this bad."

Another wave must have surged through her, because she was suddenly gripping my tunic, teeth in a tight line. She shrieked, tearing at my shirt like a wild animal.

"*Fuck*," I uttered, wanting to hold her, but instinctively pulling away.

"I'm gettin' help!" Leona shouted.

She raced away before Mae could argue. Fresh tears spilled from her eyes. "Varys, it'll pass. T-They always do—"

She let out another wail. Her body flung backward, out of my arms, her back hitting the floor before I could catch her. My breath sawed out of me, pushing frantically off the floor to lean over her.

"*Chaos.* Mae, tell me how to help." I swallowed down the thickness in my throat. "Please."

"I-I don't know." She choked on a sob. "N-No one...has ever been able to make it...s-stop."

My heart wrenched. Even I had magic and couldn't make it stop. I couldn't just reach in and take out whatever it was that was hurting her. I didn't have a single spell that would help pain. Nothing to even ease stress.

But I did have a mind. I had knowledge of exercises, meditation routines, and breathing techniques to calm the body.

And I also had an idea if all else failed. But it was an extremely *stupid* idea.

"Mae, I need you to take deep breaths. I know it's hard, but you must. In the nose, count to four, out your mouth—"

Another cry tore from her throat, sending her into another bout of panting.

"Breathe." I took her face in my hands. "Mae, *breathe.*"

"It's—too—much."

I had to get her to calm down. None of my strategies were going to work if she couldn't breathe normally.

"I'm trying to help you." Stupid, *stupid* idea. "Just please don't hit me."

I ceased her frantic breathing with my kiss.

CHAPTER 21

Varys

Mae didn't breathe beneath me, every part of her going taut. I didn't wait for her to kiss me back, didn't wait for the cool touch of her lips to respond in a way that would have me losing air too.

I broke away and rasped, *"Breathe."*

She did. The breath she took was full and deep, releasing in a slow exhale—the breath she *needed*. She took another one, and despite her still-trembling and sporadically twitching muscles, she was breathing normally again. Her shaking fingers touched her lips.

And that was about the time I started to panic.

I kissed her. I *kissed* her. I didn't want her to remember that kiss as our first, so dry and hard and passionless.

"I'm sorry." My voice cracked on the words, warmth racing through my face up to my scalp as I backed off of her. "I-I had to get you to snap out of it."

Shit Shit Shit.

"I—gods, just hit me." My pulse hammered in my ears. "I shouldn't have done that. Hit me. Hit me hard—"

"What did you do?"

"I-I kissed you." I could hardly speak. Could hardly enunciate my words. "I'm— I'm s-sorry."

226

A small laugh escaped her lips already washing back to their natural plum color. "No, you...you didn't feel the shock?"

My head jeered back. "Shock?"

"It happened the first time I touched you, too."

Her head lolled back as a groan of pain passed through her teeth. She was still hurting, but no longer losing air. I could deal with that. At least my surprise kiss had stopped her heaving.

I still felt like a bastard.

She rose to her knees, hands pressed to her chest. "There was a pulse...like the shock you feel when you rub your feet on a rug and then touch something. But different." She gulped. "Deeper."

I cleared my throat. "I didn't feel anything, Mae."

She seemed to stare past my eyes, like she had fallen in a trance, or was lost. "Not even yesterday? When we touched?" she asked.

And there was almost...disappointment in her tone. As if I *should* have felt something because it symbolized something greater to her. To *us*.

I didn't know whether to say yes, no, shake my head a certain way. But I wouldn't lie. "I didn't feel whatever it is you felt, but I cannot deny I feel many things when we touch, Mae." I swallowed, trying to wet my parched throat. "But I also want you to know that even though I feel a lot of things, I can control myself and I was only kissing you to—"

"Oh." She held up her hands. "You think you crossed a line, don't you?"

I hesitated, only incoherent words tumbling from my mouth until I gathered my senses and gritted out, "I'm not like *him*."

Him, the man who violated and touched her without permission. I had just kissed her without asking if I could and had realized quickly I was no different.

Her eyes went wide before softening, intertwining her cool fingers with mine. They shook in my hold, and the squeeze she gave my hand seemed like such a struggle. "And you never will be."

She let out another sob, body buckling inwards as she wrapped her arms around herself. For several moments, she only gulped down air. Then, her body relaxed. The pain really was coming in like waves, but I couldn't help but notice the pain had seemed to ease when I'd kissed her. Surely that was just a coincidence. She was no longer screaming, but it was obvious whatever had hold of her was not done with its torment.

When she seemed better, she pulled herself closer, and my breath hung when her hands found my shoulders. I didn't balk when her icy fingers slid up my neck and then cupped my face gingerly.

Her brows pinched. "There's a great difference," she told me through a breath. "He has never been granted permission to kiss me." She brought my face closer and…and I was lost. In those eyes, in her voice. "You, Varys Wynhart, have already received permission."

Heat roared through my veins, pulse pounding with instant desire and need. The air around her was intoxicating, stealing my breath—she could have it. "I wasn't aware of such a grant."

Her knees pressed against mine, head tilting as she studied me. She looked at me as if she was in awe of me—the same way I looked at her. "You can kiss me whenever you'd like."

That knowledge sent the pounding to places low and eager. *Chaos*, I was in trouble. Her thick lashes fluttered, eyes drawing to my mouth. She dragged that full bottom lip of hers between her teeth and I…gods, that was my favorite thing to watch in all of Xalador. How instantly disappointed I was that I'd kissed her, but I hadn't been able to taste her beautiful pout. Hadn't been able to bring it between my own teeth and tease its softness with my tongue.

"Well, then allow me to redirect my apology. I'm sorry for not kissing you in the way you deserve." I breathed in her rain and lavender scented skin. "That should not have been *our* first kiss."

She smiled, crinkling her nose and eyes. "It was *mine* though."

I went so still, she let go of my face. "What?"

The small, girlish giggle in her throat gave me the answer before she could. "I had never been kissed before."

My head dropped to my hands. Gods, that made me feel even worse. *Of course* she'd never been kissed before. She'd never trysted anyone that I was aware of, and she was Rucas Mordaunt's daughter. I wouldn't have been surprised if he had at some point forbidden her to tryst until that prick Willem Welch asked for her hand.

And if that was the case, our gazes and touches and obvious attraction, the relationship that was developing, our words...all of it made me realize that perhaps Mae was going against her father's wishes. That I was the secret affair.

A part of that excited me. It was a strange reassurance that Mae wanted me despite my previous doubts she did. That she found me worthy of her when her own family did not.

But if Rucas didn't know about us, our relationship was being built on a lie. Another damn lie that would continue to spin its fragile web until it would tear and then...and then what? This was not something she could hide forever—I would not hide and cower from her father.

"Varys," she said, a smile in her voice. "There's nothing to be—"

She hissed, her body crumbling again, ripping me from my embarrassment. I reacted without another thought and pulled her against me, settling her into a cradle. She whimpered into my shirt.

"I'm sorry," she whispered, trembling in my arms as I stroked her hair. "I didn't mean for this to happen."

"Of course you didn't mean for this to happen." I lifted her chin to meet my gaze once more. "Who in their right mind would believe you're doing this on purpose? That's absurd."

She didn't answer that and tried to bury her face back into my shirt. I held my fingers tight on her chin. "Hey. Don't hide from me. You're safe with me, and you always will be. I just want to help."

She frowned. "And I didn't want you to ever see this."

"Why?" I asked. "And what *is* this? What's making you hurt like this?"

"It's complicated," she murmured.

I eyed her, knowing she was just trying to hide something else from me. But I wondered if it was complicated because this was connected to her magic somehow.

"Well, then it's a good thing I enjoy complicated things." I gave her a small smile. She didn't return the expression, and I shrugged with apprehension. "What? I like puzzles and you're definitely one I'd like to figure out."

One dark eyebrow rose. Her jaw tightened, making her lower lip suddenly more prominent.

"I've said something wrong," I stated.

"Not wrong. It just reminded me of our conversation yesterday." She went quiet, avoiding my gaze for a long moment. But when her eyes flicked back to me, I sucked in air. Cool ire seemed to brew and swirl like a storm around her constricted pupils. "Reminded me of the answers you want."

I stilled at that. "Mae, I—"

"I wondered about that as I walked home last night," she said on a breath, teeth clenched. "I realized you probably want to know if what everyone thinks is true because Mr. Welch has said so. Seeing this today, my *flares*, my puzzle is merely whether or not I'm crazy, isn't it?"

She held my gaze. The unwarranted glare toward me elicited a cold, half-suppressed laugh to escape my throat, boiling up from where I kept my irritation at bay. I forced a hard smile. "No," I gritted out. "Don't assume so little of me."

I didn't give her a chance to respond or protest before I stood, only to scoop her up into my arms. A faint, stifled squeal escaped her throat. Assuming I'd hurt her, I snapped my head to hers, an apology on my tongue, only to find her hands over her mouth, eyes wide.

She...had squealed in surprise.

Like a little bird.

"Well," I said through a chuckle. "That was unexpected."

She still stared at me from beneath her hands. "You startled me."

I grinned. She looked so pure and sweet in my arms. Such a stark opposite from how she looked only moments before when she was scowling at me.

I promptly kissed her temple. "It was adorable."

Her hands moved from her mouth then. The skin of her cheeks had washed a light magenta. "What are you doing?"

"Getting you off this kitchen floor and to somewhere more comfortable," I told her as I carried her into the library. She was lightweight, more than I thought she would be. I didn't have long to think about it before her body tensed beneath me as another wave, or *flare*, went through her. By the time I had made it over to the settee in the sitting area, she had started to curse. I laid her down and sat on the edge, pushing the loose strands of hairs out of her face. "Just please remember to breathe."

She gave a short nod. I sighed, pulling my hand over my face as I listened to her inhale deeply. "Mae, what did I tell you at the stream when it came to my opinions of Elros citizens?"

Her eyes blinked open. "You called them pompous clowns."

I stifled a laugh. Out of everything I'd said, that stuck with her most?

"I definitely said that. I also said their opinions don't bother me." Bracing my arm against the back of the settee, I stooped down a bit. "That was me politely saying I don't give a shit what people think about me or those I care about."

She smiled. "Oh."

"And you, by the way, are definitely someone I care about." She inclined her head, exposing her neck. I grinned. "I was not able to elaborate on my opinions of you last night, but I will tell you…"

I made sure her eyes were on me. Made sure she felt the gravity of my gaze, just a flicker of the harsh burn in my heart—the wild defensive rage I felt toward the people who'd hurt her. "Out of all the words in this world that express my thoughts about you, not one of those words is *crazy*."

Her mouth parted on the breath she took. I went on, aware of the grit in my tone, "You have no idea how infuriated it makes me to hear that those words have been spoken about you, Mae. Gods damn the people who believe such tormshit. Gods damn the people who make you feel that way. And gods damn Mr. Welch, and Willem, and *anyone* who says you are crazy because they don't understand."

Her eyes had welled with tears, lips trembling. I softened my tone a touch, bending down more. "Mae, *I* don't understand. I don't have the slightest clue what is going on. What I do understand is that you are suffering from something. How in Torm does that make you crazy?"

The tears spilled from her eyes. "Varys…"

I wiped her cheeks and she leaned into my touch. "I *see* you, Mae. I see your pain. Enlighten me on what is tormenting you so I can try to understand you more. So I can help if I can. That's the only answer I want right now."

She gaped at me, her breaths heavy and slow. She pressed her hands to her chest as tremors began to overwhelm her. For a moment, I was sure it was another flare, but her expression remained baffled. "I'm scared."

My pulse skittered, brows lifting as I instantly wondered if I'd come on too strong. "Of what? Me? I'm so—"

My apology died on the shake of her head. More tears fell down her cheeks, dropping onto the cushion. She took a sharp breath, pushing harder against her chest. "I'm scared...because you are so willing to help me. So selfless for someone who has selfishly held the truth from you."

I went still.

"Because I can tell you about my illness, Varys." She sniffled. "But it's not the answers you're looking for."

My heart jumped to my throat, seeming to clog it so tightly I couldn't breathe. Could barely mutter her name.

"I know." She lifted her head a bit, wincing. "You saw more than what you let on at the stream, didn't you?"

My eyes burned. I didn't expect her to tell me here. *Now.* I'd planned on bringing it up sometime tonight.

Nodding, I admitted hoarsely, "Things just didn't add up."

Silence fell between us, and with it, the air became tense. My nerves roiled, magic tugging, muscles stringing as tight as a bowstring as a chill fell over the room. The suppressed laugh in Mae's throat didn't sound at all humored. She blinked and more tears spilled down her face, shaking hands clasping mine. "And now I need you to listen to me, Varys."

I wasn't sure how to listen, how to form a single thought as I watched her rise to her knees and take my shoulders. She took a breath, and I swore a draft raced through the room, the fire on the hearth flickering in response. No command words had been spoken, and I realized she was oblivious to how cold the room had become.

Whatever she was doing was passive. It was magic, but it was something much more.

Power.

Our eyes collided. I had to refrain from pulling out of her grasp. Because what I saw there in her captivating irises, what had replaced the radiance and tender beauty, chilled me—struck through to the marrow.

There was lightning jolting and dancing among the violet and flecks of blue.

The hairs on the back of my neck rose. "Mae…"

"I need to tell you some things, Varys," she said, her voice soft and pleading. She still held me. Tears still streamed down. As much as the energy produced a dreary, uneasy air, nothing felt evil. I had that thought at the tree, too.

It just felt…tragic.

"Things about me, about my life," she murmured. "Things I want you to know so incredibly bad. Truths. I've lied so much—"

With that, she broke.

A heart-wrenching cry tore from her throat, and with it, the warmth of the room returned, so fiercely I gasped. She collapsed on me, burying her sobs into my shoulder. "I'm sorry," she exclaimed. "I'm so sorry. I didn't want to lie to you."

I couldn't even bring myself to embrace her for a long moment. Everything I'd seen and felt over the past few days was flashing and whirling through my head like a torrent of answer after answer…

Storm magic. It was storm magic, just as I'd suspected. It didn't explain why there was a conglomerate of trapped energy surrounding a tree, but now that I had confirmed Mae's sorcerer strain, we would find out—

No. There was more to it. Mae hadn't spoken a command word. All spells had to be brought forth by command words, no matter the stream of mage.

She might have been a storm sorceress, but something strange was going on with her magic.

Still, this was progress. She was finally going to tell me the truth. And damn the relief that swelled over me. I wrapped my arms around her, rubbing her back softly. "I'm glad we could get here, Mae. There are *so* many things we need to talk about, like—"

She jolted up. Her hand pressed against my mouth so quickly I was pushed to my elbows. She leaned over me, bracing herself on the cushion beneath us. Once again, lightning ignited in those stormy eyes, banishing every thought as their ferocity blazed into me. "Don't ask. Don't speak."

The air left my chest.

She kept her hand over my lips, tears streaming down her face. "I know you want answers. I want to give them to you. I want to rip myself open and let everything spill out." And the growl in her voice made it seem like she would do just that. My throat clenched. "But I can't. Not yet. Not until I'm able to. I'm figuring that out, but I have to do that by myself."

She pulled her hand off my mouth. I stared at her, heart pounding. "Mae—"

"Please. Varys, *please.*"

I clamped my mouth shut, swallowing down my words.

"I will give you answers, Varys," she murmured. "I will tell you everything."

I held her gaze, brows furrowed. "Everything?"

Her throat bobbed. "*Everything.*" She pushed a lock of my blue hair off my forehead. "I'm not trying to go back on my word. You will get answers to every question you have about me. But I must give them when I'm ready."

"There is a difference between lies to hurt and lies to protect," Leo had said. But what was Mae protecting?

"Can you..." she paused, gulping hard. One of her tears fell to my cheeks. "Can you understand that?"

I stared at her, feeling trapped between my emotions and hers. I just wanted her to tell me. I felt disappointed that even though she seemed to trust me, something still held her back.

But how could I not be understanding? Had I not been just as terrified earlier today for her to see a panicked side of me from my nightmare? It wasn't that I was hiding anything from her, there were just parts of me I hadn't even faced myself. How could I expect her to open up about her fears and secrets when she didn't even know mine? She didn't know I suffered from crippling self-doubt, had so many inner fights with myself every single day, so lost in my head and my own insecurities I could hardly speak to people sometimes. She also didn't know I was a writer. An author of a fantasy series. She didn't know I had a personal record of reading three entire books in a day. That I liked to sing and would probably be a bard in another life if I didn't have such terrible stage fright. That I drank so much tea I practically perspired bergamot.

I didn't know certain things about her either. Her aspirations, worries, hobbies. I didn't even know what her favorite color was.

But I knew one thing. I cared for her. My affection was there even before knowing all of those things, for reasons I understood and didn't as well.

I hadn't lied to Leona when I had let it slip that I felt like I was falling in love with Mae. It scared me how much that truth had settled deep and was so undeniable. Maybe it truly was that after all of these years, the moment we were given the chance to be together, everything just clicked into place. But it had still moved fast and wild. The problem was I wouldn't brace myself when it would come to sweep me away. I would go with it willingly, plummet down, down into that love until its fire consumed every part of me.

But we needed time to learn about each other. To just be with each other.

I would start right here and give her my love piece by piece. Understanding and trust and devotion and safety.

I guided her to sit upright, gently taking her beautiful face in my hands. She inhaled sharply when I kissed her forehead, then her nose. "Mae Mordaunt, I want to know everything about you," I told her in a low murmur. "I want to know why you smile, what makes you laugh. I want to know what pisses you off so I can avoid doing so." She stared at me with wide, glossy eyes. "I want to know what makes you tick, and I want you to learn about me. Be it slow, or we drown each other in idiosyncrasies tonight over dinner and drinks, I can't wait to know you."

There was a small whimper in her throat. She said my name breathlessly.

"But more than all of that, I want you to feel safe with me." I tucked a loose strand of hair behind her ear. "I want you to know you can trust me. That is more important than any of those questions I have, and any answer you can give me. I'm sorry for not showing you patience." I offered her a warm smile. "Tell me when you're ready."

She pressed her hand to her trembling lips, squeezing her eyes shut. "I will," she vowed. "I will, Varys."

She looked up. The lightning wasn't present. There were only the glistening amethyst irises that entranced me so much. "Thank you."

She embraced me, her arms wrapping around me tightly. I released a sigh as her touch sent warmth through me and held her for a long quiet moment.

I was the first to break the silence when I asked, "Are you still hurting?"

She shook her head against my shoulder. "It passed. They always do."

She backed away and met my gaze, the muscles in her neck tense. A bashful smile crossed her features.

"What is it?" I asked.

Slowly, she wrapped her arm around mine and pulled me until we began to fall the other way—she wanted me to lay down. I chuckled, nervousness building up walls in my stomach. "This settee isn't very comfortable."

She gulped. "It's fine. I just...want you..." My blood set on fire. "I want..."

The blush across her cheeks was a deep pink and had spread down her neck and across the upper swells of her breasts. I couldn't breathe, couldn't think beyond her words. "What do you want, Mae?"

She dragged her bottom lip between her teeth, and everything low began to throb with desire.

"I just want to hold you," she told me, a tremble in her voice. "You are so kind and wonderful. I just want to hold you and I want you to hold me."

I could do nothing but gaze down at her, overwhelmed by her

request. Such a tender, lovely invitation, to just lay and hold each other. No pressures, no expectations. Just a moment of peace.

I allowed her to finish pulling me down, resting my elbows on either side of her head as the two of us shifted around until we were both comfortable.

I became aware of places where our bodies met, feeling my cheeks heat as I tried my hardest not to think about it, to just absorb her gentle touches. She seemed so small beneath me, so fragile. "Gods, I don't want to crush you."

She chuckled. "You're not. I'm fine."

Her hands roamed their way up my back, sending a thrilling shiver through me as I sunk even further onto her body. Until her hips and breasts pushed against me. I swallowed thickly, pulling my forearm under her head and letting her neck rest against it. She smiled, a hum in her throat as she continued to run her fingers over my spine. She squeezed me, nuzzling her face into my shoulder.

"Is this all right?" I murmured in her ear, hugging her back.

She nodded, and that's all the answer I received. Because when I lifted my head to look at her, her eyes were closed.

"Mae?"

A purple eye blinked open. She smiled softly. "Just resting my eyes."

"Uh-huh."

She didn't respond. Her eye closed and I watched her smile fade. She was falling asleep, and I wondered if the flares made her tired. "If you need to rest, Mae, I will watch over you."

Her smile reappeared. "I'd like that. But I do feel obligated to at least tell you about my illness and why I'm"—a yawn seized her— "so sleepy now."

"It can wait." I caressed her cheek. "Sleep, beautiful."

The smile widened, but her eyes remained closed, her body relaxing underneath mine. "When I wake, I'll tell you. But I am going to kiss you first."

My pulse skipped. "Is that so?"

She gave a lazy nod.

"Why don't I just kiss you now?" I brushed my thumb over her bottom lip. She let out a small gasp. "So you won't have any distractions."

Those sleepy eyes opened again. With a tug on my neck, I moved in. Our noses touched briefly before her lips brushed over mine in a feather-light caress, as if she was discerning how my mouth felt on hers. I couldn't stop the faint moan on the breath I released.

"Kiss me, Wynhart," she whispered.

I didn't allow another thought to form before I captured her lips with my own.

Chaos.

I forgot who I was. I forgot where I was, what I was. My gods-damn name.

Her lips were ruination, her kiss a harbinger of sweet, sweet decadence. I knew nothing but the taste of her, the way her beautiful mouth pressed against mine so devastatingly perfect.

This. This was the kiss I'd always wanted to give her. I wondered how I'd managed to wait twenty years to kiss her. How I was going to manage the moments our lips were apart when we stopped.

It seemed I'd need to figure that out quickly, because the pressure on my lips eased. I pulled away, our lips unlocking with tender release. Her eyes were closed, chest rising and falling in slow, even breaths.

Asleep.

An eerie, peaceful quiet fell over the library, my mind the loudest thing in the room.

CHAPTER 22

Mae

Maelawyn...
Why are you sleeping when you should be storming?
I feel your pain...
I feel your anger...
Reemerge, Maelawyn...
Saeör ít ölsta xera...
I do not feel pain. Nor anger.
I only feel him...
I feel him everywhere.
There's a door.
A gateway.
It leads to him. Let me go to him.

Even there in my dream state, I felt her wicked amusement trickle through me.

You have always been chaos...
You cannot answer that call...

You cannot cross that bridge...
Saeör ít ölsta xera...
Or you will be consumed...

Something skittered along the inside of my left arm, waking me with a start. I shoved my sleeve back in panic. My marks were pulsing with purple light, enveloping the dark room just like it had the first time two nights ago. With every beat, the tip of the jagged lines crawled upward. I held my breath, helplessly watching until the glow faded, leaving new dark lines just below my elbow in its wake.

I'd been right about the marks continuing to spread, but how much would they cover before they stopped? Although they were beautiful, I didn't...I didn't *want* them on my body. I wasn't going to be able to hide them forever.

But there were a lot of things I wouldn't be able to hide much longer.

I shuddered as cold dread swelled through me and I curled myself back under the blankets...

Blankets?

I had fallen asleep on a settee, but now I was alone on a bed, breathing in a woodsy, citrusy musk.

His bed.

Warmth flooded my face. I had to force myself to sit up. His mattress was incredibly soft and inviting, and that was extremely problematic for someone like me who really liked sleep—and who really liked Varys.

My memory came back in pieces, mouth tingling as I remembered the kiss we'd shared. His lips had been so warm and soft and had left my head spinning like I was drunk on a sweet and spicy wine.

I had been so close to telling Varys everything, to revealing my plans. He was someone who could help, someone I truly did trust. I had wanted to, I had felt safe to do so, and I just...locked up.

Fear had locked me up.

I thought I could do this. Even when faced with obstacles, I managed to find my way around them. I could cover my lightning marks for now. I had escaped my bedroom. I had spun my web of lies.

But tonight was risky. There was a huge possibility that I would be seen by someone part of Rucas's circle, someone who hadn't gone with them to search for Willem and Theon. Earlier today, I hadn't given a single shit about that.

But now...Now I was scared.

I told Varys I would tell him everything when I was ready, but I knew I was still lying to him. I was lying to myself as well. The fear was too strong. I was too afraid that even if my plan worked out and I was able to get away, I would still end up in Rucas's grasp somehow.

I hated myself for it. Hated that I didn't have the courage to run away, to ask for help, to reveal what I was suffering from all because I was scared.

There was also the terrible guilt plaguing my gut. I didn't want Varys to think I was just using our growing relationship as a means to escape. That wasn't my intention. I had just hoped that I could learn more about the elves from him, but I should've known the connection to him was too strong to remain purely on an educational basis.

I never should have agreed to having dinner with him, never should have allowed him to kiss me—

I shut down that train of thought. *No.* This was what I wanted. I wanted him. I wanted a relationship with him. Something that went beyond trysting and secret kisses. This was...this was *real.* I just had to figure out how to allow it to continue.

If I was going to do this, I needed to be absolutely certain I wasn't setting myself up to fail.

I was ready—I had to force myself to be ready, or I was never going to be free.

Varys was waiting for me at the end of the stairs, his smile set in an uneasy grin. I supposed it was probably because I, too, looked apprehensive.

"You've been asleep for about half an hour," he told me, holding out his hand to help me off the last step. "I hope it was all right that I moved you up to my room."

I straightened my vest, cheeks warming again as I was reminded of how nice the bed had been. "Yes, though I would have been just fine on the settee."

"Well, Leona and her mother came in and those two would have made a fuss over you." He gave a one-shouldered shrug. "I wanted you to rest."

I smiled. "You're incredibly sweet, Varys."

He slid his hands into his pockets. "Just caring for you is all."

My heart swelled. Once again, his words left such a foreign and out-of-place impression on me. He was always trying to help, to show me kindness and care. Even his kiss had been a means to comfort me.

"Thank you." He was closer now, enough I had to tilt my head to look up at him. He was beautiful. "For everything."

"You're absolutely welcome." His iconic sly smile appeared and my knees threatened to give way. He pulled his hands from his pockets to find mine, tugging me gently to come into his embrace. I did so eagerly, sliding my hands up his chest. I could feel how firm and warm it was and remembered how it had felt against my breasts when he'd laid over me. I wrapped my arms around his neck and...gods, it was overwhelming how much I wanted to kiss him. I found myself biting my lip as if it would help me suppress such heady desires.

His eyes were suddenly smoky, mouth parting. "Stop it."

I frowned. "Stop what?"

He took a breath through his nose and dipped down to my ear. My entire body sang when his hot breath graced my neck. "You," he murmured. "When you bite your lip, I..." His next breath seemed to shudder out. "Just know that biting your lip will insure you find yourself being thoroughly kissed now that I know I have your permission to do so at anytime."

I gulped as he straightened, my heart thundering, warmth whooshing and curling in sensitive areas as our eyes locked.

But that's what I wanted. I wanted to pick up right where we'd left off, for him to kiss me deeply, passionately. I wanted to know just how much he wanted me.

I let a crooked smile play on my lips. "Is that a threat, handsome?"

He didn't have the chance to respond before I dragged my lip back between my teeth.

His pupils flared and that connection between us went taut. I held my breath as his gaze trailed down my body, the wanton expression setting my skin on fire. With a soft, guiding push, he walked me backward. Back until my shoulders bumped something firm. The bookcases. His chest pressed against mine, sending thrilling shivers through my skin.

"Surely you know how much I love a good challenge," he murmured in my ear.

A breathy laugh escaped me. "I do now." He pressed against me harder, his lips grazing my temple. He was warm. Fire to my ice, and his touch was melting away every fear I'd had come over me earlier. "Look at us getting to know each other."

There was a low hum in his chest as his lips brushed my cheek. "What else should I tell you about me?" He rested an arm on a shelf above my head. "Maybe how much I've thought about kissing you against these shelves."

My pulse fluttered. "Some kind of fantasy of yours?"

His voice was strained as he said, "Something like that."

I swallowed. "I think I'd rather know how long you've wanted to kiss me in general."

He chuckled. "An agonizingly long time."

I ran my thumb along his collarbone beneath his shirt. "Was earlier not enough for you?"

He tilted his head with a smirk, then dragged his free hand down my side, stopping at my hip. He squeezed gently just as he murmured, "I don't believe I'll ever have enough of you after earlier. It's not my fault your kiss was so enticing."

I smiled, twisting my hands into the collar of his tunic. "Well, I don't want you to suffer."

His eyes went wide when I jerked him closer, lips lining up to his. We both took a breath—

The kitchen door squealed open. "Fawkes," Leona called out. "Lunch is ready."

We stilled.

"Of course," Varys muttered.

Leona stuck her head out into the room. We watched her look around, narrow eyes scanning across the row where we were currently entangled. But she only shrugged as if she hadn't seen us, then closed the door. A sigh escaped our lips simultaneously and we laughed softly.

"Come. You do need to eat," I told him.

But he didn't budge when I tried to ease him off. He only let out a low, displeased grunt.

"Varys."

With a rough exhale, he rested his forehead against the arm above me. "Not fair."

I smiled. "We do have tonight."

He didn't respond for a long moment, then pushed off the shelves. He held out his hand, sapphires ablaze. "Tonight. Yes."

Leona was cleaning her nails with a rather impressive knife when we entered the kitchen. She lifted her head, a smirk on her lips. "I hope the two of ye know there is not a single hidin' spot in this entire library."

My spine locked, warmth blasting up my face to my scalp. So she *did* see.

Varys snorted, dropping my hand only to wrap an arm around my shoulders to guide me further into the room. "There is one," he chided.

Leona's grin widened. "Where? Mae's pussy doesn't count."

I didn't know it was possible for my cheeks to get even warmer, but they did.

Varys pulled his free hand through his hair, his hold on me seeming to tense. "Hmm...No, I don't think I'll tell you, now."

She tilted her head slowly, jaw cocking. "Why not? Is it 'cause ye understand I am more than capable of embarrassin' the fuck out of ye?"

He lifted a finger. "Embarrassment is an emotion one has if he or she gives a *fuck* in regards to what is said about them to begin with." He tilted his head in the same manner. "I do not."

I bit the inside of my lip to suppress a smile. Leona's brows lifted as she inclined her head, sitting the knife down. She made sure I was looking at her before declaring, "Fawkes has a little twig dick and nothin' but tiny acorns underneath."

My jaw fell open. Varys jerked his head back with a blink, brows furrowed. "Really? You're really stooping to that level?"

Leona's grin was proud as she sat back. "The lass deserves to know the truth."

I was definitely sure my cheeks were smoking. His hand left my shoulder and for the first time, I was thankful we were no longer touching.

Varys braced his hands on the table, staring down at Leona. "You're right. My cock is the smallest in all the land."

The pause he took somehow allowed his last sentence to ring loudly in my ears until I felt as if I were shrinking.

He smiled, and the look was pure, forced innocence. "And you sleep with your sword."

She shrugged. "All great warriors sleep with a blade in hand, prepared for battle."

Varys nodded slowly, a knowing look in his eyes. "Aye, lass. All great warriors." He'd switched his normal accent to copy hers. "But only the fiercest of all do so to protect their most precious, prized stuffed unicorn."

Something like panic flashed across Leona's face. She shot to her feet. "Don't—"

"Sugar Twirl would've probably been ripped to shreds by all those goblins under yer bed if ye didn't cuddle her every night."

"Ye. Were"—in one swift motion, the knife was in her hand and then impaled into the table—"*Not* supposed to tell *anyone* about her!"

"Whoa, *whoa*, Leo." Varys lifted his hands in a placating manner. "I thought we were telling lies here?"

A roguish grin appeared as he glanced at me and winked. Leona's emerald eyes went wide, freckles now stark under the angry redness of her cheeks. And yet, she looked horrified about something still. With a big breath, she pursed her lips together tightly as if she were holding in every ounce of a tantrum, fists clenched at her sides. She blew it out in a harsh, growling huff, then plopped back down into her seat, yanked the knife out of the wood, and mumbled, "Fuck ye, Fawkes."

Varys laughed out as he took a seat across from her. Meanwhile, I was left frozen glancing between the two of them, my brain still hyper-focused on one specific part of this conversation.

Varys looked up at me. "I'm sorry, Mae. Leona's childish jokes tend to make everyone uncomfortable."

I didn't think *uncomfortable* was how I was feeling. More like...inappropriately curious.

It wasn't like I had anything to compare him to—

"It's fine. It's *fine*," I said to him—to *myself* to shut down my thoughts. "I-I'm going to continue preparing lunch."

But when I found my pie already baked, I realized this day would continue to take a weird turn. "Leona, did you finish up lunch for me?"

She looked up from her pout. "Nah, I would've burned everythin'. My mum did that. She went to fetch somethin' and will be back soon."

The pie was still warm. I guessed Leona's mother had found it and baked it for me. I had just finished the lattice top when I started flaring.

Frustration stewed until my stomach was hot. I had been so excited he was going to eat my food, that he was going to hopefully enjoy something I had made out of passion and care for him.

But my damn body...

"Do you need any help, Mae?" Varys's voice cut through my brooding so sharply, I took a breath.

I shook my head and our eyes met. The way he looked at me then had a knot forming in my throat. It wasn't desire, or lust—I'd seen those looks before. But here in this moment he just looked at me as if I was the only person in the room.

"Fawkes, ye're droolin'," Leona groaned.

He whipped his head to her. "And you're annoying."

She scoffed and went to retort but I laughed out, "You two are like a cat and dog."

Leona grinned. "That's right. I am the ferocious feline, and he's the *droolin'* dog."

I winced. I had practically walked myself into that one. Glancing at Varys, I pressed my hands to my chest nervously. "That's not what I meant."

He chuckled. "I figured you meant we bicker a lot. Similar to how siblings might."

Siblings. "Yes, that's it."

As I walked the cheeseboard to the table, I wondered why Varys and Leona didn't have *real* siblings. I knew Varys's mother had passed away and though I didn't know all of the details, it had been the first tragedy Elros had experienced. Or at least since I had been born. I knew most of Varys's timidity stemmed from that incident, but I hadn't realized until today that he still suffered greatly from that trauma. Perhaps that was why he now trained with Leona and was learning to defend himself.

My chest ached for him.

Knowing all of that, I understood why Varys didn't have a sibling. Professor Wynhart had never remarried. Leona, however, I knew was a different case. She was half-dwarf. Eryx had explained to me that dwarves never conceived children with another race. Something about them being the only race in Xalador that preferred to keep their bloodlines purely dwarven.

Maybe that was why Duros Cauldücen had moved all the way here from Gor Thorüm. Maybe he'd broken some kind of law.

I wasn't sure I'd ever seen her, but I knew Leona had a living mother and that Duros and her were still married. I wondered if perhaps it was hard to conceive other half-dwarfs, or maybe the Cauldücens didn't want another child.

I sat the sugared pears beside the cheeseboard and went to go grab the pie when Varys asked, "Wait, where did all this food come from?"

"Snow here prepared it all," Leona said. "My mum just made sure the pie was baked."

"Right, but…" Varys glanced toward the door leading into the pantry. I knew why. I had only found a few spices, eggs, a rope of sausages, and barely enough flour to make a loaf of bread. "Where did the *means* to make the food come from?"

Leona quickly explained that she and I had gone to the market after running into Professor Wynhart and learning Varys was still ill and asleep. He had given us money when I offered to cook lunch. "Snow picked out all the ingredients. She seemed eager to cook."

I smiled with a shrug. "It's something I love to do." I sat the pie down. Varys's jaw went slack. "I love baking. I love making food for people, and serving them." I swallowed, feeling a sudden weight come off my shoulders. I'd have to evaluate later why revealing my hobbies and passions to him felt like relief. "It makes me happy."

He took a breath, blue eyes wide as he looked at the food before him. I sat a pitcher down. "Leona and I got a little carried away when buying the pears. They all looked so delicious." I laughed. "So I squeezed the others I didn't use for dessert with the cider press for some fresh pear juice."

"We have a cider press?" Varys asked no one specifically, but eyed Leona.

She smirked. "Yes, Fawkes. We gifted one to yer father about four years ago for his birthday."

"I don't think he's ever used it." He sounded stunned, as if this was a feast prepared for royalty.

Uncertainty started to creep in as I poured him a glass of pear juice. Maybe he was stunned because he didn't like any of this. I hadn't even asked. "Oh, it's chicken pot pie. I hope that's fine."

"Yes, of course. It's just…well, everything is beautiful."

My cheeks warmed as I looked down to the food. I'd decorated the cheeseboard with purple thistle and white yarrow I'd picked on our way back, and had separated the slices of cheddar and smoked gouda by rows of grapes and cherries. The sugared pears I placed inside a wooden bowl I had found in the top cabinet and sprinkled them with chopped almonds. And of course I'd created a lattice topping for my pie, but had also cut out holly leaves and minuscule berries out of the dough and placed them in the corner.

Leona nodded. "Honestly, Snow. It's all too pretty to eat."

"You're quite the artist, Mae." Varys smiled.

The knot that had been growing in my throat was now a hard, painful ball. I couldn't recall the last time I had received such compliments. "Thank you." My voice was strained, but I cleared my throat to say, "But we *must* eat. Especially you, Varys."

"Oh, no, you don't have to tell me twice," he told me as I cut into the pie. A hearty, spiced scent filled the air as I plated the first slice, a thick stew of chicken, carrots, peas, and potatoes flowing out of its crust. I sat it before Varys and he once again had that look of awe. "Gods, *now* I'm drooling."

I grinned and began to move on to plate Leona's, but paused. Varys hadn't picked up his fork, and I realized he was waiting for everyone before he started. This man who had nothing on his stomach, who had helped me through my flare, had brought a smile to my face and had shown such care for me, and he was still going to wait.

I wasn't having it. I sat the fork and knife down and crossed my arms. "Eat."

His eyes went wide, then looked to Leona. She only shrugged and pointed her fork at his plate. "Ye heard her."

He chuckled as he cut into his slice, poking his fork through a piece of chicken and carrot and then took a bite. "Oh, good gods," he lauded after swallowing. "This is incredible."

Happiness bubbled up so fast I let out a laugh. "Have as much as you want."

He didn't respond as he took another much larger bite. I finished plating Leona's piece, who thanked me with a grin, then poured her a glass of pear juice before I grabbed a plate for myself.

Varys suddenly stood and walked behind me. Before I could ask what he was doing, he pulled out my chair and gestured for me to sit. "Sorry if I'm acting weird. I just don't know if I'm more in awe of the food, or you."

I stared at him. "Why me?"

He leaned in closer, hand grazing my back. "Because you are kind and beautiful. Here you are graciously serving us before yourself even though you were the one who made everything." He gently took the knife and fork from me and sat it down. "It is you I am definitely in awe of."

The knot in my throat returned. Leona stared at Varys for a moment, blinking as if in disbelief before she leaned forward and laced her fingers together. "I may not speak poetry like Fawkes here does," she said with a nod, "but I concur. Ye should've been the first to eat at this table."

I could hardly breathe through their kindness. Varys pushed down on my shoulders softly, and I obliged. He scooted me in with ease, then dipped down to my ear. "Thank you."

I swallowed back the emotion. "It's my pleasure, Varys."

I felt his mouth press against the crown of my head before he returned to his seat.

Leona lifted her glass. "We should toast to somethin'."

Varys nodded spritely. "Agreed. Mae, you choose. What are we toasting to today?"

I looked over the food on the table as if all of it could give me the answer, but I couldn't find one. It wasn't until I met Varys's gaze, then found Leo smiling at me as well, that I realized what I wanted to toast to. There was no trace of my flares or fears in that moment. If I could sit here with Varys and Leona, listening to them playfully bicker with one another, eating the lunch I had made, laughing with them, every single day for the rest of my life, I was sure I would be the happiest woman in Xalador. And I knew it wouldn't end here at lunch. That this toast was only the beginning to a friendship I wanted. *Needed.*

"Beginnings," I declared, raising my glass. "To the beginnings of this friendship."

With a bright grin, Varys lifted his own to suspend beside mine. "To the beginnings of friendship, and connection."

Lastly, Leona raised hers with the softest smile I'd ever seen on her face. "To the beginnin's of friendship, connection, and *svitoth.*"

"*Svitoth?*" I asked, and Leona giggled at my failed attempt to speak the word correctly.

"It's a word close to family," she explained. "But the family ye find. A family not bound by blood, but by companionship, respect, and...endearment."

Her pause had Varys chuckling. "You just tried to get out of saying *love*, didn't you?"

"Love is too strong of a word for how I feel about yer dumb-arse," she scowled.

Before they could begin their squabbling, I laughed out and exclaimed, "To the beginnings of friendship, connection, and found family."

We clinked our glasses together.

CHAPTER 23

We were just about to dig into the sugared pears when the door down the hallway opened and shut. Heeled boots began to click as they made their way toward us.

"Oh, Mum, we're in here," Leona called out.

A woman emerged in the doorway. When our eyes met, my heart jolted into my throat, skin suddenly clammy as my blood raced cold. As if I'd seen a ghost.

I stood quick enough my chair squealed on the hardwood, gaping at her as I rasped, "You."

She smiled at me, fixing the handkerchief wrapped around her head. "Hello, Miss Mordaunt. It's a pleasure to finally introduce ourselves formally."

Varys and Leona were looking at me with confused expressions, so I said aloud so they could understand, and so I could confirm, "You're the woman who saved my arm. You put a splint on it when Mr. Welch didn't know how."

Both Varys and Leona whipped their heads toward her, simultaneously exclaiming, "*What?*"

Leona's mother laughed out, the sound like a bell chime. "Yes, that was me. My name is Natalia Cauldücen."

I couldn't believe it. I had been so sure I only imagined the beautiful, jade-green eyed woman who had come in sometime during the night while in the infirmary and put a splint on my arm. My pain attacks brought me great torturous pain, but having my arm remain broken without any relief for hours was a different kind of agony. Mr. Welch had claimed I had head trauma, and maybe I did, but that was not the reason I had fallen in and out of consciousness. The throb had been so excruciating, so sharp it tugged at the pit of my stomach to the point I was nauseated. The only thing my small eight-year-old body could do to stop the pain was pass out.

But what had remained in my memory more than the pain, more than the words Rucas had screamed at me, was the unnerving terror brought on when Mr. Welch told me he would have to cut off my arm else it would remain lame if I lived through the infection it would cause. He'd given my parents the night to think it over, and I remained in the infirmary under his pathetic care. He only eased the pain with cold compresses and tried to get me to drink a sickly-sweet amber liquid I later would learn to be the same kind of liquor Rucas kept in his office. I didn't understand how getting an eight-year-old girl drunk was considered any form of medicinal practice.

Natalia leaned against the counter with a sigh. "I've never spoken about this to anyone except Duros. Mainly because I *technically* committed a crime."

All of our mouths fell open.

She smiled with a wink in my direction, and the look reminded me she was Leona's mother for sure. Her lashes were beautiful and thick, giving her eyes a naturally swept-up appearance. "You three finish lunch, and then I'll tell you all a story."

"Thank you for finishing up my pie," I said to Natalia as we all sat in the sitting area of the library.

"Of course. I'm just sorry I couldn't get here in time to help you through that awful bout." She sat across from Leona in one of the armchairs. "Leona said it sounded like you were in a lot of pain. Do you have those often?"

I nodded as I watched Varys take a seat beside me on the settee, instantly reminded of what had happened earlier when we were both here. Warmth blossomed through my face.

He took my hand and squeezed. "There is a reason why Leona ran to get her mother when you were flaring, Mae," he told me, a thumb stroking my hand. He looked to Natalia. "And I'm going to assume your story is going to make the path of these two topics come to the same trailhead."

"Perhaps," Natalia replied with a nod.

She crossed her legs and pushed up her pretty pink cuffed sleeves. It was then I realized her dress was all one piece besides the bib apron tied around her neck and waist. No over dress, no bell sleeves, no layers or vest or corset akin to what most Xaladorian women wore. And it was too thick to be a chemise. Just a simple, casual dress that looked much more comfortable than my wardrobe. The handkerchief around her head seemed practical as well.

I also noticed a silver brooch pinned on the left side of her apron right above the heart. A design I'd never seen before was engraved into the face of it, and there were several clay beads strung and hung across the bottom. A symbol was painted on each bead but I couldn't tell what they were or what they may represent.

Natalia tapped her nails on the chair for a moment and then began, "When I moved to Xalador from Jinya, the first thing I noticed was that Jinyan medicine and its practice is much more advanced."

That was why she dressed differently. She was from Jinya, an allied country to the east of Xalador. It was inhabited mainly by humans, but I often wondered if any halflings had settled down there as well over the past five-hundred years—since the trade agreement had been formed between the two nations. I had been told that when the humans came from an unknown place two millennia ago, some found Xalador, and some established Jinya. They were ruled by a queen and from my understanding, worshiped the earth and sky over gods and goddesses.

"From the time we are very small," Natalia went on, "we are taught about the herbs and plants that possess both healing and toxic properties. We're shown the difference in which berries can cure a sore throat and which ones will cause the throat to swell and suffocate. Physicians, or *healers* as we call them in Jinya, are those who are practiced in more severe cases. Jinyans do not go to them for common colds and seasonal coughs, nor do we even go to them for contraceptive."

My chest snagged at that. I wished I knew how to make my own contraceptive.

"We knew how to do all of it in the home. But if our child fell from a tree and broke her arm, we would take them to a healer. From there, the bone would be cared for with all the right kind of tonics and salves, but our healers are educated in how the body heals itself."

"And they know because they have studied and researched the bodies of every species over the course of hundreds of years," Varys chimed in. We all looked at him and he seemed to shrink back in his seat with a shrug. "I just thought I'd—"

"Educate us?" Leona chided. "Please, Mum, continue before Junior Professor Wynhart takes over."

Natalia rolled her eyes but the action seemed pointed at the both of them. "Yes, Varys is correct. That's another thing that is different between Xalador and Jinya. Education." My throat clenched. "Education is available to *all* who are willing to put in the time and effort. Our medicine is backed by research and science and it is certainly not based on religion." She paused. "Of course, not all physicians practice in the way Wylan Welch does. I've met several over the course of my life here in Xalador who are very educated and closer to a Jinyan healer. I don't know where Wylan received his education, but he doesn't know all that he should, and knew very little back then."

She pushed a strand of hair off her shoulder before continuing with a sigh, "When Duros and I first settled here, I saw the need for another physician based on my birthing experience with Leona. Elros's lone infirmary has no special room for birthing. Wylan wouldn't let me labor the way I wanted and he made me panic when he hurt me while checking my dilation. Then tried to give me damn blue wortseed tea to cease my anxiousness and pain." She covered her mouth for a moment. "Excuse my language."

"Mum, she's heard worse from my mouth," Leona said.

That was true, and I nodded in agreement. Leona smiled proudly.

Natalia went on, "So, of course I began to panic even more. Blue wortseed does have calming properties, but can also be harmful to the baby. He should've known that."

"So what did ye do, Mum?" Leona's smile was wicked and knowing.

Natalia smoothed the wrinkles in her skirt. "I swatted the cup away and called him several expletives before I ran out of that infirmary. All while Leona was crowning."

My eyes went wide. Leona laughed as if it was the first time she'd heard this story. "If ye ask me where I get my ferocity—"

"Dramatics, but go on." Varys grinned.

Both Natalia and Leona seethed at him. I covered my mouth to suppress a laugh.

"I get my antics, or *whatever* ye want to call them, not from my father, but from my mum," Leona continued. "I got my rage from Da." She eyed me. "It matches our red hair."

I chuckled, looking over Leona to really pick out the family traits. Her hair was just as curly as her mother's, but her eyes were more emerald than Natalia's jade. They both had tanned skin, but Natalia's was a deep gold.

"I ended up giving birth to Leona in the middle of the market in front of a crowd of people, and to this day I am at ease with that situation." Natalia inclined her head. "I would have rather given birth there than be in the care of that man. However, that put me on the path that would lead me to helping you, Mae."

I blinked. "How?"

She smiled warmly. "Because it made me want to become a physician. I knew Elros would benefit from my knowledge. Unfortunately, that's never come to pass."

"Why?"

She frowned, wringing her hands. "By the time I'm through with this story, you will understand." I glanced to Leona then, and she seemed to be intently listening just as much as I was. It was obvious she truly had never heard this part of her mother's story before. "When I made up my mind that I for sure wanted to become a physician, I began to help Malon, the herbalist. I still work for her twice a week."

I tilted my head. "Malon. That name doesn't sound familiar. Is she the herbalist behind the butcher?"

"No, that's Gertrude." Natalia swallowed. "Malon...isn't part of the merchant guild. You probably don't know her."

I shifted uncomfortably. "Oh."

Varys gave my hand another gentle squeeze. I wasn't sure why, but I was beginning to understand I would learn a lot more today than just about Natalia's act of kindness.

"Of course, I was already well-versed in the medicinal properties of herbs, but she taught me how to make them into fully functioning tonics. However, she wasn't allowed to sell them." Her stare turned hard. "Mayor Brooker has never allowed anyone but Elros's established physician to sell medicine and tonics."

"Whether they work or not," Varys growled. We all looked at him. "Sorry. I'm of course still bitter about the time Mr. Welch gave me a tonic to help with a cold I'd come down with and instead broke out in a rash he didn't know how to cure."

My eyes went wide. "Oh my gods."

"Look." He pulled back a sleeve, pointing to a part of his arm. "See where my skin is discolored right there? It's a scar—"

"Varys, I've examined that *scar* a hundred times and I've told you it's just a birthmark," Natalia said deadpan.

"It's a scar," he insisted, turning back to me with his arm still held out. "I scratched my skin so bad, I bled."

I...couldn't see anything but a slight redness to his skin. It definitely looked like a birthmark, but I nodded anyway.

"Furthermore," Natalia said, drawing out the word, "I learned a lot from Malon, but it was time to take my practice to the real thing." She stopped and took a breath. "I didn't want to overthrow Wylan. It was never my intention. I simply wanted to bring my knowledge to the table and help make the health and wellness of Elros better. I came to him and asked to become an aide. Told him all I knew, what I could do to help." Emotion began to fill her words. "Great Sky, I've practiced this story a hundred times for the day I finally saw you face to face and I'm *still* getting choked up."

My throat clenched. I didn't understand what I had to do with this story, but I knew I would in time.

She went on, "He refused. Refused to take me as an aide. Never in the thirty years I've lived here has being Jinyan been an issue. But because I didn't worship Eana exclusively, and because Jinyans are taught differently than how *he* learned, I was inadequate. I was called names I won't repeat, words I would never repeat in front of a woman. Especially you two." She pointed at Leona and I. Leona appeared stunned. "Then he learned I had been training with Malon."

She turned her head to the fire and sighed. "The merchant guild has always been hard on those who aren't members. I realized that day just how hard it can be. Malon was outcast. This was eleven years ago and most businesses in Elros still won't sell to her."

Air left me in a harsh burst. "No."

She nodded. "It's why I still help her out at her shop. Duros's business makes more than enough for us to manage, so I volunteer a few times a week to go foraging or to assist customers. She just...doesn't bring in a lot of money."

I was shaking with anger. "I am aware of how the merchant guild can refuse service to anyone they choose. But I've always been told those people had wronged the guild."

Natalia pursed her lips together. "Maybe some. In most cases, it's mainly a lack of money as...as your father requires a quarterly fee." I tensed. "In Malon's case initially, it was that she didn't *need* to journey with them to go to Latera. Everything she requires to run her herb shop is around us. Plants are found in the hills, the forests. Mushrooms under wet logs after a spring shower. She didn't require the help of a biased community, nor its greedy leader." She paused. "I'm sorry. I'm probably coming off very rude."

"You're not going to offend me," I told her. "I promise."

It was infuriating to hear the truth of the merchant guild, but I couldn't help the twisted delight wanting to curl my lips into a smile as I listened to someone speak of Rucas so harshly.

But something struck me then when I began to think of other cases like Malon. "Your family isn't part of the merchant guild either, is it?" I asked Natalia.

She shook her head. "Duros's forge is always hot, and always ready to make the finest weapons and armor. We have hundreds of established customers who come back time and time again. We've never needed to be a part of the guild."

"And we never will be," Leona scowled.

I nodded and looked to Varys. "You and your father?"

He took a breath. "Not technically. The school is funded by Elros taxes and donations. But Baron Kenrad appointed your father to make sure the school always has the supplies it needs. Tax money is pulled when we need supplies and given to Rucas. Nobody's making profit this way, and education stays available at no extra cost."

I swallowed. "So it is true then. Rucas—or, my father is against education for everyone and that's why he treats you and your father so poorly."

Varys shrugged but Leona stifled a laugh and said, "Oh, no. No, we *all* believe there's a lot more to it than that."

I blinked. "What do you mean?"

"We're getting off subject," Natalia cut in. "My point was that yes, the merchant guild controls a lot of this town, and somehow the infirmary is included. I have my theories on why, but it comes back to the day a storm blew through these hills and you were caught up in a tree."

I shuffled in my seat because I knew someone was going to ask why I was up there. The next words out of Leona's mouth were, "What were ye doin' up in a tree anyway, lass?"

I sighed. "My friend Eryx and I were playing tag. I thought he wouldn't be able to catch me if I climbed up in that tree."

I'd told the lie so many times it rolled easily off my tongue—

"You ran across the stream and a mile northward just to get away from your friend?" Varys questioned, his grip on my hand tight. "Is that really what happened, Mae?"

We locked eyes, and *shit*, his gaze was knowing. I couldn't say yes, but I couldn't say no.

Thankfully, Natalia said, "Doesn't matter why she was there. What matters is that she broke her arm and Wylan Welch didn't know broken bones can be mended. He would have had her arm amputated."

I nodded. "He told me that. I remember falling asleep, or rather passing out, believing I would wake up without my left arm."

"It's what *everyone* believed. He came out of that infirmary and practically preached his woes to all of Elros." Natalia pinched the bridge of her nose. "Gave your mother and father the night to think it over. He had the audacity to tell them that their option was amputation or he would allow the bone to stay the way it had broken and you'd have a lame arm for the rest of your life. As if *infection* was not the main worry. Your bone broke skin. You would have ultimately suffered infection and that could have killed you."

I didn't tell them I already knew that. Rucas had informed me in between states of unconsciousness that he was going to let me die for what I'd tried to do.

It had been my first attempt to escape him.

He'd hurt me that night, angered by the doll he'd tripped over when I'd accidentally left on the ground. He'd been too drunk to see it, to acknowledge anything on the floor at all.

I had been slapped and pushed, but the kind of rage he showed that night would forever haunt me. He destroyed my bedroom, broke everything I owned. Burned every doll, every picture book, every piece of clothing I had. And then he came for me—but I was already on my way out the door. I hadn't stopped running, barely remembered crossing the stream's bridge that had been there at the time. I didn't even know how I'd found my way through the twisting branches and otherworldly shadows before I saw it. A beautiful tree standing on its own. I just remembered feeling like...like this tree had been planted so I could see it. I remembered that feeling of such sureness as I began to climb.

Until now, I'd pushed away the memory of the ascend. But I'd been eight years old, small, sickly, and had climbed that tree with ease. I couldn't push down the feeling, or bury the thoughts that the tree had helped me somehow. Two years ago, I would've reminded myself that those kind of ideas were why Mr. Welch and my parents believed I was deranged, but I refused to harbor those words any longer.

There hadn't been a cloud in the sky when I'd run through the market, but by the time I'd reached that tree, the orange and pink evening had been devoured by a viscous blackness. The wind had rushed and whirred through the forest as I climbed higher, higher until I could see the darkened sky full of storm, the air thick with the smell of rain and ether. Lightning webbed and crackled in flashes of sparkling light, thunder clapping in its wake and ringing in my ears. I was eight years old, I was a young human girl, but in that moment I felt part of that storm. I held on to the branches as they swayed, not a drop of terror in my veins. The rain came down and drenched my hair, my skin, and it was like being wrapped in happiness and beauty and life.

Then the lightning struck that tree, and I was reminded how wild a storm could become. A storm could not be caged, nor controlled or tamed. That was why I loved them, after all.

My thoughts drifted to the dream I had before waking up in Varys's room earlier today. Once again, my head had been filled with riddles and metaphors I didn't quite understand.

Saeör ít ölsta xera.

I was trying to free myself, trying to do what she wanted me to do. But the more I thought over those words, the more I believed they meant something deeper. What if...what if it was telling me to free a *real* storm. Or to somehow...create one—

"Mae?"

I sucked in a breath and snapped my gaze to meet Varys's blue stare. "Did we lose you?" he asked.

Everyone was staring at me. "Oh, gods," I murmured. "I'm so sorry. I was...I was thinking about something."

"No worries." Natalia smiled. "I know you're probably very tired."

I nodded slightly looking down to the hand that still held Varys's. I was squeezing it so hard, my knuckles had blanched. I let go, but his hand chased mine and seized my hold once more, stroking light, tender caresses along the length of my fingers with his thumb. My heart thumped in response.

Natalia glanced around the room before she went on with her story. "I was there in the crowd of people and overheard Wylan's message. I wasn't going to be able to live with myself if I allowed him to amputate your arm. So I waited until he left the infirmary for the night—"

"He *left?*" Varys exclaimed.

She nodded. "He doesn't stay there. With *any* of his patients."

Silence fell over the room.

"He left sometime after midnight," she continued. "I managed to pry open a window, and climbed through. You"—she looked at me—"were in and out of consciousness, but must've heard my footsteps."

"I did."

Natalia chuckled. "How about you tell everyone the next part?"

My eyes widened. "Well, I remember you saying something softly. I think you told me you were there to help me. Then you laid a silky material over my face. I remember smelling something sweet and then...I fell back asleep."

Leona sat up and Varys shifted forward a bit. "Did you drug her?" he asked.

My blood went cold.

Natalia scoffed. "That's a very nasty question, Varys. I put her to sleep. Put her under so I could work and she wouldn't be in pain while I set her bones back in place."

I shuddered. "That does sound like something I wouldn't want to be awake for."

"It's what we do in Jinya." Natalia crossed her arms. "We use poppies and...another specific type of flower to put people to sleep." All three of us went to ask her what the other flower was, but she held up a hand. "No, no. I'm not answering that question. Else I'll have to say I committed *two* crimes."

Oh my gods.

She huffed. "It got the job done, did it not? Your arm is very much healed and functional."

I nodded quickly with a smile. "Yes. I woke up with the splint and little to no pain."

"But what happened when Wylan found the splint, Mum?" Leona asked. "He's a stubborn bastard. Did he not just rip it off?"

Natalia's smirk was devious. "I made sure someone was there in the morning to prevent him from doing anything. You see, Baron Kenrad was in town. He was actually staying at The Alderbright. I left a note for him at the front counter explaining what I had done and why I'd done it. Nothing that would give myself away, of course. But apparently, Kenrad got there just in time and stopped Wylan. Turns out, physicians from all over Xalador had begun to learn how to splint a broken bone and Kenrad knew of this practice." Natalia's face went cross. "Rucas was...was livid, Mae. I made sure I was there when this town of busybodies naturally corralled themselves back to the infirmary to see what had happened to you. Everyone was there when Rucas demanded Wylan and his family to be banished from this town for his ignorance, but Kenrad stepped in. He instead gave Wylan an ultimatum: leave Elros and resign his practice, or go learn from the Jinyan healers who had settled down in Mirefield."

My stomach dipped. "Natalia…"

She held up a hand. "It's all right. Sure, it felt like a slap in the face back then. Especially since he did go. From what I understand, Wylan is much better in his field of work now, but I will *never* step foot in his infirmary. If Leona became with child, I would deliver."

I was pretty sure Leona's eyes crossed from her mother's words. "Don't worry, Mum. I chug that contraceptive brew ye make like mead. No grandchildren for ye for a *very* long time."

Natalia rolled her eyes. "Yes, dear. Please don't remind me I'll probably be on my deathbed before I see you have children."

Leona smirked. "I won't wait that long, Mum. And if I find some pretty lass to marry, we'll adopt."

Natalia chuckled. "It's a deal, my rosebud."

I swallowed thickly. I could tell they had a strong relationship, closer to friends than mother and daughter. Such respect between them.

I didn't have that with my mother.

And I knew that if I ever had a daughter, if I was ever able to overcome my great fear of childbirth, I would make sure I had the kind of relationship I saw between Leona and Natalia. I would make sure she knew she was loved no matter what.

With thoughts of children, Leona's words came back to me. "You make a contraceptive brew?" I asked Natalia. "I have run out of the brew Mr. Welch makes and hoped I could find something else."

All eyes were suddenly on me, and that's about when I remembered I was still holding Varys's hand.

Natalia's smile was warm. "I understand. I will tell you though, the brew I make can be taken by all sexes. I think Varys has been taking it for a couple of years, so you two are well protected—"

Varys let out a loud clearing of his throat. A silent, tense conversation passed between the two of them as Leona held back a laugh, Varys's eyes wide, a slight shake to his head. Heat flooded my veins, my legs filling with the urge to get up and run. When I let go of Varys's hand, he didn't hold on this time.

Natalia pressed her lips together, an obvious apology on her face. "If you're interested, Mae, I can definitely make you some."

I didn't know how to respond for a long moment. If it could be taken by all sexes, did I really need to take it?

I shook away that thought. Of course I did. There was no guarantee Varys and I would even get that far in our relationship.

Even if I deep down hoped it would.

"That would be wonderful," I said, trying not to let the subject stay awkward any longer. "How much would it cost?"

That was still an issue for me. I'd have to find a way to pay her.

Natalia laced her fingers and shook her head. "Earth is a kind giver. She has blessed us with everything we will ever need. The plants used to make the contraceptive grow right here in these hills. Therefore, making profit off of it would feel wrong to me. Come by the manor sometime and I'll give you a bottle, and then teach you how to make it. It's easy." She leaned in closer. "And mine is much sweeter than Wylan's."

I pressed my hands to my mouth to suppress my emotions. "You're so kind. Thank you." The emotion came anyway and tears burned my eyes. "For everything. I would have thanked you much sooner if I had known who you were."

"There's no need to thank me. I'm just glad to see that you've grown into such a sweet and charming young woman." She glanced at Varys for a moment. "Our home is open to you, Mae. If you need *anything*, you come to me."

Mr. Flax had offered the same yesterday, but this was different. I knew I could trust every single person here in this room.

I nodded, taking a long, freeing breath. "I will remember that. Thank you."

She bowed her head. "Now, since my story is done, why don't you help me understand what these flares are?"

I gulped, nervousness trying to choke my words before they came out. I started with my flares, explaining to them the night when they first began. I told them how painful the attacks were and what happened sometimes when they came on. The moments I stared at nothing. The spazzing muscles—Varys and Leona had witnessed that. The three of them stayed quiet as I spoke. I was unable to look anywhere but the floor, knowing I might find unwanted pity on their faces that would only bring on the tears already threatening to form.

Varys's hand returned to mine as I spoke, and I welcomed the warmth of his palms. I was also grateful that he let me squeeze whenever I felt like my emotion might suffocate me. Eventually, his arm slid around my waist and I found myself leaning into his comfort. A soothing sensation rushed through me like warm golden honey until I was no longer anxious, no longer shaking in his hold. I was safe.

When I finished, I lifted my head to look around. Leona had curled around her knees, her intense stare full of concern and perhaps anger. She had scoffed several times when I'd spoken of Wylan Welch or Rucas. "So. Hearin' all of this makes me wonder somethin', Snow," she started. "Ye're Rucas Mordaunt's daughter. He's rich. Everyone knows that. Why doesn't he use all that money he has to take ye to someone who may know what's wrong with ye?"

I couldn't answer that question. Not without telling them of my abuse.

So I went a different route. "My flares are so random and seem to be getting worse day by day. I think my father might be scared to travel with me. On top of that, I've never been very strong. I was born frail and sickly."

Her eyes narrowed as she sat back in her seat, looking dissatisfied with my answer. She turned to her mother. "What do ye think it is, Mum?"

Natalia had turned her head to the fire. She rubbed her arms. "Unfortunately...I've never heard of anything like this."

My stomach fell. I shouldn't have hoped she would know, but I had.

"New illnesses form everyday," she went on. "That's why research never stops. We may not know what it is presently, but that doesn't mean we'll never figure it out."

"Is there anything you can do for her pain?" Varys asked.

Natalia tilted her head from side to side. "I can create a topical salve, but I don't believe this is an external problem." Her brows were furrowed when she looked back at me. "I just wish I had the answers for you now. I'm sorry, Mae."

I smiled. At least she was honest.

"What about your other afflictions?" Varys asked, sounding determined. "Do you think your flares are connected to a long term underlying illness?"

Natalia's brows perked up. "Oh, yes, you said you weren't born with these flares, but you have dealt with some sort of ailment your entire life?" Natalia asked.

I nodded. "That's right. The flares only came on two years ago."

Varys's entire body seemed to jerk beside me. I looked up to see what might have made him react like that when Natalia said, "What are your symptoms?"

My face heated, but I began to explain. Some of my symptoms were embarrassing, especially those having to do with my stomach, so I kept them vague enough to get the point across. "I've come down with several colds that nearly claimed my life. My stomach issues definitely started when I was a toddler. When I started eating solid food around two."

Leona's brow arched. "Two? From the time I popped my first tooth, I was eatin' turkey legs straight off the bone."

Natalia rolled her eyes. "You had more teeth than that, Leona."

"A very attractive image you've painted there for yourself, as well," Varys drawled. Leona just snarled.

I continued, "I was young enough I don't remember it, but it was around that age I became very ill after dinner one night. I almost died. Was in the infirmary for four days. I couldn't stop vomiting, apparently."

Natalia rose from her chair then, her eyes narrowed. Beginning to pace, she clasped her hands against her chest. "Do you remember any other symptoms?"

The sudden apprehension in her voice made my body tense. I glanced up at Varys. He too seemed concerned suddenly, as if he'd seen this kind of behavior from Natalia a dozen times and knew exactly what it meant.

"I've been told I vomited so much, my body started to shut down," I said hesitantly. "My stomach rejected all food. And then whatever illness had come over me...it left me very weak." I opened and closed my hands as I looked over the prominent veins in my fingers and knuckles. "I have always been like this because of what happened. My body, I mean."

Natalia only stared into the hearth, hand pressed to her mouth. "*Night nettle*," she said breathlessly.

I jerked my chin back. "What is that?"

"Flowers. They've been planted outside of the town gate to keep rats out of the streets."

"I've not been outside the walls much."

"But others have." She breathed in and smoothed out her dress. "Night nettle is poisonous to most species. Even their pollen can cause the skin to break out in hives. In high doses, it will kill. In smaller doses, it can do great harm to the body and leave it permanently weakened." She inclined her head. "The body rejects it through vomiting."

My stomach turned over. "I don't think that's the case. I would have had to have been—"

"Poisoned." She turned back to me, head held high. "Through drink or food."

My blood ran icy cold, ribs suddenly feeling too small for my lungs. "No. Natalia, that's impossible. I was born with this. I'm just sick."

She shook her head slowly. "That's what you've believed all these years. That's what you've been told. But I don't believe you're sick, Mae. You've been *hurt*."

Hurt.

Abused.

It was as if her very words had shattered my defenses. Stripped me raw. They'd find out about Rucas's abuse this way. They'd find out...and it'd all be over.

All of my fears came back like a violent gust of wind and morphed into fury and panic. Instincts seized me, the need to defend myself taking hold as I shouted, "No!"

I shot to my feet. I didn't give myself time to slow down and truly think about what would spew from my mouth before I continued, "I refuse to believe that! I *am* sick. It's *not* in my head, and I'm tired of you healers and physicians telling me it is. Why won't you believe me?"

Natalia's hands fell to her side. Leona's mouth parted for mere seconds before those pretty green eyes thinned into slivers of hot emeralds.

But Varys stood up behind me and took my hand. "Mae, look at me."

It wasn't like I had a choice. I felt the connection between us pull through me and demand I meet his gaze. He took my other hand and brought both to his chest. There was a serious, frustrated expression across his features. Directed at *me*. I felt like my knees might give way. I wanted to run—

"Mae, do you trust me?"

He didn't need to ask. He knew the answer. I did too. "Yes."

"Do you trust Leona?"

I swallowed. I couldn't look her way, not when she was glaring at me like a lioness about to pounce. But I knew the answer to that too. "Yes."

Varys tilted his head in Natalia's direction. "Do you trust Natalia?"

Every muscle in my body had tensed, and by the time he asked that question, I was wound as tight as a bowstring. "I do. I do. I didn't mean to yell. I'm sorry. I didn't. I'm just..."

I was terrified.

Varys hooked a finger under my chin and tilted my face up. For a moment, he searched for something, those sapphire eyes tracing over every feature. His thumb brushed the underside of my bottom lip, but it wasn't an action of desire. Whatever he found while searching my face caused that stroke on my skin to be one of care, as one would do over an old scar.

He was so gentle. So kind. I couldn't breathe around him.

"There are people in this community who lie for self gain," he said in a murmur, and I realized this was a conversation between us alone. "You know this. We have been speaking of people who commit treachery with their words. Then, there are the people they hurt with those lies. Those hurt souls begin a mean, vicious cycle of telling lies to protect themselves from being hurt again. You know this as well."

I did. Because that was *me*.

"Do you trust Wylan Welch, Mae?"

I shuddered out a breath. "No."

"I know you don't. *We* know you don't. We were listening, Mae. All three of us." He glanced over to Natalia. "I think what Natalia is trying to say is that she doesn't trust Wylan Welch either. She's not saying you are lying, or ignoring your claims. She's well-versed in this field of work and she is simply stating that what you have been led to believe may not be the truth."

My palms had started to sweat in his hands even though my blood had gone ice cold. My mouth watered as nausea sent my head spinning.

Varys turned to Natalia. "Is that what you meant?"

I didn't see her nod, but she replied, "Night Nettle has been used in dishes before throughout history...but for one purpose. It tastes a lot like black pepper." She crossed the sitting area and placed a hand on my shoulder. I wanted to apologize but she cut me off, "Mae, you are the daughter of the wealthiest merchant in Elros. A leader who has control over the livelihood of hundreds of citizens." She worked on a gulp, her next words strained. "A man who has had a hand in injustices. It is not an inconceivable thought that perhaps someone tried to get their revenge on him through you. That perhaps you were poisoned that day, my dear. Someone tried to kill you."

My stomach convulsed, and I slumped back down to the settee.

She was right. And wrong.

Because if I was poisoned, it wouldn't have been to get revenge on Rucas.

Rucas would have carried out the deed himself.

CHAPTER 24

Varys

Not long after Natalia had left did my father return home. He caught me between the bookshelves and pressed a few coins to my palm.

"Payday isn't until tomorrow," I informed him.

He adjusted his spectacles then leaned against the shelf. "You have quite the night ahead of you, am I right?"

I grinned and looked down. Four silver pieces lay in my hand. One less than normal.

"I did dock you a day's pay," he said, eyeing me. "For leaving the library unattended on the eighth."

I nodded in acknowledgement but didn't argue, pocketing the money. He didn't know what had happened at the stream on the eighth of autumn. The value of a silver coin was nothing compared to Mae's life.

"So, when will we have time to talk about what in Torm happened with you last night?" he asked as he wiped a line of dust from a shelf. Apparently, I needed to clean come work day.

I sighed, slipping a book I didn't need back into its spot. "It's a really long story. I will fill you in as soon as possible."

"I hope so." His gaze swept past me, snagging on where I assumed he found Mae sitting and waiting for me to return with books to begin her lesson. "You haven't been yourself, but I understand. New distractions can sometimes leave us feeling a bit stuporous."

I arched a brow. "Are you...calling me stupid?"

Father snickered. "Not yet." He eyed the coin in my hands. "Guess it depends on what you use that silver on."

I rolled my eyes then picked up the stack of books I had found so far. "Do you know where I can find a good beginner's literature book that isn't for a child?" I asked, blatantly changing the subject.

"No, but can I give you some advice?" I went to decline his offer, but he continued with a roguish smirk, "Read to her."

I scoffed and reiterated, "She's *not* a child."

"Doesn't matter the age." He straightened a row of books, pulling out one and tucking it under his arm. "Reading aloud to someone will progress their understanding of the Common language and its linguistics immensely. When you read aloud, you are showing the student how the word is pronounced and spelled. In all my years of teaching, this is where I start." He laid a hand atop the stack of books in my arms. "Read to her, son. Ignite her passion for beautiful words and exciting tales, and you just might find her wanting more."

My eyes went wide. "Of the book?"

He winked and walked away, disappearing around the corner.

Leona had retreated upstairs at some point, claiming she had to get ready for tonight. Whatever in Torm that meant. It wasn't like she was planning to go in anything other than her normal attire—a tunic, her plated waist cincher and bracers, greaves over her leather breeches, metal heeled boots, and Thorn strapped to her back. No matter how much she planned on drinking, and no matter if she hoped to be bedded or not.

The hour ticked by painfully slow. I learned quickly that teaching Mae how to read wasn't going to be as easy, or enjoyable, as I had hoped. She just couldn't grasp what I was teaching her. I didn't even have a chance to offer what my father had suggested before she became frustrated, so I called it quits for the day and decided to lead her upstairs to find Leo.

"Mae, you're not going to learn it all by tomorrow," I said to her softly as we came onto the landing. "It will take time and more lessons."

She only nodded, disappointment etched into her features. I knew today hadn't been the easiest on her, and I assumed she was distracted with all the new acknowledgements of her past. Even I was having a hard time not dwelling on the things she'd said when explaining to us about her pain condition.

Every word had gutted me, ripped me open from left to right, top to bottom.

I had seen first hand the pain she'd spoken about. I had answers to so many questions I had asked. Answers I'd wanted. She was indeed sick with something and that was why she seemed out of it at times, like she hadn't slept for days. It was why she was hardly ever outside and why she was so thin.

But I did not have answers for *her*. I didn't have any logical explanation as to why Mae had this pain. Why someone as lovely and kind as herself could be burdened with such a torment, she'd thought on multiple accounts of ending herself because she couldn't handle it. Those words alone had obliterated any sense of gods-damn logic. It only made me want to dive into the medicinal section of the library and become a bloody physician myself.

I just wanted to help her. In any way that I could.

And I was a fool for thinking her illness had anything to do with her reemergence. Even if her pain came on two years ago, she had been suffering for far longer. If what Natalia said was true, and Mae had been poisoned, it was entirely possible the pain was just a long term effect from that.

I had decided there in the sitting area of the library that I was done asking questions. Done wanting answers and creating hypotheses. She had made it quite clear that she would tell me the truth about her obvious power and why she had been lying to me in her own time. I would wait for that. She deserved my patience.

I opened the door only to find Leona wasn't in my bedroom. "Leo?" I called out.

The bathing room door swung open behind us.

Mae gasped and my brows shot up as Leona walked out. Lined with kohl and lids brushed with gold and green dust, Leona's emerald eyes were mesmerizing. She had also pulled the front of her hair back into loose braids and pinned them with silver combs. Chained to those combs was a string of small gold metal feathers.

She gave us both a haughty smirk, and I noticed her lips had been painted rose red. I had never seen Leona looking like this before.

"Well, you look beautiful," I told her, and I meant it. Of course, Leo was beautiful without any of the rouge and dust, she just always seemed to prefer a natural look, especially since training and working at the forge kept her sweaty and unkempt.

Leona sauntered by us back into my bedroom. "Thanks, but I'm not done yet."

She picked her pack up from the ground and dropped it onto my bed. Mae and I came up behind her and watched as she pulled out the pile of crimson material I'd seen earlier and held it against her form.

I gave her an incredulous look. "Wait, you're not going in what you have on?"

She shook her head, a feline grin on her face. "Not t'night," she purred as she dragged her hand down the hem of the dress, allowing the sheer material to melt over the arch of her hip. "I'm goin' in *this*. Displayed as the gorgeous princess I am."

Even Mae's eyes widened at that—although it could have been that we forgot to inform her that Leo *was* a princess. Either way, we both looked utterly befuddled as we stared at the woman before us.

My best friend, sister, trainer, thorn in my side...

Wearing a dress?

"Who in Torm are you and what have you done with Leona Cauldücen?" I demanded. Both Mae and Leona laughed out, but gods, I wasn't joking. "What's the occasion?"

"This is a gorgeous gown," Mae lauded, taking some of the skirt into her hands. "It's so unique."

Indeed it was. Jinyan-made—I gathered that from the sheer material. Most women's dresses were made from thick wools or linens; silk or cotton if one could afford it. But the Jinyan's had created this specific material, which was like a woven mix of silk and gauze.

"It looks even better on. Ye'll love it, Snow." Leo only smirked at me. "Ye're goin' to throw up."

I groaned and the two girls cackled. Mae volunteered to help Leona put the dress on. For a moment, I wasn't sure Leona would oblige, but she gave an eager nod and then Mae tugged her back to the bathing room. I waited and listened to them giggle across the hallway. A small smile crept up on my lips.

Leo had never had any female friends other than those she'd trysted. One in particular I thought she would marry. But both of them had been young and Leona...well, she had put in too much effort with little return. She hadn't been herself around that girl. After they went their separate ways, that was when Leona had, more or less, decided she didn't want to worry about marriage or relationships, she just wanted to do what she wanted for the time being.

I wouldn't lie and say I didn't worry about all the nights she spent at the tavern, but Leona was happy living her life like that. Problem was, that lifestyle was as fleeting as she was. If Leona was ever going to settle down, she would need someone who could fly at the same elevation she did, not someone who would clip her wings. That was why she wasn't ever interested in anyone here in Elros. All of them wanted to pin her down.

She had always met the same dilemma with friendships—besides me, of course. But I was a brother to her as she was my sister. We could talk openly to each other about most things, but there was still a line we didn't cross. Leona had a shopping habit and she sometimes bored me to tears talking about a new piece of clothing she bought and why. She loved getting together for lunch, viewing theatre shows the community drama troupe put on, enjoyed an afternoon of dice or cards, and as much as I tried to be the person that did those things with her, there were times I needed to study and be by myself.

Maybe it was selfish, but I hoped the relationship blooming between Mae and I could bring a friend for Leona as well. And as I sat there listening to their laughs, I realized I didn't really need to hope for anything. It was already happening naturally.

The giggling grew louder and my bedroom door opened once more.

I took a breath when Leona entered the room, prancing in with her arms out as if she was expecting me to bow. The same metal feathers that hung across Leona's brow made up a strap starting from one corner of the bodice and joined at the opposite shoulder. From the joining, her arm was covered by a long sheer sleeve that cuffed at the end. More feathers had been sewn around the cuff, taking on the likeness of a connected bracelet. Her right shoulder was left bare, and the bodice dipped low enough I knew to keep my eyes up.

Even though her crown was now a little crooked, she really did look like a princess in the dress.

"You look lovely. Shall I announce you?" A sly grin quirked up on the side of my mouth. "Fully?"

Her eyes narrowed, but I stood tall and deepened my voice, "Entering her majesty, *exiled* Princess to the Throne of the Great Dwarven Kingdom under the mountains, Leona Zerinyah Cauldü-cen, daughter to the exiled, *rightful* heir to the Throne of the—"

"Oh, shut it," Leona snarled. "Ye know bloody well those old goons in the mountains wouldn't so much as give me or Da any sort of title, much less make our presence known. If we ever showed up, even with me lookin' like *this*"—she ran a hand over her form—"we'd get nothin' but axes and hammers comin' down on our heads."

Mae seemed to be pondering something when I glanced to her. "*Zerinyah.* Do you have three names, Leona?"

Leo finally fixed the crooked crown. "Aye. My mum and da wanted all three of my cultures to be represented in my name. Leona, my human name, my last name's dwarven, and then my middle is Jinyan. Long story short, when humans inhabited the land now known as Jinya hundreds of years ago, a lot of them spoke a language other than Common. It's most likely the reason why those humans decided to separate from those who found Xalador—they couldn't understand each other. Unfortunately, that language is now dyin' but in an effort to preserve it and much of Jinya's history, every baby born is given a name that means somethin' in that language. Sometimes it's a word that claims somethin' over the child's life, other times it's done by looks." She grinned, twisting a lock of her curls around her finger. "Zerinyah means *red rose*. I was born with this hair color and I've made roses part of my image, I guess."

"It's the thorns," I whispered loudly.

Leona glared at me. "No, that's my sword," she snapped. "The one I'm currently thinkin' about stabbin' ye with."

I made a rude face and Leona mocked it. Mae's eyes were wide when I glanced at her. I chuckled. "She's only playing. Don't worry."

She arched an eyebrow. "Oh, I'm not. I just realized that's why you wear that rose brooch on your cloak, Leona, and why there's a rose on the pommel of your sword."

Leona smiled. "That's it, lass."

"Wait, wait, wait." I took Mae's hand. "You're not at *all* shocked that Leona just threatened to stab me?"

"No." She stifled a laugh. "I think I'm getting used to the dynamic between you two. Plus, you kind of deserved that one."

A great guffaw expelled from Leona so fast and hard she took several steps backward, buckling over as she howled with laughter.

My face warmed, but I smiled. "And here I thought you liked me."

Mae's grin turned sultry. "I do. A lot." She rose on her toes and kissed my cheek, lingering on my skin just long enough to send my pulse pounding. "You still deserved it."

I pressed my hand to my chest and feigned shock. "I'm wounded."

Her smile widened and she...*chaos*, she bit her damn lip. "I'll make it up to you tonight."

She turned back to Leona, dismissing my sensual gaze. *Tonight, indeed.* I wasn't sure how much longer I could handle this teasing, even if I absolutely loved how it made my head spin.

Leo had continued to erupt, failing to notice the searing promises exchanged. "Victors smite me, that was fuckin' funny. Hope ye're ready, Fawkes." She looped arms with Mae. "Between the two of us, I have a feelin' that yer life is about to become very interestin'."

I glanced between the two of them and smirked. "And I have a feeling I won't want it any other way."

Mae's mouth parted, eyes suddenly glossy. I didn't have enough time to study what the expression meant before Leona snorted. "Aw...ye're stupid."

I rolled my eyes, taking a seat on the edge of my bed. "Love you, too."

"Before the two of you start bickering again," Mae said with a smile. "So, you were given a middle name because you're Jinyan, but that doesn't explain all of the 'Princess to the Throne of the Great Dwarven Kingdom' stuff that Varys said."

Leona adjusted the bodice of her dress. "I'm going to assume ye don't know who currently sits on the throne of Gor Thorüm."

Mae shook her head. "I don't know much of the world outside of Elros, unfortunately. Comes with not being able to read."

"Something we are definitely rectifying," I said. She gave a small nod.

Leona sighed and plopped down on my desk chair, the flowy skirt billowing. "A bastard named Dajorn Cauldücen. He's my grandfather."

Mae gasped. "You really are a princess?"

Leona shrugged. "Da married my mum and ol' Grandpappy didn't like that too much, so Da was exiled."

"That's a hyper simplification," I stated. "But go on..."

Mae's eyes widened and Leona laughed. "Don't worry about it. After Da left, his brother became Crown Prince and they all went on to live in their prejudice, grumpy, greedy ways underground. I'll never set foot in that place. *But* I'm still a princess by blood."

"Princess of blatant intentions for tonight," I cut in with an impish smile on my face. I gestured to her exposed leg. "I'm practically your brother, but I'm *not* stupid."

Leona's hands went to her hips, the fires from our argument earlier rekindling in her gaze. "Excuse me?"

I threw a leveled, knowing look against her glare. "Who are you meeting tonight?"

Mae's brows shot upward, snapping her head toward the piping Leona. I could practically see the steam pouring from her ears.

"It's a valid question, Leo," I told her. "You're dressed up more than you ever have been before. I don't even remember you wearing dresses as a little girl, and yet you're standing before me as if it's your damn coronation day." Leona's glare died more and more with every word. I shrugged. "Who in Torm has snared your attention enough for all of this?"

There was a redness to Leona's face now—a blush. She blew out her painted lips and crossed her arms. "Orin."

My heart dropped—*plummeted* to my stomach at his name. "Are you serious?"

She pushed a curl behind her ear, pressing her lips together tightly as a smile tried to surface. "He came to Da's forge this morn."

My heart was suddenly pounding, blood iced over. "Leo…"

Mae took a seat beside me then, placing a hand on my shoulder. I knew she could tell something wasn't right, and even her voice was hesitant as she asked, "Who's Orin?"

Leona opened her mouth to speak, but I cut her off, "A stranger from out of town."

A rough laugh cracked from Leona. "As if I've never had nights rollin' around in the sheets with outsiders before. They're kind of my preferred taste, Fawkes."

"And you've never dressed like *that* for any of them." I gulped. "Leona, I told you yesterday—"

"Enough." Her warning glare sent daggers straight through me. She turned to Mae as if to merely dismiss me and continued, "Orin is a man visitin' Elros for the Fest of Change. He'd heard about Da's skills on his way into town. This morn, he brought several weapons needin' repaired and sharpened, and then even commissioned Da to make him a dagger. The two of us talked while waitin' on his repairs and I invited him out t'night." She rolled her eyes to the ceiling. "Fawkes thinks he's trouble."

Mae turned back to me. "Why?"

I cleared my throat and took a long breath, focusing on the floor. "Intuition."

Leona's glare could have made my head explode if she focused hard enough.

Mae looked between us, her shoulders tense. She clasped her hands. "Well, we're all going to be there together. So, Leona, if you start to feel uncomfortable, you can just come find us."

Leona traded her murderous look for a devilish grin. "And what will ye two be doin'?"

How did I know she was going to ask something like that?

But it was Mae who replied with a simple shrug, "Hopefully dancing."

Leona snickered and rose to her feet. "Well, that's not goin' to be near as fun if ye two don't go in pretties too."

Mae and I jeered our heads back, exclaiming in unison, "Wait—what?"

Leona laughed out and flew over to my wardrobe before I could say much more, flinging open the door even as I shouted in protest.

"Bah. Come now, ye two," she pecked. "I will be severely over-dressed."

A shirt of mine was tossed over her head. I stood to my feet and marched over, picking up the tunic she apparently didn't like. "Leona, do you mind?"

"Fawkes, out of the four tunics ye own, which one is yer best?"

I scoffed. "I can find my own—"

"Oh, ye've got this nice black one." She spun to me, holding up a long-sleeved tunic with silver grommets.

"I wear that to funerals," I said in a flat tone.

"Perfect." She tossed the shirt at me.

Mae giggled from behind. I groaned as I tossed it onto my shoulder, then looked down to my breeches—the only pair I owned —and my scuffed pair of boots. I really needed to purchase some new clothes and stop spending all of the little amount of money I earned on books and writing materials.

"Well, I should go home and change," Mae told me as she came up on my left.

A disappointment I hadn't expected immediately settled in my chest. I couldn't help but feel sad that we'd be apart for a bit.

Leona brightened. "I'll go with ye, Snow. I can help ye get ready since ye helped me—"

"Oh, I'll manage." Mae's smile was tight. "I don't even know what I'm wearing."

"You can wear what you have on," I told her.

She gestured to Leo. "She said I have to get pretty, too."

Leona chuckled softly. I only scoffed and crossed my arms. "You already are."

With a bright grin, Mae wiggled her fingers in a goodbye. "I'll meet you there."

I started. "W-What? I thought we'd go together? I can meet you at your house."

She paused at the door and said over her shoulder, "Maybe I want to surprise you."

She disappeared down the hall.

CHAPTER 25

Varys

I pulled myself from the hot bath, grabbing the towel laying over the edge of the tub. Sitting down on the chair before the dressing table, I began to dry off, eyeing the dull pink scars along my calves. Only the one on my left leg was slightly raised and bumpy. Natalia had been the one who had stitched the wound—I shuddered. I could still remember that pain as if the wound was still fresh.

In many ways, it was.

It had been twelve years since that night, but I still grieved. If I didn't have the nightmares constantly reminding me, I might have been able to heal. But the lack of my mother was still so jarring everywhere around me as well.

My father was the same way.

All of her clothes were still hung in the wardrobe in my parent's room. He had never gotten rid of them. Then, there was of course her sword on display in the library. I was currently sitting at her dressing table where I could still find bottles of rouge, perfume oils, and soaps that neither Father nor I had ever had the courage to clean out.

I knew that it was because we both had never truly let her go. Never faced our trauma. It had just sat and festered in us both as I poured all of my time into studies and him into teaching. Not once had we been to the burial grounds where her tombstone was—there was no grave. There hadn't been a body.

I was in the middle of drying my hair when someone knocked on the bathing room door. "Yes?"

"It's me," my father called out.

I wrapped the towel around my midriff. "You can come in."

The door opened, but Father didn't come in. He leaned against the threshold with his arms crossed. "I'd really like to talk about what happened to you last night."

I sighed and leaned back in the chair. I hadn't had the time to come up with an excuse, so I went with, "I took a walk in the forest yesterday and I think I may have gotten bitten by something. I don't see any marks on me though."

He inclined his head. "Which part of the forest?"

"Northern. You know I'd never step foot in the south."

He nodded. "Well, I wish you knew what happened. You had me worried sick."

I shrugged as if it wasn't an issue. "I'm fine. Definitely not sick enough for you to go beg for Mr. Welch's services though."

"I beg to differ," Father said with a sigh. "You were...you were *ill* son. I didn't think I had time to rush around town to find Natalia." He tapped his fingers on his arms. "Speaking of, I saw her as I was coming back home after my tutoring lesson. She told me Mae also had some sort of spell. Are you sure the two of you didn't catch something and give it to each other?"

I chuckled and shook my head before quickly explaining what I'd learned about Mae's illness. Father seemed to have the same look on his face that we all had upon hearing it—stunned and now aware because he too had wondered why she was so sheltered.

"If she'd been poisoned, she would have died that day," Father told me, staring hard into the floor. "People don't put low doses into things they want the victim to eat or drink if they want them dead. They would put a lethal dose. Not to mention, she was three years old. A *baby*."

"Natalia is the one who told us this." I grabbed the comb and began to work it through my hair. "She knows what she's talking about."

"I know. It just sounds a bit suspicious to me."

"Well, we are speaking of the Welches and Mordaunts here." I eyed him. "I don't trust any of them."

A smile quirked up on his lips. "Not even Mae?"

I gulped. Part of me wanted to tell him that was to be determined. "Mae is different."

"Of course she is."

I didn't expand on that conversation, shaking my head. Collecting the top section of my hair, I pulled it up into a knot and secured it with a leather cord, leaving the hair touching my shoulders down. Father uncrossed his arms and straightened in the doorway.

"You're...tying your hair back?" he asked.

I nodded, trying hard to push down how uneasy I already felt. "Leo insisted we—"

"Good *shite*, Fawkes." Leona slipped around Father and came into the bathroom. "That's a good look on ye."

"Thanks, I hate it."

"I don't see why," Father said. "We can finally see your face— *Leona*, what in the gods' name are you wearing?"

Leona laughed out, hands on her hips. "Mattis, don't be such a prude! I'm Duros Cauldücen's daughter after all."

Father turned his eyes to the ceiling. "Thank you, Formos for blessing me with a son and not a daughter."

Leona stuck her tongue out at him. Father blatantly ignored her. "I want you two to be careful tonight," he said.

I stood and asked as I stepped behind the partition, "Why do you say that? You know we always are."

He fell quiet for a moment. I pulled on my breeches and looked around the screen. Leona was looking at him too, waiting for his response.

He finally sighed, a grim twist to his mouth. "I went to the infirmary earlier today to get some help for you only to find no one there. I didn't think anything of it until I noticed half of the market was closed. My student I went to tutor today told me his mother and father left early this morning with a large group of people to look for Willem Welch and Theon Brooker. They will have been missing for a week tomorrow."

His words seized me. "Missing?"

"Both of them were seen five days ago in the market heading toward the stream, but they never returned."

Bile threatened to rise up. I didn't dare look at Leona as I ducked back behind the partition again. My damn tics took over and I was suddenly wanting to pace, hands in my freshly combed hair.

Shit. *Shit.*

The past five days and all of its chaos crashed down over me, mind whirling, puzzles clicking into place, questions being answered. Forcing the nausea down made my stomach feel like I'd swallowed an anvil. Memory pulled me back to Mae's screams, what I'd almost witnessed Willem doing to her.

What she had done to protect herself.

But Willem had been fine. I'd seen him run off with a singed hand, yelling out in pain.

"Has anyone said where they think they went?" My words were hoarse. I came out from behind the partition to find Leona had sat down at the dressing table. Her eyes met mine in the mirror, wide and knowing.

"No. Nobody knows," Father said, adjusting his spectacles. "That's why they are searching."

So that meant they'd truly been gone since the incident at the stream.

I swallowed. "Do they think they're dead?"

Leona let out a small gasp and turned to me fully. Father's head snapped in her direction. "What?"

I shook my head as realization crossed Leona's features. I knew what she was thinking. It was the same thing I was.

"What is going on?" Father asked. "Surely you two aren't *involved* in this."

I forced a laugh out. "No, of course not. I think Leona here is just—"

"I was surprised," Leona jutted in quickly. "It's been a while since we've had a murder here in Elros."

Father rubbed his chin as he glanced between us. "I don't know if they think they're dead, but they are searching for them. Problem is, do you remember what Duros was talking about?"

The hairs on my arms rose. "About the sightings of strange, elven men?"

A nod. "It's just something that has been on my mind. Nothing has been seen around here—we would know." He slid a hand over his face. "All of this being said, that's why I said to be careful tonight. Until Willem and Theon are found, don't go anywhere without your weapons. You both are skilled."

"I always bring a weapon," Leo stated.

I smirked. "But not tonight."

"Oh, no." Her smile was so devilish I was certain she'd turn into a goblin right there. "I have three on me."

She bent over and pulled a small knife from the inside of her boot. "Here."

Hiking one leg to the seat of the vanity chair, she pulled back her skirt enough to show off the holster buckled to her thigh where a gold and silver dagger was sheathed. "Here."

Father's eyes shot to the ceiling. "Good gods."

Oh, but she wasn't done yet. Her hand worked across her chest. "I've also got one—"

I cleared my throat. "You've made your point, Leo."

She laughed out. "Thought so."

"I just want you two to be careful," Father said. "You're both trained, but I just...I don't know, I have a bad feeling."

I wanted to agree. Wanted to tell him I did, too. "We will, Father."

His eyes landed on me. "Will you take your sword—?"

"*Mother's* sword," I bit out more harshly than intended. "And don't worry, I'll arm myself."

But I wasn't going to carry that blade.

Father took a long breath and dipped his head. Turning without another word, he walked back down the hall.

"That was rude," Leona muttered.

I huffed. "I know. I'm just…all over the place."

"Aye, lad." She uncapped a small jar she'd brought in, then took a small brush and dipped it into the pot. Rouge, I realized, as she touched up the arch of her lips. "I hate to ask, because I know yer head has to be spinnin'. But what do ye think about those two bastards going missin'?"

I leaned against the dressing table with crossed arms. "Something is…wrong, Leona. Something's stirring and I…I-I can feel it like grime on my skin."

She stayed quiet, staring at herself in the mirror, lips pushed to one side as if she wasn't sure of the reflection staring back.

"It doesn't feel like magic either. It feels…evil," I told her. She gave an obvious look of irritation. I scoffed. "I'm sorry if you think I'm going crazy, but ever since I reemerged, the very air feels different to me. And I know you don't care, that you're going to do what you want to do, but I felt something radiating from Orin—"

"Do *not* start—"

"No," I snapped, raising my voice. "I'm going to speak. You are going to listen, Leona."

Her brows lifted.

I pushed off the dressing table and turned, keeping my eyes on her in the mirror. She wouldn't look at me, but she sat back in her seat with her hands loose in her lap.

I huffed and gritted out through my teeth, "You have done nothing but shove my thoughts and opinions aside for the past three days." Trying to control my temper with her was like trying to cap one of the volcanos tucked between the Dragonglass Spires. "I *know* what I feel, and now hearing this about Willem and Theon, I cannot ignore it any longer." I looked at her hard. "If you are going to blow off my concerns and warnings, especially when it comes to the man you're planning on bedding tonight, be my guest. But you better watch your back."

She chuckled, hands clenching her skirts. "Right, I need to watch mine. When yer goin' to have dinner with a potential killer."

My jaw tightened. "You better have a damn good reason why you would even suggest such around me, Leona."

She just laughed again. I opened my mouth, words on my

tongue I knew I'd regret later when she said, "Ye can't tell me the same head that is constantly solvin' riddles and shite didn't immediately wonder if those two are dead because of her—the woman they attacked."

My stomach became a hard, firm knot. "It did. But it doesn't make sense. I walked her home that day—"

"What if she didn't go straight home, Varys?" Leona rose, hands on her hips. My blood raced cold. "What if she went back to the forest and found them? What if the reason she's hidin' her powers from ye is because when they find Willem and Theon, there will be signs of her magic all over them?"

I stepped back, a shudder rippling through me. "Oh my gods."

Leona shook her head, tension bracketing her mouth. "But sure, I'm a bitch for suggestin' this. Do ye know how bad it hurts to wonder? To think that the lass got so scared, she went and *murdered* them? I don't like havin' those thoughts. I want to believe Mae is innocent and yet..." She paused. "And yet, who's to say I blame her for wantin' to? Do ye know how much I hate my own attackers? I wanted to kill them, too."

I froze where I stood, my insides turning over. *"What?"*

She growled spinning from me. "I didn't want to ever bring this up. Me and my fuckin' mouth."

"Leo—"

"We don't know if they're dead. Just forget I made the comparison." She looked over her shoulder. "I'm just as confused as ye are."

My throat had gone dry. "Your questions are valid, Leona."

She faced me, her eyes glossy. "And yer feelin's are as well. I'm sorry."

I cocked my head. "But you're still meeting Orin tonight, aren't you?"

She chewed her lip, then carped to herself when she realized she'd messed up her rouge again in the process. I watched as she fixed it quickly, spun a curl around her finger to smooth it out, and smiled at herself shortly when she was done. My chest tightened, realization hitting me like a slap across the face.

"You like him, don't you?" I asked softly. "This isn't just another fun night with another stranger."

She straightened and held my gaze for a long moment. "I'll answer ye, but let me ask this first. Despite yer heart, what does that magical intuition tell ye when it comes to Snow?"

I focused on the ominous feeling. Like an ever-lurking shadow, it kept my spine rigid, senses hyper-focused and ready to throw up my wards. There were nights I sometimes meditated on the feeling only to find myself so unnerved, sleeping became impossible. But just like everything else that had to do with The ReEmergence, the need to understand was greater than fear.

But I'd never felt fearful or tense around Mae. Even when I'd seen a glimpse of her power. Nothing about Mae was evil.

But I knew what I felt upon meeting Orin. I just didn't know if the bad feelings were the same that spoke of the possible enemies lurking in the dark.

"Mae is...she's good, Leo." I looked up. "I saw her power earlier today."

Leo's mouth parted. "Oh. Well, that confirms...a whole lot, yeah?"

I nodded. "But I don't believe she knows how to use it. Not enough to go back to her attackers and kill them. She didn't seem aware of what she was doing. It was all triggered by her emotions."

She tilted her head. "Didn't ye tell me that's how sorcerers use their magic?"

A small smile lifted at the corner of my mouth. "You *have* been listening. I'm proud of you." She rolled her eyes. "Yes, but...there's more to Mae's powers than that. I will have to figure all of it out some other day but my point is, no. I don't believe Mae can use her powers to go kill two men, despite what they tried to do to her. And when it comes to the feeling of...of warning, it is not telling me to be cautious of *her*. Even amidst her lies. I just feel like I'm on the right path."

Leona nodded slowly. "Ye said yesterday that ye feel all that destiny and star courage."

"Yes."

"Ye also know that I have no faith in any Xaladorian god or goddess. I am dwarven and Jinyan, I do not have a drop of elven in my blood. I am not their child." She inclined her head to the ceiling.

"But I do believe that somethin' *bigger* has already written our story. Our destinies are set in stone and no matter what path we take, we will meet our fate."

I wasn't sure why I felt the need to look out the window, but I did. A small butterfly had perched on the window sill, and didn't seem to be bothered by the light sprinkling of rain. "I do know all of that," I told Leo.

Our eyes met and she told me through a thin breath, "I feel like that around Orin. Like I'm on the path that will lead me to my destiny."

CHAPTER 26

Varys

I took a massive breath and it came out shuddering.

I was always nervous about going someplace where I knew I'd be surrounded by people. Crowds made my stomach hurt, made me overthink, and reminded me why I enjoyed solitude and tea and books.

Tonight made me nervous for entirely different reasons.

But I did enjoy the music and the drinks, and I would enjoy my time with Mae, so I shoved those anxious thoughts down and laced my boots. When I straightened, I opened the drawer of my bedside table, reaching inside to find a small vial of amber liquid. My face was hot by the time I finished drinking my daily serving of Natalia's contraceptive brew, my mind racing through the possibilities of tonight and where it could lead me and Mae.

If she wanted it, I would give her everything.

And I knew how dangerous that was, especially knowing there was a chance she could have killed Willem and Theon. I still didn't believe that was the case, but what if I was wrong?

I didn't think I could blame her, but Xaladorian law dictated murderers be executed by beheading. To save her from that fate would cost me my own life as well.

If we were caught.

I shook off that thought with a huff, rocking to my feet. Tonight was supposed to be about romancing her. I couldn't be concocting plans to run from the law.

Looking over to Leona, I found her fussing at and straightening the little details of her dress once more, the bob of her throat telling me she too was nervous about tonight. But her grin was wide— confident.

I wished I felt that way.

The both of us were silent as we headed down the hall, coming out onto the landing. I looked over the railing of the balcony hanging over the main room to see my father below at his desk reading a letter. I heard him sigh loudly just as I began the descent down the stairs behind Leona.

When I came off the last step, a line of books on their shelf to my right were leaning slightly. I stopped to adjust them—

"Fawkes, for fuck's sake. C'mon." Leona looped her arm and tugged.

I snickered. "Sorry. Habit."

Father stood as we came out of the rows of shelves, taking another breath that ended with a sigh. "You two look great." He looked down to my hip. "You're only bringing a dagger?"

"I can defend myself with it." And magic if needed, though I'd decided to keep my spellbook here at the house. I would still be in range if I needed to use magic.

I didn't miss Father's glance to the mantle—to the sword. With a nod, he laced his fingers together, giving me an eye of scrutiny. "Can I expect you home tonight?"

Every part of me went taut and I was suddenly nervous all over again. "I...I don't know, to be honest."

Even Leona seemed surprised by that.

Father inclined his head. "Well, just so you know, whether you're back tonight or not, I may not be here for lunch." He looked away as he said, "I have a...meeting with someone."

"A meeting?"

Father didn't have *meetings* unless they were with students. Perhaps it was another student to tutor.

But the way he said it made me think this meeting was similar to the one I would be having tonight. My head was suddenly spinning.

Father adjusted his spectacles and breathed out. "Yes, and I'd tell you who I'm meeting but I don't want to ruin your night."

"So, you *are* meeting a woman." I felt like throwing up.

His head jeered back. "What? Oh gods, no. Varys, I…" He looked like he might throw up as well. "This is a business meeting."

Leo was covering her mouth, suppressing a laugh. I only let out a relieved sigh. "Then why don't you want me to know who you're meeting with?"

Father rested his arms on the table, and I noticed the letter he'd been reading over was beneath him. I couldn't see who it was from. "We will just talk about it tomorrow night over dinner. We will probably have *a lot* to talk about, so if you don't return tonight, please tell Mae that I will need to discuss things with you privately tomorrow."

Meaning if my relationship with Mae became something more than just trysting, I was not to spend tomorrow night with her as well.

"All right, I think we'll be off now," I exclaimed, snagging Leona's arm. I spun so fast, she knocked into me and growled scathing Dwarvish curses as I tried to pull her away.

"Remember to treat Mae well tonight," Father said from behind. "And be safe, Wynhart."

I stopped in my tracks. A painful lodge instantly swelled in my throat. I turned back to him, wide-eyed.

Be safe, Wynhart.

Words we had only uttered a few times over the course of the twelve years Mother had been gone. A variation of her last words to my father.

You keep our son safe, Wynhart.

And he had done just that.

Because Father had been the one who had pulled me from the log. After Mother had saved me, after she'd been dragged away, he found me screaming, bloodied, bitten, scratched, and had fought through the rest of the wolves to get to me.

He had his own scars from that night, aside from the one on his heart from where Mother had been ripped from him. A long, knotted lesion ran down his right leg from a claw that had cut through the tendon. He had a slight limp in that leg even now, and still suffered muscle pain that was progressing with age.

But he had got me out. He had kept me safe, kept me close—but from afar. Any closer and I was instantly reminded of him pulling me out of that log. I couldn't remember the last time I'd given my father a hug, a pat on the shoulder, a handshake.

"Be safe, Wynhart" had become the embrace we couldn't share.

"I will, Father," I told him, lifting my head high. "And I'll keep Mae safe, too."

Mae

My wardrobe was full of the most obnoxious gowns. Gowns with sleeves billowing to the floor. Gowns with sashes I always stepped on. Gowns with corseted backs I couldn't breathe in. All of these dresses showed off my wealth, but not...*me*. I was always buried beneath layers and ribbons and embellishments.

I huffed as I continued to search, looking over a green dress Mother had purchased because she loved the color but hadn't allowed me to wear it out of the house after I'd tried it on. Said it made me look like the walking dead.

I gave up for a few moments and sat in front of the vanity. The skin around my eyes were still puffy and dark after my flare, so I considered the assortment of face paint on my vanity; the silver and gold dust, the bright pink rouge, and the kohl.

Maybe just a little.

But I wasn't going to wear any of it because I wanted to cover up my features. Leona hadn't done that with the face paint she'd donned. She had merely accentuated the green in her eyes and red undertones of her lips.

I didn't grab the powder Mother made me wear to cover up the prominent purple veins of my temples. Varys had kissed me there earlier. He'd also kissed my plum-colored lips, so I wouldn't color them any differently tonight.

I brushed my eyelids with a shimmery silver dust I had never worn before since Mother preferred gold. Then I drew a thin line of kohl along my lashes.

Surveying my work, I couldn't help but to stare in awe at how the paint made my eyes so bold and striking. I leaned in closer to the mirror, and for a moment, just really *looked* at them. How they were purple but the inner rims were more indigo, and I had flecks of pure blue scattered through dark and light violet swirls.

I gulped as I looked over myself. At all the things Mother had always pointed out. My abnormalities, which was just her nice way of saying I was ugly. My full lips, my angular eyes, my thin, pointy nose. My white hair—the symbol of my curse.

I loved all of those things about myself.

It had never been about my own self-doubt. My anger, my sadness, my heartache had derived from loving myself and being told I was wrong to do so. It didn't matter if I thought I was beautiful. It didn't matter if I liked my long legs and prominent cheekbones. Since I was deemed cursed, my opinion about myself had been forced to match what people thought of me.

But no more. My conversation with Vamir had made me realize I was done believing in the curse, done believing I was anything other than just *different*. If I was Elven-blooded, I was from a lineage of god-made Xaladorians. I had magic flowing through my veins. I wasn't purely human.

So fuck what humans thought of me.

But the only feature I possessed that might link me to that bloodline were my eyes. Were they truly what made me Elven-blooded enough to have magic and the ability to read Elvish?

And if that was the case, why was I the only Elven-blooded person who could?

The thought made all others halt.

I stared at myself, blood racing hot suddenly. A revelation had hit me hard enough, it knocked the air from me.

"Am I the only Elven-blooded person in Xalador who has

powers now?" I asked out loud. I didn't want that question to be mixed up with thoughts that weren't my own.

And my mind landed on Varys.

I stood, my heart pounding. I'd been so focused on hiding my own powers, had I missed something about him?

Did he have powers too?

He'd shown no evidence of that. Nothing out of the usual... except...

Oh my gods.

We hadn't had time to discuss what had happened to him. Why he had collapsed on me and slept for hours.

Did something dumb.

Used a lot of strength.

"What did you do, Varys?" I rasped, locking eyes with myself in the mirror as if I could imagine him looking back at me, as if I could somehow reach him. "Does your magic make you suffer?"

Bringing my left arm up, I traced a finger over the lines of my lightning marks. I hadn't believed the two were connected, but if Varys had power and it had caused him some sort of pain or exhausted him to the point it made him sick, maybe my flares were connected to my magic too.

And if that were the case, maybe I hadn't been poisoned after all. What if I had always been sick because of my magic?

There were bigger questions going off in my mind. Why hadn't Varys told me? That question stood out the most but I didn't have any room to ask that. I was hiding my powers for my own safety. Perhaps he was doing the same.

Or maybe I was wrong. Maybe I was still some sort of anomaly. Still different. Still some sort of curse.

There was no sense in dwelling on the questions any longer. I would tell Varys about my powers when I was ready, and if he had magic, he would do the same.

Then, together, we could figure out why.

I looked through my wardrobe again, feeling a new wave of inspiration come over me. All of my gowns were pieced together, only having a completed look after I donned three to four layers. Overdresses went with certain chemises, robes went over others for a layered look. Even my everyday dresses I wore to do chores required a chemise and an overdress.

What if I merely didn't wear everything the gown required?

A silver satin skirt I'd worn only once caught my eye. Connected to the belt of the skirt was a thick sash meant to tie around and hang down in the back. With this specific skirt, I was to first don a chemise, then the skirt, then a corset vest similar to the one I was wearing, only embellished with ornate embroidery.

But what would it look like if the sash came up over my torso instead?

I quickly undressed from my traveling clothes, then slid the skirt up to my waist. Standing in front of my mirror, I took one side of the sash, flattened the material over my breast and tossed the rest over my shoulder. I did the same to the other side, then tied both pieces behind my neck. The result was...sultry. I'd never seen my body displayed like this. My entire back was exposed down to my waist. My arms were bare, and even though the thick sash covered most of my torso, it still left a thin vertical line of skin down the front where the inner arcs of my breasts were left exposed.

I smiled at how the silver made the slight lavender undertones of my pale skin pop. I felt regal, elegant. Seductive.

But I found a problem with this outfit already as I looked down to my left arm. I frowned at the lightning marks, the damn obstacles preventing me from getting away with this. But I refused to change. I dug through my wardrobe until I found a pair of black fingerless gloves Mother had purchased a few seasons ago. There were loops for my middle fingers at the tip of the V-shaped opening, and the gloves were long enough to cover the entirety of my forearms.

Lastly, I found a sheer black cape and placed it over my shoulders. The collar sat tightly around my neck and was to be pinned with a small brooch to give the effect of a choker. I picked a brooch of amethysts.

Clad in silver and black, my white hair was a beacon, but I would let it be one tonight. I let down my curls and braided the two front strands, then I pulled the top half of my hair back and secured it with a pearl-embellished hair comb, letting the rest spill over my bare back. My breath hitched as I turned a small circle and watched the satin skirt flare and tuck around my hips. This was truly the most beautiful thing I'd ever worn. And I'd chosen it for myself.

Varys

"Stop fidgetin', Fawkes."

I huffed, clenching my hands together and pulling them down from where I had started to drag them through my hair. "Can't help it."

The Nook and Cranny was wall to wall with people tonight. The two of us had been backed into the farthest corner, and the only reason I was not panicking and searching for an open space I could get to quickly was because my eyes were centered on the door. Waiting and watching to see if she would show.

Pressure clamped down on my chest. We'd already been here for a while, an hour or so. The sun had set, and the bards had played a few crowd favorites.

My hand found its way back to my face, nails on my teeth—

Leona grabbed my wrist and pulled it down. "Stop it!"

"I'm nervous," I bit out, pulling on the collar of my tunic. "She's not here."

"She will be. But bitin' yer nails is a terrible, disgustin' habit."

I sneered. "My hands are cleaner than yours."

A lewd smile rose on her red painted lips. "Not sure how long that's goin' to last after t'night."

I rolled my eyes and put my hands behind my back, returning my focus to the door. I noticed I was one of the tallest here tonight. Even the mercenaries to our left were shorter than me—wider in most places where it counted, but my elven blood had definitely given me height I could have lived without tonight.

A copper-skinned woman squeezed her way through the group in front of us, smiling as she came over. Adlin was her name, one of the barmaids and the owner's daughter. She blew out a breath and flipped her obsidian braid off her shoulder. "Busiest night I've ever seen!" she shouted over the noise. "I cleared a table on the other side for your party. Closer to the bards."

I looked to Leona who only smirked and dropped a silver piece into Adlin's hand. I was pretty sure they'd had something a few years back.

"Ye're the best, Adlin," Leona crooned loudly.

The barmaid winked and slipped the coin down into her shirt. "I've got Melissa over there waiting for you to come claim the table, but there's a group from out of town arguing with her about it."

I looked over to find Melissa indeed exchanging tense words with four Elven-blooded men.

Adlin went on, "They've booked the entire third story suite and before you arrived, bought an entire round of mead for everyone who was present."

"I told ye we needed to get here sooner," Leo growled at me.

I snorted. As if she needed a free drink on top of the many she'd have tonight.

"Yeah, so they're obviously rich," Adlin continued. She raised her voice even louder when another song began, "Better get a move on before you lose your spot."

"We'll head over," I told her with a nod before Leo dragged me away.

When we reached the table, the Elven-blooded men were still carrying on and Melissa looked like she was about to explode. With her hand firmly planted on the table she shouted, "There is not a single thing you can tempt me with to make me give up this table! Now unless you'd like me to take it up with the master—"

"We are making him a wealthier man tonight," the one with lemon-colored hair and gold eyes sneered. "Surely you understand that refusing to us is—"

His words died when he watched me take a seat. Leona continued to stand, glaring at the group for a moment before glancing to Melissa. "Thanks for keepin' our seats cozy. I'll remind my da to make sure ye get tipped *big* when we come in for mead."

Melissa grinned, gave the four a nasty look, and then marched away. One of the men stepped forward, his long red hair up in a ponytail. We locked eyes and he said, "You there. Are you...here with the others like us?"

I went still. The yellow-haired man gripped the other's shoulder, squeezing. The red-head didn't budge.

"I'm not with those who came for the Fest of Change, if that's what you're asking." Even though my stomach was flipping with anxiety, I held my head high and gaze strong.

These were *Vyl'kríev*, whether they knew it or not.

The red-head nodded. "So you're the only Elven-blooded who lives in Elros?"

It seemed like they too had realized the lack of Elven-blooded citizens here in Elros. "Not always. There were others. They've gone, moved out over the course of the last two years or so."

The group of men traded glances. I looked over their attire quickly. None of them carried a book bag or anything that might give away they had a wizard's spellbook on them, and I didn't know how I would be able to tell if they were a sorcerer or druid.

"If you have time during the fest," the red-headed one went on to say. "Stop by our tent. The Jeweler Brothers. We make jewelry— you can't miss us."

"Why in Torm would we want to do business with ye when ye've been absolute pricks to one of our favorite barmaids?" Leona asked with a scowl.

A man—another *brother*, I realized—stepped forward. He was obviously several years younger than the rest. His hair was the same color yellow as the first man, but his eyes were a bright orange. "We have our reasons for being pricks—"

The red-head lifted a hand. He turned to Leona. "I apologize. It's been a hard couple of weeks. All we want is a good night."

"Then find another fuckin' table," Leona hissed.

The four men bowed their heads. "We shall," said the yellow-haired man. "But like Ramos said"—a glance to his red-haired brother—"do come see us at our tent during the Fest. We may have...some things in common."

I nodded, but didn't say anything else. As the four walked away, the last brother who hadn't said anything kept his gaze on me beneath the hood of his blue cloak with gold trimming. I couldn't see the color of his hair, nor the bottom of his face beneath the mask over his mouth, but I would never forget the bright yellow eyes staring back at me.

Leona gave me an incredulous look. "What was all that about anyway?"

"Elven-blooded, Leo," I murmured.

Her mouth parted in understanding and she nodded slowly. She took her seat momentarily, only to stand back up. I did my best to ignore the obviousness of her pushing her chest forward. "Well, my night has started," she chimed, smoothing the material of her dress over her hip.

I followed her gaze to find Orin making his way through the crowd, his dark gaze on her alone. I pushed down the groan of irritation in my throat.

Orin met her at the foot of the table. Leona already had herself leaned against the edge, on display. He took her hand. "You look enthralling tonight, princess."

My stomach turned over. Surely she hadn't told him she was a *real* princess. All of those lingering bad feelings about the man multiplied.

Leona beamed as he took her arm. "And here I was thinking you would bring the bird. It didn't leave your shoulder earlier today."

I raised a brow hearing her speech. Her accent was..."Leona, why are you talking like that?"

She only smiled, but didn't look at me. Orin did, and there was a small curl to his lips before he quickly returned his attention to her. "Gawain never leaves my shoulder unless I tell him too. He's not much for people though, and he's probably relaxed in his cage, eating those seeds your mother gave him."

I rested my head in my hands. Even Natalia had been her usual, virtuous self around this man. Why was I the only one who felt on edge around him?

"Well, I was just about to buy myself a drink," Leona told him slowly. She was purposefully thinning her accent, removing the lilt in her speech entirely. "But now that you are here..."

I snarled at her forced elocution.

Orin chuckled, and all I could hear was the nasty twist in his throat. "I'll buy you as many as you want tonight."

"Don't give her that kind of challenge," I gritted out.

Leona only smirked. "Shall we?"

I had to bite my tongue to keep myself from mocking her as they strode away, Leona's skirt sashaying as she walked. Godsdamn princess, indeed.

Left alone at a table set for four, I was receiving side-eyes and glares from around the room. I needed at least two of these chairs. I was sure Leona wouldn't be back.

Where is she?

The bards kicked off another song, this one loud and lively. A group of people across from me cheered and rushed to the dais, beginning to form a long line. By the looks of it, many others knew what kind of dance this song required as they formed another row. The lines of people took two steps forward, then back before they flawlessly split and formed a massive circle. I winced when the dancing pushed more bystanders back, the space around me becoming tighter and tighter. Couples were up against my table. A man claimed one of the chairs, swaying in a drunken stupor as he cheered at nothing and sloshed his ale down his beard.

This was not at all how I had hoped this evening would go. For all I knew, Mae had walked up to this tavern and turned right back around in fright.

But just as I'd come to that presumption, white hair snagged my attention.

I stood up and raised a hand to wave her down. She didn't see me, *couldn't* see me through the mass. She turned around—and my pulse skipped. It wasn't...it wasn't her. But this person, this *man*, had white hair. He didn't look my way, only lifted a bony hand toward...

Orin.

The hairs on my neck rose. From where she stood in line, Leona's eyes went wide from the rim of her pint of mead. She turned to find me already looking at her, matching my confused expression.

Confusion turned to shock when more people with white hair entered the building. Men and women. I could feel the tug of my magic in my skull. I could hear every command word to every spell I knew whirl around in my mind, drowning out the conversations, the music, the beat of the drum. My nerves were roiling, but I didn't know why. They were just like Mae.

The silver eyes of Orin's friend met mine momentarily before they shifted to another. He was dressed in head to toe black and wearing an outrageous bib of emeralds. I realized he was the man who had been in front of Orin yesterday as they'd rode in on their black steeds.

Releasing a breath, I looked to Leona and Orin again. He had turned his attention back to sliding his hand up and down her exposed thigh. She was grinning, a deep red blush staining her freckled cheeks.

I looked away. She could take care of herself. She was obviously wanting whatever it was he was offering. It didn't matter if that made me unhappy.

While my focus had been on them, Orin's comrade had disappeared from my view. I found him at the front table talking to the rest of the white-haired people. It was uncanny how much he looked like Mae. The rest were similar in certain features; angular jaw structures and cheekbones, full lips, and long, thin noses that tipped up just the slightest. Their skin tones ranged from ashen-white to deep umber much like everyone else in Xalador, however, their eyes were either silver or so black I could barely locate a pupil.

None of them had eyes like Mae's—like the stunning violet and blue irises that found mine with unerring accuracy as their possessor came through the door next. Even beneath the hood of her black cloak, they shone like gemstones. She grinned as she pulled it down, her beautiful curls spilling over her shoulders.

The tavern master greeted her as he did to all women and offered to take her cloak. She nodded, unclipped it, and he helped it off her shoulders.

The air left my lungs. My throat dried entirely.

Without another thought, I was moving. I only gave a nod toward the table to Melissa as I passed—she knew to watch it. I forced my way through the crowd, practically charging toward Mae. Eyes from every direction were on her now, taking in the sight of her beauty and absolute radiance, beholding her shoulders, the sheer cape doing nothing to conceal the bareness of her back, and the thin exposure of skin down the center of the bodice displaying the inner swells of her breasts.

But she was here for me. She was *mine* tonight.

And that godsdamn dress was going to destroy me.

My very blood throbbed. Every step I took seemed to fall in place with the rhythm of the song thrumming through the air. It was impossible for me to hide the look of burning desire as I passed the last person between us. I didn't stop myself from sweeping my gaze over her form, slowly, intentionally. She only kept her focus on me, her eyes just as heated, just as full of great need.

I extended my hand toward her when a figure stepped in front of me. I stopped in my tracks.

Orin's comrade.

Mae's gaze left mine, blinking up to lock eyes with his instead. Her lips parted and she took a step away. "Oh, hello."

He took her hand, and my pulse stumbled over itself when he lifted it to his lips. Mae froze, her beautiful eyes falling to the floor as he kissed her knuckles—her hands that should have been in mine by now. The moment his mouth left her skin, she pulled it away.

"You look beautiful tonight, Mae," he purred, his accent elegant even among the deep, raspy tone of his voice.

He knew her name?

She swallowed. "Thank you, Vamir."

She knew *his*?

She looked to me again, her face heavy with an emotion I couldn't place. Vamir spun to meet my scowl. His silver eyes flickered with surprise for a moment, then he tilted his head and drawled, "Ah, it appears I've gotten between a wolf and his prey."

My insides lurched. *Shit.*

All semblance of my resolve was shredded with that comment. I took a step back, thoughts beginning to take me to where I'd been this morning. There were so many people, so little space—

Mae stepped around Vamir as if he was nothing but a piece of furniture. "No," she snapped. "I'm with him."

And she was suddenly against me, one hand on my chest, over

my erratic heart, the other on my lower back. She lifted on her toes and kissed the underside of my chin, so close to the sensitive part of my neck I shuddered.

"You merely stepped between a previous engagement." She brushed my cheek with her fingers. "I am no prey."

Vamir bowed his head. "My apologies. I misread the situation. I was delighted to see you walk through those doors, though." He gestured to the tables behind us, to where the people with white hair sat. Mae's breath hitched. "I told you earlier today I am a merchant. You seemed to be in a rush about something, so I didn't have the chance to tell you I have many hired hands and family members who are like you and I as well."

A small smile lifted on his pale lips as he looked down to her. It had me pressing a hand to her back. She leaned into my touch, her cool skin against my fingers sending a blast of warmth through every part of me.

Vamir continued, "If you find yourself free for a moment"—a glance to me—"I would very much like to introduce you to them. We are all from the same bloodline, after all."

His words were a confirmation I didn't expect to get tonight, my thoughts instantly back to the dissertation I'd read about white-haired Xaladorians being similar to those of elven descent.

"Elven," I said aloud to no one in particular. "It's an elven bloodline."

Mae's brows arched. Vamir chuckled. "Yes, elven, of course."

"Really?" she asked, taking a step toward him. "You know that for sure?"

Vamir nodded. "We are definitely not cursed as your physician has told you."

Mae looked to the floor. "No, I suppose not."

I swallowed down the tightness in my throat. He'd only been in town for a day and yet she'd had personal conversations with this man?

I couldn't help the sour taste on my tongue, the jealousy. But...these people were like her. And gods, she needed to learn more about who she was. Wasn't I determined to do that about her being

Vyl'kríev? What if by merely talking to these people, she opened up about her magic to me?

There was a heaviness in my stomach, but I lifted her chin with my finger. "Mae, maybe you *should* go introduce yourself."

Her eyes widened. "What?"

"You don't see people like yourself everyday. We can go over there together."

She was quiet for a moment as if she was thinking it over. Then she shook her head and turned to Vamir. "Maybe later tonight. I'm here for dinner, drinks and dancing." Her eyes had turned sultry when she looked back to me. "Among other things."

Before I could say another word, she took my hand and began to lead me back through the crowd. I was sure I could feel Vamir's steel gaze boring into the back of my head, but when I looked back he was no longer standing there.

CHAPTER 27

Mae

The Alderbright, the only tavern I'd ever been inside, was quiet and smelled of the rose centerpieces on each table. They served four-course meals and wines that had been aged for fifty years or more. The only music played was usually one bard strumming a lute and singing to a soft ballad, and the only dancing done was between two people, slow and repetitive.

The Nook and Cranny was the exact opposite of that.

I hadn't been inside the building for too long and was already sweating from the amount of bodies producing heat. The smell of pipe-weed stung my nose, mixing with the scents of bread, roasted meats, ale, mead, hard liquor, and dirty people. As Varys led me back to the table, I could only stare at the massive stage filled with several musicians. The music was loud enough I could feel the drum pounding in my chest, and when Varys asked me a question as we sat down next to each other I had to have him repeat it twice, which seemed to make him incredibly anxious. People were shouting, cheering, and stomping to the song. There would be no conversation between Varys and I until this dance came to an end, so we waited, watching men and women twirl around their partners, skirts flying, arms entangled, feet stepping in rhythm.

It was incredible.

Lost in thought and overwhelmed with everything I was experiencing, I watched the tendrils of smoke gathering in the air from the tables of food and the burning pipes. Up, up the smoke slithered to the ceiling that seemed to never end. There were two mezzanine floors above us, and there were people looking down to the festivities leaning over the balcony rails with happy faces.

That was another thing that separated this tavern from The Alderbright. Everybody looked like they genuinely wanted to be here.

I felt Varys's eyes on me and gave him a quick grin. I couldn't deny I loved that he'd put his hair back tonight. There was something different about the angles of his face because of it. Maybe it was because nothing was hidden behind loose strands, and now I could see how his jaw cocked slightly, how his brow came forward enough to cast a shadow over those beautiful sapphire eyes I got so lost in, and yet there was a redness under his bottom lashes I assumed was from many late nights due to studying or those awful nightmares.

The two of us jolted when a few spirited dancers collided with our table, spun to correct their step, and then rushed back into the horde laughing. The drunk man who'd stolen a seat at our table suddenly slumped over. Varys slid a hand over his face in exasperation, but thankfully two inn guards had been on standby. They trudged over and quickly removed the man from the festivities.

I winced when the drums started pounding harder, and on every other beat the entire tavern shouted "Hey!" Varys looked as if he might shrink into himself. I placed a hand on his shoulder and the smile he gave me was tight and uneasy.

I was about to try and ask if he wanted to go outside for a bit when my eyes caught two dancers stepping out of the circle of people. The two men smiled before their lips locked in a manner that made my face heat, but I didn't look away as they chuckled and kissed all the way to an area beyond the tables. Along the west side of the tavern was a row of several small rooms, the entrances shrouded by sheer red curtains swaying softly with the movement of passersby. The taller of the two men parted the material before guiding his partner inside, and I caught a glimpse of a settee and candles lit on a short table before it. As the curtain fell back in place, and I could now only make out two dark figures behind the red, I realized the small spaces were for much more private, intimate engagements.

I felt Varys's eyes on me again. He mouthed something like "I'm so sorry," but I wasn't sure why he was apologizing. Confused, I scanned the room to find what he was sorry for. His hand found mine as he shook his head and he leaned closer, loudly explaining in my ear, "I'm sorry there are so many people. It's usually loud, but not *this* loud. Not very good for conversation."

I nodded and replied, shouting over the music. "I'm fine. But do you want to go outside?"

"What?" He cupped his ears.

"Do you want to go outside?"

"You want me to go get some wine?"

"No." I waved my arms. "I'm fine."

His eyes glanced from side to side. "Wine?"

I laughed out, shaking my head. Varys pressed his lips together and then mouthed another apology.

Finally, with one last "Hey!" the music ceased. The tavern cheered and applauded for a few moments before the wave of sound died down to a constant chatter.

Varys sighed. "I'm so sorry—"

"Oh, stop apologizing." I looped my arm with his and took his hand. "I love how lively it is, but I'm glad I can talk to you now."

He smiled, leaning closer. "If you say so. But I do have one more apology." His eyes dipped down. "I'm sorry I haven't had the chance to tell you how incredible you look tonight."

I thanked him before glancing up at his hair again. "You look exceptionally handsome yourself. I like your hair. I can see your eyes better."

"Thank you, Mae." He breathed out, seeming to be disgruntled about something.

"Did I say something?" I asked.

He shook his head. "No, it's….you don't just look incredible. You look gorgeous. Exquisite. But you're all of those things in and out of that dress."

My brows lifted, but he'd already clamped his mouth closed, eyes squeezed shut. "That's not what I meant."

I laughed. "I know."

Muttering something under his breath, he stood long enough to pull his chair closer. "There are a lot of words I could use to try to describe how you look tonight," he told me, his eyes burning through every part of me, "but truly nothing would come close. So, forgive me if I'm a bit speechless."

My mouth parted. Gods, he spoke so beautifully—so beautifully about *me*. How could he claim to be speechless when I couldn't form a single thought around him at times?

Before I could answer him with the kiss I'd been wanting to give him, a barmaid rushed up to our table. She introduced herself as Melissa before joking that she was surprised Varys had someone accompanying him. Varys only rolled his eyes as he gently brushed his thumb across the top of my hand.

"What can I get you two to drink?" Melissa asked.

Varys quickly ran over a few of his favorite wines. I had never been one to drink much, especially since I could hardly stomach the smell of hard liquors. The cloying scent that seemed to ooze from Rucas's skin after a long night at the brothel. "Oh, the house mead is also spectacular if you want something other than wine," Varys told me. "But it should come with a warning because it sneaks up on you."

Melissa chuckled at that. "Varys here can attest to that. The one and only time I've ever heard him sing is when—"

Varys cleared his throat loudly, silencing Melissa. "Mae, I really think you'll like the wine I mentioned. It has notes of cherry and cinnamon."

"Wait." I dropped his hand and turned to face him completely. His eyes went wide. "I didn't know you could sing."

The way he gulped slowly made me grin. This was a secret we'd just unearthed.

He sent Melissa an unpleasant scowl. "Melissa said I sang, not that I *can*."

Melissa clicked her tongue and placed her hands on her hips. "Oh, modest Varys," she chided before looking to me. "Formos did not hold back blessing this man with pipes. I honestly don't understand why he isn't a bard."

Varys had sunk further into his seat. "Lacking the charisma, I guess," he muttered softly.

We both decided on wine. Melissa then asked us what we would be having for dinner as she slipped a menu before us. I was instantly reminded I couldn't read a damn thing, but before the embarrassment could rear its ugly head, Varys told her we would need another minute to discuss. When she walked away, Varys pulled my menu closer and began to read off the options for me. My chest snagged. I didn't even have to ask. He just knew.

"I'm getting the special. It's roast with a side of vegetables." He pointed to the very top of the menu, the first word starting with a curly letter I remembered as S from my reading lesson earlier that day.

"That sounds good. I think I'll have the same."

Varys nodded. "We get complimentary bread, so we can share that, and dessert if you'd like."

I laughed out. "Oh, no, I'll have my *own* dessert."

Varys's scarred brow rose, a sly grin lifting one side of his lips. "Aw, I was under the assumption that women believe it's romantic to share dessert after dinner."

With a sultry bat of my lashes, I gave a one-shouldered shrug. "I'm not your average woman."

He chuckled. "No, you're not. But I wouldn't want it any other way."

A broad smile broke out over my face, crinkling my nose and eyes. Varys never dropped his gaze.

"I don't think our relationship has advanced enough to share dessert," I told him.

His eyes narrowed, but he leaned in closer to me. "Oh, is that the next step for us?"

I sent him a teasing glare. "Definitely not the next. You've barely kissed me."

His jaw dropped as a laugh skittered free. "*Barely* kissed you?"

I nodded, toying with a strand of my hair. "You're going to have to kiss me at least..." I tapped my bottom lip, feigning a thoughtful expression, "Four more times before I even *think* about sharing my dessert."

My words stilled him, and the look he gave me was all too familiar. The same sensual gaze that had me feeling loose even though my limbs felt heavy. The same expression, full of such need and desire for me, had me up against the bookcases earlier today and wanting his lips on mine, on my neck. Lower.

He laced his hand with mine once more and guided me closer. "I think..." he murmured in my ear, "I can make sure you're kissed much more than that *well* before dinner even arrives."

My head emptied out, thoughts banished by his words, his voice. I barely noticed the wine that was sat before us. Melissa and Varys spoke briefly, but I was too focused on the heat between him and I. Not even the sweet and spicy flavor of the wine I began to sip on could yank me from where my head had gone.

My gaze wandered all the way over to those small, private rooms and what I might find there with him—

Varys cupped my chin and pulled me into him. My squeal of surprise was silenced when his soft lips captured mine in a strong, eager manner. The hand on my chin moved to hold the side of my face and neck, claiming me, locking me against his mouth. I didn't want to be anywhere else.

And I didn't pull away this time when the pulse between us jolted straight through me. I let it overwhelm me. Allowed myself to feel it. Let the gasps in my throat slip free as the buzzing, charged sensation caressed my bones. It was so similar to my magic. To the static and lightning I could call forth. And it felt good. Beckoned the hairs to rise all over my body.

Varys still didn't seem to notice the pulse, but it didn't matter. The way he increased the pressure on my lips made my stomach dip like I was standing on the edge of the world. I blindly reached out to find his shoulders, to hold on, gripping them tight and pulling him closer. The scent of him filled my lungs, the sweet smell of bergamot so strong I could taste it. His hands fell to my hips, fingers kneading into the material of my dress, teasing my bare lower back. I needed his skin on mine, his warmth. Reaching down, I found his hands and guided them around and under the sheer cape, pushing them against my exposed back. He sucked in a breath, but spread his hands out over my skin, stroking up and down my spine. I nearly whimpered from the scorching feeling.

When he broke the kiss, I felt a pull on my bottom lip and it dragged a jolt of heat up from my lowest, most sensitive areas. We were both breathless when we met each other's gaze.

"That's two, just so you know," he told me, his voice little more than a whisper. "Or three if you're wanting to count that terrible first kiss I gave you in panic."

I couldn't bring myself to laugh at the joke he was trying to make. Couldn't think through the heady haze I never wanted to come out of. I just wanted to kiss him again.

His mouth curled into a smile when our lips met once more. I found myself lifting off my seat so I could get as close as possible. Still, the chairs proved to be an obstacle, and that was probably for the best. I was still aware we were surrounded by people—people who were most likely watching.

I wasn't sure I cared, and it seemed Varys didn't care at all. Not as his hands roamed over my skin in ways that spoke louder than words. Not as he tilted his head and parted my lips with his sweet tongue.

Something happened then. As my sighs merged with his deep hums, my mind went...*blue*. There were so many swirls of midnight and sky and sapphire and turquoise. Every breath Varys took, with every stroke on my skin, the colors shifted.

Surely, I wasn't feeling the wine already.

I lost track of the moments that passed, how many songs began and stopped. The colors twisted until the purest, most beautiful blue I'd ever seen, filled my head and with it...a feeling washed over me I couldn't explain. It made my chest swell, as if my very soul was blooming.

But as his kiss softened, the color faded. His touch became gentle whispers on my skin until he was just...holding me. His lips stayed on mine for a beat longer before he pulled away. A bright smile rose on his face as he beheld me, murmured my name, and watched me catch my breath.

"I'd agree that's four, wouldn't you?" he asked.

I chuckled, brushing my nose against his. "At least."

"Mmm…" He took my hand and kissed my palm, then my wrist. "How come you're wearing these gloves?"

I swallowed, and it was like I could suddenly feel the lightning marks pressing against the black material. I watched him continue to kiss up to where the glove stopped at my elbow, and my stomach flipped. "I-I get cold easily."

His lips brushed my shoulder. "Is what we're doing not warming you up?"

I rolled my eyes with a smile. "It is."

"Thought so."

He brushed his lips across my collar bone and I drew in a gasp, tilting my head back. His hot breath on my neck had my nerves roiling once more. I sighed, "Your confidence is so…"

When I didn't finish my sentence, he sat back a bit quickly, his eyes wide. "Am I coming on too strong?"

"What—*no*." I laid a hand on his chest. "I was trying to say I like how bold and confident you are. I've always known you to be more reserved and quiet, so I feel like this is a side of you that is…special."

He smiled, resting his arm on the back of my chair. "I'm comfortable with you."

My cheeks burned, but I didn't shy away. I leaned into him, laying my head on his shoulder. He cuddled me close with a sigh, pressing tender kisses to the top of my head. For a moment, the two of us were silent as we listened to the bards' slow ballad.

"I was quiet growing up, yes," he stated suddenly. "Reserved. Always had my nose stuck in a book. Incredibly anxious in most social situations. I still have those characteristics, but I have…changed."

I looked up at him. "What changed you?"

He took a long breath through his nose, sending a narrowed stare toward the ocean of people. "Several things. Sure, I was a shy kid, but my withdrawn personality stemmed entirely from losing my mother and everything that happened that night. I think I found a shell of safety inside the library, within the stories told in books. But I knew deep down I wasn't meant to remain in that shell. Little by little, one experience after another, I started making small changes and then one day I…" He glanced down at me, and the look on his face made my heart skip a pulse. "I reemerged."

I tilted my head. "Like…a butterfly?"

He snorted, shaking his head. "I guess you can say I came out of my shell like a butterfly's chrysalis, yes."

For a quick moment, my thoughts drifted to the dream I'd had the night before. How my chest had split open and hundreds of butterflies had flown out of me.

"I guess my point here is…I changed because I wanted to," he said with a soft smile after taking a sip of his wine. "Sometimes people change to become a better person, other times they may find themselves so far from the person they were, they're no longer the same. And usually the ones who change for the worst never look back to see the difference, to see the destruction in their wake. When I decided to change, I became who I am today. This is who I'm supposed to be."

I smiled and squeezed his hand. "That's very admirable." It was a feat I'd been attempting myself. To change, to become something different. To get out of my terrible situation. Maybe the dream I'd had was a semblance of my own change. "It takes a lot of courage to do that. I don't think everyone has that kind of bravery."

He pulled my hand to his heart, his voice hoarse as he muttered, "You make me want to be brave, Mae."

I breathed out, gazing up at him. He only smiled and brushed his thumb across my bottom lip. As he did, that blossoming feeling in my chest rushed through me again. When my veins filled with warmth, my body went taut, anticipating a flare that would never come. Because this heat in my blood…this was different. This made me feel alive, safe, and happy. I'd never truly felt those emotions.

But I did here with him. The man I wanted and had chosen for myself.

His brows rose when I stood suddenly, wide eyes watching every move as I placed my hands on his broad shoulders. I took in the sight of his beautiful face, the way he looked up at me, the expression that spoke of something much deeper than a one night engagement. The echo of the pulse, the true meaning of the connection. In a way, it frightened me. But I was done being so afraid.

He made *me* want to be brave.

I dipped down and pressed my lips to his. The strength of my legs threatened to give way with the sigh that escaped him, and with one eager pull I was cradled in his lap. My breasts against his chest left me gasping, and the hardness I could feel beneath me beckoned my body to writhe and grind, but I resisted. We had all night to see where that path might lead.

It was another set of long moments before I pulled away. He didn't seem like he wanted to stop, his grip on me tight.

"What kind of dessert should we share?" I asked through a breathy laugh.

He only grinned and kissed me again. As long moments passed, the blues began to swirl. Around and around, from dark to light, until I was sure this had something to do with the connection to him.

Until my blood began to brew a wild storm I was begging to set free.

CHAPTER 28

Varys

I had found Vamir's eyes on us more times than I was comfortable with. He wasn't watching us particularly; he was scanning the tavern with the same pompous and studious expression. But I didn't like the way his gaze lingered on us. Didn't like knowing his focus was on us while in a heated embrace; that when my eyes were closed, his were open.

Eventually he disappeared like he had before, but I couldn't shake the feeling of being watched. I had to remind myself that I might be unintentionally associating my social anxiety and sleep deprivation with the constant menacing warning.

The fact I could feel it heavier tonight than I ever had before was more unsettling than anything.

Mae had remained in my arms, resting her head on my shoulder. Thankfully, the bards had decided to take a break, allowing us to talk about anything and everything in what felt like a game of questions. She would ask one, I'd answer, vice versa, until we knew some of each other's favorites. She had laughed when I told her the most rebellious thing I had ever done was pretend I was sick in bed so I could skip Father's lessons and read fantasy books all day.

She didn't have an answer for me when I had asked her the

same question. *"Oh, I don't know. I've never really had a reason to rebel,"* she'd told me.

The questions I asked after that seemed to come with a similar problem. She didn't have any hobbies besides baking, she'd never seen any of the drama troupe plays, had never played cards…

She…didn't seem like she had an interesting life.

Dinner came. Between the bread, butter, and the two large plates of roast and vegetables, we decided it would be easier to eat sitting across from one another. We were a few bites into our food when Leona came pushing her way through the crowd. She huffed as she sat at the head of the table, her foaming pint striking the wood hard as she brought it down with obvious frustration. "Seems like ye two are enjoyin' each other. I've done nothin' but stand in that fuckin' line."

I looked to where I believed I would find her tryst for the evening, but found no one following her over. "Where's Orin?"

"A bloody thief robbed one of his comrade's tent and then ripped it to shreds," Leona told us after taking a swig of her drink. "He went to go help but he'll be back."

I wondered if that's where Vamir had disappeared to as well. The group he'd come in with was still sitting at their table. "Did…" I glanced to Mae, who was currently spreading butter over a slice of bread. "Did Vamir go with him?"

Mae looked up at the mention of his name, and I watched her turn and look around the tavern. I couldn't help the tight feeling in my stomach.

"No, he's still around here somewhere." Leo threw her thumb to her left. "Over there, where he's been for a while."

I looked up to see Vamir, indeed, standing exactly where he'd been before he disappeared from my sight. One thing was for sure—this guy was shifty and I didn't like it.

"So, who is Vamir to Orin?" I asked, tone dripping with a bitterness I was unable to hide.

Leona stifled a snort, and her smirk was telling. She would have had to have seen the way Vamir had greeted Mae, so she probably realized I was a bit resentful. Not that I needed to be. It wasn't like Mae was here with him tonight. There was no reason for me to feel jealous of the man, but he made me uneasy. Especially about the way he looked at her. She had dealt with enough predators.

"He's Orin's boss," Leo explained. "One of the leaders for their massive tradin' company."

"So they're merchants?"

My question was for Leo, but Mae nodded. "From our conversation earlier today, I think he specializes in ancient artifacts," she told us.

I looked away, taking a long sip of my wine before I said anything I'd regret. I couldn't help wondering how she knew him and had already engaged in conversation with him.

Dammit, I *was* jealous.

"Most of their company does, I believe," Leona affirmed. "All of them are related, 'cept Orin of course. Which is obvious—no white hair."

A puzzled, but contemplative expression fell across Mae's face.

"He told me half of their group is makin' their way to Shade's Crescent," Leo continued. "They're all originally from Iarhana."

My mouth fell open. "*Iarhana?* That's on the other side of the continent. What are they doing all the way up here in Elros?"

"They heard of the Fest of Change from some people in Latera when they were makin' their way through," she explained before shifting a quick look at Mae. "Were told the festival has grown over the past few years, but also caught word that someone in the merchant guild got their hands on rare items."

My nerves tingled, sending a rushing sensation over my body. *Magic items.* I'd seen the potions in Rucas's shop, but was unable to notice if he had acquired anything else. It made me wonder if Rucas knew about Mae's magic and purchased elven items to assist her. It wouldn't be too far-fetched a thought to consider that she was reluctant to speak about her magic because Rucas had told her not to. And I knew first hand how daunting it was to go up against Rucas in any way.

Leona was staring at me by the time I shook my head from my thoughts. Mae had only continued to eat, and I was unsure she'd registered what Leona said.

"Do you know how your father acquired those elven potions?" I asked her.

When Mae looked up, her face was tight. "Rucas—er, my father purchased them in Latera on his last trip. My friend Eryx told me the market is in a bit of an uproar. There has been an influx of items people are claiming to be magical, and that they're wanting to trade these things over goods and necessities. Some are even refusing gold."

My stomach hollowed out. "Chaos. That will hurt the market *everywhere*."

She nodded. "I've already noticed that there are visitors in town for the festival who are demanding this."

"Fuck that shite," Leo scowled. "Best believe if I come to buy, I'm purchasin' with gold or tradin' with Da's weapons."

I almost smiled at her returned accent. "Problem is, how do these people know the item they're selling is truly magical?"

I knew the answer, but I needed to see if Mae did as well. A *Vyl'kriev* could use *Vid Medaes* to determine the items' arcane properties. But it was quite possible there were clever merchants who weren't mages who had gotten their hands on old antiques and were trying to sell them as magical.

"I personally think my father was swindled on some of the items he acquired," Mae said, rubbing her thumb on the inside of her left wrist. "And I think a lot of people are going to put their gold toward something false and that will cause an even bigger uproar."

"That's not going to stop merchants from taking advantage of the ignorant," I murmured.

"No." Mae lifted her glass, her violet gaze boring into the table. "It's not."

I didn't take my eyes off of her, even though it seemed she was avoiding eye contact now. "So what is your father claiming to be magical? Just the potions?"

She shook her head. "No. He purchased things I've never seen before. Strange-looking jewelry, trinkets, wax-sealed scrolls, and books—"

"Books?"

A nod. "They are...all written in Elvish."

I almost lept off the chair. I wasn't sure how many times I blinked at her before I blurted out, "Mae, we need to talk—"

"There you are, princess." Orin's words cut mine off, drawing both girls' gazes up to him.

Leona beamed. "Did anyone catch those bastards?"

Oh, so she was being herself around him now.

Orin took the remaining chair, angling it toward Leona. "Unfortunately, no," he said, scratching his stubbly chin. "But since the King's Guard arrived yesterday, I'm sure they'll find whoever it is."

I didn't continue to really listen after that, my thoughts focused on the magic items and that Rucas Mordaunt probably had elven books containing viable knowledge and historical writings. That prick hardly allowed me to step foot inside his shop for my weekly orders for the school. There was no way in Torm he would allow me to shop there. He would probably charge me outrageously as well.

But I was sitting here with his daughter. She could probably get them for me, or at least allow me inside to look at them. It would probably be the most rebellious thing she'd ever do. She would finally have an answer to that question.

Except that perhaps trysting me was the most rebellious thing she'd done. I knew she was probably going against his wishes to see me, but did he even know she was here tonight?

And suddenly I was very aware of every place on my body that had touched her. The things I had whispered to her rang loud in my ears. The thoughts I'd had and wanted.

Rucas Mordaunt's daughter. *His* daughter. The man who would do everything to see my family and our livelihood crash and burn. The reminder hit me like a punch to the gut.

I needed more wine.

Mae was watching me from the rim of her goblet, but I could barely look at her. "Are you all right, Varys?" she asked.

I took a breath. "No. But I will be."

I had to be.

"You're almost out of wine, Fawkes," Leo stated. Orin had scooted closer to her, his hand on her knee. "We were just about to grab another round."

She took Mae's goblet from her and looked inside. "You're about

out too. Want to try mine? This is The Nook and Cranny's famous mead."

Mae nodded and took a sip from Leo's pint. Her nose crinkled as she swallowed. "It's a little too strong for me," she said, handing it back.

Leona grinned, and I knew that teasing look. But before I could cut her off, she said to Mae, "Probably for the best. This mead alone could give any man the courage of a thousand kings. Or, you know, hinder nerves enough to make a shy librarian stand up on a table and sing and dance."

The look I sent her should have turned her to ash, but it just seemed to stoke her fiery grin. "I. Did. Not. Dance."

Leona laughed out, clapping her hands. "Damn! You really don't remember a thing." She twisted to Mae, and all the air left my chest. "I was *genuinely* worried for years that this man had no idea how to use his hips—if you know what I mean."

She thrusted her pelvis up in her seat.

Orin and Mae burst out into hysterics. I slid a hand over my heated face with a sigh. "Godsdammit, Leo—"

She went on. "Proved me wrong. And *while* singin'? He had the entire tavern in a fit and several lassies *beggin'* him to take them upstairs."

I yanked my wine off the table and downed what remained.

Mae's laughter rang through the air. "Our barmaid spoke of his singing, but not anything so silly. Varys, when are you going to sing for me?"

I placed the goblet down, daring a glance at her. "I-I...You don't think that's appalling?"

Her violet eyes glimmered as she laughed again. "No, I've definitely decided I cannot leave this world until I see that happen again at least once in my lifetime."

Leona stood quickly. "Next round is on me!"

She tugged Orin from his seat and they disappeared into the crowd before I could protest any further. With my elbows on the table, I rubbed my temples as I sighed in defeat. Mae smiled as she continued eating.

I clasped my hands together after a moment. "When are we going to talk?"

She paused on her next bite of potatoes, her smile fading rapidly. She sat the fork down, avoided my gaze, and gulped.

"I know you said when you're ready," I continued, feeling my cheeks heat when she frowned even deeper. "But there are things you need to understand as well. About the world, about—"

"I didn't think that's why you brought me out," she stated. "You told me you wanted to have fun. To get to know one another."

"You don't consider talking about your situation as getting to know one another?"

Her mouth parted. "I told you not to ask about it."

"I know. It's just…" I took a breath. "You spoke of the things your father—"

"I don't want to talk about him, nor his fucking store, at this dinner," she snapped. My spine steeled. I'd never heard her voice so…cold. When her eyes met mine, they were glossy and wide. "My situation is far more complicated than what you think. More complicated than my power—"

I quickly shushed her gently. "Hey, hey, let's not speak so loud about that."

Her violet gaze narrowed. "So you *don't* want to talk about that?"

"I do. But not here."

She stifled a laugh and sat back in her seat. "Then I guess you need to decide if tonight is for getting to know me or learning about my situation. I cannot permit you both. Not yet."

My insides knotted, and the smoky air became even harder to breathe. "All right," I said with a curt nod. "When you are ready, then."

Her breath hitched, and it was like I could see the invisible walls she'd thrown up crumbling down. Her shoulders slacked, the tightness to her jaw eased.

"I'm sorry," I murmured. "Truly, I meant what I said. You can tell me when you're ready. I promised, and I'm not trying to push you."

She didn't say anything. Only ran her thumb along the rim of her goblet.

I looked around the tavern. No one seemed to be interested in our conversation. "Just know this, Mae." I reached out to take her hand. "I'm only eager to know that part of you because I think you'll find our situations are similar."

She didn't let me touch her, retracting the closest hand to her lap. "No," she muttered. "They're not."

I was sure she would leave right then. Was absolutely positive I had lost her, regretting even daring to bring it up after having such a wonderful evening so far. But she didn't move. She only stared at her plate.

After a moment, she raised her head. "I'm sorry." Her voice trembled. "You don't deserve this—"

Her words were cut off by a fluttering flute, the high-pitched melody akin to an exotic bird's song. Mae perked up at it, her face brightening. She gasped, "I know this song. This is one of my favorites."

I looked over to the stage and watched people move in with excitement. But with this tune, instead of lining up or forming a circle, the people were grouping up in twos.

It was a couples' dance.

"It's silly," she said. "I know the dance by heart. I could dance it in my sleep. All sections, the steps for both people. But I've never danced it with anyone."

And as I beheld her, took in her smile and the sparkle in her eyes, a strong and warm feeling bubbled up from my chest.

I stood and rounded the table before she could even realize what I was doing. Extending my hand, I bowed my head. "Dance with me, beautiful."

Her smile came on so fiercely a laugh escaped her. Taking my hand in both of hers, she led me toward the stage.

I knew the song as well, but not for its dance.

I knew it for the lyrics and the lower line of notes to be sung beneath the main melody, creating a haunting harmony unlike anything I'd ever heard before.

Even now as the music fell over us, as the plucking mandolin melded with the reedy pipes, the hairs on my arms rose. It was both sweet and moody, and each time the chords flipped to the minor tone, I was struck with an emotion I could never truly place. Compositions like this reminded me that our Deity of Fertility and the Arts, Formos, might have created music, but Krayd, their lover, was the God of Chaos. Tales spoke of how they were inspired by Krayd when giving Xaladorians the ability to create art and song, for what good would those things be without a little deviance?

And a deviant was what Mae became the moment she stepped on to the dance floor. Her poised stature turned fluid, graceful steps falling in place with the beat, and her beautiful body seemed to fill with charged energy. When she twirled to me her eyes were wild, the violets and blues seeming brighter than normal. My heart within my chest was nothing less than a pulsing flame as she paused us away from the couples already dancing.

"It's simple," she said, and *gods*, her voice was all ice and smoke. "The steps are repetitive. By the time they start singing, you'll know them well enough."

I wasn't so sure. But as she stepped away from me, I took in the sight of her once more. That dress...I was suddenly weak in the knees and yet filled with more courage than a thousand soldiers.

"Bow," she instructed. "On the start of the next bar."

The beginning of the melody came back around. Four-quarter time. Four beats per bar. I dipped my head on one, and she curtsied as I did, the skirt of her dress fanning over the wood floor momentarily. When we rose, she stepped forward.

"Put your palms to mine," she said. "On the second beat, step in to me. On the third, step out. On the fourth, spin me."

Easy enough. And at least *I* didn't have to spin.

"But when they begin to sing, the movements change." She aligned our palms. "Just follow me."

I did. We stepped into each other, faces inches apart for a mere beat before we moved back.

"Now the spin." She guided my arm up and instructed me to act as if I were drawing a circle around her head while keeping my hand as flat as possible so she could twist around and our fingers wouldn't tangle. The first attempt was rough and she laughed through the off-kilter turn. The second was flawless, but it was her talent alone that had her twirling in a blur of silver and white.

We completed the steps again. It was a good thing the music repeated as it allowed me to practice where my feet landed and how much room to give her as she spun. I knocked into her and went to proclaim an overcomplicated apology, but she just laughed.

Before too long, I was no longer stiff in my movements or looking at my feet. I gained the confidence I needed to hold eye contact with her as we began to truly dance. With every passing moment, with every new bar, her gaze turned ardent, mirroring the heat of my blood.

When she stepped toward me during the next set of variations, she came closer than before. The air left my chest, throwing me off rhythm for a moment when her breasts pressed against me, her wine-scented breath caressing my cheeks. A teasing snicker escaped her and as she stepped back, there was a sultry swing to her hips. The spin she executed left me breathless.

In the next few steps, it seemed our hands had minds of their own. When our palms were supposed to join, hers pressed to my chest instead. Mine found her waist. It wasn't long before I noticed the other couples on the floor looking over, watching how my body connected with hers.

"It's a shame," she murmured in between moves, her voice languid as if she'd melt where she stood, "you can't feel that pulse between us."

"I still don't know what you mean," I said. She spun out, came back in quickly. "But I'm starting to wonder what I'm missing out on."

"It's like…" Our hips aligned when she came in and she stayed against me, missing her next dance steps altogether. "When I touch you, I feel more than your shirt, your skin. I feel *you*. And…" Her gaze snapped into place with mine. "I'm conducted to you."

My nerves ignited. She spun lazily, following the other dancers. When she came back to me, I asked, "Can you elaborate?"

She only smiled, pressed her lips to mine quickly, then spoke against them, "I don't think I can do that here on this dance floor."

Before I could respond—before I could even *process* what she'd said—a drum began to beat loudly. The music swept into a low drone as two singers stepped up in front of the musicians. The man played a lute, the woman rattling a tambourine.

Mae grinned. "This is my favorite part."

It was mine, too.

The singers began:

> *Come…*
> *Come…*
> *Into the briar*
> *Find dark and thirst*
> *And lover's fire*

There it was. That strange, eerie harmony that practically beckoned me to hum along.

Mae looked up to me, an almost wicked smile on her lips as she said, "Follow my lead."

> *Come…*
> *Come…*
> *Sweet lover of mine*
> *We'll dance and sing*
> *In the full moon's light*

I nodded as she turned and pressed her back against me. On the top of the bar, she swayed side to side, then stepped to her right and clapped. "You do the same, but step to the left."

"The swaying too?"

She laughed. "That depends if you want to show off all those hip movements Leona said you have."

My throat dried. "I think I'll leave that to you."

Her head lolled back against me as she chuckled. A fiddle began to play the original melody, and Mae began to move back and forth. I couldn't help but hold my breath as her hips brushed lightly against me. My face was on fire when she and I stepped in our appropriate direction and clapped. Then she was against me once more.

The music picked up, the drums building in volume until they were louder than the other instruments and seemed to fall in pace with my pulse. Every boom resounded in my chest, my stomach, the vibrations skittering over my skin.

Come...
Come...
Whisper and sigh
I'll promise my heart
If you'll be my bride

She was smiling, laughing with joy. That's all I had wanted to bring her tonight.

Her undulation became slower, more deliberate. An evident heat had formed between us, dousing momentarily whenever we stepped away to clap. The brushing of her body against me was torturous.

The next time I found her in front of me, I slid my hands to those swaying hips. Her breath hitched, but she didn't stop. She pressed herself into me and the movement was no longer soft, but a ruthless roll that had everything low begging and heavy with need.

And she...gods, she was wanting it.

The thought alone forced a curse to break free from somewhere deep down as she moved against me. She looked over her shoulder with a grimace. "Am I...making you uncomfortable?"

I shook my head embarrassingly fast. "Uncomfortable is not the right word."

Her cheeks were blushed, the aubergine undertones of her skin stark against the alabaster. "You cursed. I thought maybe I'd done something to frustrate you."

I pulled her against me a bit more, pressing a kiss to her neck, wishing the choker of her cape wasn't in the way. She sucked in a thin breath. "I'm only frustrated we aren't the only people on this dance floor."

She tilted her head back as she moved to the beat, looking up at me with those gorgeous amethyst irises. With her bottom lip between her teeth, her hips became an intentional grind.

"Fuck," I groaned softly.

Her laugh was breathy. I couldn't focus past the feeling for a moment.

The next two verses were coming around. As she continued her teasing rolls, I slipped my arm around her ribs, holding her tight against me. Sighing, she brought her arms up, wrapped them around my neck and entangled her fingers in my hair. We'd disregarded all of the dance moves, everyone around us. All, except each other and the music.

I gulped down any apprehension, rested my cheek beside her ear, and with the bards, began to sing to her:

Come...
Come...
Into my hold...
Entranced by my hands
Where they ease and stroke...

She took a breath.

Come...

Come…
Into the grove
Love me forever
And never grow old

The music went on, but she turned to me with an awestruck look. "Your voice…"

I shrugged. "It's not a talent I share with many."

"I don't understand why." She shook her head. "It's beautiful."

"Some talents are for the heart. I have another that is for the eye."

"What is that?"

Could I tell her? I felt the confession on the tip of my tongue, that I was a writer of fantasy stories, epic quests, and romances. That writing was my passion, and what I truly felt I was supposed to do. I wanted her to know every part of me. If anyone was going to find out I was an author, that *The Dragonhart Series* on the shelves were actually mine, I wanted it to be her. Before my father, even Leona.

But revealing such a secret when she was still keeping so much from me…

I couldn't tell her. Not yet.

"Dancing, obviously," I said with a wink.

She chuckled, turning away and pulling my arms tighter around her. "You're not too bad. Practice with me a few times and…"

Mae stilled in my arms. I went to ask what was wrong.

Then I saw him.

Vamir, staring straight at us from across the dance floor, a smirk on his face. He pushed off the wall he was leaning against, and the bastard began to walk our way. He crossed the dance floor, avoiding the other dancers perfectly, and stopped before us.

"See something you like?" The words snapped out of me hard, and loud enough to be heard over the music.

Vamir pressed his hand to his black ruffled shirt and raised his voice. "You insinuate too much, good sir. I was told to let you know that Orin and your friend have gone upstairs."

I couldn't help the sinking feeling in my gut. *Leona.*

"They would have told you themselves, but then saw that you two were…" There was a slight tilt to his head. "Busy. Your friend paid for another round of drinks for you two, and said to tell you both to have a good night."

I held back the scowl wanting to burn through. "Thanks for letting us know."

He turned on his heeled boots, gave an elegant wave of his garish ruby-ringed fingers, and then went right back to that wall.

Mae released a breath as if she'd been holding it. "That was weird."

"He's weird," I grumbled. "How do you know him anyway?"

"I don't." She swallowed. "Not really."

I stifled a scoff. "By the way he greeted you when you first walked in, I assumed you two knew each other pretty well."

"I think he's just overly friendly."

Indeed.

I took her hand and dipped to her ear. "Do you want to continue dancing?"

She nodded, perking back up. "We're almost to the part where we dance freely."

Freely. I chuckled. "Lead the way, gorgeous."

She glanced over to where I knew to find Vamir before pulling me deeper into the dance floor, only stopping when she was in front of the stage. Her eyes filled with determination. "You sang for me. Can I dance for you?"

I grinned. "How could I say no?"

The music suddenly dropped out, leaving only the drums to continue in their pounding. The crowd began to clap to the beat, but Mae only stepped away from me, curling her hands into the silver skirt of her dress.

She came alive.

Spun like a living cyclone around me, a smile on her lips, a laugh in her eyes. She dipped and jumped, twirling so fast I couldn't keep up with her. One moment she was beside me, the next behind, trailing a finger along my shoulders then down my arm. She whirled away before I could reach out to her.

It wasn't long before the crowd around us began to take notice, began to cheer and holler as she spun, spun, spun. With the fiddle leading back in with a quick sequence of notes, all musicians began to play once more. But no one continued to dance.

They were too focused on her.

She came around, skirt billowing around her form, arms flinging out in graceful motions as if she was made of air. Once again, she twirled around me, hands brushing over my arms in a playful manner, her grin beautiful and gleaming.

Her eyes dancing with storm.

My mouth parted as I took in the sight. She was oblivious to the lightning arching in her gaze. Panic began to swell in my chest. What if the entire tavern was seeing what I did?

But she blinked and the bolts were gone, her smile dwindling as she slowed to a stop just as the song ended.

The crowd cheered and applauded as the bards took their bow and announced a break. Mae was still standing where she'd stopped, and I realized as she pinched the bridge of her nose that something was wrong.

I took her shoulders. "Mae?"

"I'm all right." She looked up to me. Her pupils were enlarged. "Just a bit dizzy I guess. I've not danced since my pain attacks began."

I nodded. "Let's grab a nook. That way we can talk and I can tend to you if you start to feel worse."

"A...nook?"

I pointed to the row of small rooms along the west side of the tavern. Her eyes went wide. "They're sort of the namesake for this place. They're rooms for more private conversations."

She stared at the nooks for a moment longer before nodding. Taking her hand, I led her toward the first available room, drawing the curtains back and guiding her inside. This nook had a plush, emerald green settee and a low table sitting before it. Scented candles were lit on a silver plate on the table, filling the room with the fragrance of musky amber and sweet vanilla.

Mae sat down on the settee, pushing her tousled curls off her shoulders. She wiped the beads of sweat off her forehead that had formed whilst dancing.

"Feeling better?" I asked.

"Trying to." She smiled, but it seemed forced.

I guided her down so she could lay her head back on the armrest of the settee. She unpinned the tight choker of the cape and placed it on the table before us, exposing her neck and shoulders. I smiled at the flush of her skin.

But she had closed her eyes, brows pinched in discomfort. I pressed a light kiss to her forehead, "Mae, do we need to get you home?"

Her eyes popped open. *"No."*

I swallowed. I just hoped she wasn't on the verge of having one of her flares.

Breathing out slowly, she said, "Maybe we could get that next round of drinks?"

I chuckled. "Wouldn't want Leo's money to go to waste." With an uneasy nod, I pressed a soft kiss to her cool lips, then whispered, "You relax. I'll be right back."

CHAPTER 29

Varys

Leaving Mae in the nook alone made my nerves roil. I found myself looking around for Vamir, only being unable to find him once again. And for whatever reason, the tavern seemed to be even more packed now. The line was long, tight, and just...full of people. I shoved my hands in my pockets so I wouldn't bite my nails.

I made eye contact with Adlin and she quickly rushed over. "Varys, what ya need?"

"Leona apparently bought me and my tryst another round."

She grinned. "Oh, yes. She also told me that if you needed to speed this line up, you'd pay me a silver."

I sent her a narrowed look. "No, she didn't."

Adlin raised her brows and crossed her arms, tossing her body weight to one side. "I guess you're staying put then."

I clicked my tongue. "You know what? I'll give you *two* silver if you bring our dessert straight to our nook. Ask Melissa what our order is."

Adlin's mouth parted, surprise lighting up her big brown eyes. "*Varys*," she drew out my name as if I'd done something unspeakable. "You? In a *nook?*"

I rolled my eyes to stifle the instant abashment, but my cheeks began to burn anyway. "It's not like that. So two silver?"

I reached into my purse and pulled out the coin. She snatched them from me with a giggle. "I'll have you know, between you and Leona, I make damn good money."

"The pleasure is mine."

"Hope it will be." She shot a glance toward the nooks. "Wait for your drinks. I'll be back!"

I stepped out of line and found a spot out of the way to stand. There was an obvious moonshadow dealing happening at the table next to me, and a couple practically fornicating against the wall to my left. I paid no mind to either. Kept my eyes forward, arms crossed, feet ready to move. Lingering in a corner for too long or catching the eye of someone looking for a fight was how one could find themselves in trouble.

I could see the nook from where I stood. Thinking over what had transpired tonight so far, I began to grow impatient. I could hardly wait for Mae's lips to be on mine again. Adlin's response to us acquiring a nook hadn't been outlandish. Everyone knew what sometimes happened behind those red curtains.

Everyone also knew the tavern master had been known to kick out couples for doing so if they refused to get a room.

Heat began to creep up my neck. That hadn't been my intention. I had merely wanted to get Mae somewhere comfortable so we could talk and she could rest. I wondered if she thought I wanted something else.

Which, truly, I did. But only if *she* did. I would buy us a room if needed.

I caught a glimpse of Adlin's black braid before she disappeared into the kitchen. I sighed, hoping she hadn't forgotten.

Another moment passed. As I scanned the tavern, it occurred to me that I hadn't seen too many people here tonight I knew lived in Elros. Most were out-of-town guests. I thought to the *Vyl'kriev* brothers I'd talked to earlier and began to seek out the quartet of yellow and red hair—

My magic suddenly tugged and I could only take a breath before someone whispered from behind, "May your days be dark…"

Instinct seized me, hand instantly grasping the grip of my dagger, body whipping around.

There was no one there.

But there was a churning whisper creeping along the wall. I blinked rapidly when it seemed like my vision was blurring, spine wanting to lock up as I watched the tables, chairs and the people sitting in them fade from my focus. Something was trying to charm me. "*Vid Medaes.*"

Before my eyes, my world transformed into a veil of color. The arcane veins of twisted through the air like iridescent vines. But to my surprise, there wasn't any source of magic radiating from whatever was attacking me. I didn't know what that meant. I didn't know how to fight it, if I needed to fight it at all.

I got my answer when the veins shrank back, making way for something moving toward me. Terror threatened to sweep in, but my training took the lead. I threw up my wards, and whatever the thing was hit them hard. The whispers moaned and hissed as if my attacker was in pain. I rushed forward, watching the veins and how they reeled away like they didn't want to touch this thing. Even the tendrils that flowed through me seemed to tighten as I managed to back it up against the wall. The sounds fell silent, the veins falling back into the space it created—

They recoiled from around me, behind me, the strands swirling through my body attempting to go with it. I lost a breath when I felt the pull of my magic give way, *Vid Medaes* blinking in and out like it was...like it was failing.

The veins were failing.

But I was a war sage. I ripped my dagger from its sheath, spinning and slashing out with a curse. The blade connected with something, the noise reminding me of a low bell suddenly muted. I'd injured it for sure.

Before I could take a second swing, it moved away from me toward the crowd that I could see again, the whispers melding with the sound of the tavern revelry.

I gasped for air and clutched my chest as my heart thumped heavily. The veins crawled back around me as if it were a timid, scared creature apologizing for its abandonment. I canceled *Vid*

Medaes and my wards as I watched my attacker's illusion fade, the tables and chairs around me coming back into view. I slumped against the wall.

"'Ey, get lawst, ya damn busy bawdy..." Someone growled my way. I hadn't noticed the man on the wall with his woman. He was so drunk, he could hardly look at me straight. She didn't seem too interested in me. She'd dropped to her knees and was busy untying his trousers.

"Apologies," I muttered and turned away from them entirely. I sheathed my dagger as I found another spot to stand.

My limbs shook. It didn't take too long to realize there wasn't a single person that seemed to have noticed my fight with the invisible, moving noise.

I couldn't deny how damn crazy that made me sound.

"Hello again."

I jolted at the voice that seemed to come from nowhere as a man walked up to me—one of the *Vyl'kriev* brothers. The redheaded one I remembered to be named Ramos.

I stared at him for a long moment, still trying to catch my breath. Before I could gather my words, he said, "Sorry to bother you, but I wanted to inquire about your table again."

Annoyance crowded out the displaced feeling. "What about it?"

His smile was tense. "It seems you and your guest are no longer in need of the spot, and my brothers and I were wondering if we could maybe grab it now. However, the barmaid insists that you two will return and is not wavering."

"She most likely won't." I looked over to see Melissa once again bickering with the group of brothers. That poor woman. "Just tell her Varys and his guest have moved to another location and that you are free to have the table if you wish."

Ramos bowed his head. "Thank you, good sir." He paused, extending a ringed hand. "Varys, is it?"

I let out a long-suffering breath. I'd barely noticed I'd given the man my name. "Yes."

"Well, Varys. Thank you again." I nodded, but didn't shake his hand. He adjusted his tunic and cleared his throat. "Have a good night."

His movements were hesitant as he turned, like he had more to say. My speculation came true as he said, "And be careful, all right?"

Taken aback, I couldn't find the words to respond. He began to walk away again, then stopped and twisted back to me. I wondered if he was inebriated.

"Is there something else you'd wish to say?" I asked.

His fingers flexed at his sides for a moment, eyes darting left to right. Then he took a step toward me and murmured, "I can hear them too."

My skin instantly broke out in goosebumps as I took a step back. "*What?*"

"The whispers." He gestured for me to walk off to the side with him. "Do you have time to talk?"

Did I have time? How long had I been fighting that thing? Adlin hadn't returned. The bards were still on break. Mae was waiting on me, but this was something I needed to figure out. "I'm waiting on my drinks." I was surprised how shaky my voice was. "So I have until then."

Ramos nodded and led me over to an empty table in a secluded corner. He took a seat, but I chose to remain standing. I wasn't sure I could sit still.

"I saw you fighting with the enemy," Ramos stated.

I tried to take a deep, steady breath, but the air filled my lungs like stones. *Enemy.* It wasn't just a feeling. It wasn't me overthinking.

"Don't worry, nobody else saw you," he told me. "They place an illusion around their victim."

I couldn't do much but stare at him, mind racing with too many questions.

"However, I've had a spell in effect all night that allows me to see through the illusion," he went on. "I still can't see what or who the attacker is, but I'm at least able to keep an eye out for fellow *Vyl'kriev* who have fallen prey to their trap. They lure you away from the majority of the public, and before you know it you're either dead or captured."

When I took my next breath, nausea swelled. "W-Who in Torm are *they?*" I asked as I glanced around the tavern. "You seem to know an awful lot about this."

His ruby red eyes fell to the table, a solemn expression wrinkling his pierced eyebrows. "My brothers and I hail from Shade's Crescent. There are *Vyl'kriev*—"

"Stop using that word," I snapped. I finally took a seat and leaned in close. "I don't know why you would dare to speak our language when there are many people, and apparently enemies, about."

He shifted in his chair. "You're right. I don't necessarily mean to. I've found that sometimes speaking *Vylarys*—I mean, Elvish, is easier for some reason."

I hadn't thought of it that way, but I hadn't been around anyone who used the language in the two years since I'd reemerged. It was possible that all of his brothers now spoke Elvish between each other. "Let's just try to stick to Common. If we were somewhere with less ears, it wouldn't be an issue."

He nodded in agreement. For a moment, he remained silent with crossed arms, leaned back in his chair. "Forgive me, I'm trying to decide where to start. I guess there's no simple way to ask though." His throat bobbed. "You told me earlier that you were the only Elven-blooded here in Elros. That there were others, but they'd gone."

I nodded.

"Did they truly leave, or did they go missing?"

My stomach hollowed out. "They left. I'm sure of it."

"I only ask because that hasn't been the case in most towns on this side of Xalador. Especially in Shade's Crescent." Tension creased around his mouth. "Elven-blooded have been dropping like flies. Either found dead in the streets, or have disappeared."

My pulse skittered. "How long has this been happening?"

"In Shade's Crescent, about two quarters."

"Two quarters?" I questioned. "Is that why the King's Guard came so suddenly? And the taxes have raised? Why has Elros heard nothing about this?"

"I'm surprised the news hasn't made its way here. The Duke sent out word when it started becoming an issue."

I huffed. "Actually, Elros has always received news late. We're secluded, cradled in hills and thick forest. I've always worried if

King Elyon and the orc chief went to war, we'd be the last to know. But no news for half a season is alarming. It's dangerous, especially for people like us."

Ramos scratched his chin. "There's always the possibility the messenger was lost." He braced his elbows on the table and leaned in, lowering his voice. "I would assume the last thing our enemy wants is for an entire town to learn that something dangerous is coming. If they knew word was on the way, they would have intervened."

I swallowed. He had a damn good point. "And now they're here. But why now? They've had plenty of time."

"They're after magic users of course. There's been a rise of mages."

I tilted my head. "But The ReEmergence happened two years ago. Mages have had their magic all this time. Have we all truly just been keeping our magic a secret?"

Ramos shook his head. "I'm afraid I don't understand. We didn't have magic two years ago."

My blood thinned. "Wait. When did you reemerge?"

"A season ago."

I thought I might fall out of my chair. That was something I hadn't thought of—that the reason the kingdom hadn't heard any news about hundreds of thousands of *Vyl'kriev* was because they all hadn't reemerged yet.

"You seem surprised by that," Ramos said as he watched me.

"I am. I thought I received my magic upon The ReEmergence two years ago."

What if magic had been reemerged for longer?

His mouth parted. "And how did you know?"

I wasn't sure how much information I could trust him with. Telling him what stream of mage I was felt as if I were showing my hand. "Had a dream."

"Me too." Chuckling, he looked up as if he was recalling a memory. "Woke up from a nightmare screaming the command word for a fire spell and had accidentally set my room aflame."

My eyes widened. He was a sorcerer then.

"My brother woke up knowing a water spell and put the fire out.

Ruined my godsdamn personal library, but thankfully nothing else," he told me. "We were pretty sure my other brothers had magic, but they showed no signs."

"Do they now?"

"Yes. Turns out my one brother is a wizard, the other a druid. They were both missing the necessities they needed to cast."

I felt like another puzzle had clicked into place. There were probably many wizards who were unable to cast spells because they didn't know how to create their spellbooks. Druids had to use certain components to cast. "How did you all determine your stream after you reemerged?"

Ramos shifted in his seat. "We were told."

"By who?"

Ramos let out a long breath. "My brothers will be livid for telling you this. But, about three weeks after I discovered my magic, a stranger came to Shade's Crescent. He began to seek out Elven-blooded and gather us up in secret. Obviously, we were leery at first, but then a friend came back from one of the meetings with full control of his magic, so we went to the next. The stranger told us that he came to deliver news, that The ReEmergence of Magic has commenced. Then, he taught us how to cast, told us what stream we were as individuals. He even helped my si—" He cleared his throat. "*Sibling* create his spellbook. Showed my other brother what components were useful for his druidcraft. In one evening, he had washed away all apprehensions and made us truly feel like we were born to be mages. And then..." He sighed. "And then weeks later, the same Elven-blooded individuals who had attended those gatherings were found dead, or had gone missing. We fled Shade's Crescent because we were afraid we'd be next."

"Who was this man?" I asked.

Ramos pressed his lips together. "He is not a man. He is not *human*."

His statement left me perplexed. Because of course this person could be halfling, a dwarf, or even possibly an orc. But there was a serious, almost bewildered look upon his face as he muttered, "He's an elf. A *true* elf. His name is Falryn."

Great gods.

Falryn.

Falryn started with *F*.

I had wondered if the person who wrote the letter in my spell-book was an elf. It was almost too good to be true, but upon hearing this elf's name, it just felt like confirmation.

"I'd never seen anything like him," Ramos went on, eyes glossy as if he were still in awe. "When he dispelled the disguise cloaking his true form, we felt as if we had found ourselves in the presence of a god. He was tall, lithe, beautiful...intimidating. His hair was as emerald green as the depths of the seas, his eyes the same shade and yet marbled with gold. And he—he had the ears." His voice strained. "Pointed, just like you hear in all of the tales."

"Where is he now?" I asked urgently. "Does he remain in Shade's Crescent?"

He shook his head with a grave expression. "When the enemy began to murder and take Elven-blooded, Falryn fled."

I jerked my chin back. "That seems cowardice for an elf. If he's a true elf, he no doubt has magic and has had hundreds of years to perfect his craft."

Ramos shrugged. "Our enemy wants him dead more than anything. It is possible that his identity was discovered and he felt it best."

That still didn't sit right with me.

"And you, for sure, don't know who our enemies are?" I pressed. "What they look like?"

"No," he said with a defeated sigh. "I would tell you if I did. They are masters of illusion. What you faced tonight is just one of their tricks."

I raked my hands through my hair. A frustration-induced headache was building in my temples. "Has anyone decided to take action? Stand against them? I've had my magic for two years and have been preparing for the day I might have to fight for my life."

He sat back in his seat, a gleam in his red eyes. "I'm glad you asked. My brothers and I have decided to initiate a resistance and we're looking for numbers. We plan on gathering as many as we can after the Fest of Change and leaving for Mirefield."

The hairs on my arms rose. Maybe I had read too much history, maybe I had written about too many rebel groups and the like. But this sounded like the beginning of something much larger than just taking down a group of killers. Fights often came with blood and horrific grudges that split people apart, and before long, civil affairs became civil wars.

"Why Mirefield?" I asked.

"The place is practically the capital of crime and nobody knows why."

"Well, yes. So why take a group of green mages somewhere so dangerous? Everyone knows that you only dare to venture into Mirefield if you're desperate for some quick gold, or have something you can't sell in the normal market scene."

He smirked. "Aye. But we have a contact. Did you hear about the White Horse incident?"

I nodded. For many years, a band of traffickers called the Crimson Curtain had plagued Mirefield, and it wasn't until about four years ago Baron Kenrad learned why. The owner of The White Horse, a tavern similar to The Nook and Cranny but much larger, had been forced by the Crimson Curtain leader to house their band. The tavern master had been afraid their family would be killed if they refused.

But someone found the Crimson Curtain's hiding spot before Kenrad. Every single member was found in one of the rooms of The White Horse, hanging from the ceiling by their arms and split open. The leader, however, was found hung by his own entrails.

"Our contact is the vigilante who took out the Crimson Curtain," Ramos explained. "He's on the prowl once again. This time, we have a common enemy. Evidently, he reemerged as well. Mirefield residents have whispered about his new powers, have seen him spew fire. They've nicknamed him The Dragon."

My skin tingled with intrigue as I sat forward, wondering if this vigilante was actually a dragon in its human form. Perhaps he hadn't been able to use his abilities because of magic's dormancy. "So, you plan to meet with The Dragon and then what?"

"Find this enemy and put an end to their attacks."

I grimaced. That seemed much too simple. "You said you're planning to lead a group of Elven-blooded here in Elros to Mirefield. That means"—I looked around the tavern—"you've spoken to some of the Elven-blooded here? They deserve to know something might be hunting them and given the chance to fight back."

He gave a slow nod, adjusting the ring on his finger. "We've tried to inform them. Unfortunately, our warnings have fallen on deaf ears. They don't believe us."

More Elven-blooded who hadn't reemerged. I sighed. "I wish I could say I'm surprised. But unless they've seen their magic for themselves, it's hard to believe something like that. And by the time they reemerge, they will need practice before joining an initiative like yours. Meanwhile, our enemy knows how to use their magic well."

"That seems to be the case." He looked away, toward where I knew his brothers still stood trying to entice Melissa to give up the table. "There is a reason why we want that table so badly. My brothers and I hoped we would be safe this far north. But yesterday, we began to hear the whispers. We are sleeping with one eye open, avoiding back roads, and staying in public places. The table was the perfect place for us to stay out of trouble." He let out a huff. "When we saw you, a fellow Elven-blooded, were the occupier, we wondered if you wanted it for the same reason."

I shook my head. "No. If I'd known about this, we probably wouldn't have even come out tonight." I stood when I saw Adlin rushing my way. "I think I must go. Please, take the table. Come tomorrow, I will find your tent and we can perhaps discuss further plans."

He nodded and extended his hand. I shook it this time. "Stay safe, brother. Keep your eyes open and wards readied. We will speak again soon."

I bowed my head and Ramos rushed over to the table. I snickered as Melissa threw her hands up in frustration. She jabbed a finger toward me and marched off. I'd definitely need to tip her extra next time.

The four brothers sat down at the table, and my chest tightened as I watched them take a collective breath. A sign that they finally felt safe.

CHAPTER 30

Mae

I gripped the cushions of the settee again as pain swelled through me, hot and unyielding. My breath came in short pants, sweat pooling between the crevices of my breasts and dripping down my stomach, leaving the silver satin of my dress with dark, damp spots. I bit my lip hard so I wouldn't scream, and the only thing I could focus on was how thankful I was that this flare didn't come with a pain akin to the one I'd had in the Wynharts' kitchen.

I stared up at the ceiling of the nook, trying to focus on the light of the candles and the calming smell they gave off. If I could just relax enough to ignore it, maybe the flare would dissipate more quickly. Maybe it would be over before Varys returned, and I could just pretend it didn't happen. I wasn't even sure how long he had been gone.

My head seemed to empty suddenly. I couldn't form a single thought, couldn't speak or mutter a cry. I was nothing but a shell as I stared at the ceiling, the golden glow…

Darkness shrouded my vision. But there in between the swirls of black, I could see the outline of…a tree. It was a tall, twisting tree with jagged branches.

My tree. The one I had fallen from.

I wasn't sure if this was a dream, if I'd even fallen asleep. I could still feel the pain, the heat rushing through every part of me. Heat that was so different from the kind I'd felt with him. *Varys.* Tonight had been everything I'd ever wanted, and it wasn't over.

Or, was it?

Was this flare going to end my wonderful night?

Resilience robbed the pain of its sting, washing in the burn of anger. I tried to imagine climbing my tree as if I could leave all of my problems beneath me if I could get high enough.

Light flashed overhead as I climbed. I just wanted to see the sky —the storm brewing a towering anvil of dark purple and gray clouds. At the top, the space below me expanded. A glittering pool of water spread out in every direction. Rain misted down upon my face and I breathed in its fresh scent. I was in the middle of it all. As if the tree was my throne, the clouds my crown in this beautiful space where I remained. Lived.

More than that. This place was...it was mine. It was mine to have, to rule.

I willed lightning to plunge down from the sky, striking the sand with a crash that reverberated in my very bones. Excitement swelled, pleasure bloomed, joy filled my body with a feathery sensation. I could fly here if I wanted—

Crystals rose from where the jolt met its mark, their jagged points rising up out of the ground. My pulse skipped, cold dread replacing the happiness entirely.

Another bolt of lightning struck. More crystals rose.

I didn't feel like I had control over this place anymore, the clouds darkening overhead, the winds rising and swirling, out of control, out of control—

Saeör ít ölsta xera...

The crystals shattered.

Black to violet to white, my blurred vision rushed through the colors until I was once again watching the wood ceiling, the glowing candlelight, and smelling the sweet musk of bergamot.

A warm hand was in mine. I held it limply, but the moment I realized it was his, I squeezed. His breath was the first sound I heard.

Then his beautiful face appeared above me. "Are you back with me?" Varys asked with a tender, hoarse voice.

It was another beat before I could nod. I was surprised by the tears that streamed down my face as I blinked. He wiped them away before they could hit the cushions beneath me.

"How long?" I asked.

He sighed and settled back against the settee, pushing up his sleeves to his elbows. It was then I realized my legs were over his lap. "Not sure to be honest. I was gone longer than anticipated." He stared at the red curtains concealing us from the rest of the tavern. "Asked for our next round of drinks but I had to wait for them. When Adlin—one of the barmaids—finally returned, she said they had run out of wine up front, so it took her a while to retrieve some from the back. I should've just come back here." His gaze was pensive, and I watched him gulp twice before he continued, "I'm so sorry. I shouldn't have left you."

I shook my head. "It's not like you knew I'd have a flare come on."

"You weren't feeling well after dancing. I shouldn't have left you," he said again with a huff. "I promise, I'll stay beside you the rest of the night. We don't have to leave this nook if you don't want to. I even ordered dessert to be sent here directly."

I rose to my elbows with a smile. I had completely forgotten about dessert. "That sounds wonderful to me."

After he helped me sit up all the way, he reached forward and grabbed the goblet of fresh wine off the table before us, handing it to me. The sweet berry flavor was refreshing on my dry tongue.

"Do you usually become unresponsive in your flares?" he asked after a drink for himself. "You weren't like that in the kitchen earlier today."

"Not all the time. But those spells seem to be coming on more frequently." My legs were still over his lap. I thought about moving them until he began to brush gentle strokes around my knee. "Most of the time I can't recall if I've said anything, or where my head goes. If I'm moved from one location to the next, I have no memory of how I got there."

His scarred brow lifted. "*Most* of the time? So where did your head go today?"

My stomach tightened. I couldn't deny how impressed I was that he was able to see right through my words, how I couldn't hide much from him. Since I wasn't entirely sure how to explain it even to myself, I didn't know what to tell him.

But I was so tired of lying.

"I dreamed," I told him. "I think."

He opened his mouth as if to press into the subject, but took another drink of wine. "Well, I'm glad you're all right. When I came back and found you staring up at the ceiling and not moving, I...well, I thought the worst. It wasn't until I saw you breathing I calmed down and decided to just wait."

"You thought I was...dead?"

He swallowed. "I did."

Oh my gods.

My insides whirled with icy unquiet as a thought crossed my mind. What if I didn't come out of my unconscious state next time? What if I just slipped into that dream and never returned? I couldn't help but wonder if my flares were strengthening because I was dying.

The distant look on Varys's face made my chest tighten. I tried to not let myself think about his reaction when he saw me lying there. How scared he had probably been.

I bit my lip and scooched closer, looping my arms around his torso. "I'm sorry I scared you, Varys."

He sighed. "You have no reason to apologize. I only want to keep you safe and well."

I rested my forehead against his cheek. "I'm safe with you, Varys."

His tense shoulders relaxed and he pulled me closer. "And you always will be."

The warmth between us was laced with both desire and comfort. For many moments, we just held each other. The longer I stayed, the more I didn't want to leave. I was both scared and excited of where my head went when I thought of what would happen after tonight. Couldn't help to hope that I could just continue this, that this tryst wasn't temporary, that I would be here, safe in his arms forever if he would allow it.

But those thoughts spoke of more than a physical attraction, more than the connection.

I was thoroughly aware of how quickly I was falling for him.

My pulse quickened at the thought, sped up until it was pounding. And it made other areas of my body heat up.

When his lips found mine, all I knew was the want and great need to be his. My breaths came in harsh gasps as I tasted his tongue. No longer would I allow myself to focus on the pain of my sore, tense muscles. I just wanted him, around me, on me, inside of me—

Varys pulled away with a chuckle, licking his swollen lips before he pressed them to my neck. "I'm happy to know you enjoy my touch so much," he murmured against my skin.

I hummed in agreement as his mouth trailed down to my collarbone, crossing to the other side with a pull of his bottom lip.

"Oh my gods," I sighed, eyes rolling back. He only laughed breathlessly and continued his way back up to my cheek.

When we made eye contact, the connection yanked through me. Sparks danced beneath my skin, raising the hairs on my arms so suddenly a shiver seized me. He smiled with affection written in his features, placing a warm hand to my face and brushing his thumb along my cheekbone. He didn't say anything, he just seemed to take me in.

"What is it?" I finally asked.

He shook his head as if he was unsure of what to say. "I just...love looking at you."

My chest bloomed with warmth. "What do you mean?"

"You're beautiful, but so much more than that." He pushed a stray white curl off my face, then took one of my front braids into his hand. "You're a kaleidoscope of history, Mae."

That was a compliment I had *never* received, and for some reason, it felt like the most important one I would ever hear.

"Since the war," he continued. "Since we lost so much knowledge of the elven race, we've only known Elven-blooded to have bright-colored hair and eyes. Some of us have dark brown skin, others copper, or light tan like mine, but we always have those other features as well that sets us apart from others. And then there's this mystery of the people who look like you. I find the term *Pallid Cursed*—"

"A ridiculous name that shouldn't hold an ounce of merit," I declared with a roll of my eyes. "I just recently learned that it came from old religious fables probably stemmed from prejudices within the Churches of Eana. It's possible Mr. Welch told the town I was Pallid Cursed when I was born because *he* is a member of that church. He knows nothing but their version of the truth, which, as we both know, is typical for people like him."

His mouth was agape by the time I was finished. He blinked. "Mae..."

"What?"

He took my hand. "You just taught me something I didn't know."

I barked out a laugh. "Oh my gods."

He kissed my knuckles. "You're just further proving my point that you are a rarity. Because there is still the mystery of which elven bloodline you, and the others like you, derive from. Until I read those findings I spoke to you about at the stream, I was unaware of another bloodline."

I tilted my head. "Not all Elven-blooded people come from the same family's line that started over a thousand years ago, right?"

His brows rose. "Well, of course there were many families. But we are all kin to the original line—the elves that the gods created upon Xalador's inception. So, technically, yes. All Elven-blooded come from that same line."

"And mine...doesn't?"

He shrugged. "I don't have that answer. And yet, there is no denying your violet eyes. They are definitely elven, features of the god-made, and the reason you have..."

He paused. I knew what he was about to say. "The reason I have powers."

He nodded, apprehension in his wide eyes. My stomach turned over, but before I could ask him not to speak anymore of it, he went on, "All I'm saying is when I look at you, I see a thousand years of unearthed knowledge, mysteries I personally want to solve. And I'm just as excited to discover those things as I am about our...relationship?"

I beamed, heart aflutter. "Are you asking me for more nights like these?"

He cleared his throat and reached for his wine. "If you wish it." He took a drink.

Of course I did. I just didn't know how I would avoid Rucas's wrath in the process. Even after everything tonight, I hated the damn hesitation I still had. The fear that threatened to have me running. It would be so simple to just explain everything to Varys. I could get everything I wanted if I could just not be so scared.

I took a breath. "And what if...this is just temporary?"

His smile was simple, and the small shake of his head was even easier. "It is what *we* make it. I don't want it to be temporary, and it doesn't sound like you do either."

I gulped. "You want to be with me, even knowing who my father is?"

He sighed and sat his goblet down. "I don't care who your father is, but I do know that he is most likely unaware of this, or absolutely against it."

My insides hollowed out and I closed my eyes. "Both."

"And yet, you're still here."

A quivering in my bones threatened to seize my words. "I'm here because I want to be more than anything." I lifted my gaze to his. "I want to be with you. I always have."

His mouth parted. "You have?"

I nodded. "I just couldn't... My feelings for anyone outside of the suitor chosen for me was out of the question."

He swallowed. "And here I thought I'd never get you. So I..." He started to trail off. "I trysted others."

My heart sank. I knew he had trysted Elise Carrington for a while. However I wasn't sure how they'd gone their separate ways before she ruined another man's marriage.

Varys chuckled slightly. "I've always wanted you, Mae. I just couldn't reach you. I wish things had been different."

My chest swelled. "Me too. I was so busy focusing on how in

Xalador I was going to avoid marrying that pig…I couldn't reach back. That's why I need to know that what we have isn't something that is just a dream for one night."

He opened his mouth to answer but was cut off by a woman's voice calling his name.

"Dessert time," he said with a smile as he rose and pulled back the red curtain. A plate was handed to him and he sat it on the table. The tart before me was piled high with berries and sprinkled with powdered sugar, and there was only one fork.

It was silly, but I blushed when he handed me the fork first. Sharing dessert really was a whole different kind of intimacy I was sure only I understood.

"Let me ask you a question," Varys said as he sat down beside me once more. "And it's okay if you don't have a perfectly thought out answer."

I nodded as I cut into the tart. My lips wanted to pucker when I tasted the filling. It was too sour, which meant the raspberries were underripe, so the tart needed more sugar. But the crust was thick and the buttery flavor overwhelmed the tanginess of the fruit.

I handed him the fork and he cut off a slice for himself. "What kind of life do you want, Mae?"

I froze. No one had ever asked me that question. No one had ever wished to hear what my dreams of the future were.

I had to take a moment and swallow the lump wanting to form as I thought over all of my dreams and desires. I had only ever thought of them negatively, never once had believed I would see them come true.

"I want my own bakery."

Varys grinned at that as he took a bite. His nose crinkled as he swallowed. "I bet your tarts are better than this."

I snickered and continued, "I want to wake up before sunrise, prepare all of my dough for the day, bake everything and open by breakfast. I want to be so popular, I sell out right around lunchtime and spend the rest of the day shopping for dinner before heading down to the local tavern for a drink and dancing. On the days I'd choose not to work, I would enjoy a swim at the beach, or exploring a forest."

I leaned back with a sigh. It was a wonderful dream. "But I don't want to open one here in Elros. I want to leave this town for good. I'd even go as far as Elvidawn to achieve it."

Varys nodded. "You didn't mention anyone else in that dream."

I winced. "Right. It's just that whenever I've thought of the future before, it always included a suitor I didn't want. So I've never thought of a husband."

He seemed humored by that. "What about a husband who would make it his life goal to give you all that you wish and more?"

I swallowed, heat rushing to my cheeks. I couldn't deny that when I thought of Varys as that husband, my chest tightened with yearning.

"Of course, that's not to say you *need* a husband to achieve your dreams," he said with a shrug. "You're more than capable of doing it yourself."

"You're right. But I think it'd be wonderful to do life with some-one, even if they have their own dreams." I took another bite of the tart, washing it down with a drink of wine. "So, Varys, what are yours? What kind of life do you want?"

He grimaced and scratched his head. He fell silent for several beats before flattening his hands on his thighs and letting out a huff. The question had been hard for me, but it seemed exceptionally heavy for him.

"Here's the deal," he said slowly. "A couple years back, my life changed drastically and I now have several variables that are pulling me in their own direction and I can only choose one." He took a drink. "For the majority of my life, I have been studying to prove myself worthy of tutelage at the College of Elvidawn. My admission essay is nearly complete, but the college is...particular in their selec-tion. One sentence off, one punctuation mark misplaced, I won't be accepted. I'm on my twelfth draft of the damn thing and I know it isn't perfect even still."

I chewed on my lip. That sounded like my absolute nightmare not being able to even read. "Why do you feel like it's necessary to go?"

He chuckled. "I've asked myself the same question for years, and I still don't have any answer besides that I know the college will push me, challenge my mind. My love for learning and knowledge would thrive there...but I fear what I may lose."

"What's that?"

Solemn eyes met mine. "Everything else. I know that I would put so much of myself into my studies, I would forget I'm a man with desires, a family, friends. But...I'm also a man with nothing to offer this world but my mind. I don't have a trade. I was studying all those years when other men my age were saving money for marriage. If I'm accepted, I can eventually become a researcher and it pays well." He sighed, and he sounded so at war with himself. It tugged on my chest. "But if I'm not accepted, I'm left in the situation I am in now. My father pays me what he can, but he doesn't make much as it is. He wants to eventually retire and have me take over his school if I'm not accepted. But I don't have a teacher's heart—"

"Bullshit."

His eyes widened. "What?"

I smiled and laced my fingers with his. "Varys, you're currently teaching *me* how to read. I know I asked, but you could have said no. And during our lesson earlier, you were more than patient when I became overwhelmed. You're a great teacher, Varys."

His smile was tight. "I'm glad you think so, Mae."

That didn't sound very genuine.

"It's not what you want to do though," I stated. "I understand. And knowing you're expected to do something you don't want to do just to have a life is a terrible feeling."

I also understood that.

He nodded. "My father has never said it, but yes. It's an expectation. Though he's hoping I'm accepted. He's a former student, but he wasn't able to become a researcher. If I could get that far, I would have a livelihood."

He breathed out. "I have no intention of making us some temporary tryst. I just don't know how to give you the life *you* deserve though. Not yet. But I am more than willing to figure out what I need to do to keep you."

My pulse picked up its pace.

He twisted to me fully, sapphire blue eyes bright and eager. "If I'm accepted into the college, would you come with me?"

My mouth fell open. "How would we even do that? You even said you have no money. And it's not like my father would ever approve. I would have to…"

I'd have to run away.

"I know." He laughed. "It's too crazy. But your response makes me happy nonetheless."

"Why?"

"Because you didn't say no." A roguish grin lifted on the corner of his mouth, arching his scarred brow. "So either this wine is getting to our heads, or we both want to make it happen somehow."

I looked away, shaking my head incredulously. "I can't give you an answer yet."

"I understand."

"But…" I gulped and looked up into his sapphire gaze. "It isn't a no."

CHAPTER 31

Mae

Varys pressed his lips to my neck as he dipped me in the middle of the dance floor. We had just finished our dessert when another song had begun to play, and I had pulled him back out here to teach him another dance.

His forehead glistened with sweat, every part of him beaming. He laughed as he pulled me upright and I embraced him, breathing in his intoxicating musk. My heart beat wildly, the connection to him pulsing through me with every brush of skin.

"One more?" he asked above the crowd's cheering.

I had no idea what time it was, but I could feel an exhaustion starting to weigh on my bones. Thankfully, this time it wasn't from a flare.

I shook my head and kissed him. "Let's go back to the nook."

Whatever he read on my face had him lifting me into his arms, I let out a squeal of surprise, and laughter broke from him as he carried me through the crowd and back to the nook.

Once inside, he let me down to stand and drew the curtains. "You don't know how much I love that little sound you make." His voice was husky as he turned back to me, a teasing grin on his handsome face.

I ran my hands along his chest. Gods, I wanted to feel all of that taut skin underneath. "What other sounds do I make that you enjoy?"

His eyes simmered as he gripped my hips and pushed against me. A wicked and sweet heat swelled through my body as it met with his need. My breath left in a quick burst as he dipped down and murmured against my ear, "Your voice alone ruins me."

I dug my fingers into his shirt and pulled, finding his lips again. His hold on me tightened, and the deep, rough sound in his chest sent shivers down my spine.

With a quick release, I guided him backward. His fierce sapphire gaze seared right through me, his jaw fixed as if he was locking himself down. When his calves hit the seat, he sat slowly, never breaking focus as he leaned back. He lifted a finger and my stomach dipped each time he curled it toward him. I couldn't think past the gesture, of how that motion would feel against other places.

I lifted my skirt enough for easier motion, and he sucked in a breath as I slid into his lap. There was no denying the hardness I met there when my thighs graced his.

Twisting to the table, I reached for our drinks. Varys shook his head. "Thank you, Mae, but I've had enough."

His goblet was still nearly full. Mine was almost gone, and the warmth of the wine had settled low within me, lacing with my throbbing core. But I was still in control, I wasn't drunk. Neither was he, and it was then I realized that perhaps he didn't want anymore because he wanted to remain sober. I couldn't find the words or thoughts to express how grateful I was of that.

I decided to put mine down too and faced him again with a warm smile. He returned the expression, raising a hand to cup my cheek. "Are you enjoying tonight, Mae?"

I nodded, closing my eyes as I leaned into his soothing touch. He ran his thumb along my bottom lip and my body loosened at the feeling. "Very much so. I hope you have too."

"Of course." His hand moved to my bare shoulder. "Here I had planned for tonight to be about spoiling you, and yet you have gifted me with your radiance." His fingers slid along the outside of the silver tie around my neck. "You about brought me to my knees showing up in this dress, you danced for me, shared your dessert with me, and now you have me locked under your beauty."

My heart thundered as my attention was brought back to where my body aligned with his. The teasing hardness that made me want to squirm, every slight brush sending waves of ecstasy through me. I thought his hand would move lower—I wanted it to. But he found my face again and his expression turned tender, eyes full of awe. "I feel like the luckiest man alive."

I stifled a laugh and kissed the bridge of his nose. "Such a poet. Makes me wonder why you aren't a writer."

He pressed his lips together. "Well..."

My eyes widened. "Well?"

His face scrunched up and it was the most boyish expression I had ever seen him make. "I...am."

I gasped. "Wait. That's the other talent you have?"

A nod. "Nobody knows."

My mouth parted. "But you said it's a talent for the eyes."

"Oh, people have read my work." His grin turned impish. "Nobody knows it's me."

I covered my mouth with my hands as a small, excited squeal escaped my throat before I giggled. "That's amazing! Now I'm even more determined to learn how to read so I can enjoy your work."

Varys's brows had raised, and his eyes were wanton and smokey once more. "You made that sound again, Little Bird."

I ran my hands up his arms. "I'd apologize, but now that you're giving me a nickname, I think you like it."

"You'd be right." He leaned in and brought my mouth to his. A jolt of fiery ecstasy surged down to everything low when his teeth scraped against my bottom lip as he pulled away. "Little Bird."

My head fell back as a sensual laugh left my lips. He pressed his mouth to the hollow of my neck, and I felt his tongue flick against my skin. His hands trailed down my sides, to the curve of my hips. They fell to my thighs and his fingers began to make idle strokes and circles. Even through the material of my silver gown, his hand was a brand.

"Singer, writer, poet..." I mused as he worked his kiss up to my chin. "I have to wonder what other talents you have."

He chuckled against my neck. "You forgot *dancer*." Another lick up my throat had him gasping, pressing himself into me harder. "*Chaos*, you taste like rain."

A shiver worked its way through me. "Now you've got me wondering what else that tongue can do."

He stilled, his hands on my thighs stopping their circling entirely. He pulled back and his sapphire eyes were bright and blazing with desire. I watched his throat work on a swallow, and I couldn't truly feel his pulse, but I thought it might be beating in rhythm with my throbbing body. "My tongue...can do a great many things, Mae."

He slipped a hand behind my neck, angling my head until my ear aligned with his lips. His breath was hot and smelled of sweet, spicy wine and tart berries. "So can my mouth," he continued, hands moving back down to my thighs, the circles returning with eager caresses. "And my fingers and hands."

I could hardly breathe around his voice, the rawness of it drying out my throat. Everything else was damp and heated. His touch grazed upward, pulling the hem of my gown with it until his hands found my bare legs. Our embrace suddenly tightened, the connection between us becoming hot steel. He made sure I was focused, made me watch him as he glanced down, down to where his hardness pushed between my thighs and rasped, "And so can *I*."

My breath hitched.

That sly smile I loved so much appeared as he tilted his head. "It all depends on what you'd like to see demonstrated first."

I knew what this meant, what he wanted. I wanted it too. I wanted *him*. I didn't care if I was still a maiden. I didn't care if I'd never done any of this before. I wanted him to be my first, my last, my utter end.

Entwining my hands into his shirt, I gulped down every apprehension threatening to rise and breathed, "Give me all of it."

He grasped the back of my head and captured my lips. A whimper was knocked free as his taste overwhelmed me, as he flicked the roof of my mouth with hunger. My thighs and core became a pulsing fire and it was almost too much, too amazing.

I was liquid in his arms, surrendering to him wholly. Releasing all restraint on myself, I began to grind into his arousal. He broke the kiss with a gasp, eyes wide and a curse tearing from his throat. My name became a beg on his lips, but I wasn't done. I writhed and rocked, sinking my hands into his hair as our heavy breaths turned to moans.

He kissed below my collarbone and I leaned back enough to give him access to my chest. He obliged, his sweet tongue sliding down the inner swells as his hand palmed my peaked breast. I jolted when his thumb brushed over my hardened nipple. He made sure I watched how his tongue danced along my skin as he responded to my grinding, thrusting upward against the hot wetness between my legs, a growl in his throat.

I wanted more. To feel him in my hands. I pushed him against the padded back of the settee. Before he could protest, I slipped my hand between us and found the hard length of him beneath his breeches. I stroked my fingers against the material in a downward motion and greedily watched the shock wash over his face. His head fell back, blue eyes rolling toward the ceiling, and the moan that ripped from him jolted something to life within me.

"Mae...Oh gods."

I only hummed in response, repeating the motion. He hissed and writhed, chest heaving, hands clutching into the seat. I pressed my mouth to his, sucking his bottom lip as he'd done to mine.

He jeered back, laughing hoarsely. "I'm going to finish before we even begin if you don't stop."

As much as I was curious to see that, I nodded. "Touch me, then."

"What—"

I grabbed his hand and guided it beneath my skirt. "Please," I begged. "Feel what you're doing to me."

His eyes went wide and wild as I pushed into him, pleading for his touch. Another moment too long passed before I felt his graze against my inner thigh. We were both trembling, breaths coming in short as he met with the soft skin. His eyes didn't leave mine when he pressed one finger against me and the pool gathering there—and swore. The air abandoned my lungs as he stroked, my legs going taut around him. I could barely take it. The most gentle, most precise touch was ruination. A rough, sensual sound I had never heard come from me before tore from my lips, and I was suddenly someone I didn't recognize. I was everything, and nothing, and beautifully whole.

His finger was drenched with me as he slid up and down, every brush leaving me gasping his name. I moved with him, grinding myself against his touch. Heat was building, rising, and the need for that finger to plunge deep inside me every time he came near my entrance was agonizing.

Varys locked his mouth against mine...and I lost it. My hands dove into his blue hair, gripping the tresses as if they were my only anchor to this world. His stroking became harder, faster, and I kissed him in the same manner. When I circled my tongue around his, the pattern below halted—shifted to his own teasing circles. I writhed and cried out. His groans were my undoing, sweeter than any song the bards played outside our nook.

His other hand had been working its way to the side of my breast. He pulled his lips from mine. For a moment, I was damn sure those blue irises were glowing like cold-flame when he opened them, desire whirling around his fixed, searing focus. "May I touch you here as well?"

I raised a brow, a haughty smile on my lips. "Does it fall under your demonstration?"

He only grinned before his hand slipped under the sash, taking hold of my entire breast. I had never noticed the calluses on his palms, but I did now as they rubbed against my nipple. I gasped out his name as his thumb began to match the patterns he was making between my thighs.

Something was happening to me. I knew of releases, had pleasured myself enough to know what they felt like. This wasn't even close to that feeling. It was so much more.

Like earlier this evening, my headspace washed blue, but now along with it, the connection's pulse began to ripple harsh jolts through me. Every wave seemed to bring me small climaxes, but I could barely focus on my reaction to them. Because there between the blues, an iridescent string ran through an opening. It was a door, but there were no handles, no hinges. Nothing but light seeping into my consciousness, the source of the blues swirling through my head.

I didn't know why I desired to go through it. Didn't know why it was more important than the finger stroking between my legs, nor why I felt nothing but great love for that light and what lay beyond it.

"M-Mae," Varys gritted out.

His voice yanked me out of my head. I took a breath, but the air felt too heavy. I hadn't realized what had happened, that while I was focused on the pulse and the door in my head, I had started to ride his finger.

"I...I think I lost you again," he said, beginning to pull his hand away. "You dazed out. I-I wanted to make sure *this* is what you want."

I blinked and continued to grind. "Of course it is. It feels incredible."

He swallowed and nodded. "Then, we probably need to pause. We can't remain here if we want to keep going."

Nothing was making sense, only the burn and the connection to him tugging and twisting around every part of me, filling my head with the most beautiful blue light so much like his eyes.

The realization left me breathless, my chest feeling like it was blooming as joy and affection replaced the air. I didn't understand why I was seeing and feeling what I did, didn't know if it was something magical or if I was just crazy. But I trusted my heart and my head more than I trusted anything because it always showed me the truth.

I was in love with Varys.

I stopped my writhing and gazed up at him. "Where should we go instead?"

He smiled warmly. "I can get us a room for the night."

My desire jolted through me, no longer of heat, but of charged energy that needed release. I was a whirling, brewing, bottled storm that wanted—*needed* to emerge.

"I want a room," I said breathlessly. "I want *you*, Varys."

CHAPTER 32

Mae

Varys and I barely made it inside the inn room before our lips collided. It was nothing but a wild pining pulling us along, grasping at each other as we fell backward into the closest wall. My sashes were coming loose, one side threatening to slip off entirely. It didn't matter. Both of his hands were underneath them, palms smoothing over the curves of my breasts, fingers clamping down on my nipples as I ravaged his mouth.

I was breathless, sagging against the wall's surface, my mind clouded with blue swirls anytime my eyes closed. My hands found their way up his untucked shirt, and I got what I wanted. The feel of all of those delineated tendons, the ripples of tight skin proof of hard training. I had barely made it to his ribs before he let out an exasperated grunt, pulling away only to rip his tunic over his shoulders and toss it aside, down to where I had hastily thrown my cape.

My knees wanted to cave in. The gods had to have crafted him themselves. His chest heaved, muscles bowing and flexing. I was almost daunted, as if removing his shirt made me remember how tall he was. Made me realize that I was moments away from being underneath all of this strength. I suddenly felt so…delicate. But he would be gentle. I knew he would be. I trusted him.

I let my eyes slide down to his carved abdominals, sucking in a breath at how they curved into a beautiful vee before disappearing below his pants. My head lolled back against the wall. "You're gorgeous, Varys Wynhart."

He grinned and the next kiss he gave me was his thanks. His mouth worshiped mine, moaning as his tongue slipped across my bottom lip. He pressed himself into me, and I finally explored his bare chest, his broad shoulders, and the swell of his biceps.

But I wanted more. The strain in his breeches had my nerves begging, but I couldn't get close enough, couldn't settle it against me just right—

He read my mind. His hands gripped my thighs and he yanked them up, tossed my legs around his torso, and ground his need into mine. I cried out his name. The lash of pleasure whipped through me so hard I let go of him, but he didn't let go of me. He was like steel, his grinding unyielding. His mouth gaped as he watched me writhe.

"I want you so bad, Mae," he gasped, and the moan that left his lips brought me to the sweet edge of rapture. I wasn't sure how he managed it, but one sash slipped away from my breast. He pushed me higher, lowering his lips to my nipple. Those blue eyes flicked up to mine, glazed with lust as his tongue slipped out and over the peak.

"Oh, gods..." I murmured. He licked it again, and a jolt of ecstasy raced down, connecting with the wet heat between my thighs where he still ground into me as if he were already inside. *"Fuck, Varys."*

My eyes closed, and as my heart pounded, my headspace shimmered with the richest blues of sky or ocean. When he took my entire nipple into his mouth and began to suck, my release shattered through me. I shouted, nails digging into his shoulders to a point I feared I would hurt him. But he didn't stop, he only switched to the other breast. It was too much—it wasn't enough. Only when I went limp and pleaded his name did he cease in his teasing.

I was gasping, my climax still sending surges of pleasure through my body, colors swirling with every spasm and drawing a moan from my lips. He gripped me tightly as he pulled me away from the wall and carried me to the bed in the far corner of the room. I barely had time to take in the little dresser and nightstand before I was laid back. The room was lit with a small chandelier of candles I could see from my position.

The mattress dipped as Varys crawled over me, his mouth on mine before I could take a breath. His body sank into me, heavy and hard, and *gods* I could lay under him for eternity. I pressed kisses to his chest, tasting the sweat on his skin as I ran my fingers down his arms. He groaned my name, whispered how much he wanted me. How much he needed me as he continued to push into the soft flesh between my legs. I couldn't take it anymore.

"Varys," I whimpered. "Take me, please."

A shuddering groan escaped him. He spread my legs with his knees, and my thighs clenched in anticipation. His hands were fiery on my skin as he pushed my skirt up. My breath left me as he bent my knee and brought his mouth to the inside of my thigh. My core begged for those lips to find their way up, but he kissed his way down, down until he found my ankle. He pulled off the slipper on my foot, and I grinned when I realized what he was doing— undressing me, but in a slow, worshipful way.

He repeated the steps on the other side, then crawled back up, kissing my breasts as he passed. His hands slid to my neck and he whispered, "Can I untie this now?"

My heart skipped a beat, but I nodded. He found the sash end and pulled, the makeshift bodice falling apart around my torso. Slowly, he dragged the material away before sitting back, eyes wide and smokey as he surveyed me. With a hard-set jaw, he began to unbuckle the belt around his waist, his heated gaze never leaving mine. The belt sagged, and so did his breeches. My mouth went dry as my eyes dipped down to where his waistband now hung loosely around his hips, revealing the start of the shock of coarse hair I knew would lead me to that wild abandon.

My head lolled back to the mattress as I bit my lip. There was a low rumble in his throat.

"My turn, Little Bird," he purred as he dipped back down. He tugged on my chin, unlocking my lip from my teeth, and in one swift motion took it between his own. I hissed, his tongue running along the fullness of it before he began to suck. My body arched in response, the drags of his mouth yanking wild bursts of pleasure through me.

With a wet release, he murmured, "Tell me what you want."

My eyes had closed and those blues turned to something deep and dark, beckoning me to some place of decadent desire, tempting me with a remedy that would ease the building ache, quench my ardent thirst. "I want…"

My hand roamed, finding that vee, the line of his pants, the hair that brushed roughly against my palm. I slid my way between his hips and the waistband and Varys went still, then jerked when I wrapped my fingers around his cock.

My breaths became wild pants, our eyes locking as I muttered with a voice that wasn't my own, "I want you inside me."

He let out a breath, a shiver rushing through him as I glided my hands up and down his warm shaft.

"*Chaos. Mae.*" He could hardly speak, hardly breathe as I stroked. I loved watching him writhe for me.

But he didn't let me continue for long. He took my right hand and kissed my knuckles, lips sliding to my wrist as his fingers found the glove's end at my elbow. He slipped it off, then removed my left hand from around him. He stripped the glove free with a smile, his mouth dipping to press against my wrist.

He paused.

"What the——" His eyes focused on something on my skin, and another beat too long passed before I realized.

I ripped my arm back without a second thought, air locking in my chest.

He blinked in surprise as he backed away. "Mae, what is that?"

Oh gods, how could I have forgotten? If he saw what lay beneath the glove, I would have to tell him everything. *Everything.* I hadn't prepared. I hadn't——

"It's a scar." I couldn't stop the lie as it rolled off my tongue.

But he knew better. He *knew*. His bright blue eyes that had been full of nothing but affection and longing went hard and cold. "No, it's not."

I swallowed, the sudden pain in my chest threatening to rip my heart in two. "It's not," I muttered.

His brows furrowed, tension bracketing his mouth. "What is it then?" Each word was tight. "Why were you hiding it?"

My eyes stung. I shouldn't have waited so long. Shouldn't have let fear get in the way of us. But by the time I worked up the nerve and decided what I would say, Varys rolled off.

Panic sliced through me as I scrambled upright. "Varys. Oh, gods." I reached for him and gripped his arm before he could stand. The pounding heat had iced over and there was nothing but dread twisting my stomach. I couldn't lose him. "Varys, *please* let me explain. Don't—"

"Why do you keep lying?" His voice was raw with emotion. He wouldn't look at me. "I told you I want this. I want you, and everything we're going to be. I haven't been worried about how fast we're moving, how fast I'm…" He pressed his lips together, silencing his words. The corners of his glossy eyes started to blotch with red. He whispered, "Leo was right. I'm being reckless."

He shrugged away my touch and stood. I lost control over myself. I didn't care if I was half-dressed as I went after him. "No, no, no, Varys. I'm sorry."

He didn't seem to be listening as he ripped his shirt from the ground. "You would bed me. You would share yourself and your dreams, and your smile." He strapped his belt back on. "You say you trust me, and yet you lie to my face."

I could hardly think, barely form words. Cold waves of nausea swept in. "It has to do with my powers. I should have shown you sooner. Look. *Please.*"

I held out my arm—

"Why show me *now?*" He whirled to me, and I couldn't stand the hurt on his face. "Why bother when you won't even allow me to explain how I can help you?"

The tears fell down my face as I quickly tied the bodice back around my neck. "I know. I *know*, Varys. I-I lock up. You don't understand how terrified I am."

His brows furrowed deeper as he inclined his head. "That's where you're wrong, Mae. I do."

Without another word, he pressed his thumb and pointer finger together before his face as if holding a quill. Closing his eyes, his hand twisted, and when he flung his arm outward, the candles in the chandelier extinguished and the room went dark. I let out a breath as something raced up my arm—an exhilarating heat that didn't bring pain.

"Give me your answer, Mae," his voice rang out from the darkness. "Tell me you're *Vyl'kríev*."

The Elvish word filled me—I *felt* it fill me like a cool drink of water that quenched all confusion. I took a gasping breath because I knew what it meant, its importance, even though I had never muttered it from my lips, nor heard it from another's. Knew it didn't translate to just *elf blood*, but an individual who carried the blood of the elves who came before us and their gift of magic.

And I was one of them.

It was as if I'd had a cloud fogging my mind and now...now there was nothing but clarity.

In a voice I hardly recognized as my own, I declared into the darkness, and to the man I loved, "I am."

Blue light enveloped the room as two glowing orbs blinked into view. Eyes. *His* eyes were shining and glittering, staring at me with such intensity I thought I might crumble beneath them. A breath was the only thing I heard before, "*Çruthi*."

His eyes shut once more, cutting off the light, but in its wake...I gasped.

The surrounding darkness twinkled with dots of light. I was standing in sky and stars, wading in a sea of blazing comets and colorful distant galaxies. I spun in awe, no longer able to tell where the walls began or where my feet met the floor.

"Magic," I rasped. "You have magic, too."

I turned, finding Varys's half-lidded glowing azure eyes gazing at me. Faint silvery-blue streams of energy rippled beneath the skin of his face, hands, and arms. The sight of him brought me to an edge of terror and adulation, and the display of power demanded my shaking knees to give way. I was reminded as I hit the floor that I was witnessing the gift given to the god-made elves. The magic of the silent gods.

Varys made no sound as he walked over. I thought perhaps he might have been gliding. He knelt before me, lifted my chin. I stared up into his glowing eyes, burning like a sapphire star in the center of one of those galaxies currently swimming around us. He was beautiful, majestic and ethereal.

I didn't know what to say. I wasn't sure if I remembered how to speak. It was as if every word that came to mind wasn't enough, wasn't right.

But he was *Vyl'kriev*, as was I. We didn't have to speak in Common.

"…*Jdimen*."

Forgive.

A sob broke free. "*Jdimen ni, Varys*."

Forgive me, Varys.

The hand on my chin tensed before sliding softly to my cheek, the other finding the back of my neck. His fingers were warm and velvety, and the energy radiating from him made me feel at peace.

Inches from my lips, he breathed the words like lyrics that would be forever engraved on my bones, "*Ethi vö ath, aríma*."

There you are, beloved.

I broke. Crumbled into his arms as his words seemed to ignite the connection between us. I could see all of the blues again, my mind lit with a fire the same shade as his eyes. The iridescent string pulled and tugged me toward that door. I was hypnotized, gasping against him as I reached, reached…

I couldn't open it. Couldn't go through it. There was still no handle, no hinges. But I could feel the heat of the flame, taste the sweetness of his kiss on my tongue. I didn't understand why something I knew was somehow connected to the man I loved remained out of reach. As if I wasn't allowed to have it.

It made me cry harder.

Varys smoothed his hand over my hair, shushing me softly as I sobbed against his chest. "All is well, little bird," he whispered. "Please don't cry. You are safe."

I could hardly force the words out. "I know." I choked back a cry as I wrapped around him tighter. "I'm safe with you. I know."

My eyes lifted to his, still beaming with magical light. He wiped my face. As I reached out with my left hand to cup his cheek, the energy under his skin reflected streams of dim light over my wrist, illuminating the lightning marks. The initial touch sent one of those pulses he couldn't feel surging through me, and I wondered now if the feeling was our magic reacting to each other's, sparking like flint striking steel.

He leaned his face against my hand and for a moment, I just gazed at him. Took in every expression on his face, soaked in his ferocity and kindness. He was intelligent and clever, and he made me laugh and smile like no one else could. His words moved me, whether they were spoken to educate, or to soothe, or breathed against my skin to rouse my desire. Looking at him like this, with his power displayed, was like seeing him for the first time.

I loved him.

"No more secrets," I murmured. "No more lies. I'm *yours*, Varys."

He smiled. "We have a lot to talk about first."

I nodded, pulling his hand to my lips, kissing his knuckles and fingers as if I let go, he would vanish. I couldn't bear the thought. I knew right then I would go wherever he went. I would follow him to the edge of the world. It didn't matter what my fear told me or what my trauma wanted me to believe. He had given me a reason to live, a reason to *fear* death. And maybe that was why I had still hesitated, still locked up. I had never feared my end. My end would bring relief from pain, freedom from Rucas. Being with Varys meant I would have to endure those things, and I would have to fight for everything I wanted.

I would. I would fight for him, for us. For myself.

He helped me to my feet. Stepping away, he cast his spell once more, the energy flowing beneath his skin flickering brighter for a moment. The stars and galaxies faded, leaving Varys's eyes as the only source of light. He overturned a fisted hand and unfurled it slowly. There in his palm was a glowing turquoise butterfly, its wings laced with rivulets of purple.

"Nen ath Vyl'kriev."

We are Elven-blooded.

The butterfly fluttered off his palm toward the finger I extended. When it perched, bolts of lightning webbed across its flapping wings. My chest bloomed.

"Nen völat orö'hith."

We have reemerged.

A breath left me. I had heard that word in my dreams, in my head. The woman in my consciousness had demanded it, just as she had demanded me to free the rising storm inside.

"What does it mean?" I asked as the butterfly crawled up my wrist. It paused and Varys tilted his head curiously. I blinked and the butterfly was gone. In place was Varys's hand gently grabbing my arm and turning it over. "To reemerge."

"The ReEmergence of Magic has begun," he told me, his fingers trailing over the jagged lines. "I have spent the last two years training and learning everything I can about our ancestors and their magic. Preparing for what may come."

I shivered when his touch caressed the inside of my elbow, right where the lightning marks stopped. "What's coming?"

His glowing eyes met mine. "Enemies."

My stomach hollowed out, spine locking in place. "What—"

The air around us curled with a growling whisper. Varys cursed, and before I could take a breath, he shoved me back. I caught myself against the mattress.

"Ignaes!" Varys yelled, pointing to the chandelier. One by one, the candles' flames flickered to life, lighting up the room once again. He shifted into a guarded stance. *"Sçölith!"*

A strange glowing circle of runes and shapes manifested before his outstretched palm along with a wall of transparent blue energy. "Mae, throw up your wards," he implored with urgency. "They've not made their way inside yet."

My *wards?* I had no idea what he was talking about.

The droning whispers became laden with words in a language I couldn't make out. Varys whipped around frantically, the dagger gripped tight in his hold. "Your wards, Mae."

"I don't know what that is." I crawled backward to where the wall met the bed, pressing myself against the hard surface. "Varys, I don't know how to use my magic."

The whispers ceased suddenly, but out of the silence came a curdling scream from below. Then another. Another, until they were met with shouts of many. Boots began to pound on the floors beneath us—people were running. Claps and thuds of objects hitting the ground joined in the shrill crash of glass shattering.

My breaths came fast and hard, heart thundering against my ribs. Varys hadn't turned from the door, his own body heaving. With another curse, he rushed forward and slung the door open. People were running by, to their rooms or from them I couldn't tell, screaming and trampling over each other. Their words brought the answer to what horror had transpired.

"They're dead!"

"Gods speak, they've been killed!"

Varys plunged himself into the chaos, holding out his hands to stop a frenzied woman in her tracks. "What's happened?"

"Three men are dead," she cried. "Slit across the throat."

With that, she rushed away. Varys closed the door and pivoted to me, pulling the dagger from his belt. He held the blade before him, muttering another command word, but I couldn't focus on anything except my stomach and the saliva gathering in my mouth from the onset of nausea. Only when a spark ignited from his hands did my attention turn back to him. I watched as glowing red Elvish runes began to etch into the face of the blade, spelling out *Álaçarna. Fire.* When the last rune appeared, the red glow brightened until each was burning like metal freshly pulled from a smelting furnace. With a quick smirk, Varys muttered, "Good to know that works."

I was surprised to see he could sheath the knife, expecting the red-hot runes to set him aflame. He didn't seem surprised at all as he came to the bed and crawled to me.

"Dias na ni." Come to me.

I scrambled into his arms and clutched onto him tight. He pressed a kiss to the top of my scalp as his hands quickly moved around my head. Something cold and metal fell against my collarbone. Looking down, I saw he'd hung a necklace around my neck. I didn't have time to inspect the jewel set in the center of the pendant before he said, "This will protect you. Stay here."

My insides dipped. "W-What? Where in Torm are you going?"

Warmth was spreading across my chest from where the necklace lay. Varys rolled out of bed, shoving his tunic back into his breeches. "I need to go find out what happened—"

"Varys, three men are *dead*."

"Yes." His jaw locked. "And those were the whispers of our enemy."

Like a warning toll of death.

I went to stand. "Then I'll come with you."

"Mae, no." He came at me again, pressing my shoulders down and forcing me to sit. "You just told me you don't know how to use your magic."

"I know, but—"

"I told you I'd keep you safe." He squeezed my shoulders. "This is how I'm going to do so. I know how to use my magic, but not against this. I can't promise I can protect you down there."

"Then stay here instead."

He bent down until our eyes were aligned. "Too long have I waited around for answers about the threat of an adversary. We have reemerged. I have to know why that means people want us dead."

My eyes fell to the floor. "What if you don't come back?"

"Mae, I'll come back—"

"What if you don't come back?" I gripped my hands in his shirt.

He let out an exhale and his strong arms wrapped under my shoulders. "If I don't return, go to the library," he whispered before pulling away. He raised his head, his weighty gaze severe. "You will always find sanctuary at the library."

Before I could say anymore, he spun from me and stalked out.

***

It felt like he had been gone for an eternity even though I knew it had only been ten minutes or so. There was no way in Torm I could just sit around and wait for him, but it wasn't like I could do anything else. Pacing made me feel better, so I walked up and down the length of the bed repeatedly, listening for his voice or any sign of danger.

Our room was on the second floor, and I had already opened the window to look for an escape if needed. There were many ledges where I could find purchase, but one slip and I would be done for.

Frustration ate at me as I walked around aimlessly. I felt like a coward. I was capable of using magic, I just didn't know how to bring it forward.

He left you.

The sudden voice jolted me, compelling me to spin and find where it had come from.

I've never left you, she purred. ***And yet, you still aren't free.***

My pulse sped up, the burn of anger surging with it. "What do you want?"

Saeör ít ölsta—

"Shut the *fuck* up!" I shouted, nails digging into my palms. "I'm sick of your riddles. If you won't tell me exactly how to free myself, then leave me *alone*!"

A sensual laugh filled my ears. ***I cannot leave you alone. I cannot leave*** **you.**

I shook my head. "What do you mean?"

Why don't you look for yourself?

I turned to the dresser where a small table mirror stood beside a bucket of water, there for guests to wash their face. "In the mirror?"

She didn't respond. Slowly, I made my way over, heart fluttering as I dipped down to gaze into my reflection.

Black eyes met mine.

I shrieked, stumbling back onto my ass before I scuttled away. My eyes. They were void of my purple irises, as if my pupils had expanded over the color and whites. Panic coursed through my bones, seizing my mobility.

"What have you done?" I seethed. "What have you done to my eyes?"

Our eyes.

Icy dread swam up, freezing me to the floor. I opened my mouth, but words could not emerge. Not a single sound could be mustered.

I feel your pain…
I feel your anger…

The voice went silent, as if it were thinking.

You believe you are safe with him, but only I can truly help you. So, why not let me take over for a while?

Tears blurred my vision. "*What?*"

Pain suddenly sliced through my arm, up my shoulder and neck. I cried out as the burn overwhelmed everything in me, back arching off the floor, left arm lifting involuntarily to the ceiling with veins glowing an incandescent violet.

A glow so similar to the magic I had seen Varys display tonight.

You are not where you should be. You cannot open that door. Not until you free the storm.

Not until you free me.

CHAPTER 33

Varys

I had never seen this much blood.

My stomach lurched at the sight of it, but more so because of whose blood still trickled down, pooling under the table and chairs Mae and I had occupied several hours earlier.

Ramos. Two of his brothers. Throats sliced from ear to ear.

The table, their food, and pints of mead were sprayed with red. And I couldn't help but feel like Ramos's blank gaping stare was focused on me alone.

But I wasn't the only one in the main room looking on in horror. Most of the tables and chairs had been flipped over, goblets, mugs, plates, and baskets scattered, drinks sloshed across the floor. The tangy, metallic smell of blood mixed with the bittersweet stench of spirits and ale was willing the bile to rise up my throat.

I breathed in through my nose and out my mouth slowly. The cuts across their necks were clean, which meant something thin and probably small was used. The way their bodies sagged against the chairs suggested there hadn't been much of a struggle. This was a quick job. A targeted job.

I already knew that. Ramos had told me he and his brothers felt like they were being hunted.

But where were the hunters?

A hand clapped my shoulder. Reflexes took hold before I could take another breath, hand gripping the dagger as I whirled around, blade cutting through the short distance between me and...

The damn bastard.

Vamir didn't seem fazed by the dagger I still held inches before his face. His head tilted like a pigeon watching the market, eyeing the blade and its fiery runes.

"No need to get all jumpy," he crooned.

I glared and yanked my dagger down. "Apologies."

Vamir's silver eyes glanced side to side. I looked over my shoulder to see the remaining crowd now whispering, eyeing me and the dagger. I quickly sheathed it.

"I was actually coming to inform you of what happened," Vamir told me, his focus returning to the dead. "Since it seems you were preoccupied when this occurred."

I tried to ignore the thoughts constructed by that comment. He had watched me and Mae all night, it was possible he had watched us ascend the stairs to the room I purchased too.

Vamir read something on my face, and a faint smirk curled up the corner of his bloodless mouth. "There was no warning. One minute the bards were singing a very touching ballad, the next those men"—he waved his hand as if the bodies were nothing more than an uncouth inconvenience—"were bleeding out. Tragic, really. They seemed to be enjoying themselves."

I breathed in slowly again. I couldn't lose my stomach here. "Were the murderers caught?"

Vamir picked at his sleeve, the ruby rings on his fingers almost the same color as the blood. "Not that I know of. But it's odd. There had to have been three murderers. They were killed at the same time. Very same moment. And yet, no one saw anyone behind them. No one saw *anything* at all. It was almost as if..." He paused, lips thinning. "The murderers had been invisible."

I knew that already. Whatever had tried to attack me earlier in the evening had remained unseen as well.

I didn't press on the subject. Not to him. "If there are killers still on the loose, I think it'd be best if I return to my room for the night. Thanks for informing me."

With one last glance to the brothers, I went to turn.

"So, she's safe?" Vamir questioned in a low voice.

My spine locked, irritation setting my tics off. I flattened my hands against the sides of my legs, but my fingers still tapped with impatience. "Yes," I gritted out.

"Good." He inclined his head. "Please, keep it that way."

He bowed, white hair spilling forward before he began to walk away.

A burning, seething resentment boiled up from the pit of my stomach, every part of me tightening as I spat, "How do you know her?"

Vamir's smile was all too innocent. "Honestly, I met her this morning."

I took a step toward him, narrowing my gaze. "You seem to have known her for longer than that with the way you initially greeted her tonight."

A short, acidic laugh left him. "Can a man not simply tell a woman she looks beautiful? Or are you insinuating that Elros citizens are so uncivilized that it is unheard of? Are you people of the hills known more for things like..."

He eyed the three brothers.

I scowled. "You make her uncomfortable."

His brows flew up as he blinked. "Do I? I assumed because we share the same bloodline, she and I might understand each other a little more. In the same way you might understand the Elven-blooded like you."

I opened my mouth to retort, but a realization seized my words.

Did he not realize he was *Vyl'kriev* as well?

What if he hadn't reemerged yet?

I breathed out my nose, shoving down my frustration. Maybe this was simply a misunderstanding. "People say Mae is cursed, but I know that's not true. What is the origin of your bloodline that is so different from mine?"

Vamir's face was unreadable as he fell silent.

I continued in a low whisper, "Afterall, you are *Vyl'kriev* aren't you?"

He chuckled, the broad grin revealing his almost too sharp teeth. "You may be intelligent, but not very wise."

I jeered my chin back. "Excuse me?"

Vamir looked around the tavern. It had pretty much cleared out, which was the only reason I'd chosen to speak in Elvish. "To announce you are what you are," he said with distaste. "How do you know I'm not your enemy? You just gave yourself away."

I crossed my arms with a smirk. "Same as you. Only Elven-blooded can understand our language."

Vamir frowned. "Indeed. I guess you have your answer then."

Voices rose from the entryway. We both looked over to find seven guardsmen walking into the tavern. I decided I would take my leave.

"Stay safe, *yrçen*." I nodded to Vamir, trying not to make the Elvish word for *mage* sound too condescending.

His smile was sly as he fixed the collar of his black ruffled shirt. "And you as well."

I had just reached the landing of the second floor when emerald eyes met mine. She was still in the dress, but her hair was tousled, rogue smudged, metal feather headpiece off.

"Victors' sake," Leona gasped before rushing toward me. I wasn't expecting her to wrap her arms around me. We rarely hugged. Her eyes were wide when she looked up. "Folks were yabberin' on about a murder. Said some Elven-blooded had been split wide. I couldn't find ye. Orin went lookin'."

I was taken aback hearing Orin cared enough—cared for *her* enough—to make sure I was safe. There was no denying the scent of ale and sex as if she'd bathed in it, the typical scent on her after nights here at The Nook and Cranny. Tonight was the first time it had ever bothered me.

I shoved off the thoughts. "I'm all right." Taking her shoulders, I dipped down to her eye level. "Three Elven-blooded were murdered downstairs, Leo. The brothers we met."

She swallowed. "Ye said those brothers were magic—"

I cut her off with a nod. "Let's not speak aloud about *that* here. We'll discuss more with Mae. She's waiting in our room."

Her brows rose as she stepped away. "Does that mean...she knows?"

I gave a curt nod. With a guiding push on her shoulder, I began to lead her down the hall. "We need to get out of here. Let's grab Mae and get back to the library for the night. We can figure out the rest in the morning."

There was a slight hesitance in her next step. "Orin will be lookin' for me."

I didn't know how to respond to that, so I chose not to as I reached to open the door. The hairs on my arms bristled when the knob didn't turn. It was locked.

I hadn't locked it.

Pounding on the door, I called out, "Mae? It's me and Leo."

If it was merely that she had fallen asleep, I would apologize for the rude awakening later. I wasn't taking any chances with a murderer—or three—on the loose.

But there was no answer. No response. The seconds that ticked by were excruciating.

"What's wrong?" Leona asked.

My stomach began to curl, chest tightening. "Mae, open the door." I pounded again. "Mae, please."

Nothing.

With a quick pitch forward, I bashed my foot into the door. Then again, shouting her name. Again, fear and frenzy in every kick—

"Fawkes, *stop*." Leo grabbed my arm. "Let me before ye hurt ye'self."

She moved back further, hiked up her skirt, rushed ahead and threw her foot upon the lock itself. As metal crunched, the door flew open.

We rushed inside, and the air left me when I found the room empty. The window was wide open, allowing a chill wind as cold as my blood to circulate around the room. There was no sign of her past the unmade bed and abandoned satin slippers. The nausea I had felt earlier swelled up my throat as I bounded toward the window, looking up, down, around. She was nowhere to be seen. Gone.

"*Dammit!*" The shout scraped my throat as I whipped back to Leo.

Her eyes went wide with concern. "Where is she?"

"She's gone." I barreled past her, rushing for the door. "Someone either took her, or she left."

And I didn't understand why she would leave.

Unless she was hiding more from me.

PART III: AWAKENING

Skin.

I liked having skin.

I liked the feeling of her pounding heart. The fluttering of her eyelashes. The brush of curls along her delicate spine holding up such a fragile body.

A body that wasn't mine. Not yet, but soon.

Where…am I?

"Somewhere safe," I told Maelawyn, her voice resonating deep from within our shared consciousness. I felt her panic bubble up as she looked around, seeing the canopies of orange and red trees far beneath us through our eyes. She wanted to scream, but couldn't. Her throat was not her own.

Where have you taken me?

The demand in her voice was so like mine, a reminder I was merely a reflection of her. "Just above this world to watch and wait."

Thunder rumbled, its deep growl echoing off the hills breaking up the clusters of trees. The great storm I was brewing wasn't strong yet, but Maelawyn still looked on in awe. Lightning skittered under her flesh in response. She wanted to storm, to break free and swirl with it.

It wasn't time.

Why can't I move? What have you done with me?

"I am keeping you safe. I can't allow you to throw your body around so carelessly. It is fragile, like a pupa."

I offended her with that comment, but she still seemed more interested in getting down. *Let me go.*

"I cannot do that."

Give me back my body.

"It's my body. You have merely been preparing it for me."

Her stunned silence was palpable.

"I'd be grateful," I went on, "but you've kept it so weak, allowed it to fracture so it can remain human."

Stop it. This is my body, and I am *human.*

"You still believe that? Even though you know you're *Vyl'kriev*? You are no fool, Maelawyn. You are no human, either."

She didn't respond for a long moment, and I could feel how my words pressed in until realization washed over her like a sudden downpour of rain. Her heart began to pump harder.

What am I then? Her words were little more than a breath.

"That's not the right question."

Then tell me what I should be asking.

I sighed. "It is not about what *you* are, it is about what *we* are."

The only sound heard was the next clap of thunder, eliciting a flock of birds to take flight, cawing in panic as they flapped toward the south. Smart creatures. They knew what kind of storm was coming.

I don't understand, Maelawyn finally said, her voice wavering.

"Do not lie to yourself. It is written in your blood, carved into your bones. Every word in *Vylarys̀* has been laid upon your tongue since the day you were made. You know what I am, what *we* are."

I could feel how she quaked.

I don't. Please. I want to know. I want to understand.

"We are chaos. We are reckoning. Storm given form, lightning and thunder incarnate."

Please.

A sob echoed through our shared headspace. I knew she hurt. I knew she was angry and sad.

But I couldn't hate those emotions. They are what created me after all.

I beg you.

I didn't give her an answer. If I did, she would know the truth.

And I was so very close to shedding this skin.

CHAPTER 34

Varys

My body shook as I knelt before the pile of ashes, clutching her cloak the tavern master had given me before I had set out to search for her. Burnt ribbons of silver material identical to her dress lay within the ash, along with the necklace. The chain was broken, melted at the clasp, but the pendant itself, unscathed.

Footsteps bounded down the alley behind me, the clank of a metal heel I knew too well. Leona knelt beside me, now dressed in her normal attire she'd left at the library.

"She's not in the market," she told me as she handed me my book bag. The red ruby in Thorn's crossguard cast a red dancing glimmer on the ground, reflecting what little light the stormy sky promised for today. "What's that?"

I took a piece of the material in my hand. "It *was* her dress."

Her mouth fell open, green eyes widening in horror. "Ye...ye don't think she—"

"There's not enough ash for a body." I gulped, disturbed by the fact I even had to explain such a thing. "But she may have been taken and someone burned her clothes to hide evidence."

As I stood and tossed the cloak over my shoulder, something tumbled to the ground, clinking against the gravel in front of Leo.

Two keys. One ordinary, the other set with a green jewel in the bow. When I picked them up, the ornate key was warm in my palm.

"Looks like Mae was carrying a magic item," I remarked.

Leo seemed focused on something else entirely. "Her cloak has pockets?"

"Apparently so."

"Damn. I want pockets in my cloak," she muttered.

I stifled a chuckle and handed the key to her. "Can you confirm what kind of jewel this is?"

Examining the stone, her freckled forehead creased. "What is it about ye lately, Fawkes? Findin' things with stones ye can only find near my grumpy grandpappy's personal quarries."

My brows rose. "I thought it was a peridot or something."

"Aye, but it's not." She held the key in the sun, and it was then I saw the dark speckles throughout. "It's called *vivastine*. Just another stone that the dwarves dig deep to find. It's very lightweight and easy to cut. Cheap, cause there's so much of it down there under Drake's Spine."

I shook my head incredulously. "This key has to be ancient. It's magical. There's no one *making* magical items right now, and yet they just popped up one day."

She handed the key back to me. "Think ye're probably goin' to have to find that elf ye told me about if ye want those answers. But first, find Snow. Did ye go to her house?"

I nodded, pocketing the keys in my bag. "First place I checked after the library. The house was dark and all the doors were locked. If she is there..."

My words trailed off because if she had simply gone home and hadn't answered the door, after everything we had done and been through at the tavern, then she was definitely hiding more from me. My stomach hardened at the thought. I couldn't accept that possibility after our night together, after the embraces and caresses we had shared. More than once had I made myself dismiss the thoughts of how her fingers had felt wrapped around me, how she tasted like sweet rain. How I had almost found completion each time she sighed my name.

I had to find her. Had to know it all wasn't a lie, a mistake.

"What if she's not here, Varys?" Leona asked after I'd remained silent. "What if someone took her and she's no longer in Elros."

I ran a hand through my hair, sighing. "If that's the case, whoever took her are probably cohorts of our enemy. If we don't find her within the hour, I will turn my search to another."

"Who?"

I held up the pendant. "Ramos told me to swing by their tent today to discuss our next plan of action. They're jewelers, and I just so happen to be in need of a new chain."

Leona blinked at me. "Fawkes...the jeweler brothers are dead."

I gave her a sly, clever smile. "Ah. Three of them, yes. There were four brothers at the tavern last night."

***

It was only about eleven o'clock in the morning when the sun disappeared behind dark gray clouds. The winds sliced through our cloaks like icy daggers, and the look of the thunderhead over the market and its low, bizarre and lumpy clouds that had produced on its underbelly made my senses tingle with alarm. Those strange formations were usually the sign of a particularly strong storm. It wasn't but a few moments after I took note of the brooding sky when thunder rolled overhead and rain began to pour down.

Leona and I rushed for the closest alcove. I wiped my eyes just as the door behind us opened, and realized we were huddled under the entryway of Mr. Flax's bakery.

The halfling dipped his head out. "You two want to come in where it's warm?"

Smiling down at him, I said, "Thank you good sir, but we'll be all right."

I had always liked Mr. Flax. He had treated me and my father well even though we weren't part of the merchant guild. Had even thrown in a loaf of bread for free here and there.

"It's coming down hard," he remarked, looking up at the sky. "Was sunny just an hour ago. But good business for me. People tend to start craving hot pies when it rains."

A warm feeling spread in my chest, his words reminding me of

Mae's amazing baking. The air smelled like her skin, and as I watched the clouds flash with light, I swallowed down the undeniable yearning. I longed to be with her, to find her. All I wanted was to just be next to her as we discussed The ReEmergence, together discovering this new world that affected us.

I felt Leona's stare drilling into me. She gave me a tentative smile and said quietly, "We'll find her, Fawkes."

I went to nod when Mr. Flax asked, "Find who? You've lost someone?"

Leona and I exchanged glances. I often wondered if halflings meant to eavesdrop, or if they really did have naturally good hearing. Either way, I hadn't met a halfling who wasn't as curious as a child, and I reminded myself a lot that if I were that small, I would be constantly looking up and listening to make sure I wasn't trounced upon.

"A good friend, yes," I told him. "You wouldn't happen to have seen Miss Mordaunt around, have you?"

Mr. Flax's deep brown eyes went wide. "Mae's missing now?" He wrung his hands. "Gods speak, I hope she's all right."

By the use of her first name, I realized he was a friend of hers as well. "She went missing from The Nook and Cranny last night."

He gripped his flour covered shirt at his chest. "I pray she hasn't found the same fate as Willem Welch and Theon Brooker."

Heat swelled in the pit of my stomach. "What fate? Did the search party find them?"

His eyes were grave as he shook his head. "Ah, you've not heard. The two were found dead in the market early this morning."

Shock rushed through me, stealing my breath as I snapped my head to Leona. She mirrored my expression.

Dead.

"How early this morning?" I asked the halfling, barely able to speak.

"Apparently, after midnight."

Around the time Mae disappeared.

My body went cold as my thoughts raced through everything Leona and I had spoken about the day before. What if all this time,

Willem and Theon had been in hiding in fear of Mae finding them?

What if she had left the tavern because she saw an opportunity to finally strike them down?

I didn't want to believe that. And a part of me refused to.

"Mr. Wynhart?"

Mr. Flax's voice snapped me out of my head and I took a massive breath.

Leona's hands were on my shoulders. "Ye look faint, lad."

I *felt* faint. Nausea had returned and I didn't know if I could hold it back for much longer.

"Sorry," I muttered. "Long night."

Leo stepped back and Mr. Flax opened his door wider. "You sure you don't want to come in?"

I shook my head, swallowing. "We should probably continue our search for Mae. I won't be able to rest until she's found."

His salt-and-pepper brows furrowed, the umber skin of his forehead wrinkling. "I don't think my heart could take it if something happened to her."

I locked focus with Mr. Flax. There was something like desperation on his face, but as he studied me the expression turned optimistic. "But I know you'll find her, Mr. Wynhart," he told me. "You care for her—it's written all over your face."

I did. I cared for her more than I had allowed myself to. Ever since Leona had told me I was being reckless when I confessed I was falling for Mae, I'd kept it to myself. But between the sensual words we had whispered, within the strokes I'd left on her skin with my lips and tongue, I had shown her just how much I cared. How much I wanted—*needed* her. Not just physically, not just temporarily. I didn't care that we had moved quickly. I knew for a fact that I would never leave her, never hurt her. She would be safe and cared for, and I would always make sure of that.

Because I loved her.

But I didn't want to feel any of it. Not right now. Not when there were so many uncertainties. I owed my heart that much, didn't I?

I bowed my head. "Have a good day, Mr. Flax. I—"

"You know," he interrupted me suddenly, "it's probably inappropriate for me to say this…"

He urged me to stoop down to his height. I obliged and he glanced toward the market momentarily before he came closer, eyeing me as he whispered, "I'm not entirely sure about that family. The Mordaunts. Fantine and Rucas, I mean."

Leona made a sputtering sound with her lips. "Damn pricks."

Mr. Flax's brows rose upon her curse, but he nodded in agreement. "Mae has *always* been an absolute treasure. I've never known another person like her. Sometimes I feel like she is both sunshine and rain, and not truly meant for this world. She's an excellent baker and yet that stubborn man she calls Father refused my proposal of Mae absorbing this bakery when it's my time to leave this world."

My heart snagged at that. "She dreams of owning her own bakery."

"I don't doubt it. She's got talent." He swallowed. "Sometime when she was younger, I got this rather odd feeling that I should look out for her as much as I can. However, I'm not getting any younger. I'm a hundred and thirty-five this year. So I've just managed to keep her in my shop longer, lending my ear if she ever needed to talk, teaching her recipes and techniques. Maybe it's just these old eyes, but more than once I've seen bruises on her arms under those pretty sleeves."

I stared at him, his words stilling the beating of my heart. "What do you mean?"

Tension bracketed his mouth. "Long, dark lines around her wrists."

My breath faltered.

"Last summer, she came into the store with a limp. She'd claimed she had fallen from one of her flares, but I saw that bruise." His eyes darkened. "Looked like a boot to her calf."

The rattling in my bones was something I'd never felt before. With it came a raging heat, overpowering the uneasiness in my stomach, taking control of all thoughts. I could no longer look at him, at Leona. Couldn't hear either of them. All I knew was the unadulterated, cold fury washing through me, wave after wave of a sickening realization.

I didn't recognize my voice, the darkness of it as I asked, "You think she's being abused?"

Mr. Flax gulped and nodded as he held my gaze, his features just as hard and grim as my own. He pointed a finger at me. "You're a good man, Mr. Wynhart," he started. "When she is found, and I pray that she is, I implore you to take this information and use it to protect her."

A gave a short nod. "I will, sir. Don't you worry."

He sighed, rubbing his knuckles. His voice flooded with emotion, "I fear keeping that to myself all these years may have cost her life. But I was...terrified that if I spoke up, and it not be the truth, it would cost me mine."

I rested a hand on his shoulder. "You are not to blame."

He shook his head, whispering, "Silence can be the deadliest weapon of all. I have lost enough to know that." He took a deep breath and inclined his head. "Find her, Varys."

"I will."

He didn't say anything else as he turned and slipped inside his bakery.

The rapid beating of my heart returned. Avoiding Leona's awaiting gaze, I spun toward the rainy market and stalked away, out from under the alcove.

"Fawkes," Leo called from behind, a warning in her voice.

I wasn't listening. The cold rain hit me, drenching my hair and face. I barely felt it. Barely heard the thunder clapping above. My head shook involuntarily, as if I couldn't believe this. But I wasn't surprised. Not a damn bit. What I'd seen and heard in the alley with Rucas and the Whitakers should have made me aware that his villainy didn't stop there.

But was it just Rucas? Was it her mother, too? Was there more to what she had told us about the Welches? The Brookers?

Questions hit me over and over like bricks to my head. Every single person in power in this blasted town was connected to one another through money—through the merchant guild. How long had Rucas been able to hide his abuse because of who he had paid off to keep quiet? Who else had he abused?

Maybe that's why Mae was so scared. She didn't know how to get herself out.

Leona's boots clinked behind me as she ran around, hands raised in a placating manor. She had lifted her cloak over her head. "Varys. Please stop, just for a moment."

I halted, biting out, "What if she's scared to be with me because she knows her father will hurt her?"

Leo's mouth parted, but she didn't answer. I stepped in closer, keeping the conversation out of earshot from the people rushing about around us.

"I think that's it." My jaw tightened. "That's probably why she's hiding now—"

"Varys, *don't* let this get in the way of the possibility that Snow may be in danger—"

I let out a cruel laugh. "Leo, she's in danger *anyway*."

She gulped, nodding. "Then we continue to search for her. We find her, and get her out of whatever situation she may be in." She took the hood of my cloak and pulled it over my soaked head. "Breathe, Varys."

I did as she told me, inhaling the chilly, stormy air. "I will find her," I promised. "And when I do, if I find out Rucas has indeed hurt her...I swear, Leo. I swear to every silent god that I'll do anything I can to get her out. I will risk *everything* to set her free."

CHAPTER 35

Varys

Up and down the streets we searched, dipping in and out of shops, knocking on doors and asking around. No one had seen her. Most barely even knew of the murder at The Nook and Cranny, however that didn't surprise me. The majority of patrons last night were visitors, so we decided our next stop was their campgrounds, though I wasn't expecting much luck, especially now that it was pouring. These people would be preoccupied with the mud and leaking tents, not a missing person.

We were just about to head down yet another alley when my stomach grumbled painfully. A heavy exhaustion had settled in my muscles. I had officially been up for twenty-four hours and I didn't see sleep in my immediate future.

I stopped in my tracks. "Leo, go get some food."

"What?"

"Go rest." I raised my voice over the thrum of the rain, turning to her. "We won't find her on empty stomachs. You go first."

Her leg armor clinked as she shifted her weight to one hip and crossed her arms. "And what exactly will ye do?"

"Continue searching."

"On an empty stomach. Right." Her lips pursed. "Fawkes, do ye know what Snow would do if she learned you weren't takin' care of ye'self searchin' for her?"

I smirked. "She'd probably be mad."

"Good. That brain of yers is still workin'. So—"

"I'll be fine," I insisted, hoping she didn't hear how my insides argued. "You go eat and then we'll switch out. I'm heading for the campgrounds."

Leo pressed a hand to her waist cincher, grimacing. "I'm honestly too hungry to argue with you any longer."

I laughed out. "Go. We'll meet up—"

She cut me off. "At Da's tent. He's comin' into town early to set up for the fest. Meet me there."

I agreed, and for another moment she stood looking up at me. With a swallow, she said, "Don't use yer magic unless ye have to."

"I won't," I promised.

"Ye're tired. Ye haven't eaten."

"Leo." I placed a hand on her shoulder. "I won't."

Another beat passed before she nodded and turned, metal boots clinking against the rocky wet road as she strode back into the still bustling market.

The bell struck noon, and it seemed the temperature dropped with every chime. I had pulled Mae's cloak over my own for extra warmth, but both were soaked. I didn't mind being wet and cold, I just worried how long my book bag would keep the water from my spellbook. I held it against me as I walked, making sure both cloaks covered it more than anything.

I knocked on another door belonging to a family my father knew. I couldn't help but eye the foundation of the house as I waited. Homes in this area were notorious for collapsing because of too much rain. This family was at the bottom of the hill on flatter land, but I hoped the houses on their shared hillside would last.

I moved on when no one answered. My eyes had started to burn from lack of sleep, so I found a bench to sit for a moment, letting my head fall back to the icy rain to promptly rouse me.

Metal swished and clanged off to my right, drawing my attention to a group of guards rushing between a group of houses and around a corner. The moment the last guard disappeared, someone in a blue cloak stepped out from under an alcove and into the pouring rain. I froze, knowing for certain there hadn't been someone there before. A shivery awareness rushed through me, making my hairs stand on end. *Magic.* The person had just cast a spell, or I was feeling the reverberation of one that had ended.

I quickly looked down, making sure my hood would cover the glow of my eyes and prepared to cast *Vid Medaes*—

Metal sharp and cold pressed to my neck. My spine went rigid as thin fingers wrapped around my bicep, someone's cold breath in my ear. "Ya move so much as an inch, I'll run this blade across ya throat." A young woman's voice. "Why're you following me?"

I kept my breaths steady, tried not to swallow. A bob of the throat would guarantee a nick. "I'm not," I gritted out, finding the pommel of my own dagger beneath my cloak. "If you didn't want to be seen, you shouldn't have stepped out of that illusion spell, *yrçen.*"

She seemed to still behind me. "Wha's your name?"

"I don't give that kind of information away to people who hold knives to my throat."

"What if it's a matter of your name, or I cut ya?"

I sucked in a breath. She sounded young. A teenager. Probably scared of her new powers, thus she was jumping to violence to protect herself in the only way she knew how. "Varys."

The dagger left my throat then, and the girl stepped back with a, "Oh, shit. You're that man."

I stood and spun to her, having to tilt my head down quite a bit to make eye contact. She wore a black mask over her mouth and nose, but it was her eyes that made me pause. Bright yellow irises parallel to a gilded moon. I immediately looked her over, recognizing the blue cloak with gold trimming she wore.

Ramos's remaining sibling wasn't a brother at all.

A sister.

"Sorry," she muttered, stepping back. "That's embarrassing."

I went to laugh, but…this young teen who barely came past my rib cage had managed to put a dagger to my throat, and could have killed me before I had even processed a thought. *That* was embarrassing.

"Don't worry about it. I apologize for alarming you," I told her, running a hand through my hair. "I'm looking for someone, but oddly enough, I've been searching for you, too."

"Why?"

"Hoping for some answers. Have anywhere we can talk?"

She glanced around, yellow eyes seeming to brighten when lightning flashed. "You know I could have killed you?"

"No need to rub it in." I lifted my hands. "I just want to talk."

Another beat passed before she nodded. "Follow me."

Wards readied, I did.

I was surprised when Ramos's sister passed the Jeweler Brother's tent, eyeing the large red and white sign that read something about fine jewelry from Shade's Crescent. Instead, she began to lead me toward the mass of campgrounds. We stopped before a small tent that looked like it had seen better days. She lifted the flap, and after she gestured me forward, I ducked my head and went in. At first glance, I could tell she had been the only one here. There was barely enough room for the two of us, but it was dry. She sat down on the bedroll, and I took a seat just inside the flap.

When she pulled the hood of her cloak down, the mask came with it. It took everything in me not to audibly gasp as I looked upon her face for the first time. She'd been sliced open from the corner of her mouth to the middle of her cheek, the wound stitched together in a very impromptu manner. My first thought was that she had probably been injured at the tavern, but it wasn't swollen and the yellow-green bruises around her skin indicated this wound was a few weeks old at least.

I tried not to focus on the injury, drawing my eyes to the shade of her hair. Where Leo's was the shade of copper with fiery undertones, this girl's hair was a summer sunset, the exact color of flame. And even pulled back into a high ponytail, it cascaded well past her hips.

"M'name is Amerilys. Go by Meri, though," she said, speaking out of the unscathed side of her mouth. Her lashes flicked to the wound. "Got this a few weeks ago. Don't know if Ramos mentioned it."

"He didn't," I said carefully. "I'm terribly sorry about your brothers. Very glad you're all right."

Meri sighed through her nose. "My twin felt it coming. Told me to hide. Now, I'm just trying to survive. Been avoiding the guards 'cause someone told them about me—that I was related to them. I need to leave sooner rather than later, so I spent the morning selling the entire stock of jewelry and tools to a jeweler here in town."

My brows shot up. "You sold your business?"

"No." She sounded amused. "Was my brothers' business. What's a fourteen-year-old going to do with a bunch of stuff like that?"

Fourteen. She really was just a kid.

She went on, "Sold it all for a lot of money and I'm going to use it to get back to Mirefield."

I folded my arms. "Because The Dragon is there, right?"

Her catlike yellow eyes narrowed. "Yeah. He's got a place I can stay a while."

I nodded slowly, not knowing exactly how I felt about this fourteen year old girl traveling to such a dangerous city to meet with a vigilante. "This is what your brothers wanted?"

She shrugged. "Don't care. The only reason I've had to travel with them is 'cause Father died three seasons ago. Bear got 'im. Cadoc, my twin, was only starting his apprenticeship when we were forced to flee Shade's Crescent, so he couldn't take care of me. I begged Ramos to stay with me, but Syrus..." Her face hardened. "He made us all go."

"Ramos told me there were killers after you all. Sounds like you *needed* to go."

"Yeah, and look what that got 'em. Dead anyway. Even Cadoc."

I bit my lip. "I'm so sorry—"

"Honestly? Don't bother," she snapped. "I'm better off without them."

I grimaced, but didn't push her. There was obviously a feud in this family I hadn't been aware of, and had no reason to get in between now.

She shrugged her cloak off completely, revealing the too-big men's tunic she was wearing tucked into a pair of dirty, ripped pants. But there on her hip was a holster of sorts. Two leather strips connected to the belt she wore and holding a small leather bound book. Ramos had told me one of his siblings was a wizard, so I wondered if that was her spellbook. If so, I definitely needed to get a holster like that so I could quit carrying my book bag everywhere.

"So, you're here for a reason," she stated as if to say *get on with it.*

I nodded. "Before everything that happened last night, Ramos and I had spoken about The Dragon's agenda."

She tilted her head from side to side. "More Ramos and Syrus's agenda. The Dragon is just willing to help."

My optimism dwindled a bit. "Do you think now that they have passed, he'll still be open to discussing things further?"

She shrugged. "You'll have to find him first."

I sighed. "That was my next question. Do you know where he lives?"

She let out a high pitched laugh. "He doesn't *live* anywhere. He resides in places. First place I'd look is The Chaste Cat."

"What's that?"

She grinned as much as she could. "It's where all the rakes go 'nd spend their coin."

I gave a slow nod in understanding. "So a brothel. He's there a lot?"

"Yeah, but it's not like that." She scrunched her nose. "He's got some sort of agreement with the headmistress. Defender of the entertainers there or something. He's not a regular, if you know what I mean."

I cleared my throat, then changed the subject, "It'll be a start. Thank you."

Taking a quick glance around the tent, there was only a small pack leaning against the farthest support pole. Mirefield was a good week on foot from Elros. If there were rations inside, there couldn't be much. Since she had just acquired a lot of money for selling her brothers' wares, I figured she could probably get more on the way. But did she know what to do if she encountered wild animals? Traffickers? She was already injured.

I would worry myself sick if I didn't at least offer. "My companions and I will be leaving within the next couple of days. You are more than welcome to join us. Traveling with a group is much safer."

She ran her fingers through her long ponytail, and I took note of the crescent moon ornament pinned where the hair was gathered. "Thanks, but no. I've spent a season and a half running only for my brothers to wind up dead. No offense, but I don't trust you. Don't trust anyone right now. I've got my ways of remaining unseen, 'nd that will get me to Mirefield just fine."

"That's fair," I said slowly, thoughts snagged on a few of her words. "Is it some sort of invisibility spell you speak of?"

She snorted. "Oh, please. You've got to give me more credit than that. If another mage had *Vid Medaes* active, they'd spot me. That spell's only good for those without magic."

"So what is this spell? Is that how you escaped the enemy at the tavern?"

She nodded. "It's called shadow walking. You probably noticed I stepped out from under a dark alcove 'nd I could be seen again. If there's a shadow, I can walk into it 'nd hide—that simple. And I can move from shadow to shadow."

My eyes went wide. "Is it exhausting?"

She lifted her palms. "Was at first, I guess. Just got good at it."

"Can you teach it to me?"

Her nose twisted, and she stated curtly, "No."

"Why?"

"Because it's the spell that has kept me *alive*. I'm not about to give it away. I don't care if our great ancestors, or whatever, shared their favorite spells like they did recipes. Nowadays, magic is going to become a lot like the merchant market—knowledge 'nd items are sold for a pretty price, or you might find some shady shit in the black market."

With that, she reached behind her back and pulled out a stick about as long as her forearm. I had to refrain from snatching it from her, knowing exactly what it was by the raw quartz wired to the top and the Elvish runes carved into the wood.

"That's a wand," I breathed.

She wobbled her head proudly. "That's right. Got this *in* Mirefield. That's where a lot of the good stuff is. Been saving its charges for something special."

Almost every reputable mage I had read about had carried wands or a staff back in the first age. They used them as an extension of their magic, storing several charges of one spell inside so they could use the magic later without using their own energy. Crafted from things of nature, a wand's body was made from twisted roots or sturdy twigs, where large branches made staves. In the illustrations I had seen, they were often decorated with clay beads, small stones or crystals, leaves and vines, or feathers, attached to the body with string or wire. The embellishments used were merely for aesthetics, bringing a personal and creative touch to the instrument.

But the most important process of creating either a wand or staff was enchanting the chosen foci, which was usually a translucent gemstone like quartz. Once the spell was cast, the foci was attached to the head of the instrument, and the runes for whatever spell laid within was then carved into the wood.

The runes on Meri's wand read *Álaçarna'Çor. Fireball*. "Is that a pretty strong spell?" I asked in awe, glancing at the crimson beads braided into the burlap tassels hanging from the top.

She shrugged. "Don't know. Haven't been able to use the wand yet, 'nd I haven't learned the spell."

"Just be sure you don't use the wand unless necessary, else you may not be able to re-enchant it."

An annoyed expression crossed her face, reminding me that most people found me a bit of a know-it-all when I became informative. "Yeah, got it," she said as if it was obvious. "But hey, listen, if that's all you needed to speak about, I really do need to leave. Have some things you may want, though. Some of my brother's stuff."

Reaching over to her pack, she flipped open the flap and pulled out three books, laying them before me. The top read *Uthörium's Glory*.

"Ramos bought these from that Mordaunt Treasures the other day," she explained. My pulse skipped. "He was intending to rebuild his book collection he set aflame back home. Books are heavy though. I don't want to carry any around 'sides my spellbook. So, they're yours."

I bowed my head. "Thank you. My father and I actually own a library, and have collected many elven books."

She nodded. "Well. Nice to meet you and all. Maybe we'll see each other in Mirefield."

"I feel like I'd be doing your brother a disservice if I don't at least offer to accompany you on your journey."

"Nope. I'll be fine, 'nd if not, it's not your problem."

I took that as my time to leave. "The offer remains open," I said as I placed the books inside my bag. Something glimmered at the bottom, snagging my attention and reminding me of the other reason I had wanted to seek out Ramos's sibling. I picked up the pendant and its broken chain. "You wouldn't happen to have any way to fix this? I can pay a silver."

I held up the broken necklace. Her yellow eyes went wide. "That's a pretty stone. Unfortunately, no. I sold all the chain—*wait.*" She reached back inside her pack, feeling around for a moment before she pulled out a spool of leather cord. "Kept this 'cause the tent leaks." She pointed to a stitching right above her. "You can have some of this. Won't charge you."

She didn't give me time to respond before she unraveled a long strand's worth, ripped it off the spool and handed it to me in a clump.

I sighed. "It'll get the job done."

She shrugged. "If you want a chain, I can point you to the jeweler I sold my brothers' wares to."

I shook my head, knowing exactly who she had probably sold to. A man named Mr. Lovis who was part of the merchant guild and had never been affordable. "Thank you, but the cord will do for now."

She grinned. "Is it a betrothal necklace?"

I chuckled, lacing the cord through the pendant's bail. "It is a gift for the woman I love. There's some sort of protection spell on it."

I knotted the two ends together and held the necklace up, frowning in disappointment. The leather was just too plain for the elegance of the pendant. Even in the dim light due to the ongoing rainstorm, the small iridescent jewels still glinted with rainbows.

Meri looked on to the jewel with fondness in her eyes. "She's a lucky lady then. To have someone who wants to make sure she's always protected."

I blew out my bottom lip, feeling the weight of her words. "Unfortunately I've been terrible at protecting her so far. She went missing last night and I'm afraid something has happened to her."

She tilted her head. "Is she *Vyl'kriev?*"

"Yes."

"Then she'll be all right." She pointed to her cheek. "Got this when bandits attacked our wagon a few weeks ago. Do you know why he cut my mouth and not my throat?" I shook my head and she continued, "This group of bandits are *tongue lurchers.* They wear the tongue of those they kill, and are all mute themselves. Some wicked mentality that has something to do with the silent gods." She rolled her eyes. "Anyway, they were trying to cut out my tongue, 'nd in the squabble, cut my mouth instead."

My stomach knotted, reminded that Duros had spoken of the bandits roaming north. I wondered how far north that meant. "I'm so sorry. Was this somewhere in the Great Plains?"

"Yeah, outside a little town north of Fairegrove."

Shit. That meant there were bandits in the lower forests of this region of Xalador.

"But here's the point I'm making—no one helped me when the bandits found us. My brothers made me sit in the wagon while they fought them off 'nd had been too distracted to notice the man who'd snuck around 'nd crawled inside. If I could have fought with them, we could have beaten those bandits faster. I *know* how to use my magic. It was unfortunate what happened to my face, but I'd rather my cheek injured than my tongue. Had he cut it out, I couldn't have cast the spell that killed him." She pointed to the necklace. "Your lady can protect herself too, you know. If she's *Vyl'kriev,* then she has magic. You have to allow her to be powerful, or she never will be."

I pursed my lips with a nod, impressed with her advice. Even though Mae's circumstances did require my protection, and I was also aware that she didn't know *how* to use her magic, I wholeheartedly believed that she was incredibly powerful. She had only displayed mere fragments of her magic. Sparks in her eyes. Gusts of wind around me. She was a bottled tempest, and when she learned how to unleash her storm, I was fully prepared and eager to watch her take on the world.

CHAPTER 36

Varys

The rain had slowed into a gentle mist, but the wind was colder. I knew if the temperature continued to drop, we might see a dusting of snow.

Searching the campgrounds was quickly becoming a complete waste of time. Meri searched with me, stopping at every couple of tents to ask people she knew if they'd seen Mae. Most just pointed to Vamir's caravan, where many white-haired men and women sat around a fire. So after Meri said her farewells, I decided to pay them a visit.

Coming into their camp slowly, I gave a friendly wave to the first person who made eye contact with me. A middle-aged looking woman with silver eyes and tawny skin, her white hair tied into a loose ponytail. She nudged the man next to her and he looked up from his bowl of whatever he was eating. It was in that moment every other person in the circle turned to me. I halted when they rose in unison, hands clutching daggers and swords at their waists.

"Hello there," I called out, raising my hands to hopefully placate them. "I'm a friend of Vamir's. I was hoping I could ask you all some questions."

"Seldszar," a younger woman said toward her comrade with the bowl who had remained seated. Seemed he knew his companions

407

could handle a fight if there was to be one, so he hadn't bothered to rise. "This man was at The Nook and Cranny last night," the young woman said. "Vamir definitely knows him."

Seldszar took another bite of his stew, and an uncomfortable silence stretched before he swallowed and glanced up to me again, long white hair falling over his russet brown shoulders. "What's your name, friend of Vamir's?"

"Varys," someone else answered for me, their voice a velvet rasp. I tried not to show my annoyance, turning to face Vamir and Orin as they walked into the camp. "Excuse my family's unwelcomeness. Most are pretty sleep deprived, especially Seldszar here."

Seldszar rolled his steel-toned eyes. "We just don't like strangers walking into our camp so casually."

I bowed my head. "I apologize. I'm just in a hurry to find my friend."

Vamir's focus flicked to mine, holding his head higher. "I'm assuming that means you haven't found Miss Mae yet?"

"No," I replied with a sigh, my stomach dropping. "Came here to see if she'd found refuge with your family."

Orin came to stand beside him, the large falcon on his shoulder studying me with black beady eyes. I told myself to relax and absolve the guarded feeling that immediately seized my bones whenever Orin came near. "I'm sorry Gawain and I haven't had much luck either," he said, and it sounded genuine. He petted the bird's head. "Usually Gawain can find someone quickly, but with all this rain, your friend's scent has probably been washed away."

A cynical laugh almost escaped my throat. I imagined it would be hard to find someone whose scent *was* rain.

"Thank you for your help anyway. We'll find her." Although, it seemed a little bit of my hope dwindled every time I said those words.

"Do you know of anyone who might hurt her? Or hold her captive?" Orin asked.

Her father came to mind immediately, but I barely had proof of that. As much as my anger wanted to usher me all the way down to Mordaunt Treasures and demand answers, I knew our enemy was the larger threat here. I just didn't know where to start. What questions to ask, who to ask, and if asking those questions would even be the smart thing to do.

Orin and Vamir were still awaiting my response, and I wondered if they knew about the disappearances and murders. Leo had told me they had traveled all over Xalador.

"Where was your caravan last? Before traveling to Elros?" I asked them.

Vamir and Orin traded glances, the crew behind them narrowing their eyes almost completely in sync. The raptor ruffled its feathers, scattering droplets of water.

"Besides the smaller settlements on our way here, we were in Fairegrove," Vamir replied, looking me up and down. "What does that have to do with Mae?"

"When you were there, did you hear of anything involving murders?"

The older woman who had been sitting next to Seldszar frowned, a hand covering her pale lips. Vamir's face tensed as he looked over to her.

"Actually, yes." He motioned me forward with two quick curls of a finger, eyeing his family, all of them solemnly focused on the older woman. "Let's not talk about that here. My brothers and sisters have been through a lot."

As I followed Vamir and Orin back into the market, the three of us were quiet. I felt as if I'd struck a nerve with his family, and the guilt had settled into my stomach like clumps of iron.

Vamir finally sighed, stopping on an empty path. "Haritha," he started, "the older woman that was sitting beside Seldszar, lost her husband—my uncle—to the people hunting Elven-blooded a few weeks before. It's why my family reacted the way they did when you entered the camp. We aren't the most trustful bunch right now."

I swallowed. "I understand. I'm terribly sorry for your loss. I only brought it up because of the murders last night. I'm terrified something has happened to Mae."

"When those three at the tavern were killed last night, my

family…" He let out a long breath, flexing his long, varnished fingers. "They don't want to stay here much longer. They're on edge. I am trying to assure them this Fest of Change will be worth the gold."

"It will be," I assured him. "The merchants have a phenomenal take home every year."

Vamir smiled slightly. "Good. I believe it will bring the kind of cheer my family needs."

We both glanced at Orin who had seemed to be waiting to redirect our conversation. "On the subject of Mae, I think it's time to begin looking outside of Elros," he suggested. "Has a search party been formed?"

I shook my head. "I don't think anyone knows she's missing except us and Leona."

I left out Mr. Flax.

Vamir's brows rose as he inspected his fingernails. "And her father."

There was a dropping sensation in my chest, my eyes widening. "What?"

He gave a simple, one-shouldered shrug with an elegant flip of his hand. "I told him this morning when he came back into town. Apparently one of those two men they set out to find, only to wind up dead, was her future husband." He chuckled. "I told him I had no idea she was promised to anyone, since she obviously has a lover."

Shit.

"He told me he had no idea she had a lover." Another laugh. "When he discovered it was you, well, I realized I probably shouldn't have said anything."

By the time he'd stopped talking, I had gone still. My mouth opened to respond, but nothing came. I wasn't entirely sure *what* to say, what to *do*. I could only stare at him, panic creeping through my veins, my bones.

"So, did the father send out a search party?" I barely comprehended Orin's question.

Vamir nodded. "He has a group of men searching for her."

The panic changed to something else entirely, and I had to press my teeth together as if to hold it back. It wasn't fear, it was a deep sense of dread as if I *knew* what was coming.

I needed to think. Needed an inkling of a lead on her. *Godsdammit*, if they found her before I did—

"I have to find her first, Vamir," I bit out, a darkness returning to my voice. I held his wide gaze. "And I need you to make sure that if you happen to find her before I do, you bring her to me."

He frowned. "Mae is Rucas's daughter."

"I don't care," I growled. "You may be on good terms with him, but he is not trustworthy."

His head tilted, silver eyes narrowing. "On what accusations?"

"You're just going to have to trust me. Whether Mae is in the hands of her father, or of those hunting us mages, she is in danger."

"Says you," he remarked. "Her father is quite worried about her."

"Is he worried about her, or is he worried about her revealing the truth?" I snapped, shaking my head. "You have no idea what you've done."

"What *I've* done?" he asked with a coy chuckle, pressing a hand to his chest. "It's not my fault you fucked the wrong father's daughter."

Silence fell between the three of us. I held his glare. Matched it with my own. A single step toward him had the falcon's beak pointed in my direction.

But Orin held up a hand with a clearing of his throat. "Boss, if I may," he said slowly, eyeing Vamir. "I know we've dealt with our fair share of crooks, but I trust Leona, and she trusts Varys."

I blinked in surprise as the two delivered a silent conversation, and whatever had been said had Vamir snarling.

"I can give her protection as well, you know." He crossed his arms. "She'll be safe with someone who understands the prejudices against her."

I shook my head. "How do I know you won't just turn her over to her father?"

A proud smirk lifted the side of his lips. "You're just going to have to trust me."

But I didn't. I couldn't. Even if his words made sense, I couldn't shake the feeling he was saying them just to persuade me. I'd seen the looks he'd given her at the tavern. They had been a mirror of my own.

Right now wasn't the time to argue over love affairs. I needed Mae safe, and that meant away from Rucas entirely. Vamir was obviously amiable with Rucas despite my accusations against him.

"I'm sorry, but I can't trust anyone close to Rucas right now."

Vamir's eyes glinted with ire.

I had to stand my ground. "And if you won't heed my request, then I will demand it—if you find her before I do, you *will* bring her to me."

His gaze traveled down my form, nostrils flared. When he met my cool stare once more, he smiled. "And what will you do if I don't?"

My chin dipped as heat flooded my veins. Every command word to every spell I knew surfaced in my immediate thoughts, that snobbish grin of his faltering as he studied my face.

I knew what he found there: A visage of pure, unyielding protectiveness for the woman I loved.

She was *mine.*

Nothing was going to stand between me and finding her.

Nothing.

"I won't need to rend her from you," I told him, my voice dark and crisp. "I will not have to destroy everything in my path to get her back. She will go where she feels safe—that much I know. But if you value her at all, you will do as I say."

His chuckle was breathy as he flipped his white hair off his shoulders. "Your suggestion is wide off the mark, but I do value her greatly."

I swallowed. "Good. Us mages need allies, and since Mae is a fellow mage…"

My words trailed off as I watched his silver eyes widen after a few blinks, surprise spreading across his features.

I lifted my chin. "You did not know?"

"It is…unexpected." A glance to Orin.

"Why?" I shook my head. "Mae is Elven-blooded, just like you. Like me. Magic is reemerging across Xalador."

Vamir didn't respond, falling silent, eyes searching the ground as if he'd find something there.

"Boss?" Orin asked.

Vamir stepped away, turning from the both of us. Another beat passed before he murmured, a hiss in his throat. "If I find her, I will bring her to you, Varys."

I didn't move, didn't breathe. His sudden change of heart was like whiplash.

When he looked back at me, the smile on his face was so genuine, I wondered if I had imagined this entire confrontation.

Maybe I…had.

"You're right," he said, his voice coaxing my nerves. "She needs protection at all costs."

With a quick jeer of his head back toward their camp, both he and Orin bowed in farewell and began to walk away.

I didn't follow. I didn't need to.

I just…trusted him.

He would keep her safe.

He would.

CHAPTER 37

I heard the bell strike two, and with every toll my eyes grew heavier, every blink burning with exhaustion and worry. Turning yet another corner, a heavy sigh laced with defeat left me as I took in the sight of the burnt-orange octagonal tent with gold tassels—Duros's tent for the fest. My stomach churned painfully, begging for food, when I breathed in the smell of meat and herbs.

Take care of myself. I had to. I had two women, and one watching over me from the stars, that would scold me until my ears bled if otherwise.

Upon entering the tent, my eyes caught the array of weapons and armor on display. There was nothing more unique than dwarven craftsmanship. One could simply look at a weapon and know just by the geometric, symmetrical designs and the use of mixed metals that the blade, axe, or hammer was crafted by a dwarf. They prided themselves on their reputation for having the finest weapons and armor in all the land.

Duros was a prime example of this. It was obvious he had been working tirelessly. No two blades were alike, and they lay along the table on stands branded with Duros's crest: a single hammer above an anvil.

I looked on in awe of a dual-sided battle axe. The leather handle was fashioned with small gold and silver studs, and there was a long spike between the two heads on either side. The socket was engraved with braided designs surrounded by diamond and triangular shapes. All of it perfectly symmetrical, and so very similar to the markings I had to draw when creating a spell's *eçor*.

There was a sword with a wide blade next to the axe, also engraved with fine lines cutting down the edges, the pommel set with a rough smoky quartz. Leo emerged from the back of the tent just as I lifted it, surveying the dark metal of the blade.

"Helped Da with that one," she told me, coming closer. "Thought about polishin' the stone, but liked how rough it was compared to the rest of it."

"Agreed."

"Named it *Wit's End.*"

I raised a brow. "Why?"

She pursed her lips in annoyance and glared up at the sword. "Because I was at my *wit's end* gettin' that stone set into the damn thing."

I was about to scold her for that terrible pun when Duros came in from behind me, carrying a few logs of wood. His turquoise irises gleamed as he met mine, setting down the logs quickly to grasp my hand with a firm grip. "Varys, lad. Ye look like ye've slept on a bed of bricks."

"He hasn't slept at all," Leo cut in.

"I'm more hungry than anything," I muttered.

"Well, lunch is brewin'." Duros patted my stomach hard enough to make me lose a few breaths. "Feel free to lay yer cloak by the fire."

I bowed my head in thanks and quickly untied Mae's cloak from around my neck, then mine, and walked over to the blazing logs. The fire felt like summer as its warmth kissed my cold face. I knelt and held my hands as close as I could comfortably, skin tingling as the blood returned to my frozen fingers.

It wasn't long before my kneeling position became taxing, so I took a seat on the ground, resting my chin on my fist. Between the warmth and the comfortable position, my eyes closed, and sleep swept in——

Thunder clapped and jolted me awake, the flail of my legs almost knocking over the bowl that had been placed in front of me. A warm chuckle came from beside me, and I found Natalia sitting and eating.

"Soup's still warm. You were out for only a few moments," she told me, handing me the bowl of what looked like beef stew. "Eat."

I thanked her and didn't allow it to cool before I began to scarf it down. I would deal with the burn on my tongue later, eager to continue searching for Mae.

But the food settled heavily in my stomach and after I finished my second helping, sleep found me once more. At some point, I laid down on the ground, ignoring the dampness and smell of mud.

My mind remained dark and undisturbed, and I was unsure of how much time was passing. I couldn't rouse myself enough to care.

Then, I was walking…

Along the bank of the stream I strode, muscles heavy and tingling. A cool hand held mine, pulling me along. Her hand.

There she was, as beautiful and mysterious as ever, tugging me to trek deeper into the forest. *"Dias çlina ít xera,"* she murmured in my ear, heating my skin…

Time stretched, and I wasn't sure how we'd ended up back at the fallen tree. The air around me was just as tense as before, but Mae seemed to dance among it, flitting around me. Her lips pressed to mine, then to my neck, her hands roaming up my shirt, mine down her slender body…

Her hair tangled among the crisp leaves, violet eyes closed, plum lips parted in sweet rapture. I couldn't feel the chill of the air anymore, nor the pressure of it. Not when the fire between us blazed.

"I *love* you," I murmured in her ear.

Her legs wrapped around my hips, pushing me deeper inside. The feeling of her consumed me entirely, and I moaned nothing but her name, like lyrics of the most beautiful song I'd ever sing.

Maelawyn…

Maelawyn…

A song of storm and sky, of something dark, dangerous, and divine.

"I'm going to find you," I promised, brushing my lips against her temple.

Her eyes opened…

Everything within me went entirely still as I stared down at her. The air began to stir, the wind rustling the leaves and trees around us as I blinked and blinked, hoping she'd return to normal.

She didn't. Her eyes remained black as if I were staring down into pits of the abyss.

My breaths came in short. No. *No*, this wasn't right. She was——

"**You will not find her**," a voice echoed in my head. "**She is exactly where she is meant to be**."

Mae's chest cracked open. I launched myself away just as a bolt of lightning struck her body, incinerating her flesh.

All that was left was ash.

I screamed for her, crawling wildly back to what was left, scooping the dust into my hands. Agony blazed a hole through my chest, splitting me open until I too began to wither away, crumbling into nothing.

From our ashes, butterflies scattered, free to fly away from the storm building, its darkness devouring the world…

"Fawkes? 'Ey, ye awake, lad?"

A hand touched my shoulder. I wasn't sure how that was possible since my body——

No, I could feel the touch. I was aware of my arms, my legs, my feet. My heart pounded against my ribs as I slowly opened my wet eyes——I had been crying in my sleep.

Leona was looking down at me, face pinched with worry. I took a shuddering breath. "It…was all a dream."

She offered a comforting smile. "Yer mum again?"

As I started to sit up, the nausea that had never truly gone away returned with a vengeance. I coughed through it, then replied, "No. This was…"

I wasn't sure what I had experienced. I wasn't even sure when I had fallen asleep. Everything had felt so real, as if a single blink had taken me from here on the ground, to the forest, then to my end. I could still feel her lips, still taste the lavender and rain on mine. I had made love to her.

Then watched lightning destroy her.

But I had not called her by her name. I had said something else. A name that felt like…truth.

"Maelawyn," I whispered.

A slight wind ruffled the tents, like the name on my lips had commanded it.

"What did ye say?" Leo asked.

I shivered. "I need to continue my search."

We were quiet for a few moments as I gathered my wits. I pulled the two cloaks from the edge of the cinders, relieved to find them both dry and warm.

Leona swallowed when I looked at her. "Ye know ye were out for two hours."

I sighed. "Figured as much. I'm still exhausted."

Her face scrunched. "While ye were out, I looked all over this bloody town. She's not here, Fawkes. I don't think she's in Elros anymore."

I nodded, stomach hardening. A huge part of me had already realized that. "I think I know where to look."

I stood and began to tie the cloaks around me. "We need to go back to the tree."

Leona stared at me for a long moment, as if she was processing a realization. "All right. But first things first."

She turned and grabbed a small wooden box off the workbench, handing it to me with a slight grin. "I told ye the other day I was workin' on somethin'. Ye know how I am about my random gifts."

I did. Leona was probably the best gift giver I knew, but I didn't just receive them on my birthday, or within the wreath she always made for me on Hearthswreath. She gave spontaneous gifts over the course of the year, and I always told her as I did now, "I swear Leo, one day I'm going to get you something so amazing, it'll make up for all the gifts you've given me."

She, like always, rolled her eyes and said, "Hurry up and open it." But this time added, "Just…don't hate me."

My brows knitted in confusion, but I lifted the top of the box. Inside was a bundle of black leather straps, fastened together with brilliant steel rings and rivets. I realized it was some sort of belt when I flipped over the plate-style buckle and blinked in awe of the trillion-cut sapphire embedded into the face of it.

I didn't have to ask what the belt was for. Leo had grabbed a sheathed longsword, then took the belt from me and slid the scabbard into a small loop attached to the many straps. "It's a sword belt. First one I've made."

She motioned for me to stand before her, then showed me how the straps wrapped around my waist twice. She adjusted it, pulling it tighter at one of the rings, and then I finished buckling it.

Leo stepped back to survey me, crossing her arms. "I made a damn good lookin' belt, aye?"

I chuckled. "Yeah, you did." I rested my wrist on the pommel of the sword, for the first time feeling comfortable with one at my side beyond training. "Thank you, Leo. It's perfect."

"Not yet." She tapped the sapphire. "There's a reason I chose a sapphire, and not just 'cause it matches yer hair."

I smirked. "It's my eyes, isn't it?"

She scoffed. "The belt is universal. I made it that way because eventually, I want to see Krystan's blade on ye. *It* matches the sapphire."

My chest tightened as Leona's eyes shifted back and forth, searching my face for the grimace I knew she would find. She took a step forward. "Why do ye still doubt ye'self?"

I breathed out my nose, frustrated old fears continued to keep me back. "I couldn't explain it if I tried."

She was quiet for a few breaths before she placed a hand on my arm. "Ye'll never be ready if ye don't allow ye'self to be. Ye didn't get to decide when ye'd reemerge." She said the last word a bit quieter. "But ye can decide what ye goin' to do now that ye have."

I inclined my head with a soft sigh. Those words had been said to me a thousand times, or some variation of them. They had never been able to intervene and destroy the self-deprecation and anxieties, no matter how badly I wanted them to. Leona was my trainer and best friend—it should have been enough. Unfortunately, my issues were deeper, born of grief and trauma I still faced everyday along with the nightmares that often tormented me.

But I didn't have time to sort them out. Not when so much was at risk and Mae was in danger.

"When I leave for Elvidawn, I'll take Mother's sword," I vowed, surprised by the steadiness of my voice.

Leona's eyes widened. "And when do ye plan to do that?"

A fluttery feeling had replaced the tightness in my chest. "When I find Mae."

Her shoulders slacked, hands falling to her sides. "That soon? What if ye find her today?"

I shrugged. "All I want is her safety. If that means I leave Elros today, so be it."

"Without supplies? Use yer head, Varys." She smacked my chest lightly. "Ye can't leave town without food."

"I know that. I'll figure it out. I promise."

Her mouth parted, freckled face flushing red. "B-But...yer father. The library." She gulped. "What about...what about me? We had planned on leavin' *together,* Fawkes. I'm comin' with ye."

Taking her shoulders, I dipped down to her eye level. "I still want that. I want to leave this wretched town with you *and* Mae."

She huffed, and I knew she was uncomfortable with how impulsive I was being. She was used to me being the stable one with all my plans, my life determined.

But since my reemergence, nothing in my life had been stable.

"You just have to understand something, Leo." I lowered my voice. "If I find her in the clutches of our enemy, we will have to run."

Her jaw tightened. "Where will we go?"

"Mirefield."

She squinted. "Ye want to leave Elros for fuckin' *Mirefield.* Do ye have a death wish?"

"There's a *Vyl'kriev* there seeking alliances. We will be safer with him." I paused, squeezing her shoulders. "Promise me something, Leo. If we're ever split up, I need you to promise that you will still travel to Mirefield to find The Dragon."

Her brows rose slightly. "What?"

"Promise?" I asked again.

She nodded slowly, interest swirling in her emerald eyes. "No matter what. Mirefield to find The Dragon."

———

Leona buckled Thorn onto her back as I helped myself to yet another bowl of Natalia's stew, hoping it would keep me from getting hungry in case our venture led us elsewhere. The drizzling had returned, but what was worse was the wind. We were just about to head out when a strong gale swept inside the tent. Duros shouted a stream of Dwarvish curses as some of his displays blew over, running over to quickly pick up the daggers and axes that had toppled to the ground. It wasn't a few moments before another gust rushed inside, taking a support pole with it. None of us were fast enough to catch it as it fell on top of Duros.

"*Da!*" Before Natalia and I could reach him, Leona had already barrelled over a table. I was reminded of her natural strength when she lifted the pole off her father without so much as a wince, a few coughs and angry sounds telling us he was fine.

"Bah, don't worry ye'self, rosebud," Duros told her as he brushed himself off. "It'll take more than that to do yer ol' Da in."

She grinned, but couldn't reply before another gust blew in, the collapsed side of the tent billowing and flapping. There was no way to keep the rain out on that side, so Natalia and Duros asked us to keep an eye on the wares while they went to purchase lumber for a new pole. We agreed, even though frustration and impatience prickled my skin. Every passing moment was another away from Mae, another reminding me she was still missing and possibly in danger.

Leona sent me to the back after I had apparently paced the length of the tent one too many times. I untied the laces of my boots only to retie them tighter, checked the straps and buckles of my belts, adjusted the collar of my shirt under the cloaks—finding anything I could to keep my mind off the fact that we were not already on our way to find Mae. My chest pounded hard enough I wondered if my ribs could hold it in much longer.

Leona greeted someone out front, welcoming them into the tent and quickly explained the pole situation.

"Hoping to trade for a new dagger," I heard a man say. "Didn't know *you'd* be here."

The man's voice was familiar, but something about it made my annoyance flare.

I stepped out, eyes locking on Eryx RothHall standing before one of the tables. His amber-brown eyes widened, only to heat with sudden anger. I didn't have time to react before he pulled his shortbow from his back and loosed an arrow. It flew past me, its point striking another support pole.

Metal sang—I knew the tune too well. Thorn had been unsheathed.

But Eryx had already nocked another arrow and stepped out of Leona's reach. I drew my own sword, although I wasn't entirely sure why I needed to.

"*Where is she?*" Eryx yelled from behind the fletching. "I know you're hiding her, so tell me where she is."

CHAPTER 38

Varys

"Put down the bow, RothHall," Leona demanded, Thorn extended in his direction.

"Not until I see Mae," he said, eyes like thin slivers of amber. "I've been all over town, knowing she'd be with you, Wynhart. Your little game of hide and seek is over."

I chuckled. "It's not my game. I've been looking all over to find her as well."

The tension on his bow loosened a bit. "You're lying. Her father said she'd be with you."

I rolled my eyes. "Well, it's not the first time Rucas Mordaunt has lied about the wellbeing of his daughter."

Eryx's expression pinched. "What are you talking about?"

"Put the bow down"—I sheathed my sword—"and I'll tell you. There's no need for this. It's a misunderstanding."

I quickly glanced at Leona, her eyes wide and infuriated. Apparently, that had given Eryx the wrong signal and he released the arrow. It whistled as it flew by, landing yet again on the support pole behind me.

"Eyes on me, Wynhart," Eryx growled. "Or the next one won't miss its mark."

The next one would miss if I used my wards, however doing so would reveal a secret I was not ready to share just yet. Especially with him.

"Tell me where she is," he demanded.

"I don't know," I said a little softer, raising my hands. "But I'd be very open to talking about what happened last night if I didn't have a bow pointed at me."

Eryx sneered. "I think I can believe that. You don't ever *stop* talking."

I stifled the smirk wanting to rise. "Let's not be petty when we have a mutual friend in danger."

He blinked, as if the last few words released him from an enchantment. "Danger?"

I pulled the flap to the back of the tent, revealing the empty area. "She isn't here, so how about we chat?"

It was another beat before he lowered his bow, keeping an uncertain gaze on Leo. Only when Eryx slid the arrow back into his quiver did her arms slack, lowering Thorn's point to the ground with a displeased expression.

"We should discuss things in the back," I stated.

"I'm smarter than that, Wynhart," Eryx snapped. "We leave our weapons out here."

———

There was a cot in the back area which Leo quickly claimed, laying out like a lazy cat. Eryx and I remained standing, facing each other across the space with folded arms. I found myself digging the heels of my boots into the ground, dreading the confrontation coming as Eryx glared at me from beneath his dark green hood.

With a tilt of his head, he began, "There are some things I don't quite understand. Not that they really matter, but I've been hunting for a week in the forest and when I left, Mae for sure was not seeing you. She knows better."

My eyes narrowed. "Knows better? Because Rucas hurts her?"

Eryx's chin jeered back—I had hoped that would catch him off guard. "Excuse me? What do you mean by that?"

"Exactly what it sounds like."

His mouth parted on the sharp breath he took, which told me he knew nothing about Rucas's alleged abuse. Relaying that information could work to my advantage. I doubted Eryx would stay in good graces with Rucas if he knew, and as much as I was beginning to despise this guy, I needed allies right now more than anything.

I exhaled, loosening the tension of my shoulders. "I only learned today, and I don't know for how long. But it could be one reason she would be in hiding."

"You told me she was in danger."

"Yeah. *Rucas* might be the danger."

An incredulous expression tightened his features. "She told you this?"

I shook my head. "I learned it from a trustworthy source."

"I'll be the judge of that," he snapped. "Who was it?"

I held his gaze for a moment as annoyance threatened to raise my temper. "I am not a man of gossip. This person doesn't deserve to be pulled into this, but they wouldn't have said anything to me if they didn't care for Mae."

"Then until I see it, or Mae tells me herself, I'll take your words as hearsay."

I jerked my chin back. *"Why?"*

He uncrossed his arms with a stifled laugh as if my question amused him. "Mae is practically my sister. I've been in and out of the Mordaunt's home my entire life and I've never seen anything like what you are claiming."

I let my head fall backward in an attempt to compose my frustration. "You really think someone as proud as Rucas is would make the abuse known?"

He shook his head in disbelief and looked away. "Mae would have told me."

"I doubt that," I muttered. "She's not one to reveal her secrets so easily."

That typical disdain for me I'd seen multiple times flickered in his eyes. "Ah, I guess you know all about her now that you've fucked her."

My veins rushed with heat. Leona sat up, but I eyed her before she could lash out. This was the second time today I had been accused of "fucking" Mae. Twice now had the term been used to degrade me, to question my integrity, to claim me as some kind of pervert and put me on the same damn level as Willem and Theon.

Holding Eryx's glare, I entwined my fingers behind my back and stepped toward him. "So…" I let the word hang for a moment, the grit in my voice deep and cold, "That's what makes me the threat in this situation. Mae and I have a relationship that her abusive father and overbearing pretend-brother don't approve of."

Eryx's jaw tensed, and he too stepped forward. "You. Touched. Her." He jabbed a finger into my shoulder. "That absolutely makes you a villain in my eyes."

Fury ignited in my chest. I opened my mouth to retort, but Leona objected, "Ye're a bloody idiot, huntsman." Standing, she pushed herself between us, hands on her hips as her head tipped back to seethe up at Eryx. "Ye've villainized the wrong man, but don't worry. The sick fuck who violated Snow is dead, along with his accomplice."

He looked down at her, face twisted in disgust as if just looking at her made him nauseated. "What are you talking about?"

I pulled Leona away from him and replied, "If you've turned a blind eye to the abuse of her father, I guess I'm not surprised Mae doesn't trust you to know about Willem Welch's attempts either."

Shadows seemed to dance behind his dusky gaze, brows pinching as he leaned in closer. "Attempts at *what*?"

The last word bit out like a threat, so I made myself as clear as possible. "Willem has tried to rape her more than once. A week ago, he tried to do so for his last time with Theon Brooker's help."

His face contorted into molten rage, glancing between us as silent as death. Then, he knelt as he slid his pack from his shoulders, reaching inside to grab something, tossing it at me in a blur of silver and magenta. I caught it, fumbling to keep my hold on it.

My spine went rigid, fingers tightening around the thin wire. I recognized it immediately, but now that it was in my hand, I could feel the warmth of magic radiating from it.

The circlet Mae had been wearing that day in the shop before the events of the stream.

"Does that story of yours have anything to do with this?" Eryx inclined his head. "It was laying on Willem's body when *I* discovered both him and Theon dead in the market early this morning. Placed there as if to make some kind of fucking point."

My breath left me in a shudder.

A muscle feathered in his jaw. "What's going on, Wynhart?"

Every word I knew in every language I spoke was suddenly unattainable. My pulse began to thunder in my ears as I merely stared between him and the circlet.

Mae...

This was evidence. This proved she truly murdered Willem and Theon.

I had always considered myself a man of good morals, but at that moment, I wanted to do nothing but get rid of the circlet. Hide it somewhere so that no one would find it ever again and Mae would remain innocent.

"What is that?" Leona asked me as Eryx tried to take the circlet back.

"It's Mae's." I held on to it, pulling it out of Eryx's reach. "S-She was wearing this...that day."

"That day, before she killed them?" Eryx asked. "Did they try to hurt her and she killed them?"

"I...I don't know—"

"Don't give me that bullshit," Eryx snapped, swiping a hand in the air before yanking the circlet away from me. "You know a lot, and it's time to speak up."

I held up my hands as if to slow things down.

I needed everything to slow down.

I couldn't think fast enough and there were so many questions. Not enough answers.

"She was wearing it at the shop, but I don't recall her wearing it at the stream. And Willem and Theon—they *were* alive when I got there, but ran off." I swallowed, sweat forming on the back of my neck. "Injured. Mae defended herself."

Shit. That was too much information.

She had defended herself with her magic.

I backpedaled, fumbling over my words. "S-She said she'd kicked and hit them."

That had been the very first lie she'd ever told me.

"I-I don't know what happened after I left her that day," I told him. "But I don't believe Mae is capable of killing those two."

Eryx's chin lowered. "Not alone, no. I think she had help."

My mouth parted when I met his amber glare. "Why do you think I have anything to do with it?"

"Your sudden stuttering speaks for itself."

I snarled, but Leona warned, "Watch yer mouth. Varys doesn't have anythin'—

"You wanna know why I was out hunting that night we had our first encounter?" Eryx interrupted, his voice changing to a much more inquisitive tone. "When I found you two in the forest around midnight with a cold torch?"

My stomach turned over.

"I've been having to hunt much more than usual because I've come back with *nothing*. There isn't any wildlife for miles. I've found animals slaughtered, a bite in a full-sized buck that belonged to neither wolf nor bear. Something is happening in these hills, and I believe whatever happened to our game has helped Mae as well."

I shook my head. "You're accusing me—"

"Not yet," he snapped. "Thing is Wynhart, whether or not you had anything to do with this murder, you know there is something bigger going on. Something that explains cold torches and lights from nowhere."

My eyes closed, legs tingling with the need to run. I felt Leona come closer to me.

Eryx went on, "And I think that something will also explain the condition I found Willem and Theon's bodies in as well." His head cocked. "Maybe you can explain why there were bites up Theon's arm, skin and muscle removed in..."—his nose scrunched in disgust—"...chunks."

"Some sort of animal?" Leo asked as if it were obvious. "A wolf?"

"No," Eryx replied gruffly. "There are usually long drag marks with a wolf bite. There was nothing like that present, even in the larger wound on his neck. Probably bled out from that alone. Wasn't until I inspected Willem I found the truth."

A haunt replaced his hard expression. "The bites were small and round—*human*. Willem's mouth was covered in blood, and there was flesh between his teeth."

My eyes went wide. Leona cried out, "Willem *ate* Theon?"

Eryx nodded. "It appeared so. Sometime after that, he was stabbed in the heart."

"What kind of pure fuckery did they get themselves into?" she asked, looking to me as if I had the answer.

Eryx's gaze bore into me as well. "Some sort of dark magic, I'd presume."

"There's no such thing as dark magic…" But my words trailed away.

It was the truth that the elves' magic was not generally evil. There were tales and historical writings about criminals of old using their magic for misdeeds, but because the gods and goddesses of Xalador were still present and governing our world, the elves simply knew better than to violate the rules in place, and specifically, suffer Elethros's judgment.

However, those rules among other disagreements were why Lithia, Goddess of Death, sought out to create her own race to begin with. And the magic given to them was dark and wicked indeed.

My world started to tip, legs weakening. Every thought became a disturbing realization, knotting my stomach in a way that couldn't be untied. I took a seat on the cot and everything I had ever learned about magic and the evil the elves faced during the war hit me at once.

Oh gods.

It was power Mae did not possess—*couldn't* possess. Because the things Eryx had spoken of pointed to a magic not of the elves, but of those who annihilated them.

The dryamorn.

When I looked back up, anxious to explain my revelation, I found Eryx scowling down at me. "I watched that ball of light manifest in your hand the other night, Wynhart."

Anger and panic collided, the muscles in my neck taut as I stood slowly. "You've got it all wrong. I don't have the kind of magic that killed Willem and Theon."

He sneered. "Do you think Mayor Brooker will give two shits about what kind of magic you have? All he wants is justice for his son."

"And I have the answer to that!" I shouted. "I'm the one with questions now. Did Willem die *before* or after he ate his friend?"

Eryx's chin jeered back. "Of course he died after. No one can…" His words trailed off, expression hardening. "No one can come back to life."

I shook my head. "No," I breathed roughly. "But in the war, the elves were beaten by magic they did not know how to counter. Not only demonic power, but the ability to raise the slain to fight again."

Eryx was right about one thing: I did know there was something bigger going on. Mornish or demonic power would explain why I couldn't see through the illusion at the tavern, why we could hear dark whispers swirling in the air. Our enemy was the same as it had always been.

"Willem was a monster, but he wasn't a flesh eating fiend," I told Eryx. "The only race that can compel another to do something against their wish, or create undead, is the dryamorn and their Torm-given necromancy."

Leona's eyes went wide and horrified. "Ye're not serious, Varys."

I nodded and Eryx threw up his hands, scoffing. "You're out of your godsdamn mind, Wynhart, if you expect me to believe that dryamorn still exist."

"You can believe whatever you want, but yes." Standing, I adjusted the two cloaks around my neck. "And if there are dryamorn in the area, I can't waste anymore time."

I started to move toward the flap leading to the front of the tent when Eryx blocked my path, crossing his arms.

I frowned. "Let me pass, Eryx."

He only cocked his head. "What are you playing at?"

"Nothing," I insisted, feeling Leona's presence as she came to stand beside me. "Mae couldn't have been the one to kill Willem and Theon, no matter what happened between the three of them."

"I don't think she's the one who killed them. I said I think she had help." His amber eyes narrowed. "Funny how I start revealing strange occurrences and you suddenly start spouting off about monster myths."

I shook my head with a scoff and tried to walk around him. "Do what you want with the information you have on me, but I'm finding Mae—"

Eryx's hand met my chest.

"No." His voice was all shadow, his glare like amber cinders. "You are not."

My nostrils flared. "Move."

"Don't escalate this to somethin' ye can't get out of, huntsman," Leo warned from behind me.

He sneered, fingers digging into my shirt. "I'm giving you one last chance," he muttered. "Tell me where she is, or I'll put you down and find her myself."

"I've already told you. I don't know."

Rage warped his features as he let go only to swiftly reach behind his neck, under his cloak hood. The silver sheen of a small dagger was the only thing I saw before reflexes kicked in and I threw my hands up, shouting, "*Sçölith.*"

Eryx sank his dagger down toward my face and met with my wards just in time. I only felt the resistance as my wards absorbed the strike, the blade bouncing off like the wrong side of a magnet. With a harsh breath of surprise, Eryx stumbled backward.

I didn't have time to stop her before Leo rushed him. He barely dodged the swing of her fist, coming around with the dagger. My pulse skittered when the edge of the blade sliced across her arm, blood staining her white sleeve. She cursed through it, fist going for his face again, this time finding its mark on his mouth. The strength of her blow caused his grip on the dagger to falter, and when it fell to the ground, I kicked it to the other side of the room. He let out a growl and shoved Leona down. I couldn't react fast enough to catch her as she tumbled to her back. The thud of her head against the ground lit my chest on fire with rage.

I gripped Eryx's shoulders. "Stop—"

His fist sank into my stomach. Pain flooded my insides and for a moment, I wasn't sure I remembered how to breathe, trying not to tip over, my training kicking in. Staying hunched over left me vulnerable, so I backed away, raised my hands, gasping through the nausea.

Eryx wiped his bloody lip. "Rucas always said he didn't like the way you looked at his daughter. Tell me, Wynhart. What kind of dark magic illusions did you use before you raped her?"

The world halted around me.

And then my rage erupted, ice and fire coursing through my blood, seeping up from my very bones, to the tip of my tongue, and rolled into one lethal command, *"Śiçaevr."*

Eryx's eyes went wide as he watched my hand begin to glow white. A thin layer of ice glazed my skin, thickening as I curled my fingers into a fist. I didn't give him a moment to react before I rushed forward, a guttural growl tearing from my throat as I struck him, and I was unsure if the deep cracking sound was the ice breaking or his jaw.

He toppled backward into the main side of the tent. I stalked to him, the spell sustained, forming fresh ice along my knuckles and fingers. Before he could rise, I grappled him, gripped his arms and unleashed an icy fury. Frost crystals crawled over his wrists, through his jerkin and froze him to the ground. He hissed around his bloody teeth and tried to throw me off, kneeing my spine. I held his glare with one of my own and extended the shards of ice until they covered his arms wholly, frost biting into his skin.

Eryx writhed as I backed off him, his arms bucking against the frozen bonds. "I'll kill you!"

I rushed back for Leona, helping her sit up. She seemed a bit dizzy, but stood with my support. As we passed Eryx, she took a long deep breath and spat on him. *"Fenoth.* Smugglin' in a fuckin' blade when we had no weapon."

Eryx snarled, pushing against the ice again. "That's a lie when you know *he* has magic."

I pulled her along, ignoring the next set of curses and accusations spewing from Eryx. Grabbing my sword and dagger, I turned and told Leona, "Get Thorn. Then, run."

CHAPTER 39

Varys

Lithia, Goddess of Death, hated her elven children.

And so after Xalador's conception and the creation of the elves, Lithia tried to create beings that would only worship her. But without the powers of her brethren, her attempt was disastrous, creating the abominations she called dryamorn. The creatures crawled on all fours, could only live in utter darkness; blind in the sunlight. She put them in the Evershade where they bred like animals, feeding on whatever they could—even if it meant their own kind.

When the dryamorn began to find their way to the surface and kill the elves, the gods discovered Lithia's deceit. She was cast out, stripped of her godhood, and forced to live among her abhorrent spawn.

Unfortunately, somehow, Lithia found the Gate to Torm. It was written that Torm was on another plane entirely, a world overrun by demons and devils, monsters of one's worst nightmares.

Lithia and the demon king, Duagvin, became lovers. He promised to give the dryamorn powers to counter the magic of the elves. She promised him Xalador.

After a long, ruthless battle that went on for almost a century, Lithia claimed victory. For five years, she and Duagvin ruled, the dryamorn and the demons overwhelming Xalador like an invasive parasite. I hadn't been able to discover how she was finally over-thrown, how she, the dryamorn, and all the demons of Torm were banished to the Evershade. All I understood was that it was done so by something, or someone, with immense power.

And now that magic had returned, logic would dictate that the magic barrier keeping them inside the Evershade would strengthen, so how in Xalador were the dryamorn escaping?

Catching my breath, I let my head fall back against a wall inside the abandoned shack. More than once Leona and I had found our way here, whether it was to escape bullies or just to discuss secrets. Several times she had cried here because some girl or boy broke her heart, and I had come straight here to vent about Elise's betrayal. It wasn't anything special, but it was the only place in town that wasn't my house where no one would find us.

After our confrontation with Eryx, we figured it would be the least conspicuous place. I had made sure we were inside before canceling Śíçaevr, releasing Eryx from the ice from where he still remained across the market. As much as I would have preferred him to stay there all night, I was afraid the spell would drain my energy —and I didn't think Natalia and Duros would appreciate it if I left him in their tent.

However, I was also aware it was only a matter of time before Eryx told the right people about me. My time here in Elros was coming to an end rapidly.

Leona sank down against the same wall, pinching the bridge of her nose. We were inside what was probably once a commons room. The shack had been abandoned years ago from a mudslide. Half of the building still remained underground. Oddly enough, it had kept its warmth. The windows were filthy and covered in webs both old and new. A large tree spider had made the furthest window its home and had already made a nest for her eggs. Come spring, the spider would be dead, her children hatched and gone to find their own place in the world for their short life span. This shack though, would remain. It wasn't like anyone helped the family who had once owned the place. They hadn't been a part of the merchant guild, that was for sure. I knew that not because I had known whoever lived here, but because it was obvious—people who worked under Rucas didn't live in shacks. They didn't live in the neighborhood where mudslides were a hazard, the cheap land with too many hills and not enough space.

After several moments of nothing but our rapid breaths, I said, "I'm sorry, Leo."

She looked up, taking another few gasps of air. "Why? Not yer fault that dumbarse tried to kill us."

I sighed. "I know, but I should've jumped in with magic sooner. I'm…hesitant. I'm never sure when it's the right time, I'm exhausted and don't want to use a spell then be unable to walk straight, and I don't know how to fight with it just yet."

She chuckled. "Ye froze him to the fuckin' ground. Seems like ye know what ye're doin'."

I slid a hand over my face. "Maybe. But that was only after I lost my temper. Even before then, I didn't know whether to stay diplomatic or knock him on his ass."

"Aye." She extended her legs out, pointing her toes to stretch as much as she could in the metal plated boots she wore. "To be honest, I'm rusty and back there proved it. No offense, but I've been trainin' ye so much, I haven't had time to work on my own skills. I need to train m'self back up."

I grimaced. "Fighting with fists isn't exactly your style, Leo. Don't be so hard on yourself."

"Ye're right about that, I guess. If I'd had Thorn, he would've never touched me."

I agreed and scooched closer, pulling her arm closer to examine it. She protested. "Just let me look," I insisted.

"It'll need stitches, that's for damn sure."

I nodded. "How's your head?"

"A bit scrambled, but no more than it already was." She winked. "I'll be all right."

"Well," I started, helping her to her feet. "I don't want to stay here too long. We need to—"

Leona swayed forward, catching herself against me.

"Fuck that hunter," she groaned.

I gave a curt nod, tasting the bitterness of anger on my tongue as I helped her sit back down. We weren't going anywhere for a while.

"Rest," I told her, trying not to sound too defeated. "While you do, I'll try to wrap my head around this dryamorn information."

"*Och*, ye want me to stay dizzy?" She grinned and laid her head on her knees. "Only jokin'."

I sat before her, unpinned the cloaks, then pulled my book bag off my shoulder. "When your father told us Baron Kenrad had written to him about *strange elven men* the other day, I'd wondered if it was the dryamorn. Thing is Leo, we don't know what the dryamorn really look like."

"Da always told me stories to spook me. Always talked about their fangs and horns and wings."

I nodded. "But they were created by Lithia, who originally helped create the elves. It's very possible that the dryamorn look like elves, like *Vyl'kriev*. They may very well be blending in with society, able to hide their monstrous features."

A visible shiver went through her. "The thing that attacked ye at the tavern, and what killed the jeweler brothers…Ye think it was a dryamorn?"

"Yes." I pulled out my spellbook, flipping through the pages to make sure everything was dry. "Ramos said our enemy's magic cannot be seen with the spell we use that allows us to recognize magical auras or see through illusions. The dryamorn's magic is not of the veins—it's not arcane. It's Torm-magic borrowed from demons and devils, and purely evil. That's why the elves had a hard time combating it, especially necromancy. How do you kill something that's already dead?"

She gave a one shouldered shrug. "Set it on fire?"

I snorted. "I'm sure they figured that out eventually, but there's other magic the dryamorn possessed which led to the elves' demise. Especially compulsion—strong enough to take control of even the dragons."

Her freckled forehead scrunched incredulously. "If they have mind control, why aren't they usin that instead of illusions to kill folks?"

I grimaced. "I don't have that answer. I wish I did. It terrifies me because my mind is all I've got."

She scoffed. "Cuttin' ye'self short. Again. Besides, I'd think it'd be much harder to take control of a powerful mind, yeah?"

I nodded, hoping she was onto something. "I do have a theory, but not sure it makes sense since the dryamorn's magic isn't of the veins. I have been wondering if magic is reemerging inconsistently."

Leona's brows rose. "What do ye mean?"

I shrugged. "It's just a theory, but one I'm serious about. It would explain why I still have trouble holding small spells, but then something lethal like I cast on Eryx doesn't drain me a bit. Mae's magic also seems to be a little out of her control."

"And how would one fix this if it's true?"

With a sigh, I opened my book bag once more. "I think I'll have to find this Falryn character and ask him. Maybe we'll get lucky on our journey to Elvidawn and cross paths."

Pulling out the rest of the books inside my bag, I sifted through the three Meri had given me. When I got to the one on the bottom, the title caught my eye.

Ít Nánöweth. The Nexus.

"Oh," I murmured, opening to the first page. "Interesting."

Leona leaned in. "New book?"

"I didn't get to tell you. I found the missing jeweler brother." I grinned. "Sister, actually. Meri is her name."

"And she gave ye these?"

I nodded. "Coincidentally, they were purchased from Rucas's shop. That man has no idea what he has, especially this find."

She looked over the pages like she always did. I swore it because she was hoping she would discover she too could read Elvish some-day. "What's it about?"

"Nexi." I wasn't sure why, but my pulse picked up. "They were a group of powerful mages whose magic drew from an elemental plane."

She blinked. "What?"

I chuckled. "In my understanding, a nexus was an individual who had become a conduit, or bridge, between the material plane and the plane of one element. There were four of them: the Nexus of Fire, the Nexus of Water, the Nexus of Earth, and the Nexus of Air. They could only cast magic within their specific element."

"Like an elemental sorcerer."

I nodded. "Yes, but where sorcerers draw their magic from the veins through their blood, nexi drew their power from the planes. That's why they were conduits. While they were *Vyl'kríev*, they were...*made*. At conception, or at least that's what I've always understood." I held up the book. "I'm assuming that process can be found in here."

Opening the book, I quickly scanned the pages to see if I could find a spell or instruction. Turning a sheet, I stilled. Drawn onto one entire page was an immaculate *eçor*.

"It's a binding spell," I said in awe, then read aloud, "*At the age of magical maturity, the spell must be cast over the nexus to create a bond, else the nwív will take sentience and besiege its host to bring its elemental wrath upon the world.*"

"What's that word?" Leo asked, then tried to pronounce *nwív* and was unable to do so.

I took a breath. "That's a pretty complicated question. It's an incorporeal, magical being created for the sole purpose of connecting the nexus to the elemental plane."

Leona cringed. "And what's the age of magical maturity?"

"About four."

When Leona's eyes widened, I laughed.

"Ye're tellin' me there were probably *elskairv* settin' their little friend's toys on fire because they wouldn't share?" she asked.

I showed my palms. "It probably happened, but magical maturity doesn't mean all-powerful mages at the age of four, because magical aptitude is determined by the strength of the mage."

She still looked uneasy. "So...these nexi were created and had to have a spell put on them when they were toddlers, else this magical creature would take over and try to destroy the world?"

I scratched my head. "That's what this says at least. But all four of the nexi had to have been successfully bound to their nwív. I'm sure that was a very supervised process. Doubt the elves, nor the gods, wanted elemental wrath to be brought upon Xalador."

Leo rubbed her chin. "What happened to the nexi?"

"All of them died in the war."

"Is there a chance that some of these Elven-blooded people will reemerge as a nexus?"

Her question made me pause. "Not likely. I think. As I said, they had to be created, so I'm sure that's why there won't be any more nexi. No one in this age would know how to create them—"

"Varys, there *is* a real elf still wanderin' around Xalador accordin' to Ramos."

I gaped at her. "Oh my gods. You're right."

She tapped the book. "And, *ye* may know now."

I shrugged. "I suppose, but I don't think I'll be creating nexi. Sounds like a lot of power to be thrust on someone, and at such a young age. They must have had reason to create them back then."

Leona snapped her fingers. "Maybe to combat the dryamorn, since they were given magic from Torm. If the nexi draw their magic from another plane, does that mean their magic comes from the veins, or whatever?"

I tilted my head side to side. "One would argue that the veins flow through all. Even other planes of existence."

"But ye said earlier Torm-magic isn't of the veins."

Nodding, I said, "You're right. So, maybe nexi magic isn't either."

I flipped through the next few pages, eyes widening when I found yet another *eçor*. "Krayd's chaos, it's a banishing spell."

Walking to the center of the room, I sat down and laid the book before me. "During the war, the elves used a lot of banishing magic on demons and devils."

"What's the purpose of a banishin' spell?"

I didn't respond right away, instead reading over the passage, bewilderment overwhelming my thoughts. "It sends a creature back from whence it came. According to this spell, it casts out the nwív from the nexus's body, returning it to the elemental plane where it stays and waits to either be bound, or to gather strength to take over the nexus again." I motioned toward my bag. "Hand me my spellbook, please."

Leona did so, and once it was in my hands, I laid it beside the open book and turned to a blank page. For many moments I worked, writing down the instructions, bringing forth my casting circle, then beginning the process of constructing the *eçor* for the binding spell first. I could skip a lot of the mental work since whoever had written *Ít Nánöweth* had included the correct *eçors* for both spells. So this time, it was as if I was simply tracing the images into my spellbook.

Only, I couldn't cast them now. Besides being too exhausted to cast beyond learning the spells, both of them were too powerful. The *eçors* were much more complex than any of the spells I knew now, and had command phrases instead of just simple words.

From within my soundless casting circle, I noticed Leona perk up just as I finished copying the banishment spell. She waved her hands and pointed toward the window. As the glow of my spellbook and casting circle faded, a deep trumpeting sound flooded the shack, blaring from the market. My breath left in a burst as I jolted to my feet. That was no ordinary horn; a sound we had not heard in years. The announcement that a criminal was to be tried.

The rain had ceased, but the puddles remained. I pulled Leona along, an invisibility spell cast over myself and extended to her by holding her hand as we walked into the market and avoiding splashing that would no doubt give us away. A crowd had already gathered, their voices churning the air with an ominous resonance.

Leo's grip on me tightened when someone walked by and looked in our direction, their eyes looking past us. When they were out of ear shot, I said, "No one can see us. Promise."

She didn't respond. We came to the edge of the crowd, and it didn't take long to realize we were too far away to really perceive what was happening.

"Hate to be this person," Leona murmured. "But I'm too short to be this far back."

She couldn't see me nod, but I did, guiding her away and into an alley. I knew where to go so we could see everything and remain out of sight with or without my spell cast. Mr. Haynes, a carpenter, always left his ladder around the back of his shop, and the building's roof had a perfect view of the market.

The alley was clear—unsurprisingly, since the majority of Elros was in the market—so I let go of Leo's hands and dismissed the spell. Her eyes were wide as she watched our bodies return to normal.

"Don't know how I feel about that just yet," she said with a grimace. "But it seems it's not as taxin' as it was the first couple times ye've tried that spell. Ye even cast it on me too."

I eyed her. "Just another point to add to my wild magic theory."

"Just another point to add that ye cut yourself short."

I shrugged, then we climbed up to the roof, crouching down on the back slope and peering over. Everyone had gathered around the platform where Elros officials held town meetings.

But instead of a city official, Rucas Mordaunt stood before the crowd. He wore a gaudy blue doublet over a red shirt with a matching blue cape. An orange flat cap sat on his bald head, the massive white feather pinned on the side ruffling as he raised his hands to silence the murmuring. I wondered if he wore the ugly thing to hide that head wound I had given him a few days back.

"People of Elros," his voice boomed. "I stand before you in Mayor Brooker's stead with a heaviness in my heart I've never felt before. As most of you know, Willem Welch and Theon Brooker were found dead in the market after many days of searching."

Prayers to the gods for the deceased began tumbling from the lips of many. Leona glanced to me with a roll of her eyes, but I couldn't focus much past the group of guards off to the side, ready to climb the stairs up to the platform.

Rucas's face twisted with anger. "Hours ago, I would have given you all a much different speech, a eulogy in remembrance of two men whose lives were cut too short. Instead, I must address this wonderful, peaceful town with horrific news." Any remaining whispers in the crowd died out. "Willem and Theon did not die in an accident, they were viciously, *brutally* murdered."

A communal gasp washed over the people.

Rucas's voice cut through, "And within the same hour they were discovered early this morn, three of our out-of-town guests were killed at The Nook and Cranny. These thugs struck while we slept, while our children were in their beds. They took advantage of our shadowy alleys, our houses tucked in between hills, and brought a death this town has *never* seen!"

Cries and shouts tore from the crowd, families huddling closer, others lifting their fists in outrage.

"Where is this killer?"

"Elethros bring down your judgment!"

When the crowd's volume began to rise once more, I asked Leona, "Why is Rucas riling up the crowd like this? He's doing nothing but mongering fear."

She didn't respond, only gave me a shake of her head, expression as tight as our grip on the roof ridge. The crowd began to roar.

"Good citizens!" Rucas bellowed, lifting his hands once again. "I hear you. I feel your sorrow, your anger. It is the same as *mine*."

The audience erupted.

"Yes!"

"Silence the killers!"

"Find them!"

"You question your safety." Rucas growled. "Your peace has been challenged. So allow me to give it back."

My jaw tightened upon his words. How dare he stand in a position to give *anyone* safety and peace when I knew what he did to his daughter. To Mrs. Whitaker. To so many people who stood before him even now.

Rucas nodded to his left, signaling two guards to climb the stairs. They carried up a wooden block with the top center carved down to a smooth notch, and sat it in the center of the platform. Someone was then pushed onto the landing, hands bound, a burlap sack over their head.

My breath sawed out. "Leo, they're executing someone."

She had gone utterly still. "They won't try them first?"

The alleged criminal didn't struggle when a guard shoved them to their knees. With a mocking grin on his face, Rucas pointed to the person beneath the sack.

"This is justice!" he cried, and the people cheered. "This town is not one of crime and trouble, but *this* is what we will do to those who try to decimate our security."

He allowed their applause to continue, surveying the crowd with his head held high and proud—a false king observing those who blindly bowed at his feet. Because that's who had gathered closest to the platform. Members of the merchant guild, their spouses, children. People who lived in The Flats.

Rucas lifted a hand, placing a finger on his lips to shush the noise. "Before we begin, I must warn you all of the insanity that will spill from this murderer's lips." A chuckle started in his chest, head shaking incredulously. "This person claims they used *magic* to kill last night."

The people erupted with laughter, but the breath I took was thin. Leona's hands raised to her mouth as she twisted to me. "Fawkes...what if it's a dryamorn?"

I didn't respond—I was suddenly looking at the stranger differently. The long-sleeved shirt and black pants they wore were too loose to make out their sex, but I could tell they were thin. Their hands were behind their back, and the bag covered their neck so I couldn't make out the color of their skin.

All I knew was that this person was either *Vyl'kríev* or a dryamorn if they claimed to have killed with magic. The former didn't make any sense, unless—

"Mae..." her name fell from my lips.

She wasn't in the crowd.

She had been missing all this time.

Leona's head started to shake. She took my arm, squeezing it. "Varys, no. It's not her. It's *not her.*"

"*Magic!*" Rucas shouted, and the citizens laughed louder.

I couldn't move. Couldn't breathe.

He spun to the guard standing behind the criminal. "Remove the hood."

Panic seized me. Jerking away from Leona, I didn't think before I jumped up, one foot on the roof ridge and readied to rush down. Time seemed to slow, focus narrowing in on the guard who walked toward the knelt person. I didn't want to watch, but I couldn't take my eyes off the hood.

Leo's hands twisted into the back of my shirt. "Varys, wait a second."

"If it's her, I'm going down there," I declared.

"Ye'll break yer fuckin' legs is what ye'll do," she growled. "Hold on."

The roar of the crowd rattled my bones, angry shrieks slicing the air. As the hood was removed, blood left my face only to rush back to my cheeks in confusion and ill-timed relief.

"It's…another *Vyl'kriev*."

The middle-aged, Elven-blooded man glared into the crowd with lime green eyes.

A *Vyl'kriev* murdered another *Vyl'kriev?* This wasn't making any sense.

"Behold the filth who murdered those three men at The Nook and Cranny. Alas, whoever is responsible for Willem and Theon's death is still at large." Rucas sneered at the criminal. "Tell them how you did it, *elf*."

My blood heated at Rucas's remark, but I dismissed it when I realized this one *Vyl'kriev* might reveal The ReEmergence of Magic.

He was silent for several breaths, murderous eyes still fixed on the crowd. When he glanced toward Rucas, the guard behind him stepped forward and braced his shoulders. His face contorted with anger as he tried to shrug the guard off.

"Stop your struggling and speak," Rucas demanded.

The *Vyl'kriev* rolled his eyes. "I sliced their throats while I was invisible."

My head fell back in frustration. More laughs sounded from Rucas and the crowd.

"Show us then," Rucas mocked as he looped his thumbs under his belt and leaned back. "Show us how you can turn invisible."

I shook my head, watching it play out powerlessly. "Dammit."

"Fawkes, dryamorn could look like Elven-blooded," Leona reminded me. "Ye told me that earlier."

I blinked. "I did say that."

Chaos, I was counting on it now. It all came down to how he'd use his magic, if I would hear whispers as he conjured, or if he would use Elvish to command his spell. I found my hands gripping the pommel of my sword, feeling as if I was on the edge of a world about to shatter on one bated breath.

With a lift of his chin, the *Vyl'kríev* cried out, *"Neváçína."*

Gasps washed over the gathered citizens when his body disappeared from sight. My heart plummeted to my stomach, eyes closing. I had just used that spell.

He was one of us.

"I still have him!" The guard behind the criminal shouted, his hands seeming to cup the air. The other guards rushed onto the platform, feeling around to grip the invisible man. When his body returned, his gaunt face showed no emotion, even as several guards grabbed at his crimson hair, his clothes, and pinned down his legs that were already kneeling.

Rucas glanced between him and the crowd with wide, stunned eyes. He seemed unsure of what to do for a moment before he snapped his fingers. "Gag him!"

As the guards moved, a terrified expression rose on the *Vyl'kríev's* face. He shrieked, "I must be granted my final words!"

The guards stilled, looking to Rucas for direction.

He sneered at the man. "You can say them with your head on the block."

Any light left in the man's eyes flickered out as he was hauled back. The crowd chanted viciously as one guard put his boot in the *Vyl'kríev's* back and forced him over the block. Captain of the guard, Dominik Rochester, made his way to the platform, pulling his sword from its scabbard.

"Speak now, or die with your words on your tongue," Rucas hissed.

The *Vyl'kríev* glared forward, lifting his chin off the notch. He snarled, "My final words are merely a message from my leader." A bead of sweat rolled down his face. "We have reemerged."

I took a breath through tight teeth, spine going rigid.

He went on, "We are among you—those who can cast spells of the ancient elves."

No.

"The ReEmergence of Magic has begun. There is *nowhere* left to hide."

No. No. *No.*

An apparent fear swept over the audience below as my world started to spin. If this *Vyl'kríev* made the people scared of us—

"We killed your precious citizens!" he shouted. "And we will kill again!"

Shrieks rang out from the crowd. People began to back away.

Rucas gritted his teeth and snapped his head to Captain Dominik. "Shut him up!"

The sword rose.

In a panicked fury, the *Vyl'kríev* jerked against his bindings and the hold on him, his last breath screaming, *"May your days be dark, and your victims blind!"*

The sword came down.

Silence stretched.

The head fell, blood spraying across the platform floor.

Enemy.

Our enemy was *Vyl'kríev.*

I couldn't breathe.

I didn't understand.

The citizen's screams swelled into a chant, repeating the words over and over, *"Death to magic! Death to magic! Death to magic!"*

CHAPTER 40

Varys

"Go home," I told Leona, ducked behind a flipped cart. "Gather what you need and tell your parents everything. I'll meet you there."

Guards were already going door to door, rounding up Elven-blooded for questioning. The front gate had been shut, the city closed for entry or exiting. We could already hear the screams, the shouts of protests no doubt from the outsiders here for the Fest of Change.

This was all so wrong.

We were leaving Elros *tonight*. I wasn't going to wait around to see what today's execution would lead to when it came to Elven-blooded. In a few words, that criminal had villainized every single one of us. People were still chanting *"Death to magic"* in the market circle, the words mixing with pleas. If this mentality spread beyond Elros, those words would be the start of a dark future for every *Vyl'kriev*, the blood of the elves smearing the land as history repeated. Another genesis for another genocide.

Whoever these enemy *Vyl'kriev* were, they obviously had no idea the damage they had caused. Or maybe they did, and I just didn't understand.

I swallowed down the uneasiness in my stomach once again. I

hadn't been able to hold back the purge after watching the beheading, and I couldn't deny that I was afraid—there was just no time to let it consume me.

"What are ye goin' to do?" Leona asked.

"I have to tell my father." I swallowed. "He deserves to know, especially if I'm caught."

"Varys, they'll go to the library first. Ye're one of the only Elven-blooded who's an Elros citizen." Her voice filled with emotion. "Ye go home and ye might as well be handing ye'self over."

Metal boots clanking against the ground drew closer before a pounding on a door just down the alley. We threw up the hood of our cloaks and began to move further down the way quickly. A thick fog had settled over the town after the rainstorm, and it couldn't have come at a better time. We could use the decreased perception to our advantage.

"I'll use my invisibility spell if I need to," I murmured to Leona.

"The invisibility spell that criminal just said he used to kill?" she asked wryly.

I didn't respond, only turned the corner. We could make out three figures ahead, and by the shape of their form, I could tell at least two were guardsmen. There were a few stacked boxes before us, so we scrambled behind them to listen.

"That necklace s'been in ma family for four generations!" a woman yelled. "I'm not no Elven-blooded, why badger me?"

"By order of Mayor Brooker, all items that are claimed to have magical properties shall be confiscated immediately," the soldier declared.

The blood left my face. I peeked around.

"And who's a'claiming this necklace be magical?" the woman demanded. "I gots no ol' man, no munchkins running and fibbing 'bout me. How do you know it's magical?"

The guards shifted and were quiet for a beat too long. Finally, one stated, "We don't."

"But," the other said slowly, "we've been given orders. If we have reason to believe something is magical, we are to take it in for evaluation. If it's not magical, we will return it to you promptly."

The woman took a step back. "You're bloody thieves, the lot of you!"

"Madam, we don't want any trouble." Even from where we hid I could see the guard had placed his hand on the pommel of his blade. "Failure to hand over this item will be considered resisting authorities and you will be arrested as suspect in the murder of Willem Welch and Theon Brooker."

My breath hitched and my feet took a few steps forward involuntarily, the need to help this woman overwhelming what was the smart thing to do. I only stopped when Leona grabbed my arm.

The woman sighed. "Fine. You'll see. No magic."

The chain clinked upon the guard's outstretched gauntlet, and I took that as a sign for us to turn and find another way.

Down the next alley, Leona said, "Bet ye they aren't searchin' the Flats."

I frowned. "Bet you I know who's going to be *evaluating* these items, too. Isn't it interesting that Rucas Mordaunt suddenly becomes a seller of magical goods just a few days before the Fest of Change where merchants will be selling items that are no doubt being confiscated at this very moment?"

Leona's next step was hesitant. "But…why?"

"I don't know. Nothing is making sense to me at the moment. We just need to leave as soon as we can."

She breathed out. "Varys, what about Snow? Are we still goin' to the tree?"

A lump grew in my throat. "If I can make it to your house in one piece, then yes. We will go there before leaving Elros."

"And what if she's not there?"

We came to the crossroads of a few different backroads, one specifically that would lead me directly to the back door of the library. This was where we would part.

I turned to her, swallowing back the emotion. "I will never stop searching for her, but I will never find her if I'm imprisoned. I have to trust in her powers. I have to trust that she is where she is supposed to be."

"*Nevắçína.*" I cast the invisibility spell as I entered the library from the back door, creeping inside quietly. The house was too still. I could tell something was off, and when I came into the gathering room, dread pooled in my stomach. The guards had been here.

Papers and books were scattered across the floor. The contents of my father's messy-yet-organized desk had been shoved to the ground, students desks overturned, drawers emptied.

I rushed further in, taking in the sight of the rows of bookshelves. Books were in piles, off their shelves, some open-faced with pages bent. I rushed back to the section where we kept our elven collection. I wasn't surprised, but that didn't prevent the dismay— everything was gone. They hadn't left a single book. I could only thank my ability to read so quickly that I had read every one of them at least three times through.

I looked up the stairs leading up to my bedroom. Everything seemed quiet up there as well. The moment I stepped up to climb, a faint, distant groan from above snagged my attention.

Keeping the spell sustained, I ran upstairs. Slipping into my room, I pulled my sword from its sheath, huffing at the mess. My mattress had been flipped up, my blankets crumbled on the floor. The bookshelves had been left bare of any elven book, the books in Common scattered. A few personal items were missing—a chunk of quartz, my dagger, the uniquely shaped empty bottles I'd kept just because they looked neat. It was like whoever had given these guards their orders had told them to go into citizens homes and round up everything that looked shiny, dangerous, or had weird script.

When another pained sound rang out, my pulse stammered. I recognized it too well. I found him laying among the splintered wood of what was once my writing desk, covered in parchment and ink. There was no sign of anyone else, so I canceled the spell. A growl tore from my father's throat, his own sword lifting.

"Who's there?" he growled. His eyes softened once he realized it was me. "Varys. Thank the gods."

"Who did this to you?" I knelt down and helped him to a sitting position. "The guards?"

A nod. "They came for you, son. You and magical items." He

wiped the blood from his lip. "Took on five men. You would've been so proud. I still have a little in me."

I swallowed, glancing down at the scrapes on his arms and legs. "More than a little. Anything broken?"

"Just my pride, I think. The old damn leg injury got the best of me." He sighed. "Help me to the bed."

I fixed my mattress and threw my blanket over it before helping him limp to the bed. Once he was sitting, I started to tend to his wounds, removing his tunic and not surprised to see his back had taken the most bruising.

"I was listening to the trial from inside the library," Father told me as I grabbed some fresh rags and a pitcher of water. "They're after every Elven-blooded because this one crook stated you all are dangerous. It's a mindless accusation."

I nodded, and he winced as I pressed a wet rag to a slice across his shoulder. "There's...a lot going on, Father. Why did they attack you if I wasn't home?"

He went still beneath the rag. "They came in without warning. Stated the place is public so they could come in as they pleased. Tried to tell them that was only during school hours, but of course that didn't mean anything to those tyrants."

An angry heat flooded my veins. "So they came in and when they didn't find me, they took what they thought was magical."

"Yes," his voice wavered.

I pressed the rag to another scrape, wiping off some ink as well. "I'm surprised they didn't arrest you."

"They kicked my ass. That's all they wanted."

Wringing out the rag, I said, "I'm sorry I haven't been home."

"I'm glad you weren't home to get arrested." He smiled. "But go on."

"I have to leave Elros. Tonight at the latest. But I actually came to tell you something."

Father's face rippled with perplexity. He folded his arms. "Did you have something to do with Willem and Theon's murder?"

I shook my head and stepped back. "But I think I know what killed them. I don't know if this group of Elven-blooded is entangled with them, but I know that if I don't get out of Elros, I'll be hunted down and killed either way. Either by the mayor's orders, this group of Elven-blooded…or by dryamorn."

My father's jaw parted. "Varys, what—"

"I can hear them. Their whispers." I stood straighter. "I know Willem and Theon were killed from dark magic only the dryamorn possessed. I know this because I've been learning all I can about the elves and what happened in the war…by reading the elven books."

His eyes went wide. "You can read them? How?"

I swallowed. "You have to understand, Father. I never told you because I was concerned about the very things happening as we speak. I was trying to protect you. Magic has reemerged within all Elven-blooded Xaladorians." I held his stare. "If not now, soon."

Father stood shakily. "Tell me."

I took a heavy breath, and hoped I wouldn't regret this proclamation. If magic hadn't been a deadly secret before, it absolutely was now. But he deserved to know.

"I reemerged two years ago. I'm a mage, Father. I can cast magic."

He went still for only a moment, obviously surprised by my words. But as a sly smile so like my own rose on his mouth, I wondered if he was genuinely surprised at all.

"I know."

A span of uncomfortable quiet settled in the room, mainly because I had no idea how to respond. The only thing I could do was stare at him, trying to read if he was just saying he knew to lessen his own shock, or if he really, truly, knew.

"What do you…..*How* do you know?" I finally stammered out at length.

A shit-eating grin replaced his coyness. "You *told* me."

My chin jeered back. "No, I didn't."

He chuckled, adjusting his spectacles before clasping his hands behind his back. "You told me when I found you puking your guts out after you'd *apparently* used a spell for too long and it made you sick."

I froze. I knew my memory had been hazy that night, but not so much that I'd forgotten things I said. "Oh my gods. I really told you all of that?"

He shrugged. "Honestly, at first I thought the sickness was making you a bit bonkers. But then last night, I overheard your conversation with Leona about how you believed something evil was stirring and how your magic could feel it."

I pinched the bridge of my nose. "Well, shit."

"Well, shit indeed."

The hand he placed on my shoulder was light, as if he didn't feel like he could allow the full weight of it. I exhaled through my nose as I looked at him. "There's so much to discuss, but I don't have a lot of time. Mae disappeared last night. That's where I've been, searching for her since midnight. She's a mage too."

He frowned. "Ah, so your tryst with Mae..."

I took a breath. "It was everything, Father. Until it wasn't. I fear she has met a fate like those killed last night, but I'm not going to stop until I find her. I just couldn't leave with a good conscience knowing you would be left wondering where I went."

I reached inside my bookbag, pulling out my spellbook. Handing it to him, I said, "I found this in Mother's chest the day I reemerged. It's her journal, but evidently it had been a spellbook all along."

Father cocked his head. "That's not Krystan's."

I grinned, and merely waved my hand over the cover, murmuring, *"Çliöça."*

Father *jumped* when the spellbook changed, the violet aura of the illusion school shimmering and billowing as that journal so familiar to us presented itself. He ripped his spectacles from his eyes as if they were making him see things, hand clasping his mouth as he stared and stared.

After a moment, I cast the spell again, returning it to my spellbook and opening it to flip through the pages of instruction and *eçors*. The letter from *F* slid out, and I knew it was another sign to read it—to maybe learn more about the person who'd written it.

"This was inside the book when I found it that morning." I unfolded the crease, watched another tally mark appear at the bottom, and began to read to him.

Father remained frozen as he listened, toward the end sitting back down on my bed to steady himself. "W-Who is *F?*"

"I wasn't sure for a while, but last night I found out his name may be Falryn."

My father's eyes widened. "Falryn? Like that man who used to come into the library almost every day?"

My pulse skittered. *"What?"*

He placed his spectacles back on. "Falryn. Tall, Elven-blooded man with long emerald green hair."

My jaw fell open. That matched the features Ramos had spoken about. "I believe so," I said in awe. "He used to come here?"

A nod. "You were very young though, which may be why you don't remember. He's the reason we had that collection of elven books, Varys."

I couldn't believe what I was hearing. "When was the last time you saw him?"

He showed his palms. "It was a few years before your mother died." He eyed my spellbook. "I wonder if Falryn gave Krystan that letter and she placed it in her journal."

I shook my head. "Mother would have placed it in the journal maybe, but it fell out of the spellbook."

"You think Falryn placed it there? But how?"

"Magic," I said simply. "Falryn is an elf, Father. A *true*, pure-blooded elf."

He took a sharp breath, and I explained everything Ramos had told me. Father rubbed his chin in thought for a long moment.

"I think you need to find Falryn," he told me.

I nodded. "I think so, too."

Father sighed, combing his hair back. "You truly must leave tonight?"

"Yes. I'll be with Leo. She's currently saying her own goodbyes."

As he wiped off the blood from his lip, I came to sit beside him. "Father, I want you to leave Elros as well. Maybe not tonight, or even weeks from now."

"Varys, the library—"

"Things will get worse, Father. I will be gone, and they won't stop trying to drag my whereabouts out of you. Someday, I will be the head of our family, no matter how small we are at the moment.

To protect our future, I need you to do this. I need us to stay together."

He stared at the ground, a minute shake to his head. "I don't…I don't think I could leave this house, Varys."

Looking up, his eyes fixed on the door leading up to the attic. "But maybe I've held on for too long." He gestured me to follow him. "Come see."

They'd taken everything.

Everything.

Mother's chest was empty of her armor, her jewelry, her hair accessories, her favorite books. The guards had rummaged through other chests up here, extra blankets and Hearthswreath decor strung across the attic, a few ornaments shattered.

We weren't a family of much, but the things we had we loved. Cherished.

Father started folding an old quilt I used to love making a fort with. I could do nothing but stare at the empty chest, knowing if they had come for those things two years earlier, they would've taken my spellbook.

The pounding rain on the roof above us filled in the silence of the attic as I continued to search around, still hoping to find things to no avail.

I let out a growl. "You know I can see magic? None of what they took from her chest was magical."

Father exhaled. "I figured as much, and when the Baron gets here, I'm sure we can get everything back. But if we don't…" He shrugged. "You are right, Varys. Everything is about to change. I can't continue to hold on to the past. Not justifying what they took, but maybe this was some sort of cruel shove for me to finally give in."

He swallowed and rested against a wall, tipping his head back. "Do you want to know what my meeting was about?"

My brows rose. Between everything that had happened, I'd forgotten.

"King Elyon has raised taxes to pay for more security for all towns and cities across Xalador."

"So the King is aware that something is stirring," I murmured.

"Perhaps. But these raised taxes are affecting everyone. For years, Baron Kenrad has allowed us to be tax exempt, as we are fulfilling a great need for our community. However, I was informed last week that he can no longer afford to allow that." He paused and held my stare. "I'm broke, Varys. I cannot pay taxes and have money for food and necessities. We have lived by a thread for years, and this will ruin me."

My eyes burned. "You shouldn't have started to pay me."

"Oh, *psh*. What good a father am I that doesn't make sure his son has money of his own? However, I was still met with two options —sell the house, or get a loan."

My stomach turned over, and it was like I knew before he even said it. "A loan. You're not saying—"

"I meant to meet with Rucas Mordaunt and ask for a loan, yes."

I could hardly breathe around his words. "Please tell me you didn't."

He sighed. "Well, turns out Rucas was unable to meet with me today because he had to run a criminal trial, so no I didn't."

"Good, because I'm not allowing you to give that man anymore money. Not when he hurts the woman I love."

Father's eyes went wide. "*What?*"

I lifted my head. "I'd rather you sell the house. I'd rather you come with me on the road to Elvidawn then give a single fucking silver to that man."

Father looked around the attic and nodded. "Then it's decided. I will take my earnings and buy a cart at the Fest of Change. Then, I will pack up and come to you, wherever that may be."

"Mirefield. I don't know for how long, but my first destination is Mirefield. I have a possible confidante there, a fellow mage, that can help me."

He looked uneasy about Mirefield, but didn't protest. "Then you best hurry and pack."

I nodded, taking one last glance at Mother's chest. "Hopefully you can at least get her armor back. We can't *replace* that. It's a good thing we still have—"

My words failed. A terrible, horrific realization hit me like a cold, painful wave.

"No," I started breathlessly, my legs moving involuntarily even though my knees threatened to cave. "No, No, *No.*"

Father called my name, but I was already out of the room, barreling downstairs. We had been so concerned with the things in my room, in the attic, we had forgotten about the most valuable thing we owned—*I* owned.

They could have taken anything but that. *Anything.*

My heart sank into the hollowness of my stomach, a great hole that had been dug out by words, adversities, tragic understandings, and fear. Just as empty, as vacant as the hearth mantle where my mother's sword had been in its display case.

Gone. The sword was gone.

CHAPTER 41

Varys

As my knees gave out, so did the fight in me.

My head fell back when I hit the floor, blood surging with fiery fury. I barely heard Father come into the room, stepping up behind me. Barely heard him murmur, "They took it. They really did."

A great anguish stirred and swelled, a scream scraping its way up my throat. From the hollow place I erupted, roaring at the ceiling, ensuring I was loud enough for my rage to pierce through those storm clouds shrouding the sun, dominating the thunder, and echoing off the hills. I wouldn't stop until I knew my scream had been heard all the way up into that infinite field of stars. Where I usually looked for counsel, for guidance, but today only found what I knew I needed to say.

As my voice died out, a silence fell over the library. My fist pounded the ground, tears spilling free, unlocking the words I'd kept in chains somewhere deep inside.

"She deserves to be here as a mage instead of me."

They were the words that summed up everything I believed about myself. My spellbook had been her journal. She had been a great warrior who would have stepped into the role of a war sage effortlessly.

Instead, fate decided that she would die, and I live. I had hoped that my reemergence would give me some sort of clarity and would help me see that I wasn't worthless. I was supposed to be powerful, so why did I feel so powerless?

I laced my fingers together and pressed them down on the crown of my head, still looking up at those imaginary stars, still waiting for something to tell me what to do. But the gods were silent. So was my mother.

"Tormshit," my father's voice broke from behind. "That is *wrong*, Varys. Complete shit. Don't you *ever* say that again."

He knelt before me, taking my shoulders. I avoided his stare, my jaw aching from clenching so tight.

"You hear me, son?" He shook my shoulders. "Your mother would have been *livid* if she heard you say that."

"If she was alive, she would have been a mage." I choked back a sob. "You know that, right? My elven blood is from her. She would have reemerged as well."

He gave a curt nod. "I do understand that. I understand that if she were still here today, I would have gained two incredibly powerful mages in my family. *Two*, Varys. Because her becoming a mage wouldn't have prevented you from this ReEmergence. So why would you say something like that?"

Lips quivering on the breath I took, I could hardly speak through my words, "I'm…I'm f-failing. I've read every book about using my magic but it amounts to nothing if I don't know what I'm doing." I coughed, rubbing the hot tears from my face. "I don't even know how to save the woman I love. I'm nothing."

Father cut in to protest, but I kept on, finally looking up to him, "I always felt unworthy of the sword. I knew I wouldn't be able to use it as my own until I had all the answers. Until I wasn't failing. Now it's gone." I shook my head. "She wouldn't have failed, though. Mother always had the answers. Even now I find her guidance when I'm unsure of my next step."

"So what is she saying to you now?" he asked.

"I don't know," I bit out.

"Listen, Varys." His words lit something on fire within me. "What is your next step—?"

"I.Don't.Know!" I yelled, fists clenched to my chest. "It's not like I can hear her voice." More tears fell down my face. "She's dead."

"No," my father grit out, taking hold of my shoulders. "No, Varys. She's not."

The hands on me gripped tighter before he yanked me into an embrace. For a moment, I didn't move—didn't know *how* to move.

"I've got her spirit right here in my godsdamn arms," he told me.

My breath hitched.

"She's not a ghost lurking around to give you advice. I would know." His voice cracked, but he fought through it. "Her spirit has lived on in *you*. I see it everyday. The same determination. The same care for those you love. The same smile, the same strengths. Stop denying yourself of your power. You have always been worthy, my son. You have always been *enough*."

My chest buckled on the cry that ripped from me escaping. I could no longer hold my head up, allowing myself to sink into my father's embrace. Slowly, my arms found their way around him, and something inside me broke and mended all at once.

"You know your next step, son," Father assured me as he pulled away. "Sword or no sword, you must leave Elros. You are in danger here. I have no doubt that you will take the knowledge you have of this ReEmergence and help other mages outside of Elros. Xalador needs you, Varys."

I wiped my eyes, sniffling back the last of my tears, and nodded. Not because I was any less afraid, but because I was ready to move forward. Ready to prove to *myself* I was a mage. I didn't need a book stating I was, nor did I need all of the answers in the world. I was a mage because I had reemerged, because I was simply Varys Wynhart, son of Krystan and Mattis Wynhart, Elven-blooded and...

It was my godsdamn destiny.

"This isn't over yet," Father said as we stood. "Whether our walls are here, or somewhere else, we have not fallen. That sword belongs to you, Varys. You better believe we haven't seen the last of it." He lifted his chin. "I'll make damn sure of it."

After quickly gathering some clothes in a pack, I came back downstairs to say a final farewell to Father. But as I stepped off the last step, lightning struck somewhere close by, illuminating the room with a bright flash. The clap of thunder that followed was deafening, shaking our walls. The sound of falling rain swelled from soft to hard and pounding, and I noticed we could no longer see the market through the windows beyond the wall of water.

The storm that had been brewing all day was here.

Our shutters began to flap and rattle as wind swept through the streets. Father and I glanced at each other as I came back into the gathering room with tight teeth. I knew what both of us were thinking. This house had stood strong for years, but would this be the season an autumn storm would claim it?

"You sure you're leaving *tonight?*" Father asked.

I grimaced, another flash of light filling the room with light. "I mean, I have to—"

Before I could finish my sentence, there was a pounding on the front door. I whipped around with a snarl, my anger still burning hot. "They've come back."

Father pointed behind us. "Get to the backdoor. Go out that way."

I hadn't packed rations, hadn't said goodbye. I wasn't ready—

Thunder crashed in an explosive resonance as if lightning had split the town apart. We both hit the floor, covering our heads, shielding our eyes as glass shattered. A branch had snapped from the tree outside and fallen through a window.

Father jumped up and limped over, taking hold of the wet tree brush and pushing. "Water's coming in!"

There was another pound on the front door. I seethed forward, ripping my blade from its sheath. Father called out for me to stop, but I was done with visitors today. If someone else was here to take my things, or arrest me for a crime I didn't commit, I wasn't going down without a fight. Not this time.

As I came into the entryway, the winds picked up. The next knock on the door had me growling, rushing forward in a march. I yanked the door open and the winds blew in. Lightning flashed, brightening the space between me and our guest—

My breath left in a harsh gasp, sword falling from my hand, metal shrieking as it hit the ground. More flashes of light lit up the sky, illuminating the bare figure before me. She was drenched with rain, white hair clinging to her porcelain skin and hardly concealing her breasts and the lower regions of her body. But it wasn't her nakedness that made me step back into the house as if I'd seen a ghost. It was the way she looked at me, chin tilted down, glaring through my very soul with pitch black eyes. Gone were the whites, the amethyst irises so full of radiance. They'd been replaced by a void as deep and haunting as they had been in the dream I'd had earlier.

She raised a hand, and those dark lightning-like marks lit up with an incandescent purple glow. Lifting one finger, she pointed at me, and I didn't know if I should run or stay frozen in fear.

"You know what lies in the eye of the storm," she said, her voice cold and wicked.

With that, she closed her eyes and her body began to tremble. Her lashes fluttered, and when her gaze found mine once more, her violet irises presented themselves again, now mere slivers around her enlarged pupils. She took a step toward me, arms reaching out. I stepped back on instinct.

"Varys," she said in a high-pitched rasp. *"Graešta ni…"*

Her eyes rolled back as her body tipped forward. The air sawed out of me as I lunged for her, catching her limp form in my arms.

Mae was murmuring in her unconscious state as I lay her down on my bed, every word in Elvish, but so quiet and jumbled. I pulled my blanket over her, then brushed her wet curls up off her body, twisting the hair into a loose bun to lay against the pillow. She was still quivering, her plum lips practically colorless.

"She's ice cold," I said, pressing a hand against her cheek.

Father remained in the doorway, seeming a bit too uncomfortable to walk in and unsure of what he could do to help. "What is happening to her?"

I turned to him, a lump growing in my throat. "I told you. I don't know how to help her. I don't know what's going on."

"Do you think Natalia could help?" he asked with a shrug.

I was about to say no, but remembered Natalia had helped Mae before when she had fallen from the same tree that was somehow connected to her magically. "Maybe."

The windows rattled, quickly reminding us of the violent storm still raging. Mae let out a groan as high-pitched as the whistling wind. I sat beside her, instinctively shushing her as if it would help calm her. "Mae, you're safe. I'm here."

Father let out a sigh. "You can't take her in that condition."

"I know."

I wouldn't be leaving Elros tonight after all.

"I will watch over her tonight. See how she is in the morning." I traced a finger down her face.

Father sucked in a breath. "If those guards come back—"

"I have ways of hiding us." I gave him a hopeful grin, waving my hands. "Magic."

He nodded. "Well then, I've got a window to patch. I'll see you in the morning."

"Goodnight."

When the door clicked shut, I let out a long, shuddering breath, raking my fingers through my hair. My head was so...empty. I had no answers, but I didn't have the energy to ask questions. Nothing mattered except that I'd found her—or, she had found me.

I went to my wardrobe and grabbed a tunic. I was wearing the only pair of pants I owned, so I figured I could probably create a make-shift skirt out of the small, lightweight blanket I used in the heat of summer. She didn't have any shoes, so I would carry her to the Cauldücen's.

I was just about to lay the items at the foot of the bed when the winds outside came to an abrupt stop. A chill slivered down my spine, but not because of the sudden calm. I *felt* the eyes on me.

"Such a strange feeling, this pulse," she purred behind me. "Just a glimpse of you sends her heart pounding."

I turned, my own heart slamming against my chest. Black eyes met mine, staring up at me with a small, but absolutely insidious smile. With one blink, the rain stopped falling as if something had sealed the sky shut. A hair-raising silence fell over the room. Over Elros entirely. The stifled breath I took was too loud.

A hum started in her chest as she rose into a sitting position. I stepped back cautiously when she got to her knees, movements fluid and graceful. A predator about to pounce.

"Mae?" I forced out.

Her smile broadened. "Your voice is so pretty."

But *her* voice...it wasn't right. Gone was the sweet rasp, replaced with something deep and dark.

"Y-You're not Mae, are you?" I asked, taking another step away, keeping my focus on her mouth. I could hardly stand to look into her eyes.

The shake of her head was unsteady and heavy, as if she was sure how to use her neck. "I'm *Maelawyn.*"

I sucked in a breath. That name. The voice I'd heard in my dream was *hers*, whatever *she* was.

As the blankets fell away from her hips, she looked down, curiously taking in her form. It seemed she had never seen anything like it before. The lightning marks had spread up her arm, to her shoulder and left side of her chest, and seemed to go behind her as well.

"What have you done with Mae?" I asked hoarsely.

"She's here," she told me, stroking her hands along her body. "She just let me take over for a while. She's weak."

A chill swam through me. "What are you? A demon? Succubus?"

Her black eyes narrowed, nose curling. "You humans are so dense," she growled, her voice as dark as the thunderhead. "Always quick to assume something is a monster when it is not of the material plane."

I could only blink at her, forcing myself to breathe. "I apologize," I said cautiously, spreading my fingers wide, gulping as I tried to find the *right* words, not knowing what she would do to me, to Mae. "I didn't mean to offend. You are within my friend's body."

"*Friend?*" she asked. "Come now. I am consumed by need in your very presence." She ran her hands over her form, down her legs before stroking up to her breasts. I struggled to shut down the thoughts, my blood roaring. This *was* Mae's body after all. "You are no friend, Varys Wynhart. Not to her. Not to me. Not to us."

Us.

"You speak as if you are separate from her, but are you truly?" I asked. "If you have such desires for me, her emotions must have a hold on you."

A sly smile lifted her paled lips. "For now, but I do not resent them. I was made by her emotions, and they are strong. Thus, so am I."

"So, Mae is a sorceress," I stated, spine locking when she drew closer to the edge of the bed. "It's been written that a sorcerer's magical aptitude is determined by how controlled their emotions are. So, are you result of unbridled emotion?"

A cackle started in her throat, and as she tipped her head back to laugh out, thunder boomed, rattling the windows, the walls. I went still as stone, a terrible realization flooding my head.

The thunder had been no coincidence. It had been in sync with her laughter.

"I am storm. I am ruin," she told me.

A gale rushed against the window, the lock threatening to give way.

"You're commanding this. The storm," I said in a whisper. "You aren't casting a spell."

She only grinned, the lightning marks on her arm lighting up in a violet glow. "I have no need for magic."

"But she is *Vyl'kriev*—"

"I know what she is!" she screeched, leaping off the bed. I stumbled back. "Only a *Vyl'kriev* could be *made* into what we are. Only a *Vyl'kriev* could make *me*."

She spread her hands apart, fingers bending and twisting in a wicked dance. Small sparks flickered before they streaked out, connecting nail to nail. A buzzing, crackling sound filled the room, the current of light casting glittering flecks along my walls. It was beautiful, but I was terrified of the puzzle piece that had suddenly clicked into place before she could ever continue to explain herself.

I pulled out *Ít Nánöweth* from my book bag, denial tumbling from my lips.

No.

How was this possible?

"I am a nwív," Maelawyn declared. "I am the element of storm. I am chaos and beauty intertwined. I am power. I am change."

My eyes burned with tears of awe, and as the answer rolled off my tongue, I felt as if the very world shifted beneath the weight of it. "Mae is a nexus."

CHAPTER 42

Varys

The bridge between our world and an elemental plane.

The perfect, physical embodiment of a storm.

That was what Mae was.

But how had she been *made?*

It didn't make any sense. When she was conceived, magic had not yet reemerged, and nexi were created with a spell.

A spell neither Rucas Mordaunt, nor Fantine could cast.

I looked over her white hair, her full lips, her beautiful angular eyes. Features Rucas did not possess. Maybe she had gotten her lips from her mother, but all other characteristics were not that of a Mordaunt.

Chaos.

I had to steady myself on the back of my desk chair. I had missed something.

"How were you made?" I asked in a breath.

The nwív let the lightning between her fingers flicker out, then flipped her white curls off her shoulders. "Her mother and father of course, though I barely recall the first light. My clearest memories begin at the first spark—an emotion I would only later understand as fear. Then, I learned of anger, then yearning." She paused, and for a very short moment, she looked more like Mae than she had since showing up at my doorstep. "Sadness."

She lifted her chin. "I didn't know of joy until recently. One day, the storm plane stopped thundering for the first time ever. The rain turned to a pleasurable mist. I could almost feel it." She grinned. "It was just the right kind of power I needed. It gave me the strength to become what I was made to do."

I swallowed. "And…what will you do?"

That demented expression washed over her face again. "Free the rising storm."

My stomach turned over, reminded of what the book spoke of. How an unbound nwív could take over its nexus completely and unleash its element upon the world.

Another thought formed and demanded my attention. I wondered how that might feel. To be taken over by something.

Would it be painful?

"Her flares…" My hands snapped to my mouth, tears blurring my eyes. She had lived with so much pain and it had been her nwív trying to break free.

But she wasn't completely gone yet. The nwív said she had only taken over for a little while.

With a careful step toward her, I asked, "Is Mae gone?"

"She is here."

I breathed out the breath I held. "Can I speak to her?"

Thunder rumbled as her lips turned down. "Why?"

I reached out my hand slowly. "You are in her body. She must be very confused. If you will allow me to explain her situation—"

"It is far too late for that," she snapped. "I am no chrysalis. I am the end."

I still held out my hand, forcing myself to look into her black eyes. This was Mae, and I couldn't deny that. If she was a nexus, her nwív was a part of her and crucial to her power. "What do you feel for your nexus, Maelawyn?"

The question seemed to stump her. She stared at my outstretched hand. "She is everything to me."

"Do you love her enough to let me make her smile," I asked,

unable to hide the desperation, "to bring her *joy* again? Even if it is for the last time?"

Lightning crackled along the edges of her midnight gaze. "You will not free her. That door is closed."

I wasn't sure what she meant, but I didn't necessarily need to. I just needed this delay. If I could get Mae back, I could tell her what was happening and then maybe figure out how to bind her before the nwív took over completely.

I stepped in and took hold of her icy fingers. Her breath hitched, but she didn't pull away. "What…is this?"

I smiled, bringing her closer. "*Dias na ni,* Mae. Just for a moment."

The winds roused once more, another flash of energy glittering in her gaze. "She will not—"

Her eyes closed on a rattled breath.

And when her lashes flicked up, there were those glittering amethysts staring up at me. I almost crumbled at the sight of them, breathing out, "Hello, Little Bird."

Mae

I had been running.

Away from the pain. The fear.

From *him.* Rucas.

My abuser.

My villain.

The shroud of opalescent haze began to diminish. The warm feeling in my hand was distant, but the connection told me it was him. Slowly, as if walking through the last bit of fog, the outline of his face appeared before me, and I took a breath with my own lungs.

His hand gripped mine tighter, and I leaned into his pull. One step at a time, I came into him. Strong arms wrapped around me, lifted me, carried me over to a soft surface. I realized it was his bed, and understood I was probably in his bedroom, but I wasn't entirely sure how I'd gotten here.

I felt his warmth leave me for a brief moment before a wool-like material draped around my neck and head. His hands guided my arms beneath more of the cloth that smelled like bergamot—like him. Then, something soft was wound and tightened around my hips, falling over my cold legs.

He had dressed me. I hadn't even realized I'd been naked.

"Where did you go, Mae?" His voice filled my very soul, but my name...

It's not right.

"Mae," I whispered. "Is that...who I am?"

A pause. "Is that who you *want* to be?"

I didn't know the answer to that.

"I want to live."

The softest touch pressed to my temple, and it wasn't until the sound of his lips releasing I understood he'd kissed me. "How can I help you do that, Mae?"

I looked up to him, blue eyes reflecting the warm glow of a candle. Reaching up, I cupped his face with my hands. "Let me change."

His hold around me tightened. "Do you know what takes hold of you, *aríma?*"

I nodded. "Maelawyn."

She was...

...everything.

She was who I was supposed to be.

His features darkened. "Do you know what you are?"

"I am a storm."

It was the only answer.

"You are a nexus, Mae," he murmured in my ear. "You are beautiful. And powerful. But you are those things on your own."

He was wrong. "No. I need her. She's going to kill him for me."

His muscles tensed. "Who is she going to kill?"

My eyelids felt so heavy, my bones like lead. I was little more than sludge on a river rock.

A pupa in a chrysalis...

…breaking down…

…getting ready to fly…

"Rucas," I muttered. "He knows."

The haze was coming back. I wasn't sure I could hold on for much longer.

Varys tilted my chin up, made me look at him. "Stay with me, Mae. What does he know?"

A thunderous pounding started in my mind.

I could hear every boot hit the ground.

My breath left me in a small screech. "He's here."

"What—"

Men began to yell, bashing in wood and metal. I pushed my hands over my ears.

So loud…

It was too loud…

"What in Torm?" Varys shouted. His presence left me as he stood. I wrapped my arms around my body, shielding myself.

"Varys."

The door flew open. I screamed as their heavy feet marched into the room, as if their soles were crushing my skull. Varys took a surprised gasp—

He yelped.

My eyes flew open just in time to see him drop…

to

the

…ground.

A figure stood with a large weapon in his grasp.

Varys's eyes were closed.

He was…

I screeched his name, tumbling off the bed, crawling to his side.

Violet flooded my vision, heat rushing through my veins.

A hand grabbed my arm.

The calluses rough.
His grip like **iron**.
"You little witch…

…it's time you die."

My world went dark.

I was fourteen years old.
  Father was drunk.
  He was always drunk.
  And I knew that when the room was permeated and soaked with the scent of ale, pain was in store for me.
  I'd priced something wrong at the store. Sold it for too little. Cost him gold.
  His eyes were lit with rage. He had me cornered.
  One slap across the face.
  Another.
  I shouted for Mother to help. She didn't come.
  She never did.
  I didn't know where the scourge had come from until it came down across my belly
  But I managed to slip under his legs. S c r a m b l e out of the house.
  I ran that day. The first time I'd run away.
  Just like I had run from him today.
  *I couldn't go to my tree. He'd already found me there once, when I'd climbed so I could be on top of the world and watch the **storm**. When I had fallen and* bled.
  Such a powerful child.
  I didn't know where I would go.
  I just had to run.
  But he was faster. His men were faster, with their horses and dogs.
  He'd called it his new toy as he'd scourged me across the back.
  Hard enough to hurt.
  Gentle enough to heal.

I had learned that day that I was not chaos.
I would never be safe from my father.
The storm could not protect me.
Not yet.
Not until I was the storm itself.

Muffled voices stirred me from my slumber.

"Rucas," the voice was familiar, but I couldn't place it. My mind was too

f ʳa ᴄ t ᵘ ᵣe ᵈ

"Please. Don't do this."

"Do you not understand what she is? She's one of *them*."

"So what if she is?" Eryx. It was Eryx. "Rucas, she's your daughter—"

"She is no daughter of mine!"

I opened my eyes to find I was on my knees before my iron chair, my wrists tied up to the top rail. Unfamiliar eyes met mine from a chair at the dining table. My pulse skipped when the man rose, grinning with yellowed teeth.

"Boss. She's awake."

Breaths coming in short, ragged bursts, I tried to twist myself around and find my friend.

"Eryx? Help—"

The skin of my back ignited with a fiery pain, overwhelming every part of me for an agonizing moment. When my scream came, so did the realization.

Rucas had that scourge again.

There was a scuffle behind me, Eryx's shouts of protest echoing across the dining room.

"Rucas, I made sure Varys would be imprisoned." He growled out. "That's what you wanted."

Everything in me shrank.

I pulled against the bindings, tears blurring my eyes. *"No!"*

I barely registered the hand on my shoulder before the next lash came. Eryx shouting my name mixed with my screams, footsteps racing toward me

"Get him out of here!" Rucas demanded.

"*Mae! I'm sorry!*" Eryx cried out before the front door slammed shut.

In the silence, I wept.

"For every lie you tell, another lash." Rucas words made my blood ice over.

I could hardly breathe through the throbbing pain of my back, every inhale stretching my injured skin. I repressed my whimpers and cries, listening to Rucas's footsteps as he paced behind me.

Someone was watching from the hall. Big brown eyes full of tears.

"Sorry," she muttered.

Mother.

"I'm so sorry."

The scourge snapped. My body jolted on instinct, but I bit my lip to hold back my yelp.

"This isn't how I hoped you'd go, girl." He chuckled darkly. "I wasted too much coin paying those two. Thought they would take care of it so I wouldn't have to."

My stomach turned over, bile rising up my throat.

No.

The stream…the stream had been…

…*planned?*

"What I can't figure out is how you managed to kill them," he went on. "Where did you get your powers, fiend?"

I didn't want to answer. Anything out of my mouth would mean another lash. To Rucas, to my mother, I lied about everything, even when I was telling the truth.

And he knew that.

"Answer me," he growled.

I sucked in a breath. I would speak the truth anyway. "I didn't kill Willem and Theon."

I hadn't. I knew I had nothing to do with it.

I braced myself for the scourge, but his hand swung across the back of my head instead, forcing my forehead into the iron chair. I cried out as pain lanced through my skull, a trickling warmth running down the bridge of my nose.

"I won't ask again," he told me. I hadn't realized how close he was to me until his fingers dove into my hair, ripping my head to the side. Terror took hold of me, ragged cries escaping as…

…his lips trailed across my neck.

"You get your devilry from Varys's cock?"

I squeezed my eyes shut, trying not to think about where his hand lay as I searched within, my very soul crying out.

Help me.

Please.

The air whistled as the scourge came down, the lash sending violet stars through my eyes and searing pain up my spine. I shrieked, fingers wrapping tighter around the chair, eyes burning with hot tears.

I'll give you everything.

Another lash came down.

Then another.

Everything?

My entire body jerked forward with each blow, heart pounding in my ears.

Everything. Just…

I could feel my blood running down my back in streams.

"You're done with your lies, wretch."

The next lash undid me. Even braced against the chair, I couldn't hold on.

Just kill him.

"Beg for the block girl. I won't stop until you do."

I was going to die.

I was n o t h i n g.

Kill him.

KILL HIM.

My veins began to glow, the pain that coursed beneath my skin just as hot and agonizing as the lashes. A wild screech tore from my throat, yanking against the bindings. My body was on fire, but there was a new release climbing to the surface of my skin.

Take my pain.

Take me.

Free me.

Say it.
You know the words.
The rope around my wrists turned to ash.

The whipping stopped.

Mother gasped out. "Her eyes! Rucas—"

She was cut off by my screams, the pain of both ice and fire, burning up every nerve. Purples warped my vision, a violent fury taking over as I pulled on my hair and clawed at the floor like an animal.

Say it!
Free the rising storm.
My outer vision went white, like it did when Willem was forcing himself on me. When he tried to rape me.

When my father paid for me to be **murdered**.

Another scream ripped from my throat, filled with all of my rage, **destruction** rising up from my very bones.

Free it!
I had never felt so ~~dead~~.

I had never felt so ***alive***.

"*Saeör…*" I screamed, lungs roaring, fingers curling **wickedly**. "*Saeör ít ölsta xera!*"

I shattered.

Lightning exploded from my hands, blasting in all directions, burning jagged trails into the wood floor. The line of fires were only alive for a moment before they flickered out, leaving behind the smell of ether and a terrifying silence.

And the pain…

All of the pain was gone.

But

so

was

I…

This was freedom...?

I hadn't expected freedom would feel like this.

As the command expelled from her lips, and I emerged from the storm plane, I was suddenly overwhelmed by a sensation I had never felt before. It was sharp and hot along my back. My heart beat quickly in response, stomach turning over, hands and toes clenching.

"What is this?" I gasped. My knees were trying to buckle.

I felt...weak.

The remnants of her thoughts vanished as I reached behind me, feeling around for whatever was making my body feel this way. The touch elicited a hiss through my teeth, fingers dampened with something warm and wet. When I pulled my hand back, I found my fingers coated with red.

My body went taut. I had only seen this through her eyes.

Blood.

Her blood had been spilled. That was dangerous magic if done with the right intention. Like what had happened when she fell from that tree some time ago.

Gritting my teeth, I wiped the blood off on my legs and looked up to lock eyes with him.

Her abuser.

Her villain.

He hadn't been there at first light. He didn't look like the one who had made me.

And still, she called him Father.

To me, he was my initiator. All of her fear and anger and sadness. All of the emotions she had for this pathetic human had fed and given me strength to rise up. It wasn't until her reemergence I believed I could.

He was terrified standing before me now, clutching something with long, dark strings and knots. The ends of the knots were red—bloodied.

"What is this...agonizing feeling?" I asked him.

His head shook. He didn't respond.

"It's hot." I took a breath and it brought another lash of heat through my body. "It burns. It brought blood."

His lips trembled. "What are you—"

"*Answer me,*" I demanded. "Only then will I speak to you."

He took several steps away from me, a whimper in his throat.

"Pain," someone else said from behind.

I turned to find the woman she called Mother standing on the edge of a long, dark space. "You are in pain," she told me.

Pain.

Maelawyn spoke of this often. Would always tell me how much it hurt whenever I tried to possess her. She had started to call them *flares* and *pain attacks*. I never understood.

I did now.

If she felt this pain all the time, I could understand why she had begged for death. Why in her last moments she had pleaded for me to take over. How she had wanted for it all to stop.

But I didn't want it to stop.

It made me angry and sad, and such strong emotions would brew another storm.

I pointed at the man named Rucas, glaring. "You did this to me."

"Demon. You're a demon," he whined. "I always knew you were cursed."

Thunder rolled with my laughter. I didn't give him a response, stepping over the pile of ash around me. When my true form had dominated her body, the clothing she wore had burned away, and her cloud-white flesh had turned to a beautiful violet that glittered as if I was made of diamond dust. Delicate cords of energy entwined with the lavender hair cascading from my head, arching and jumping over my breasts and stomach with every step I took toward him.

He held the weapon out, muttering something I didn't care to pay attention to. Walking brought more pain. I wanted to scream. My eyes burned with tears—something else I had never experienced before.

But these new sensations only made me stronger.

"Before I release my storm upon this realm, I must carry out the task I agreed to," I told Rucas directly. Eyeing the mother, I said, "This is your final warning. Leave this place if you know what is best for you."

The woman's eyes widened before glancing at Rucas. He snarled. "Don't you dare."

Her lips trembled, arms wrapping around herself. "Do you know? The truth?" she asked me.

I wasn't sure what she meant. "I know nothing but what I am meant to do."

The woman looked dissatisfied by my answer, but quickly rushed toward the kitchen.

"You *bitch!*" Rucas yelled, marching toward her as she fled for a side door. She let out a cry, flung the door open, and ran out.

I wasn't taking any chances at him thinking he could do the same. I held out a hand and brought forth my lightning, fingers curling around the bolts and forming it into a ball I instantly tossed in front of him. When it met the floor, blinding light flashed before thunder rang out through the room. Rucas pushed his hands over his ears as he stumbled backward, falling into the iron chair.

Interesting.

I understood Maelawyn had attachment to this chair. Had always chosen it over the others around the table. It was made of iron, of metal—something lightning conducted to.

He began to rise, but I threw out a long chain of jolting energy, commanding and guiding it to wrap around his neck. It touched his skin and he cried out, sitting back down and going as still as stone.

A chuckle left me as I circled around to face him, grinning at his terrified expression. He glanced down at the crackling snare. "I should have killed you in your crib."

Another laugh started in my chest. "You still think you are speaking to *her*, don't you?"

Panic filled his eyes. "You're...not Mae?"

I smiled. "I am storm incarnate, the embodiment of chaos. You should have already known that by her *true* name. You *all* should have."

I raised my hands to the ceiling. Rucas shuddered in absolute terror as my feet left the ground, my lavender curls lifting off my shoulders, dancing around my head in the wind billowing from all directions of the room. Plates were knocked from the shelves in the kitchen, books were torn from their cases, the pages from within ripping out and flying around. I spun my hands above my head in an enchanting circle, manifesting dark clouds to form as bolts danced over my knuckles.

"Witness the power that slept inside the one you called daughter." The air smelled of ether. My skin tingled in pleasure as the energy flowed underneath. *"Maer."*

Rain.

The clouds released, water pouring upon us. Rucas shouted when the rain hit the energy band around his neck, loosing sparks and jolts and shocking his skin.

"The daughter you beat and maimed." My hands came together. *"Ladrön."*

Thunder.

The room shook as a loud clap rumbled. Rucas stared

up at the storm, tears running down his face. "Oh *gods*," he whispered.

There was a low thrumming in my veins. A warning of what was coming. I lifted my hand straight to the storm in the ceiling. "The daughter you foolishly diminished daily, only to discover seconds before your end that she is no curse, no demon. She is power. She is rain, thunder..."

A streak of lightning shot down from the storm, connecting to my fingers, crackling and buzzing as it filled my body with incredible power. I let it flow naturally through my veins and tendons, spidering over my bones before it found its exit—the tip of the middle finger of my left hand; the end of the mark of the nexus. The energy gathered in my hand.

"She is *wyn'kevlla.*"

Lightning.

I descended, letting the lightning flit around my fingers. His breathing turned more shallow as I came closer, kicking his legs out only for the ring of lightning around his neck to shock him once more. Unadulterated fear contorted his face, and as a shudder went through him, his pants became dark and damp. Liquid began to drip down the chair, onto the floor. He clamped his lips together, eyes squeezed shut.

"Please," he begged, chest rising and falling as heavy tears fell down his face. "I'm her father. She wouldn't do this to me. "

I tilted my head. "You are not her father. And she wants to live."

His eyes went wide as my hands fell to the arms of the iron chair. The energy connected to the metal, sparkling bolts racing along the rails and posts, and then jumped onto Rucas. His body convulsed, arms and legs flailing as my lightning surged through muscle and marrow. Smoke rose from his flesh, filling the room with a thick and putrid scent. His unseeing eyes never rolled backward, never left mine, mouth gaping open in a scream that never came.

And then my first troth to my nexus was fulfilled. His body slacked, toppling forward. I let it fall to the floor and didn't give it another thought before I exited out the side door. Lifting my hands to the storm swirling above me, I commanded a bolt of lightning to strike down upon the house. Flames roared to life upon impact and began to burn and devour the walls and windows.

I ascended into the sky and watched as the house turned to ash—something she'd wanted. But her body had not been the kindling as she had hoped, it had been the spark.

CHAPTER 43

Varys

A great, ear-splitting boom rattled me to my senses. I curled into myself, shielding my head with my hands as the ground quaked around me. When the clamor died out, not a moment passed before the smell of smoke began to permeate the air.

Panic rose as I shot to my feet. I was in a dark room, unbound and hurting everywhere. Despite my foggy, disoriented mind, my survival instincts took over, but when I went to yank the sword from my hip, I found nothing there. Whoever had brought me here had disarmed me, and upon that realization, another wave of alarm had me patting myself down. I sighed in relief to find my book bag still around me. A quick glance in told me everything important remained, including my spellbook. They'd only taken the obvious weapon.

"*Wyn.*" The ball of light manifested and hovered over my outstretched palm. I flicked it to the corner of the room, the space illuminating before me. An unfamiliar four-poster bed was in the center of the room, the quilts bunched up as if the owner had kicked them off. A small side table with a lone candle sat to the left of it, along with a fairly large wardrobe. The other side of the room was filled with chests and boxes, perhaps storage. There wasn't anything on the walls. No shelves. No books.

Turning, the door snagged my attention. I went for the handle and tugged, only to find it locked. There was a vanity to my left filled with items I assumed belonged to a woman, including several hair pins I could use as a lock pick. I took one decorated with a cluster of yellow and green jewels and turned back to the door.

But my plan failed before it could even begin. This door was locked from the other side, similar to the kind used in the prison, and I was obviously not in a jail cell.

Pinching the bridge of my nose to alleviate the ache in my head, I turned to find something that would tell me whose room this was. Nothing felt…familiar. I didn't know anyone who particularly liked this grassy, almost yellowish green color the bedding possessed. The garish gold and red floral design along the crown molding screamed of a wealth I'd never known. Looking closer to the things on the vanity, I found an uncapped jar of silver dust, next to a pile of glittering jewelry as if their owner had tried everything on but hadn't put them away. None of it I recognized enough to solve whose room I was in.

When I went to turn toward the wardrobe, my leg bumped the vanity chair. A vest that had been hanging over the back slumped to the floor, and my pulse skittered when I went to pick it up. *Gods*, my hands knew the texture of the material before touching it, face heating as I remembered all too well how my fingers had run over the ornate designs as I had kissed her on the settee in the library.

This was Mae's bedroom.

And as if the very thought of her had been a key, everything became suddenly clear. I understood why my head was pounding, recalling the moments with Mae before Rucas and a group of men had broken into my home hitting me over the head with a club—I would have to obsess over my carelessness later…

Because the room was now filling with smoke.

A haze veiled the ball of light, tendrils of smog dancing among the shine. The breath I took tasted like ash, and the next felt like I had breathed in cindering sand, triggering a set of coughs to overwhelm me. My eyes began to burn as I backed away from the door, looking down in horror at the dark smoke billowing in from underneath.

Cursing into my sleeve, I ran for the window and prepared to break my way out. Surprisingly, it was unlocked, and when I looked down into the Mordaunt's yard, I realized why. It was a straight shot to the ground. There was nothing along the house to find purchase on.

The tree about two of my arm's length away was the only safe way down, and I could jump to the nearest branch. I had an escape.

But I couldn't ignore the voice in my head demanding me to use the little time I had to save some of Mae's clothes, especially since she had nothing on the last time I saw her. It was reckless, and I wasn't even sure of her circumstances, but I rushed for the wardrobe anyway and threw the doors open. After finding a burlap sack, I grabbed a simple looking dress, then a purple tunic I knew I had seen wear, and stuffed them both in. In a drawer, I found a pair of black pants and socks. My chest twinged at the knowledge that I was leaving things behind that might be important to her, but the smoke was too heavy now. I was out of time.

I grabbed a pair of boots I found under the bed and tossed them and the bag of Mae's clothes out the window, barely missing someone below who was currently placing a ladder along the wall. I stepped back in surprise when the rails hit the window sill.

"Mr. Wynhart?" A female's voice called urgently from below.

I peered over and found Fantine Mordaunt waving me down. Everything from confusion to bitterness swam through me at once, distrustful of the ladder; whether or not I would begin to climb and she would sabotage its balance—

The groan of buckling wood snared my attention, and I barely got a glance behind me before the ceiling caved in. Splinters and ash consumed the room, hot toxic smoke quickly pluming toward me as I bounded over the window sill. Flames engulfed the very spot I had been standing, roaring out into the open air above me as I descended down the ladder.

"Quickly," Fantine cried.

I stepped off the last rung just as a loud snap sliced the air. Fiery planks and stones began to crash down from the roof. Fantine screeched for me as I took off, my sprint little more than stumbling hurdles as the mass of smoldering wood and brick toppled down to the ground.

Once I was safe, I sank to my knees and hunched over, coughing to clear my lungs of smoke. I barely took note of the crowd currently gathering around the house.

Fantine came to stand before me. A thank you rose up my throat, but I hesitated. I *was* thankful—she had just saved my life. But another question came out instead, one she even seemed to expect. "Why?" I asked through a rattling breath.

Her lips parted as if to answer, but she was cut off by a man shouting her name. A middle-aged blond rushed toward us. I recognized him immediately, ire igniting in my chest as hot as the flames engulfing the Mordaunt home. Wylan Welch stopped before us, ignoring me entirely—and I him. I had locked down many words over the years I knew would easily escape if I engaged in even the slightest amount of small talk with him. Instead, my focus slid to the group of bystanders cresting the front yard of the Mordaunt home. Some of them faced the house, horrified by the scene.

Others faced the opposite direction, looking up.

My eyes widened. Stretching to the left and right, and encircling the house entirely was a wall of rain. Not a single drop splashed outside the knife-edge perimeter, and I didn't need to cast *Vid Medaes* to know this was magic's doing.

Something was preventing this area of The Flats from being touched by rain. Something wanted the house to burn.

Not something. Someone, I realized as I got to my feet. *Mae's nwiv.*

"Where's your husband?" Wylan asked Fantine. "Mae?"

Her focus remained on me. "The house," she muttered, eyes glazed and unblinking. Afraid.

The same fear that overwhelmed me upon her words.

Wylan's face contorted with fervency as he spun from us. "Men! The house! Search the house before it comes down!"

The smoky air I breathed in filled me with dread, sinking into the marrow of my bones and taking over my feet. Mae's name left my lips, the step I took charged with desperation.

"Wait." Fantine's command was soft, but brutal. She gripped my arm in the same manner, the hold speaking of a plea she hadn't yet said. "She's not in there."

The relief that wanted to rise was stifled when someone shouted, "We found him!"

A whimper tore from Fantine's lips as she snapped her head back toward the house, dropping her grasp on my arm. My skin broke out in goosebumps as I watched three men pull someone out of the burning home, laying the man on the ground a few feet before us, his eyes wide and unseeing. Dead.

Rucas Mordaunt was dead.

Gasps washed over the bystanders, words of condolences on several lips. Fantine didn't move from her spot, didn't run to him. She only stared down at her husband's lifeless body, chin lifted high.

"You asked me *why.*" Her whispered words were for me alone.

I could only respond with a nod, unable to avert my eyes from Rucas's body...

From the jagged burn marks covering his still smoking flesh.

The knot in my stomach seemed to liquify and spill into my veins, turning my blood thick and cold. I could hear people muttering questions I believed only I had answers to.

When I looked back at Fantine, I realized I was wrong. She knew. She knew Mae was the one responsible for this.

An intense tremble overcame her hands at her sides. "Krystan used to say her hair was like moonlight. She adored my daughter in a way I never could."

The next breath I took was thin.

She looked up to me once more, brown eyes lined with tears. "Mae went east," she said so softly, I almost didn't catch it. "Toward the stream."

East.

The nwív had probably gone back to the tree.

I bowed my head in thanks and muttered, "I'm sorry."

She shook her head. "Don't be. She did what I couldn't."

"What?"

She looked back down at Rucas, and the glare in her tearful gaze was one I would only give my worst enemies. "She saved herself," she said.

Halfway across the stream, the harsh rapids I had greatly underestimated pulled me under. Both bags I was carrying above my head to keep dry were ripped from my grasp. The rushing water tossed me around as I fought to the surface, managing to blindly latch onto the straps. I gasped when my face hit the cold air and found my footing on the rocky bottom once more. Tossing the bags around my shoulders, I waded with burning arms to the other side.

My knees hit the bank, and the breath I took felt like sharp, icy knives instead of air. My stomach became a hard knot as I crawled to a tree with a wide, dense canopy. Being under a tree during a thunderstorm was a terrible place to be, but I needed a moment to collect my thoughts.

Everything was drenched. Mae's clothes and shoes, the loose parchment, my quill, the three elven books, including *Ít Nánöweth*.

My spellbook.

Body quaking and chilled to the bone, I peeled my spellbook open, bracing myself for what I would find. My brows shot up in surprise when I found the paper to be wet and fragile, but the ink was not running. Every *eçor*, command word, and instruction was exactly how I had written it, as if I'd burned the information to the page instead.

Breathing a sigh of relief, I quickly cast *Thryng* over my spellbook, pulling the water from the books and dispersing it to the mud, then I did the same to the other books hoping to give them a fighting chance. Even though the rain was still coming down incredibly hard, I cast the spell over myself as well, if only for a moment of reprieve from the cold.

On my way to the stream, I had rushed right by the library without a second thought of my father's whereabouts. Now, I realized he had to have been home when Rucas and his men attacked. Had they imprisoned him? Had he escaped? Not knowing those answers was terrifying.

But where I had gotten my recklessness from my mother, all of my stubbornness and quick-thinking came from my father. I had to believe he was all right. Better in a jail cell than dead.

Back into the icy rain, I ran down the bank of the stream, searching for the path leading to the tree. Leaves swirled around as twigs snapped off branches and pelted down on my ducked head, the timber bowing and thrashing in the winds.

Finally, the falls came into view just to the right of the path that would lead me to the tree. Before I knew it, I was thrown to my ass by a strong gale and splattered with mud. Scrambling to my feet, my focus snagged on something ahead. I went still as stone.

It was only about two or three feet tall and seemed to be composed entirely of wind. Tendrils of billowing air made up its arms, and the small glowing lights were the only features reminiscent of a face. But when I went to take a step toward it, a dark hollow formed in the center of its whirlwind body, moving as a mouth would.

I cringed against the shrill, howling voice, unfamiliar with the language it spoke. Every indistinguishable word left me anxious as if the language itself told me I was in the presence of something beyond my understanding.

The wind creature sent another gale in my direction. I threw up my wards before it could reach me, the air dispersing in all directions. Another gust hit the wards again, and the creature let out a howl before whirling into the forest.

Down the path leading to the tree.

I winced, forcing down the uneasiness in my gut telling me to turn back. As I mentally kept my wards raised, I slowly trudged through the mud and reminded myself that the creature I just faced was only a start of the strange things we would see come from The ReEmergence. I couldn't let my nerves get the best of me now.

But when I turned for the path, my pulse skipped over itself. The winding trees, the thick brush—the entirety of the passage had been swallowed by total darkness. Not the darkness of night, but by billowing, ominous clouds as if I had just walked into the edge of a thunderhead. My skin crawled, nerves tingling with unease at the feeling something was watching through the shroud.

Pulling out my spellbook, I turned to a page with shaking fingers and read over the command phrase one last time. The banishing spell. A spell that would most assuredly kill me if I tried to cast it.

But I had no weapon. No other plan. Nothing but a fool's heart, the gall of a warrior I was not, and the love I had for her.

It was enough.

Because I was also a mage. A reemerged *Vyl'kríev*. And the only person in Xalador who could save Mae from her nwív.

It was enough.

I was enough.

So I plummeted into the black.

CHAPTER 44

Varys

I had believed I'd learned of true darkness the night Mother died. I had learned of the cold, paralyzing darkness I knew as fear and uncertainty. I had learned of the darkness that came with my nightmares, the shadows and blurred images of claws and fang. The darkness of inescapable death.

This was darker.

It was unending. It had devoured my *Wyn* spell, negated the magic entirely. Each blind step I took sent a swell of nausea through me, not knowing where my feet would land—if they would at all. Since entering this dark cloud, I hadn't noticed any of the terrain I had encountered before. Leaves didn't crunch beneath my feet, and my hands hadn't found any low twisting branches. It was as if the winding path simply didn't exist anymore, or something was changing the landscape entirely. I didn't know which one was more disturbing.

I had thrown up my wards, but knew if I kept them sustained for much longer I would drain myself of energy I might need for whatever awaited me on the other side. Still, the use of them kept me from turning back entirely.

I couldn't be scared.

I knew how much more scared she probably was.

And that was what I focused on as I pressed forward, ignoring my stomach wanting to purge, the sweat rolling down my face and pooling in the groove of my upper lip. It didn't matter how dark it was, didn't matter how this frightened me to the core. Not being able to save her, the possibility that she was gone. Dead. I was terrified of that. Losing her…I didn't know if I could come back from that.

My breath left me in a gasp when light flashed ahead. It came with a low buzzing thrum, and I stilled when it webbed out along the darkness. Thunder rolled a few seconds after the light flickered out.

Krayd's chaos. I shuddered.

I really was inside a thundercloud.

It didn't make any sense. The temperature was too cold to even brew a normal thunderstorm, much less one that could form and remain on the ground.

None of that mattered, and I knew I would have to stop questioning what wasn't logical. Mae was the Nexus of Storm. I was still trying to wrap my head around the fact that storm was an element —that there might be *more* elements Xalador was unaware of—but if this was the truth, and the nwív was what it said it was, then the magic, the power, that was present didn't follow rules of nature. It *made* them.

And if I managed to bring Mae back, save her from her nwív, she would no doubt be one of the most powerful beings in all of Xalador.

Another streak of lightning sparkled off to the left, twisting through the black. A curse spilled from my lips in a whisper. Even a slight brush with one of those bolts would no doubtedly kill me. My wards were only as strong as I was.

But the light illuminated the area long enough I could see the outline of trees ahead. I breathed out a sigh of relief, facing my feet in that direction to run—

Light crackled behind me, and the chilling feeling of being watched returned. I realized the light had traveled from in front of me, to the left, and was now behind me. Circling me.

Peering over my shoulder, I found the jolting energy had merged into a form similar to the creature of wind I'd confronted earlier. Its glowing eyes seemed to seethe at me as it spoke in what I assumed was the same foreign language, its voice a low hum that made my chest and ears warble strongly, forcing me to hunch over myself.

Its light blinked out and the darkness resumed. I went still again, too cautious to move or step toward the trees. The only sound was the distant thunder and my shuddering breaths.

Suddenly, a frictious sensation roamed over my body. The hair on my arms stood in response, and when I turned my head, it seemed my blue hair wanted to cling to the back of my tunic. *Static.*

When the sensation increased, I took off toward the trees. Behind me, the creature roared. Lightning flashed and struck the ground, shaking the earth beneath my feet as I ran in a stumbling mess. Brisk air hit my face when I frantically leaped out of the dark clouds, arms and legs flailing as I went down. My body slammed into leaves, instantly cracking my wards. I rolled uncontrollably over sticks and roots, my book bag and Mae's pack walloping me in the face. I finally stopped, groans breaking free in gasping yelps as pain raked down my body and head.

Biting through the sting of the scrapes along my limbs, I forced myself to my knees, then to my feet. Stumbling backward, I caught myself against a bark surface and when a pressure began to push down on me, I knew exactly what I leaned against.

Through a shaky breath, I brought my wards back.

The same eerie peace I had felt before imbued the clearing. It wasn't raining, and the leaves on the ground were dry, crunching beneath my feet when I moved. It seemed the storms of late hadn't touched this place at all. As if nothing had changed.

But something was different indeed. The air was chilly, and yet I felt warmth racing over my skin. There was a pleasant buzz in my head, as if I had sipped on a sweet wine for hours but felt no clouded judgment. I had experienced similar sensations when I was around or casting magic, but this was much stronger.

"Vid Medaes."

When the colorful veil of the veins fell down before me, I had to remind myself to breathe. I had never seen anything like the energy swirling around the clearing, warping the colors of the veins, bending the ley lines in the same direction off to the right. I followed it, my eyes widening.

It looked like a tear in the air near the earth, the edges encrusted with iridescent crystals, large enough for someone to step into, but I didn't think anyone would do so willingly. Not when it looked like a portal to some sort of darkworld.

I backed away, canceling my spell to find out where this tear had manifested. I was both unsurprised and greatly disturbed when I found myself looking at the roots of the fallen guardian oak tree.

A throaty, feminine chuckle rang out behind me. I spun to search for the nwív, the laugh too malicious, too dark to be Mae's. A resonance from above whirred and thrummed as low as the pulse in my ears. I lifted my gaze—and went still. Terror froze me, heart plummeting to my stomach and slamming against my chest all at once.

But I couldn't look away.

She hovered in the wind above me, shrouded in dark flashing clouds as black as the eyes seething down at me in rage. I barely recognized it was still Mae's body she possessed, for the porcelain color of her skin had been replaced with a rich shade of violet, glimmering like her body was made up of stars.

And her white hair, the one thing that set her apart from everyone in Elros, the proof of the mysterious elven bloodline, the hair my mother had said shone like moonlight, was now a lavender color that just seemed so out of place. Her curls were lifted, frizzy and entwined with jolting streaks.

The nwív's terrifying beauty was one I could not look upon in awe of. Not when her very existence manifested a painful truth.

"My, my, you are impressive," she purred laconically, twirling a sphere of sparks between her fingers like a toy. "Such a shame your endeavors were futile."

Every bone I possessed felt like they had disintegrated, the hot, jagged blade of agony slowly driving into my chest, the passage of *Ít Nánöweth* repeating in my head.

The nwív will take sentience and besiege its host…

It had happened. I was too late.

I shook with fury, but repressed the sobs. Blinked back my

burning tears. I wanted to scream, I wanted to tear this thing apart for what she'd done.

But I couldn't. I wouldn't. Destroying her would destroy what was left of Mae as well.

"I didn't come here to fight you, Nwív," I muttered, my ire clanging through me—the only sword I would unsheathe tonight. "So just let her go."

The nwív tilted her head. Considered me as she slowly descended to the ground, the clouds around her settling against her erogenous zones and billowing down her back like a cape. Her hips swayed as she strolled my way. I didn't move when she stopped inches before me, lust evident in her eyes even within the black. She traced a finger down my arm, her touch sending small shocks over my skin.

"She is gone, Varys." Her chin dipped as she breathed, "It's just me now. *Maelawyn*. Need to start calling us by our true name, *aríma*."

A smile that was too much like Mae's lifted on her lips, sending flashes of heated images through my mind. How she had smiled just like that during our stolen moment inside the nook at the tavern.

I stepped away, hands out. "I don't want you. I want Mae."

Her smile fell, the seething glare returning. Lightning crackled across her black eyes before she spun away from me, plumes following, and the whirls and twists of her body became in sync with the wind blowing around us. Her back arched, arms falling behind her as she stepped with pointed feet.

Dancing. She was dancing like Mae did.

Streaks of energy raced under her violet skin as she faced me again. "I told you earlier I loved my nexus, for how could I not? She is me as I am her." Her black eyes narrowed. "But she was suffering. Always begging for a death only *I* could bring her. She *wanted* to be free of the pain."

A snarl curled my features. "Did she know that *you* were the one causing her pain?"

Her chin lifted, jaw tensing. "She didn't need to know."

Baring my teeth, I snapped, "You tricked her. She allowed you to change her because you made it seem like she was nothing unless you took over." I stalked toward her. "I won't tell you again. Give her back, or I will end you."

Her head tipped back as she cackled. Twirling on her toes, she leaped into the air, and gave no warning before her wind rushed into my wards and broke through them. I fell to my back, brain feeling like it had been slapped and overturned within my skull. Tendrils of air whipped around me before I could get up, coiling around my torso and arms, lifting me off the ground. I shouted as I was flown toward the dark sky, struggling against a force I couldn't see. My stomach tumbled as the wind brought me above the trees.

When I finally halted, I didn't dare look down. The tendrils of air held my shaking arms out, feet bound at the ankles.

The nwív came to float beside me, her cold hand curling around my chin and forcing me to look her way. A sultry smirk played on her lips. "I don't know why you are so eager to get her back when I am right here. I am her true form."

I ripped my face from her grasp, turning my head away. My traitorous pulse sped up when she came closer. The press of her body against me was too familiar, how it seemed to curve into all the right places as if we had been created from the same mold.

"My desire for you is just as strong and real as hers was," she murmured, hands running down my chest.

Avoiding her void-like gaze, I gritted out, "And I told you. I don't want you. I want Mae. *My* Mae."

My words seemed to fall on deaf ears, but she untangled herself from my body and turned to the horizon. My stomach lurched.

With a grin and a sweep of her arm outward, she purred, "Behold. This storm is my troth to my nexus. How she will receive my thanks for freeing me." The black marks up her left arm flickered with violet light. "I will wash away all who brought her harm."

Every muscle in my body went taut, breath sawing out. We were facing Elros. A curse tumbled from my lips as I watched the slow churn to the dark and menacing thunderhead hanging low over the entire town. This storm would be violent—deadly. And as much as it alarmed me, my chest also ached. This storm was created by a nwív, which was a sentient embodiment of Mae's emotions. All of her pain, her fears, every tear she had shed.

This storm was how she truly felt on the inside.

Gods, I had to do something before she went too far. Before anyone got hurt—

The nwív raised her hands. Thunder rolled and rumbled in the distance—like a toll of warning, it seemed. Her fingers curled, her breaths labored with small groans in her throat. Jolts jumped around her glittering knuckles and between her hands, and when the winds shifted and rushed toward Elros, time seemed to slow.

Chaos.

I knew what she meant to do.

Panic burst through me but I couldn't move. Couldn't shout fast enough. My pleas for her to stop were drowned out by a low reverberating pulse, thrumming, thrumming, provoking a rattling pain in my ears and chest. I felt like I might explode, might shake apart. I couldn't cover my ears, couldn't hunch over to protect myself.

Everything quaked as if the very world trembled in fear.

Then as a high-pitched wail tore from her throat, a mass of lightning bolts struck the earth, leaving explosions in their wake, and the town began to burn.

"Stop…"

I was too far away to hear the screams, the shouts of many. The cries of children. Was too far to see if my home burned, if Father was—

"Stop it!" I yanked against the bindings of wind. "This isn't what she would have wanted."

"It seems you don't know her as well as you thought you did," she told me with an exasperated voice. "It is what she's *always* wanted."

My throat went dry, and I blinked as if her words had ripped off a mask I hadn't realized I donned. Recalling the conversations Mae and I had at the stream, in the library the night I had fallen weak from using too much magic, even last night when we had discussed our dreams of the future…

Mae hated this town, and for good reason. She hated this town for the same reasons I did, the same reasons Leo, my father, Duros and Natalia did. Its faults and injustices had been its downfall.

But there was good in Elros. There were honest people. Hard-working people. There was joy and laughter in the market. There was warmth and good food at Mr. Flax's bakery. There was music, dancing, and thrill at the tavern. Things I knew Mae loved. That she wouldn't want to see destroyed.

With every breath, the roaring pulse in my ears increased, face and neck on fire with anger, solidifying my decision. This display of hate, of malice…

I let out a shuddering breath.

To save her and Elros, I would have to banish the nwív, despite the consequences. Despite what might happen to me.

"She may have wanted those who hurt her to suffer." My voice shook. "But not at the cost of those she cared about."

The nwív had remained facing away from me, her body swaying in the air as she panted.

She slumped over, her body visibly shivering. "But people like *him* outnumber the good."

As she brought her hands closer to her face, the clouds around her dispersed…

Revealing her torn, bleeding back.

My insides hollowed out as I stared with wide eyes, the long, swollen lacerations revealing what had happened without even asking. She had been scourged, whipped across the back, right upon the lightning marks running down her spine.

"Her body is too fragile," she muttered with a cold growl.

"Rucas…" My blood ran hot. "He hurt her."

She straightened, glaring across the hills and trees, eyes set on Elros once more. "He did. Before I put an end to him."

Streaks of light began to crawl down her fingers again. I watched blood trickle down her spine, to the back of her legs, over-whelmed with the innate need to…

Help.

I stifled a gasp, clenching my teeth as if it would hold back the realization—disclose her weakness.

"Maelawyn, you're hurt," I said softly. As soft as I would speak to an injured animal. "But I can help you."

According to the banishing spell, I had to make physical contact with the host. If I could just get her to trust me, to take my hand.

I tried to pull against my shackles of wind as I stated, "Her body isn't ready for the kind of power you are trying to cast and if you destroy it, you won't be able to remain on this plane."

She snarled, whipping back to me. "She was ready. I made sure of it. These wounds are to blame."

"You cannot ignore that your nexus was a sorceress. The rules of the gods-given magic she possessed still apply, and her magical aptitude never developed." I held her gaze, focusing on the concern I had for Mae's bleeding body in hopes she would read it in my eyes. "I promise, if you let me go, I can heal you with a spell I have, and then you can continue to fulfill your troth."

The statement left a grime in my mouth, my blood seeming to thicken as my deceit solidified. This wasn't Mae, but it was her face.

And I was lying to it.

For a long moment, the nwív only stared at me. Then with a slow nod, she came forward. My wrists became unbound as she murmured, "I know you don't agree with my motives, but I also know I can trust you."

I nodded and reached for the nwív's hand, the beginning of the banishing spell's command phrase on my tongue—

"I'm safe with you and I always will be, right?" she asked

My entire being went rigid.

Those words…I'd said them to Mae before. They were a vow, a promise I'd made that she would always find shelter with me.

I didn't know how to respond as she tilted her head, observing me. This was a test, one I hadn't prepared for.

"Yes, you are—"

Light flickered before my eyes, followed by a sizzling snap. My body jerked in surprise, and the moment I yanked my hand away, a thin cord of charged energy began to wrap around me, radiating with heat.

She moved away, her tinkling, sinister laugh sending my heart pounding. The lightning marks up her arm lit in a bright violet glow. "Do not lie to me, *aríma*. My elementals have eyes. They've seen the *eçor* in that spellbook of yours."

My scalp prickled with unease. *Elementals.* She must have been referring to the strange creatures I had encountered, recalling the feeling that something had been watching me through the black clouds. It was one of the first things I had read about the nexi and their power—the ability to cast great elemental magic, and to summon beings of the plane they were connected to. But from what I understood from the passages, there had to be a way for the creatures to come through. Some sort of door or—

My blood ran cold.

The portal I had seen at the base of the tree.

That was how they were coming through. It was an entrance to the storm plane. She had somehow ripped a hole into Xalador's very existence. Gods knew how many had already come through—how many more would before the night was over.

"Do you think me a fool?" the nwív asked when I didn't respond. "You're a wizard—you cannot heal me."

I swallowed, the hairs on my arms rising. I wasn't sure if the beads of sweat that formed on my forehead and under my arms were from the heat of the current, or my fear. I was hundreds of feet up in the air and I could not move.

She knew I had deceived her, and I was about to pay for it.

"You mean to banish me," she hissed.

My breaths turned ragged as my terror turned to acidic fury. "I came here to save Mae," I snarled. "To free her. And I will do whatever it takes."

Another laugh left her lips, mocking. Annoying. It sounded nothing like Mae's—at least that's what I kept telling myself.

"Because you love her?" she chided.

"Yes," I rasped, anger gnawing. "I do—"

The next breath in my lungs was cut short, my vision going white as if something had punched me in the face and then filled my body with a million stinging hornets. The sensation stopped just as quickly as it began, leaving me heaving and nauseated, my blurry vision focused between the cord of light around me and the nwív watching me with a grin on her face.

Shocked. I had been shocked.

"Did you know that the nexi are forbidden to love?" She asked airily.

I sucked in a breath. My mouth parted. "What—"

"Love hinders a sorcerer's magic, always holding sway over their decisions, threatening to disturb their primitive power and innate capabilities. So when the gods created the nexi, they determined a nexus cannot be bound by anything but their nwív." She sighed with a shake of her head. "You are fighting for something that can never be."

My tense muscles locked even tighter as rage swelled. "That's *tormshit!* And I'll defy anything, any *god*, who stands between us. No matter the cost."

Thunder rolled. Lightning flashed across her black gaze.

"You are a hindrance, Varys Wynhart." Her world-ending growl ran my blood cold. "The cost is your *life.*"

The light flickered out, and the wind holding me in suspension was suddenly ripped out from under me.

A heavy gasp tore from my throat, my stomach shrinking.

No.

My arms flailed, hands grasping to hold on, only finding air as she pulled away.

And I began to fall.

I screamed, my arms still stretching…

For her.

For the woman I had hoped was still in there. The woman I loved.

"Maelawyn!"

Those black eyes just stared down, watching me drop back toward the canopy of trees.

Falling to my death.

"No! *Please!*"

The force of air yanked the bags from my shoulders, the contents spilling out. Pages of my spellbook and the other tomes flapped as they fell.

This was it.

No one was coming to save me. I couldn't even save her.

Branches snagged on my tunic, my shoulder clipping a limb, flipping me over to fall face first.

Forgive me. I was trying to free you.

My vision blurred.

I love you.

I squeezed my eyes shut, arms out as if they would break my fall—

I never hit the ground.

The bag of Mae's clothes dropped to my right, and the books hit the ground one by one, leaves scattering as they slammed down.

But I didn't.

I had stopped falling.

I was floating on wind a few feet above the earth for only a moment before the air dispersed and I dropped to my face, coughing through the tuft of dirt I inhaled upon landing.

Alive. I was alive.

The nwív shrieked above me, thunder blaring and echoing across the dark forest. I looked up just in time to see her flying toward me, sparks jolting off her violet skin.

"*How?*" she screeched. "How are you *still* reaching her?"

Her.

The air filled my lungs like I was breathing for the first time.

Mae had saved me.

It was all I needed to gather my wits. I stood on shaking knees, muttering, "*Sçölith,*" just as the nwív descended beneath the tops of the trees. *Eçor* spinning, the thin blue barrier began to manifest before the tips of my trembling glowing fingers—

I cried out, stinging hot pain raking up my right arm. My spell failed entirely, and as the magic ebbed, dizziness settled in my head.

Dammit. Without my wards, I was—

The nwív slammed into the earth, and it was obvious in the way her knees buckled Mae's body didn't react well to the force. Bright sizzling energy blasted in my direction. I ducked, only for it to veer off entirely. She missed.

"If you don't stop this, you're going to kill yourself and your nexus!" I roared.

Her chest caved in with every breath. The emission of her power had brought a visible heaviness to her body, mouth slacked as she gasped. Fingers curling, she tried to manifest another energy orb. It flickered out before it ever began.

"How did you reach her?" She straightened, baring her teeth. "That door is *shut*."

Her words tugged on a memory. She had said something like that to me before. Spoken about a door and seemed angry about anyone trying to open it. Mae had never spoken of a door but had asked if I felt some sort of connection between us.

Whatever that connection was…maybe it was the only thing anchoring Mae to this plane.

I dug my heels into the ground, ready to spring into action. "Perhaps you've simply underestimated your nexus. If she's still getting through, perhaps you were wrong about her disinterest returning."

As I suspected, my words angered her. "*She* is gone." Her breathing became heavier as a scowl twisted her features. "She doesn't care about anyone or anything anymore. Not even you."

"I refuse to believe that."

Her skin glittered with energy as she seethed. "Then you will die in denial."

A rough, pained sound escaped her lips as she clenched her fists and threw her arms to the sky. Thunder cracked above.

Blood dripped from her nose.

"*Stop!*" I rushed for her. "Please, you'll—"

With a scream, her arms thrust forward, and my world exploded with light. I lost control over every part of me, my jaw paralyzed in a gape as jolts of lightning danced and burned through tissue and bone, body humming and jerking.

Falling to the ground was a distant concern. I didn't know if hours passed or mere seconds, my mind dark and unfeeling.

She was standing over me when I came to, one foot on my chest, wheezing through the streams of blood running from her nose and eyes. Her fingers flexed, arms stretched down to me as she grimaced through tight teeth. "You just won't die."

I didn't move. Didn't try to escape her wrath as the jolts along her fingers flickered, drawing more blood from her nose. Every instinct within me demanded I use my wards, to protect myself against the next bolt that would surely kill me. But I wouldn't waste precious energy I would soon need. Because as she stepped down harder on my chest, and I became prey under a predator's claws, she seemed too focused on what she thought was her victory to remember.

The banishment spell required the two of us to touch.

"Sorry for the disappointment." I clutched my pounding chest, muscles so tense I thought they might snap. "But I won't be dying until I know she's been saved. You're welcome to try again then."

She let out a frustrated growl, hands reaching to wrap around my throat.

Perfect.

I caught her wrists, gripping them tightly. Her black eyes went wide with surprise, a sob escaping her lips as my strength overwhelmed her. I pulled her down to her knees, moving to sit on mine. Her touch became charged, sending little shocks along my skin. I hissed through them, ignoring the spasms in my muscles.

The jolts dwindled, and the look in her eyes was full of knowing —an understanding that she had lost. "You will see, fool. She is a chaos that will never be tamed."

I didn't drop my gaze from hers, hoping somewhere behind the black, Mae was staring back. With a snarl and a shuddering breath, I declared, "Then, I will love her wildly enough, she never will be."

As thunder echoed through the forest, and the clouds flashed with glittering light, I pulled Maelawyn closer. I didn't know what would become of me, if this was going to hurt, if I would simply burn into nothing.

She was right.

Maybe the cost of her freedom was my life.

"*Ethari, vatha….*" *Ground, confine…*

A garish yellow aura went forth and wrapped around her form, circling back to me, rooting us both to the clearing ground.

"*…yrçae wyn.*" *…arcane light.*

The nwív shrieked and cried out, writhing to break free. My eyes burned but I could not blink. Tears fell down my cheeks.

The spell's *eçor* appeared below us, and as the aura swirled upward it took the leaves on the ground, throwing them around us as if we were in the center of a twister. The nwív's screech melded with the whistling air, and I watched as the violet of her skin blanched.

And then everything began to shudder.

I didn't know if the roar in my ears was my pulse or my own scream as I jerked in response to the agonizing, searing pain in my right arm. I could feel the veins ripping through me, yanking on my skin. My strength waned, but the last phrase burned on my tongue, demanding to be muttered. I locked eyes with the nwív as her violet locks turned white, gritting out, "*Krievas, xutha. Íjaç gasi zaryn.*"

Veins, bind. Banish this blight.

All I knew was pain. My shouts became wails, my head splitting open, spine breaking in two. I found myself begging, praying to some god I'd never worshiped—something arcane and of a higher power—to make it stop.

Let me die. Let me die.

Let her go. Let her live.

When those black eyes cleared, and wide glistening amethysts stared back...I accepted my fate.

I wanted nothing more than for her to live. To be free. To achieve those dreams she'd spoken of at the tavern.

I was giving her a second chance.

I love you, and I always will.

Maybe I would go wherever my mother was.

Maybe to the stars, where I would forever watch over Mae, *my* Mae, my beautiful little bird fly away and live the life she wanted.

I welcomed death as the last of the nwív vanished, and Mae toppled to the ground.

My eyes closed, my mind went dark.

And the spell finished.

CHAPTER 45

Varys

"Godsdammit, Varys. C'mon."

The lilting voice was far away, echoing like it was down a long hall.

"Please, wake up."

"She's lost a lot of blood," another voice said, this one warmer, the accent more like mine. "I need to get these wounds stitched before infection sets in."

Hands gripped my shoulders, shaking me. I couldn't open my eyes or move my body in any way. I was…disconnected still.

"He seems to be stable," the warm voice said before I heard a series of clinks and shuffles. "Here. Put this under his nose."

Something cold was pressed against my upper lip. On the next breath I took, an acrid smell hit my senses. Irritation flooded both my sinuses and head, but it jolted me awake. The moment my eyes shot open, intense nausea overcame me, and I barely managed to roll onto my side before my stomach heaved.

Then I felt the pain.

Every part of me hurt. My muscles ached upon movement, but nothing was worse than the tender sting running up and down my right arm. I could barely breathe through every throb.

Someone pulled me to them, reclining me back into their hold.

506

Light from a lantern cast a gold sheen through the darkness of night, reflecting in the emerald green eyes I knew very well. Leona let out a heavy sigh of relief with what sounded like a repressed sob.

"Fuck, ye scared me," she said. I hissed through clenched teeth when she took hold of my injured arm. "What in Torm happened?"

She helped me prop it up against my chest. The smell of charred flesh churned my stomach, but the sight of my arm drained the blood from my face. Starting from the center of my palm and stopping before my elbow, my skin was shredded as if I'd been sliced into by a blade with a serrated edge, and within the gashes, jagged Elvish runes had been etched into my flesh along with deep lines and circles.

I blew out thickly. The *eçor*. Part of the spell's *eçor* had been cut into my arm.

But I was still alive. I had survived casting the banishment spell. *Krayd's Chaos.*

"Mae," I gasped, forcing myself upright. "*Ieth shöni. Lla rö et?*"

I barely registered the Elvish words—*Oh gods. Where is she?*—leaving my mouth, only understanding I probably sounded like I had lost my mind when I came face to face with Natalia. She raised an eyebrow, then glanced down at the unconscious woman in her arms covered by her cloak.

My pulse quickened as I took in the pearly skin of her face, no longer glittering or shrouded in clouds, her white hair fanning over the leafy ground of the clearing.

A sob broke free. I had done it.

Her chest rose and fell, sweaty forehead crinkled in distress. The sight of her made me forget the pain of my arm entirely, pulling myself closer. I went to take her, but stopped when I found Natalia eyeing me, face full of confusion and concern, dress covered in Mae's blood.

"What happened here?" she asked severely.

Leona came to my side, a hand on my shoulder. "Mum knows. About the magic."

Natalia lifted her chin. "Yes."

Keeping a hand on Mae's cheek, I swallowed. "Mae is a nexus."

Leona sucked in a breath. "I'd wondered—when ye read that book…"

I glanced to her. "I didn't think it possible until it was too late."

Still looking confused, Natalia went to speak when Mae let out a sharp whimper, pulling her knees up as she shivered. I was instantly reminded of the clothes and shoes I'd brought from her house.

Picking myself up off the ground, despite a protest from both Leo and Natalia, I hobbled across the clearing, searching through the darkness for the books and bags that had fallen. Leona followed with the lantern, finding Mae's clothes while I continued to search for the books. She had just returned from helping her mother dress Mae when I found *Ít Nánöweth*. As I bent down to pick it up off the ground, I found myself overly cautious, as if the book itself would transform into the nwív.

"I don't like it here," Leo stated as she took the book from me. "Why do I feel like I'm walkin' through sludge?"

I had hardly realized. The pressure was still present, but had seemed to weaken.

Mae was weak as well.

And if the pressure was coming from the storm plane—

"Varys. Leona. We need to leave," Natalia's urgent voice called out from the dark. "I need to tend to Mae *immediately*."

"Go with my Mum," Leo said. "I'll find the rest of yer things."

My stomach dipped. "My spellbook. If you find nothing else—"

"I'll find it." She handed me the lantern. "Go."

Holding my arm against my chest, I trudged quickly back over to Natalia. Mae was shuddering, her murmurs a mix of jumbled Elvish words and my name. Ignoring the burning of my injury, I handed Natalia the lantern and scooped Mae into my arms.

"You're hurt, Varys," Natalia objected with a scoff.

"I know. But she's mine to look after now." I cradled Mae close, pressing a kiss to her ear. "Hold on, Little Bird. You're safe. You're free."

PART IV: FLIGHT

CHAPTER 46

Varys

TWO DAYS LATER…

"Found that note in the display case on yer mantle," Leona told me as I folded the piece of parchment. "The sword was gone. Think yer father took it?"

I shook my head, avoiding her eye contact. She hadn't said a word to me since our massive argument the day before.

After taking a deep breath, I said, "When the guards came for me and attacked my father, they took the sword then as well."

I cleared my throat of the knot trying to form, shifting around on the edge of the guest room bed before gently squeezing Mae's hand. Over the past two days, I'd been finding her cool touch every time my emotions got the better of me. I was a wreck.

She hadn't woken up yet.

I could practically feel the steam pluming from Leona's ears, and when I finally glanced over, she was seething into the fire on the hearth. "Fuckin' bastards. Krystan's blade isn't magical." She paused. "Right?"

I nodded—though, I didn't necessarily have proof of that. I'd never cast *Vid Medaes* on it. I hadn't even held the thing in my hands. "Unfortunately, that doesn't seem to matter now that the leaders of this town gave the guards orders to use personal judgment."

She folded her arms, muttering under her breath. "Wouldn't have been able to take it if ye'd been carryin' it."

My chest twisted with hurt, adding to the brimming anger toward her. She caught my glare and swallowed, an apology on her face that wouldn't come until she had cooled off. One I wouldn't accept until *I* had.

She crossed the room, sliding the pack on her back to the chair in the corner where I'd been sleeping. "Grabbed all the clothes ye own and yer bedroll. Ye'll need furs for our journey. I'm sure ye can borrow some."

I shuddered. I hated sleeping under furs.

"Thank you," I said, and I meant it. But Leona walked out without another word.

I stifled the frustrated growl in my throat by bringing Mae's knuckles to my lips. I hated miscommunication, I hated arguing, I hated losing my temper. But most of all, I hated the isolation that came with it. It seemed this argument had been coming, given me and Leona's little spats over the course of the last several days before the tavern. But when she had discovered what happened to my arm, that I'd never told her about arcane decay, and how the spell could have—*should* have—killed me, it had been the final stroke. She had blown up over breakfast yesterday morning after I'd found myself unable to stomach much, still dizzy and exhausted, and hardly able to use my dominant hand to eat.

"Well, I'm not fuckin' spoon feedin' ye," she'd said, dwarven accent thick and punchy. *"Ye did this to ye'self."*

I didn't find her statement fair. For once, I had used my magic for more than just lights and ice. I had saved the woman I loved, and the entire town of Elros. Maybe even Xalador. I had yet to see the aftermath of the nwív's storm. Leona had said that a few homes had burned, trees had been ripped from their roots, and roofs were damaged. But we would never know if the nwív's storm would have become large enough to wipe out the entire land. I believed she would have tried, despite destroying her nexus's body in the process.

I wasn't looking for a pat on the back, wasn't looking for pity. I did what had to be done, and it had felt right. But Leo wasn't one to talk an argument out with me. She dealt with her problems by herself, which left me in my head.

My head was the last place I wanted to be right now.

However, I could understand her other statement—I *fucked up* my sword arm. She had put her time and sweat into training me for two whole years, and injuring it put us back several steps. It would heal, and I would work on strengthening it again. Would even use my left to the best of my ability if needed. But it might not ever be the same, especially with the arcane scars already beginning to form.

I had seen enough depictions in elven books to know what I could expect. The scar usually took on a pigment close to the color of the mage's natural features. I wasn't surprised to see the blue coloration of the healing tissue when I had unwrapped the bandages this morning.

I squeezed Mae's hand again. She lay on her side under the orange and red quilt with several pillows propped behind her tailbone to prevent her from rolling to her back. An infection had set in her wounds, no doubt from dirt and sweat, and she had run a fever on and off. However, that wasn't why she hadn't woken up.

Her mind seemed trapped. She'd had some sort of fit come over her, had screamed about crystals and butterflies and storms. I had felt terrible relief after witnessing her thrashing on the bed. It had been the most activity out of her since Natalia and Leo found us in the forest.

Two days unconscious. Almost three nights. I feared this was how she would remain, that she'd die like this.

That I hadn't saved her after all.

Sighing, I left Mae's side for a moment to see what Leo had brought in my pack. With Orin's help, she had been sneaking in and out of town, searching for my father and listening to news. After the execution of the *Vyl'kriev*, the main gate had been shut, but they had kept the gate to the east open since the stream was the main water source. Yesterday, they decided to close it after a few people tried to escape. *"The Mayor has gone absolutely mad trying to find who killed his son,"* Natalia had ranted after Leona returned yesterday. *"Doesn't he realize he's holding all of those people hostage?"*

It was criminal. Even the King's Guard were following Mayor Brooker's orders. The only thing keeping the riots at bay was the promise that the Fest of Change would still happen two days from now, and would be extended. It was a trade off: if one could remain in Elros until Theon and Willem's murderer was found, they would have a chance at making more profit than they'd made at the Fest of Change in prior years. However, if the guards were still confiscating goods they claimed might be magical, there were probably a lot of people left without wares.

I could feel something bad was about to happen, but for the first time in my life I just…didn't care. *Couldn't* care. I was Elven-blooded and that meant I had a chopping block with my name on it. All that mattered to me was Mae and our journey to Elvidawn. We would escape through the southern forest, despite my vow to never venture through that part of northern Xalador again.

I stepped behind the partition to change, pulling on a clean, light blue tunic and a pair of loose pants I usually wore to bed. I had still been in my vest, breeches, and sword belt—hadn't even taken off my boots. Just as I thought about how nice a bath sounded, Mae let out a small whimper. I promptly returned to her side, placing my hand to her forehead to make sure her fever hadn't spiked again. Her body had cooled ever since Natalia had placed some sort of salve on her stitches before wrapping her upper torso completely with strips of cloth.

I wanted her to rest if she needed it. But I also couldn't suppress the desire to hold her, to talk to her and answer all the questions she would have upon waking. I just wanted her to open her eyes and tell me…I had done the right thing.

I wanted her to know I loved her.

There was a knock on the doorframe. I stood quickly and Natalia sighed as she came in. She had already scolded me a good ten times over the past two days for hovering over Mae.

"Dinner will be ready soon," she told me, rounding the bed to Mae's backside. "How about you take an hour to rest?"

"I am resting," I assured her, gesturing to the chair in the corner.

She snorted, tossing her hair behind her shoulders. "Varys, I spent the majority of my time breastfeeding Leona in that chair. I know how uncomfortable it is."

I only shrugged. "I promise I—"

"Go take a nap on the settee downstairs," she cut me off with a smile that didn't reach her eyes, her words a gentle but stern bidding.

With a wince, I admitted, "Natalia, I...I can't leave her side. I'd get less rest being away from her." I swallowed, body already humming with anxiety at the very thought of not being here if something happened.

Natalia didn't respond, too busy unwrapping the cloth and checking Mae's back. She frowned, eyes blinking shut slowly with a long breath out her nose.

"What is it?" I asked.

After adjusting the handkerchief around her forehead, she pulled out a pair of shears from her apron. "I wish she would wake up. She needs water and food."

When she cut a long strip of cloth from Mae's back, my stomach tightened. There was a yellow-white fluid among the old blood stains. "Is that...coming through her stitches?"

A slow nod. "She needs fresh dressing."

When her eyes flicked up to mine, I took that as my cue to turn and give Mae some privacy.

The short, thin sound of snipping was the only thing heard for several moments. Mae didn't seem to like what Natalia was doing, and when she cried out softly, I braced myself against the doorframe to force myself from turning around.

"Done," Natalia announced, allowing me to come back into the room. Her body was twisted from me, and as she pulled the apron over her head, it was obvious she was trying to hide the amount of fresh blood stains from me as she immediately rolled it into a ball.

"Tea?" she asked with a sigh, tossing the apron into the pile of dirty cloth.

I swallowed with a nod, and she eyed me when I went right back to Mae's side. As we waited for the kettle to whistle, silence fell between us, and I found myself staring into the dying flame on the hearth as a means to keep my heavy eyes open.

Truthfully, Natalia was right. The chair wasn't comfortable and I knew I hadn't slept much. Every cry, every whimper Mae let out, I was up and by her side, caressing her face and hair as if it would soothe her. I hoped it would.

Once the kettle was hot, Natalia poured water into two cups fixed with tea bags. "It's not bergamot, I'm afraid," she said as she scooped several large helpings of honey into each cup. "But I figured a nice cup of chamomile might soothe the nerves."

I thanked her as she placed the cups down on the side table to cool before sitting down in the corner chair.

Mae let out another whine. I pressed a kiss to her forehead, frowning at the pained expression on her face even in her unconscious state.

My chest squeezed. "She's not getting any better, is she?"

Natalia didn't have to say it. As she rubbed her forehead I knew the answer; she was just as stressed as I was.

"I'm doing everything I can," she said, taking her cup of tea. "I promise I am."

"I know."

I was just afraid it wouldn't be enough.

I could feel her eyes on me as I stared down at Mae, as I held her hand once more. Natalia sucked in a breath. "Varys, dear…"

When her words trailed away, I glanced back. "What is it?"

She gripped the handle of her cup. "I know I'm not your mother…"

"You are my family, Natalia." I gave an assuring nod.

Her jade eyes glistened as she pressed her lips together. "And you are as close to a son I'll ever know. I have just wanted to talk to you about something, but I have never known how to bring it up."

I shrugged. "I'm an open book. What is it about?"

She took a heavy breath. "Your romance with Miss Mordaunt."

My stomach fluttered, and the smile that rose couldn't be stopped as I gazed down at the woman laying on the bed.

"I love her." My words were the most simple thing to ever roll off my tongue.

"Oh, that is evident," she teased. "I don't think you hover over your books as much as you do her."

Any other time, I would have laughed. Maybe even gave a roll of my eyes.

Her comment only made my chest ache, as if she reminded me of why I hovered. Why I felt the need to be beside Mae as much as possible. "I almost lost her."

Her gaze fell to her lap as she murmured, "I know."

I went on, "And I'm terrified I still will. We have already endured so much. I feel like we're a bit star-crossed."

"I don't believe that at all." Another coy expression washed over her features, but I didn't think she was teasing. She just…knew something I didn't. "Would you like to hear a tale I told your mother several years ago?"

"Please," I said with a nod.

She placed her tea on the side table and leaned forward. "This is the Jinyan tale of the lovers, Earth and Sky."

I swallowed, heart picking up in its pace as I held Mae's hand and brushed my thumb over her cool and soft fingers.

Natalia began, "When the world was brought into existence, Sky took his first breath. At the very same time, a great boom rang out from below, the first beat of Earth's heart. She looked up to the stars and clouds, and he looked down to the flowers and fields. And so with the first breath, and the first pulse, love dawned.

"But they could not be together without destroying what had been determined by their Makers. So Earth erected mountains high enough to touch Sky's clouds. Sky brought down rain to Earth's grassy plains. Their frustrations and yearnings gave life and yielded fruit to the realm that would become Jinya."

Natalia clasped her hands and held them to her chest, releasing a romanticized sigh. "It was not enough. They could not bear to look over all they had created and still not be one. They begged their Makers to let them touch somehow. 'Your connection would lay this world to waste,' the Makers told them, 'We forbid it.'"

I found myself squeezing Mae's hand tighter, a knot trying to form in my throat. This was folklore, a faerie tale. But I had found myself picturing me and Mae in this story, and I realized that's exactly why Natalia was telling it to me.

"Accepting their fate, Earth and Sky wished for habitants to occupy the beautiful realm they had created. And so, the Makers guided a group of humans across the sea to the shores of Jinya all those years ago, and our great ancestors were told by the Makers if they worshiped Sky and Earth, every Jinyan would be granted a love so great, it would transcend time and all planes of existence. We sit in the grass and lift our hands to the sky in worship, so that we may be the connection between the lovers who would never be."

I sucked in a breath. "That was beautiful."

Natalia nodded. "It is, but there's more to this tale I want you to know about." She tilted her head side to side, as if she was trying to determine what to say. "There have been Jinyans who have taken this story so seriously that they devoted their entire life to worship, and then became angry when they were not granted such love. Then, there have been other Jinyans who never worshiped Sky and Earth, and were granted such a love anyway."

I raised a brow. "So, the story is fictional. But that kind of love exists?"

She smiled. "Yes. I've seen it."

I chuckled. "You and Duros."

"Not necessarily." She gave a one shouldered shrug. "I love Duros. He has my entire soul. But this is something quite...supernatural." She eyed me. "Lovers who find each other without having to search. Simply experiencing a sensation that lets them know their other half is nearby."

My mouth parted, heart beginning to pound as I looked down to Mae's hand, thinking about the *pulses* she felt whenever she touched me. The first time we had touched, she'd reacted as if static had sparked between us.

Natalia's smile warmed. "I've seen the way your eyes lock with hers. The other day in the library was quite a sight."

My cheeks heated. "What do you mean?"

She took a sip of her tea. "I can't explain it. You hadn't told me the two of you were trysting, and yet I just...*knew*. There was a naturality to how you sat beside her, how you looked at each other."

She laughed. I swallowed down the yearning starting to build in my chest, palms beginning to heat against Mae's cool hand.

"But it didn't just start now that you're adults, Varys," she continued. "Oh, *no*. Even as a child, you would hide in your mother's skirts, but if Mae Mordaunt came around, the two of you couldn't keep your eyes off each other. Krystan always believed it was because you were fascinated by Mae's looks. I told her exactly what I'll tell you now: I believe you and Mae have been granted the elven equivalence of the Jinyan folklore, and that Mae is your *Fated*."

My pulse skipped. "Fated?"

A nod. "I believe it even more so now that this ReEmergence of Magic has come into play. You've not come across the Fated in all of that elven history you've been reading?"

I blinked. "No."

She pulled her lips to the side of her mouth. "Hm, I learned the term from Duros actually. As the Crown Prince, he was taught everything the dwarves knew about the elves, which wasn't much. When I had told him the story of Earth and Sky, he'd said it reminded him of the elves' Fated. Of course, the elves called it something else, and the dwarves spoke of it in a very derogatory way." She rolled her eyes. "Called them Fated Fucks."

Acid churned in my stomach. "Why would it be used negatively?"

Natalia huffed. "The one thing I learned about the dwarves is that they pride themselves on culture, but a lot of them mock the culture of the other races. It's one thing Duros spoke about putting an end to when he became King. But..."

"Fate had other ideas," I said with a curt nod.

She feigned a dramatic gasp. "Varys Wynhart, look at you. Talking as if you actually believe in destiny."

"The idea is growing on me a little more each day."

She winked. "I don't doubt it, now that you may have a Fated and all."

My cheeks heated. "We'll see."

For a moment, I pondered whether or not I could deduce which Elvish word meant the kind of love Natalia was speaking about. *Aryn* meant fate—

"*Arynáthi*," I gasped.

Mae stirred, letting out a small whimper. The hair on my arms rose.

Natalia stood, eyes wide as she stared at me. "Say that word again."

My eyes burned, but I obliged. "*Arynáthi*."

We both watched Mae, waiting to see if she'd move again. She didn't. But Natalia had come to my side, her shaky hand on my shoulder.

"Your eyes lit up just for a moment when you said that word, like the spark of a firesteel," she told me.

I gave a slow nod. As stated, the language of the elves was magic. If spoken as a command and with intention, a word in Elvish could cast a spell.

But there were some words that *held* power. Words that over-ruled, forced hands, made bargains or destroyed covenants.

Arynáthi was such a word. It was a binding of two souls, allowing them to connect on a more intangible level as if their psyches were one. I had even read their senses were heightened for each other, aromas and tastes stronger, voices like sweet songs, and a simple touch brought a sensation that had been described in text as *euphoric*.

But I wasn't so sure Mae and I were *Arynáthi*. Besides my lack of faith in fate, there was one other thing I had never experienced.

I didn't feel a bond.

I didn't even feel the pulses. Her voice and scent and taste was my undoing, but because I loved her. And I had fallen for her by myself, without a bond. I wasn't so sure I wanted a bond like that.

Because what if I started to question what was real, and what were just moments of fate?

"You all right?" Natalia asked, pulling me from my thoughts.

"Y-Yes." I took a breath, running my hands through my hair. "Do you think there's a downside to that kind of love?"

Her jade eyes lowered to the ground. "That would depend on what you believe. There has been speculation that the higher power —the creator of Xalador and its silent gods, the Makers of Jinya and Sky and Earth—are the same deity."

My breath snagged at that. "Really?"

A nod. "Our ancestors spoke of them to be bored trickster gods with too much power who chose to create worlds only to toy with them. There are stories about Jinyans who did acquire a Fated, but had a hard time keeping them."

Pressure clamped down on my chest. "What do you mean?"

"Fated aren't star-crossed lovers. They are *destined* to be together. But the stories speak about many trials in their lives, as if something wants them to prove their love can stand no matter what." Her eyes were full of alarm when they met mine. "A love so easy is so vulnerable. There may always be something that will try to rip it apart."

Nexi are forbidden to love, Mae's nwív had told me. Maybe it was that simple. We had always been forbidden to be together. But we had overcome every obstacle so far, hadn't we?

Looking down at Mae, I wasn't so sure we were out of the woods yet.

"Fated or no…" I took a steadying breath. "I love her, and I don't need the gods, the Makers, or some other higher power telling me I do."

CHAPTER 47

Varys

It wasn't long after Natalia and I finished up our conversation when Mae had another fit. More screams about shattering crystals. Her fever had spiked, and Natalia determined the infection had abscessed under several of the stitches. She made me leave the room so she could drain the wounds.

I wandered downstairs to clear my head, and had sat down on the settee in the commons room for just a moment before exhaustion overwhelmed me, the tufted pillows tempting and promising a deep sleep I truly needed. I rested dreamlessly, only waking to a harsh pounding on the Cauldücen's front door.

The hearty conversation in the dining room stopped. Duros and Leo rose from their chairs, faces like stone. He took the handle of his warhammer, sliding it off the table effortlessly as she spun to me, tossing her head toward the stairs and whispering, "Go."

I didn't allow myself to question what was happening before I rushed upstairs, turning when I got to the landing to see if Leo had followed. She had stopped and was waiting at the bottom, watching the door, listening.

She began to ascend quickly, urgency crossing her features. "Guards," she mouthed

Shit. Shit.

My panicking focus flicked around, as if I would find the answer of what to do somewhere in the hall. "What do we do?"

"I don't—"

"Mae's immovable." I didn't mean to interrupt, my head spinning, words coming out before I could hear myself. "There's nowhere to hide. Leona, there's—"

"Varys, stop." She took my shoulders. Duros shouted downstairs as the front door slammed open.

Leona bit her lip in thought for just a moment before an idea seemed to spark. "Remember when we got drunk that one night and decided to play hide and seek?"

Her words caught me off guard. "What? I-I used—"

"Think ye can win again?"

Frustration flared. I'd cheated that night by using an illusion spell. "You want me to use *magic?*"

After everything she said. After all of the arguing. After she knew how much pain I was in.

She swallowed, a sudden redness to her eyes. "I just want ye *alive*," she breathed.

Before I could respond, she took off to her bedroom. Shaking off my irritation, I slipped into the guest room and shut the door.

Natalia straightened, placing her mortar and pedestal down on the table. Whatever was in the bowl masked the stench from Mae's wounds. "Varys, what in Xalador—"

"There are guards here." I could hear several voices of men downstairs now, the clanging of metal on the stone floor.

She wiped her hands on her apron before pulling it off and tossing it at the foot of the bed. "Stay here. Hopefully Duros and I can chase them off."

I nodded and closed the door behind her, bracing myself against it. My heart pounded as I weighed my options. I knew this spell well. My magical aptitude was beyond its simplicity. But I couldn't ignore the unknown consequences of using magic so soon after almost dying from using a spell beyond my strength.

I had survived though. Couldn't I...celebrate that feat? I had done something that should have been impossible. Had beaten the odds. It wasn't because I had managed to pull it off, it wasn't because I was lucky. I was capable. I was confident in my magic. My power.

I thought of the image in my head—a dark, dusty broom closet. That's all those guards would find upon opening the door in search of an Elven-blooded or magical items.

Palms facing the door, I spread my fingers wide, shoulders bunched up to my neck. Then I twisted my hands in opposite directions and felt the inward flow of magic as the veins snuffed the fire in the hearth, shrouding the room in darkness.

"Çlïöça Sam."

A deep purple aura whirled around the space, the spell's *eçor* blinking as it materialized before my palms.

But there was a different illumination among the magic. Something new. I choked on my next breath, panic swelling through me as I took in the sight of the arcane scars, now gleaming in the same bright blue as the glow of my eyes when casting.

My alarm shifted to the distant arguing downstairs, Duros shouting about their lack of magic items, Natalia's scoffing as they probably pushed past her anyway.

Then, they began to climb the stairs.

I heard Leona's door open. She growled something in Dwarvish —something about how their mom should have swallowed them instead.

The door to the guest room opened.

He was young, ginger-haired, no facial hair. Probably sixteen or seventeen. Possibly his first week on the job.

I didn't breathe. Any sway in my arms could disrupt the illusion. I silently begged Mae didn't let out a sound.

Even with all of the spell-light, I knew he could only see the illusion I had created. His gaze flicked around, staring at the broom in the corner, down to the tuft of dust in the pan I had imagined Leona had been too lazy to throw away.

The guard's eyes slid up to the exact spot my face would be if he could see me. My pulse skittered when they stayed, squinting as he leaned in.

I stifled the gasp. He was looking right at me.

If the spell was working, there should have been no way he could see me.

Unless…my scar's glow was affecting the illusion somehow.

It shouldn't have mattered. The spell was blocking all light. Even the low amber glow of dusk coming through the lone window.

He gripped the handle of the blade at his hip, glaring as he stepped further into the room.

My stomach plummeted, knees threatening to give way.

Oh gods. No. Please, no.

Just as I thought he would reach out and touch me, he huffed, shaking his head. "Fuck, I need some sleep," he mumbled, turning away to shout, "Looks like just an old broom closet over 'ere."

The door shut, darkness falling around me once more. My chest rattled as I breathed out, heart pounding in my ears so loud I could hardly hear where the guards had gone. It felt like an eternity before I heard boots clanking on the other side of the door. Leona mouthed off something else in Dwarvish as the guards descended down the steps.

I didn't dispel the magic, not even as my arms began to tingle, until Leona opened the door. She looked me over, at the scars' glow beginning to fade. "They know she did it, Fawkes. They came 'cause they're lookin' for her."

CHAPTER 48

Varys

Wanted. She was wanted, with a bounty on her head, for the murder of Rucas.

Duros had managed to get the information out of the guards, feigning a promise to bring her to them if he found her himself. It was the only thing to get them to leave. Evidently, someone had seen Mae's nwív fly away after calling down the lightning bolt to strike the Mordaunt home, and had told the mayor they were afraid the Pallid Curse had overwhelmed Mae Mordaunt.

The mayor ordered her to be found, to be brought back to Elros and executed. Without evidence, he had also gone as far as holding her accountable for the death of Theon and Willem. I had a terrible suspicion Eryx RothHall had told him she was involved after finding that circlet. I didn't know if he would betray her.

Either way, we needed to leave, needed to escape and never look back.

But we couldn't until she woke up.

After reading the last sentence on the last page of *Ít Nánörweth*, I closed the book with shaky hands and began to rub my temples to alleviate the ache in my head from the information overload and exhaustion. My heart pounded as I looked down at Mae, taking in her features.

When the nwív had first presented herself, and told me what she was, I'd wondered how Mae had been made a nexus. Upon reading the process, it confirmed a chilling fact.

Rucas Mordaunt could not have been her real father.

What I didn't know was if it confirmed that Fantine had an affair.

I couldn't blame her if she had, honestly. And after seeing the way she had looked at Rucas when they pulled his corpse from the burning house, the words she had said to me about not being able to save herself like Mae had…Fantine was no doubtedly abused by Rucas, too.

But since knowing nexi were created with a spell, and eighteen years ago magic had not yet reemerged, that meant Mae's father had to have been a real elf. After finding out Falryn had been here in Elros years ago, I had to wonder if he had fathered her.

However, if Fantine had slept with an elf, it also meant she knew what Mae would become. *Had to* have known. The spell to create a nexus was done so during the *act* of conceiving a child. Which meant one of three things:

Fantine Mordaunt willingly conceived a child knowing she would someday grow up to be a powerful nexus.

Or, Fantine Mordaunt *un*willingly conceived Mae and had no idea what she would become—which would mean the elf had disregarded everything the elven culture stood for.

Or, Fantine Mordaunt was also not Mae's parent.

The latter raised the hairs on my arms, but…*gods*, Mae looked nothing like Fantine either. And if it were true, why had the Mordaunts adopted a baby if they had been so negative toward her white hair?

That was also a conundrum. I had always assumed Elven-blooded people took on the traits of whatever parent was Elven-blooded. My mother had blue hair like mine. Mr. Flax's late wife had bright orange hair, and all their children had shades of the same fiery colors. The jeweler brothers had similar shades of reds and yellows.

According to Ramos, Falryn's hair was emerald green.

Was the white hair really some kind of curse? Tainted moments in the bloodline? Because if Vamir was right about there being another bloodline, like that dissertation from the college I had read stated, then who in Torm were Mae's parents?

I wasn't so sure I would get any answers tonight, and the questions about her parentage weren't the only ones I had after finishing *Ít Nánöweth*. A lot could be answered if she would wake up, especially whether or not she had figured out how to use and control her powers.

She would need to use them to close the *chasm*.

That's what the tear in the world had been, the portal to the plane of storms. A nexus could open chasms to summon elemental monsters to aid them in their endeavors. This one would need to be shut, and Mae was the only one who could do so.

Sitting the book aside, I took Mae's hand and pressed a gentle kiss to her wrist, right upon the lightning marks. How I wished to just lay beside her. Hold her. I didn't want to cross any boundaries, didn't desire anything more, but I wondered if my presence would comfort her while she slept.

Or maybe that was just wishful thinking on my part.

Another blink had my eyes closing for longer, and the heaviness in my body from lack of sleep tugged me down to lean on my elbow. The extra pillow Mae wasn't lying on bunched up around my arm, tempting me with much-needed rest even more so. Just a few moments…I could take my eyes off of her for a few moments—

"Wake up." Someone was shaking my shoulders. "Varys. Wake up."

I jolted upright, and on the first breath I took, a foul and noxious smell hit my senses. My stomach lurched as I got to my feet.

Mae shook as beads of sweat rolled down her face, dampening her hairline. Natalia took one look at her back—and stepped away. "Great Sky, this is…"

I came around, trying my best to ignore the smell.

"*Fuck*," I hissed around the instant knot in my throat.

She was…

This was…

Black ooze seeped through her dressing, mixing with pus and blood dripping down to the mattress. This was no ordinary infection.

"Poison." Natalia rushed to her, rummaging through the tools in her apron. "I don't understand."

She cut through the cloth to reveal the wound, and I lost the strength in my knees. Her veins beneath the skin across her shoulders, down her tailbone and backside, and through her upper thighs were black, even those beneath the lightning marks.

"Poison was not present two days ago," I blurted out as Natalia frantically snipped away the stitching.

"I don't know." She let out a sob. "Varys, I just don't know."

The last snip of the first set of stitches let the wound spread. A watery mix of discharge and the dark matter seeped out of the wound. Mae let out a shout, and for the first time in several days, she moved, hands thrashing as they went for her back—

"Varys. Hold her."

I barely heard Natalia's voice, my exhausted mind narrowed in on Mae's screaming, the way her spine bended, face locked in agony. My hands gripped my hair, panic rising.

"She's going to hurt herself. Varys. *Hold her.*"

With a steadying breath, I took hold of Mae's arms and held them to the mattress. Her skin was dangerously hot. "Mae, darling," I whispered in her ear. She just screamed again. "Mae, you're safe. You're—"

Small jolts danced under the contact of our skin. I sucked in a breath, backing off quickly. Time seemed to slow as I watched Natalia go in for another set of stitches, *metal* scissors open for another cut.

"Natalia, don't!"

I threw myself over Mae, into Natalia, knocking us both to the ground just as sparks lit up the room. White smoke rose from the small flames around Mae's body only lit for a few seconds before they died, leaving spots of the mattress in ashes.

Leona and Duros rushed in as Mae continued to thrash. Duros helped his wife to her feet, and when they turned back to the bed their wide eyes stared at the burns, the purple light of Mae's lightning marks. She was fighting. Somewhere in that trapped mind she was fighting for her life.

"Mum," Leona whispered as she watched. "Can ye help her?"

Natalia's face was full of fear and complete…*loss*.

"The scourge would've had to have been tipped with poison," I said, hoping to kick start some sort of plan as I climbed back into the bed. "Remember, Mae has been poisoned before." I snarled. "I have no doubt Rucas was the culprit behind that, too."

"Perhaps…" Natalia swallowed. "But her symptoms sounded like the use of night nettle. This poison is thicker and has coagulated her blood as if she has been bitten by a snake or spider." Her hands shook as she felt Mae's forehead, grimacing. "Varys, this is beyond my skills."

I shook my head in disbelief, holding Mae on her side so she couldn't flip to her back. The smell of her infection churned my stomach. "Natalia, you are the best healer I know. We *all* know. There's no one—"

"Varys, I know my limits." She had picked up her scissors. "The best I can do is try to drain the poison but…it has spread." Her grave eyes met mine, then her daughter's. "If you two can hold her, and let me know if she may shock me, I can get these stitches out. It's the only thing I can do."

I didn't hesitate to pull Mae closer, folding her arms against me tightly. Leona pinned her legs down.

"No sparks?" Natalia asked as she leaned in with open scissors.

I shook my head, and she snipped open the next row of stitches. Mae went taut in my arms as more of the ooze trickled out. I buried her face in the nook of my arm when she screamed, ignoring the pain when she pushed against my arcane scars. Her legs tried to kick, but didn't budge as Leona held them.

The smell…it took everything in me to not pull away, to not breathe too deeply or I would taste it.

Natalia cringed. "I shouldn't have stitched her shut. *Godsdammit.*" She snipped away another row and as more curses spilled from her lips, Mae screamed. The next set of snips had her convulsing, her shrill cries ripping me in two little by little by—

I snatched Natalia's wrist. "Wait," I pleaded. "J-Just wait. She's in pain."

"Varys, let me go," Natalia demanded. "You're not yourself. I must concentrate or I can accidentally hurt her. Your lack of discretion right now is a distraction."

Her words sliced through me, a parallel of the nwív's. *You are a hindrance, Varys Wynhart.*

It was Leona who ripped my arm back. I apologized and held Mae against me again. On the last row, the wound opened and Mae's entire body shuddered before another screech undid me completely.

"*Stop, stop, STOP!*" I didn't even know what I was saying. Every sense of logic had flown out the window. I couldn't bear to see her in so much pain. Even after everything she'd been through, everything I did to save her, she was still hurting. And her screams, her cries...

Natalia tossed the scissors on the side table in frustration, then pointed at a darkened spot inside one of the larger slashes. "Do you see that? It's necrosis. This poison has started to eat away at her."

My blood thinned. "How do you—"

"I have to cut it out." Natalia lifted a thin knife from the pocket of her apron. "And I don't know if I can."

Leona swallowed. "Then, maybe it's time to take her to another physician—"

"*To Torm with that!*" I exploded, head whipping to her. "We take her to the Welches, they will throw her bleeding body on a chopping block."

She glared. "I wasn't suggestin' that. Don't act like I'm not on yer side."

It didn't feel like she was at that moment, not as the anger I felt toward her became as toxic as the poison in Mae's blood.

Before I could respond, Natalia's breath hitched. She was staring down at Mae with wide, alarmed eyes, two fingers beneath her chin. "Duros, get Varys out of here."

I went cold. "Wait, why—"

"Now." Natalia stood, eyes on her husband. "We're losing her."

Everything in me began to deteriorate. "*No.*"

My chest wrenched, tightened so harshly I could no longer breathe. I shook her in my arms. "Mae. Mae, come on. You have to wake up."

I felt Duros come to the edge of the bed. Felt him take hold of my arm. The pounding of my heart ached as I looked down to her lifeless face, images, sweet memories flashing before me. I was losing her. I was losing her.

My Mae.

The woman I loved. The woman I'd vowed to give everything to. To have a future with.

Dreams of dancing and baking, of loving, of growing…they were slipping from my fingers, sand in my palm.

Dying. Dying with her.

I screamed. I held on to her tightly as Natalia yelled for her husband to move. He began to pull—and something possessive and feral erupted inside me. I let out a shouting growl as I yanked myself out of his grasp. *"Ölsty naev! Ölsty naev!"* *Wake up.*

I couldn't fight Duros's strength. He ripped me from her, and Natalia immediately began to push her hands against her sternum. I fractured, legs forgetting how to walk. I just continued to scream for her.

I didn't even realize I had been guided to the hall. Didn't realize the door had shut behind me. I barely acknowledged Leona's hands on my shoulders, the words she spoke before racing down the stairs.

All was silent in the hallway, but the impending death was screaming.

We are all cursed with something.

They were the only words consuming my thoughts. I had shut down, absolutely numb and emptied out. The dwarven time-teller downstairs told me I had been sitting, staring, waiting, for two hours.

That day at the stream, I told Mae what I believed my curse was. I thought I was cursed with always asking questions, and then always finding the answers. But these past few days had proved me wrong. Even now, I didn't know if she would die tonight. I didn't know if Natalia could save her.

I had been here before. Uncertain of the fate of someone I loved.

Maybe *that* was my curse. I had never believed in fate or destiny, so I was cursed with ill-fate. Forever destined to lose those I loved. To always reach for my goals and never take hold of that prize. To be teased with the possibility of an *Arynáthi* only for my lover to be ripped away.

And if that was the case, if that really was my curse, nothing could change fate now.

I had fallen asleep, no longer able to stay awake—no longer *wanting* to, either—when I heard rapid thuds on the stone floor, then someone running up the stairs.

A voice called out, "Mum, I have somethin' that might help!"

Leona.

"Somethin' that might save her life."

CHAPTER 49

Varys

N *eśta Philam.*

That's what the faded label read on the small bottle of golden-red liquid in my hands. The health vial Leona had brought back from her quick trip to Vamir's camp. No one knew she had even left. It was both surprising and a relief Vamir and his family had avoided having their stock taken by the guards.

Breaking the wax seal on the cork, I popped the vial open. A strong smell of overripe fruit and earth wafted up to me.

Duros leaned in, taking a sniff for himself. His auburn mustache curled around his scrunched nose. "Smells like some gowk brewed up some moldy berries in an ol' boggin' keg."

"It was probably created centuries ago." I twisted the vial to view the back. After reading the instructions listed, I asked Leo, "Did Vamir give any guidance when you purchased this?"

She shook her head, unpinning her cloak from its rose brooch. "Nope. And I haven't paid for it. Not yet."

When I looked at her in confusion, she turned from me. I knew her words no doubtedly meant something more, but I would have to ask later.

"I'm sorry I couldn't help more," Natalia said, sniffling back a sob. She was still at Mae's side, apron covered in black filth and blood.

"You've done enough," I assured her. "Thank you."

"It will help her?"

I swallowed. "If it works like the potions I've read about—"

"It will," Leo cut me off and stated firmly. "It has to. I won't let this be her fate."

Her words stole my breath.

She had gone all the way to Elros, had risked getting caught, to bring this back.

This was the change of fate I didn't think would happen.

My best friend had always been a believer in destiny. It was fitting that she was the one who had taken fate into her own hands —then probably told it to fuck right off.

However, I knew that this wouldn't just give Mae another chance. Would this change my fate as well? Leona's?

Ours, I realized.

And I suddenly believed right there, as I crawled onto the bed, as I took Mae's limp body into my arms, that this was changing fate for all. Changing it for the better. It had to.

Tipping Mae's head back, I pressed the lip of the vial to her mouth.

"Varys, wait," Natalia warned. "She might—"

"She won't choke." My confidence was suddenly bursting like a hundred fireworks as I held up the vial once more, showing off the back label, all of it written in a language she couldn't understand. But I could, and that felt like destiny, too. "Says right here."

She nodded and leaned forward, clasping her hands. "May all higher powers across the realms be with us tonight," she murmured. "Please, do not remain silent."

It was the first time in a while I acknowledged a prayer. Let the words repeat in my head as I lowered Mae's bottom lip with my thumb. She let out a small, breathy whimper. "Hold on, my love," I whispered. "Just a little longer."

The potion glinted as it poured over her tongue, falling like shimmering red and gold dust instead of liquid. The scent seemed more pleasing as the potion spilled down her throat, as if the fruit within had been restored to its original ripeness.

"*Victors*, look!" Leona cried out, standing.

I blinked in shock as the veins along her throat began to light up in a bright ruby, the glow spreading through every vessel. Her lightning marks lit up at the same time, filling the room with a violet luminance.

I carefully shifted her in my arms to view her back. I didn't know what word fell out of my mouth in exasperation, nor in what language, as I watched the scourge wounds begin to glow the same ruby red, the light rushing through her tainted veins. All of the blood, pus, and residue of poison vanished as if it had never been there—was simply *dismissed*.

And then the edges of each wound began to sparkle gold. Mae's closed eyes squeezed, her teeth clenched, a pained sound in her throat. I didn't breathe as I watched the redness of the skin fade, the bruises disappear, and the sparkle crawl over the injured tissue. Something was happening beneath, and it seemed to make Mae uncomfortable for only a moment before the light began to dim, revealing new, *healed* flesh.

The last wound mended, and I lifted my eyes to find Leo. I saw the small break in her face. The relief. She let out a breath, quickly wiping her face of the tears that had fallen.

My chest clamped. I had been selfish. Mae was important to Leona, too. Their budding friendship was something I wanted for them both. Leo had been just as worried when she was missing, just as terrified. We had searched for her together.

And then for me to get hurt as well. I had ignored her feelings, took her anger toward the situation as an attack on my integrity. She had said some things that hurt, but I had hurt her as well.

When her gaze met mine, I knew she felt the same as I did— none of that mattered right now.

Mae had been healed.

Our friend had been healed.

"So," Leo started, her voice strained. "That's it then. Ye gave her all of it, yeah?"

I winced at her question. "Yes, that was all of it." Taking the bottle, I read over the instruction again. "There's nothing here stating whether I should give her the whole thing or just a drop."

"I'm just…glad it worked." She gave a smile that didn't meet her eyes before turning from me entirely. "Mum, Da. I need to talk to ye alone."

The emotion in her voice had my pulse picking up. I lay Mae down to the mattress just as the three of them stepped into the hall. A cry broke the quiet, and I almost didn't recognize the sound, from who it had come from. I had only heard it a few times in my entire life.

My stomach twisted upon the realization. "*Leo.*"

I wasn't fast enough. The doors to Duros and Natalia's master suite slid shut with all of them inside. I could no longer hear her cries, but knew something was very wrong.

***

"She'll talk to you later today," Natalia had told me when she found me outside the suite. *"Go ahead and get some rest. Dawn will be here in just a few hours."*

I didn't know how she expected me to do that when I knew Leona was upset, and that there was a great possibility Mae would be waking up soon. So I found something to eat, bathed, and welcomed the morning sun while starting another read-through of my *Dragonhart Series* using Leona's personal copy. I liked to keep my mind refreshed of the plot, hoping that someday I would have time to write the third book. Maybe after we started a new life in Elvidawn—a dream, and not at all what was really happening. We would be on the run to hopefully find sanctuary in Elvidawn. We had little money and I didn't know how far my silver would go. I hated feeling like I might still fail, that leaving Elros might be a fate worse than staying.

No. I couldn't think that way. Not when Mae's head was on the line.

Dawn's sky splashed pink and yellow light on the manor floor, and it was just bright enough my eyes stung in response. My legs felt like I had chained anvils to them with every step up the stairs.

When my feet hit the landing, my eyes begging to close, I found myself at a pause. It was quiet in the hall. Too quiet for someone like me whose head wandered in silence. My thoughts were nothing but a whirlwind of chaos and trouble right now.

With a deep breath, I forced myself to walk toward the guest room. Mae was still asleep, but it seemed she had stirred at some point, for her arms were now relaxed over her head in a pose that reminded me of something she had done when dancing. Natalia had dressed her in the purple tunic and black pants I'd brought from her house. She looked more alive now than she had just an hour ago, face relaxed, her chest rising in a normal, effortless manner, and there was a color to her skin I had never seen before. It made me wonder if the potion had cured more than just her wounds, that maybe it had also cured her of the lingering effects from being poisoned years ago.

Smoothing my wet hair back, I made my way over to the chair to sleep. The moment I sat down, I became hyperaware of the returned silence. One look at Mae's face had everything hitting me at once.

The tavern. Her disappearance.

The jeweler brothers. Vamir. Orin. Meri. Eryx.

The execution.

Mother's sword.

Rucas. Fantine.

The nwív and the price I'd paid to save this woman before me.

I hadn't processed any of it. I'd been holding on to a thin lifeline. Every moment I had learned something new. Something terrifying. Something distressing. It was both information overload and emotional reckoning.

I didn't remember slumping to the ground. Didn't know how long I struggled to catch my breath, my arms wrapped around my knees, squeezing, squeezing as if the strength of my arms could compress everything overwhelming me into a pulp. I felt nothing and yet *everything*. It was a monster that had been slowly eating me alive, that knew to go to my head first. Question after question with no answers. So I doubted myself, I was no longer in control, and then to overcompensate, I became reckless. I had been desperately reaching for some fucking sanity.

It was a trauma response.

The last time I lost someone I loved, and my life spun out of control, I had been too young and vulnerable to prevent myself from crashing. This time, I gave everything, had pushed myself over an edge to make sure it didn't happen again.

But this wasn't just about Mae. It was the state of the world. The feeling of this brink of disaster. I felt all of it alone, as I was now. Though, I was glad she was still asleep. Didn't want her to see me like this.

It was another several moments before I unlocked my knees from my chest, wiping my face of the hot tears. I dragged myself to the window, drew the curtains back and opened the glass pane, hoping if I breathed in the fresh morning air my panic would wane. But my heart wouldn't slow, my breathing still short and rattling. I could sleep this off, but the sound of another few hours in that chair made me nauseous.

I looked down to the bed—a bed that was big enough for three people if they all cuddled close—and crawled in.

I kept my distance, my body above the quilt, arms folded against my chest. If she found this inappropriate when she woke up, I would deal with the consequences then. I just needed to rest—

Mae let out a sleepy sigh. My eyes shot open, and I turned to find her rolling onto her side, hand reaching toward me.

"M-Mae?" I whispered, going still.

There was no response as her slumbering body shifted around to get comfortable. I couldn't help the smile that lifted my lips as I reached out to her extended hand and stroked my thumb over her fingers, the feeling of her skin on mine igniting a fire in me. *Gods*, she was exquisite even when sleeping.

And…I allowed myself that thought.

I allowed the desires I had temporarily buried, too focused on whether or not she would be here right now, to resurface. I wrapped my hand around hers, feeling her pulse against mine. She was alive. Healed. She was safe and free.

My pounding heart slowed, the tightness in my chest easing. It was as if this simple touch washed away all of the panic I had felt just moments before. She might have been everything her nwív said she was, born to be a bridge between our world and a plane of chaos and destruction, a walking storm. But within my own storms constantly striking me down, she was the eye. She was where I found peace. No wind, no rain, no chaos. Just her there in the middle of it all.

I watched the rapid movement of her eyes behind her lids, her forehead scrunching every once in a while, but it didn't seem to be out of any kind of pain. I wondered if she still dreamed as she had when she was injured, that maybe that had nothing to do with her injury at all.

A muttering of Elvish woke me out of a short doze. My pulse skipped as I found her closer, one hand upon my chest, her face buried in the crook of my arm. I didn't want this to become something she wasn't comfortable with, so I started to roll out of her reach. She followed me, a sound of sleepy protest escaping her mouth. My chest swelled with undeniable delight. She *wanted* me close. She could feel my presence.

Chuckling softly, I slipped beneath the quilt and pulled her closer, her form naturally fitting against mine. Whether or not I believed in the possibility of her being my *Arynáthi*, I wholeheartedly believed she was made for me, and I her.

"I don't know if you can hear me," I whispered in her ear, "but I have so much to tell you, *aríma.*" My nose brushed her temple, my skin tingling in response to her warm breath along my collarbone. "We need to run. We've got to get out of here."

I traced my fingers along her jaw set in a sleepy agape. "I'm going to give you the life you deserve, Mae. I don't know how, but I'm going to make sure those dreams you shared with me are fulfilled."

A yawn overwhelmed me, my eyes blinking heavily. Laying my head down on the pillow, I continued to whisper, "Wake up so I can hold you. So I can show you just how much I've missed you, Little Bird. Wake up, so we can fly away together."

As I began to doze off, a fear wanted to rise, my mind conjuring dreadful thoughts that would no doubt plague me in my sleep. I was still terrified she would never wake up, even after everything we'd done to bring her back.

I couldn't stop the tears forming as I pulled her against me tighter, holding on to the hope that maybe my touch, my voice, had reached her. Just as my world began to fade to black, something fluttered in from the open window. I didn't know if it was real, or if I was already dreaming.

There was a butterfly perched upon Mae's white hair.

CHAPTER 50

Maelawyn

y mind was shrouded in beautiful storm clouds and streaks of opalescent light. No longer did I dream of shattering crystals. There was no more pain. I had never felt more at peace.

For the first time in what felt like an eternity, the lights flickered out. The clouds dispersed, and my mind tumbled into darkness. But it wasn't the darkness I'd known before, where I had found the true meaning of fear and agony. This was rest. True rest. A sleep bringing a warmth like I was wrapped in a chrysalis, safe and secure.

It didn't last long, though. My mind became aware of an outside light piercing through the black, and I only understood my eyes were closed when my senses began to awaken as I did.

I lay on my side, vision blurred and groggy. The sun cast a warm glow into the room through a window. Red-orange curtains swayed in the gentle, cool breeze blowing in from the open pane. Curtains I didn't recognize, but I hadn't had much time to look over the inn room before…

Well, before what exactly?

The thought seemed to wake up more of my senses. I could hear the crackling of wood on a fire, and birds chirping outside. There was a sound I could only assume was something heavy clanging on metal in the distance, and a murmuring of voices outside the room. The quilt I lay beneath was thick and soft, and I was pretty sure the blanket in the room had been thin and scratchy.

I went to rise despite the heavy feeling in my body. That was when I felt the presence behind me, the arm laying over my hip, the rise and fall of someone's warm breath against my neck. Alarm shot through me as I twisted and rolled to face them.

My pulse skittered, the sight of him before me stealing the air from my lungs. He lay resting on his folded arm, the faintest of snores in his throat. A sleepy pink tinted his cheeks beneath strands of messy blue hair.

"*Varys,*" I whispered, my voice like gravel. His name on my tongue awakened everything in me still sleeping. The smell of bergamot and woodsmoke elicited a hunger only he could satiate as his scent flooded my veins with heat. The connection to him tugged and evoked images of everything we had done in the tavern, those sensual and passionate moments the last I could recall before...

I didn't know. I didn't even know if we were still in the tavern.

Careful not to wake him, I slid his arm off my hip and rose to a sitting position. An aggravating buzz of displacement set in as I looked around the room, recognizing nothing. There was a chair in the corner and a fairly large hearth at the far end of the room. The top of the side table was covered in several types of flowers and herbs, some of them shredded inside a mortar and pestle.

My eyes snagged on a small empty bottle, stomach flipping when I read what was written on the label. Written in Elvish. *Nesta Philam. A health vial?*

Someone had been hurt.

I took the bottle into my hands, a question rising. *Did I get hurt?*

Was that why I couldn't remember anything past the tavern? Was that why I was here? Was this some sort of infirmary?

I wasn't going to get answers until he woke up. I placed the bottle down and turned to Varys, shuffling back beneath the quilt. Cuddling close, I reached up and brushed my fingers over his cheek, chuckling under my breath when I found his skin prickly instead of smooth.

"Varys," I said. I still couldn't speak more than a whisper. "Wake up, handsome."

He didn't stir, so I pulled myself closer, our lips only inches apart.

"Varys." I stroked his cheek again, tracing down his relaxed jaw, to the side of his neck. I pushed myself up and leaned over his ear, barely able to keep my hands from sinking into his hair. "Wake up. *Ölsty naev.*"

A gasp tore from his throat, his body going taut. Bright blue eyes snapped open up to meet mine. I grinned as he blinked and blinked, breaths coming in harsh bursts.

"M-Mae?" he asked frantically.

The panic in his voice sped up my pulse. "Hello."

Shaking hands cupped my face, fingers entangling in my hair almost to the point of pain. My eyes went wide at his grip, the severity of his expression.

"Is it—is it really you?"

I gave a nod. "Of course it is, who else would it—"

Varys captured my lips with his own, muffling the surprised squeal in my throat. I wasn't able to catch my breath before he rolled on top of me, holding me to his body as he kissed me with a passion I'd never seen. I melted into him, wrapping my arms around his neck, my legs around his torso, pressing myself against his pelvis.

But he didn't move on me, didn't push back. He broke the kiss, gasping, his eyes wide and glassy.

"*Mae,*" he rasped before pressing his lips to my forehead, then my nose and cheeks, the stubble on his chin scratching my face. "Thank the gods. You're awake."

He kissed under my jaw, every thought threatening to vanish as his lips glided over my skin. But my focus was too hung on his behavior, and the fact that my name didn't sound the same anymore.

As if…he wasn't saying it correctly.

"Varys." I tugged on his hair to make him pull away. He only gripped me tighter. "Varys, darling, why are you kissing me like I might disappear?"

He went still, breathing into the crook of my neck. When he lifted his eyes to mine, there was…*gods*, I couldn't place a single emotion swirling in his gaze.

"Because," he whispered. "You're *alive*."

Alive.

His words banished the throb of my core. Something wasn't right. My memories were nothing but fragments. "What do you mean?"

Varys studied my face for a moment before sliding off me and sitting up. "*Um…*" He pulled a hand through his hair. "Mae, you've been asleep for three days. Well, technically about four but—"

I sat up quickly, hands pressing into the mattress to steady myself. "No, last night…we…" It all seemed to be so distant. Like a dream I could hardly remember. I looked around the room, to all the furniture I didn't recognize. "Where am I? What's going on?"

I had crawled off the bed before he could answer and rushed to the open window on legs tingling with sleep. Pulling the curtains back, I found myself high up on a second story, gazing out to a long downhill yard of thick grass billowing in the gentle wind and stopping before a forest edge. The same pine and oak trees I was familiar with crested the property, expanding a few miles in every direction. But looking to the west, I could see the hills surrounding Elros, the faintest outline of barns and houses.

"You're at the Cauldücen's manor," Varys told me from behind.

"Leo's house," I said absently, coming back to him. "How did I get here?"

His eyes darted away for a moment, and on their travel back to mine it seemed a haunt had been swept into his gaze. "What is the last thing you remember?"

The hairs on my arms rose upon the tone of his question, and it was then I saw the dark circles under his lower lashes, the bruise along his jaw I hadn't noticed. His right arm and hand were wrapped in bandages. "The tavern, of course. With you and the room…" I trailed off, shifting uncomfortably as heat washed through my face. A soft reminiscent smile lifted on Varys's lips.

But desire hadn't been the only thing we'd discovered in that room.

"Magic," I said. "You told me you're a mage, and I realized I was as well. We are *Vyl'kríev*. And I was about to show you—"

I froze. The lightning marks…they had spread even more. Holding my breath, I traced them from the tip of my middle finger, down to how they splattered across my palm, to my wrist and beneath the cuff of my tunic. I pulled the entire sleeve up to my forearm and gasped. They went beyond my elbow now. Unlacing my tunic collar in a frenzy, I looked under to see if they had gone to my shoulder. Another breath left me. Like branches stretching toward the sun, the lines extended across my heart.

Varys cleared his throat. "They're down your spine as well."

"What?" Arching my back, I looked over my shoulder. I couldn't see what he was talking about. "How do you…"

My pulse pummeled as a realization dawned on me. My marks hadn't spread yet when we were at the tavern, in the room where I had shown him hidden parts of myself and let him touch me where no one else had.

But my memories were so…

"Oh my gods, I'm forgetting something, aren't I?" The words tumbled out of me. Confusion crossed his features, matching exactly how I felt. I swallowed, face burning from embarrassment. Not because of what I believed had happened, but…how in Xalador had I forgotten? "Did we have sex?"

His blue eyes went wide, a stifled and gasping half-laugh escaping. Then that side smile I loved so much appeared, coy and sensual. "Would you slap me if I said *unfortunately, no?*"

A wicked heat curled everything low, warming my neck and cheeks. "No." I grinned.

His languid gaze dipped, catching on the exposed upper swells of my breasts. I didn't cover myself, my own eyes tracing over where the shirt he wore went taut against the muscles beneath.

When he looked away, it seemed he had to force himself. "We

were…cut severely short that night in the tavern. Of many things." He let out a long breath, sliding a hand over his face. "And nothing is less important to me than the other, however, we needed to discuss The ReEmergence of Magic in greater detail. And I wish we could have before…everything happened."

I sat back on the edge of the bed. "And what happened exactly?"

That disturbed look returned. "What do you understand about your powers?"

I shook my head, cupping my hands in my lap and running a thumb over the lightning marks on my palm. "Not much. These marks glow sometimes. I have lightning beneath my skin."

"And?"

I shrugged. "I don't know. I don't know how to make it appear. I don't know how to use it."

He chewed on his lips in thought for several moments before waving his hands as if wiping a slate clean. "Let's just start from the beginning." He winced. "Did your powers manifest for the first time at the stream?"

I swallowed with a nod, quickly realizing now that Varys and I were aware of each other's magic, I would need to revisit everything that happened. Again. Something on my face had Varys scooting closer and taking my hand into his left—the one that wasn't wrapped.

He already knew that I'd used magic to defend myself. What he didn't know is that it had been completely out of my control.

"It came on like a flare. Pain shot through my arm right as he was going to…" I snapped my eyes shut. "Then the light hit him and they both ran."

Varys rubbed his chin in thought, "If your powers manifested during a moment of great defense, it makes me wonder if others' have reemerged and they don't know it because their powers haven't been triggered yet. I didn't have that kind of experience."

I stared at him. "I think you may have to help me understand what this ReEmergence is."

He blew out a breath with a nod and began to break down the details about an event called The ReEmergence of Magic, and how

I was one of thousands of Elven-blooded Xaladorians whose lives had been altered at the same moment. He told me of his theories, of how he had spent the majority of the past two years reading every elven book he could get his hands on, learning about the elves'—no, *our*—history.

He told me about our enemies, that there were *Vyl'kriev* like us who were killing mages, and how he was almost positive the dryamorn were escaping the Evershade somehow. He went on to tell me about the elf who evidently still roamed Xalador. An elf we needed to find so we could get answers.

He paused as if to allow me to catch up. Or maybe it was because I obviously seemed focused on something else entirely.

"Any questions so far?" he asked.

"You said The ReEmergence happened two years ago," I said slowly, knowing the next thing I said would be difficult to convey, "And I reemerged through a defensive reaction. But I've…had to defend myself at other times and didn't gain power then."

Varys's face fell. He squeezed my hand. "Like from your father?"

For a moment, I wasn't sure if I heard him right. But as my mouth parted, unease rose quickly like I was in a room filling with water and there was no exit.

"I know," he said, and there was an underlying coolness to his tone that had my stomach dropping. "You have people watching out for you. *Good* people. Mr. Flax warned me."

I stared at him, every breath harder than the last. A deep shiver began in my bones. "How did he know?"

Varys moved his arm around my shoulders. "He had grown concerned after seeing bruises that didn't look self-inflicted. I put two and two together."

My shaking hands found my mouth. I gaped past him, looking at nothing, nothing but racing, painful images and harrowing memories. Every slap, every push, every twang of hunger; the blurring tears in my eyes just as hot and laced with the same dread.

The shivering erupted into an uncontrolled shake, sobs scraping out on the break of my throat. I buckled over, face in my hands as an entire life of torment spilled from me in tears and wails. No longer did I have any reason to hold any of it back.

But with it came—

"I'm going to be sick."

As I went to the floor, Varys leaped to his feet, dashing over to a bucket of water he quickly turned over into the hearth. It doused the fire, but not the heat in my body as bile rose and rose. He got the bucket to me just in time.

For several long minutes, I purged, mostly dry heaving because there was nothing in my stomach. It didn't matter. My body had been holding this back for days—*longer*. Years.

I coughed and gagged, all of my anxiety rushing to my chest. I couldn't breathe through the thoughts, the fucking fear I still had. Into the bucket, I screamed until my face was hot, my vision red and white.

Finally, I collapsed back, finding a warm body pressed against me. I didn't realize he had hold of my hair—had pulled it back and held it while I vomited. A strong arm wrapped around me and he pressed my head to his chest.

I lost track of the moments that ticked by. How long he held me there against him, rocking me back and forth until my breathing returned to normal.

"I'm sorry," I sobbed.

"No, no, no." He took the bucket and placed it aside. My cheeks heated with embarrassment. "Mae, you have always apologized for things you should not be apologizing for."

I sniffled, wiping the moisture from my nose. "But I *am* sorry. I should have told you."

Brushing my sweaty hair from my forehead, he asked, "How long?"

I didn't need him to clarify. I knew what he was asking. "All my life." He tensed behind me, and I took a shuddering breath. "My first memory…I was about four. It just got worse."

Varys's grip on me tightened. He didn't move or speak as I began to tell him about my father's abuse. Every word fell from my tongue in discombobulated heaps he seemed to still understand. I told him about my vanity, how I barred my door with it because Rucas might have forced himself on me. Like Mother. How my nights smelled of liquor and sweat.

Varys finally understood why I hadn't let him walk me home that day after the stream, that I was hiding our exchange from Rucas entirely.

I told the truth to every lie I had spun.

And it was supposed to be a release, one I had wanted for years. But I only felt worse about myself.

"I've…always lied to avoid his wrath. I may have a few good people watching my back like Mr. Flax, but Rucas has the merchant guild. People indebted to him. I've always worried if any of them saw me at the wrong place, with the wrong person, they'd tell him sooner than I could hide it. So I lied to protect myself from that happening."

I tried to twist to him, but his embrace was too tight. "I never wanted to hurt anyone. Especially you. That day at the stream, when my powers manifested…" I sniffled and wiped a tear from my cheek. "I didn't know how long I had, especially when the marks showed up. Rucas has looked for every justified reason to harm me. He's never found one, but this? I have power, something to defend myself and I was certain if he found out, he'd kill me before I learned how to use it."

Varys's forehead dropped to my shoulder. I squeezed my eyes shut, continuing, "He's been trying to get rid of me for years. When Natalia told me I'd been poisoned, I realized it was Rucas who probably did it."

"*Fuck.*"

The tears began to flow again. "I just wanted…" I trailed away and forced myself around to him. My breath hitched when I saw the tears rolling down his face as well. I wiped them away. "I wanted to live the life I chose for myself. I hate that you got wrapped up in this, but it's because I wanted *you*, too. I was selfish."

"No," he said sternly. "You aren't."

"But I am, Varys. Every lie was to get what I wanted—"

"So what?" He pulled me against him. "Stop apologizing for wanting, Mae. Stop apologizing for your desires. Be selfish. You were *abused*." His breaths turned harder. Angry. "Fuck him. I hope he rots in Torm. I hope that when he died, he…"

He trailed off, eyes fluttering shut, lips pressed in a thin line. As if he'd made a mistake.

My pulse sped up along with my head. Did he mean…?

I remained frozen before him, waiting, staring as the swell of suspense rose from the greatest depths of my soul.

"Varys, tell me." My words were both a demand and a plea.

He lifted his head, and the look on his face spoke of shackles breaking, a cage opening, my fear flying out like trapped butterflies and birds.

His throat bobbed, squeezing my hands. "Rucas Mordaunt is dead."

He held my gaze, the tendons in his neck as if he were waiting for an eruption from me.

But I said nothing.

I felt nothing. No sadness. No reminiscence. I didn't suddenly wish that things could have been different.

He was dead.

Gone.

"Good," I muttered, my voice unwavering and certain.

I was free.

But Varys's gaze was wary, his hands moving to my face, locking our eyes. "You…you killed him, Mae."

My mouth fell open on the startled breath I took, and the emotional void began to fill with dread. *"How?"*

Standing, he crossed the room to the corner chair, bending down to his bag and pulling out a familiar looking book.

I held the air in my chest as he handed it to me. In an instant, the book began to glow just like it had the first time among the stack of books I had carried to Rucas's shop several days ago.

Ít Nánöweth. The Nexus.

But there was no ringing in my ears. No pain in my arm. It simply shimmered and felt warm in my hands.

"It's never glowed like that for me," Varys said in awe. "It must sense the presence of a nexus."

My eyes went wide, breaths becoming uneven. "You mean…I'm a nexus?"

He gave a slow nod. "And I don't believe Rucas was your real father."

And then everything in me went still.

"We have a lot to talk about."

———

I couldn't stop shaking, gripping the edges of the tome as if I would just crumble into nothing if I let it go.

I didn't know who I was anymore.

I didn't know who my parents were.

The alleged affair, the reason that gave Rucas some skewed justification to harm me...It was the truth. He had been right about Mother laying with another to conceive me.

It was all written in *Ít Nánöweth*. My father would've had to have had magic and cast a spell at conception. And we only knew of one person who had been here in Elros eighteen years ago and had such abilities—the elf. Falryn.

But was Falryn the only elf who had been wandering around Xalador for decades? Only Mother could tell me the truth, and I didn't know if I cared to ever see her again.

Was that why I had white hair? Were all of us Elven-blooded with white hair truly cursed in some way from a wrong deed done during our conception?

I had practically shut Varys's voice out as he continued to explain how my nwív had overwhelmed me, how he had fought her in the air, how she had opened some sort of hole in the world called a chasm. My heart pounded in my ears louder than his voice.

But the description of my black eyes jarred an obscure memory of seeing myself in the mirror at the tavern. "That's when it happened," I told him, cutting him off.

From where he sat across from me on the bed, he tilted his head and waited for me to explain myself.

Walls built up around my stomach. "That's when *she* took over."

"She." He swallowed. "Your nwív?"

It had been her all along. She had coaxed me into believing if I set her free, I would be freeing myself. Instead, she had locked me in my own mind as she tried to destroy Elros. Tried to destroy the man I loved. She had killed Rucas.

But I...

"I can't hear her anymore."

His brows shot up, body going tight as a bow string. Then he stood, hands out in front of him like he was trying to stop time. "You...knew about your *nwív?*"

His question hung in the air for a beat. I watched the expressions on his face shift, incredulity washing to revelation.

My mouth went dry. "I didn't know that's what she was—"

"You *heard* her though," he snapped. "For how long?"

My hands went to my mouth, neck and cheeks rushing hot. "I'm not sure."

His expression hardened with hurt. "When were you going to tell me?"

Fresh tears stung my eyes. I didn't know how to respond. This looked like another lie.

But it wasn't.

"When were you going to tell me you could hear her?" he asked again through tight teeth. "You said you knew nothing else about your powers, and here you've lied again—"

"*No.*" I shot to my feet. A deep pain lanced through my chest, a knot instantly growing in my throat. "When were *you* going to tell *me* about magic? About The ReEmergence? About this whole fucking thing?"

He blinked, chin jeering back as he stared down at me.

I raised my voice. "I fully understand why you chose to keep it to yourself because I know you were waiting to make sure it was safe to do so. Which is *exactly* what I did and you *know it.*" My frown deepened. "How dare you continue to chastise me?"

He shook his head, and his shoulders fell as his gaze went to the floor. He tucked his wrapped hand to his chest. "Mae, I'm—"

"*Maelawyn.*" I lifted my chin. "Use my *real* name."

He took a step back, eyes widening, something like hesitance flittering in his gaze.

"I'm no longer Mae Mordaunt," I told him through the knot in my throat. "I don't think I ever really was. Whoever she was, she's gone now."

And the power I felt in my real name demanded my voice to be heard.

"She's gone with the lies, with Rucas, and with weakness. I feel like I've woken up and I'm something else. I'm still me, but I will no longer answer to *Mae*, nor do I carry that family name."

Silence fell between us.

Then he nodded, shoulders falling like he had accepted something. "Maelawyn…"

My heart began to pound.

"I'm sorry," he said. "That wasn't fair of me."

It was another beat of quiet before I sighed softly. "I don't think either of us have been fair to each other."

He came back to the bed, slumping as he sat down.

"I just…I saw what you became," he murmured. "I saw what your suffering had created." His blue eyes lifted, ablazed with honesty. "I care about you, Maelawyn. I only wish you had felt safe enough to tell me so I could have done everything within my power to prevent her from taking over."

My chest tightened. "And I wish I didn't have this power."

His mouth parted.

I shook my head. "I'm not like you, Varys. I'm not excited about my magic. I'm scared and…" My aching throat threatened to silence me. I swallowed it down hard. I wanted him to understand. "What if the nwív takes over again? You said she could come back."

He took *Ít Nánöweth* into his hands, opening to a page containing another *eçor* similar to the banishing spell. This one however was a *binding* spell. Pointing to the elaborate, circular design, he said, "I will have to figure out how to cast this spell before that happens. It binds you to your nwív so she is a part of you."

I nodded, feeling a bit more calm. "All right. When can you start?"

He winced. "Maelawyn, I'm not strong enough yet. Or rather, my magical aptitude is not advanced enough. Casting that spell might kill me."

My brows pinched. "Why? You cast the banishing spell just fine, right?"

His lips thinned. Something about the way he pulled his wrapped hand closer, as if to protect it, invoked a question in my head. My pulse quickened

"Your hand…" I stared at the bandages. "What's wrong with it?"

His face fell. "I wondered when you were going to ask."

"Why haven't you told me yet?"

His throat bobbed. "Because I'm worried about how you'll react."

With a huff, I took his arm gently and pulled back the sleeves of his tunic. He was bandaged up to his elbow. "Can I look?" I asked.

He nodded, but his eyes wouldn't meet mine as I began to unravel the bandages. Once uncovered, it revealed gashes starting in his palm, up his wrist and to his lower bicep. All of the wounds glowed like a dull blue ember, and were shaped like Elvish runes.

The breath I held came out with trembling lips. I ran my fingers lightly over the damage, and I could feel him quivering lightly as he said, "They're arcane scars. When a spell is cast beyond a mage's aptitude, arcane decay ensues and…"

He didn't finish. I filled in the rest. "This looks like pieces of the banishing *eçor*."

My eyes stung with hot tears I couldn't prevent from falling. He was wounded to save *me*.

"*Why?*" I questioned, letting go and putting space between us. "You could have *died*. Why would you do that?"

Our eyes locked, his suddenly like deep pools. The connection between us began to sing and burn bright, coiling around me until my blood ran warm and languid.

"Do you not know?" he asked.

I went still as I watched his disposition begin to change, until I could see nothing but a declaration on his face.

"Maelawyn," he breathed. "I love you."

My entire world went utterly quiet as chaos erupted inside of me. The shake in my bones turned violent. I could do nothing but bury my face in my hands.

It wasn't the right time. Not when I was such a mess.

Not when I was a walking killer.

"Do you not feel the same?" he asked through a breath that seemed hard to take.

"I do," I said through a cry. "But Varys. I could have killed you. I-I can't…"

I shook my head back and forth, over and over, unrest and panic pulling me under crashing, roaring waves. I barely heard Varys say my name, my chest caving in and out. I couldn't breathe. I couldn't—

"*You need to stay away from me!*" I screeched from under my hands.

"Maelawyn—"

"*No,*" I sobbed. "I'm not good for you. I can't…be with you. Not until I'm bound."

I couldn't think past the black eyes in my head, glaring with a wolfish grin. I was a monster. I was an awful, lying, torrential monster.

"That could…" Varys began, the mattress bowing as he slid off. "Maelawyn, unless we find Falryn, it could be weeks, several quarters…maybe even years before I can cast that spell without repercussions."

I lifted my head, tears rolling down my face. This was my punishment. My consequence. "So be it."

Varys's mouth parted. He stepped away from the bed. I looked away, unable to stand the hurt on his face. The betrayal.

"No…" he started. "No, *no.* After everything?"

I squeezed my eyes shut, avoiding the stare that would pull me back in. "I've hurt you so much. I don't deserve you—"

"Stop it," he snapped, stalking back to me. I turned away, but his hand slid under my chin and guided my face to his again. "You think you don't deserve someone who wants to take care of you? To help you and keep you safe?" I whimpered, my body wanting to lean into his gentle touch as he lifted my chin and brushed the tears from my face. "I *love* you, Little Bird. Tell me what you want, what you need. You are in my life now, and I am in yours."

His lips pressed to my cheeks, kissing away the moisture. I needed him to leave. To go. Or I was going to lose it. I wasn't used to someone wanting to know what I wanted. Even what I needed felt selfish.

"I just…I need you to go." His hand on my chin froze. I quickly softened my meaning. "I need some time to catch my breath. To think about all of this."

Despite how still he'd gone, the hurt in his expression, his hand left my face. Nodding, he stepped away once more, backing up all the way to the door. The connection loosened—I already missed its hold.

"Then I'll give you that," he said, voice strained. "I set out to free you. I'm not here to give you another cage."

CHAPTER 51

Varys

Sitting at the dining table, I opened and closed my right hand, testing the strength of it. Making a fist made the hand shake and pulled on tendons still extremely tender. There was no way I would be able to hold a sword, much less the cup Natalia placed in front of me. I grabbed it with my left and drank down the water inside in one gulp.

"You sure she's not hungry?" Natalia asked slowly.

I let out a sigh. "I think the potion cures a lot more than just wounds. Might have filled her empty stomach enough. Don't worry. She'll eat." I chuckled. "She loves food."

"I'll take it to her anyway, then."

The front door opened and Leona's heavy, exhausted huff echoed through the entryway as she trudged in. Pulling the blacksmithing apron over her head, she tossed it in the laundry basin near their water supply.

"Promise I'll clean that, Mum," she said as she sat down—right beside me. "Smells like burnt shite and a man's balls."

She smelled like burnt shit and a man's balls.

Natalia scoffed, dramatically plugging her nose. "Makers' sake, girl. It's a good thing I'm done in this kitchen. How about you go bathe before that stench kills your best friend?"

Leona whipped her head to me, her eyes wide and daring. I lifted my hands and shook my head. "I'm not saying a godsdamn word."

She grinned with a bit of her tongue between her teeth as she billowed the collar of her tunic to cool off. "Nah, see, Mum. He's smart."

I stood then, and she watched me through narrowed eyes as I rounded the table and sat across from her instead. With a smug smile, I laced my hands behind my head and sat back. "Smart indeed."

Leona rolled her eyes. "Oh so funny, Fawkes—"

I cut her off with a forced dry heave. She let out a scowl as her mother laughed out.

"I'm going to take this food to Mae," Natalia told us, carrying a bowl of stew. When she winked at her daughter, Leona's back straightened.

A familiar tension returned, and even though silence fell over the room, the words we had spoken out of both anger and confusion rang loudly as if they'd been stored within the walls.

But after everything that happened last night, I hoped she was ready to—

"I'm not leavin' with ye and Mae," Leo announced.

Her words were like a slap across the face, jarring my entire being. "W-What?"

She crossed her arms, blowing a curl out of her face through her bottom lip. "I have accepted a job within Vamir's caravan. I'll be workin' alongside Orin as a sellsword of sorts."

A hard lump grew in my throat. I swallowed it down.

"I'll get to do what I want to, and that's fight." She sounded as if she was still trying to talk herself into it. "I plan to do that for a while and when I've made some money, I'll come find ye and Mae. Hopefully in Elvidawn."

She waited for me to respond, but I was unable to. It felt like she was running away from our problems—running away from *me*.

"Ye're mad," Leona stated after I merely stared down at the table for several moments.

I didn't know if anger was what I felt. I was…crushed. "What about the pact we made?"

She shrugged. "Things change. It's not like ye're leavin' for Elvidawn 'cause of college."

"I have to leave now. And just a few days ago, we decided we'd go to Mirefield first—"

"*Ye* decided," she snapped. "Leavin' Elros has always been on yer terms. Yer conditions, yer plans."

I scoffed. "At one time, it was your *belief* in fate that if it became my time to go, you would as well. It's not like I ever kept you from leaving, Leona. You never had a reason."

"Well I do now." The last of her words died on a break in her voice. She looked away, a growl in her throat. "Fucks sake, I'm so tired of cryin'. If it weren't so close to my quarterly visit from *Mother Red*, this wouldn't be so damn hard."

My brows shot up. She meant she would start bleeding soon.

I cleared my throat. "Well, anything I say right now may sound insensitive—"

"No," she snapped. "Fuckin' speak yer mind."

That was easier said than done—I might as well be handing her a dagger to stab me with. "I think despite your menses…this is just *hard.*"

She sniffled, wiping her nose on her sleeve. "It is." Her eyes lifted to mine. "So, Snow woke up?"

I raised a brow, her shift in the conversation unexpected. "Yes."

"How is she?"

I blew out slowly, almost unsure of what to say. "She's well. In good health. She's just needing some time to think after learning about her powers."

Leona nodded but didn't respond. In the silence that stretched, something tugged on my memories of last night. How Leona had told me she hadn't paid for the potion.

Not yet.

I sucked in a breath. "Leona. How much was that potion?"

Her features buckled, head dropping to the table. "Five hundred gold…or workin' for Vamir to pay off my debt."

I jolted to my feet, slamming my hands on the table. "*No.*"

With a harsh cry, she barreled away from the table, darting for the front door.

I chased after her, refusing to let her run away from another damn problem.

For a woman in metal heeled boots, she was quick. Or maybe I was too exhausted.

I found her on the outskirts of the forest, up past the manor where the land suddenly dropped off the side of a cliff. It had been a few quarters since I'd made my way over here. I smiled up at the cloudy sky that stretched on for leagues, the thick forest below continuing until it faded from our sight due to the mist from the shores of the violent Serpent Sea.

Leona was sitting up on a boulder we often sat on together. Any other time, I would be able to climb up there with ease, but without the use of my right hand, I would have to remain below.

"I never got to thank you," I said loud enough she could hear. "I feel like an ass."

She let out a long huff. "Ye're not an arse, Fawkes. I am." She sniffled and lifted her chin off her knees. Her face was swollen and tear streaked. "And not because of the decision I made. I don't regret that one bit. I couldn't let her die. But…"

Looking down, she reached out her hand. "I don't know why the fuck ye're still down there when ye know I'm half dwarf and can pull ye up without breaking a sweat."

I chuckled. "Just giving you space."

"I don't want it. Get up here."

I took her hand, bracing a foot on a crevice in the boulder. In one tug, Leo hoisted me up to the top, steadying me as I found purchase on the boulders rounded surface. Sitting with my shoulder to hers, I waited for her to continue.

"I have to be honest," she started. "I like Mae. I really do. And I have always hoped ye would get her, Fawkes."

My stomach turned over. I couldn't necessarily say she was mine yet.

Leo went on, "But I've been worried for ye. Ye fell in really deep, really fast." She swallowed. "Ye've been so reckless lately. I was scared she was goin' to hurt ye. And then…ye did get hurt."

I looked down at my arm. "That wasn't her fault though."

"I know." She huffed. "And, I'm sorry I got angry about ye savin' her. It's not like I wanted her gone. I just saw that fuckin' wound and…" She pinched the bridge of her nose. "I hate to see ye hurt. Ye're my brother, my best friend. I want ye happy. I realized I wasn't mad at ye. I wasn't mad at Mae. I was angry with the situation. It's not fair that someone as selfless and carin' as ye are has to go through so much shite."

The hairs on my neck lifted, Natalia's word of the hardships Maelawyn and I might endure to prove our love ringing like a bell in my head.

Leo went on, "By the time I realized I was angry for the wrong reasons, we started to lose her." She sniffled, voice filling with emotion again. "My brother was goin' to lose the woman he loved. The woman he'd risked his life to save. Suddenly, everythin' was all for naught. And I…*I* was goin' to lose a friend." She held both of her fists to her chest. "Somethin' lit on fire in me last night. Right here. Felt like my heart was burnin'. I don't know whether it was the Victors, the gods, fate itself…but I started runnin' back to town. We needed a miracle, so that meant magic." Her eyes squeezed shut. "It was goin' to be my ultimate apology. 'Sorry for bein' a bitch, here's to prove I love ye both.'"

As the tears dropped down her face, my eyes welled with moisture. "Leo."

She wiped her cheeks. "I had planned on breakin' into Rucas's shop to find somethin', but I can't read Elvish. So, I went to Vamir and Orin." She crossed her arms. "Wasn't until I told him it was Mae who was injured that he backed down from twelve hundred gold."

I blinked. "Is he nuts? You could buy four houses in The Flats for that price."

She shrugged. "Ye know how he is. A snob. Said it's rare 'cause no one knows how to make them right now."

Well…he was probably right about that.

"So he offered five hundred gold and"—she scoffed—"that's the amount Da makes in three years. I knew I couldn't even ask my folks for help."

The next part of the conversation only hung in the air—the part where she accepted the offer to pay off her debt.

"It'll be good for me, I think," she said. "I don't regret this decision."

She turned to me, placing an arm on my shoulder. "Don't tell Mae what I did though, all right? She'll get mad, I know she will, and I don't want her pissed at me, too."

I held her gaze for a long moment before taking her hand in mine, squeezing it. "I'm not pissed at you, Leona. I just wanted you to understand why I chose to use that spell. I have a fierce need to protect those that I love. It's something I know I got from my mother, but I also found that in *your* training. You would do the same, Leo. As a matter of fact, going to get that potion and handing over your freedom for a few years to save your friend is the same kind of recklessness you have scolded me for." I shrugged. "What's the difference?"

She squeezed back before dropping my hand, a small smile on her lips. "Ye have something to live for."

I frowned. "What?"

She looked back out to the vast horizon. "Ye've always known where ye wanted to be two seasons from now. Ye have an idea of a future. A goal in mind. Even if things change and ye get off course, ye know what ye want." Her smile widened despite the glisten of tears still lining her eyes. "It's admirable. I wake up everyday and I don't have a focus. I don't know what I want. I'm nineteen and all of the people my age have already settled down. I feel like my life hasn't even begun."

I hadn't known she felt that way. I did sometimes too. I was a year older than her and hadn't married or started a family yet either.

But I had been working toward my future, even if it felt obscured. Discussing my dreams with Mae felt like the beginning of the rest of my life.

Yet, here I was at a crossroads once more.

Leo rested her arms and chin on her knees, a melancholy sigh escaping her. "I was just frustrated because I thought ye were riskin' it all for a few moments"

I shook my head. "Leona, I didn't risk my future to save Mae's life. I risked my life to save Mae because she *is* my future."

I hoped.

Leona lifted her head. "I know that now," she murmured. "And that's why this'll be good for me. I suddenly have a goal."

I closed my eyes. "What does this mean for Orin and you?"

Her shrug came too quickly. "He proposed, so—"

"*What?*" My heart dropped into my stomach. "You're joking."

She shook her head. "Don't worry. I haven't given him an answer yet." She sighed, and the sound was full of so much frustration. "I just…wish for more. Even at the tavern, the moment Orin and I stepped into that bedroom, I just fell into the same motions I always do. And he was just like every person I have ever slept with. Maybe I'm bored. Maybe I choose borin' people. I don't know."

My stomach was in knots. "I wish more for you too, though I have to say I no longer see him as a threat."

She rolled her eyes. "Maybe I'll find some cute mage lass on my adventure and tell Orin to hit the road."

I snorted. "I think I like that better for you, but I may be biased."

As we both laughed, I wrapped an arm around her shoulders. She leaned into me, and for a long moment we just stared out. I wasn't sure if she was thinking the same, but I was reminded as I looked as far as my eyes could see that this was only a small part of Xalador, and that the journey awaiting us would no doubt take us a distance I currently couldn't fathom. Eventually, we could end up so far from each other, it would possibly take a season or two to catch up.

What if I never saw her again?

The thought ripped through me, eyes burning as tears began to form. "I hate this."

She looked up at me. "So do I."

"I'm going to miss you terribly."

She cupped my face. "Ye'll have Mae."

The tears fell. I couldn't tell her. Couldn't tell her that I might not.

"But I'm goin' to miss ye too, Fawkes." She wiped the tears from my cheeks. "Leavin' Elros doesn't feel like leavin' home, but leavin' without ye does."

"Then don't go," I gritted out. "We can just run and figure out how to pay Vamir back later."

Her freckles disappeared beneath the red of her cheeks. "We have enough enemies, Varys. We do not need more."

I wanted to say I didn't care, but she was right. "Then once we make it to Elvidawn, I will save every extra silver I can to get you out of debt early."

"Ye have to get to Elvidawn, settle down, and buy Mae a house first."

Every word about Maelawyn was a deeper thrust of the dagger embedded in my chest.

"I'll be fine, Fawkes." She settled against me more. "Just promise me that ye'll keep trainin', don't blow ye'self up with magic, and ye'll take care of Snow. If I know ye're doin' all of that, then I'll rest easy at night."

With a deep, steadying breath, I nodded. "I promise."

Leo sat up then, a grin on her face as she hopped down from the boulder. "All right, get yer arse down here."

I blinked in confusion and watched her pull two wooden swords from underneath a bush—the same swords we'd used at the beginning of my training.

I grinned and slid down myself, barely catching the sword she tossed me. I hissed under my breath when it met with the tender skin of my arcane scars, switching it to my other hand.

Leona's chin dipped, a roguish smile on her lips. I would miss that look—the expression informing me I was about to get my ass handed to me.

Lifting her sword and crouching into a defensive position, she purred, "Let's see what that left hand can do."

CHAPTER 52

Maelawyn

When I had opened the door to the Cauldücen's bathing room, I had not expected to be met with complete darkness. Quickly realizing what the burning lantern outside of the door was for, I lifted it from the wall and held the light inside.

There were stone stairs leading down into a cavernous room. I knew the Cauldücen manor had been built into the side of a cliff, and knew dwarves could craft entire rooms from stone. When I reached the bottom, it seemed Duros had decided to leave this space natural and raw.

The latrine was on the far wall along with a basin of water. There were dozens of candles sitting around a wide, shallow pit, and to my left was a space with some kind of lever and spout embedded into the stone walls. The damp air smelled of minerals and earth, and had notes of the same crisp and sweet scent of rain.

I quickly determined this was my favorite bathing chamber I had ever been in.

Kneeling, I took one of the candles and lit it with the lantern fire. One by one, I ignited the others until the room was bright with warm candlelight. It all would have been so peaceful, but I couldn't hear anything from upstairs, and the sound of my breathing bouncing through the room only reminded me I was alone—something I had asked for out of a moment of uncertainty, but now wasn't sure I wanted. I hated myself for hurting him, my fight-or-flight response making me so damn indecisive when fear overwhelmed me.

I realized the shallow pit was the tub, but there was no water. Another strange spout was on the side of the wall, the lever currently pointing down. Bracing myself, I slowly pulled up—

Water roared as it plunged into the pit. I let out a screech in surprise, immediately pushing the lever back down. The water stopped falling, and the amount that had pooled below drained into a small, round metal grate I hadn't seen before.

The door to the bathing room opened. I turned to find Leona walking down the stairs. "Damn, I hoped ye had already washed up," she said.

I winced. "I'm sorry, I haven't even started."

"No worries. I just smell awful."

When she stepped off the last step and came to me, I suddenly understood what she meant. Sweat dripped from her hairline, dampening her shirt around her armpits and the cleavage of her breasts. She had pulled her curls into a very tight bun, but the short and frizzy ones had escaped.

"You can go first," I said, stepping aside. "I was trying to figure out the tub anyway."

Leona's head tipped back with a laugh. "Ah, I forget there are people who haven't been shown how to use a faucet. Dwarven mechanism. Pull the lever up to release the water but make sure to cover the drain hole first."

She pointed to a flat stone I hadn't seen beside the tub, perfect for the size of the small grate. I took it, reached down into the tub and settled the stone on top of the drain.

"How does this all work?" I asked. "You don't have to go to the stream every other day for water?"

Leona shook her head as she unbuckled the waist cinch around her. "Nope. There's an underground spring within the cliff this manor was built into. Da ran metal pipin' through the house that allows spring water to come to each faucet. Pullin' the lever pumps water from the spring. Then beneath the tub and shower, Da cut out a drain that washes out somewhere into the forest."

I tilted my head. "What's a shower?"

Leo grinned and pointed to the space with the first spout I'd seen. "It's a stand up bath. I use it for quick wash-offs. But in Gor Thorüm, it's supposedly the most amazin' bathin' experience, especially since they have broilers and can heat their water."

I turned to her. "You don't have a broiler here in the house?"

Leona laughed again. "Oh, no. Da says those rooms are *massive* with several fires and all burned by coal. So, we still have to boil our water if we want a hot bath. Today, I'm good with a cold one."

I nodded. "I actually prefer cold baths. I don't think I realized until now it's because I'm the Nexus of Storm and cold baths remind me of rain water. It's probably why my skin is always cold too."

Leona rubbed her chin in thought. "Well, if ye like rain, maybe ye should take a shower and I take a bath? That way we both get cleaned."

I agreed and she led me over to the shower area. It wasn't until I got closer I noticed the floor wasn't flat, but was slightly caved in toward another small drain.

Leona took hold of the lever and pulled up. Instead of a gush, the water came down in sprinkling streams. "Go ahead. I gotta go get more soap."

As she rushed back upstairs, I quickly took off my pants and tunic and walked into the space. The moment my feet hit the cool, wet ground, chills rushed along my body. I stepped under the stream of water and sighed as I wet my hair, breathing in the spring water's scent of minerals and earth.

The door opened and closed. I brushed the water from my eyes to find Leona carrying down a basket. She reached in and handed me a bar of soap with lavender and rose petals encased in the solidified beeswax. "There's a towel in the basket as well," Leona said before pulling her tunic off. "Oh, and I figured ye wouldn't want to put on the same clothes so, I brought ye one of my chemises. Might be a little big on ye, but it's just to sleep in."

I thanked her and began to lather the soap in my hair. Lost in relaxation, I barely noticed Leona had gone stiff when she'd pulled off her breeches. "Fuckin' dammit," she huffed.

"What's wrong?"

With a sigh, she tossed her pants and tunic into a corner. "I knew it was comin' but I was hopin' that bitch would stay away for a few more days."

My head jeered back. "What…bitch?"

"Mother Red," she said over her shoulder as she headed to the bath. "I got my bloods."

I grimaced. "Oh, I'm sorry."

She shrugged as she started the water and stepped down into the tub. "Bah, I'll be all right. Not like I'm the only person in the world who has to deal with it."

I looked away. "I haven't bled in several quarters."

The water sloshed as she turned to me, resting her arms up on the ledge. "How come?"

I shrugged. "If you would have asked me that a week ago, I would have told you it's my Pallid Curse. But now? I'm not sure what to believe. Maybe it's because I'm a nexus. Maybe it's from all the stress on my body."

She nodded in understanding. "There was one time, back when I started gettin' serious about my trainin', I didn't bleed for a whole season." She pushed off the side and dipped her head under, grabbing her own bar of soap when she came back up. "Point is, Mother Red is an absolute cunt. It's goin' to be such a bummer on the road."

I rinsed the soap from my legs. "Well, just know I'm more than willing to help you. I'll even do your laundry if your cramps get bad."

Leona's mouth parted, her forehead wrinkling as her brows turned down sadly. "I'm sure ye would. Ye are so kind Snow, and I'm really happy to know I have ye as a friend."

My pulse skipped. Why did it sound like she was about to tell me something bad?

Leona ran the soap over her neck and collar bone. "I guess

Varys hasn't had a chance to tell ye. I'm not goin' to be leavin' with ye two after all."

My eyes went wide. "Why?"

She stretched. "I acquired some debt and to pay it off, I now have a job. I will be leavin' with my new boss after the Fest of Change."

Finished with my shower, I pulled the lever down and walked to the basket, taking a towel. Disappointment tugged at my insides. She was the closest friend I'd had since Kendra. "How long will you have to work?"

She shrugged, palms up. "Depends on how much Vamir pays me—"

"*Vamir?*" I exclaimed. "You'll be working for Vamir?"

Leona took a large breath and held it as she submerged beneath the water. She was under for long enough, I started to tiptoe toward the ledge.

The water's surface splashed as she came back up gasping, a smile on her face. "Victors, that's refreshin'. Will ye hand me a towel?"

Pulling herself from the tub, she sat on the side of it and gestured for me to do the same after I gave her the other towel. I moved aside one of the candles and sat, patting my body dry.

With a sigh, Leona said, "Aye. I'll be workin' alongside Orin and protectin' the caravan from their many wolf and bear encounters, along with the possible bandit attack." Her smile didn't meet her eyes. "It will be good for me. I've always trained to fight, but I don't have much experience. Now I will."

I nodded in understanding as I dried my hair. "Well, I hope everything goes well and you're able to pay off your debt quickly. I must say, I am sad. I was really looking forward to getting to know you more."

Her chest puffed as her lips clamped together, as if she were holding something back. "I'll…" She cleared her throat. "I'll meet up with ye and Varys as soon as I can. Will ye promise me somethin', though?"

"Of course."

She took a breath, blowing her wet curls off her face. "Varys can take care of himself. But I just worry about him sometimes. Promise me ye won't let him do anythin' stupid."

Her words made my stomach turn over. "Like…cast a spell that might kill him."

Tension formed between us.

"I didn't mean—"

"No," I said. "I'm not going to let him do anything like that ever again. I can't handle knowing he almost died because of me." A knot lodged in my throat. "And that's why I chose for us to not be together right now."

"*What?*" she breathed.

"I don't want to hurt him again." I crossed my arms over my breasts. "But until I'm bound to my nwív, I might. I want to be good for him. I want to deserve him. But I'm not any of those things. I'm a liar. A monster."

She stared at me for a long moment, her lips pressed together and eyebrows pinched as if she were thinking hard.

"Do ye want to know *why* Varys can't love a liar?" she asked.

Her words knocked the air from my chest, but I nodded. She looked off, as if she were viewing a scene playing out before her.

"A wolf pack killed his mother," she began. "A pack that found him first. He hid inside a hollowed log, and got stuck inside. He was mauled. Still has a few scars, like the one through his eyebrow. But the only reason he'd even found himself in trouble was because he lied about how far he would go into the forest."

The hairs raised on my arms. I pulled the towel around me tighter.

Leona went on, "He became severely claustrophobic. It's why he likes that big bedroom of his and opens windows often when he's overwhelmed."

My chest tightened as I thought back to how I found the window in the guest room open this morning and wondered if he had been anxious because of my condition.

"For a while, he closed himself off from others," Leo told me. "He was very shy as a boy, but that just got worse when she died. Even around me, he was quiet. Let me decide what we'd do, where we'd go. Krystan had been my trainer, but I'd gone on to teach m'self. I think Varys stuck beside me because he knew I had a sword." She sighed. "When he became of trystin' age, he started tryin' to work on himself more. Heal a little. Nobody cared that he was shy or awkward, but I don't think he liked bein' like that. Mainly, I think he knew if he didn't start presentin' himself in public more, he was goin' to miss his chance with you."

My cheeks warmed. "There were many years, I don't think I saw him more than once a quarter."

She nodded. "Unfortunately, by the time he felt comfortable with who he was, had accepted himself and all his quirks, he felt ye were completely out of reach and around that same time, another came forward with interest." Her eyes rolled. "Elise Carrington. She was sweet and at the beginnin', gentle with Varys's trauma. I don't know all of the details but she did help him heal."

I swallowed down the bitterness. I had no room to be jealous, not now, not then. It hadn't been his fault I couldn't have him.

"However," Leona continued. "Varys was very busy with his studies. He couldn't drop everythin' when she wanted sex all the time. Then, one day, he found her ridin' a married man's cock."

I frowned, a heaviness on my heart. "I heard about that. I didn't realize that's how things ended between them."

Leona gave a nod with pursed lips. "Apparently, she was only usin' Varys to cover up the affair." She sighed. "Varys learned a lot in their romance. What love was, wasn't. What he wanted and didn't. It wasn't their breakup that hurt him the most, wasn't even her unfaithfulness. It was the lies."

My eyes burned with tears. "Then I'm right. I shouldn't—"

"No. Ye're *wrong*." She took my hands in hers. "Ye lied, yes. About a lot, yes. But ye did so to protect ye'self. And I know for a fact Varys sees the difference, even if he didn't originally. Ye may have lied, but ye aren't a *liar*, Mae. Ye're a survivor."

Her words struck me, and the breath I took was full and gasping, as if I had been underwater, drowning and struggling to reach the surface.

I had survived.

Eighteen long years of abuse and neglect.

Unexplained illnesses.

Assault.

Agonizing pain due to an inescapable transformation.

But I had *needed* that change. It had been hideous, frustrating, terrifying. I had morphed into a monster born of hate and suffering.

And yet, love lay beneath. Varys had seen that. Varys had fought all of my ugliness because he knew who I really was. That rising storm hadn't been my nwív. It had been *me*. My true reemergence had been becoming the woman I was now, releasing the old shell I had created for survival.

I'd broken free of my chrysalis. Why was I still so scared to take flight?

"Ye love him."

My breath hitched, but I nodded.

She grinned as she stood, reaching into the basket and tossing me a soft chemise. "Then, allow ye'self to, Snow."

CHAPTER 53

Varys

I sighed as I let the coins fall back into my purse. I had twelve silver pieces. In Elros, that could get me about a week's worth of food. Our journey to Mirefield on foot would take at least a week if we didn't stop, and we would have to. I had a feeling this was going to be pretty hard on Maelawyn. I was not going to be able to afford a room at an inn every night along the way.

"You haven't touched your food," Natalia said to me as she came to sit across from me. The chicken and potatoes were amazing, but my stomach tumbled with too much worry to feel hungry.

"I'm trying," I told her, pocketing my coin purse. "I know I need to eat."

"Between you and Mae, I've made too much food." She sighed. "She hasn't eaten either. I'm hoping that she'll come to dinner after their…" Her words trailed away as she looked toward the hall. "Ah, speaking of."

My pulse quickened as I looked over my shoulder. Maelawyn and Leona giggled about something under their breath as they came into the room. Leona promptly left her side to sit down next to me. "I'm starved," she groaned, snatching a leg off the roasted hen in the center of the table.

Maelawyn smiled warmly as she stopped before the stairs. Her wet hair lay in loose curls over one shoulder, her face still dewy from the bath, giving her skin a lustrous and silky appearance. She had obviously borrowed the chemise she wore from Leona. The skirt was too short and only came down to her knees, and the bodice was too wide in the shoulders, making one side slip down with every small movement.

"Mae, dear, are you going to eat something?" Natalia asked.

Maelawyn's eyes had lingered on mine. I watched the way her throat worked on a gulp, and didn't dare to let my gaze travel down where I'd already seen the hint of her peaked breasts beneath the thin material.

"I'm not very hungry," she responded, finally taking her eyes off me. "And I'm not exactly dressed for dinner."

"*'m nawt eether*," Leona uttered through a full mouth, tugging at her own chemise. She swallowed before continuing. "We're all family here."

Maelawyn's smile widened. "Thank you. For everything. Truly." She bowed her head. "I wouldn't be here if it weren't for all of you. I'm just still feeling a little disoriented and going to turn in early."

I nodded. "Let us know if you need anything."

She turned to climb the stairs, but paused, twisting back to me. "Will you be joining me in bed?"

Heat blasted through me like I'd jumped straight into the fire on the stove. Leo choked on her food. Natalia cleared her throat and removed herself from the dining room entirely.

Maelawyn slapped a hand over her mouth. "Oh gods. No. *Shit.* That's not what I meant." Her face washed a deep magenta as her hands moved frantically as if they would help her find the right words. "Are you going to sleep in the bed beside me like you did last night since there isn't another bed? Because that's fine. I'm *fine* with that. I just didn't know if I should leave the candle lit in case I fall asleep before you..."

She went on, and I couldn't help but laugh. I had never heard her ramble before. She didn't even notice when I rose and walked to her, voice dying out when I took her shoulders.

"Don't worry about it, Little Bird." I kissed the top of her head. "I'll be taking the settee tonight."

I felt her body slump beneath me, as if that disappointed her. "Oh."

"Get some rest." I guided her toward the stairs. "We have a long journey ahead of us."

She didn't respond as she ascended. I had to force my eyes away when she reached the top of the stairs—that godsdamn chemise was short indeed.

Duros had come in from outside when I returned to the table. After gulping down a pint of mead, he announced, "I know what I'll be sayin' to get me rosebud out of this agreement."

Natalia smiled down at her husband as she massaged his shoulders. "Come up with something convincing?"

Leona let out a long breath. "Mum, Da, I appreciate it but—"

"I won't be havin' me daughter start her life in debt," Duros said. "We make extra at the fest every year. Whatever we bring in, I'll be offerin' as a down payment if he accepts I bear the cost."

Leona frowned. "The money ye earn at the fest is for the winter."

"And we'll be fine, rosebud," Natalia assured her daughter. "My garden was very fruitful this year thanks to the rain. All we'll need is meat, but if we need to go on a bread and vegetable diet until spring, we can do that."

"*Ye* can do that," Duros grumbled. "If we run out of coin for meat, I'll be goin' huntin'."

Natalia chuckled. "You said that during the terrible blizzard we had three years ago and the moment you stepped out of the manor, you decided my vegetable stew wasn't as bad as you remembered it."

We all laughed. Duros crossed his arms. "Fair point, Nat." He looked to his daughter. "What ye did Leona was brave and commendable—"

"And I would do it again, Da. That's why I have an issue with ye takin' on the debt." She took his hand, emerald eyes hard and serious. "Ye and Mum have given me so much, and have taught me that there is no greater joy than to help someone in need. It's time I put my skills to work and help people, 'cause that's what I'll be doin' in this caravan. Protectin'. Servin'. I know I was upset and scared yesterday, but this will truly be good for me."

I found myself no longer listening. Just a few hours ago, she had told me she hated leaving. Now it seemed she was excited.

Everything was moving too fast. *Changing* too fast.

They continued to talk as I excused myself from the table and walked into the kitchen. Just as I had breathed in the sweet aroma of the air, Natalia let out a shout and rushed in.

"Almost forgot my pie," she murmured as she passed me, grabbing a hot pad, and pulling a golden pie from the stone oven. A dark, fruity filling bubbled out of the lattice. After she placed it on the counter to cool, she went to the basin and began to wash the dishes.

"I'm surprised you aren't up there with Miss Mordaunt," she said to me.

I shrugged, eyeing the pie. "We had a bit of a disagreement earlier. I'm giving her some space."

Chuckling, she said, "Well that's good, given you were practically on top of her for four days straight."

My cheeks heated, her words instantly compelling me to think about things I shouldn't. Natalia knew it too, her face scrunching with a playful smile—an expression that reminded me she was Leona's mother.

The thoughts didn't go away though. Not when I moved to the bathing room, not when I washed my face with cold water and shaved. Not even as I sat on the edge of the stone tub for a moment trying to swallow down the knot in my throat that had formed from hearing the last of Leona and Duros's conversation.

I was being selfish. I felt like I might lose my best friend. I wanted us to leave Elros together.

I wanted Maelawyn.

Gods, I wanted her.

I couldn't stop thinking about how her skin felt on mine, how her breasts had felt against my palm. Couldn't get her moans out of my head, my name a beg on her plum lips. The way her body had bent and writhed as my fingers dipped in and out of her.

She'd been so godsdamn wet.

My pulse was pounding, blood surging with need as I sat on the settee in the commons room and stared into the fire on the hearth. If I didn't shut down the thoughts, if I didn't remind myself that she didn't want the same right now, I was going to be up all night.

Returning to the dining room, I found my food still on the table. It was cold now, and although I hated to waste, I tossed it into the cinders still burning in the stone oven. Natalia was washing up the last of the dishes.

"I'll get mine," I told her.

She shook her head and took the plate from me. "You should be sleeping."

"I'm going."

When I turned, my eyes snagged on the pie. There was only one slice left, big enough for probably two people.

Or one person who hadn't eaten all day and had a bit of a sweet tooth.

Natalia scoffed as she watched me place the slice on a clean plate and grab a fork. "You barely ate your dinner, but you're going to eat dessert?"

I chuckled and headed for the stairs. "It's not for me."

"Who is it?"

"Me," I said.

"Come in."

Maelawyn's soft invite sounded hesitant, so I only cracked the door and peered inside. She was busy shifting around and tossing the quilt over her more.

"I have something for you," I told her.

Her eyes brightened and she waved me inside. "Shut the door behind you," she said.

I swallowed, but did so. Her smile was bright as she took in the sight of the pie, inhaling in awe. "Really?"

I nodded. "I know you said you're not hungry, but—"

"You brought me dessert." She took the plate. "You remembered."

"That…you love sweets?"

A nod.

I laughed. "Of course I did. I love—"

I cut myself off, pressing my lips together tightly. When Maelawyn's smile fell, my stomach went with it.

"Varys." The breath she took was thin. "You can say it."

My chest wrenched. I looked away, combing my hair back as I sat on the edge of the bed. "I didn't mean to."

She didn't respond.

"But…" I smiled warmly as I watched her cut into the pie with her fork. "Thank you."

My words seemed to catch her off guard, the metal fork clinking against the plate as it slipped from her fingers. "Oh gods. I didn't thank you for—"

"No. Thank *you* for allowing me to express my feelings despite yours."

Her eyes went wide.

I continued, "I just don't know if I feel comfortable speaking those words right now. I don't want to make things worse between us."

Her breaths became shaky, and I worried I was *already* making things worse.

"That's why I want you to say it," she said quietly. "I need your reminder as I work through my head that you're still going to be there when I'm ready."

I swallowed. "You understand that's…very confusing for me?"

She looked away, placing the plate down. "You're right. I'm sorry." She pulled her legs to her chest beneath the quilt, resting her chin on her knees. "I don't want to hurt you, Varys."

"You won't."

"I *did*." She jabbed a finger toward my arm. "I cannot allow that to happen again."

I took the hand extended toward me. "Mae, it's—"

"Don't call me that."

I winced. "Sorry. Habit."

She nodded. "It's not that I don't like Mae anymore, it just hasn't felt *right* since I woke up," she told me. "Every time you say

Mae, I feel like you're talking to someone else. You're not talking to…" When her eyes lifted to meet mine, I could have sworn I saw a flash of light like distant lightning behind her enlarged pupils. "Me. Maelawyn, the Nexus of Storm. That's who I am."

I nodded slowly, my skin pimpling with goosebumps. Her name didn't seem the same to me either anymore, as if it was now a pennant of her power.

With a steadying breath, I leaned forward. "We have both had a pretty taxing day. I don't want it to end in tears." I picked up the plate of pie, handing it back to her. "I want to see you smile."

She did, and when she took a bite of the pie, her grin spread.

"Gods, you're adorable," I said, and she chuckled. "If Leona were in here, she'd call you a pixie."

She took another bite. "Why?"

I tapped my chin, trying to remember a certain faerie tale Leo had told me. "Something about a group of faeries discovering sugar gave them a high and would steal sugar cubes to sell in their faerie blackmarket. And the faeries against the usage of sugar called those who ate it *pixies*."

She laughed out, cutting off another piece. "I would definitely be a part of the pixies if I were a faerie."

I lay back, hands behind my head. "I wonder if we'll see faeries with The ReEmergence of Magic."

"That would be amazing."

I nodded. "I'm not sure what all The ReEmergence entails, but I don't think we'll know until we travel into other areas of this world."

"I have to say"—she put the plate back down—"Besides having to escape because people want us dead, I am excited to see the rest of Xalador. I've never been outside this town."

"Not even once?"

"Nothing past that tree." She winced. "Which reminds me…"

Reaching behind the pillows, she pulled out a familiar book. My eyes widened when *Ít Nánöweth* began to glow again.

She rolled her eyes. "Apparently, it's a bit dramatic and is going to glow *every* time I come in contact with it." She handed it to me as I shifted to lay on my side instead. "I read it all."

My mouth parted. "Already?"

She nodded, an excited smile rising on her face. "I couldn't stop. Not only was it about my powers but…" She sighed. "Varys, I can *read*."

My chest swelled. For me, waking up one day and learning I could read Elvish had been exciting, but I already knew how to read Common, a little Halfling, and some Dwarvish. I hadn't realized that this part of our reemergence had changed Maelawyn's life. If everything around us had been written in Elvish, how different would her life have been?

"I have a couple others in Elvish you can read as well," I told her.

"I'd love that." She stretched out her legs beneath the covers, the tips of her toes almost touching my ribs. "But about *Ít Nánöweth*. It's more about the history of nexi than a guide. However, I learned about this." She held her left arm up. "It's the mark of the nexus, the *çirö*. It's a magical mark to display what I am, but also has the ability to open and close chasms."

My breath hitched. "You think you can close it?"

She tilted her head back and forth. "I don't know yet. But I want to try. It's my fault it's even there." She tossed her wet hair over her shoulder and began to braid it. "When I was eight, I fell from the tree and broke my arm. It was an open fracture; my bone broke through my skin, which bled. If I understand correctly, a chasm is created by spilling a nexus's blood and then commanding it to open by intention."

"You're saying that's when the chasm opened?"

Her forehead pinched. "I'm not sure. Is it possible that my blood and the magic within it stayed dormant all these years?"

I rubbed my chin in thought, thinking back to the first time I went into the clearing and felt the pressure. I quickly told her about my first experience with the tree. "Something had been there long before the chasm was opened. The place was riddled with magic. Your nexus power is not of the veins, so perhaps you're correct. Maybe your blood spilled and created the ability to open a chasm, but couldn't until The ReEmergence."

Maybe The ReEmergence wasn't just for the descendants of the elves. Maybe it was a reemergence of *all* magic.

She nodded. "So I reemerged and my nwív acquired the ability to overwhelm me. When she did, she went to that dormant spot of magic and opened the chasm. I do speculate she used more of my blood to help the spell though." She sucked in a breath and glanced at the empty potion bottle still on the side table. "I get my memories back in waves, and this one is still in fragments, like I'm looking through a broken window. But I remember Rucas whipping me."

I went rigid. "I…forgot to tell you."

Or perhaps I had chosen to forget. How I'd lost a piece of my very soul seeing that black ooze. The scent, the terror, the unadulterated primal rage that had ripped from me when she began to die.

She merely shrugged—she didn't know the extent of it. "It's probably better I remember this way instead of finding out among…" She blinked and shook her head. "Everything else."

I would tell her when I knew I wouldn't have the urge to wrap her into me and never let her go. She didn't want that side of me right now. So I buried the knowledge.

"I think that's when I freed the nwív with the command words," she told me.

I tilted my head. "What command words?"

"Saeör ít ölsta xera."

Free the rising storm. Words the nwív had spoken to me as well.

She sighed, running her fingers along the *çirö* on her arm. "If it's all right with you, I'd like to try to close the chasm tomorrow before we begin our journey. I feel like it's the only right thing to do."

I smiled. "I think that's a very brave and wise decision."

She looked away. "I'm…trying. I'm scared, and I don't know how to use this power yet, but I'm ready to start learning how. I can't be afraid of it." She lifted her chin. "When I woke up today, I felt like I had changed. I *am* a nexus. There's no point in running away from it any longer, not when we have enemies and dryamorn hunting us."

"And I'll be here through it all. If you want."

She nodded. "I do. We are different streams. I'm an entirely different magic. But we are still *Vyl'kríev.* We need to stick together."

"Agreed." I sat up and stood to my feet, taking the empty plate from her. It dawned on me she had eaten the entire piece in three or four bites. If I hadn't been such a terrible baker, I would have tried to bake her another. "Well, get some sleep. We'll be doing a lot of walking on our journey ahead unless we find a stable and I'm able to buy a horse."

I had no idea how I was going to be able to buy a horse with twelve silver.

Maelawyn's nod was slow and hesitant. With a smile, I took her hand and pressed a kiss to her knuckles. "Good night, Little Bird."

She swallowed. "Good night, Varys."

I began to turn, releasing her hand. Her hold on mine tightened. My pulse skipped in pleasant surprise as I met her eyes once more, warmth spreading from where our skin met.

Her face flushed and for a moment I didn't think she would say anything. Then, "I don't want you to go just yet."

A spark of hope ignited within me.

"I don't want to be alone. Can you just…" She gave a one shouldered shrug. "Stay. We can talk. Or read."

I grinned, and as my body felt like it might start floating away, I was sure this was the happiest I'd ever felt. "I can go get those other elven books. Maybe I can find you more dessert."

Her mouth fell open. "Stop trying to seduce me."

I blinked. "What?"

"What?" She winked.

I narrowed my eyes, glaring playfully as I dropped her hand. "I'll be right back."

"Do you want a bite?" Maelawyn asked as I placed the other two elven books Meri had given me down on the side table. I had found a tea cake Natalia had made for breakfast earlier today.

"No, thank you." I chuckled. "I thought you weren't one for sharing your dessert anyway."

"That was before…" She trailed off, taking a bite. "This is delicious."

Before. Before everything at the tavern. Before, as she had said, our relationship advanced to a level where she *would* share her dessert. We had gotten there. Had shared a berry tart before I tasted it on her tongue.

How could we be on that level but not be together?

The thought irritated me, and I didn't want to be irritated with her. She was obviously very confused right now.

I had grabbed Leona's copy of *The Dragonhart Series* downstairs and headed over to the corner chair with it. Maelawyn watched me from the end of her fork.

"Which book should I read first?" she asked.

I opened my book, finding where I had left off. "Well, unfortunately I haven't had a chance to read either of them. I believe *Uthörium's Glory* is an elf's recollections."

She picked that one up. "I don't think I care. I'm just so excited to read."

I smiled. "I'm happy for you. And I'm sure on our journey, I can continue our reading lessons in Common."

She nodded, and we fell into a content silence as we began to read our choices. It reminded me of the times my father and I would sit and read together, but this had an air of intimacy and peace I'd never felt with anyone before.

It was…something I had imagined doing with my wife someday.

I found myself not reading, glancing up from beneath my lowered lashes, absolutely lost in her beauty. One side of the chemise hanging off her shoulder, her knees hiked up to support the book in her lap. The golden glow of the evening sun's light giving her features a warm coloration, darkening those beautiful plum lips, her bottom currently between her teeth as she read. She bit her lip in focus, I realized, but she also did so when flirting. With her sitting there in bed, looking absolutely stunning, reading a book…I wasn't sure I knew the difference anymore.

"Gods," she suddenly muttered. "I don't know what's so glorious about this Uthörium. All he's done is try to fuck a dryad and hunt faun for sport."

I jerked my chin back. "Krayd's chaos, I'm sorry. I wouldn't have suggested it to you if I'd known the content."

She laughed, closing the book. "It's fine. I think I was just expecting a story."

Her eyes trailed downward to the book in my hand. Head tilting, she asked, "What are *you* reading?"

My fingers gripped the edge of the pages, stomach fluttering as I glanced down to the words written across the page. I knew I only had seconds to come up with a decent answer, or I would have to tell her I was reading something written by *me*.

"A…book," I said, instantly regretting ever responding.

"Obviously," Maelawyn drawled dryly. She put her book down and pulled the covers off. My heart drummed as she walked over with a devious grin and I was too distracted by the sight of her bare, slender legs, I didn't have time to react before she snatched the book from my hands.

She frowned as she looked over the cover. "Aw, it's in Common."

A breathy, nervous laugh rattled my chest. "Yeah. It's called *The Dragonhart Series*."

She flipped through the pages. "What's it about?"

I winced. I was sure that was my least favorite question of all time. How was I supposed to summarize my entire book in a few sentences?

"It's about a woman who discovers a secret about the enemy dragon kingdom when she finds one in his human form." I shrugged. "There's adventure, mystery, political intrigue, and romance."

Her eyes glistened with delight. "That sounds like an incredible story." She tapped her lips in thought. "But I must ask something…"

She leaned down, bracing the arms of the chair on either side. I swallowed as I watched her dark brows angle, eyes narrowing as they stared into mine, jaw cocked in an untold annoyance. That look on her face was by far the most intimidating she'd given me yet.

Because I was *thoroughly* attracted to it.

"The series," she began, "is called dragon *heart*, like what beats in our chest?"

The thing currently pounding in mine.

"Or," she continued, "is it *hart*, like the Elvish word for *soul* and half of the meaning of *your* surname?" She grinned. "It's a bit on the nose, Wynhart."

My eyes went wide beneath her growing smile. She'd figured it out. Originally, I had swapped *heart* for *hart*, my sixteen-year-old mind believing it to be clever. No one had ever caught on. When I'd reemerged, my last name had taken on a brand new meaning. *Wyn* was light, *Hart* was soul. I'd always found it interesting that Wynhart was not my mother's family name, but my father's—my non-Elven-blooded father.

Hart also coincidentally fit the title of my series as well, *Dragonhart* meaning *Dragon soul*.

Chuckling, I took a deep breath. "Fine. You caught me."

She straightened with a happy shout and threw a celebratory fist in the air. I pressed a finger to my lips and shushed between snickers.

"I'm not ready for a lot of people to know I write this series," I told her. "Not even Leo—it's her favorite. But it became a bit popular and I had to make three extra copies of each book for the library alone so people wouldn't fight over who got to borrow them first."

She placed a hand over her chest. "I solemnly swear I won't tell a soul if..." She pushed the book into my hands. "You read it to me."

"What?" My entire body locked up, clutching the book as I stared up at her. These words were not just a story, but my rawest thoughts and ideas. Some of the main character's personal views were my own, but how would she feel about me after listening to the sadistic plans of the villain?

I started to sweat. Could I really read my romance scenes out loud to a woman I hadn't slept with?

"Please?" She asked when I didn't respond, smiling softly. "I want to hear your story. And maybe someday, I'll be able to read it again for myself."

Something about her words jarred my memories, recalling the conversation I had with my father. *Read to her*, he had told me. *You may find her wanting more.*

I looked away before I knew I would get lost in her amethyst gaze, snickering under my breath. "Fine."

She beamed, rushing back to the bed. She abandoned her plate of cake to the end table and climbed in. I couldn't help the massive grin on my face as I sat on the other side of her. We huddled close, and despite my hammering heart, I opened to the first page and began, "Once upon a time—"

"Oh my gods," she snorted. "That's so cheesy…"

Her words trailed off when she noticed the disgruntled look on my face. Her hand clamped over her mouth.

"I-It's fine," she said with a wince. "Go on, it's fine."

My nervousness now doubled, I rolled my eyes and continued slowly, "Once upon a time, there was a girl who could not feel the touch of another human. Unfortunately, it was what she wanted more than anything else in the world."

Maelawyn's breath left her, mouth parting. "That's…" She looked up at me, her eyes now glossy. For a moment, she only stared up at me and…I wondered if she had already figured out that the main character was written after my own struggles, how I had also spent years unable to feel much of anything. "That's a beautiful opening. Please. Keep going."

I pressed a kiss to her forehead and she settled against me. I read to her until the glow of the evening sun faded from the room, welcoming in sleep for the both of us.

CHAPTER 54

Maelawyn

No longer were my dreams filled with shattering crystals and screaming. I dreamed of rain, light and refreshing. I dreamed of dancing in it as lips pressed to my neck.

You love him. Allow yourself to.

Leona's words seemed to echo in my head like a lullaby, reminding me of his warm presence beside me. Every breath was filled with his incredible scent, tugging me further into peace. It made waking up effortless, my heart racing to see him again.

I had fallen asleep with my head on his chest. Not because the story wasn't captivating. Varys was as incredible with words on paper as he was in speech, but I had been greatly reminded last night that his voice was intoxicating. Mixed with the heat of our bodies and the exhaustion of the day, I didn't stand a chance.

Neither did he, it seemed. He had fallen asleep at some point too and had never moved to the couch. Our legs were entangled beneath the quilt. His arm was still wrapped around me, the injured one laying limply across his stomach.

We had left the window open all night again. The hairs rose on my arms as I realized the same misty rain I'd seen in my dreams fell outside, permeating the room with a light humidity. I imagined what it might feel like on my skin, wondered if Varys would dance with me in it.

It didn't exactly feel like coincidence that the rain was the same here as it had been in my head. *Ít Nánöweth* had spoken of how my emotions affected my powers since a nexus was a reformed sorcerer. How the Nexus of Air had changed the direction of the winds with a simple huff, and how the Nexus of Fire had set a house aflame from an angry outburst. Varys and I hadn't been able to discuss how my sorcerer magic and nexus power worked together, and there hadn't been much within the book on both.

All I knew was that this rain was like the soft, languid peacefulness I currently felt in bed with Varys. I rolled back to him, laying my head on his firm chest once more.

He stirred then, taking a deep breath as he buried his face in my hair, pressing tender kisses to the top of my head.

"I could get used to this," he murmured, his voice just above a whisper.

I hummed. "Me too."

His body went taut beneath me. "You…you mean that?"

I rose to my elbows, hovering above him. His blue eyes were still glazed with sleep, his jaw tense as his hands found the curve of my waist.

"I do," I told him, brushing a strand of blue hair from his cheeks. The pull of the connection was tantalizing, my mouth a whisper from his. "I'm just…terrified, but—"

Unable to hold back any longer, I captured his lips. A relieved sound left him as his arms wrapped around me. I melted against him, reminded of the blues in my head as they washed behind my closed eyes. With every turn of the hue, our kiss deepened. His grip on me tightened, and our breaths became heavy as the color of the morning sky at early dawn darkened to the darkest shade of midnight. A color that promised desire and passion.

A breathy whimper left me as his hands kneaded the thin material of the chemise like he was desperate to tear through it. I gasped his name on the small release for air, and he replied with a groan, kissing me again fiercely. He sucked my bottom lip between his teeth, his tongue flicking over the pout as I sighed and sank my hands into his hair. I pulled myself onto him, pressing my hips into his hard need. He ground out my name, my *real* name, and my body lit on fire. My name held power, but on his lips, it held power over *me*.

He broke the kiss only to trail his mouth down to my neck. "Move on me, *aríma,*" he whispered in my ear.

I lost a breath when he rocked against me, his cock like steel between my thighs. The hands on my hips moved beneath the chemise, cupping my ass. I moaned and did what he told me to do, grinding myself against him.

"That's it," he coaxed. "Use me, Maelawyn."

I rolled my hips in a circle, pushing myself into him harder, every touch just a breadth too far from that spot. His pants…I needed them off. I needed his skin on mine.

As if he'd heard my thoughts, he pushed me up, pulling my chemise over my head as I straightened, now naked before him. I didn't have a chance to remove his tunic before it was tossed to the floor and I was flipped to my back.

Our lips crashed into each other again, hips perfectly aligned. A gasping moan tore from the deepest part of me when he slid his thigh up and began to move it up and down my slit.

He grasped the back of my neck, holding his lips to my ear. "What do you want, love?" he asked, a growl in his voice.

I could hardly breathe around the heat, the pleasure. "I want you to touch me."

His tongue ran across my collar bone. "Tell me where."

My face scorched. "Everywhere."

He met my gaze, a small grin on his reddened face. "I plan on it. But if you have no preference…"

He removed his leg, shifting to his side. His hand trailed down my stomach, and my head fell back when he traced the curve between my thigh and center, my dripping entrance trembling with anticipation. His thumb slid between my crease, grazing the bundle of nerves as another finger dipped into me. His body loosened on the gritty moan that scraped from him.

"*Fuck,*" he snarled. "I love how godsdamn wet you get for me."

I let out another whimper, watching him as he focused on the finger sliding in and out of me. His thumb drummed on my bud, dragging sighs and stifled screams from my lips when he applied quick pressure. *Gods,* he knew how to build me up, my climax already so close.

But I wasn't sure it would be fair if I came when he hadn't. Not even at the tavern.

With the hand closest to his breeches, I found his waistband. His eyes went wide when I began to pull them down, letting his cock free.

My mouth went dry. I had felt him, but I never...I had never looked. My breaths came in harsh bursts as I took his length into my hand and began to stroke. He bit his lip, head falling back, the thrusts of his fingers quickening.

"You're perfect," he said between his teeth. "I just...don't know how long I'm gonna..."

I clenched around him, and a broken shout was forced from his gaping mouth. I pumped harder, hands sticky with his pleasure.

He nipped beneath my chin. "*Chaos*, I...I can hardly handle it."

I jerked, his patterns below quickening. Heat was rising, my back uncontrollably arching into his touch, needing more and more.

"I don't want you to handle it." Another stroke up him had him growling my name. "I want you to *lose it.*"

His moans became pleas, voice dying out, eyes squeezing shut as his mouth gaped. He buried his face in the crook of my neck, roaring as he spilled over my hand. My own climax shot through me, but with it my arm began to burn—

Thunder cracked when a bolt of lightning struck a tree outside, a bright flash enveloping the room. We both jumped in surprise, but I screamed, gasping as my heart began to pound painfully, raising the hand still drenched in him to my chest.

"*No!*" I shouted. My climax faded with the thunder echoing over the distant hills. "No, no, *no.*"

Varys shot up. "W-What's wrong? Hey." He cupped my face. "It's all right."

"It's not." I sat up as well, pressing myself against the head-board. "Varys, that was *me*. The lightning strike. When I…"

I let out a sob, unable to finish the words. Realization spread over his face. He glanced down and took my arm.

"Look."

I sucked in a harsh breath as I took in the sight of my slightly glowing lightning marks. The *çirö*.

Tossing the quilt around, I searched for the chemise, pulling it back on when I found it.

Varys stared at me, at the chemise, his features taut. "I…you don't want to continue—"

"Are you kidding me?" I panted. "I'm out of control. I'm using my powers without knowing, they're being triggered by my…" I gulped, cheeks heating. "Emotions."

I stood up, knees still shaking from my pleasure. I didn't face him as I said, "I don't want to hurt you."

Varys let out a harsh breath. "Maelawyn—"

"I'm sorry." I wrapped my arms around myself, staring out at the pouring rain. "I was scared before, but now I'm absolutely posi-tive that until I can get control of my magic and bind myself with my nwív so I don't become a fucking monster, I can't"—I clenched my teeth—"*you* can't be with me. We have to remain—"

"Don't say friends," he bit out behind me, his voice laced with anger. "Godsdammit, *don't* say we're just friends. What we did just now? I don't do that with friends." His voice rose. "I don't do that with just anyone either."

I shook my head. "I wasn't going to say that."

"Then tell me, Maelawyn. What are we?" His voice chased away the remainder of the warmth in my blood. "If we're not two people in love, and we're beyond consorts, then what are we?"

I shook as I stared out the window, watching the gale rush through the trees below. Lightning flashed. "Stop…"

"Stop what? Talking to you?"

"*Stop*…" Thunder rolled.

"Loving you?"

"Just *stop!*" I screeched, spinning back to him and whipping my arms down at my sides. Thunder cracked the air as my *çirö* lit up brightly, jolts racing down my arms, buzzing and sizzling along my fingers.

Varys remained on the bed. He hadn't jumped, hadn't flinched. Had remained unmoved besides the tears filling his eyes, his gaze stoic as he watched the energy until it flickered out.

I lifted my shaking hands to cup my mouth, looking at the man I loved so much but couldn't have.

"Stop," I said through a cry. "We're just *stopped*. At a pause. *Please*."

Varys blinked and his tears fell as well. "I'm sorry."

"You don't know how bad I want you, Varys," I told him. "How badly I want to be yours. How much I…"

I dropped my head to my hands and wept. The mattress groaned as Varys got off, and I felt him stop before me. He took my chin and lifted my gaze to his.

"You can say it," he said, repeating words I had spoken just last night.

I shook my head. "That wouldn't be fair."

He swallowed, releasing his hold on my chin, both hands cupping my cheeks instead. His arcane scar felt rigid against my skin as he studied me for a moment, an endearing smile on his lips.

"When you say those words, let them be a command to release all restraints." His nose touched mine. "For you. For me. For *us*. Be it a year, or five moments from now. My love has no time limit."

Varys

Hoisting the pack on my shoulders, I turned to face the Cauldücen family. I wasn't sure how I was supposed to speak through the knot in my throat.

With Maelawyn's hand in mine, I took a steadying breath. "Well," I swallowed, "I guess we're off then."

Natalia was the first to break, stepping away from Duros to take my shoulders. She embraced me tightly. "This isn't a goodbye," she said sternly. "You know that right?"

I nodded. "I will write." I glanced at Maelawyn. "Maybe we both will."

Maelawyn nodded with a smile as Natalia moved to her, hugging her as well.

"Thank you," Maelawyn murmured. "For everything. Even all those years ago."

"Of course, my dear."

Backing away, Natalia looked toward her husband, wiping her face. Duros nodded and she told us, "When Leona is finished with her job, we've decided to sell tha manor."

It seemed even Leona had been unaware as she snapped her head toward her parents.

Natalia went on, "The age is changing. We feel it best to move into a city where we are more welcome and not so isolated. Elros was a great escape from Gor Thorüm until…"

"Until it wasn't," Duros said, finishing her sentence. "We'll be usin' this next year to sell wares and belongin's we don't need. And we'll use our profit on tha house to both move and hopefully pay off Leona's debt."

Leona's lips spurted as she blew out. "Da, I—"

"It's our decision, rosebud." He crossed his arms. "And for our safety as well."

Leona didn't argue further, turning back to me. For a long moment, we simply stared at each other. She cleared her throat and looked at Maelawyn. "Promise?"

Maelawyn let out a small laugh, her hold on my hand tightening. "I promise, Leo."

I glanced between the both of them, unsure of exactly what promise they meant. My thoughts were cut short when Leo rushed me, throwing her arms around my torso, her face in my stomach. Smiling warmly, I let go of Maelawyn's hand for a moment and hugged her back firmly. She let out an annoyed huff when I kissed the top of her head, but didn't pull away, squeezing me.

"See you soon, Leo," I said. She only nodded into my shirt. I took a breath. "Love you."

She jabbed me in the ribs. "I fuckin' love ye, too, ye big oaf."

We pulled away. Duros shook my hand, "Don't worry about yer father, lad. I'll find 'im." He leaned in, murmuring, "Wouldn't be surprised if he's gone to tha baron."

My brows lifted, reminded of the note he'd left that stated he was with friends. "I hope so then. Maybe he's explaining—"

"Let's not say anymore." Duros held up his thick hands. "Thing about secret missions is ye don't talk about 'em."

I chuckled. "Of course."

After another several moments of goodbyes and tears, I turned from my second family, and Maelawyn and I took the first step of our great journey. It took everything in me not to turn back, to rush and give them all another hug, to beg Leona one last time to come with us.

Natalia was right. This age was changing. I needed to accept it and press on.

Maelawyn kept close as we ventured through the thickwood, keeping our heads down and eyes keen for any guardsmen. I hoped I would be capable of an invisibility spell if we ran into trouble.

The leaves were too wet to crunch beneath our feet which made for a quieter passage through the forest, only the sounds of wildlife and distant groaning trees breaking the silence. Morning mist clung and dampened our clothing. Both of us were without cloaks after my unfortunate mishap at the stream, and the Cauldücen's had none to spare. We would have to buy some at the next town, along with more rations. Natalia had graciously given us two loaves of bread, a quarter of their cheese wheel, and some fruit, along with five gold pieces. She had found out I had little money, and I had practically had my ears ripped clean off from her scolding. It was enough money to get us across the Serpent Sea and if I could be frugal, get us an inn every few nights. I had been so terrible in the past with my money and was kicking myself for it.

Maelawyn seemed in awe of her surroundings and hadn't really looked down from the canopies. In an effort to make conversation, I asked, "Which tree do you like best?"

She hummed in thought. "I guess I like whatever kind of tree I fell from."

"That's a guardian oak tree, like that one," I pointed to a younger oak, its branches only now beginning to twist. "Their branches grow to be several feet long before twisting, and because they often grow close together, it's always hard to tell where one branch ends and another begins. Your guardian oak was probably only a hundred years old or so, so it hadn't connected with others."

Her eyes were wide when I looked back to her. "A hundred years?"

I nodded. "See that one?" I pointed to another further from us, its trunk extremely wide and smoothed from weathering. "I would guess that one has been standing for several hundred years. The guardian oaks along the edge of Aldeon Forest north of Elvidawn are probably a few thousand years old."

"That strange, gated dead wood you see on the map?"

I nodded, lacing my hands behind my head. "I hope to see that forest someday, even though it's dead. I can't wait to see the sea and Drake's Spine. It's unfortunate we won't get to see any of the southwestern parts of Xalador. I've heard from travelers over the years that it's absolutely incredible."

Maelawyn was smiling up at me when I finished talking. I grimaced. "Sorry, I'm talking too much."

She shook her head. "I love to listen to you talk, Varys. I find it brings me joy listening to how passionate you are."

My cheeks heated. "I'm just happy I'll get to share all of that with you, Maelawyn."

She opened her mouth to respond when a gust of wind blew through the forest. On instinct, I pulled her behind me, unsheathing the blade on my hip and throwing up my wards.

"Stay behind me," I said.

"Why?" She stepped out from behind my arm. "It's just a little wind—"

I couldn't react before another gale swept into us, knocking me back. "*Maelawyn, look out—*"

She was still on her feet. From where I sat on the ground, I watched the wind billow around her, catching the strands of her white hair. She had held up her left hand, *çirö* glowing with violet light.

Before us, a wind elemental materialized, but instead of a small formless creature, this one was a wisp of air taking on a feminine shape. Her hair plumed like smoke as she descended to the ground.

"Ieth, Hara Nánöweth dö Xera," Oh, *Great Nexus of Storm,* she said, her voice a whispering sigh. "I have finally found you, our Great Ruler."

Thick air spilled over the leaves like fog as she knelt and bowed her head. For Maelawyn.

"R-Ruler?" Maelawyn stared down at the elemental with wide, astonished eyes. "I'm a nexus, not a superior."

The elemental gave a slow nod. "Yes. You are storm incarnate, the controller. We bend to your commands."

Maelawyn pulled her arm back, holding it to her chest as her body went taut with apprehension. I stood to my feet and came to her side, placing a comforting hand on her shoulder. She leaned into it.

"We?" she asked. "There are others like you?"

"Yes, many who take my shape, others who take a different form. Some smaller than I, some taller than these trees. *All* are yours."

Maelawyn reached up and found the hand on her shoulder, gripping it. "Where are they?" she asked with a broken voice.

"Most are in the storm plane," the elemental said as if Maelawyn should already know. "You can reach them through the chasm just beyond this wood."

Maelawyn released a breath. "Can they teach me how to shut it?"

The elemental's spectral head tilted. "Why would you want to do that? You summoned us to this plane."

"I didn't."

Stepping forward slightly to face her, I said carefully, "Maelawyn, I think your nwív did."

She frowned, a determined expression crossing her features. "Then all of you must return to the storm plane immediately so I can rectify my nwív's mistakes."

The elemental rose slightly. "I beg your pardon, Great Nexus.

But are you no longer in need of us to aid you in the defense against the dryamorn?"

The word snapped through my entire being. I didn't think before I stepped in front of Maelawyn, cutting into their conversation. "*Dryamorn?* The nwív knew about the dryamorn?"

The elemental had no features, no expression to show anger. But as the tendrils of air billowing around her lifted and swirled up behind her, taking aim like a scorpion's stinger on the verge of attack, I knew I'd pissed her off. "How dare you step before our Great Ruler—"

"Ah, no." Maelawyn waved her arms, pushing me behind her with a bump of her hips. "He means no harm. He's my..." She paused. "He's with me."

My head tilted back slightly, frustration biting. I couldn't focus on how much that hurt right now.

The elemental's wisps fell back to flow beneath her, a ghost-like hand gliding over her chest with a bow of her head. "Apologies, Great Nexus."

Maelawyn twisted to me, nodding at me to go on. I blew out a breath, suddenly unsure of every question in my head. "The nwív said nothing about the dryamorn. She had confrontation with them?"

"Yes," she hissed. "They have taken an interest in the chasm. Some have tried to force their way through with their dark magic, but only a nexus or those of the plane can enter and leave."

"What would the dryamorn want with the storm plane?" Maelawyn asked.

"*Us,*" the elemental replied. "We are powerful and there are many of us." She seemed to look directly at Maelawyn as she said, "We can be protectors or absolute destruction. Whatever you command."

"An army." My stomach turned over. Maelawyn's head whipped toward me, eyes wide with understanding of the power she held.

She could summon soldiers for *war.*

The elemental gave a slow nod. "If it is what our nexus requires of us. We are loyal to you and only you, but some of our younger elementals are still developing a sentience, and those without great will are vulnerable to the dryamorn's compulsion. That is what we fear may happen if they manage to break through."

"Then I must close it," Maelawyn said with finality. "We can't allow the dryamorn to obtain numbers knowing what they did to the entire elven race in the last war."

"If you wish." The elemental's head dipped. She floated above us, a wisp of air wafting deeper into the forest. "Follow."

CHAPTER 55

Maelawyn

Ruler. Commander. Controller.

The weight of the responsibilities I now possessed pressed down on me as we followed the elemental deeper into the forest. The trees were no longer of pine needles among the few guardian oaks scattered around. We were now in a labyrinth of winding branches, some twisting around like lovers holding hands. Every guardian oak in this part of the wood was massive in girth, their red and orange crowns so thick we could no longer see the cloudy morning sky.

Chills broke over my skin when the clearing came into view, snapping me out of my thoughts to focus on Varys's nearly one-sided conversation with the elemental once more.

"You aren't speaking the language another elemental I encountered spoke," Varys said to her as we came into the clearing. "Why do you speak Common and Elvish?"

"We are transcendent beings who know multiple languages," she sneered. "Perhaps it did not find you worthy of conversation, *Vyl'kriev.*"

Varys blinked in surprise, looking to me for my response. I pressed my lips together to hold back my laugh, his eyes narrowing in a playful glare.

"So I guess *you* find me worthy of conversation?" he asked the elemental, but smirked at me. "Since you're using Common."

"You mean something to our Great Ruler." The elemental paused. "And I like your blue hair."

I laughed out as Varys combed a loose strand out of his face. "Well, thank you. I'm Varys. Do you have a name?"

The elemental stopped before the base of the guardian oak tree. "I am air. An elemental to serve the nexus in her bidding. I do not need a name."

He tapped his lips in thought. "How about…AeElla?"

The elemental didn't respond before she vanished, her whispering voice echoing, *"Dias çlina ít xera, Maelawyn, ieth, Hara Nánöweth."* *Come into the storm, Maelawyn, oh, Great Nexus.* *"We are waiting."*

I turned to him, reaching up to run my fingers over his scalp. "I like your blue hair, too."

He snatched my wrist with a grin, purring, "Is that so, 'Oh, Great and Powerful Nexus?'"

I bit my lip, knowing well what it did to him and drinking in the expression on his face as his blue eyes dipped to my mouth. Reality hit me too soon—I had a chasm to close and a nwív to bond with before I could entertain those thoughts.

Twisting out of his hold, I began to walk into the clearing. I froze on my next step as a pressure fell over my skin, weighing down on me like a heavy blanket. I hadn't been here for a while, but I had never felt *this*. "Varys, do you feel that?"

He nodded. "I believe it's the force of the chasm." He muttered the command words, and the spinning *eçor* and blue aura of his wards appeared. "If it gets too much, you can get behind my wards."

He winced as we stepped closer to the tree, but I found it becoming lighter as the glow of my *çirö* began to brighten. I held out my arm, and as I closed the distance between me and the tree, my arm became a radiant beam. My breath left me in a gasp, squinting as the light enveloped the clearing, my blood hot and surging. My ears reverberated with a low hum, rising to a high pitched whine. A mass of swirling energy began to appear at the base of the tree.

"That's the chasm!" Varys exclaimed over the noise.

I stared in awe as lightning danced along the crystalline edges, reminding me of a cracked geode. The whining hum diminished, and the glow of my arm died out, leaving my skin tingling and warm. Thunder rumbled from within the swirling portal, but I was too focused on the iridescent crystals bordering the chasm. The same crystals I always saw in my dreams. Looking at them felt like both a bad omen and as if I'd solved some sort of puzzle.

Varys's wards yielded to me as he placed a hand on my shoulder and pulled me through the shimmering blue aura. I gave him a tense smile as I looked up into his glowing eyes. "I think I have to go in."

A nod. "And I don't think I can go with you."

I closed my eyes, fear creeping its way up my spine. I had to be brave. I was the Nexus of Storm, the bridge between our world and the storm plane. A ruler. "Am I…a queen?"

His laugh was breathy as he took my hand, warm and tingling from the effects of his wards. "I most certainly think you are."

I blushed. "I meant in the storm plane."

He shrugged. "I don't have that answer. But if you're the ruler of the storm plane, I think you get to decide what that makes you."

I gulped. "That's a lot of pressure for someone who almost died yesterday."

"It's not your mortality that determines your strength. It's what you choose to do with the strength you have." He gave a comforting smile, the blue aura of his wards seeming to brighten when he did. "Trust me. I'm learning that, too."

My insides tightened, stomach feeling like it was coiling itself around my spine. I gazed into his eyes, the connection wrapping around me too. "What if I don't come back?"

"You have to come back. A bridge has two sides and your side belongs over here."

"But what if something goes wrong and I get stuck over there?"

He huffed. "I don't want you to ask that question."

My pulse quickened. "Then come with me. If I'm the ruler of the storm plane, surely I can allow you to come through."

Shaking his head, he pulled the hand he held to his chest, a pulse racing under my skin upon contact. "When I was fighting your nwív, there was a moment where you managed to break through."

I frowned. "I don't remember that."

"I know, but you did." He tucked a stray white strand of hair behind my ear. "I had a thought then about that connection to me you always talk about. That maybe it had been your anchor to this world and helped you get through to me."

My chest swelled. The connection had always felt like a chain or string tying me to him. Maybe it was a lifeline as well.

"You feel that connection for a reason," he murmured. "I don't know why I don't. But I have no doubt it will help lead you back home."

He let me go and I stepped away with a nod, knees shaking as I turned toward the chasm. I began to walk, focusing hard on the connection. It seemed to pull from behind, from where he stood and watched. Varys, the man I loved. My sanctuary.

"Home…" I whispered.

Not Elros. Not even Xalador.

Varys was my home.

A sound scraped up my throat, a whimper and a growl. No longer could I hold myself back from the connection pulling me. Just for one moment, for one beat of my pounding heart, I could allow this.

I whipped back around, relinquishing my restraint. The connection yanked my feet into a run back to him. Varys's eyes went wide as he staggered back, the *eçor* blinking and allowing me to come through his wards once more. I jumped and he barely caught us both as I threw my arms around his neck, legs around his torso, and kissed him hard.

He gripped my ass with a sigh, breaking the kiss only to push me up, head leaned back. "Arms on my shoulders," he told me in a whisper. "I've got you."

I did what he said, placing both elbows on either shoulder, supporting myself on his strength as I looked down and kissed him again. My headspace washed a beautiful blue, as bright and stark as his gaze and I knew I could stay here forever.

But he broke the kiss, and the blue began to fade. And yet, as his grip on me tightened, the connection strengthened until I could focus on *nothing* but him.

"Listen to me," he implored.

I nodded.

He lowered me to the ground but didn't let me go. His mouth moved to my neck, the hairs on my skin lifting as his bottom lip grazed up to my ear. "You are *mine*," he whispered.

The possessiveness in his voice made my blood surge with need. *"Yes."*

He kissed behind my ear, down my throat, a hand cupping the underside of my breast. "Mine to hold, to protect, to love."

My head fell backward. *"Varys."*

"And I'm going to do all of those things, *aríma*." My heart skipped, the Elvish word feeling even more right than it ever had. "You have to stop being scared and *let me*." The gritty sound in his throat made me weak in the knees. "Let me love you. *Please*."

My eyes met his illuminating gaze for only a moment before his lips pressed to mine. He didn't let it last long, breaking it roughly and turning me toward the chasm.

"Come back." His demand was full of passion, filling me with courage. "Come back to *me*."

I rushed forward again and didn't stop until I was inches from the swirling portal. I didn't turn around, but I kept one mental hand tightly clutched around the chain leading back to him and stepped into another world.

In one moment, I was surrounded by trees and greenery, the next I was sucked through the portal and my world expanded tenfold. I'd never stepped a foot outside of Elros, and yet here I was on an entirely different plane of existence.

And I had been here before.

I stood upon glittering water I didn't sink into, so still it was as if it was a sheet of glass. It went on for an eternity in every direction, reflecting a source of light I couldn't see. There was no sun, no moon or stars. It was all just *sky*.

Gentle mist fell upon my face from the rolling purple and gray clouds above, lightning dancing within.

This place…I'd seen this place in my dreams.

The water swished beneath my feet as I took a few steps forward, looking back at the chasm. There were no crystals on this side, but instead of a dark swirling portal, it was a golden shimmering opening.

I looked up and my gaze snagged on a ray of blue light shining down from a cloud.

Just as I thought to investigate, a gust of wind whipped through my hair. I turned to find AeElla materializing before me. She dipped her head. "I am glad to see you made it, Maelawyn."

I bowed my head as well, catching my reflection in the water. My breath hitched as I looked at my skin, now violet and shimmering. My braided hair was a deeper purple, strands of flickering light within the plaits. But my eyes…

"They're like hers," I murmured. "Why are my eyes *black*."

"I do not fully understand myself," she told me, "however I believe it gives you the ability to see in complete darkness."

Well…that would be useful when it was storming, especially at night.

"Is this my true form?" I asked, taking note of the rain beginning to fall a bit harder.

"That depends." My spine locked upon the booming voice from above, heart tripping over itself before it began to pound. My bones quaked, looking up to the sky as it went dark. Churning clouds tumbled down like a mountain of smoke, swirling far ahead of me and AeElla. I wanted to run, to scream, but found myself only able to watch as AeElla's wisping tendrils of air swept around me.

"Do not be afraid, nexus," she told me as the clouds formed into a masculine body, towering over us like one of Elros's larger hills. In a knelt position, lightning webbed across his torso, his massive umbrous head dipping down to bow.

"My lightning comes to serve," he announced, his thunderous voice echoing through the plane.

I dropped my knees to the water on instinct when his hand moved forward. More dark clouds tumbled down from his palm, dozens of small, formless lightning elementals materializing before me.

AeElla floated away and joined other air elementals like herself, all of them floating beside a smaller kind swirling among short, ever-turning funnels—wind elementals.

The water below me began to ripple and I sucked in a breath as something splashed up from beneath, drenching me. Dancing upon a swirling column of water was a small childish figure. It waved to me before jumping back into the water like a fish, joining others like it as they dipped in and out of the never-ending pool and circled around all of us.

Gods, I couldn't even estimate how many elementals there were now. I was completely surrounded as they lined up in attention. Facing *me.* They had come for me, to see me, their commander.

My heart was pounding, blood cold as ice.

"There are many more of us," the lightning elemental told me. "Hundreds as mighty as I, in every elemental this plane of storm possesses."

My breathing became rattled, overwhelmed by his statement as I tried to imagine this entire plane filled with such beings. "Where are they now?"

"They are here, but elsewhere." Lightning crackled across his face, seeming to dip as a small smile would. "They stayed back. We can tell you are frightened, Great Nexus."

I waved my hands. "No, No, I'm not…scared."

"Then why is the rain so cold?"

I blinked in realization, holding out my marked palm to catch the drops of rain that fell like icy pellets around us. My emotions even held sway over the weather here. Had I been accidentally determining the weather of Elros too? Was that why it rained every time Rucas hurt me? Why there was a thunderstorm during my pain attacks?

It was all beginning to make sense, but as the rain became a wall of water, I knew I was even more terrified now.

"Sorry," I whispered, wrapping my arms around my wet body as if it would help me grasp hold of my reality. I closed my eyes and instead found the connection to Varys, still alive and warm as ever. I focused on it, feeling for the line I knew was anchored to him. I was safe. I could be strong.

This place was a part of me. At one time, I had believed this was where I was meant to be. Maybe someday, I would feel that way.

The rain stopped falling entirely as I took a deep breath. I stood once more, lifting my head. Even though none of them had eyes, I felt all of them staring, waiting for their *great ruler* to say something. I wondered if they understood I had barely grasped being a nexus and that being in a leadership position for another plane of existence was something I would have to work toward.

"It is a great honor to witness this place," I said after I mustered every kernel of courage I possessed. "Please forgive my apprehension."

"To speak for all of us," the giant elemental began, "*we* are honored to finally be in the presence of our Nexus of Storm."

Sounds of agreement from the other elementals rang through the area, of wind and bubbling water, crackling light and rumbling thunder. Sounds I was so familiar with, hearing them all at once continued to calm me. A smile lifted on my lips.

Nature's chaos had always been my lullaby.

"To answer your question regarding your appearance," the elemental went on. "You will be able to take on this form at will once you are bonded with *her*."

I blinked. "You mean my nwív? Where is she?"

"She is formless and without power, renewed and waiting to be bound. She waited too long and was full of such destruction. The plane of storm has not seen light for a very long time."

Guilt seemed to hover over me like one of the dark thunder clouds. Did that mean my nwív made the elementals suffer here? "I will never allow my nwív to become what she did again. I know this, because *I* have been changed. I am no longer the woman who created such a monster."

Thunder rumbled across the plane, and the elemental dipped his head. "I do not believe a monster is what she became, for you are not a monster. Your nwív's actions were the result of a monstrous world."

"Perhaps." I sucked in a breath. "And the true monsters of

Xalador are threatening to invade this realm if I do not close the chasm. Can you tell me how?"

"You bear the mark of the nexus. You already have everything you need, and much more."

I looked down at the *çirö*. "I don't know how to use my powers though."

"You are a nexus. You do not use your power. You *control* it."

I didn't know how that was supposed to help me. "I don't have to say anything to close the chasm? My friend Varys told me spells are cast by speaking command words."

The whole plane had gone silent, every elemental so still, even the swirling of wind and splashing of water had ceased. It seemed I had said something wrong.

"You do not need a word to close the chasm, no," the elemental told me. Even in the deep, otherworldly sound of his voice, I could sense a confusion I didn't understand. "But I must ask, as we are *all* wondering, why do you refer to Varys as your *friend*."

My pulse thumped heavily. Did they know we were…what we were? "He is my friend, even if we are more."

The elemental's head cocked to the side, "Very much more, since he is your *Arynáthi.*"

CHAPTER 56

Maelawyn

One moment I was gaping up at the lightning elemental. Next I was on my back in the water, staring up at the purple clouds and the ray of blue light beaming down. As blue as his eyes, a hue that often filled my headspace when I kissed him.

Arynáthi.

I'd fallen over as if something had struck me. Something had.

Arynáthi.

I only knew what it meant because of my passive understanding of Elvish.

My fate bound lover.

The elementals rustled around me, whistling and gurgling voices asking among themselves if I was all right. I could only remain in the water, drowning in my thoughts.

This was what the connection meant. This was what drew me to him in common places, what locked our eyes when we felt each other near, what made me hungry for his touch, his scent, his voice. Why I felt the pulse, why I fell for him so quickly and so hard.

I knew some of it was magical, especially after discovering he was a mage as well. But now it all felt like a trick.

Another lie.

Tears fell down my face, dropping into the water.

I had believed he was someone I had chosen for myself. Instead, it seemed he had been chosen *for* me.

I loved him, but were my feelings only because I was fated to him? By whose orders? The gods? The elves?

Was his love for me an order too?

AeElla appeared above me. "Great Nexus, are you well?"

No. *No*, I wasn't.

But I needed to get back to Varys so I could…

I didn't know.

"I just need to go." The words shot out of me, water sloshing as I got to my feet, barely supporting myself on shaking knees. Quickly bowing my head, I said, "It has been a pleasure to meet all of you. I am determined to learn how to use my magic and find someone who can bind me to my nwív as soon as I can."

I turned to the chasm again, readying myself to race out.

"You are *leaving?*" The lightning elemental bellowed. "You have only just arrived."

"Y-Yes, I must return to my…to my *Arynáthi.*" My heart pounded, the word on my tongue setting my skin on fire.

The elemental raised a hand to the ray of blue light casting down from the clouds behind the chasm. "As you can see, he is well."

My eyes went wide. "I don't understand."

"You are the bridge between the material plane and this one, Maelawyn. Anything attached to you has been given access as well. However, his way is shut. He cannot come through."

"Why?"

"We do not know. Only your nwív did."

My blood pounded in my ears as my frustration hit its peak. I was so confused. So tired of riddles.

Thunder cracked through the air as I spun from the elemental, rain pouring down.

"You understand that if you close this chasm, you will not be able to return unless another is opened…" the elemental called out as I reached the chasm. I didn't respond as I stepped inside, barely hearing his final words.

Something about a *plane diamond.*

Going through the chasm felt like something gripped me by the shoulders and pulled me through a doorway to the other side. It was that simple.

But nothing that I was about to face was simple.

Varys was sitting down against the fallen trunk of the guardian oak, a book in his hands, his wards glimmering. His glowing eyes were wide and bright when they met mine. "You're back already?"

I could only stare at him, trying to ignore how the connection tugged and beckoned me to his side. I couldn't tell anymore if it was the reason I wanted him to touch me, or if I truly desired that. My entire body tightened as I tried to resist, heart pounding so hard I could barely breathe. I managed a nod, and he stood, slipping the book into his bag.

"What happened?"

"A lot."

"I just sat down." His voice held a bewildered air. "You've only been gone a moment."

Any other time, I would be fascinated. I wasn't sure I cared right now.

He started to come to me, the *eçor* blinking as it had earlier to allow me through—so he could touch me. I didn't know if I could handle that right now. When he went to take my shoulders, I crossed my arms looking away.

"Maelawyn?"

"I'm fine." My words shook. I wished he could read what my body was trying to tell him. To leave me alone. Maybe instead, he was reading that I wanted him to strip me bare and take me right here.

Which of those thoughts was how I truly felt? I didn't know.

I barely comprehended his words as he asked, "Did you learn how to close it?"

"Not really," I murmured, turning to the chasm. "But I have to try anyway."

Holding out my left hand, the *çirö* instantly lit up. I held it there for a long moment, but nothing else happened.

I let out a frustrated huff, dropping my arm. "I don't have any idea what I should do."

Varys came to my side, hands on his hips in thought. "Well, it's of magic, but not necessarily elven magic. When we want to dispel, we say *Löth Medaesí—*"

"There's not a command word for this."

"I know. But it may work similarly." He guided my arm back up. "In order to dispel magic, we have to use magic. Maybe if you tried using your powers, you'll find the answer."

I rolled my eyes. "Your riddles are just as confusing."

He frowned. "Put magic in, make magic stop," he droned, stepping back. "Just trying to help you."

I exhaled through my nose slowly, focusing on the portal instead of the fact that with his annoyance toward me, the connection loosened.

Inching closer, I watched how my *çirö* brightened. The chasm's pull on my arm was strong, beckoning me back inside.

Close. Close now.

I kept a tight mental grip on my intention, even as the chasm tugged harder and my lightning marks became a beacon. I couldn't pull away even if I wanted to, conducted and locked to the force. Varys called out, asking if I needed help. I didn't respond, *wouldn't* respond, honing in on my intention entirely.

Close.

Frustration rose with a swooping groan under the whistling wind. My palm and middle finger began to burn, heat surging through my arm much like a flare. But there was no pain.

Close! Dammit, close!

As if invisible fingers curled around my wrist, I was yanked in harder. Instinct took over, the feeling too much like the way Rucas used to pull on me. I resisted, ripping away with a shout.

Like flint striking steel, a great burst of light sprang forth, thinning into a crackling streak of energy and connecting with the portal. A high pitched whine shrieked through the forest, rising,

rising until I was sure my ears would bust, until Varys and I both screamed.

But as power surged through me, I felt the force recede. I was pulling now, watching the crystalline edges grow inward and shrink down until the chasm was nothing but a pierce through our world. The shrieking died out, an echo lingering.

Something cold and glassy hit my palm. I closed my fist around it—energy whooshed, blasting outward, throwing me to my back. And then all went silent.

The pressure of the clearing ebbed until it no longer pressed down on my skin. Varys dropped his wards and rushed to my side, helping me sit up. "Are you hurt?"

Besides feeling frazzled, I wasn't injured at all. "No."

"How did you do it?" he asked as he helped me stand. "Did you use your power?"

"I didn't use power, no," I told him, overturning my fist and opening it. "I think I took it."

There in the center of my palm, sparkling above the sheen of my glowing *çirö*, was a cluster of small iridescent crystal points, its dark-turquoise, greens, and purples the same as which had been on the edge of the chasm. The same in my dreams.

Varys peered over my shoulder. "What is that?"

I stared at the space where the chasm had been, memories tugging on what I'd seen within the plane. All was told.

What I probably missed.

"I'm not entirely sure but…" I held the cluster closer to my chest, running my fingers over the smooth, glassy surface of the point in the very center. "I wonder if it's a plane diamond."

"A what?"

I winced, placing the crystal in my pocket. "An elemental tried telling me something about a plane diamond, but I rushed out."

Varys's scarred brow lifted. "What happened in there?"

My pulse picked up. "I just got scared."

Not a lie. But not the whole truth.

When he took my hand, I told myself not to pull away. He smiled. "I'm proud of you. I know all of this has you scared, but you have shown incredible bravery. You did what you came to do even though you had no idea how you were going to do it." He kissed my knuckles. "I have no doubt in you, Maelawyn."

I closed my eyes before the tears could begin to well, whispering a thank you. Varys's lips touched mine—I turned away from him.

His breath hitched. "Are you all right?"

I shook my head. "I'm just ready to leave this place. We should start making our way to Mirefield."

Both of those things were also not lies. But…half truths could be just as damaging. *No more secrets*. I'd told him no more.

I watched as he hoisted the pack up on his shoulders, the connection somehow choking the words in my throat even as it continued to loosen. How was I supposed to start this conversation?

"We'll take the southern forest path," he told me, voice laden with pent up frustration. For *me*, I realized. "I don't particularly like that way, but it's the most wild, so it will have places to hide if we need to."

He began to make his way across the clearing and I…

I knew I was losing him.

"Varys, stop."

His head perked up and he turned to me. I had stopped in the center of the clearing.

I didn't know what I was doing. What I would even say to him. All I could focus on was the words he had spoken to me before I entered that chasm. When I had been so sure that our love could work.

"*Mine,*" he'd said. "*You're mine.*"

"*Let me love you.*"

"*Stop being so scared.*"

I could if only I knew I wouldn't hurt him.

If I knew our love was real.

The words tumbled from my lips. "I know why you can't love a liar."

He blinked, chin jeering backward. "What?"

"I know how you were hurt." I was already breathing hard. "By Elise Carrington."

Varys scoffed as he let the pack fall to the ground once again. "Maelawyn, none of that matters now—"

"But it does." My voice went hoarse. "I lied so much."

His head tipped back on the massive breath he took. "And I forgave you for everything. I know why you did so."

I nodded. He came into the clearing more, but I found myself stepping away. I needed to get all of this out before he touched me again. "Just know I'm suffering the consequences for all of my lies. I have lied so much that the world decided to lie to me."

The way he studied me with a hard, incredulous expression threatened to drain my thoughts clean of any words to come. But I continued, "Everything I've ever known about myself is a lie. My father wasn't my true father. My mother had lied about that all of these years. Maybe it's a learned behavior. She lied out of survival as well."

His lips parted, face falling. "Maelawyn—"

I held up my hands. "I need to get this out. I need to talk."

He nodded quickly, another step toward me. I closed my eyes, pressing my lips together, focusing on all I wanted to finally say. "I'm not Mae Mordaunt. I'm Maelawyn. I'm not just a human with white hair. I may not be human at all. I'm *Vyl'kriev,* but even more than that. I'm a nexus, and it seems like I haven't stopped learning about myself even now. Even after all of that." The tears broke free of my closed eyes, running down my cheeks. "Lie, after lie, after lie."

Varys had stopped before me, his presence warm, the connection pounding as fast as my heart. I went on, "Then, there was you. And after a life of deceit, I finally had something I believed was true. My heart and head have never lied to me." I stifled a whimper. "But I should have known they would betray me as well. I don't have power over myself. I never have."

I lifted my chin, opening my tear-blurred eyes, meeting those sapphires ablaze with tender affection. "I'm sorry if I'm not making much sense."

He shook his head vigorously. "No, *no.* I don't care if it doesn't make sense right now. We can figure that out later." He took my shoulders, and the touch sent shivers down my spine. "This is good. You're talking to me. You're not clamming up. That's all I want, Maelawyn. Don't avoid me because you think I won't understand. Just *talk.* Let me in."

I swallowed, my very bones shaking. "Do you want me to be—"

"Honest? Yes."

"No." I sucked in a breath. *"Blunt."*

His hands moved to my face, cupping my cheeks. "Please."

My breaths turned shallow, the words pushing past the knot in my throat. I moved his hands from my face, pushing them to his chest, and steeling my gaze as I said through a rattled breath, "We are *Arynáthi.*"

Nothing in the clearing moved, as if the world had stilled upon my words. Varys stared down at me, even his expression unchanged.

Then a bright, radiant and ecstatic smile lifted on his lips as he began to laugh. He buckled at the waist, his chuckles laced with something about Natalia.

Heat blasted through me. I placed my hands on my hips. "Why are you *laughing?"*

"Because I'm happy." He straightened and took my hands, the last of his laughs dying with a sigh. "Did you think I'd be upset?"

I gaped at him, and it took him another moment too long before it seemed to click.

"You're upset," he said with a bob of his throat.

My head began to shake. I looked away, sifting through my emotions. "I don't know."

But I did know, and I was tired of pretending I didn't know what I wanted.

I crossed my arms. "How do I know that our feelings for one another are real?"

He combed his hair back with his fingers. "What do you mean?"

Turning from him, I paced forward, moving my hands around as if it would help me explain myself better. "Something or someone decided to write our name in the stars, binding us as lovers before we could ever make the decision for ourselves. So, how do I know that the love I have for you isn't because fate told me to love you?" I steadied myself on a tree, sliding my fingers along the smooth bark. "And how do I know your love is true—"

"Because I can't feel it."

I snapped my head over my shoulder. "What?"

His shoulders squared, head tilted back to the sky. "I told you earlier. I don't know why I can't feel that connection you speak of. Magic is reemerging inconsistently and our *Arynáthi* bond is of the gods' magic. I can only assume that part of *my* magic hasn't fully reemerged yet." He huffed. "Maybe it's because I've been so damn resistant to the idea of destiny and fate."

For a moment he only watched the sky as if there was something up there looking back. Maybe the stars beyond the blue sky that decided we were made for each other.

Then his eyes closed, head dropping in what looked like defeat.

No. Release.

"Maelawyn, I love you."

My heart stumbled a beat, tears welling.

"And I don't feel a magical jolt when I touch you. I don't feel something telling me you're in my presence." His eyes found mine, jaw tight. "But I cannot deny that I have a connection with you. It is of companionship, affection, and desire."

His voice lowered to a rasp. "And I cannot deny that when you touch me…" He lost a breath, retracting the step he'd taken as if he was trying to restrain himself. "I am enchanted by how your skin feels on mine."

My blood heated, and I found myself pressed against the tree. I was holding myself back as well.

"Nothing about my love is forced. It's not an obligation." He paused. "I'm not another cage, Little Bird."

I blinked and my tears fell.

"I don't need to be your *Arynáthi* to know I love you, and if the day comes that I suddenly feel that bond, I can promise you won't even know the difference."

His name left my lips in a sob. Thunder rolled in the distance.

He went on with a shake of his head. "My love is not a lie, and I don't think yours is either. I think you're so distrustful of this world because of what you've gone through that this looks like another trick when really…" Emotion strained his voice. "Fate knew there was something powerful between us and gave us a *gift*."

I wiped my face with shaking hands. "I've just always been confused about the connection."

He nodded. "I understand. But you told me you've always wanted me. Was that before you felt the connection, too?"

His question made me take a breath, clearing all confusion. He had always been able to do that with his words. "Yes," I whispered. "I did want you then. When the connection started, I leaned into it. I always followed wherever it took me because I knew it would lead me to you."

A smile lifted on the side of his lips.

"It's not a chain," I realized, smiling too. "It's a compass."

He laughed, and the sound was full of so much joy.

I went on, feeling like light was rising up from within me, "It's a thread I can follow back to safety. But it's not forcing me to love you."

His breathing turned heavier.

"I already do."

That restraint was still on him, even when his features broke. "Say it," he pleaded.

I remembered what he had told me. I held the command.

"I..."

The words didn't seem right all of the sudden. The *Common* didn't feel right.

We were *Vyl'kríev.* We were *Arynáthi.*

With a pounding heart, I gathered the Elvish words and declared, "Varys...*Śí arí vö.*"

His body went rigid, chin dipping and eyes suddenly ablaze with desire. But he still didn't move, as if he was waiting to see if I would take it back.

I only grinned, letting the tears run as free as I felt. *"Śí arí vö."*

The breath in his chest released with a soft growl as he came at me, crossing the clearing in long, powerful strides. I braced myself, prepared for his strength to overwhelm me. But as he crashed into me and took my face into his hands, his kiss was gentle; filled with all of the love he'd restrained. We fell backward, and I was pinned between him and the tree behind me. As I wrapped my arms around his neck, the hands on my face moved down, one to my waist, the other pulling my thigh up and locking a leg around him.

His tongue parted my lips, and every swirl had me gasping with unbridled moans.

His lips moved to my neck, teeth scraping as he pressed into me harder. A whimper slipped free when he nipped at the soft skin beneath my chin. His hand roamed up my shirt, thumb stroking my peaked nipple and sending teasing shivers down my spine. The connection seemed to rumble with his low groans as I writhed and rocked against the strain in his breeches.

He put space between us for a moment to pull my tunic over my head. The crisp morning air kissed my skin, tightening my already aroused breasts. He wasted no time, yanking me up in his hold higher and dipping down to my nipple. My head fell back against the tree, and I sighed his name as he sucked and licked, moving from one side to the other. I ran my fingers through his soft hair, grinding myself on any place his body met mine.

His tongue swiped up to my neck and he inhaled. "You still smell and taste like rain, *aríma*."

I grinned. "I hope that's a good thing."

"It is." He lowered me to my feet only to take hold of my arms, pinning them above my head. My heart tumbled as a roguish smirk lifted the corner of his mouth. "It just has me intrigued."

I tilted my head. "About?"

"Whether or not you taste like rain…" When his eyes trailed downward, my thighs clenched.

Oh gods.

Keeping his eyes on mine, and one hand on my wrists, he slipped his other beneath my pants and cupped my center. I jolted, a cry escaping my trembling lips. He watched me intently, his stare glazed with hunger as one finger dipped into my wet core and filled me. In and out, he slid and stroked only for a moment before pulling his hand up, raising it between us. I took a thin breath as I looked at the slick wetness of me on his finger, and my heart began to pound when his grin returned. He wrapped his lips around that finger and my mouth went completely dry as I watched him suck me off.

"*Fuck,*" I whispered.

He swallowed, unceasing the intensity of his gaze as he hummed in approval. "I was right." Freeing my wrists, he stepped back just enough to steady himself, mouth gaped as he hooked his fingers under the waistband of my pants. "And I want more of you."

My breathing turned heavy as he dropped to his knees. As he pressed wet kisses along my stomach, his hands explored my thighs and ass, slowly moving my pants down inch by teasing inch. His lips grazed the top of my pelvic bone, running over the patch of hair there with his eyes flicked to mine. I was quaking, gripping onto his shoulders in anticipation. My pants now down to my knees, he ran his mouth up my leg, then licked between the crease of my thigh and my throbbing core, the heat of his breath staving off the chill of the air.

In one quick movement, his tongue found its mark. I bucked in response with a gasping moan as he dragged up my slit, then back down to my entrance. Languid heat pooled into my trembling legs.

His pattern changed and began to circle around the bundle of nerves there. Between the involuntary sounds and sighs, I looked down. My breath caught in my throat when I found him watching me, his eyes narrowed. He released for just a moment, spreading my folds with his fingers. "Angle your hips toward me, gorgeous," he said, lips slick with my wetness.

My pulse skipped, but I nodded and pushed against the tree more. The bark scraped against my back and brought an almost pleasurable sting as I tilted my hips, my trembling center lining up with his mouth. "That's it," he purred. My heart tumbled.

With an eager groan, he flicked my exposed bud with his tongue. My body lit on fire, lashes of ecstasy ripping through me. And it seemed as though he was waiting for something as his eyes shifted between me and something above us—the sky. Just as I started to feel the build of my climax, he obviously found what he was looking for on my face, a smug grin appearing before he took my swollen flesh between his lips and began to suck.

A rough shout broke from me, hands slamming down on his shoulders and fingers digging into his shirt. He only sucked harder, the satisfied hums in his throat as if he could do this all day. I whimpered and gasped with every pull of his mouth; every lick, every swirl, every suck evolving the sounds to cries of sweet rapture.

My body slacked against the tree, losing grip on his shirt,

finding his hair instead. His hands moved around to grip my thighs, holding me in place. I was so focused on the feeling, I didn't realize I had closed my eyes until I began to see blues dancing in my mind—

"Look at me."

I gasped and glanced down. Varys paused and pressed a kiss below my navel. "I want your eyes on mine the entire time I'm doing this to you."

I gulped. "And…what will you do if I look away?"

He grinned. "Are you challenging me, Little Bird?"

My laugh was short and breathy. His expression hardened as I held his gaze and scraped my teeth over my bottom lip.

"Perhaps I am." I closed my eyes. "Make them open again."

Nothing happened for a moment, and the anticipation became agonizing. I listened to how he breathed, inhaling through his teeth, exhales shivering as they warmed the apex of my thighs—

A hand forced my knee to bend and give way. I dropped, was caught in his arms and flipped over; dipped to the ground like he had done on the dance floor at the tavern. My back hit the forest floor softly, braided hair tangling with the autumn leaves, and before I knew it, my boots were off with my pants and my hips were lifted to his mouth.

And then he ravaged me.

Every bit of air in my chest abandoned me as he drove his tongue into my entrance. I cried out, overwhelmed by waves of hot pleasure raking and curling as he licked. No longer could I keep my eyes shut, too in awe of what he was doing. He watched me writhe, and I watched him consume me.

Lifting his head, he paused, his cheeks pink and lips glossy from my pleasure. I almost let out a plea, a protest before he said, "I love you."

With trembling lips, I whispered the phrase back to him. He smiled lovingly and dipped back down, murmuring against my slit, "Come for me, *aríma*."

I didn't get a chance to catch my breath before his tongue darted back out, the instant contact to my bud making my body jerk. It was too much, the sensation like fire, like *lightning*, every swipe sending intense, hot jolts surging through me. My body arched and bent away, I couldn't take it—

Varys's forearm pushed against my stomach, forcing me back down. I screamed, pleading his name as he flicked harder and applied more pressure. He thrust a finger of his free hand inside me, sliding down to the knuckle, curling up and hitting a part of me I didn't even know existed. My eyes went wide, my mind wiping all words and thoughts as I came, hard and explosive. He locked my legs around his neck as my body shuddered, hands needing to grab, to grope. I dug my nails into the leaves, the dirt and grass. Wave after wave crashed and burned through me as the sky above spun, the gathering clouds flickering with light.

Varys didn't stop with his torment, still thrusting his finger in and out, still hitting that spot. I couldn't believe how fast I was building back up, just as quickly as the clouds swirled and the sky darkened. He was touching and stroking everywhere I wanted and yet, not enough. I needed more, I needed the heat rising from the deepest part of me to set me aflame. Greedily, I began to rock against his tongue, as if it were the flint to my steel. He moaned as thunder rolled across the forest and the two sounds spoke of everything within the *Arynáthi* connection.

A gentle breeze rushed over us, bringing with it the smell of rain, the promise of a storm I couldn't stop. I didn't want to stop it. Didn't want to stop what he was doing to me.

So I didn't.

My *çirö* lit up and I sunk that hand into his hair, pushing his face against me more as my hips undulated in great swells. His eyes flicked up to mine, a look of simmering surprise as he obliged to my need. I moaned loudly, wildly, running my other hand over my body, my nipples, feeling beautiful and sexual. Alive and powerful.

With his name laced with a scream, lightning shot down with my next release, connecting to the earth beyond the wood. An ear-splitting thunder mixed with my cry of pleasure, the ground rumbling beneath us. Varys went completely still. He sat up on his knees, head tilting back to the sky. *"Chaos."*

My body slacked, and rain broke from the sky.

With wide blue eyes, he overturned his palm, catching the drops in his hand. Goosebumps rose on my skin as the rain sprinkled down, cooling the lashes of heat still surging through my body. He splashed the collected water over his head, pulling his fingers through his wet hair with a smile before he crawled up to me and captured my lips with his. I could taste the sweetness of rain, of *me*, on his tongue. I gathered up the material of his tunic, breaking the kiss only to yank it over his head.

He took my face into his hands. "I want you," he murmured, running his thumb over my bottom lip.

"I'm yours." I pushed him up to his knees, wrapping my arms around his neck and pressing my breasts against his bare chest. "How about you go and grab one of those bedrolls?"

He didn't move, breaths gritty as he ran his lips over mine. For a moment, I was sure he would take me right here on the forest floor —maybe I wanted that. But he nodded and made his way over to where he had dropped the pack.

I wrapped my arms around my wet body, hyper-aware of my nakedness. And yet, I had always been comfortable here in this clearing. This place, where I had escaped many times when I needed peace in my life, and how even after the fall, it had remained so sacred to me. I didn't feel naked here. I felt liberated and eager to explore myself and my desire with the man I loved.

I took an easy breath, and the rain turned to a light mist. Varys finished laying down one bedroll and fur blanket. He sat down and kicked off his boots, then unfastened the sheathed sword from his hip, eyes on me the entire time. "*Dias na ni,*" he muttered.

I shivered and stood, pulling my wet hair out of its braid as I walked over. The furs brushed my knees as I knelt before him, sliding my hands down his broad chest speckled with raindrops to his belt. I held his gaze, a sensual grin on my lips as I unbuckled with deliberate leisure, watching his nostrils flare with impatience. His fingers dug into my hips, breaths heavy and shaky. Tossing the belt to the side, I pulled his breeches down and over his hard length. As he finished pulling them over his ankles, I took in the sight of him. Breathing through the nervousness suddenly trying to threaten our moment, I let my eyes wander over every detail, pausing on a long scar on his hip, another across his upper right thigh.

He followed my gaze, pointing to the one on his hip. "Training. Leo got me when I didn't parry quick enough." He chuckled and went to point at the other, but paused. "I'll tell you about the others another time. I don't want to ruin anything."

I nodded and stroked the side of his face, brushing away drops of water. "You're absolutely beautiful, Varys."

He smiled and brought my lips to his, wrapping me in his strong arms. My pulse sped up as our bodies connected, his cock sliding between my thighs, teasing my entrance.

He kissed down the side of my face, to my ear. "You tell me when you're ready," he murmured.

My stomach knotted, head falling back. I wanted this. I wanted him. But despite myself, I shook with unease. I closed my eyes and tried to focus on the connection, the blues, and the heat of my core. How I throbbed, my body needing so much more of him.

But I…

"I'm nervous." My cheeks heated.

His lips pressed to the soft skin beneath my chin. "I can tell. It's all right."

Thunder rolled, echoing off the hills. "What if I lose control?"

I met his gaze. He studied my face lovingly. "You won't, because you're already in control of this situation, Maelawyn. You lead *me*."

I swallowed, not knowing how I was supposed to do that when he would be on top and inside of me. "What if it hurts and my powers—" I cut myself off. "I'm sorry, I'm being foolish."

He shook his head. "No, you're not."

Sitting back, he pulled me against him. I breathed in his scent in an attempt to calm me down as he stroked my back. The rain only fell harder.

Varys kissed the top of my head. "You have lived a life where everything you've ever wanted only brought you consequence. Even now, you believe you may get hurt, or hurt me, if you give in to your desires. You're still scared."

I nodded, a knot in my throat. "I'm sorry."

"You have nothing to apologize for. Especially not in this situation." He lifted my chin. "We don't have to have sex—"

"No, I want to." Lightning flashed above us.

Varys glanced up with a smile. "Your desires, your wants…they are powerful, Maelawyn." Still having hold of my chin, he ran his thumb across my lip and slid his free hand into my drenched hair. "You are a chaos that will never be tamed."

I blinked as if released from some enchantment. I had heard that before, but I couldn't remember where. Another flash of lightning enveloped the sky, followed by a roar of thunder. The hair on my arms bristled as something began to rise from the depths of my entire being. As I stared up at him, I could see specks of light dancing in the reflection of his gaze. It was from the lightning crackling in mine.

Tightening his grip on me, he breathed against my lips, *"Storm, vi Arynáthi."*

I lost it.

Everything wild and carnal within me broke free. I flung my arms around him and captured his mouth, stifling the gasp in his throat as I instantly pinned his tongue between my teeth and began to suck as he had between my legs. His sweet moans fueled a sudden, unfamiliar need of dominance. I wanted to overwhelm him, wanted him to succumb to me. I had always felt so powerless. But here with him…I was on top of the world.

With a fierce release of his mouth, I pushed my hands into his chest and guided him to his back. His eyes were wide with wonder as he went down, watching me with heaving breaths as I straddled him. I kissed along his collarbone, licking the rain from his skin, savoring the water on my tongue like the finest wine. When my *çirö* lit up once more and my power surged through me, I knew if I could somehow tap into this feeling, this sense of strength and highness…I would never question my magic again.

I felt every pound of thunder, every jolt of lightning. I moaned loudly as I writhed against his stomach, his skin teasing my drenched entrance. His hands palmed my breasts, fingers tugging on my nipples as I used his body to ease the ache between my thighs.

"I'm in control," I told him, the rain falling harder.

He nodded, water trickling down his face. "You are."

With a sensual grin, I pulled up on his shoulders, holding on to his strong arms to balance myself as I spread my legs and aligned my hips with his. I found his warm cock beneath me and guided it to my entrance. My body tried to tense when I felt him there. But I was in control. I was the leader.

Both of our mouths gaped in awe, breaths uneven and hard. Holding on tight, I began to lower myself.

My stomach curled, a whimper of pain escaping as I took him, the stretching bringing an expected sting. Curses spilled free, thunder roared, the hurt intensifying as he slid in, and in. He held his breath, hands on my hips to both support and guide.

"I know. I'm sorry," he said when I hissed. "You're doing so great, love."

I shook as I went lower, the fleeting feeling of both pleasure and pain overwhelming every thought. I forgot what day it was, where we were, so lost and completely entranced by him.

Finally seated at the hilt, I waited for the sting to ebb, burying my face in his neck and focusing on the deep and hot throbbing. How his cock stretched and filled me, every pulse sending shivers down my spine with the chilly rain. He whispered that I was loved and safe as I kissed along his wet jaw.

Knowing what I would need to do next, I pushed up slightly, and moved back down, gasping when the tip of his length touched a spot deep inside, sending hot, tingling barbs of pleasure through me.

Varys's breath left him with a moan, eyes fluttering backward. "*Fuck*, I can't..."

Still sliding up and down, I asked with a tilted head, "What?"

He hissed, gritting out through his teeth, "*Mine.* I can't believe you're mine."

I hummed, pressing my lips to his ear. "I'm yours, Varys Wynhart. And you're mine."

His breaths came harder as I adjusted myself to gain traction. No longer in need of his shoulders to support myself, I pushed him to his back softly. His eyes gleamed as they fell over me, and I began to move faster. Every rise and fall of my hips had both of us sighing deeply, breaths short and rough. I found a rhythm and a perfect angle that allowed me to hit that spot each and every time. My head fell back as I rocked, listening to his perfect moans and deep growls. With his hands gripping my hips, I felt him arch before he thrust up into me. I cried out, thunder clapping. He drove into me again, and the force of it sent fire shooting through every nerve. The rain became large, pelting drops, drowning out our sounds of pleasure. I only moaned louder to rival it.

He continued to thrust. Harder. Deeper. My climax was building again, and I couldn't help but to circle my finger between my slit.

"Oh gods." He watched me stroke myself, his chest heaving, his hips moving faster. "Keep going, Maelawyn."

Every inch left me breathless. Raindrops dripped down my breasts, onto his hands as he teased my nipples. His pounding was unbridled, my legs tightening as the spot inside me heated up, a new kind of climax I'd never felt before building, surging in great waves.

Varys glanced up to the sky, blinking the water out of his eyes. The smirk that crossed his features was devious before I was flipped to my back, and in one easy motion, he slid himself back inside. I cried out as he spread my legs wide, and one more thrust had me shattering. I didn't know what I shrieked, what language left my lips, I just seeped into him as his hips continued to move in easy, deliberate waves, each entry sending hot flashes of pleasure scorching through my body as I came and came.

One more powerful, consuming thrust had him rearing back, roaring my name as he spilled into me. I watched with wide eyes and could have sworn his own glowed with blue light as he collapsed, catching himself above me.

For several moments, we only panted, still unable to catch our breath. Our gazes met and the tender kisses we shared slowed our racing hearts. We held each other tight, wet with rain and pleasure, neither one of us reaching for the furs.

As the rain stopped and the clouds receded, we both fell into a peaceful quiet akin to the calm after a storm.

CHAPTER 57

Varys

I wasn't sure how long we had been laying there, looking at the sky in total silence, both of us in complete bliss. Our legs were still entangled, hips still aligned so perfectly I could slide inside if she so desired. Her head lay on my chest as she breathed deeply.

I was…*chaos*, there wasn't a word in any language I knew that could describe how I felt. I was absolutely ruined, and yet whole.

I brushed her white hair, stroking the top of her head. I wanted to lay here like this for the rest of my mortal life.

But we needed to go. We were supposed to be halfway across the southern forest by now.

I caressed her back, her skin like cool marble. I was almost sure she'd fallen asleep. "Maelawyn?"

My voice had her stirring, legs moving and pressing the softest parts of her to my hardness. A lovely sigh escaped her lips as one purple eye blinked open.

"Fall asleep on me?" I asked.

"No, I just…" She didn't finish.

I chuckled. "Same. Are you cold?" I reached for the fur blanket, but she shook her head. I traced my fingers down her upper arm, following the marks of lightning. "I only ask because your skin is so cool."

Her mouth turned down. "I know. I'm sorry."

"What? You have nothing to apologize for." I squeezed her, pressing a kiss to her temple. It was actually warm there. "I love your skin. I love how it's icy against me. I'm always burning up."

She grinned. "Well, I love your skin. You keep me warm." Her lips pressed to my mouth, then my chin. "You're the first to love my cold skin. That's why I apologized. People always balk at my touch."

"Ah, so it's a secret then."

She tilted her head. "What is?"

I pushed her up gently, only to roll onto her, lips pressed to her neck. I slid my tongue down, causing her to buck. My cock throbbed against her in response, but I continued to the crevice where her shoulder and neck joined. "You have secret warm places on your beautiful body. Right here." I brought her arm up and kissed the inside of her elbow. "There." I dipped down to her heart, kissed it, then moved to the underside of her breast. I let my tongue do the work there and she hissed my name. "All of those places are very warm and get warmer the lower I explore."

Her breathing turned rapid as I pressed my lips to her sides. "There." To beneath her navel, a soft hum in my chest. "Definitely right there."

"Varys," she gasped.

I chuckled, hanging over her midriff. Sliding a finger between the contour of her inner thigh, I followed how it connected with her soft center. I stroked up and down, again on the other side, watching the skin of her legs flush. I flashed a grin her way, licking my lips as if to show preparation. Her body trembled, eyes begging for me to taste her.

Instead, I moved lower, bending one leg. I darted my tongue under her knee. "Oh, so warm here."

"You damn tease." She chuckled.

I arched a brow. "That's not what you were wanting?"

Those amethyst eyes narrowed, simmering as she spread herself wide, sliding two fingers down, around the engorged bud there. "You're no fool, Varys Wynhart."

I swallowed and in one quick movement, I entwined my arms around her legs, yanking her to me. The laugh that slipped through her lips turned to a moan as I pressed my lips against her wetness before I—

"Varys, stop."

Her body stilled. I lowered her hips to the furs. "What? What's wrong—"

"Do you hear that?"

There was nothing, the forest as quiet as it had been since we arrived. Birds chirped in the distance. Leaves rustled in the light breeze.

Maelawyn had already found her clothes, yanking on her pants before throwing mine to me.

I pulled them over my legs. "What do you—"

She shushed me, her purple eyes filled with terror. With a shake of her head, she cupped her ears. She'd had a similar reaction to sounds when her nwív was trying to take over. I wondered if this was another passive power she had.

Her eyes went wide, mouthing the words, *"Growls."*

My heart stumbled and I didn't press any further as we finished dressing. Wolves? Here in this part of the forest? I'd already expected we would come across some on our journey. Had already given myself a mental inducement that I wasn't that helpless little boy stuck inside a hollow log anymore.

After gathering the bedroll, I strapped on my belt and attached my sword to it. Boots on our feet, I drew my blade in my left hand, murmuring, "Keep close, love."

I'd dropped our supply pack somewhere close to the edge of the clearing. We couldn't leave without it. "But if I tell you to run, then—"

A mass of fur launched into our path, between us and our supply pack, barking viciously. Maelawyn screeched, and I held out my blade, wards readied on my tongue. I didn't expect to look into the eyes of a hound.

Something was hunting us. It just wasn't wolves.

Another set of barks rang out from the right, two more hounds joining the one before us. I looked around, seeing nothing above nor ahead. *"Sçölith!"*

My wards went up before us, arcane scars glowing bright blue. Maelawyn's breath came in short bursts, hands flexing.

"Come on, come on," she whimpered urgently.

She was trying to make sparks.

From behind a tree, a guardsman stepped out, an arrow already nocked in his bow and prepared to shoot.

"Maelawyn, get back!"

About a dozen other guardsmen came from nowhere, and my stomach dropped as they all released their arrows, hitting my wards one by one. Maelawyn instinctively dropped to her knees, covering her head.

When the last arrow struck, my wards shattered. I gasped and stumbled back. *"Run!"*

With a wild shout, Maelawyn leaped to her feet and rushed away. I steadied myself, ignoring the burn of my arcane scars, and ran after her. The dogs nipped at my ankles, their teeth tearing through my pants. Anxiety rose up my throat, the same wet heat of their foul breath on my skin, conjuring memories—

Claws caught my right arm, scraping into the arcane scars. I screamed in pain, the burn so intense I tumbled to the ground. The hounds barked in my face as I tried to find a grip on my sword.

Someone stepped on the blade, and the dogs backed off. I opened my eyes to look up into the face of Dominik Rochester, Captain of the guard. He held his blade to my throat. "Still scared of dogs, Wynhart?"

Anger burned through my veins like acid. "The hounds, or the mangey bastard I'm looking at?"

The point of the sword pressed in harder. "Quiet. You so much as mutter another word, I'll remove your head right here."

I tried to slow my breathing, every exhale pressing my skin to the sword. I could only hear distant barking and guards shouting across the wood. My qualmish stomach churned as I tried to search for Maelawyn out of the corner of my eyes. I couldn't see her.

Then she screamed, and the entire forest lit up with an incandescent spark. Dominik cursed, screaming for his men to pull back. Two rushed to my side and went for my arms, yanking me off the ground. I sucked in a breath, a command word on my tongue—

Dominik's fist was the last thing I saw before my world went black.

Maelawyn

When I came to, my world was dark, but not because my eyes were closed. Something was over my face, tightened around my neck to the point I could hardly breathe. It was then I realized the gag in my mouth, the cloth tasting like moldy bread and sour fruit. My breaths came in quick, panicking bursts, every inhale smelling of burlap and piss. I tried to raise my hands, only to find they were bound behind my back, chains around my wrist.

They'd imprisoned me.

I erupted with terror, screaming and yanking against the chains. I tried to call for Varys, the gag forcing my tongue down. I couldn't even speak in Elvish. I kicked, pounding my feet on the cold floor. *Let me out, Let me out!*

My heart sank into the depths of my stomach when I heard the jangling of keys before a door opened. I could hear footsteps coming forward, the vibrations of their boots on the floor beneath me. Hands gripped my arms, pulling me to my feet. I screamed again, kicking out—

"Stop squirmin', you fuckin' cunt," a voice snapped near my left ear, "or I'll snap yer legs."

I suddenly didn't think I cared. I just wanted him to stop touching me.

"She's not going to need them where she's headed." I did recognize that voice. My stomach tumbled. *Mr. Welch.* "I hope the blade is blunt for you."

My blood ran cold. Where was I...

They grabbed my arms again, dragging me up a flight of stairs. I tried to speak, to scream for help, struggling against the chains.

"Maelawyn?" someone asked as we passed them.

Oh my gods.

Varys.

I shrieked, planting my feet on the ground. The men were too strong.

"Maelawyn!" His voice broke. *"NO! Maelawyn! No, No, No!"*

I could hear him pounding on metal—a jail cell. He was locked up too.

"You fucking bastards! I'll kill you! Maelawyn!"

My eyes burned with tears, his voice fading behind a door slamming behind me. I didn't know where they had taken me.

Until I heard the crowd.

They were chanting, angry voices filling the air, feet stomping. "Death to magic! Death to magic!"

I was dragged up another flight of stairs, so cold with fear, I was numb. The men stopped and I was shoved to my knees.

The crowd went silent. My breaths quickened, chest quaking as I wept.

"We should have known eighteen years ago when she was brought into this world we'd be dealing with a demon," Mayor Brooker's voice rang out. "After the murders of her promised, his beloved friend, and her own father, we had a hard time tracking this vile woman down."

My body went taut. I didn't kill Willem and Theon. Neither did my nwív. I screamed, desperate to make my voice heard—

A fist struck me in the stomach, knocking the breath from me. I choked on the gag, trying to refill my lungs through my nose.

"She killed five of our guardsmen when we found her and Varys Wynhart in the woods outside our borders. They both will die for their crimes tonight," Mayor Brooker continued.

Nausea rose up my throat. I *killed* those guards, and hadn't even realized it. I had just exploded with fear. Had I passed out? Is that how they had captured me?

I realized why I was gagged, why they kept me bound and a burlap hood around my head. They thought my magic was like Varys's. But I didn't need my hands, nor my mouth to conjure my magic.

I focused on my fear, imagining rain as icy as my blood felt, winds whipping violently through the town, thunder so loud people shook when it clapped…

Nothing happened.

"But do not worry, citizens. She cannot harm you now. We are thankful her father collected many potions, keeping them so these mages could not use them."

Lies.

"And that he acquired one that nullifies their magic."

My heart skipped.

"We turned her wretched magic against her."

I shuddered. The gag. The gag tasted of sour fruit.

The potion was on my tongue.

But Rucas wasn't *Vyl'kríev.* He couldn't read what was on the potions. That meant that by some chance the potion had been labeled with Common.

Or that they had a *Vyl'kríev* on their side.

Someone ripped off the burlap sack from my head. The bright light of a hundred torches in the night pierced my eyes, pain lancing through the back of my skull. The crowd began to shout at me, angry curses spilling from their lips.

"Kill that demon bitch!"

"Send her to Torm!"

I stared in horror, chest caving in and out with sobs. There were people I had known my entire life in that crowd, people I'd had conversations with as I bought their wares in the market.

All of them now glaring up at me, eyes reflecting the flames.

But the ones I really cared about? They weren't here. Varys was locked up, set to die next. Mr. Flax was not in the crowd, nor was Eryx. I realized…I was glad they wouldn't see this.

I looked down and my world began to spin. I was before the block, stained with the blood of the criminals before me.

My bladder loosened, warmth running down my legs like the tears on my face.

"She is powerless," the mayor bellowed.

I was.

I had always been.

Time slowed, the pulse in my ears louder than the chanting of the crowd. I paid no mind to the rest of the lies, nor the command to end my life. A foot pressed into the small of my back, forcing my neck to rest on the notch of the block. I stared at nothing, felt nothing. I just screamed.

For myself.

For Varys, my *Arynáthi*, his name nothing but muddled wails.

I should have told him I loved him sooner.

I should have run away with him sooner.

He was wrong. Our love, the thing I had wanted more than anything, came with consequence after all.

A shadow cast over me. A sword lifted.

I was going to die.

Shutting my eyes, I held tight to the connection that would lead me back into his warm arms. I hoped wherever death took us would allow us to be joined there forever.

A clang rattled my senses. For a moment, I thought it was the clock tower bell, or maybe the sound of the sword slicing through me.

But the next noise had my eyes opening. A gurgling cough to my left. It was at that moment I realized the sword was on the floor of the platform. And I wasn't dead.

Someone toppled to the ground, hands still clasping their bleeding neck. Captain Dominik's eyes were wide as red pooled onto the landing.

Another guard fell to the platform floor. Then another, blood spurting from the slice in their throats. The crowd began to scream in horror, parting from the center for a spontaneous appearance of green smoke.

I lifted my head off the notch, jaw going slack even with the gag. Silver eyes met mine with icy mockery as their owner emerged from the green smoke and flew into the air, *nothing* holding him in suspension. He hovered above us, a silhouette before the bright moon in the sky, and I sucked in a breath as I watched his eyes begin to burn a deep ruby.

"It has been a pleasure, Elros." Vamir's rasping voice crawled across the market.

I didn't understand.

What was he—

The green smoke burst, and as it expanded outwards over the market circle in a cloud of wafting haze, screams of pain curdled the air. A shocked shriek left me as I watched the skin of the people in the crowd bubble up in sickening blisters before it simply slid off their bones. A man tumbled to the ground, blood pooling from a face no longer attached. Torches fell, some were thrown, dropping onto tents and roofs. In mere seconds, the town began to burn.

I scrambled up, pushing past the fear and quaking in my legs. Someone gripped me from behind. Terror seized me. I slammed my head back into their chest, but it only made their hold on me tighten. I screamed and fought—

The gag was cut, the cloth slacking in my mouth. I spat it to the ground, saliva drooling down my chin. When the chains broke from my wrists, I gasped, spinning around to find another white-haired man, his eyes glowing the same red. The dagger in his palm dripped with blood.

"If you want to live, you'll come with me," he growled. "Vamir wants you *alive.*"

I didn't respond, my focus snagged on something else entirely.

Under the chaos, under the screams and violence, there were whispers. Rasping, curling whispers.

I turned back, looking up to Vamir. He was commanding another group of people now, pointing in several directions.

Those people…

They were all *Vyl'kríev,* their hair like a rainbow among the fire and blood.

Vamir was the leader of the Elven-blooded criminals who had been slaughtering their own.

Who were currently hunting us.

Vamir…

Vamir was the enemy.

CHAPTER 58

Varys

The next kick at the cell bars rattled my legs, my throat in ribbons from screaming for her. I hadn't stopped. I couldn't stop. Not until I got free and could save her.

A guardsman laughed as he walked by. I growled, rushing the door again. "Keep laughing!" I was nothing but fire and anger and absolute terror. "You bastards will fucking pay for—"

The area exploded with fiery light, blasting me backward. I landed on my back, my shoulders jarred from the strain of my bound wrists behind me. The building shook from another blast further down, the next shaking the ground beneath me. With ringing ears, I blinked through my dancing vision until it cleared. My breath hitched.

A massive hole had been blown into the prison, exposing the cell to the night air permeated with smoke. Buildings burned, flames licking the starry sky. Screams of pain and anguish filled the air as people ran through the streets.

I forced myself to my feet and rushed to the cell door, pressing my cheeks between the bars to see if I could determine what had happened down the hall. The other blasts had destroyed multiple cells, releasing their prisoners. Most were Elven-blooded.

"Hey!" I yelled. "Down here! Let me out!" Of course the explosion near me hadn't conveniently blown *my* cell out. "Someone help!"

None of them turned to me. I repeated the words in Elvish. One boy glanced my way. His mother picked him up and ran out.

I couldn't blame them. Who knew how long they'd been wrongly imprisoned as I was.

I had to think of something. I had tried to freeze my shackles off already. They'd known to bind my hands to prevent crucial somatics.

They had gagged her though. At first I wondered why they hadn't gagged me as well, if they knew we commanded our magic with words. Then I realized they probably gagged her not to prevent her magic, but to prevent the truths she would speak on that platform. If she had even made it to that platform before the town was attacked.

By who though? By what? Was it the dryamorn? Our enemy *Vyl'kríev?*

"Varys?" came an urgent voice. My chest swelled in relief as my father's face emerged from the dark hallway. He rushed to me. "Oh, thank the gods. Let's get you out of here."

Keys jangled as he pulled them from his pocket. I grinned. "How is it you have keys to the prison?"

He chuckled, picking a key and inserting it into the lock. "Pulled them off the unconscious—or, possibly dead—guard back there."

The lock didn't budge on the turn of his wrist. He picked another key. Same thing. "Let me try your shackles at least."

I turned around, sticking my hands through the cell bars. The first key unlocked them.

"Krayd's Chaos, Varys," Father exclaimed, "Whatever have you done to your arm?"

I rubbed and massaged my wrists, careful of the still bleeding claw mark across my arcane scars. "Long story. I would love to chat about it over tea, but let's get me out of here first."

Father nodded and tried another key. "Dammit. None of these keys are for your door."

I rubbed my temples. "Of course they aren't. That would be too easy."

"Do you have a spell?

I huffed, shoving my hands in my pockets. "I could try to freeze the lock and you could break it but it may take time we don't..."

My words trailed off as my fingers brushed over something deep within my pocket. It was thin and metal. Warm like magic.

I knew what it was. Had forgotten I pocketed the magical key when it had fallen from Maelawyn's cloak several days ago. "Too easy..." I murmured as I pulled it out.

"You had a key?" Father asked as I snaked my arm through the bars, inserting the key into the lock. One turn of my wrist, the mechanism clicked. I pushed on the barred door with bated breath, relief flooding through me when it swung open.

I grinned, taking the key from the lock. "That's going to come in handy."

My father's eyes were wide. "I'll say—"

Another explosion cut him off, this one across the market. We stepped over rubble, into the mass of people running about, all of them avoiding a green smoke in the market circle before the execution platform.

My eyes widened with terror. Four bodies lay beside the block. I rushed up the stairs, stepping around a pool of blood on the landing. Three guardsmen were dead along with Captain Dominik, throats sliced just like the jeweler brothers.

But besides the old blood stains on the notch, there was nothing fresh. Somewhere among the chaos, Maelawyn was still alive.

Maelawyn

Elvish words I understood and hundreds of citizens did not rang out around me, bringing fire and sparkling projectiles. I was pushed through the chaos with a harsh grip on my arm as rubble fell and the ground shook below. My body was moving like it was supposed to, but my head screamed just as loud as the shrieks of death and horror around me, demanding me to run away from this man.

But what would he do if I tried?

My gaze fell on a child in the streets screaming for his momma, blood on his hands. She lay beside him, eyes blank and unseeing.

Help.

I needed to help that baby—

The white-haired man yanked me back to him. "Don't," he snapped. I hadn't even realized I tried to drift. I lost a breath, along with my view on the boy.

A group of *Vyl'kríev* rushed by, eyes wide when they looked to my captor. "T-There's no one else in this direction, Seldszar, sir," one told him.

"Then group up with the others in the market. I'll block this way off."

All of them nodded and began running. I couldn't help but notice they all looked terrified.

He continued to pull me with one hand cast backward. More green smoke billowed from his fingers, creating a wall of fog behind us.

They were trapping everyone in the center of the market.

"Where are you taking me?" I asked.

Seldszar didn't answer, hands grabbing both of my arms and pushing me forward harder. I was suddenly thrown back to the jail cell, to the many times Rucas had gripped me like this, to Willem's squeeze before he—

As if a veil of fear had been ripped away from my eyes, I shrieked and kicked backward, nailing him in the groin. He lost his breath and his hold on me. I launched into a desperate flight, but he managed to grab hold of me again, this time around the waist. I dug my nails into his arms, screaming for help. My struggling made us tumble to the ground, and for a moment I believed I was free.

But his dagger hovered over my chest. All of his weight came down on my hips, locking me to the dirt road. His silver eyes lit up ruby once more. "Don't think I won't cut you, girl. Vamir said *alive*. He didn't state what condition."

I locked the air in my chest, telling myself not to scream. There was no thunder, no lightning. I was sure the potion was still affecting me.

Just as he moved the dagger to my shoulder, something flew into his. He cried out, tumbling off me. I rolled away quickly, scrambling to my feet and looking down to the arrow protruding from Seldszar's shoulder. I recognized the pheasant fletching immediately, head snapping to my savior.

I cried out, rushing to him. *"Eryx!"*

His arms flung around me, pulling me into an alley. "Run," he told me. "I'll catch up."

I stopped on the outskirts of a farmer's estate, off the road leading to the stream. Knelt behind a wagon of hay, I tried to catch my breath. I could still hear the shrieks and cries from the citizens in the market, the fires washing the night sky in an orange glow, and in my moment of pause, *everything* sped up.

Tears streamed down my face, images of melting skin plaguing my mind. I was still drenched in my own piss, the smell overwhelming the scent of smoke on my clothes. I shivered, my blood like ice in veins from absolute terror.

I could still feel the texture of the block's notch on my neck, the vessels there pumping hard as if…they knew I had been seconds from decapitation.

Pain and qualm surged through my stomach. I vomited on the grass, lungs heaving from my attempts to remain quiet. When I knew nothing else was coming up, I crawled under the wagon and wrapped my arms around myself.

"Mae!"

I cried out loud enough Eryx heard me. He ran to the wagon, taking my arms and pulling me out from under. "We need to get to the stream—"

"The gate's closed." I pointed with shaking fingers. "We can't get out."

"I know a way out. Just follow me."

He covered me with his cloak and guided me through the farmer's field, behind a stable, past an orchard of apple trees, until we reached the log wall spanning the border of Elros.

Eryx left my side for a moment, grasping the trunk of one log and moving it aside, leaving a gap in the wall just large enough to slide through. "Saw that Cauldücen girl do this once."

I perked up. "Leo." The Cauldücen's didn't know Elros was under attack. "That's where I'll go."

I took Eryx's shoulders. "I need you to do something for me."

His brows pinched. "What—"

"Find Varys Wynhart." My eyes burned. "Find him and come to the Cauldücen manor. I'll be safe there."

He scoffed. "I'm not going all the way back there to risk my life for that bastard."

I frowned, glaring up at him. "That bastard is my *Arynáthi* and I demand you find him."

He blinked. "Your *what?*"

I hadn't even realized I'd spoken Elvish. I lifted my hand, showing off the *çirö*. "I'm a mage, Eryx. Like Varys. And like all of the people that have been imprisoned, some being slaughtered at this very moment."

His jaw tightened. "Mages are attacking the town—"

"We are not the same. Find Varys, Eryx."

He stared at me, at the lightning marks. "And what if he's already dead?"

I swallowed, the burning in my eyes turning to angry tears. "Then don't come looking for me."

Coming up the hill and into the manor's front yard, I began to shout for Leona. My legs and chest burned from running, lungs feeling like they may collapse as I did, knees buckling. I caught myself, heaving, shouting for Leona again.

Ahead, the door swung open. Leona and Duros stepped out, and I thanked the gods they were both wielding their weapons of choice and in armor. She called my name and rushed toward me.

"Oh my gods, Snow." Leo knelt before me, pulling me upright. "Speak to me, lass. What happened?"

I could barely breathe. "The…town…the town is…"

"Under attack," Duros finished for me. "I can taste tha smoke in tha air."

Gripping his axe, he started back down the hill.

"Where's Fawkes?" Leo asked, her grip on my shoulders tightening as my hands clutched her white tunic. "Mae, where's Varys?"

I stifled a sob. "I don't know. We were…we were captured."

Her emerald eyes went wide with fury.

"I…" A cry broke free. "They were going to cut off my head."

Her face fell, jaw dropping. "*Victors*…And Varys is still—"

"I don't know." I shook my head, over and over because I didn't know, *I didn't know.*

Duros shouted something in what I assumed was Dwarvish. Leona's head snapped up. She cursed, pulling on my arms. "C'mon, Snow. Get up." Her breaths turned uneven. "They're comin'—"

A shriek tore through the night sky before it ceased in the same devastating moment.

We snapped our heads around. Back to the manor.

Natalia's wide eyes were fixed on us. Blank.

Lifeless.

Her head went limp to one side, body hanging on a bloody dagger protruding from her chest. The blade tore from her with a gruesome, wet rip, and as she fell to the ground, her attacker stepped into the moonlight.

Orin.

CHAPTER 59

Maelawyn

Leona's scream pierced the night sky as she ripped away from my hold on her. She launched into a dash, but was cut off by Duros and pushed back. With a violent cry he barreled across the yard, axe lifted to swing. Orin sidled to the side of the house, disappearing into the dark southern forest with Duros following, his tormented shouts fading away.

Leona ran to her mother's side, dropping to her knees into the pool of blood. Her hands shook as they pressed to the wound. "Oh, Mum…" Her voice broke, head tilting back to the sky as a sorrowful wail ripped from her.

I clasped my hands to my mouth, fresh hot tears streaming down my face. Devastation settled in as I kneeled beside Natalia, a woman who had been so headstrong and compassionate.

She had saved my life *twice*. She hadn't known me, not really. I had barely known her. And yet, she had welcomed me into her family as if I had been there for years. I wasn't sure I realized until now how…*loved* she made me feel. And I wasn't even her daughter.

Her daughter—the woman who now clasped Natalia tight, face buried in her shoulder as she cried. I came to Leona, wrapping an arm around her. I didn't know how else to comfort her, if this was what she even needed. I knew nothing I could do would ever be enough, but I held my friend tightly as she mourned.

Until drums began to beat.

No, not drums. Footsteps. Boots marching through leaves and—

"Leona," I started under my breath. "Someone's coming."

She clutched her mother's body tighter, blood staining her arms and torso. She didn't move.

I pulled on her anyway, the footsteps pounding in my head to a near painful point. "Leona, I'm sorry." She shoved me off. "Leona, *please*. We need to go."

"No." Her voice was so hoarse. So broken.

My breaths turned rapid as the footsteps quickened. I pulled on her again. She only pushed me away.

"Stop!" I cried. "I'm not going to let you sit here and die."

Branches snapped. I squinted, straining my eyes in the darkness, looking beyond the shadows of the trees ahead down the hill. Maybe it was just someone coming to help—

Something shot over us, drilling into the front door of the manor. A crossbow bolt.

"Leona!" I screamed, holding out my hand and leaning into my fear, searching for those sparks I knew lie beneath my skin. Nothing.

Several men's voices shouted from the edge of the forest. Another bolt shot over us. I crawled backward, unadulterated terror surging up my spine, my throat, coming out shrieking, *"Leona!"*

Slowly, her head lifted as if she was waking from a long sleep. Gazing forward to the forest, her wet eyes turned hard and cold, no longer of fire and emeralds—the forge had been snuffed.

Rocking to her knees, with Natalia's blood on her hands, she reached for the handle of her blade—and unsheathed it with fervor. The intense ring echoed across the yard to the trees surrounding. A sound of warning, her stare into the darkness a promise of violence.

She began to stand, a strained cry in her throat as if pushing up the weight of a mountain. Her tears glinted silver in the moonlight, lips quivering as she held her blade out.

I sucked in a breath. I knew what she was going to do. "Leona, no," I pleaded. "Let's just—let's just go."

She didn't even seem to hear me. She only snarled, her breaths heavy, murderous gaze fixed on the men approaching us rapidly.

Then, she began to recite, "Bones may shiver, mind may shake…"

Several men tore from the edge of the forest, racing uphill to the manor yard.

"Steel your heart, turn fear to flame…"

Their crossbows were loaded and aimed.

"I am a Cauldücen."

Swords and axes lifted. I could only watch as Leona's stance shifted, head held high, hands gripping the handle of her sword tight.

"My heart knows *no* fear."

With a deafening war cry, she rushed them. The air locked in my chest as her blade made contact with the first, ultimately knocking the man's weapon from his grasp. She came back up and in one clean slice, his detached head thudded to the ground. Bile rose up my throat.

With light steps, she twirled to the left, meeting with another's axe and sending the attacker back by the strength of her sword alone. Her blade sank through him, pulling it back just in time to spin out, ducking her head under an oncoming charge. She moved as if… as if this was a dance. But not one of grace and joy, but of reckoning and fury, her music the clang of steel and pounding of boots.

I backed myself against the house, heart pounding and spine rigid. Three more men rushed out from the brush, axes and clubs raised. She twisted, stomped toward them and released a scream that sent shivers over my skin and fresh tears down my face. I was terrified of her.

And so were these men.

Drenched in blood, her face shattered in sorrow and pain, she charged with her sword high, her chest and arms vulnerable and yet these men stepped *away* from her. As if they were not the monsters on the battlefield.

The last man fell in pieces, his blood painting the trees behind him. And then there was no sound beyond her heaving. Her sword fell from her shaking hand to the ground where bodies lay scattered in her wake. At last, she turned to me—to her mother's body—and as blood ran down her face as easily as sweat, she dropped to her knees and screamed, her words of a language I didn't know.

Whatever they translated to, they were full of pain and promise.

Varys

Smoke burned my eyes and throat as we ran with the screaming citizens. From what—who—we did not know.

The green fog-like substance had billowed into the streets and formed a wall, cutting off all exits and any chance of escaping whoever was attacking Elros. We were forced to run around or jump over bodies in the streets, skin peeled off the bone.

"This way, Varys!" Father called, leading me into an alley that seemed to be clear. We found a wall of flame cutting us off instead.

Leaning against the back of a building, I paused just enough to quiet my panic and look around at the chaos. Everyone was being forced into the market circle. The attackers were drawing citizens out of their homes by setting the town on fire, but keeping everyone in one area with the threat of the acidic clouds.

There was no way out. No escape.

With a lost and terrified expression, Father looked at me. *To* me. For answers I didn't have.

But I wouldn't die. Not like this. Neither would he.

"I'll figure this out! Just stay close!" It was an empty promise, but it brought hope back to his face.

We found a pile of rubble and dropped down behind it. Casting *Vid Medaes,* I focused on the green cloud. The veins seemed to warble as they flowed around it, but if I could just focus a little longer—

I cried out, my arcane scars burning. *"Dammit!"* I yelled, holding my arm to my chest.

Father's brow pinched. "Your magic hurts you?"

I shook my head. "I'm just injured. It'll heal. I just don't understand why something so simple…"

My words trailed off, hands instinctively patting the book bag I always had on me.

Gone. My book bag was gone, along with my spellbook.

"No, no, no…" Repeating the words over and over, I spun, as if I would find it on the ground. As if it wasn't missing entirely. "Oh my gods, my spellbook is…"

In the clearing, I realized. With my pack of clothes and money. At least I knew where it was, if it was still there.

"I know where it is, but because I'm so far from it, I can't use magic for very long." I huffed, a roll to my eyes. "Quite the inconvenience when we're about to die."

"We're not going to die." Father shrugged off the pack on his back, kneeling. "You're a mage Varys, but you forget."

He opened the pack and reached inside, his entire arm disappearing completely. I blinked in confusion. "What is—"

"I met with friends. Didn't you get my note?" He winked. "I found Baron Kenrad. He has known about The ReEmergence since Shade's Crescent was attacked last quarter."

My eyes went wide.

"I wish I had more time to explain." His arm began to pull out. "I left when Mae showed up at the library that night, knowing that if I found Kenrad, I could get it back."

In my father's grasp, the blue jewel of my mother's sword glinted in the firelight. I lost a breath as he continued to pull it from the pack before placing it in my hands. "Let's talk about the night your mother died."

Maelawyn

The smell of gore and blood, shit and piss, was thick in the humid air, so heavy I could taste it.

Leona's screams had died down to sobs, but she hadn't risen.

Her sorrow was palpable, every cry pulsing through me. I had been sitting against the house for so many moments I'd lost count, racking my brain of something to say. I had nothing. I had never suffered a loss like this.

But she was my friend. She had been there for me in moments where I felt lost. I could try to do the same.

Rising, I began to cross the yard to her, every step churning my stomach. Every step feeling stronger than the last.

Bones may shiver, mind may shake, but steel your heart and turn fear to flame.

I repeated the verse, the one she had recited before slaughtering the men who came to kill us. The one she had told me she held close after being assaulted.

As I knelt down, placing a gentle, cautious hand on her shoulder, I focused on my fear and breathed through it.

Rain, cool and refreshing, began to pour down.

Leona went silent, slowly tipping her head back. The blood washed from her face as she blinked up at the sky, then looked at me.

"Is this…yer doin'?" she asked.

I swallowed, feeling the surge of my power rushing through me, a heat in my blood that for once didn't burn. "I think so."

I was a storm, but as Leona cried out and wrapped her arms around me, I knew I could be her calm.

"I'm goin' to kill him," she muttered.

Her words stole my breath, but the nod I gave was easy. "I know," I whispered.

"I…" Her sob shook her entire body. "I slept with him."

My heart sank for her as I held her tighter. "I'm so sorry."

I didn't even know what else to say. That kind of betrayal was vile, and I wouldn't dare hold her back from the revenge she deserved.

She lifted her head. "My da…my da should be the one to bury my mum." Tears spilled down her face as she turned back to her mother's body. "Let me just…"

Leona's eyes went wide, her grief turning to absolute terror. *"What the fuck?!"*

I snapped my head back as Leona started to scream and crawl backward. The blood left my face, my own scream tearing from my throat as I stared through the sheet of rain into the glowing ruby eyes of the woman shambling toward us.

Natalia.

The gaping hole in her chest was still bleeding.

And she was still dead.

CHAPTER 60

Maelawyn

Leona screeched, taking hold of her blade and standing. Both of us began to walk backward downhill—

Something snagged my ankle, throwing me face first to the ground. I looked back and my breath sawed out of me. Gripping my foot was the hand of one of the men— one of the *dead* men. His angry eyes glowed the same color Natalia's were.

"Leona!" I screamed, kicking my other foot into his face, nose crunching beneath my boot.

Her sword came down, slicing the hand clean off from the elbow. The dead man didn't seem to mind, not as he quickly tried to grab Leona with his other. Another slash removed its head and the body fell back down.

I scrambled to my feet and began to run with Leona. We had just reached the edge of the forest when something cut through the air past me and into her. She was thrown back with a sharp yelp, and I lost a breath at the sight of the crossbow bolt protruding from my friend's shoulder.

I snapped my head around, finding another dead had risen, his insides spilling from his abdomen as he reset the crossbow in his hands. With his jaw agape, eyes unfocused and whirling around uncontrollably, he pulled back the bowstring and set his finger on

650

the trigger. I held out my left hand, focusing on my fear, finding the sparks beneath my skin. My fingers began to glitter with jolting energy, *çirö* glowing, and before he could release the bolt, I sent the energy outward in a strand of white light. On contact, the body jolted before bursting into flame, and as it fell to the ground, a laugh rang out from the brush.

Vamir stepped into the yard, his silver eyes glowing the same ruby red as all of the undead. "I *knew* you were something different," he crooned. "Something...special."

I ran to Leona's side, pleading for her to get up. She groaned and hissed in pain.

"A nexus," Vamir went on. "I wonder what Lithia will think about that?"

Varys

Rain had started to pour down. I gripped my mother's sheathed sword with all the strength I possessed, as if I let it go again, I'd never get it back.

My father stared at me long and hard, eyes glossy under his spectacles. "There is a reason your mother didn't make it out alive. Between me and her, we could have killed a few wolves, enough to get away on horse. But what I saw...what Krystan saw...she knew one of us was going to die."

His words brought images I didn't want to remember at the moment. There was enough fear and confusion racing through me.

He swallowed thickly. "It should have been me. It *should have* been *me*. But if I'd argued with her decision, all three of us would have been dead. You remember wolves, son. But I remember *monsters*."

Someone shouted nearby before a blast lit up the street over. We jolted up and were about to run the other direction when we realized...the *rain*. The rain had doused the fire blocking the path.

We had an exit.

Running down the alley, we didn't stop until we came to the log wall bordering Elros, a section of it in splinters. It seemed someone else had escaped this way too.

Running into the forest, I faced the direction I knew would lead me back around to the Cauldücen's, stomach turning over with a terrible realization.

I'd lost Maelawyn again.

"Wynhart!"

Father and I flipped around to a figure rushing toward us. Anger whipped through me, teeth bared as I cried out the command word for my wards, shoving my father behind me. I would have recognized that green cloak anywhere.

Eryx halted before the glowing blue aura. "What in Torm are you doing?"

I huffed a laugh, shrugging off the pain in my arm as I sustained my wards. "The last time I saw your face, you were trapped under my ice, vowing to kill me."

His jaw tensed. "That was before I watched Rucas flail the skin off my friend's back."

I snarled. "You *watched*—"

"Don't get it fucking twisted." Dark eyes settled on me. "I tried to stop him and was imprisoned instead. Only got out 'cause of that explosion."

I crossed my arms, mentally keeping my wards raised. Doing so burned like tormfire, but I let my ego sing for a moment. "So, what you're saying is *sorry?* For threatening me and accusing me of being someone I'm not?"

He scowled. "Do you want my help or not?"

I scoffed. "No thanks."

He threw up his arms, turning back toward the forest. "Fine," he called out over the rain picking up in strength. "I'll just tell Mae you're dead."

His words snapped through me, throwing off my concentration and dispelling my wards entirely. "Tell me where she is."

He halted, looking over his shoulder with a mock on his lips. "Thought you didn't want my help?"

My anger tipped over the edge, the step toward him filled with fury—

"You don't need his help, Varys," Father said from behind. Coming up beside me, hands tucked behind his back in his astute, instructional disposition, he nodded to both of us. "He's already practically revealed where she is."

Eryx straightened. "What are you talking about, old man?"

Father's expression turned cross, chin dipped as he looked to Eryx from the rim of his spectacles. "Oh, come now. It's quite simple." He pointed to the muddy footprints under Eryx's feet. "We can deduce that you came from the forest to the east of Elros, since your prints lead all the way back. The only thing beyond there is the Cauldücen manor. I wouldn't be surprised if Varys here has made Ms. Mordaunt fully aware that she is absolutely safe there."

My mouth parted, eyes flicking to Eryx. "Is that true?"

With a shake of his head and crossed arms, Eryx muttered, "I pinned you as a bookworm, not a tracker."

"There are many things you can learn in a book, Mr. RothHall," Father said as if it were obvious. "This, however, is just common sense."

I couldn't hold back the snort, pressing a hand to my mouth as Eryx seethed at me. That was godsdamn hilarious—

"You could have figured it out just as easily, son," Father told me, brows raised in a dignified manner. "Better to think with your head when someone is being unreasonable."

I pressed my lips together. I knew that. I'd used the same kind of tactic on Rucas multiple times. Maybe that's why Eryx annoyed me so much—similar personality.

With a growl under his breath, Eryx grumbled, "Come on."

As he stalked back toward the forest, I turned to my father. "You're coming, too, right?"

He placed a hand on my shoulder. "I'm not." I opened my mouth to protest, but he went on, "Kenrad is in Revyk, at an inn there. We have things to discuss. Plans."

I shook my head in confusion. "What kind of—"

He pressed a finger to his lips. "I cannot say. Not aloud. Not to you."

His words tugged on my memories. Duros had said something similar before Maelawyn and I had left the manor.

"But I must finish what I was trying to tell you earlier." Voices began to shout beyond the fence, and we started moving again. Eryx seemed to wait for us before continuing on as we got closer.

Stopping under a tree, out of the rain, Father reached inside the pack, pulling out the bound tome of pages I knew as his own personal record book, the one he used to write important notes to himself. "I, too, have done my research in secret, son. And I found the creatures closest to what I saw that night."

He pulled out a page folded within, a drawing of a large wolf-like creature as big as a bear, with yellow eyes and teeth the size of my hand. The eyes of every nightmare I had ever endured.

"Let me give you one last lecture." He looked at me the same way he always did when he wanted me to listen close and carefully. "You told me magic never went away. That it was only dormant in the blood of elven descendants. So what does that mean about creatures of magic?"

"My findings suggest it varied from creature to creature," I told him.

"What about the creatures of Torm?"

I swallowed, nervous about where this conversation was headed. "The monsters Lithia created were banished with her." I shook my head. "Father...*nothing* has been able to escape the Evershade for over a millennia until The ReEmergence began. And that's under the assumption that the barrier holding those fiends inside is weakening as magic returns." I held his gaze. "They were just wolves—"

He gripped my shoulders. "Varys, they–were–*monsters*. Forget the books. Forget the studying for a moment and just..." He loosened his grip. "Listen."

I shook my head, taking the drawing in my hand. "Father... these are *dire wolves*. They were the Guardians of Aldeon Forest, and the High Druid could beckon them to aid him. A High Druid that perished with all of the elves in the war."

My heart began to race the more I tried to convince him this was wrong. Because...what if it wasn't?

"Why would dire wolves attack Mother?"

He folded the drawing in my palm. "If anyone can discover the truth, Varys, it's you." He lifted his chin. "You told me the other day it was time to leave Elros. You were right. But in a time of great change, stars align, fate speaks, and destinies are unraveled. I have found my place in all of that, but we must part ways for now."

My mouth slacked, the knot in my throat becoming impossible to swallow down. "When will I see you again?"

He smiled, glancing up at the sky. "Only the stars know, Varys."

He embraced me, and as tears began to fall down my face, mixing with the drops of rain on my skin, I clutched onto him tightly.

"Be safe, Wynhart," he told me.

I nodded, but the words were not enough. They never had been. "I love you, Father."

His body went taut in my arms before his chest shuddered with a sob. "I love you, son."

Stepping back, I hadn't noticed he'd grabbed hold of the sword, pulling it from my grasp. "Hold out your hands."

I did so, and he laid the sheathed blade in my palms. My chest tightened as my father declared, "You are Krystan Wynhart's son. A warrior of the blade and the gods-given magic. Go now and protect those you love as she did for you." Heavy tears poured from both our eyes as he uttered, "Draw your sword."

With a courageous breath, I gripped the handle and with one sharp pull, unsheathed the blade. The ring of steel resonated off the trees surrounding us.

And then before our eyes, my arcane scars began to glow as the sword burned white-hot.

The air in my chest left in a burst as we watched the tip of the blade begin to curve, Elvish runes burning into the steel, engraving up the edge. The sword hadn't been pulled in twelve years, but it had never looked like this. It was changing from a longsword to an elven scimitar, a weapon I had only seen in books, but knew from the many descriptions that the elves who used such blades relied on a dexterous style of fighting.

A weapon of *my* finesse.

As the glow faded, I read over the inscription of the runes. *"Adönes na fich rys"*.

Courage to bring change.

A chill barreled down my spine. It was perfectly balanced and lighter than it had been originally. The handle fit in my palm as if it had been made for me.

But out of everything that I had just witnessed, nothing was as magical as the realization that it did not hurt to grip it in my right hand. My injured hand. The coolness of the handle even seemed to ease the arcane scars on my palm.

I couldn't speak. Nothing I would say would come out right anyway.

My father gaped in awe. "I knew the sword had been passed down through her family, but…"

Slipping the scimitar back into its sheath, I found it also formed to the blade perfectly. I attached it to my belt once more, then lifted my head for the first time as a fully realized war sage.

Maelawyn

"I'm only giving you one option."

Every direction I turned to run they were rising. Rising as if they'd never fallen. Even the legless were up on wrists, balancing the top half of their corpse, crawling and scraping toward me and Leona through the rain. I couldn't breathe hard or fast enough to stop the pounding pain in my chest, arms drawn in tight as if making myself smaller would prevent them from getting to me.

"You will come with me and join the rest of us." Vamir's fingers bent and curled at his sides.

I understood raising the undead was something he was doing with magic, but it hadn't clicked in my head yet. "You're a… necromancer."

Vamir just grinned.

My stomach turned over. *Shit.* We had all been so damn blind. "You killed Willem and Theon."

A wicked, breathy laugh cracked out of him. "You know, sweetling. It would have been you."

My body went rigid.

His hands raised and the undead stopped in their walking. "But, being *Pallid Cursed*"—he bobbed his head in a mocking fashion—"it just…wasn't enough. This town didn't give a single drop of rat shit about the poor Mordaunt girl. So, when I discovered your dear daddy was just so *eager* to kill you off, and he'd paid those cretins to do the job, I figured it might start some sort of distraction *at least.*"

My eyes went wide, thunder rolling. His head tilted and…there was something wholly different about him suddenly.

"But then you surprised the fuck out of me." He clicked his tongue. "Not only were you like me and my kin, but you were a mage. It was perfect. And then you were so determined to make sure *you* hadn't been the one that killed them, you left yourself open to be framed. And if the entire town found out it was *magic* and not"—he flipped his wet hair off his shoulders—"*me*, well, then we create prejudice and this town was just *waiting* for someone to blame."

Leona had stood to her feet, groaning as she leaned on the pommel of her blade. "Shut him up."

I barely heard her, his words swirling in my head like a riddle. "You and your *Vyl'kriev* followers killed other *Vyl'krievs* to make me look like I was a murderer?"

"Oh, it's not all about you, dear." His hands began to bend again. "My *mage* followers are killing everyone who defies me and my kin so that *mages* become Xalador's new, great enemy."

I stepped back, glancing around at the undead that had begun to move once more. Leona was staring with wide eyes. "'May yer days be dark, and yer victims blind,'" she recited hoarsely. "Ye're usin' these mages to blind us from the real threat."

His smile widened with a roll of his eyes, raising his arms and twisting his black-varnished fingers like a puppeteer. "Come on, girls," he purred. "When will you figure it *out?*"

Throwing his arms forward, the undead began to charge. A

shriek caught in my throat as Leona grabbed my hand and forced me into a run beside her. We bounded into the southern woods, and so did the undead.

Guttural growls bellowed close behind, our pace faltering as the ground turned to thick mud and wild brush. We sprinted over a hill, ducking under limbs and jumping over fallen logs. Leona's cries deepened with every fall of her foot. Her running slowed and she let go of my hand. I halted, barely catching her as she began to tip.

"Keep runnin'," she urged.

I shook my head, gasping. "I won't leave you to die, Leona."

"Oh, I'm not done yet," she growled. But as she held out her blade, she yelped, a shaking hand flying to the injury. Blood dripped from the bolt in her arm, gushing with every movement she made.

The undead were closing in, Vamir hovering behind them. "And here I thought the dwarven Princess of Gor Thorüm would be more sturdy," he chided with a shrug. "Thought her mother would be too."

Leona's growl turned rabid, charging forward into the risen army. Vamir's hand flicked, and the first undead she made contact with ducked under her attack and threw her backward.

I went to rush for her when someone grabbed my arm and flipped me to the ground. My face slammed into dead leaves and mud before I was forced to my back and yanked by my ankles to my attacker.

Fear shank its cold fingers into me, gripping my spine and freezing me in place. This…wasn't real. I refused to believe this was real.

His cold fingers gripped my thighs in the same manner he had that day, forcing my legs apart. The gasping scream in my throat broke free as I kicked and bucked against Willem Welch, whose head wobbled limply and dead eyes stared right through me, ripping me right back to his assault at the stream.

I threw my fists and kicked. He growled in response and dipped down to my face, the smell of days-old rot on my neck as his foul, dry tongue licked my cheek.

A cry tore from my throat before I screamed for Leona, for Varys, *anyone*, as his teeth snapped like a dog near my chin. But as the ice-cold fear washed through me, it began to ebb with heat. The same kind of heat I used to feel with my pain attacks. The same hot agony I had felt right before I shocked him last time.

But this time…this time I was done.

The jolting power rose to the surface as I lifted my shaking glowing arm, every intention set on sending the charge through him again. But my eyes caught the ruby glow of Vamir's, and with an angry shout, I sent the streak of lightning blasting into his chest instead.

His body shuttered before it fell, and the undead fell with him. Willem toppled off.

Leona gasped as she watched the army slump around her, spinning to shuffle toward me. I stood with a sob, clasping onto her. "Come on, let's—"

A shrieking scream pierced through my mind. I forced my hands to my ears, teeth clenched until it died out.

Did you truly believe this was part of your power?

Footsteps pounded in my head like they had before. Pounding like I was being kicked over and over again.

The voice wasn't mine. It wasn't my *nwív's*.

Vamir began to rise from the ground, face scrunched in pain for just a beat before his eyes opened.

Black. Like mine were in my true form.

The skin of his face became taut against the bones beneath, veins seeming to cloud with ink. He grinned, his teeth no longer blunt and straight but two rows of sharp fangs, and as horns surfaced from the crown of his head, Leona took a rattling gasp. "Varys…" Leona growled. "Godsdammit, I should have remembered."

My head continued to ring, whispers speaking in a language I didn't know. Something of Torm.

"He's a necromancer." Leona's sword rose. "Because he's a dryamorn."

Vamir's laugh rang like bell tolls in my head, along with my *Arynáthi's* words, *"There have been findings…which trace Xaladorians with white hair to be similar to those of elven descent."*

Similar.

But different.

"We are of the same bloodline, after all," Vamir had told me at the tavern.

And I wasn't lying.

I began to run.

I didn't slow down, not even as Leona began to chase me.

Everything clicked into place as Vamir's voice still slithered through my head.

Your white hair is not of your Elven-blood, sweetling.

I ran. And ran.

No. I didn't want to hear him say it.

Tears poured, the rain falling harder. I couldn't be...no, I wasn't—

You may have that gods-given, wretched power. But you are one of us…

THE REEMERGENCE CHRONICLES WILL CONTINUE IN
TO IGNITE THE FLAMES WITHIN

ACKNOWLEDGMENTS

I truly don't even know *how* to begin this. The fact that I'm writing an acknowledgements page is just mind blowing to me. It took me six years to write this book, but I've had the dream to become a published author, some way or another, since the very first little story I wrote in kindergarten when my teacher handed me a blank sheet of paper with lines to practice my handwriting. I stapled together probably thirty of those little stories by the end of my kindergarten year, then moved on to sheets of printer paper at home, then to notebooks, then to this amazing thing called a computer where I kept secret folders of fan fiction and short stories. It was all a dream I thought would never become a reality.

Now it is.

And I couldn't have done it without the amazing people in my life.

I want to thank my incredible creative partners over the years. To my Sprint Queens. To everyone who I've talked to about this book and who have taken their time to read any amount I've thrown at them.

To my incredible beta readers. Every single one of you made this book a reality, and gave me the courage to publish this book with every comment you made, whether it was about a mistake, or how you wanted to stab my villains. I have laughed and cried over your comments. Thank you for being patient when I intended to have the draft I gave you done early 2021 and the pandemic depression consumed me. Seriously. Thanks for sticking around.

To another group who stuck around: my reader group. I started posting snippets and throwing around sneak peeks, desperate for someone to take me seriously. You all did. I feel like I have a small fandom every time I post and it's just incredible. Thank you for liking my posts and watching my crazy lives.

Thank you to those who have helped support me financially. To my *Buy Me a Coffee* supporters: Linda, James, Steve, Sierra, Krystal, Heather, and Whitney. Thank you for supporting me when I had nothing to give to the world yet. Your contribution helped support the concept art of Varys, Mae, and Leona I commissioned.

To my family who has also helped financially, and has encouraged me to keep going all these years.

To my mom and in-laws who have watched my kids when I needed to edit, and when Lance and I took our vacations for some R&R and for me to finally see the scenery I wrote about in this book.

Also, yes. My mom read my book before anyone. Mom, sorry my book was your first "smutty" read. Also, you're welcome.

And last but certainly not least, thank you to my incredible husband, Lance. I think it's important to note that Lance was originally a writer on this project, and there are pieces in this story that were his brainchild, including Varys and Leona's original character concepts. Even though I became sole writer, and changed a lot, the world of Xalador continues to be ours. This book is for you. You are the reason I have healed, the reason I live, and the reason I reemerged into who I am today. Thank you for pushing me, thank you for reading that awful fan fiction you found on my laptop and encouraging me to continue writing, thank you for loving me with everything you have.

PRONUNCIATION

CHARACTERS:

Mae (she/her): MAY
Varys (he/him): VAIR-ISS
Leona (she/her): LEE-OHNA
Eryx (he/him): AIR-IX
Rucas (he/him): ROO-CAS
Fantine (she/her): FAWN-TEEN
Mattis (he/him): MATT-ISS
Krystan (she/her): KRISS-TAN
Duros (he/him): DUR-OHS
Natalia (she/her): NA-TAWL-YAH
Vamir (he/him): VAH-MEER
Orin (he/him): OR-IN
Maelawyn (she/her): MAY-LAH-WIN

Mordaunt: MORE-DAUNT
Wynhart: WIN-HEART
Cauldücen: CAWL-DOO-KIN
RothHall: ROTH-HALL

PLACES:

Xalador: EX-AL-AH-DOOR
Jinya: JIN-YAH
Elros: EL-ROSS
Latera: LAH-TAIR-AH
Livohka: LIVE-OH-KAH
Fairegrove: FAIR-GROVE
Mirefield: MIRE-FIELD

Aldeon: AL-DEE-ON
Elvidawn: EL-VI-DAWN
Hakdvar: HACKED-VAR
Iarhana: EYE-AR-HA-NAH
Gor Thorüm: GORE THOR-OOM

THE SILENT GODS:

Eana (she/her): EE-AH-NAH
Lithia (she/her): LITH-EE-AH
Elethros (he/him): EL-EH-THROSS
Formos (they/them): FOR-MOSE
Krayd (he/him): KRADE
Willa (she/her): WILL-AH

CREATURES/BEINGS:

Nwív: NWEEV
Dryamorn: DRY-AH-MORN

ACCENTS

Leona/Duros "Ye" when saying "You" is "Yeh"

For full pronunciation list, please see C.N.Maxwell's website.

ABOUT THE AUTHOR

C.N.Maxwell is an Epic Fantasy Romance author living in Texas with her family. When she's not writing, she's obsessing over her comfort shows, shipping characters that will never canonically be together, and listening to Sleep Token's entire discography on repeat. She loves to sing, play piano and guitar, doodle, travel, and daydream of worlds she'd rather live in.

facebook.com/C.N.MaxwellAuthor

instagram.com/author_c.n.maxwell